# A GAME OF THRONES

## THE GRAPHIC NOVEL

### VOLUME 3

# GEORGE R. R. MARTIN

# A GAME OF THRONES

## THE GRAPHIC NOVEL

**VOLUME 3**

ADAPTED BY DANIEL ABRAHAM

ART BY TOMMY PATTERSON

COLORS BY IVAN NUNES

LETTERING BY MARSHALL DILLON

ORIGINAL SERIES COVER ART BY

MIKE S. MILLER AND MICHAEL KOMARCK

BANTAM BOOKS · NEW YORK

GAM
v. 3

Painting on page vi by Michael Komarck.
Paintings on pages 2, 32, 62, 92, 122, 152, and 182 by Mike S. Miller.

Published in the United States by Bantam Books, an imprint of Random House, a division of Random House LLC, a Penguin Random House Company, New York.

Bantam Books and the House colophon are registered trademarks of Random House LLC.

ISBN 978-0-440-42323-2
eBook ISBN 978-0-345-53860-4

Printed in the United States of America on acid-free paper.

www.bantamdell.com

9 8 7 6 5 4 3 2 1

*Graphic novel interior design by Foltz Design.*

Visit us online at www.DYNAMITE.com

Follow us on Twitter @dynamitecomics

Like us on Facebook /Dynamitecomics

Watch us on YouTube /Dynamitecomics

Nick Barrucci, CEO / Publisher
Juan Collado, President / COO
Joe Rybandt, Senior Editor
Josh Johnson, Art Director
Rich Young, Director Business Development
Jason Ullmeyer, Senior Graphic Designer
Keith Davidsen, Marketing Manager
Josh Green, Traffic Coordinator
Chris Caniano, Production Assistant

25.00
3/8/14
NRN

113989704

# CONTENTS

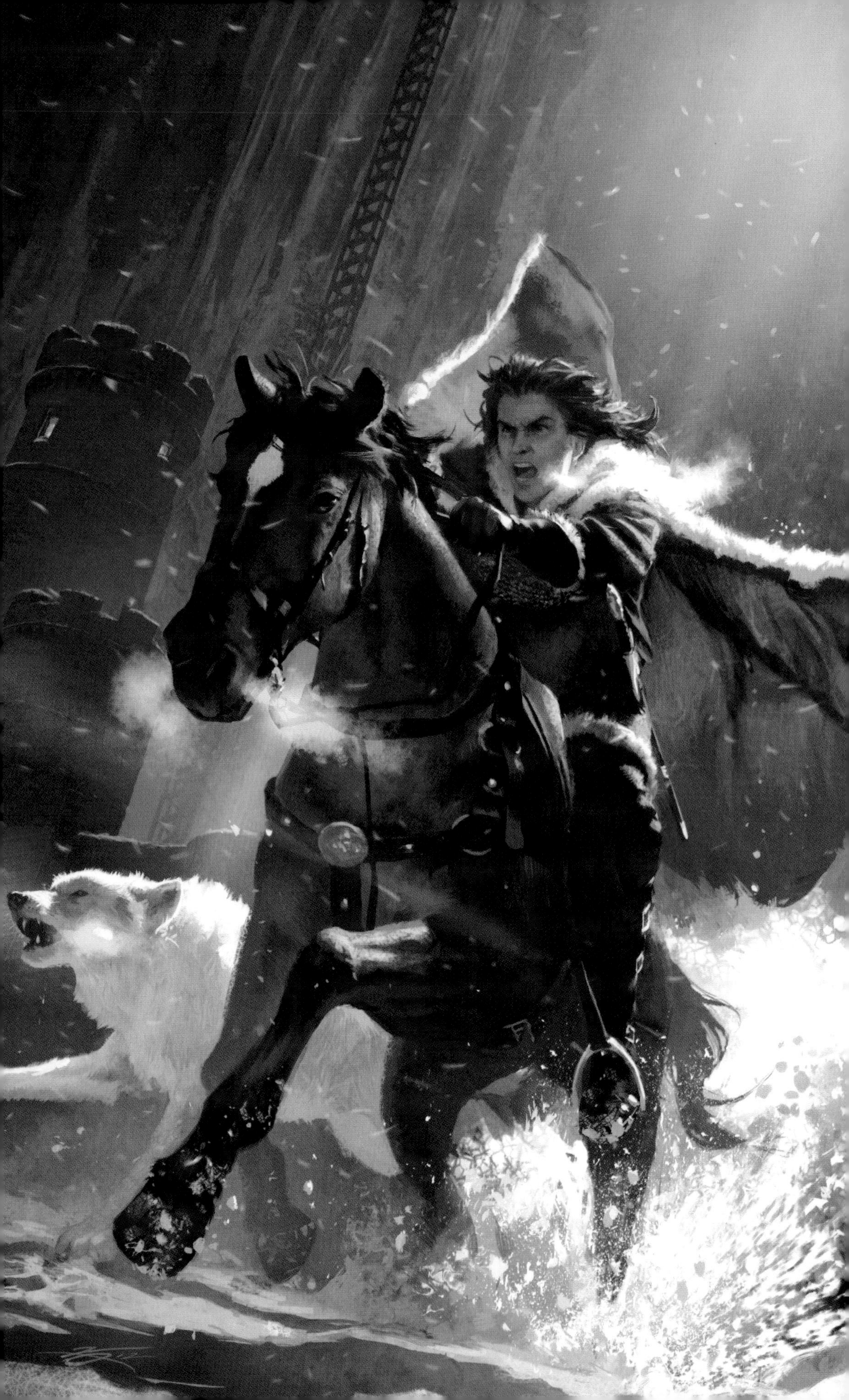

# A GAME OF THRONES

## THE GRAPHIC NOVEL

VOLUME 3

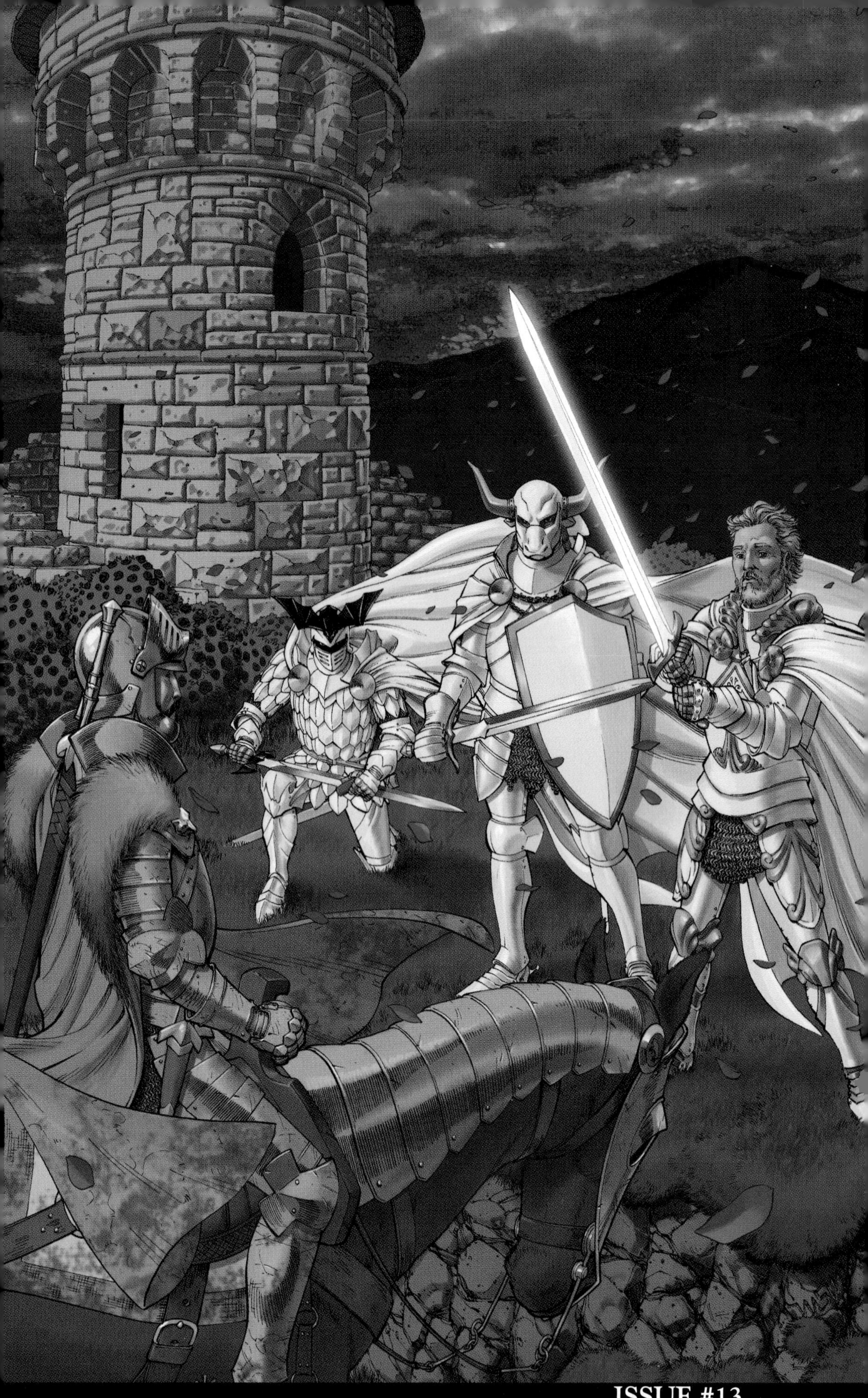

ISSUE #13

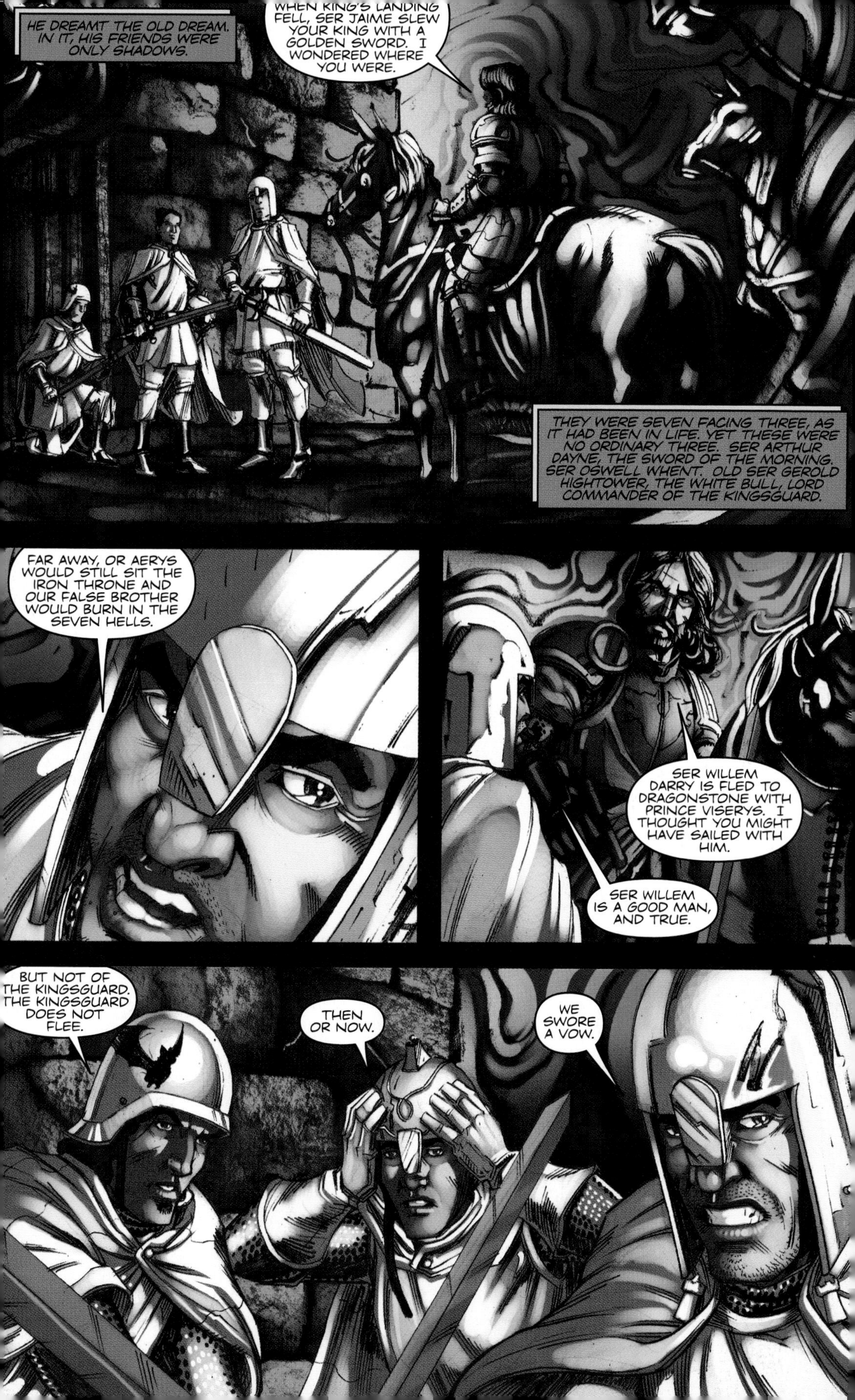
HE DREAMT THE OLD DREAM. IN IT, HIS FRIENDS WERE ONLY SHADOWS.
WHEN KING'S LANDING FELL, SER JAIME SLEW YOUR KING WITH A GOLDEN SWORD. I WONDERED WHERE YOU WERE.
THEY WERE SEVEN FACING THREE, AS IT HAD BEEN IN LIFE. YET THESE WERE NO ORDINARY THREE. SER ARTHUR DAYNE, THE SWORD OF THE MORNING. SER OSWELL WHENT. OLD SER GEROLD HIGHTOWER, THE WHITE BULL, LORD COMMANDER OF THE KINGSGUARD.
FAR AWAY, OR AERYS WOULD STILL SIT THE IRON THRONE AND OUR FALSE BROTHER WOULD BURN IN THE SEVEN HELLS.
SER WILLEM DARRY IS FLED TO DRAGONSTONE WITH PRINCE VISERYS. I THOUGHT YOU MIGHT HAVE SAILED WITH HIM.
SER WILLEM IS A GOOD MAN, AND TRUE.
BUT NOT OF THE KINGSGUARD. THE KINGSGUARD DOES NOT FLEE.
THEN OR NOW.
WE SWORE A VOW.

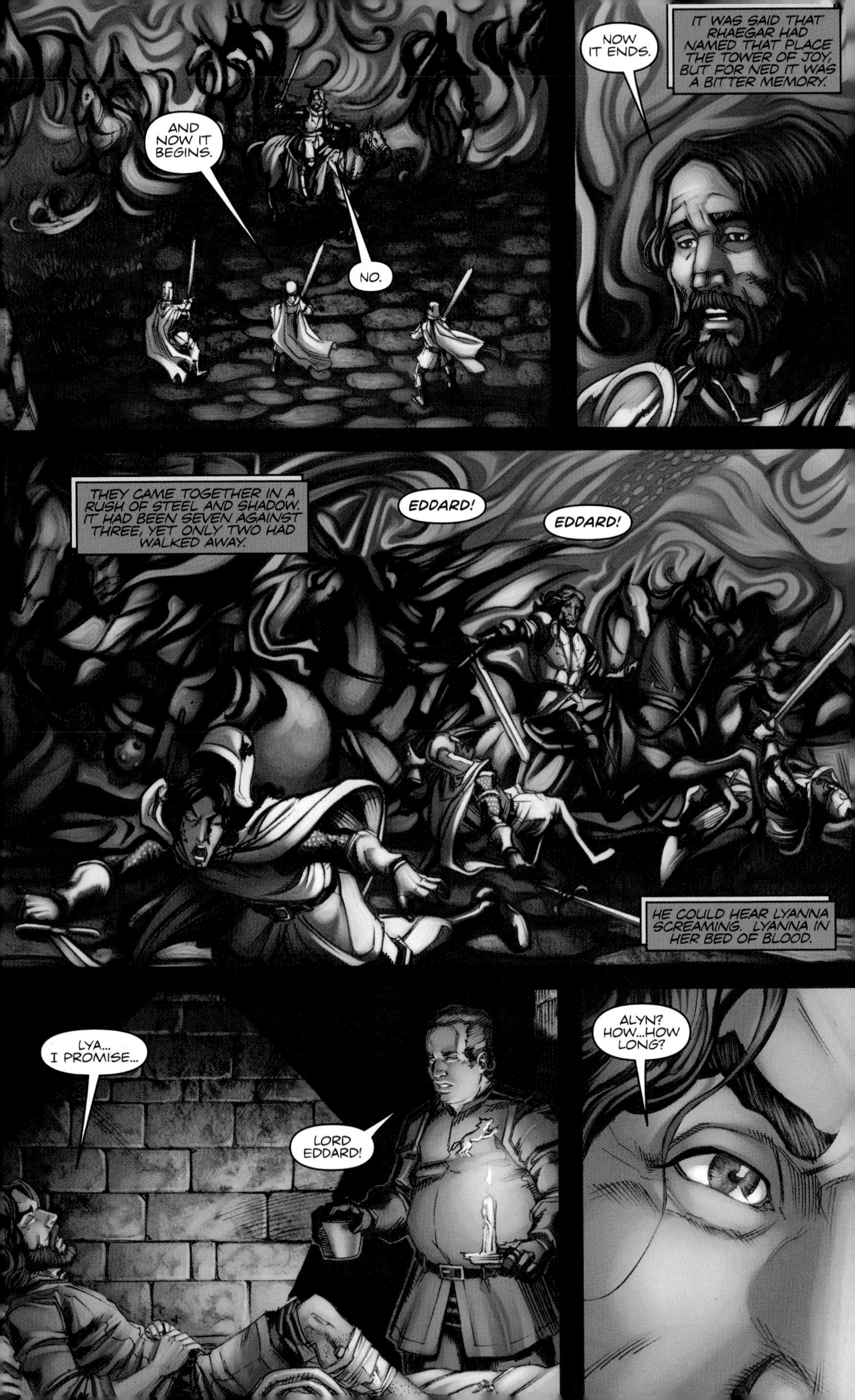
AND NOW IT BEGINS.
NO.
NOW IT ENDS.
IT WAS SAID THAT RHAEGAR HAD NAMED THAT PLACE THE TOWER OF JOY, BUT FOR NED IT WAS A BITTER MEMORY.
THEY CAME TOGETHER IN A RUSH OF STEEL AND SHADOW. IT HAD BEEN SEVEN AGAINST THREE, YET ONLY TWO HAD WALKED AWAY.
EDDARD!
EDDARD!
HE COULD HEAR LYANNA SCREAMING. LYANNA IN HER BED OF BLOOD.
LYA... I PROMISE...
LORD EDDARD!
ALYN? HOW...HOW LONG?

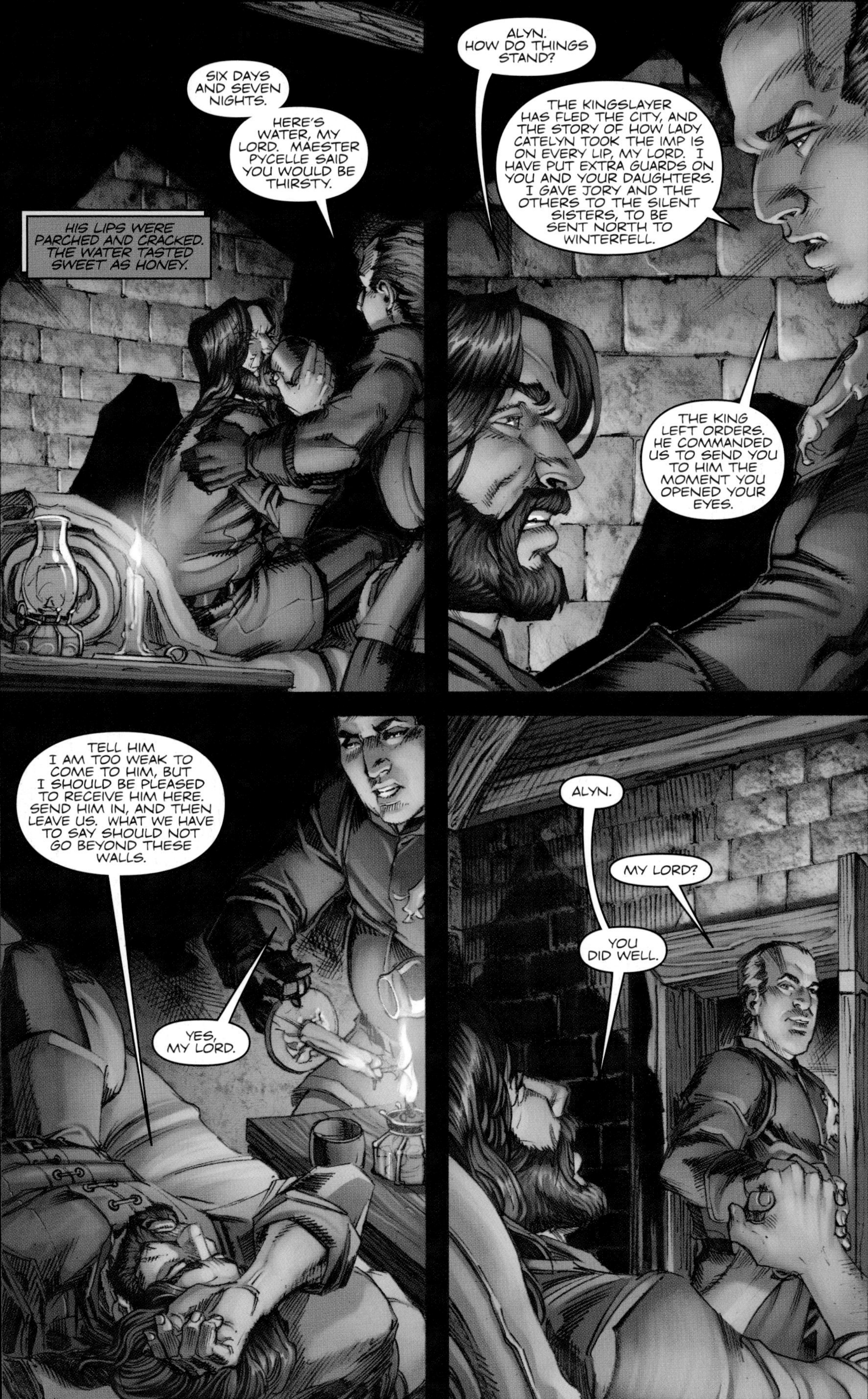
SIX DAYS AND SEVEN NIGHTS.
HERE'S WATER, MY LORD. MAESTER PYCELLE SAID YOU WOULD BE THIRSTY.
HIS LIPS WERE PARCHED AND CRACKED. THE WATER TASTED SWEET AS HONEY.
ALYN. HOW DO THINGS STAND?
THE KINGSLAYER HAS FLED THE CITY, AND THE STORY OF HOW LADY CATELYN TOOK THE IMP IS ON EVERY LIP, MY LORD. I HAVE PUT EXTRA GUARDS ON YOU AND YOUR DAUGHTERS. I GAVE JORY AND THE OTHERS TO THE SILENT SISTERS, TO BE SENT NORTH TO WINTERFELL.
THE KING LEFT ORDERS. HE COMMANDED US TO SEND YOU TO HIM THE MOMENT YOU OPENED YOUR EYES.
TELL HIM I AM TOO WEAK TO COME TO HIM, BUT I SHOULD BE PLEASED TO RECEIVE HIM HERE. SEND HIM IN, AND THEN LEAVE US. WHAT WE HAVE TO SAY SHOULD NOT GO BEYOND THESE WALLS.
YES, MY LORD.
ALYN.
MY LORD?
YOU DID WELL.

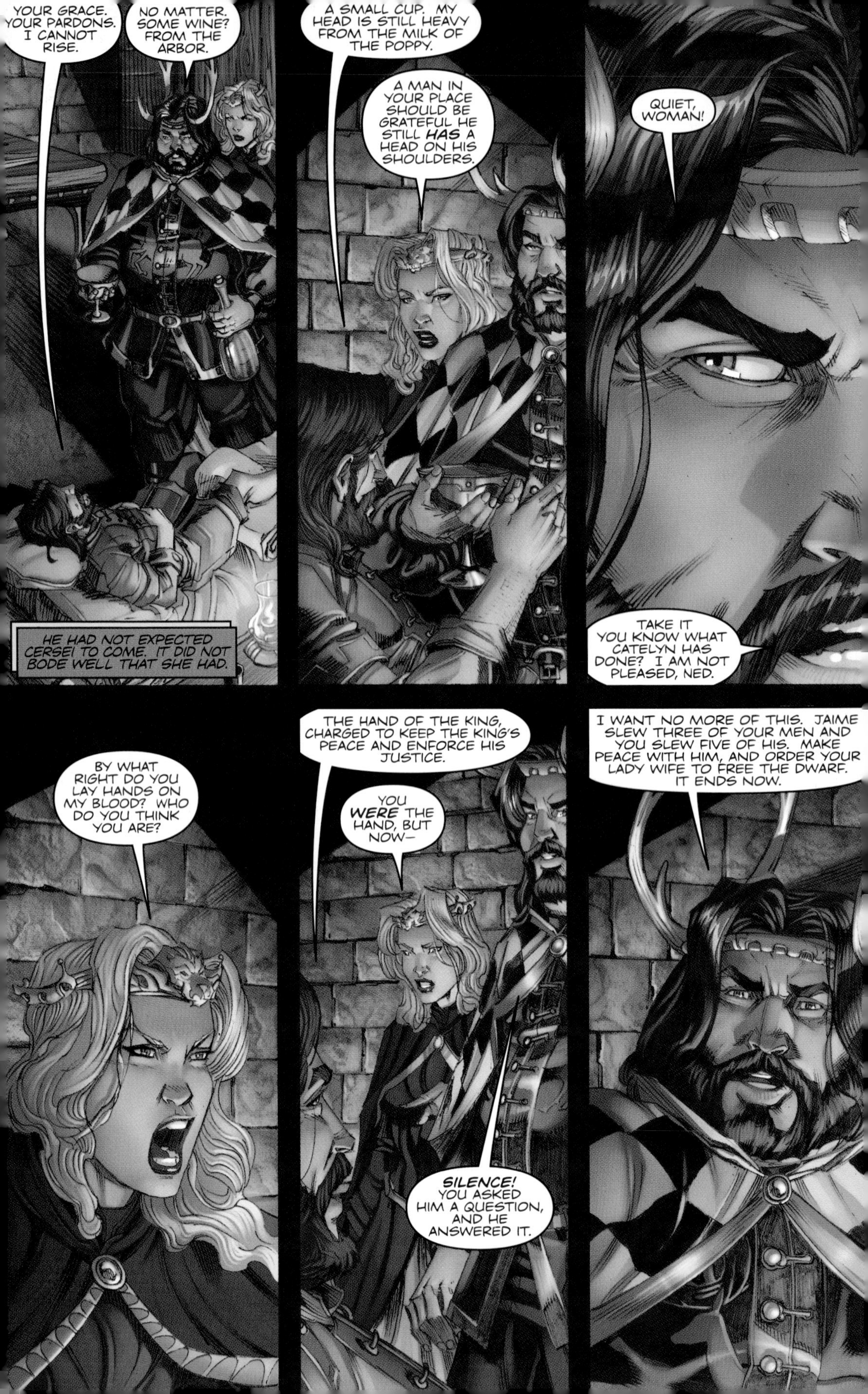
YOUR GRACE. YOUR PARDONS. I CANNOT RISE.
NO MATTER. SOME WINE? FROM THE ARBOR.
HE HAD NOT EXPECTED CERSEI TO COME. IT DID NOT BODE WELL THAT SHE HAD.
A SMALL CUP. MY HEAD IS STILL HEAVY FROM THE MILK OF THE POPPY.
A MAN IN YOUR PLACE SHOULD BE GRATEFUL HE STILL **HAS** A HEAD ON HIS SHOULDERS.
QUIET, WOMAN!
TAKE IT YOU KNOW WHAT CATELYN HAS DONE? I AM NOT PLEASED, NED.
BY WHAT RIGHT DO YOU LAY HANDS ON MY BLOOD? WHO DO YOU THINK YOU ARE?
THE HAND OF THE KING, CHARGED TO KEEP THE KING'S PEACE AND ENFORCE HIS JUSTICE.
YOU **WERE** THE HAND, BUT NOW—
**SILENCE!** YOU ASKED HIM A QUESTION, AND HE ANSWERED IT.
I WANT NO MORE OF THIS. JAIME SLEW THREE OF YOUR MEN AND YOU SLEW FIVE OF HIS. MAKE PEACE WITH HIM, AND ORDER YOUR LADY WIFE TO FREE THE DWARF. IT ENDS NOW.

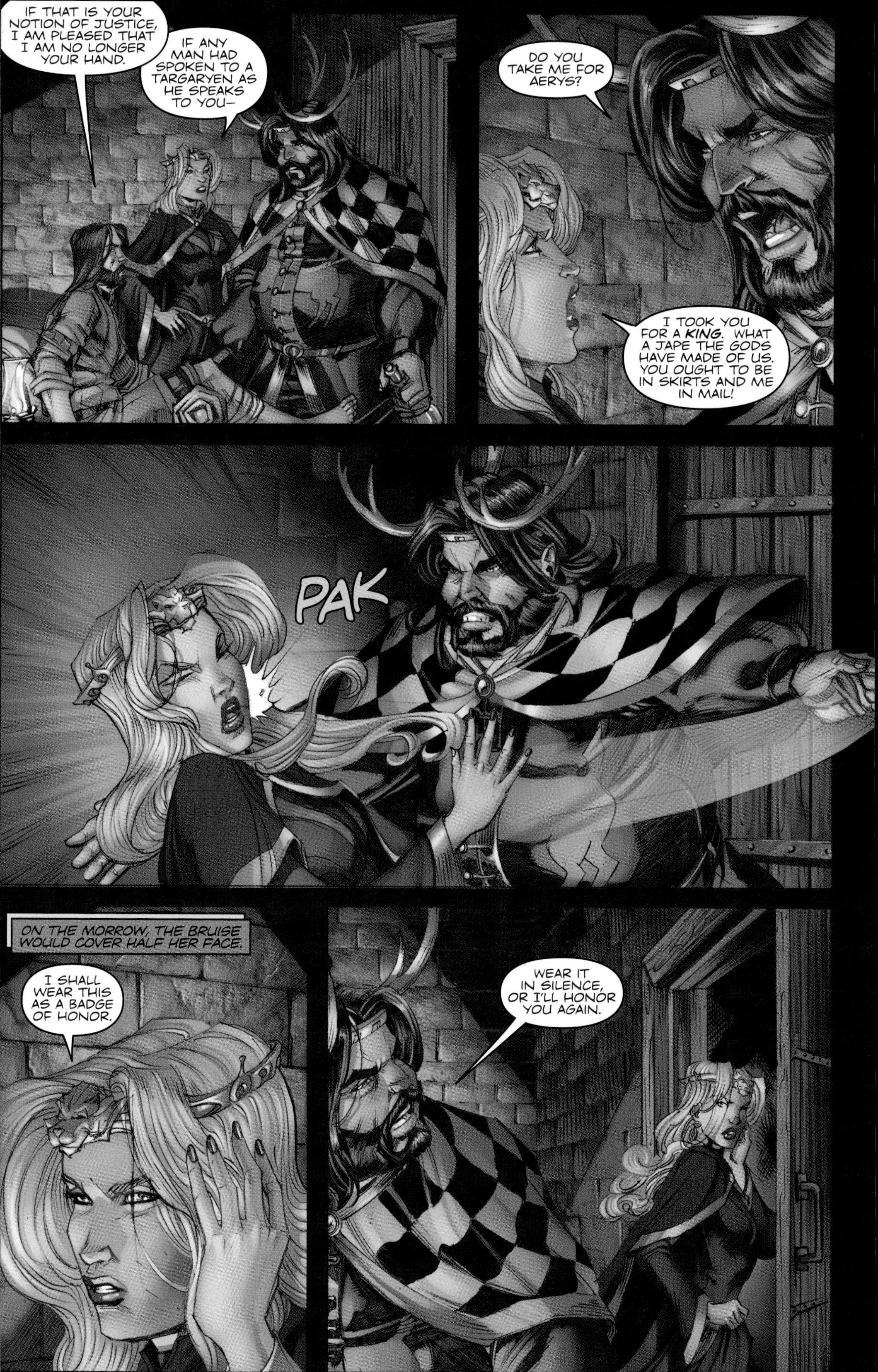
IF THAT IS YOUR NOTION OF JUSTICE, I AM PLEASED THAT I AM NO LONGER YOUR HAND.
IF ANY MAN HAD SPOKEN TO A TARGARYEN AS HE SPEAKS TO YOU–
DO YOU TAKE ME FOR AERYS?
I TOOK YOU FOR A KING. WHAT A JAPE THE GODS HAVE MADE OF US. YOU OUGHT TO BE IN SKIRTS AND ME IN MAIL!
PAK
ON THE MORROW, THE BRUISE WOULD COVER HALF HER FACE.
I SHALL WEAR THIS AS A BADGE OF HONOR.
WEAR IT IN SILENCE, OR I'LL HONOR YOU AGAIN.

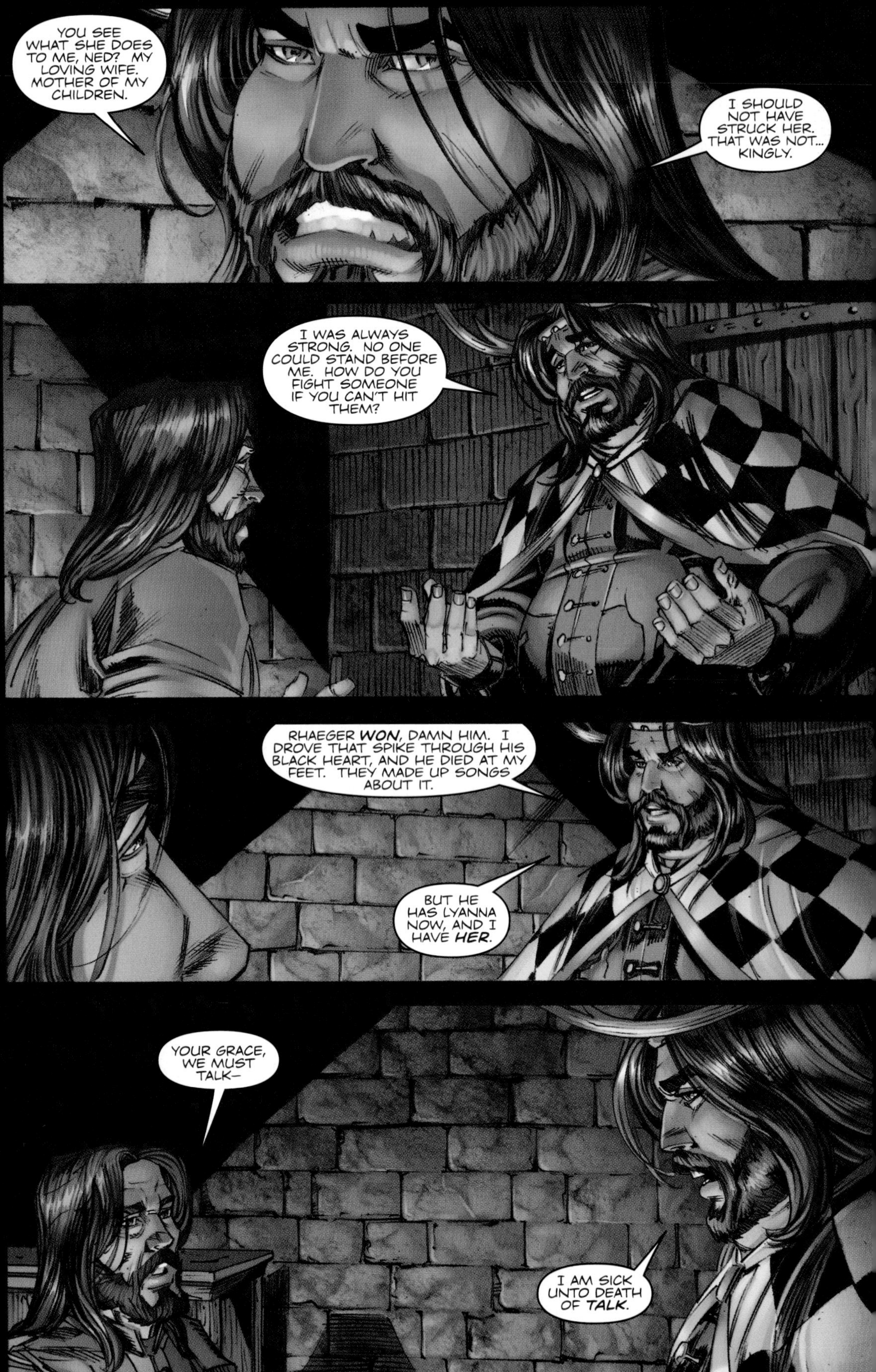
YOU SEE WHAT SHE DOES TO ME, NED? MY LOVING WIFE. MOTHER OF MY CHILDREN.
I SHOULD NOT HAVE STRUCK HER. THAT WAS NOT... KINGLY.
I WAS ALWAYS STRONG. NO ONE COULD STAND BEFORE ME. HOW DO YOU FIGHT SOMEONE IF YOU CAN'T HIT THEM?
RHAEGER **WON**, DAMN HIM. I DROVE THAT SPIKE THROUGH HIS BLACK HEART, AND HE DIED AT MY FEET. THEY MADE UP SONGS ABOUT IT.
BUT HE HAS LYANNA NOW, AND I HAVE **HER**.
YOUR GRACE, WE MUST TALK—
I AM SICK UNTO DEATH OF **TALK**.

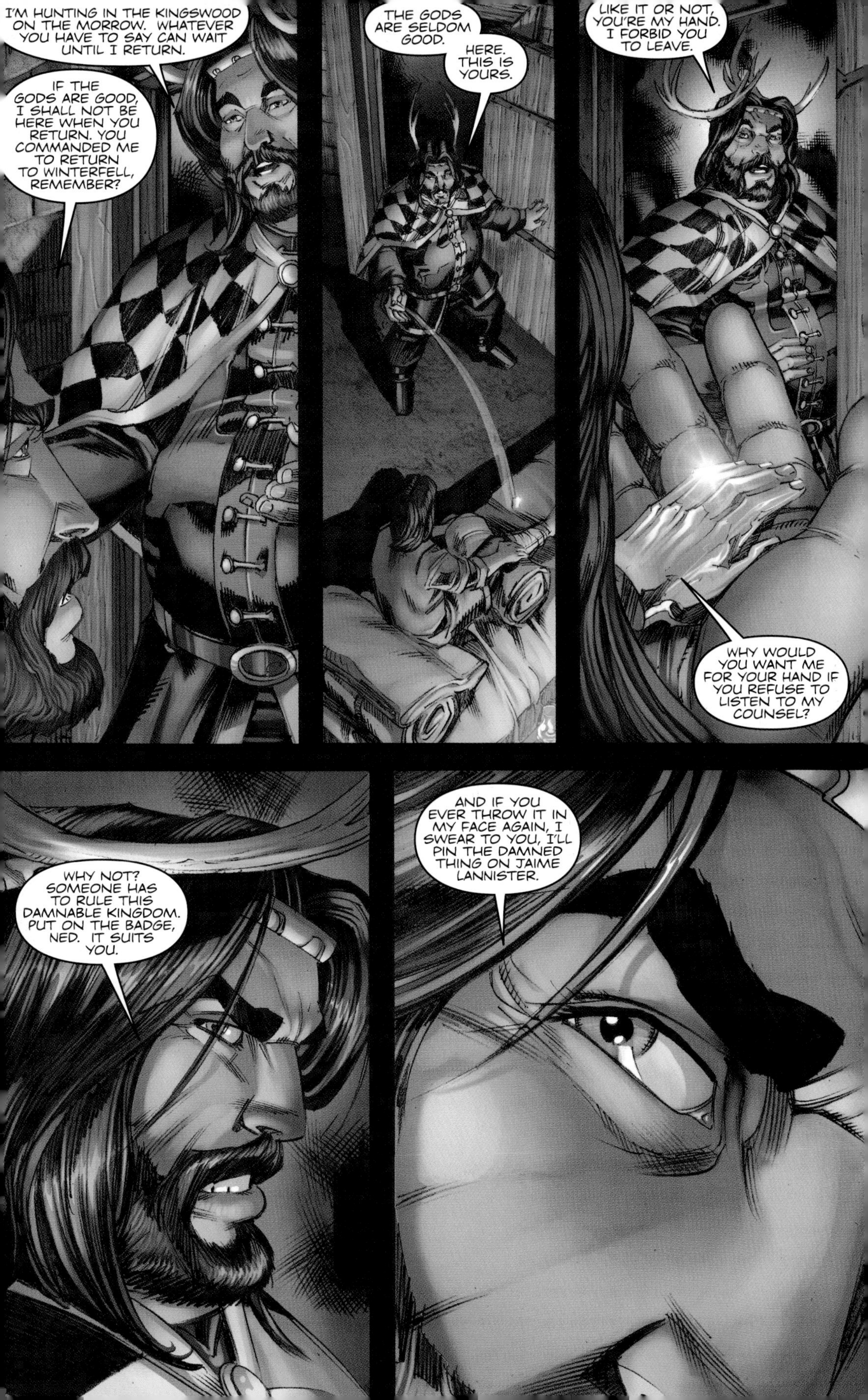
I'M HUNTING IN THE KINGSWOOD ON THE MORROW. WHATEVER YOU HAVE TO SAY CAN WAIT UNTIL I RETURN.
IF THE GODS ARE GOOD, I SHALL NOT BE HERE WHEN YOU RETURN. YOU COMMANDED ME TO RETURN TO WINTERFELL, REMEMBER?
THE GODS ARE SELDOM GOOD.
HERE. THIS IS YOURS.
LIKE IT OR NOT, YOU'RE MY HAND. I FORBID YOU TO LEAVE.
WHY WOULD YOU WANT ME FOR YOUR HAND IF YOU REFUSE TO LISTEN TO MY COUNSEL?
WHY NOT? SOMEONE HAS TO RULE THIS DAMNABLE KINGDOM. PUT ON THE BADGE, NED. IT SUITS YOU.
AND IF YOU EVER THROW IT IN MY FACE AGAIN, I SWEAR TO YOU, I'LL PIN THE DAMNED THING ON JAIME LANNISTER.

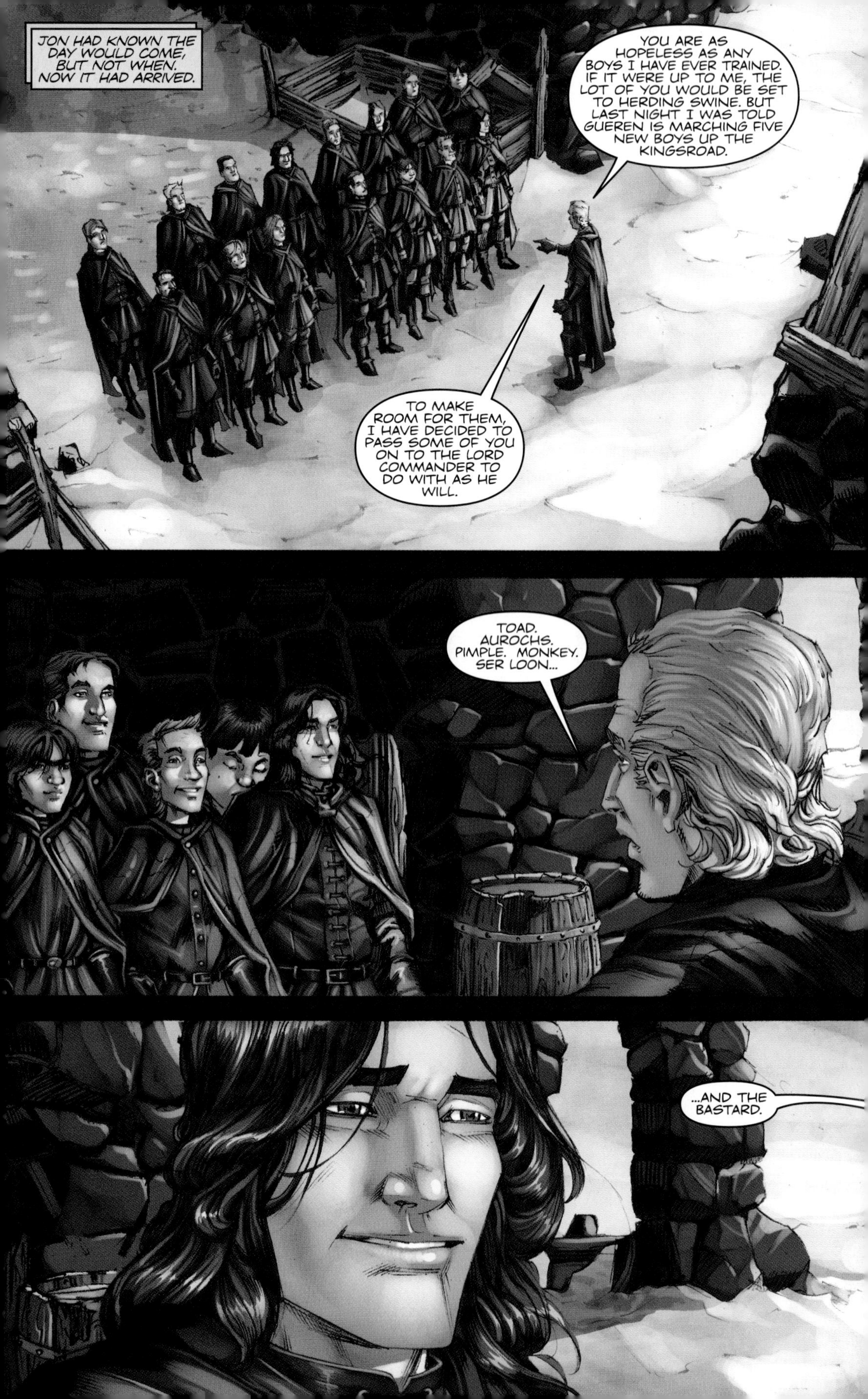
JON HAD KNOWN THE DAY WOULD COME, BUT NOT WHEN. NOW IT HAD ARRIVED.
YOU ARE AS HOPELESS AS ANY BOYS I HAVE EVER TRAINED. IF IT WERE UP TO ME, THE LOT OF YOU WOULD BE SET TO HERDING SWINE. BUT LAST NIGHT I WAS TOLD GUEREN IS MARCHING FIVE NEW BOYS UP THE KINGSROAD.
TO MAKE ROOM FOR THEM, I HAVE DECIDED TO PASS SOME OF YOU ON TO THE LORD COMMANDER TO DO WITH AS HE WILL.
TOAD. AUROCHS. PIMPLE. MONKEY. SER LOON...
...AND THE BASTARD.

WHOO!

BE QUIET, YOU IDIOT.

THEY WILL CALL YOU MEN OF THE NIGHT'S WATCH NOW. BUT YOU ARE BIGGER FOOLS THAN THE MUMMER'S MONKEY HERE IF YOU BELIEVE THAT.

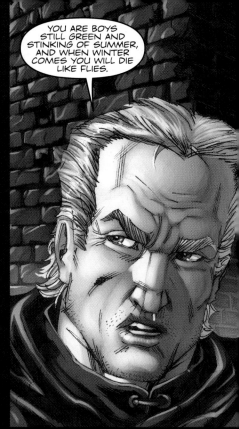

YOU ARE BOYS STILL GREEN AND STINKING OF SUMMER, AND WHEN WINTER COMES YOU WILL DIE LIKE FLIES.

AND WITH THAT, SER ALLISER THORNE TOOK LEAVE OF THEM.

THAT NIGHT, THREE-FINGER HOBB COOKED A SPECIAL MEAL TO MARK THE OCCASION, AND THE LORD STEWARD HIMSELF LED THEM TO THE BENCH NEAR THE FIRE.

DO YOU THINK THEY'LL KEEP US TOGETHER?

I HOPE NOT. I'M SICK OF LOOKING AT THOSE EARS OF YOURS, PYP.

YOU'RE CERTAIN TO BE A RANGER, TOAD. THEY'LL WANT YOU AS FAR AWAY FROM THE CASTLE AS THEY CAN. IF MANCE RAYNER ATTACKS, LIFT YOUR VISOR AND HE'LL RUN OFF SCREAMING.

I HOPE I'M A RANGER.

YOU AND EVERYONE ELSE.

NOT EVERYONE. IT'S THE BUILDERS FOR ME. WHAT USE ARE RANGERS IF THE WALL FALLS DOWN?

THE OLD BEAR'S NO FOOL. YOU'LL BE A BUILDER, HALDER. JON WILL BE A RANGER. HE'S THE BEST SWORD AND RIDER AMONG US, AND HIS UNCLE WAS THE FIRST RANGER BEFORE HE—

BENJEN STARK IS STILL FIRST RANGER.

JON! ARE YOU GOING TO EAT THOSE?

THEY'RE YOURS, GRENN.

THE REST MIGHT HAVE GIVEN UP ALL HOPE OF HIS UNCLE'S SAFE RETURN, BUT HE HADN'T.

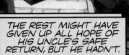

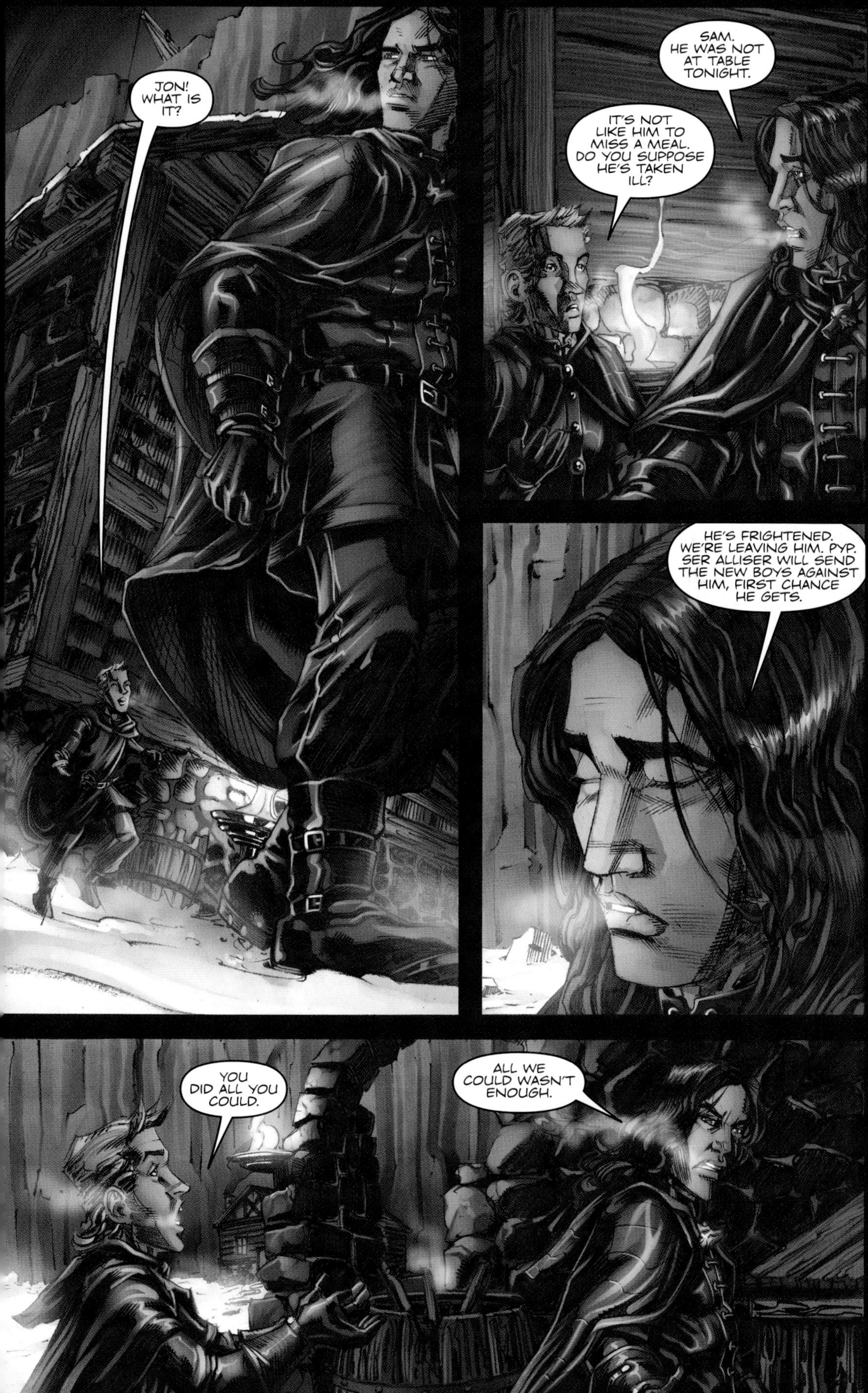
JON! WHAT IS IT?
SAM. HE WAS NOT AT TABLE TONIGHT.
IT'S NOT LIKE HIM TO MISS A MEAL. DO YOU SUPPOSE HE'S TAKEN ILL?
HE'S FRIGHTENED. WE'RE LEAVING HIM, PYP. SER ALLISER WILL SEND THE NEW BOYS AGAINST HIM, FIRST CHANCE HE GETS.
YOU DID ALL YOU COULD.
ALL WE COULD WASN'T ENOUGH.

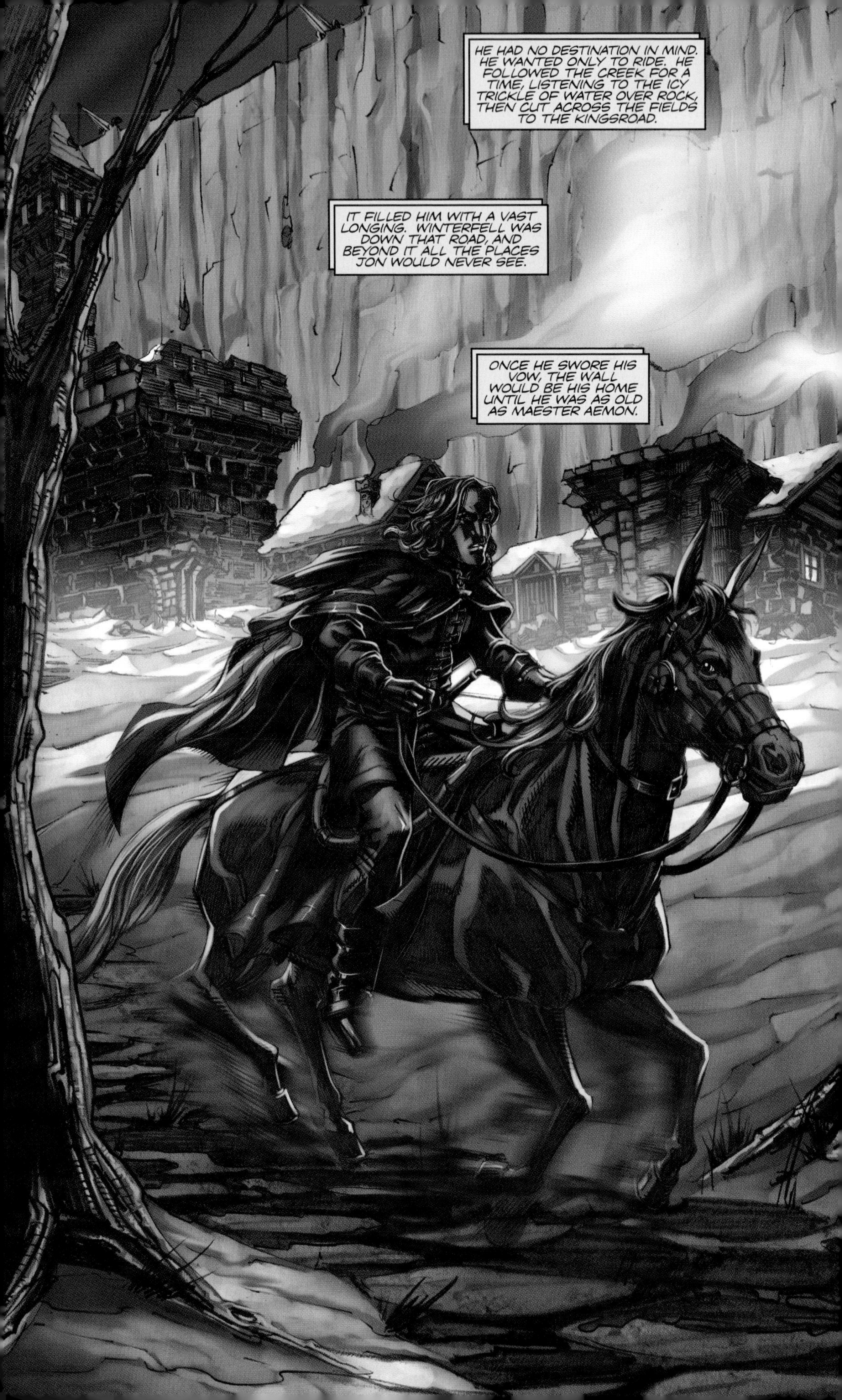
HE HAD NO DESTINATION IN MIND. HE WANTED ONLY TO RIDE. HE FOLLOWED THE CREEK FOR A TIME, LISTENING TO THE ICY TRICKLE OF WATER OVER ROCK, THEN CUT ACROSS THE FIELDS TO THE KINGSROAD.
IT FILLED HIM WITH A VAST LONGING. WINTERFELL WAS DOWN THAT ROAD, AND BEYOND IT ALL THE PLACES JON WOULD NEVER SEE.
ONCE HE SWORE HIS VOW, THE WALL WOULD BE HIS HOME UNTIL HE WAS AS OLD AS MAESTER AEMON.

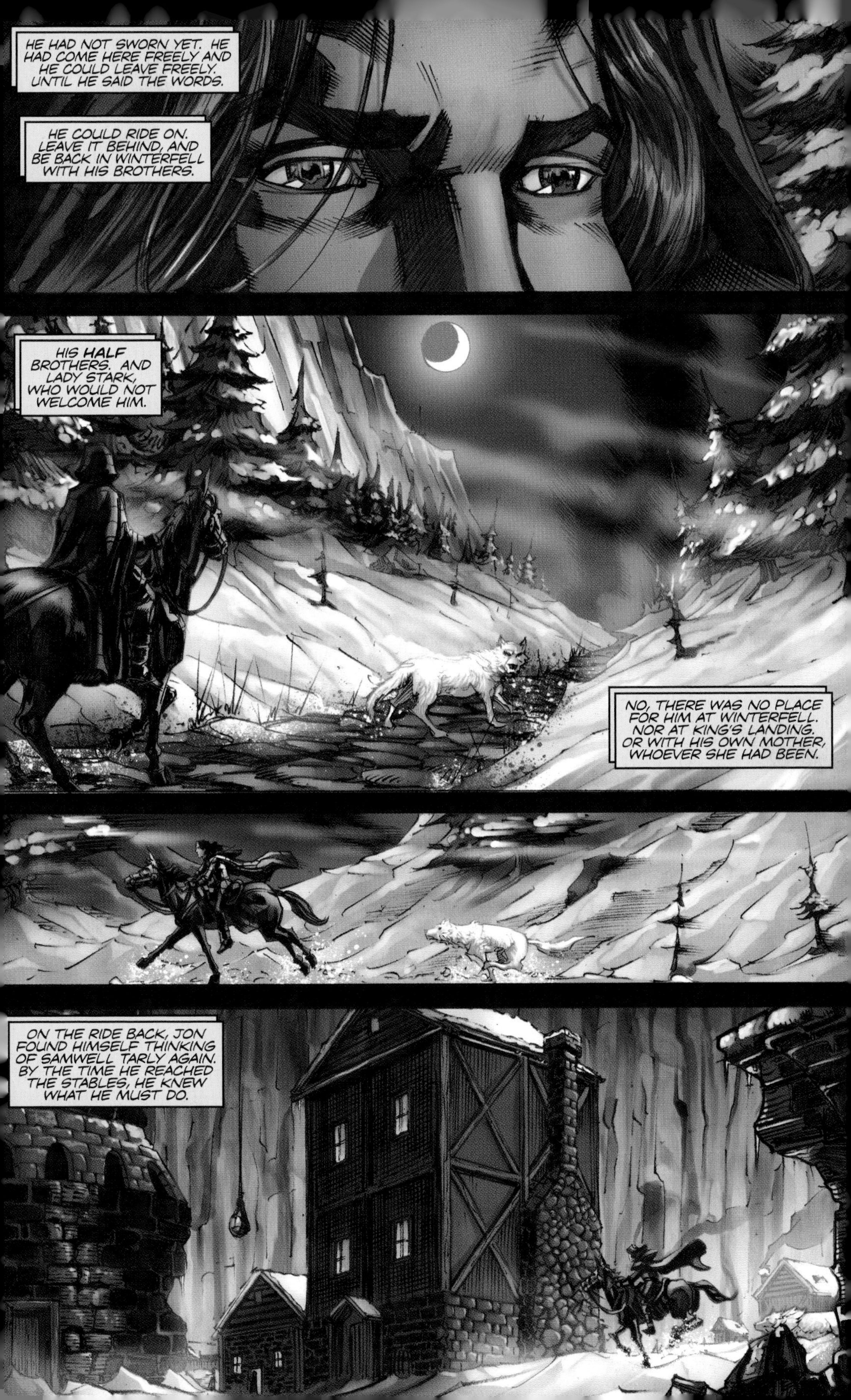
HE HAD NOT SWORN YET. HE HAD COME HERE FREELY AND HE COULD LEAVE FREELY. UNTIL HE SAID THE WORDS.
HE COULD RIDE ON. LEAVE IT BEHIND, AND BE BACK IN WINTERFELL WITH HIS BROTHERS.
HIS **HALF** BROTHERS. AND LADY STARK, WHO WOULD NOT WELCOME HIM.
NO, THERE WAS NO PLACE FOR HIM AT WINTERFELL. NOR AT KING'S LANDING. OR WITH HIS OWN MOTHER, WHOEVER SHE HAD BEEN.
ON THE RIDE BACK, JON FOUND HIMSELF THINKING OF SAMWELL TARLY AGAIN. BY THE TIME HE REACHED THE STABLES, HE KNEW WHAT HE MUST DO.

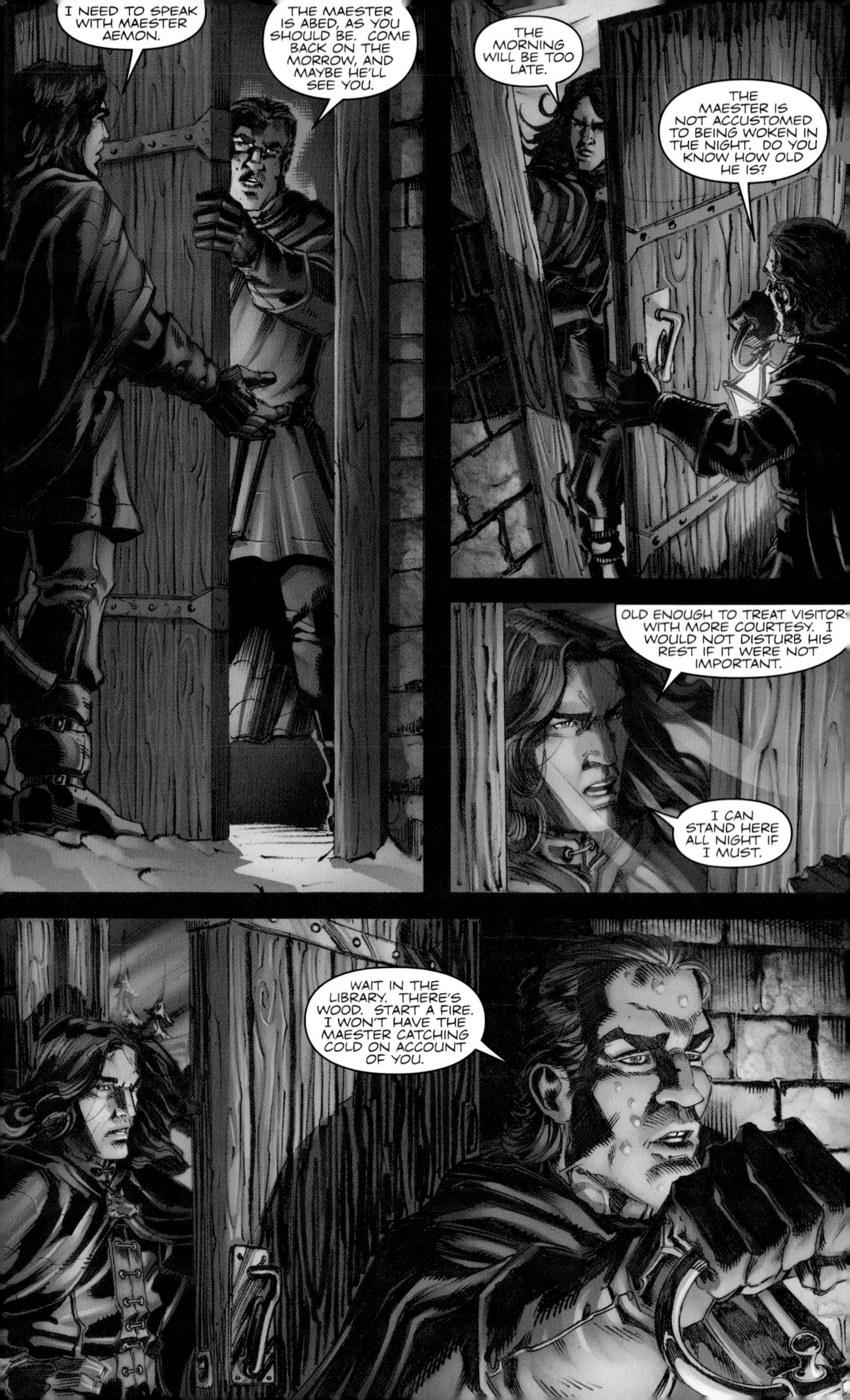
I NEED TO SPEAK WITH MAESTER AEMON.
THE MAESTER IS ABED, AS YOU SHOULD BE. COME BACK ON THE MORROW, AND MAYBE HE'LL SEE YOU.
THE MORNING WILL BE TOO LATE.
THE MAESTER IS NOT ACCUSTOMED TO BEING WOKEN IN THE NIGHT. DO YOU KNOW HOW OLD HE IS?
OLD ENOUGH TO TREAT VISITORS WITH MORE COURTESY. I WOULD NOT DISTURB HIS REST IF IT WERE NOT IMPORTANT.
I CAN STAND HERE ALL NIGHT IF I MUST.
WAIT IN THE LIBRARY. THERE'S WOOD. START A FIRE. I WON'T HAVE THE MAESTER CATCHING COLD ON ACCOUNT OF YOU.

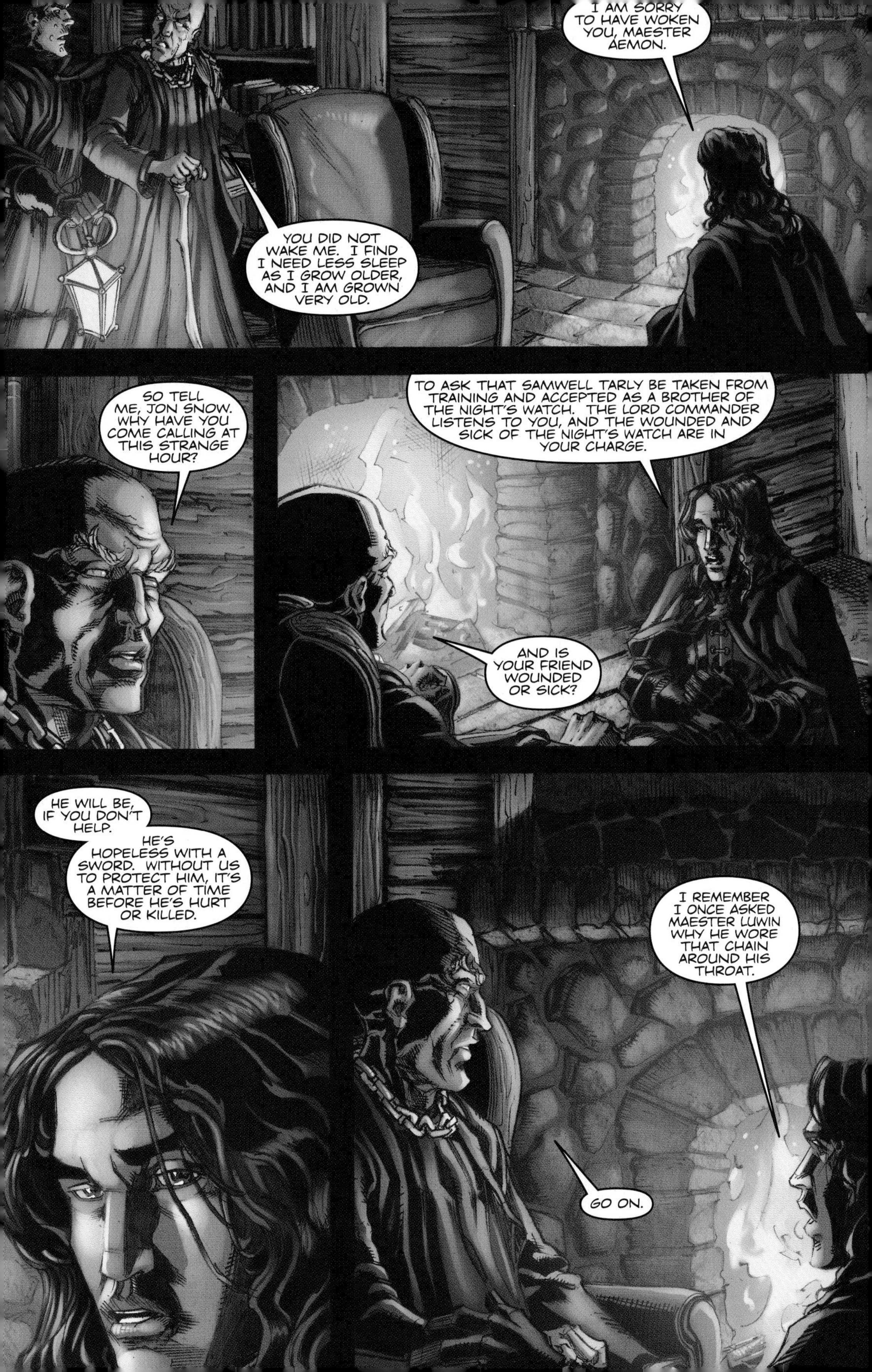
I AM SORRY TO HAVE WOKEN YOU, MAESTER AEMON.
YOU DID NOT WAKE ME. I FIND I NEED LESS SLEEP AS I GROW OLDER, AND I AM GROWN VERY OLD.
SO TELL ME, JON SNOW. WHY HAVE YOU COME CALLING AT THIS STRANGE HOUR?
TO ASK THAT SAMWELL TARLY BE TAKEN FROM TRAINING AND ACCEPTED AS A BROTHER OF THE NIGHT'S WATCH. THE LORD COMMANDER LISTENS TO YOU, AND THE WOUNDED AND SICK OF THE NIGHT'S WATCH ARE IN YOUR CHARGE.
AND IS YOUR FRIEND WOUNDED OR SICK?
HE WILL BE, IF YOU DON'T HELP.
HE'S HOPELESS WITH A SWORD. WITHOUT US TO PROTECT HIM, IT'S A MATTER OF TIME BEFORE HE'S HURT OR KILLED.
I REMEMBER I ONCE ASKED MAESTER LUWIN WHY HE WORE THAT CHAIN AROUND HIS THROAT.
GO ON.

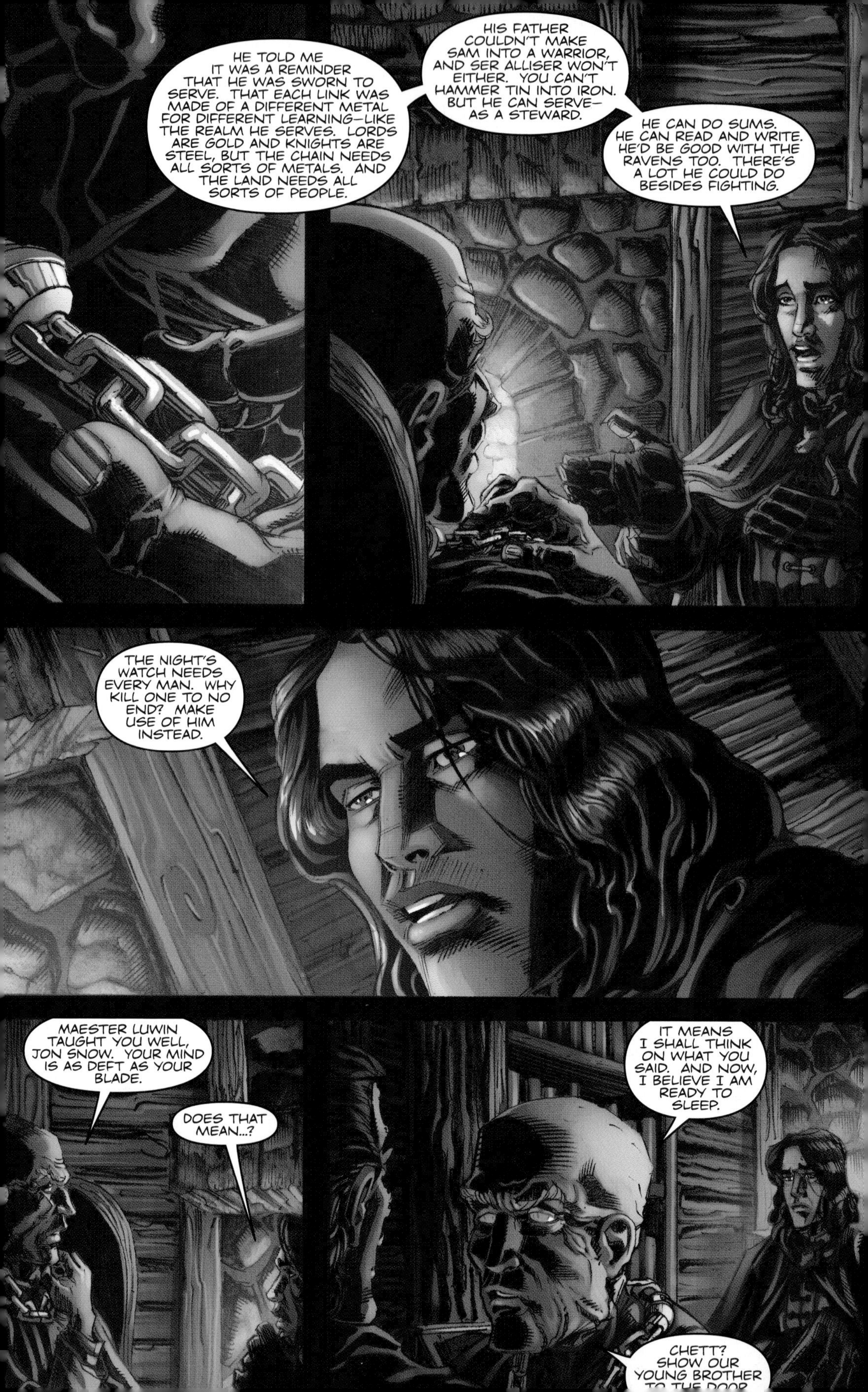
HE TOLD ME IT WAS A REMINDER THAT HE WAS SWORN TO SERVE. THAT EACH LINK WAS MADE OF A DIFFERENT METAL FOR DIFFERENT LEARNING—LIKE THE REALM HE SERVES. LORDS ARE GOLD AND KNIGHTS ARE STEEL, BUT THE CHAIN NEEDS ALL SORTS OF METALS. AND THE LAND NEEDS ALL SORTS OF PEOPLE.
HIS FATHER COULDN'T MAKE SAM INTO A WARRIOR, AND SER ALLISER WON'T EITHER. YOU CAN'T HAMMER TIN INTO IRON. BUT HE CAN SERVE—AS A STEWARD.
HE CAN DO SUMS. HE CAN READ AND WRITE. HE'D BE GOOD WITH THE RAVENS TOO. THERE'S A LOT HE COULD DO BESIDES FIGHTING.
THE NIGHT'S WATCH NEEDS EVERY MAN. WHY KILL ONE TO NO END? MAKE USE OF HIM INSTEAD.
MAESTER LUWIN TAUGHT YOU WELL, JON SNOW. YOUR MIND IS AS DEFT AS YOUR BLADE.
DOES THAT MEAN...?
IT MEANS I SHALL THINK ON WHAT YOU SAID. AND NOW, I BELIEVE I AM READY TO SLEEP.
CHETT? SHOW OUR YOUNG BROTHER

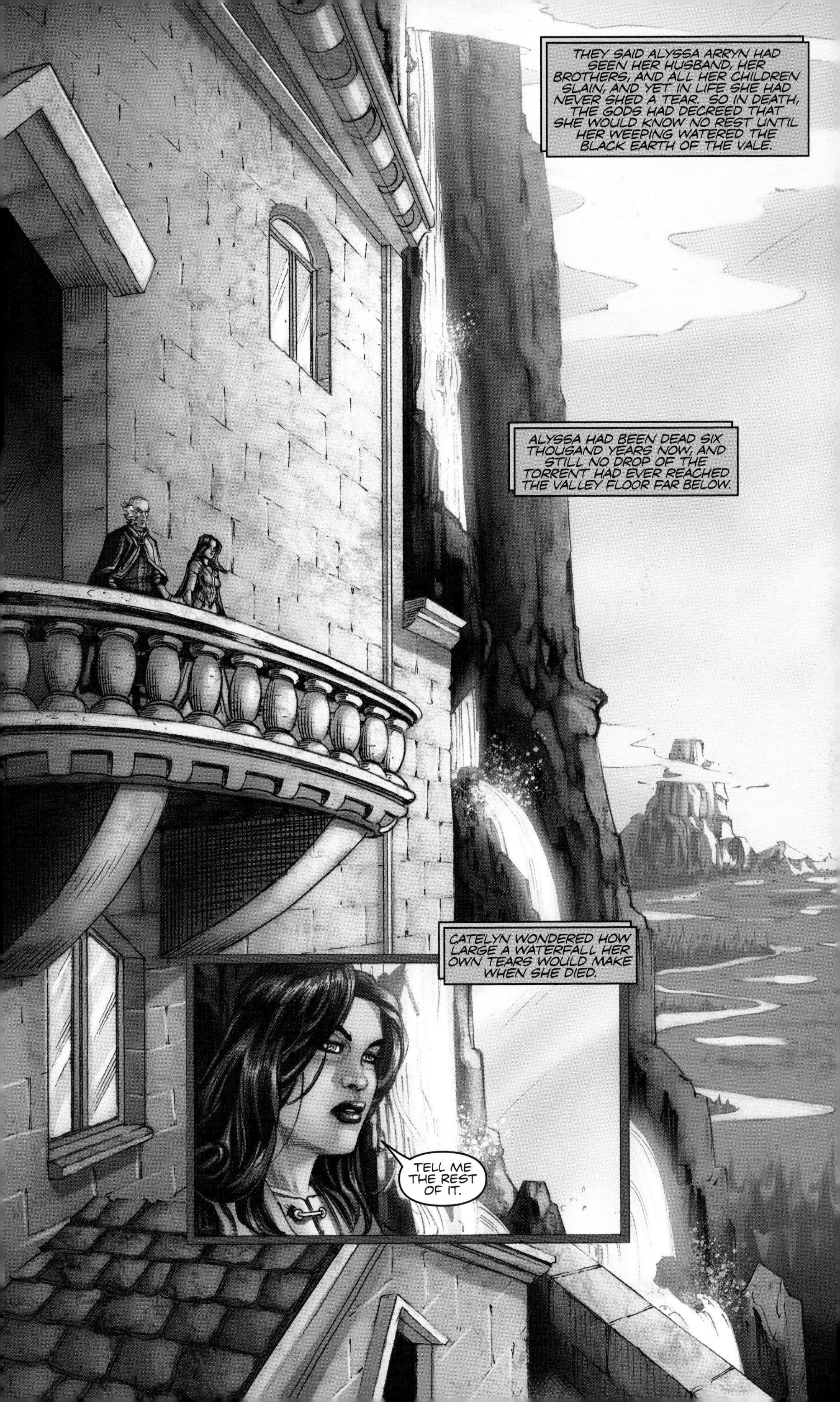
THEY SAID ALYSSA ARRYN HAD SEEN HER HUSBAND, HER BROTHERS, AND ALL HER CHILDREN SLAIN, AND YET IN LIFE SHE HAD NEVER SHED A TEAR. SO IN DEATH, THE GODS HAD DECREED THAT SHE WOULD KNOW NO REST UNTIL HER WEEPING WATERED THE BLACK EARTH OF THE VALE.
ALYSSA HAD BEEN DEAD SIX THOUSAND YEARS NOW, AND STILL NO DROP OF THE TORRENT HAD EVER REACHED THE VALLEY FLOOR FAR BELOW.
CATELYN WONDERED HOW LARGE A WATERFALL HER OWN TEARS WOULD MAKE WHEN SHE DIED.
TELL ME THE REST OF IT.

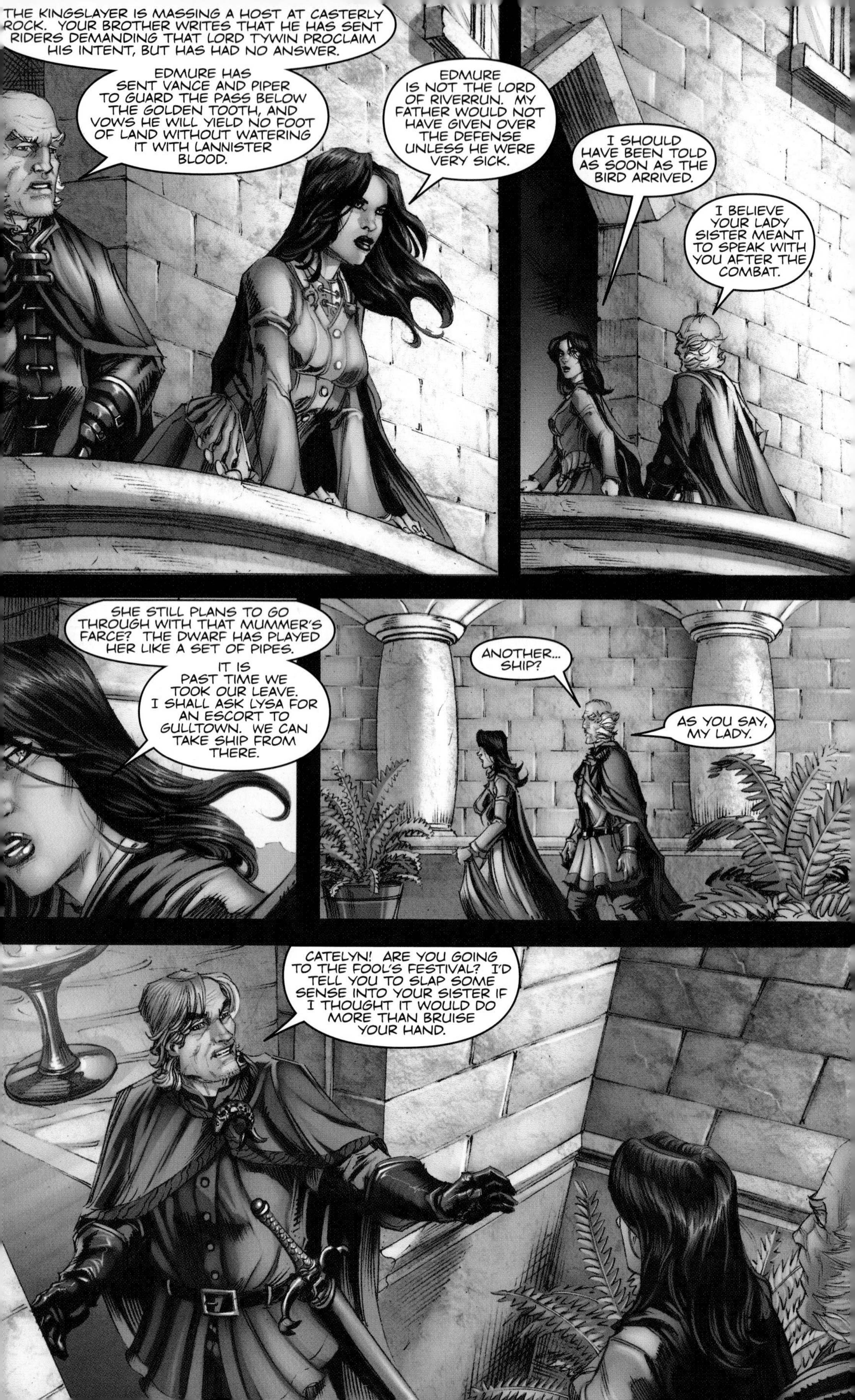
THE KINGSLAYER IS MASSING A HOST AT CASTERLY ROCK. YOUR BROTHER WRITES THAT HE HAS SENT RIDERS DEMANDING THAT LORD TYWIN PROCLAIM HIS INTENT, BUT HAS HAD NO ANSWER.
EDMURE HAS SENT VANCE AND PIPER TO GUARD THE PASS BELOW THE GOLDEN TOOTH, AND VOWS HE WILL YIELD NO FOOT OF LAND WITHOUT WATERING IT WITH LANNISTER BLOOD.
EDMURE IS NOT THE LORD OF RIVERRUN. MY FATHER WOULD NOT HAVE GIVEN OVER THE DEFENSE UNLESS HE WERE VERY SICK.
I SHOULD HAVE BEEN TOLD AS SOON AS THE BIRD ARRIVED.
I BELIEVE YOUR LADY SISTER MEANT TO SPEAK WITH YOU AFTER THE COMBAT.
SHE STILL PLANS TO GO THROUGH WITH THAT MUMMER'S FARCE? THE DWARF HAS PLAYED HER LIKE A SET OF PIPES.
IT IS PAST TIME WE TOOK OUR LEAVE. I SHALL ASK LYSA FOR AN ESCORT TO GULLTOWN. WE CAN TAKE SHIP FROM THERE.
ANOTHER... SHIP?
AS YOU SAY, MY LADY.
CATELYN! ARE YOU GOING TO THE FOOL'S FESTIVAL? I'D TELL YOU TO SLAP SOME SENSE INTO YOUR SISTER IF I THOUGHT IT WOULD DO MORE THAN BRUISE YOUR HAND.

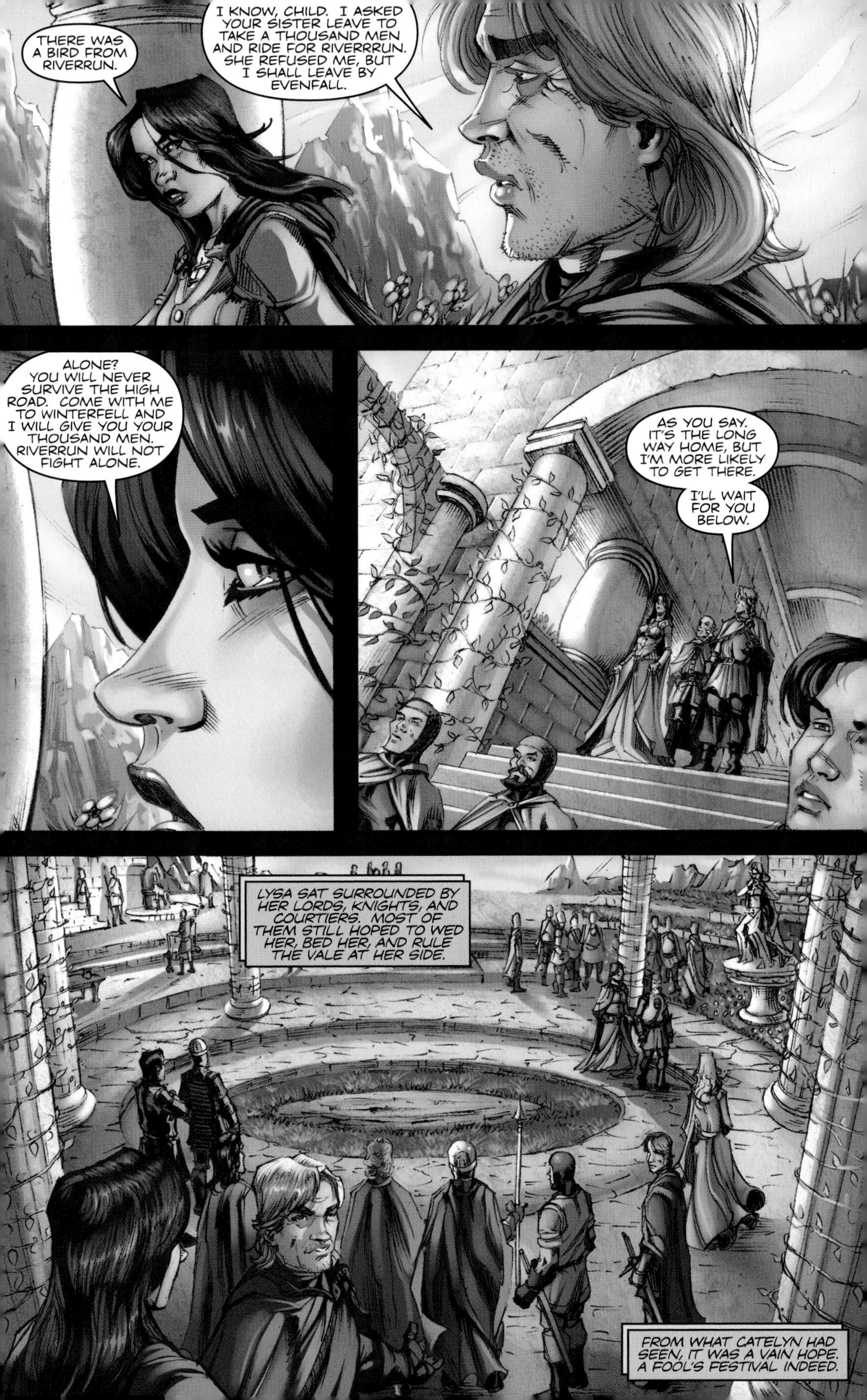
THERE WAS A BIRD FROM RIVERRUN.
I KNOW, CHILD. I ASKED YOUR SISTER LEAVE TO TAKE A THOUSAND MEN AND RIDE FOR RIVERRUN. SHE REFUSED ME, BUT I SHALL LEAVE BY EVENFALL.
ALONE? YOU WILL NEVER SURVIVE THE HIGH ROAD. COME WITH ME TO WINTERFELL AND I WILL GIVE YOU YOUR THOUSAND MEN. RIVERRUN WILL NOT FIGHT ALONE.
AS YOU SAY. IT'S THE LONG WAY HOME, BUT I'M MORE LIKELY TO GET THERE.
I'LL WAIT FOR YOU BELOW.
LYSA SAT SURROUNDED BY HER LORDS, KNIGHTS, AND COURTIERS. MOST OF THEM STILL HOPED TO WED HER, BED HER, AND RULE THE VALE AT HER SIDE.
FROM WHAT CATELYN HAD SEEN, IT WAS A VAIN HOPE. A FOOL'S FESTIVAL INDEED.

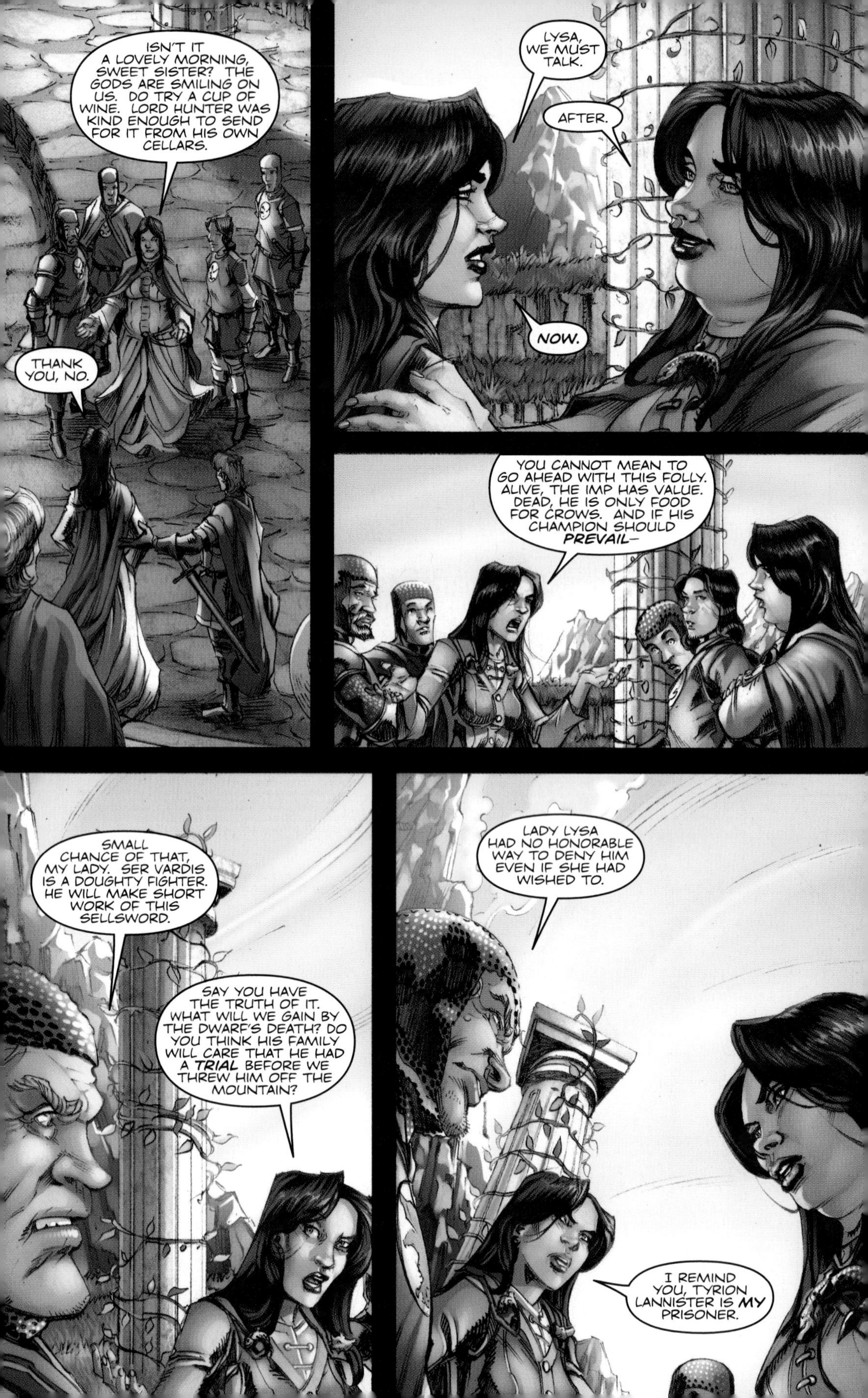
ISN'T IT A LOVELY MORNING, SWEET SISTER? THE GODS ARE SMILING ON US. DO TRY A CUP OF WINE. LORD HUNTER WAS KIND ENOUGH TO SEND FOR IT FROM HIS OWN CELLARS.
THANK YOU, NO.
LYSA, WE MUST TALK.
AFTER.
NOW.
YOU CANNOT MEAN TO GO AHEAD WITH THIS FOLLY. ALIVE, THE IMP HAS VALUE. DEAD, HE IS ONLY FOOD FOR CROWS. AND IF HIS CHAMPION SHOULD PREVAIL—
SMALL CHANCE OF THAT, MY LADY. SER VARDIS IS A DOUGHTY FIGHTER. HE WILL MAKE SHORT WORK OF THIS SELLSWORD.
SAY YOU HAVE THE TRUTH OF IT. WHAT WILL WE GAIN BY THE DWARF'S DEATH? DO YOU THINK HIS FAMILY WILL CARE THAT HE HAD A TRIAL BEFORE WE THREW HIM OFF THE MOUNTAIN?
LADY LYSA HAD NO HONORABLE WAY TO DENY HIM EVEN IF SHE HAD WISHED TO.
I REMIND YOU, TYRION LANNISTER IS MY PRISONER.

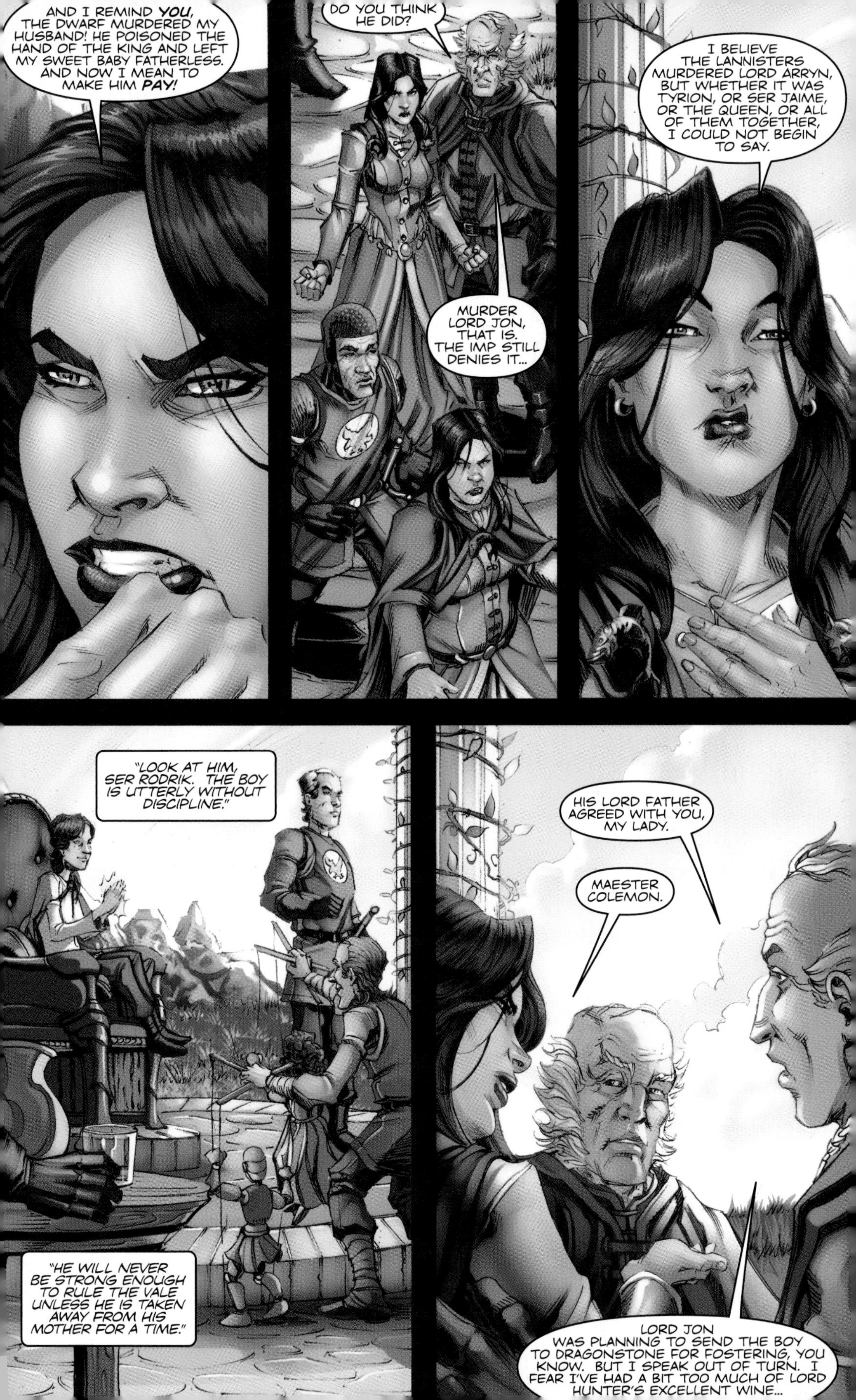
AND I REMIND YOU, THE DWARF MURDERED MY HUSBAND! HE POISONED THE HAND OF THE KING AND LEFT MY SWEET BABY FATHERLESS. AND NOW I MEAN TO MAKE HIM PAY!
DO YOU THINK HE DID?
MURDER LORD JON, THAT IS. THE IMP STILL DENIES IT...
I BELIEVE THE LANNISTERS MURDERED LORD ARRYN, BUT WHETHER IT WAS TYRION, OR SER JAIME, OR THE QUEEN, OR ALL OF THEM TOGETHER, I COULD NOT BEGIN TO SAY.
"LOOK AT HIM, SER RODRIK. THE BOY IS UTTERLY WITHOUT DISCIPLINE."
"HE WILL NEVER BE STRONG ENOUGH TO RULE THE VALE UNLESS HE IS TAKEN AWAY FROM HIS MOTHER FOR A TIME."
HIS LORD FATHER AGREED WITH YOU, MY LADY.
MAESTER COLEMON.
LORD JON WAS PLANNING TO SEND THE BOY TO DRAGONSTONE FOR FOSTERING, YOU KNOW. BUT I SPEAK OUT OF TURN. I FEAR I'VE HAD A BIT TOO MUCH OF LORD HUNTER'S EXCELLENT WINE...

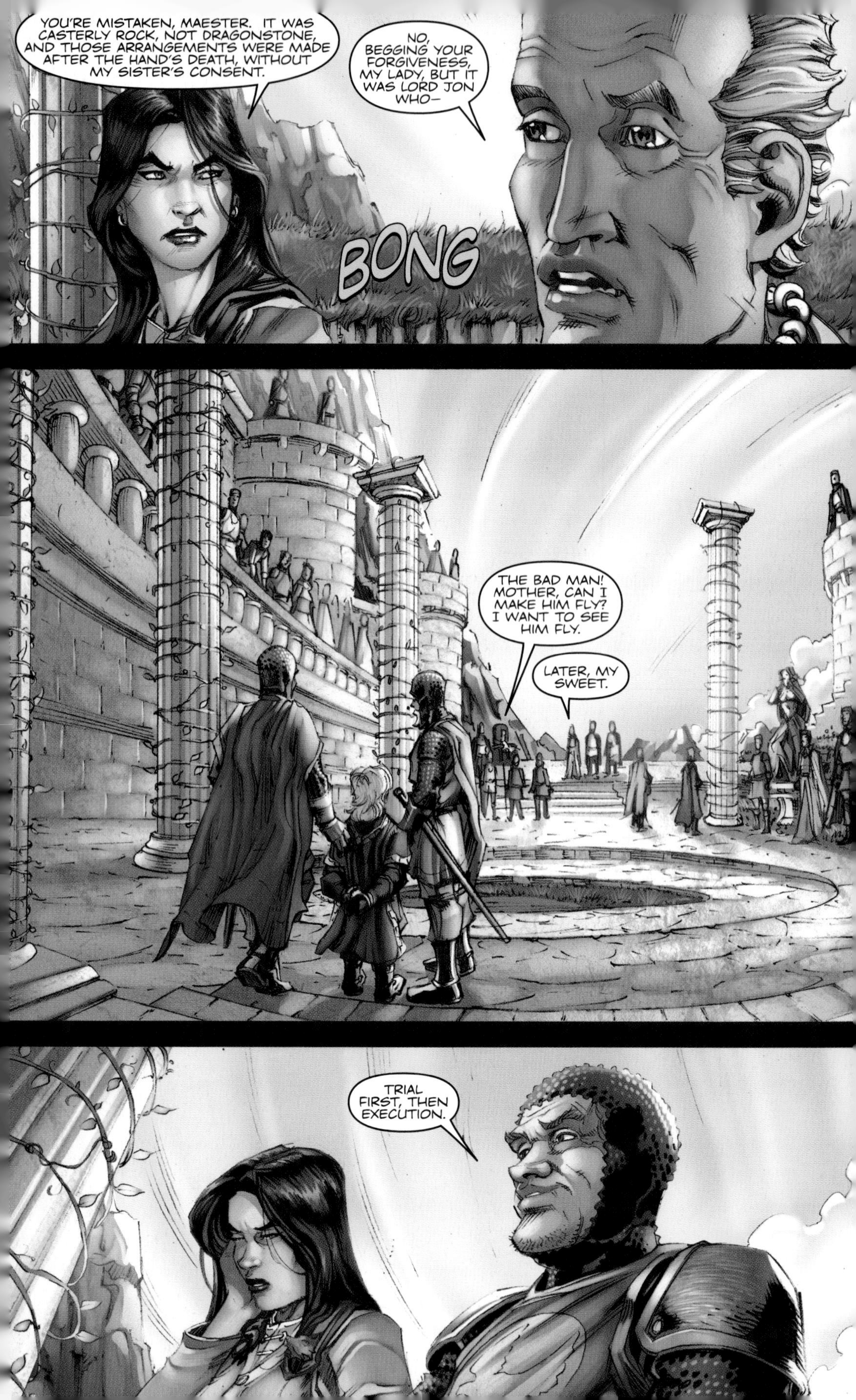
YOU'RE MISTAKEN, MAESTER. IT WAS CASTERLY ROCK, NOT DRAGONSTONE, AND THOSE ARRANGEMENTS WERE MADE AFTER THE HAND'S DEATH, WITHOUT MY SISTER'S CONSENT.
NO, BEGGING YOUR FORGIVENESS, MY LADY, BUT IT WAS LORD JON WHO—
BONG
THE BAD MAN! MOTHER, CAN I MAKE HIM FLY? I WANT TO SEE HIM FLY.
LATER, MY SWEET.
TRIAL FIRST, THEN EXECUTION.

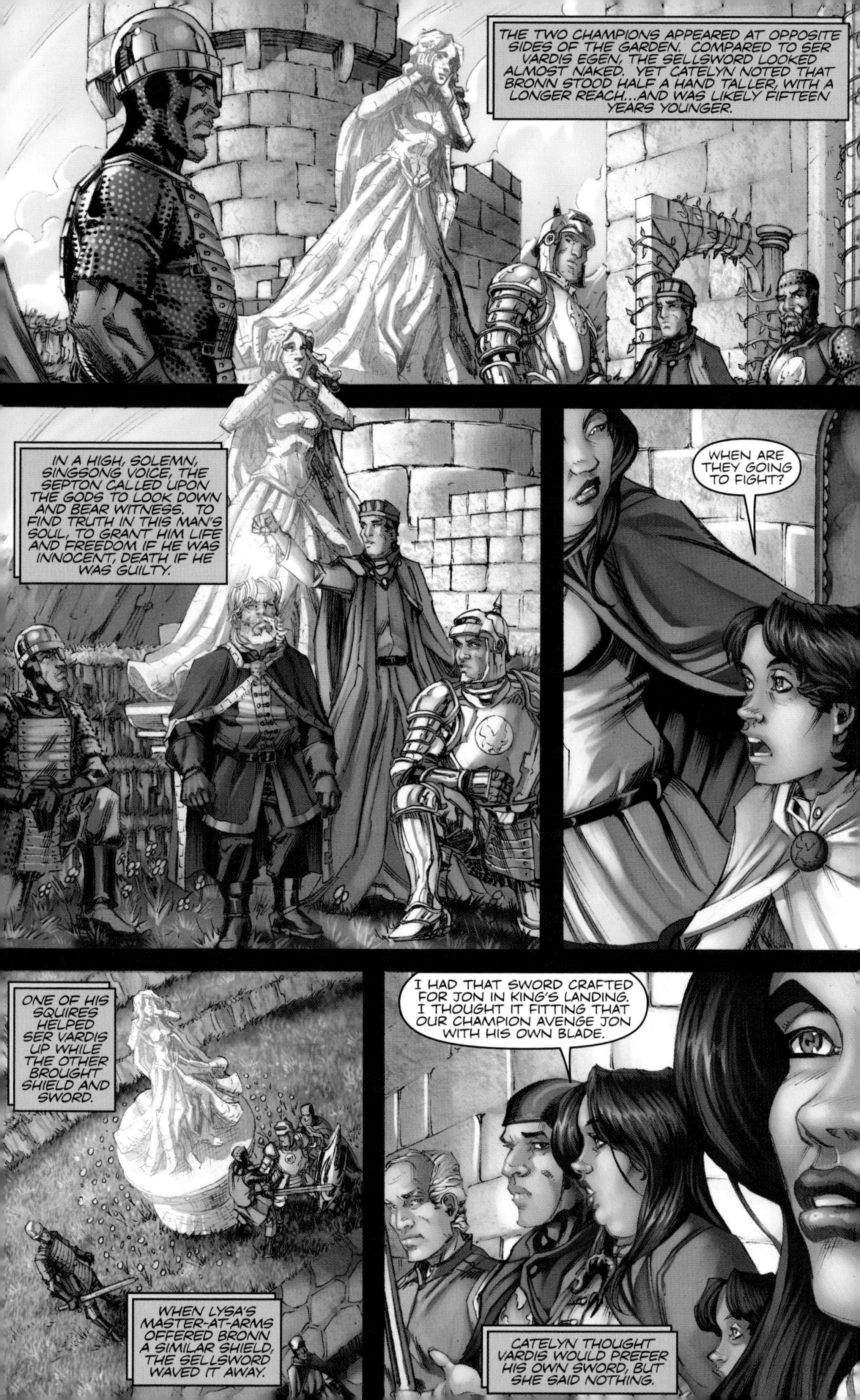
THE TWO CHAMPIONS APPEARED AT OPPOSITE SIDES OF THE GARDEN. COMPARED TO SER VARDIS EGEN, THE SELLSWORD LOOKED ALMOST NAKED. YET CATELYN NOTED THAT BRONN STOOD HALF A HAND TALLER, WITH A LONGER REACH...AND WAS LIKELY FIFTEEN YEARS YOUNGER.
IN A HIGH, SOLEMN, SINGSONG VOICE, THE SEPTON CALLED UPON THE GODS TO LOOK DOWN AND BEAR WITNESS. TO FIND TRUTH IN THIS MAN'S SOUL, TO GRANT HIM LIFE AND FREEDOM IF HE WAS INNOCENT, DEATH IF HE WAS GUILTY.
WHEN ARE THEY GOING TO FIGHT?
ONE OF HIS SQUIRES HELPED SER VARDIS UP WHILE THE OTHER BROUGHT SHIELD AND SWORD.
WHEN LYSA'S MASTER-AT-ARMS OFFERED BRONN A SIMILAR SHIELD, THE SELLSWORD WAVED IT AWAY.
I HAD THAT SWORD CRAFTED FOR JON IN KING'S LANDING. I THOUGHT IT FITTING THAT OUR CHAMPION AVENGE JON WITH HIS OWN BLADE.
CATELYN THOUGHT VARDIS WOULD PREFER HIS OWN SWORD, BUT SHE SAID NOTHING.

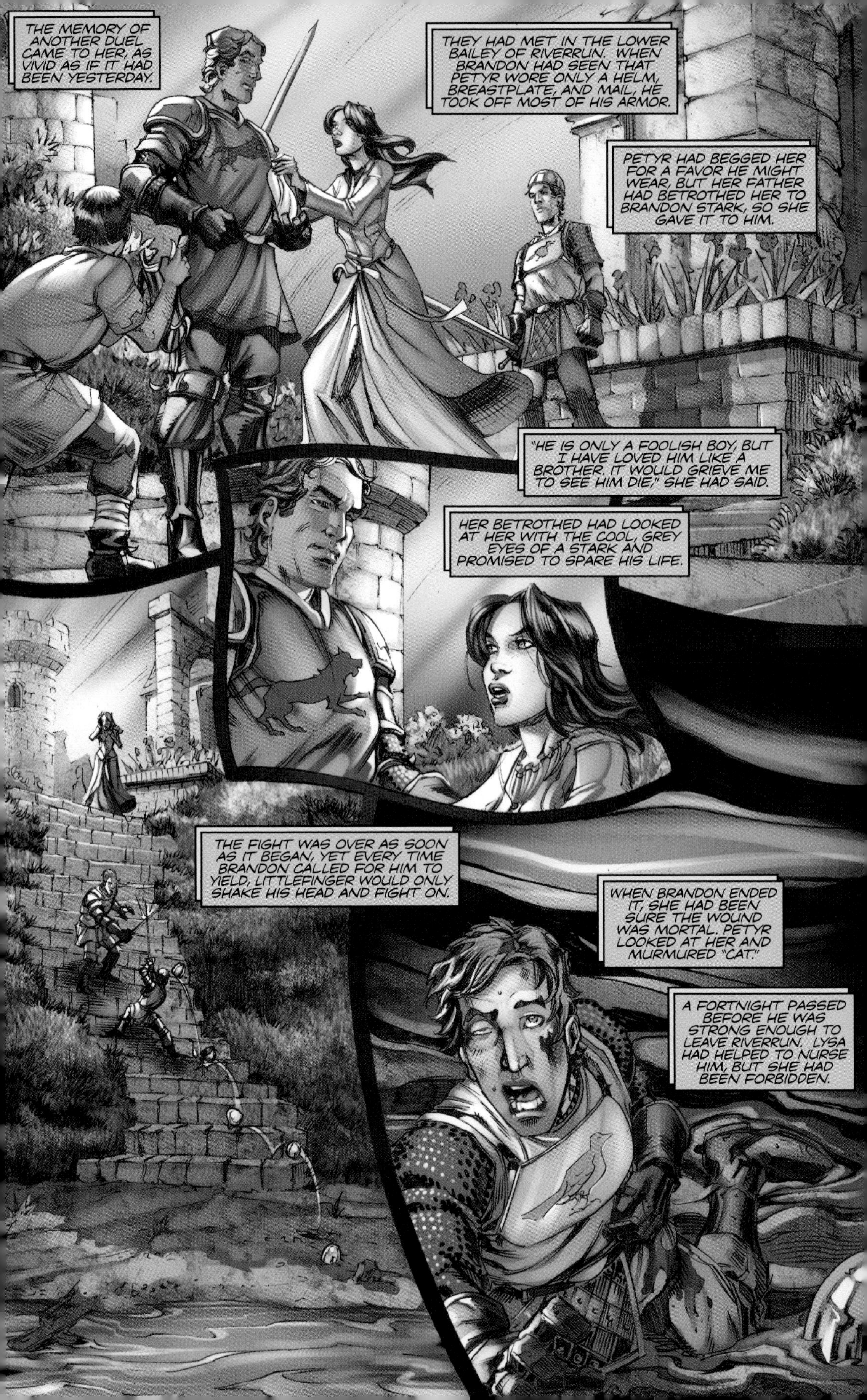
THE MEMORY OF ANOTHER DUEL CAME TO HER, AS VIVID AS IF IT HAD BEEN YESTERDAY.
THEY HAD MET IN THE LOWER BAILEY OF RIVERRUN. WHEN BRANDON HAD SEEN THAT PETYR WORE ONLY A HELM, BREASTPLATE, AND MAIL, HE TOOK OFF MOST OF HIS ARMOR.
PETYR HAD BEGGED HER FOR A FAVOR HE MIGHT WEAR, BUT HER FATHER HAD BETROTHED HER TO BRANDON STARK, SO SHE GAVE IT TO HIM.
"HE IS ONLY A FOOLISH BOY, BUT I HAVE LOVED HIM LIKE A BROTHER. IT WOULD GRIEVE ME TO SEE HIM DIE," SHE HAD SAID.
HER BETROTHED HAD LOOKED AT HER WITH THE COOL, GREY EYES OF A STARK AND PROMISED TO SPARE HIS LIFE.
THE FIGHT WAS OVER AS SOON AS IT BEGAN, YET EVERY TIME BRANDON CALLED FOR HIM TO YIELD, LITTLEFINGER WOULD ONLY SHAKE HIS HEAD AND FIGHT ON.
WHEN BRANDON ENDED IT, SHE HAD BEEN SURE THE WOUND WAS MORTAL. PETYR LOOKED AT HER AND MURMURED "CAT."
A FORTNIGHT PASSED BEFORE HE WAS STRONG ENOUGH TO LEAVE RIVERRUN. LYSA HAD HELPED TO NURSE HIM, BUT SHE HAD BEEN FORBIDDEN.

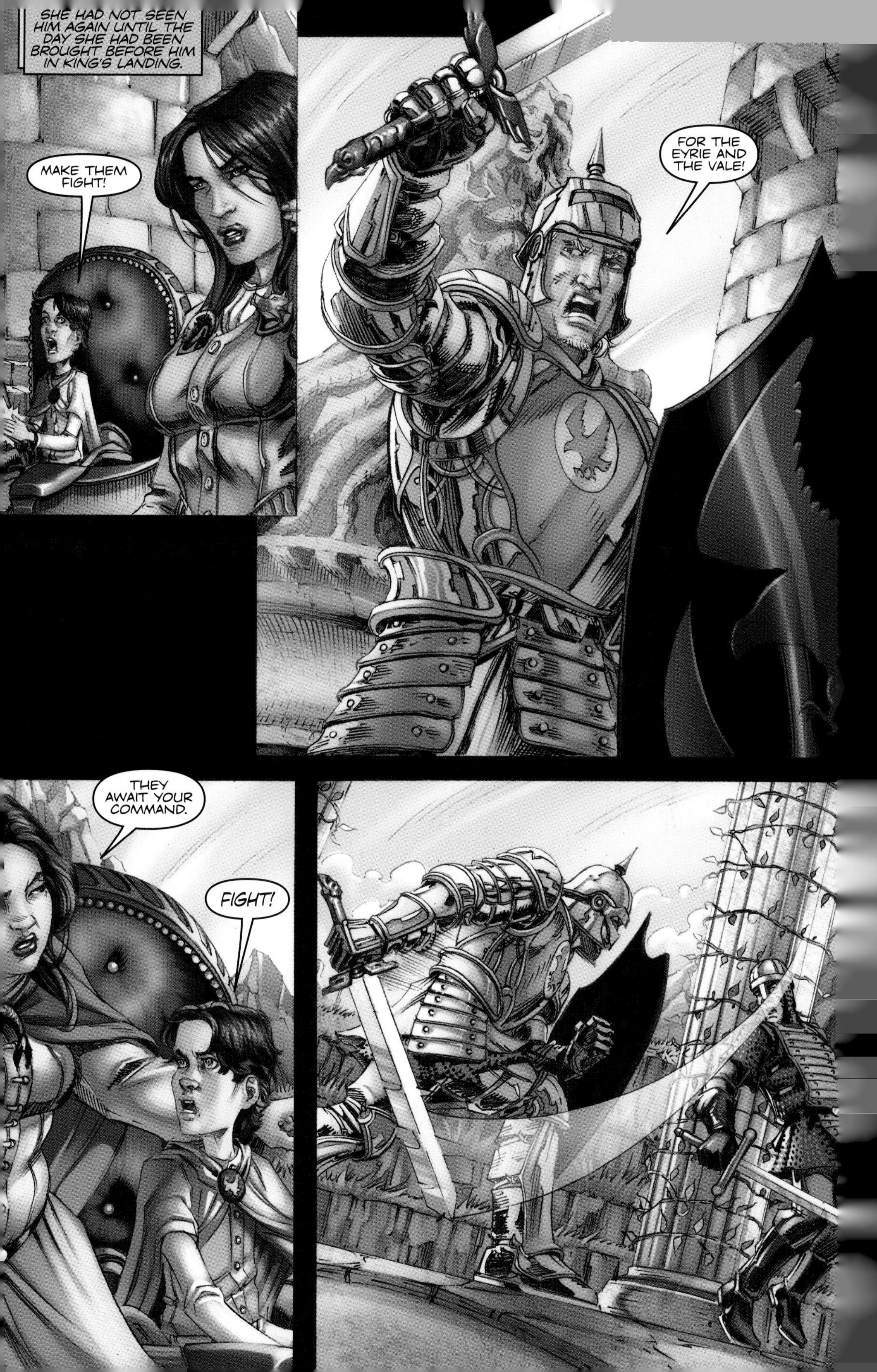

SHE HAD NOT SEEN HIM AGAIN UNTIL THE DAY SHE HAD BEEN BROUGHT BEFORE HIM IN KING'S LANDING.
MAKE THEM FIGHT!
FOR THE EYRIE AND THE VALE!
THEY AWAIT YOUR COMMAND.
FIGHT!

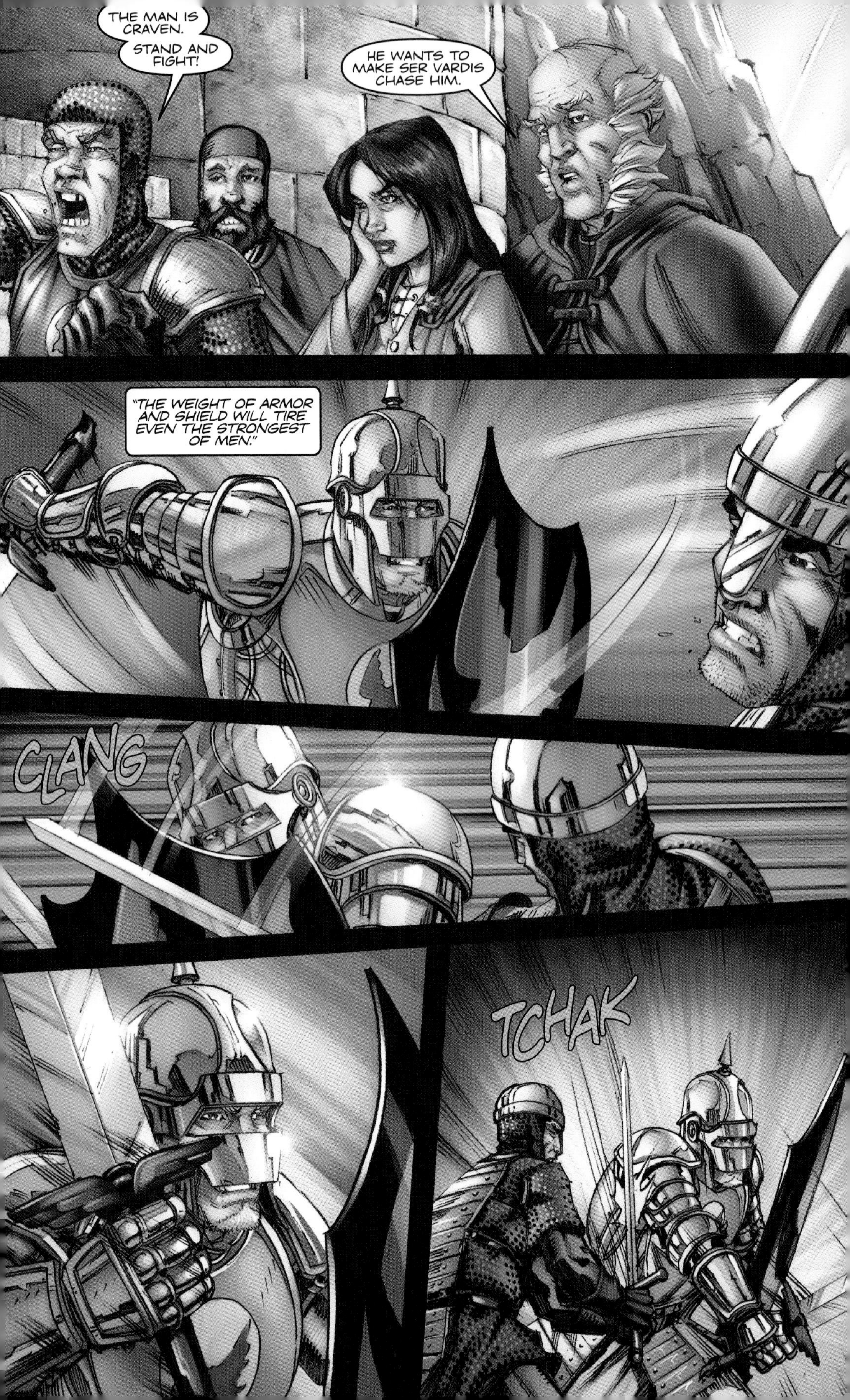
THE MAN IS CRAVEN.
STAND AND FIGHT!
HE WANTS TO MAKE SER VARDIS CHASE HIM.
"THE WEIGHT OF ARMOR AND SHIELD WILL TIRE EVEN THE STRONGEST OF MEN."
CLANG
TCHAK

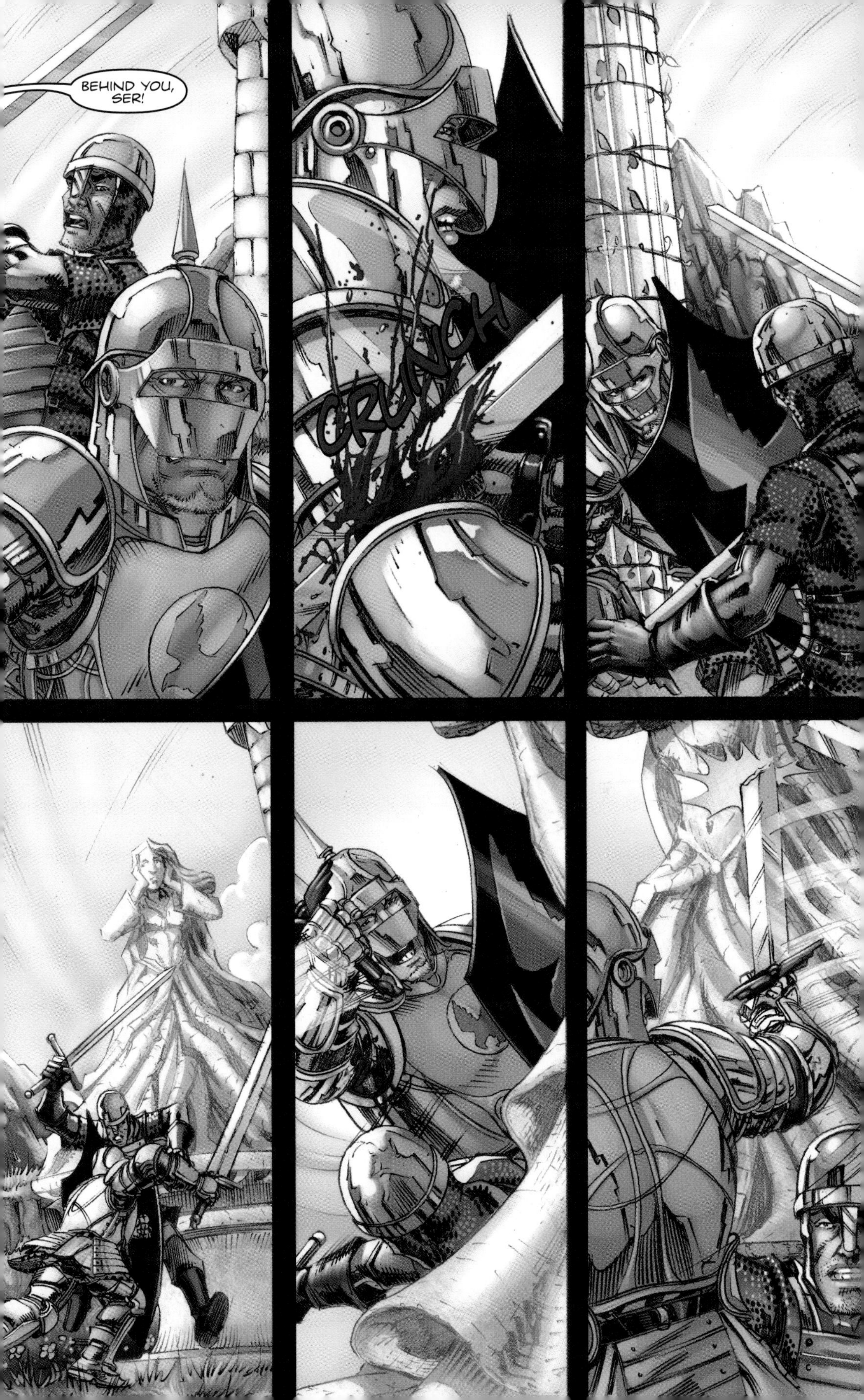
BEHIND YOU, SER!
CRUNCH

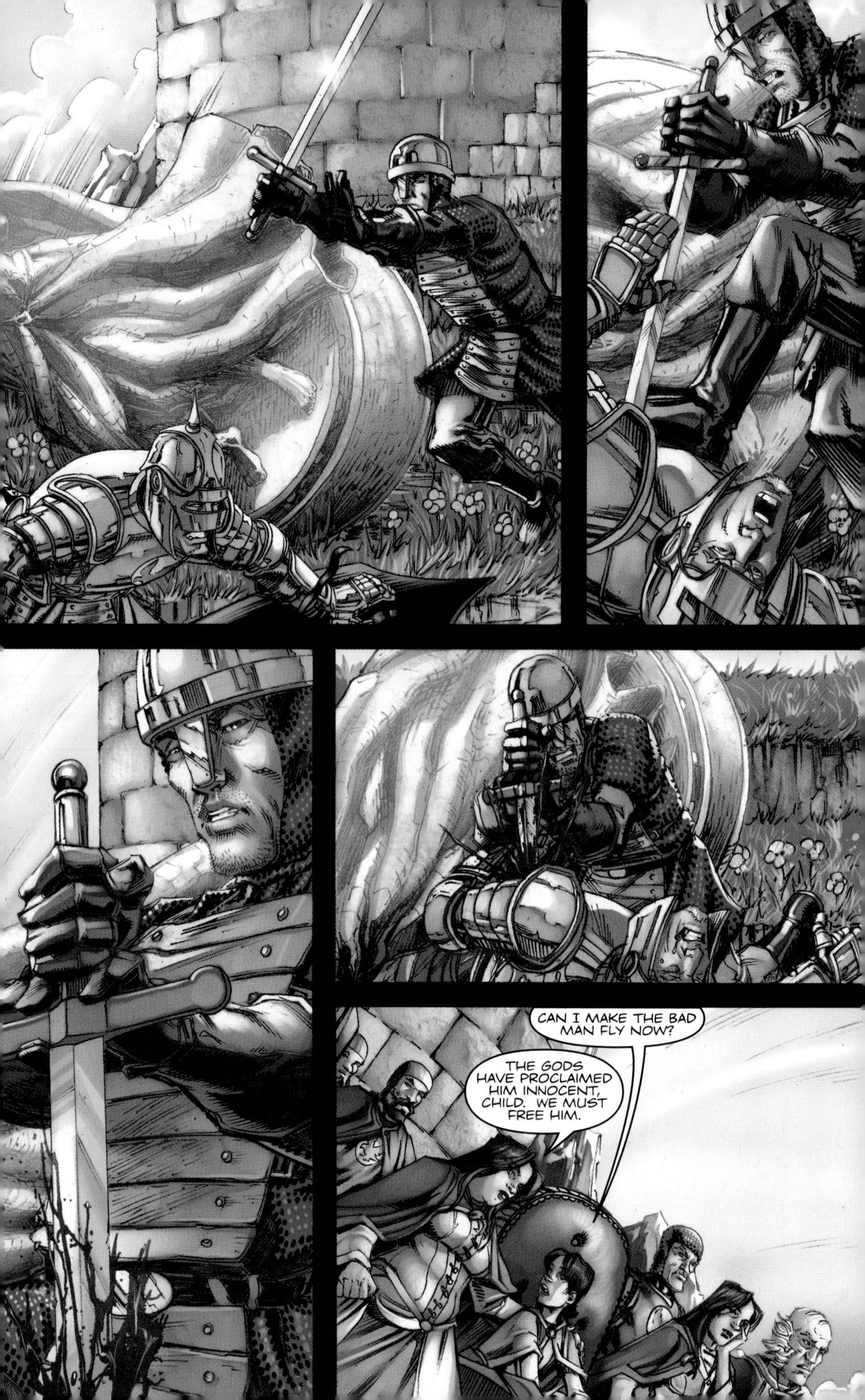
CAN I MAKE THE BAD MAN FLY NOW?
THE GODS HAVE PROCLAIMED HIM INNOCENT, CHILD. WE MUST FREE HIM.

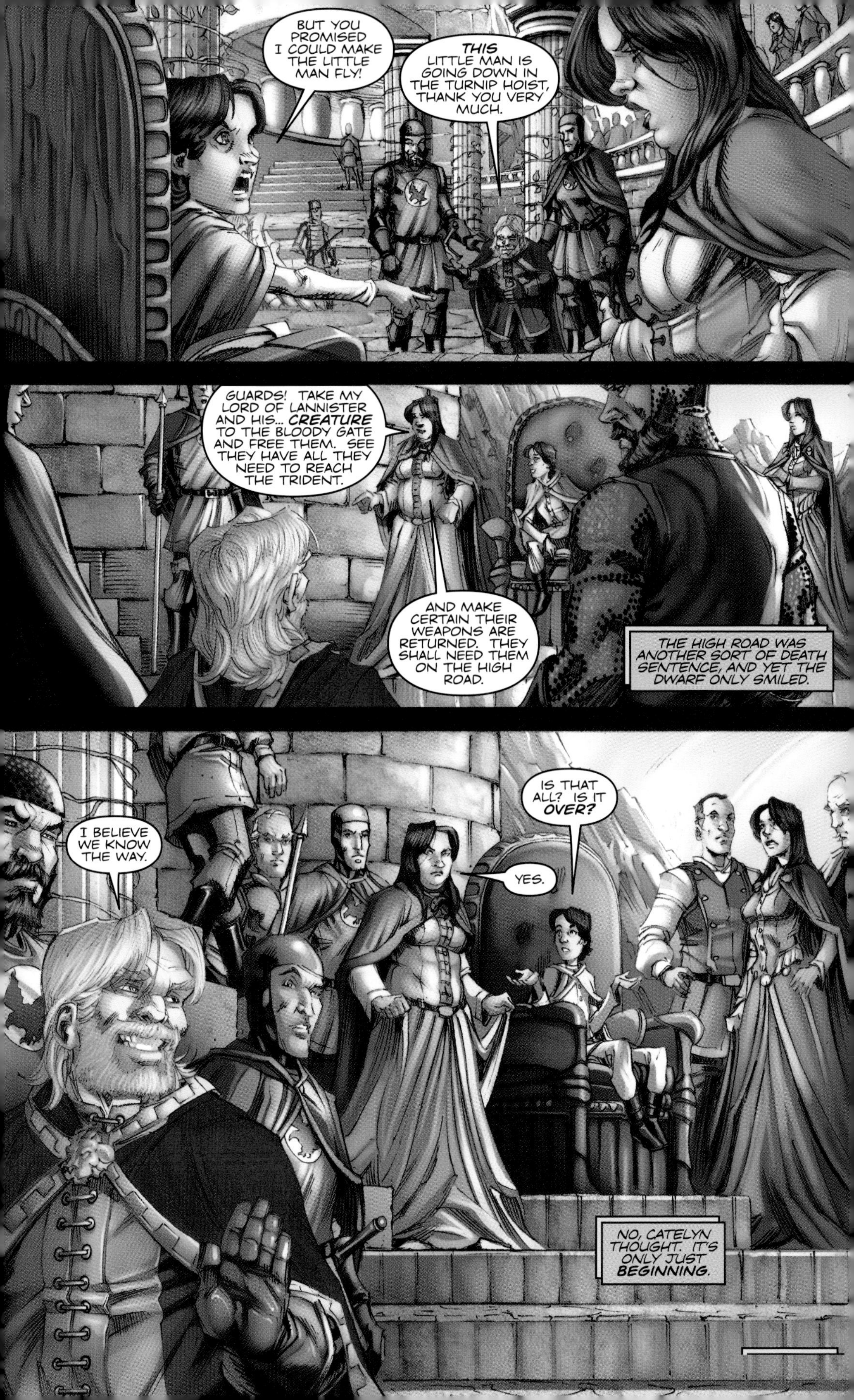

BUT YOU PROMISED I COULD MAKE THE LITTLE MAN FLY!
THIS LITTLE MAN IS GOING DOWN IN THE TURNIP HOIST, THANK YOU VERY MUCH.
GUARDS! TAKE MY LORD OF LANNISTER AND HIS... CREATURE TO THE BLOODY GATE AND FREE THEM. SEE THEY HAVE ALL THEY NEED TO REACH THE TRIDENT.
AND MAKE CERTAIN THEIR WEAPONS ARE RETURNED. THEY SHALL NEED THEM ON THE HIGH ROAD.
THE HIGH ROAD WAS ANOTHER SORT OF DEATH SENTENCE, AND YET THE DWARF ONLY SMILED.
I BELIEVE WE KNOW THE WAY.
YES.
IS THAT ALL? IS IT OVER?
NO, CATELYN THOUGHT. IT'S ONLY JUST BEGINNING.

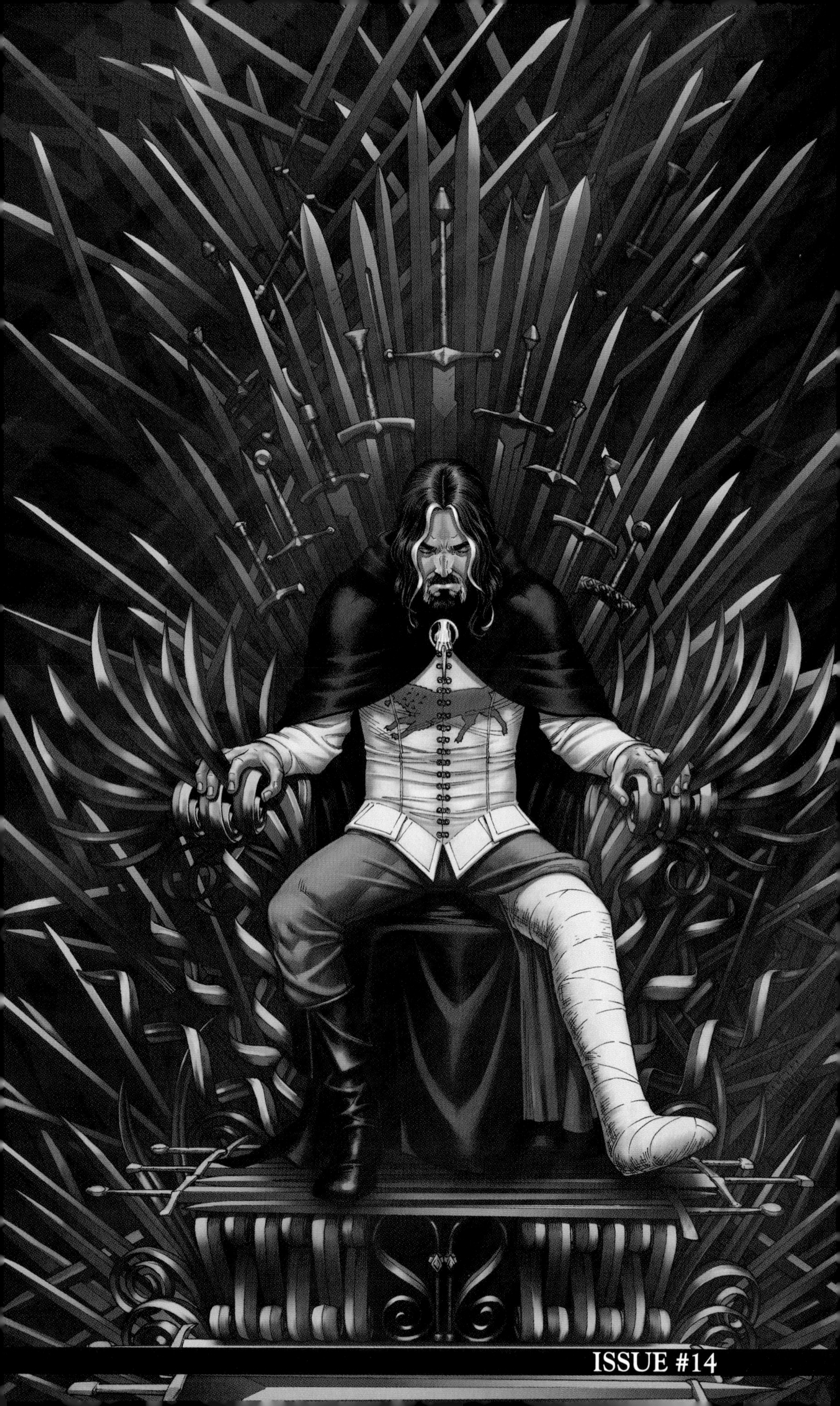

ISSUE #14

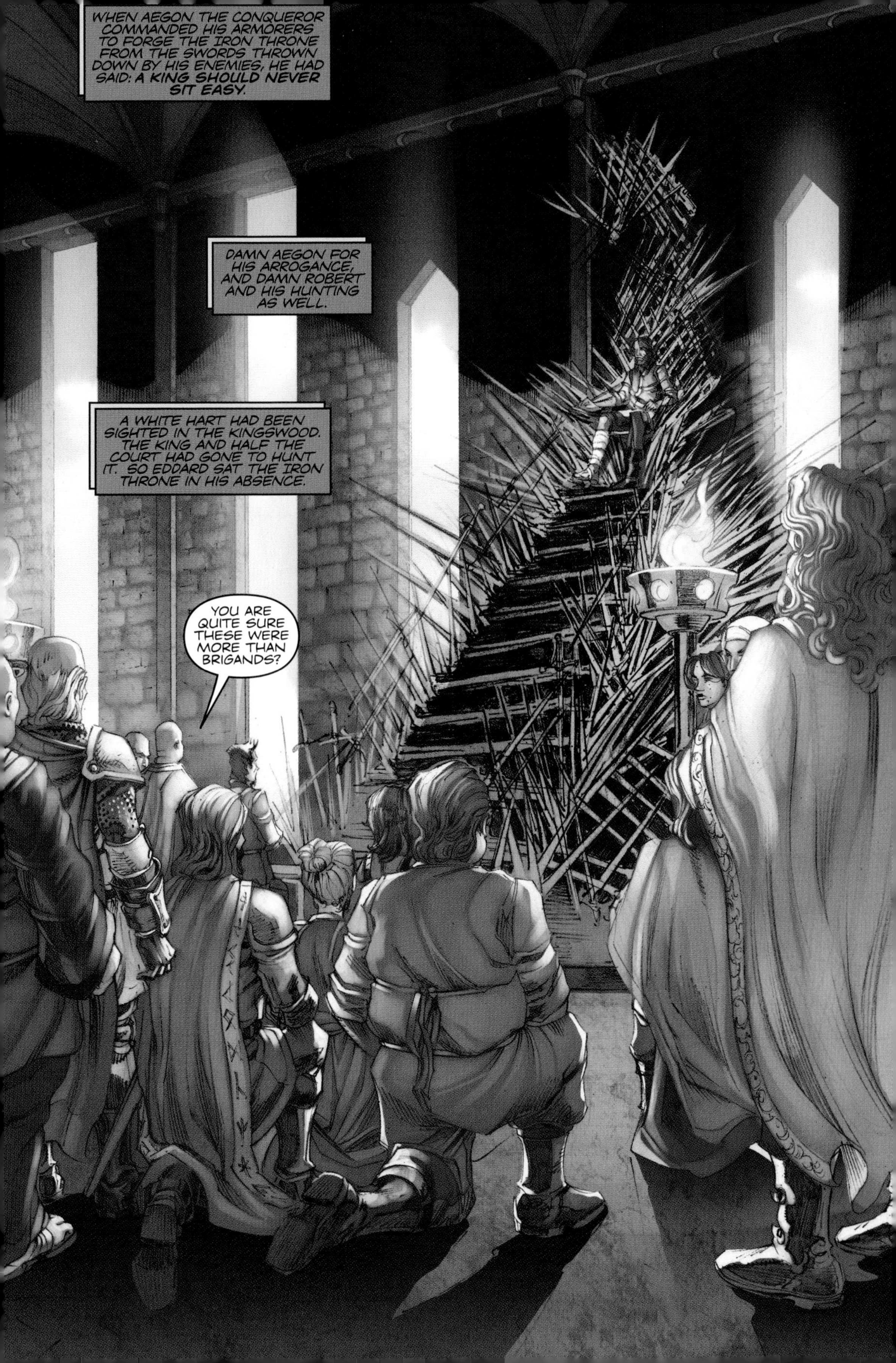
WHEN AEGON THE CONQUEROR COMMANDED HIS ARMORERS TO FORGE THE IRON THRONE FROM THE SWORDS THROWN DOWN BY HIS ENEMIES, HE HAD SAID: A KING SHOULD NEVER SIT EASY.
DAMN AEGON FOR HIS ARROGANCE, AND DAMN ROBERT AND HIS HUNTING AS WELL.
A WHITE HART HAD BEEN SIGHTED IN THE KINGSWOOD. THE KING AND HALF THE COURT HAD GONE TO HUNT IT. SO EDDARD SAT THE IRON THRONE IN HIS ABSENCE.
YOU ARE QUITE SURE THESE WERE MORE THAN BRIGANDS?

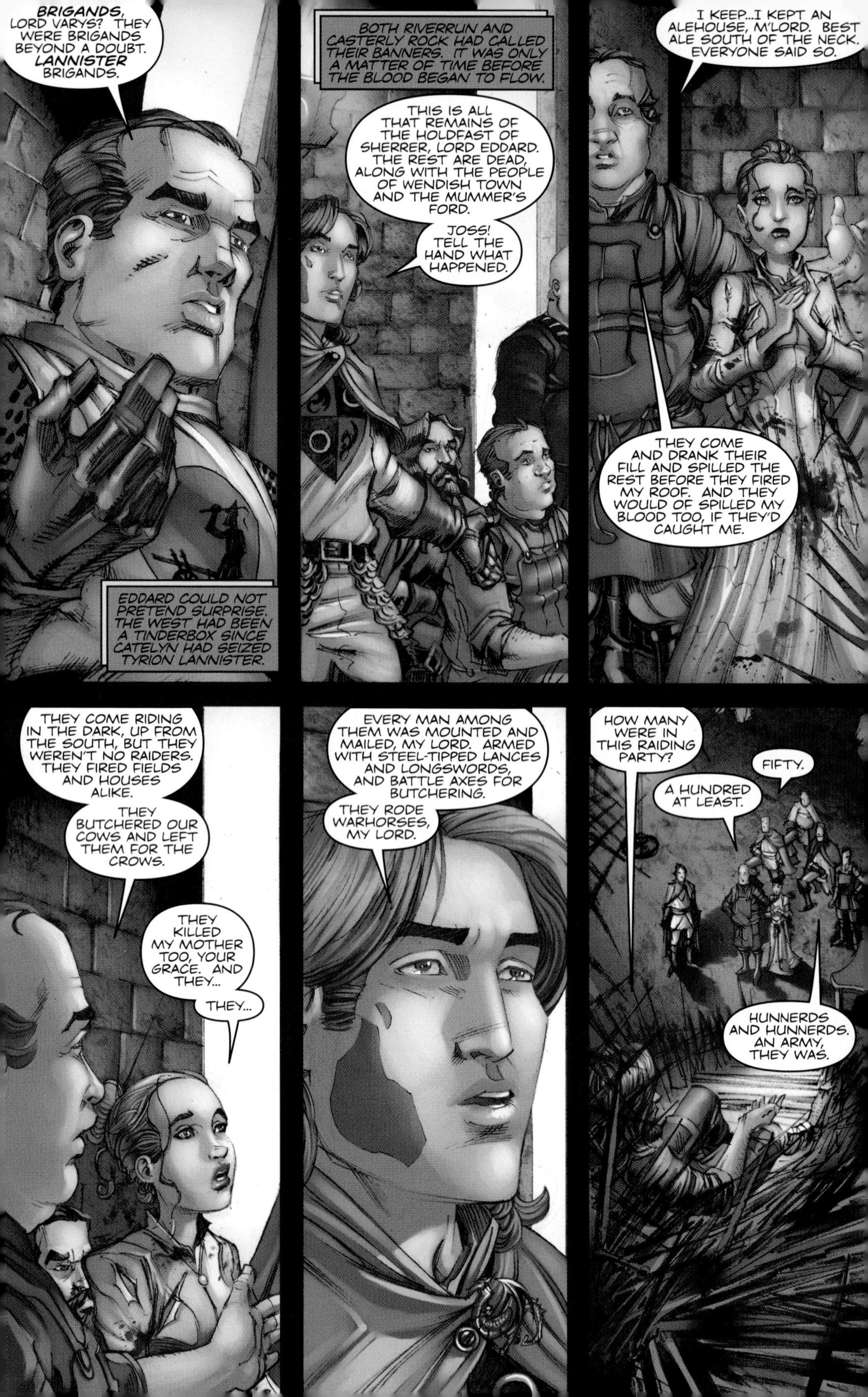
BRIGANDS, LORD VARYS? THEY WERE BRIGANDS BEYOND A DOUBT. LANNISTER BRIGANDS.
EDDARD COULD NOT PRETEND SURPRISE. THE WEST HAD BEEN A TINDERBOX SINCE CATELYN HAD SEIZED TYRION LANNISTER.
BOTH RIVERRUN AND CASTERLY ROCK HAD CALLED THEIR BANNERS. IT WAS ONLY A MATTER OF TIME BEFORE THE BLOOD BEGAN TO FLOW.
THIS IS ALL THAT REMAINS OF THE HOLDFAST OF SHERRER, LORD EDDARD. THE REST ARE DEAD, ALONG WITH THE PEOPLE OF WENDISH TOWN AND THE MUMMER'S FORD.
JOSS! TELL THE HAND WHAT HAPPENED.
I KEEP...I KEPT AN ALEHOUSE, M'LORD. BEST ALE SOUTH OF THE NECK. EVERYONE SAID SO.
THEY COME AND DRANK THEIR FILL AND SPILLED THE REST BEFORE THEY FIRED MY ROOF. AND THEY WOULD OF SPILLED MY BLOOD TOO, IF THEY'D CAUGHT ME.
THEY COME RIDING IN THE DARK, UP FROM THE SOUTH, BUT THEY WEREN'T NO RAIDERS. THEY FIRED FIELDS AND HOUSES ALIKE.
THEY BUTCHERED OUR COWS AND LEFT THEM FOR THE CROWS.
THEY KILLED MY MOTHER TOO, YOUR GRACE. AND THEY...
THEY...
EVERY MAN AMONG THEM WAS MOUNTED AND MAILED, MY LORD. ARMED WITH STEEL-TIPPED LANCES AND LONGSWORDS, AND BATTLE AXES FOR BUTCHERING.
THEY RODE WARHORSES, MY LORD.
HOW MANY WERE IN THIS RAIDING PARTY?
FIFTY.
A HUNDRED AT LEAST.
HUNNERDS AND HUNNERDS. AN ARMY, THEY WAS.

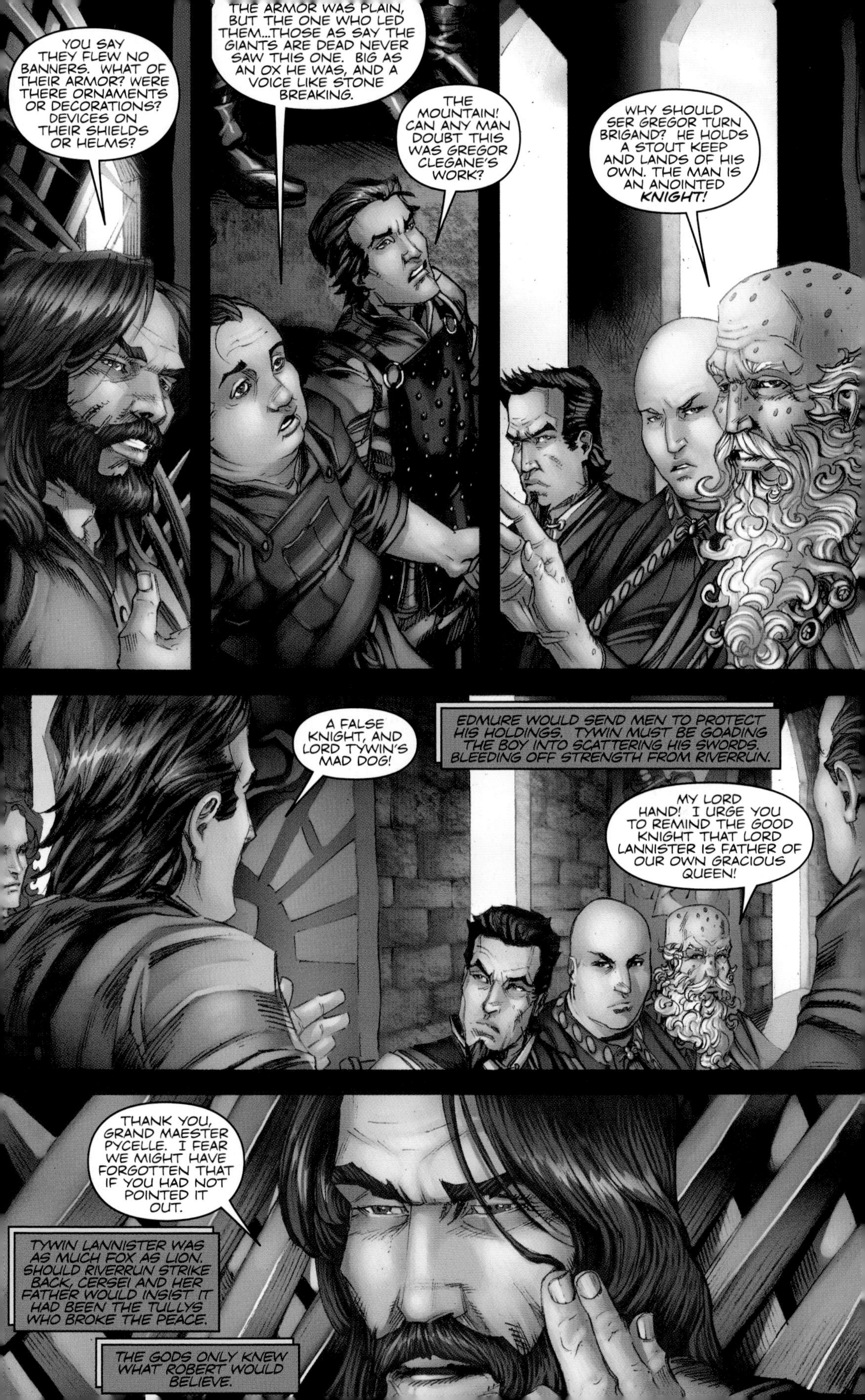
YOU SAY THEY FLEW NO BANNERS. WHAT OF THEIR ARMOR? WERE THERE ORNAMENTS OR DECORATIONS? DEVICES ON THEIR SHIELDS OR HELMS?
THE ARMOR WAS PLAIN, BUT THE ONE WHO LED THEM...THOSE AS SAY THE GIANTS ARE DEAD NEVER SAW THIS ONE. BIG AS AN OX HE WAS, AND A VOICE LIKE STONE BREAKING.
THE MOUNTAIN! CAN ANY MAN DOUBT THIS WAS GREGOR CLEGANE'S WORK?
WHY SHOULD SER GREGOR TURN BRIGAND? HE HOLDS A STOUT KEEP AND LANDS OF HIS OWN. THE MAN IS AN ANOINTED **KNIGHT!**
A FALSE KNIGHT, AND LORD TYWIN'S MAD DOG!
EDMURE WOULD SEND MEN TO PROTECT HIS HOLDINGS. TYWIN MUST BE GOADING THE BOY INTO SCATTERING HIS SWORDS. BLEEDING OFF STRENGTH FROM RIVERRUN.
MY LORD HAND! I URGE YOU TO REMIND THE GOOD KNIGHT THAT LORD LANNISTER IS FATHER OF OUR OWN GRACIOUS QUEEN!
THANK YOU, GRAND MAESTER PYCELLE. I FEAR WE MIGHT HAVE FORGOTTEN THAT IF YOU HAD NOT POINTED IT OUT.
TYWIN LANNISTER WAS AS MUCH FOX AS LION. SHOULD RIVERRUN STRIKE BACK, CERSEI AND HER FATHER WOULD INSIST IT HAD BEEN THE TULLYS WHO BROKE THE PEACE.
THE GODS ONLY KNEW WHAT ROBERT WOULD BELIEVE.

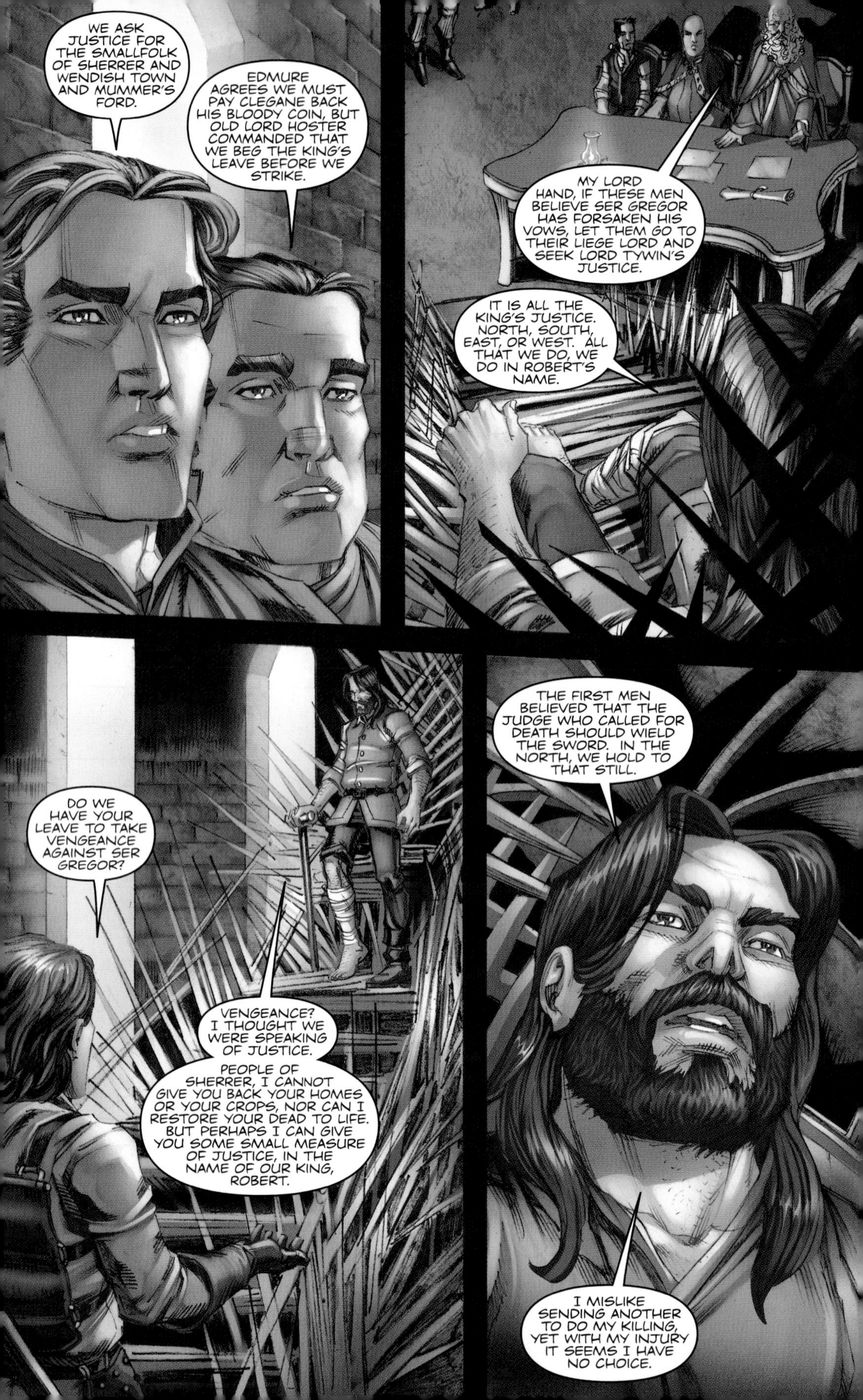
WE ASK JUSTICE FOR THE SMALLFOLK OF SHERRER AND WENDISH TOWN AND MUMMER'S FORD.
EDMURE AGREES WE MUST PAY CLEGANE BACK HIS BLOODY COIN, BUT OLD LORD HOSTER COMMANDED THAT WE BEG THE KING'S LEAVE BEFORE WE STRIKE.
MY LORD HAND, IF THESE MEN BELIEVE SER GREGOR HAS FORSAKEN HIS VOWS, LET THEM GO TO THEIR LIEGE LORD AND SEEK LORD TYWIN'S JUSTICE.
IT IS ALL THE KING'S JUSTICE. NORTH, SOUTH, EAST, OR WEST. ALL THAT WE DO, WE DO IN ROBERT'S NAME.
DO WE HAVE YOUR LEAVE TO TAKE VENGEANCE AGAINST SER GREGOR?
VENGEANCE? I THOUGHT WE WERE SPEAKING OF JUSTICE.
PEOPLE OF SHERRER, I CANNOT GIVE YOU BACK YOUR HOMES OR YOUR CROPS, NOR CAN I RESTORE YOUR DEAD TO LIFE. BUT PERHAPS I CAN GIVE YOU SOME SMALL MEASURE OF JUSTICE, IN THE NAME OF OUR KING, ROBERT.
THE FIRST MEN BELIEVED THAT THE JUDGE WHO CALLED FOR DEATH SHOULD WIELD THE SWORD. IN THE NORTH, WE HOLD TO THAT STILL.
I MISLIKE SENDING ANOTHER TO DO MY KILLING, YET WITH MY INJURY IT SEEMS I HAVE NO CHOICE.

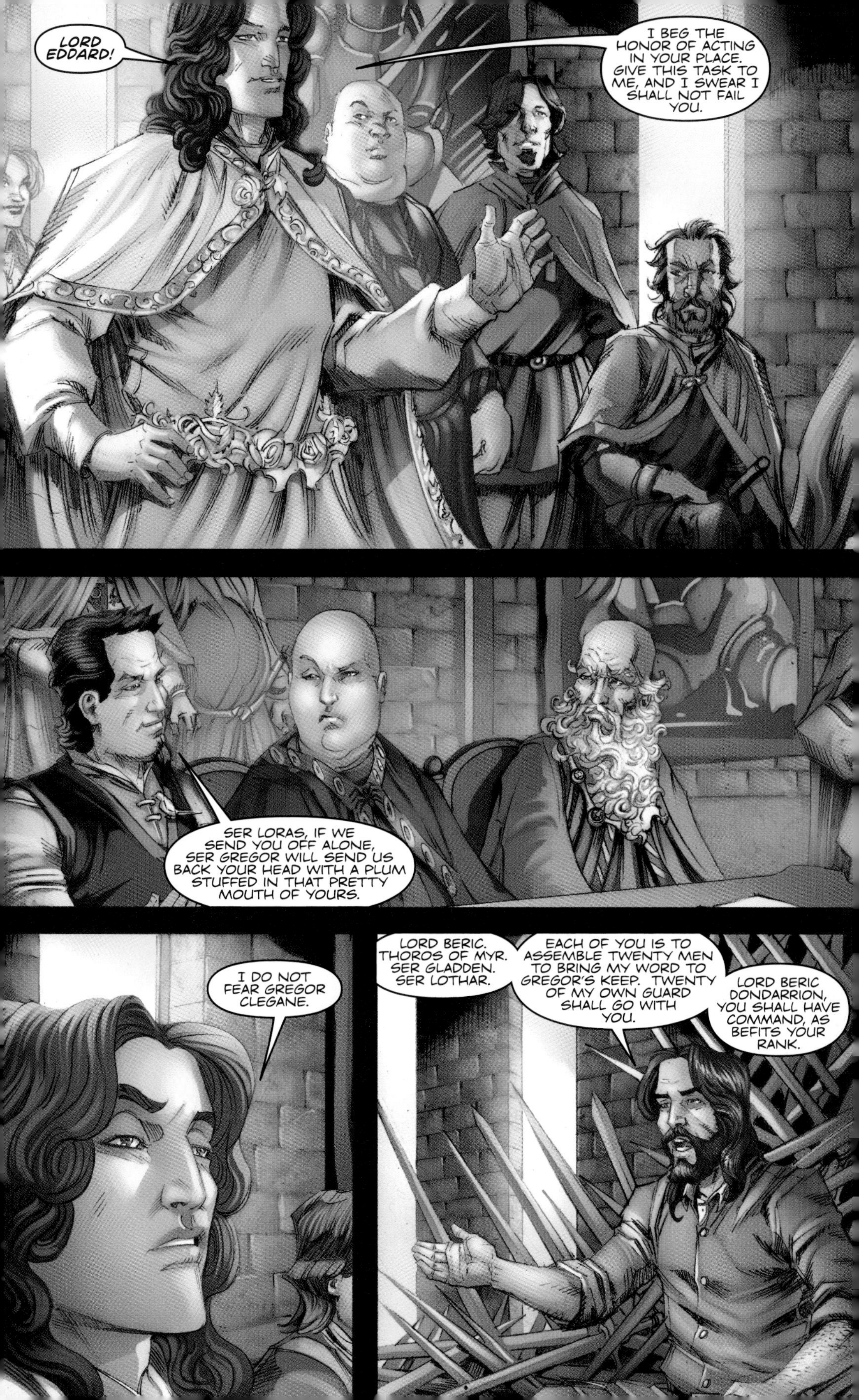
LORD EDDARD!
I BEG THE HONOR OF ACTING IN YOUR PLACE. GIVE THIS TASK TO ME, AND I SWEAR I SHALL NOT FAIL YOU.
SER LORAS, IF WE SEND YOU OFF ALONE, SER GREGOR WILL SEND US BACK YOUR HEAD WITH A PLUM STUFFED IN THAT PRETTY MOUTH OF YOURS.
I DO NOT FEAR GREGOR CLEGANE.
LORD BERIC. THOROS OF MYR. SER GLADDEN. SER LOTHAR.
EACH OF YOU IS TO ASSEMBLE TWENTY MEN TO BRING MY WORD TO GREGOR'S KEEP. TWENTY OF MY OWN GUARD SHALL GO WITH YOU.
LORD BERIC DONDARRION, YOU SHALL HAVE COMMAND, AS BEFITS YOUR RANK.

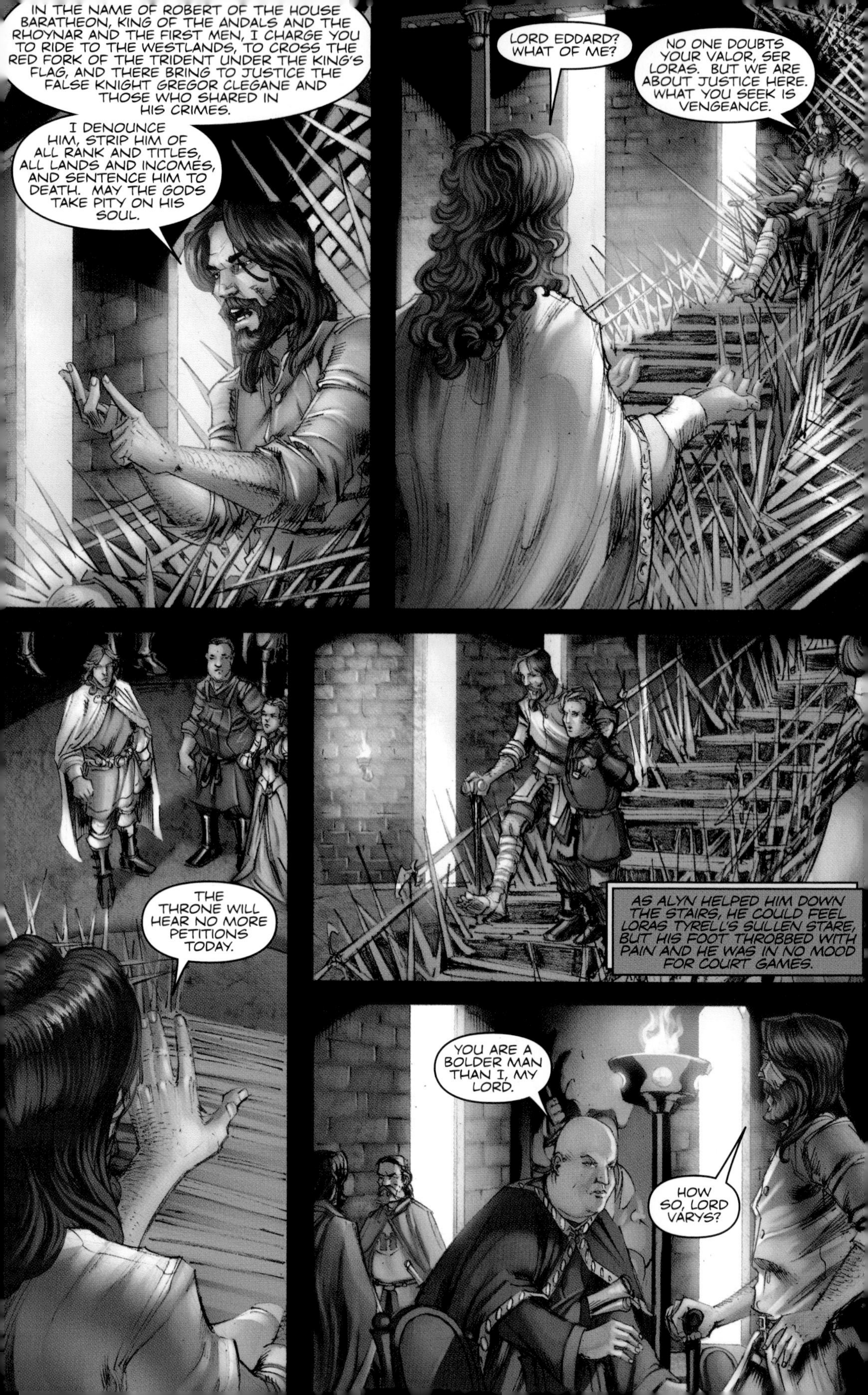
IN THE NAME OF ROBERT OF THE HOUSE BARATHEON, KING OF THE ANDALS AND THE RHOYNAR AND THE FIRST MEN, I CHARGE YOU TO RIDE TO THE WESTLANDS, TO CROSS THE RED FORK OF THE TRIDENT UNDER THE KING'S FLAG, AND THERE BRING TO JUSTICE THE FALSE KNIGHT GREGOR CLEGANE AND THOSE WHO SHARED IN HIS CRIMES.
I DENOUNCE HIM, STRIP HIM OF ALL RANK AND TITLES, ALL LANDS AND INCOMES, AND SENTENCE HIM TO DEATH. MAY THE GODS TAKE PITY ON HIS SOUL.
LORD EDDARD? WHAT OF ME?
NO ONE DOUBTS YOUR VALOR, SER LORAS. BUT WE ARE ABOUT JUSTICE HERE. WHAT YOU SEEK IS VENGEANCE.
THE THRONE WILL HEAR NO MORE PETITIONS TODAY.
AS ALYN HELPED HIM DOWN THE STAIRS, HE COULD FEEL LORAS TYRELL'S SULLEN STARE, BUT HIS FOOT THROBBED WITH PAIN AND HE WAS IN NO MOOD FOR COURT GAMES.
YOU ARE A BOLDER MAN THAN I, MY LORD.
HOW SO, LORD VARYS?

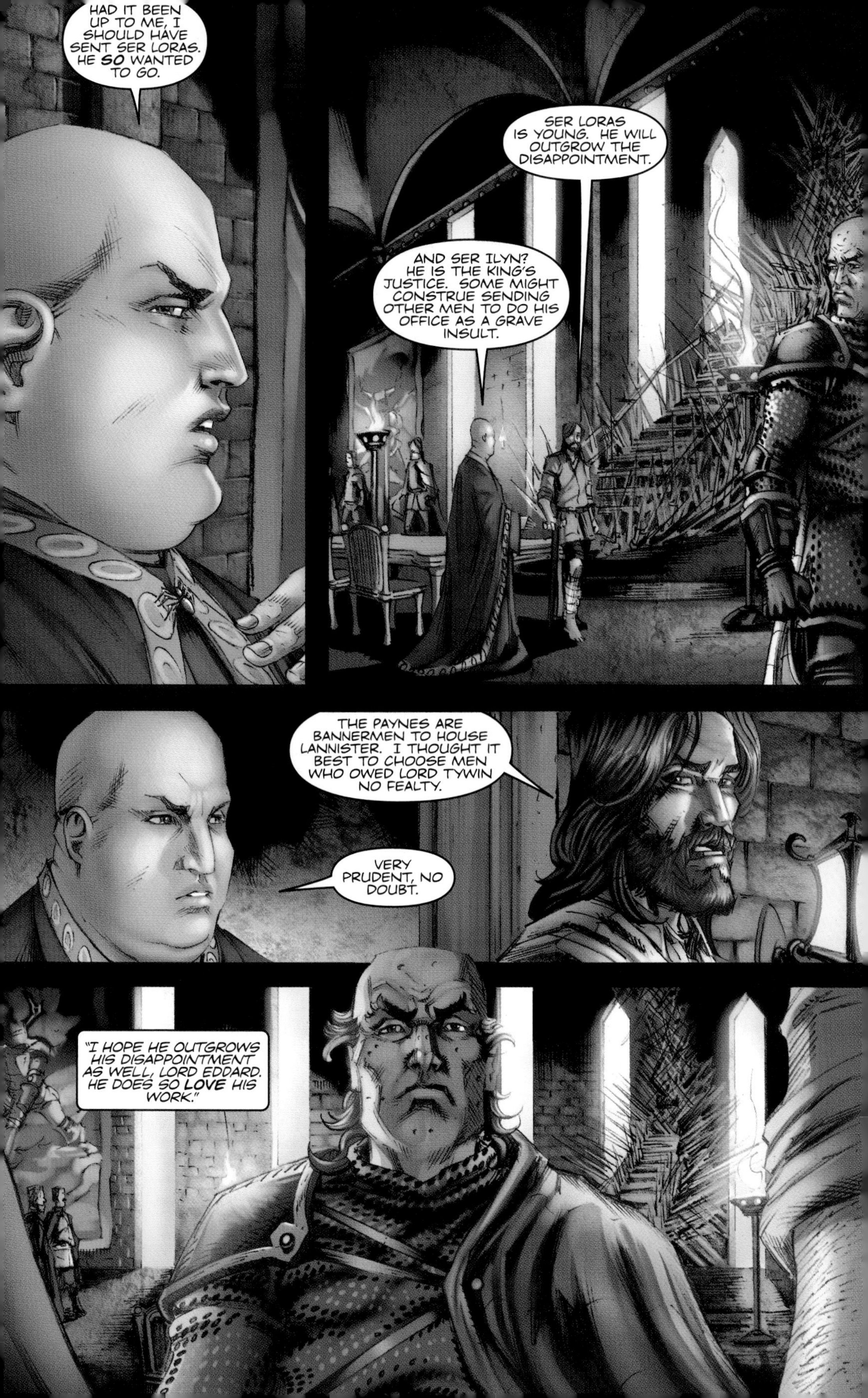
HAD IT BEEN UP TO ME, I SHOULD HAVE SENT SER LORAS. HE **SO** WANTED TO GO.
SER LORAS IS YOUNG. HE WILL OUTGROW THE DISAPPOINTMENT.
AND SER ILYN? HE IS THE KING'S JUSTICE. SOME MIGHT CONSTRUE SENDING OTHER MEN TO DO HIS OFFICE AS A GRAVE INSULT.
THE PAYNES ARE BANNERMEN TO HOUSE LANNISTER. I THOUGHT IT BEST TO CHOOSE MEN WHO OWED LORD TYWIN NO FEALTY.
VERY PRUDENT, NO DOUBT.
"I HOPE HE OUTGROWS HIS DISAPPOINTMENT AS WELL, LORD EDDARD. HE DOES SO **LOVE** HIS WORK."

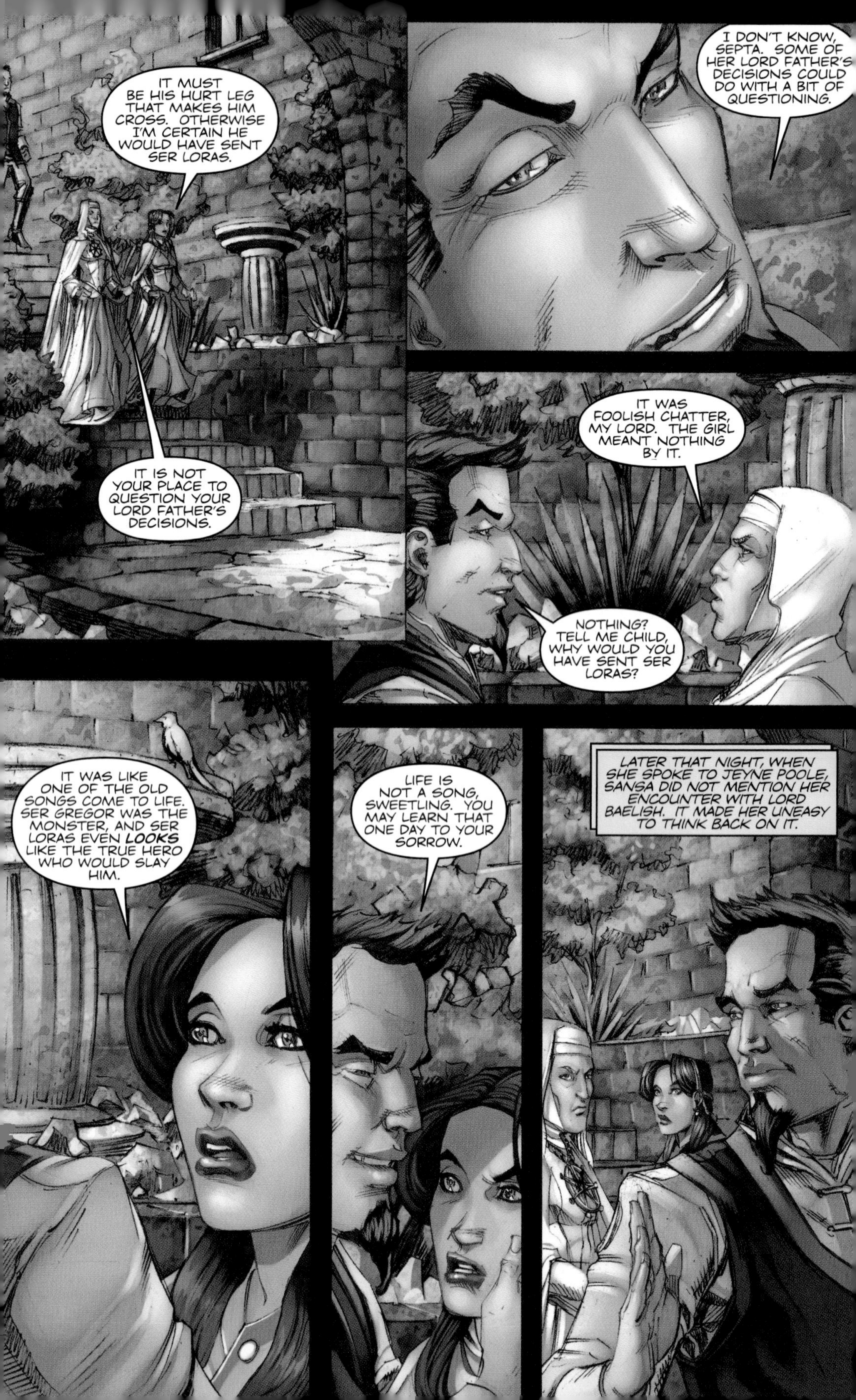

IT MUST BE HIS HURT LEG THAT MAKES HIM CROSS. OTHERWISE I'M CERTAIN HE WOULD HAVE SENT SER LORAS.
IT IS NOT YOUR PLACE TO QUESTION YOUR LORD FATHER'S DECISIONS.
I DON'T KNOW, SEPTA. SOME OF HER LORD FATHER'S DECISIONS COULD DO WITH A BIT OF QUESTIONING.
IT WAS FOOLISH CHATTER, MY LORD. THE GIRL MEANT NOTHING BY IT.
NOTHING? TELL ME CHILD, WHY WOULD YOU HAVE SENT SER LORAS?
IT WAS LIKE ONE OF THE OLD SONGS COME TO LIFE. SER GREGOR WAS THE MONSTER, AND SER LORAS EVEN LOOKS LIKE THE TRUE HERO WHO WOULD SLAY HIM.
LIFE IS NOT A SONG, SWEETLING. YOU MAY LEARN THAT ONE DAY TO YOUR SORROW.
LATER THAT NIGHT, WHEN SHE SPOKE TO JEYNE POOLE, SANSA DID NOT MENTION HER ENCOUNTER WITH LORD BAELISH. IT MADE HER UNEASY TO THINK BACK ON IT.

I HAD A DREAM THAT JOFFREY WOULD BE THE ONE TO TAKE THE WHITE HART.

DID HE TOUCH IT WITH HIS HAND AND DO IT NO HARM?

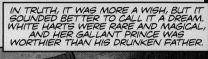

IN TRUTH, IT WAS MORE A WISH, BUT IT SOUNDED BETTER TO CALL IT A DREAM. WHITE HARTS WERE RARE AND MAGICAL, AND HER GALLANT PRINCE WAS WORTHIER THAN HIS DRUNKEN FATHER.

HE SHOT IT WITH A GOLDEN ARROW AND BROUGHT IT BACK FOR ME.

"I SAW YOUR SISTER THIS AFTERNOON WALKING THROUGH THE STABLES ON HER HANDS. WHY WOULD SHE DO A THING LIKE THAT?"

I DON'T KNOW WHY ARYA DOES ANYTHING. DO YOU WANT TO HEAR ABOUT THE COURT OR NOT?

I DO, BUT ARE THERE ANY LEMON CAKES?

THERE WERE NOT, BUT THE KITCHEN YIELDED HALF A STRAWBERRY PIE THAT WAS ALMOST AS GOOD. THEY ATE IT GIGGLING AND GOSSIPING AND SHARING SECRETS.

AND SANSA WENT TO BED FEELING ALMOST AS WICKED AS ARYA.

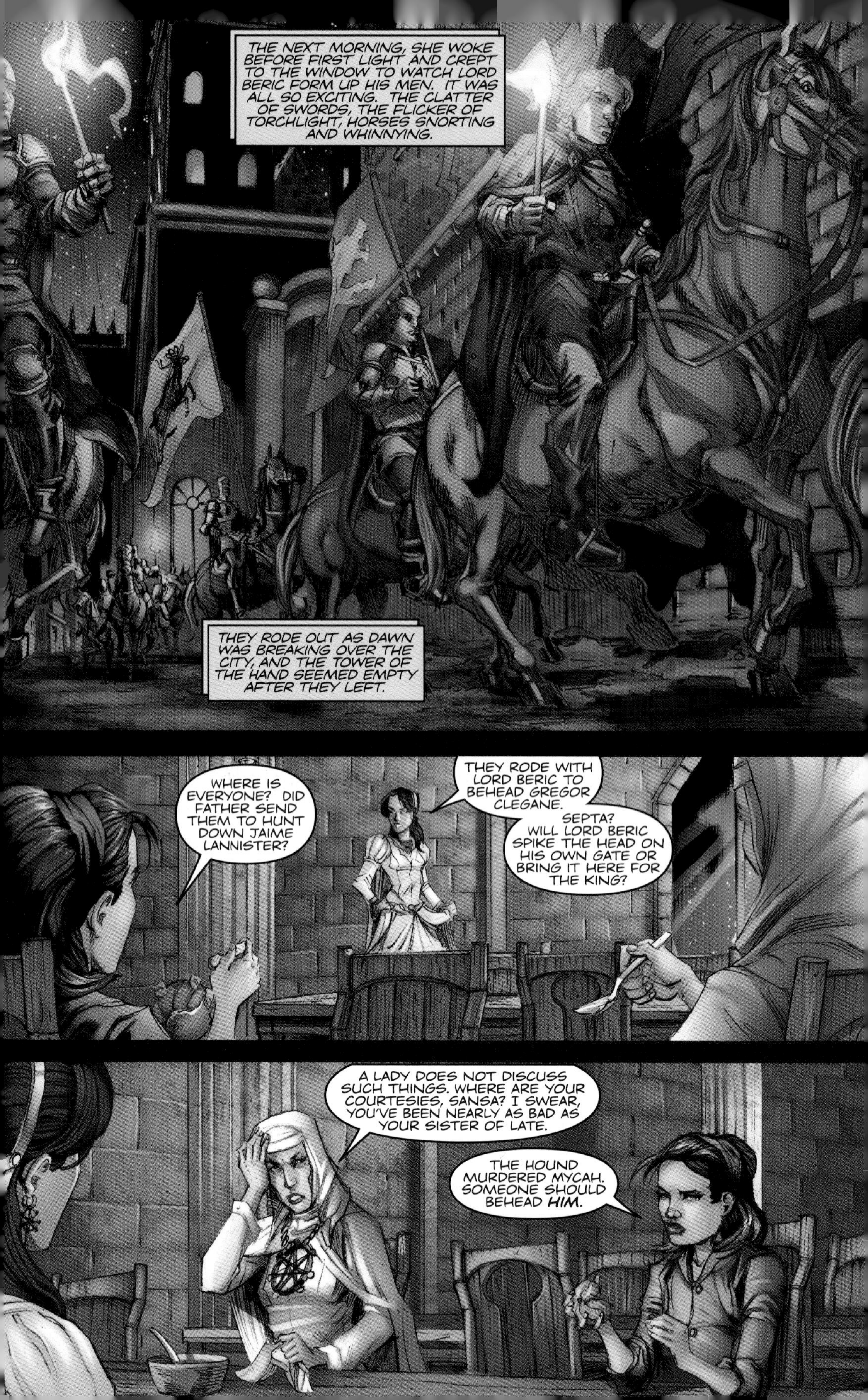
THE NEXT MORNING, SHE WOKE BEFORE FIRST LIGHT AND CREPT TO THE WINDOW TO WATCH LORD BERIC FORM UP HIS MEN. IT WAS ALL SO EXCITING. THE CLATTER OF SWORDS, THE FLICKER OF TORCHLIGHT, HORSES SNORTING AND WHINNYING.
THEY RODE OUT AS DAWN WAS BREAKING OVER THE CITY, AND THE TOWER OF THE HAND SEEMED EMPTY AFTER THEY LEFT.
WHERE IS EVERYONE? DID FATHER SEND THEM TO HUNT DOWN JAIME LANNISTER?
THEY RODE WITH LORD BERIC TO BEHEAD GREGOR CLEGANE.
SEPTA? WILL LORD BERIC SPIKE THE HEAD ON HIS OWN GATE OR BRING IT HERE FOR THE KING?
A LADY DOES NOT DISCUSS SUCH THINGS. WHERE ARE YOUR COURTESIES, SANSA? I SWEAR, YOU'VE BEEN NEARLY AS BAD AS YOUR SISTER OF LATE.
THE HOUND MURDERED MYCAH. SOMEONE SHOULD BEHEAD **HIM**.

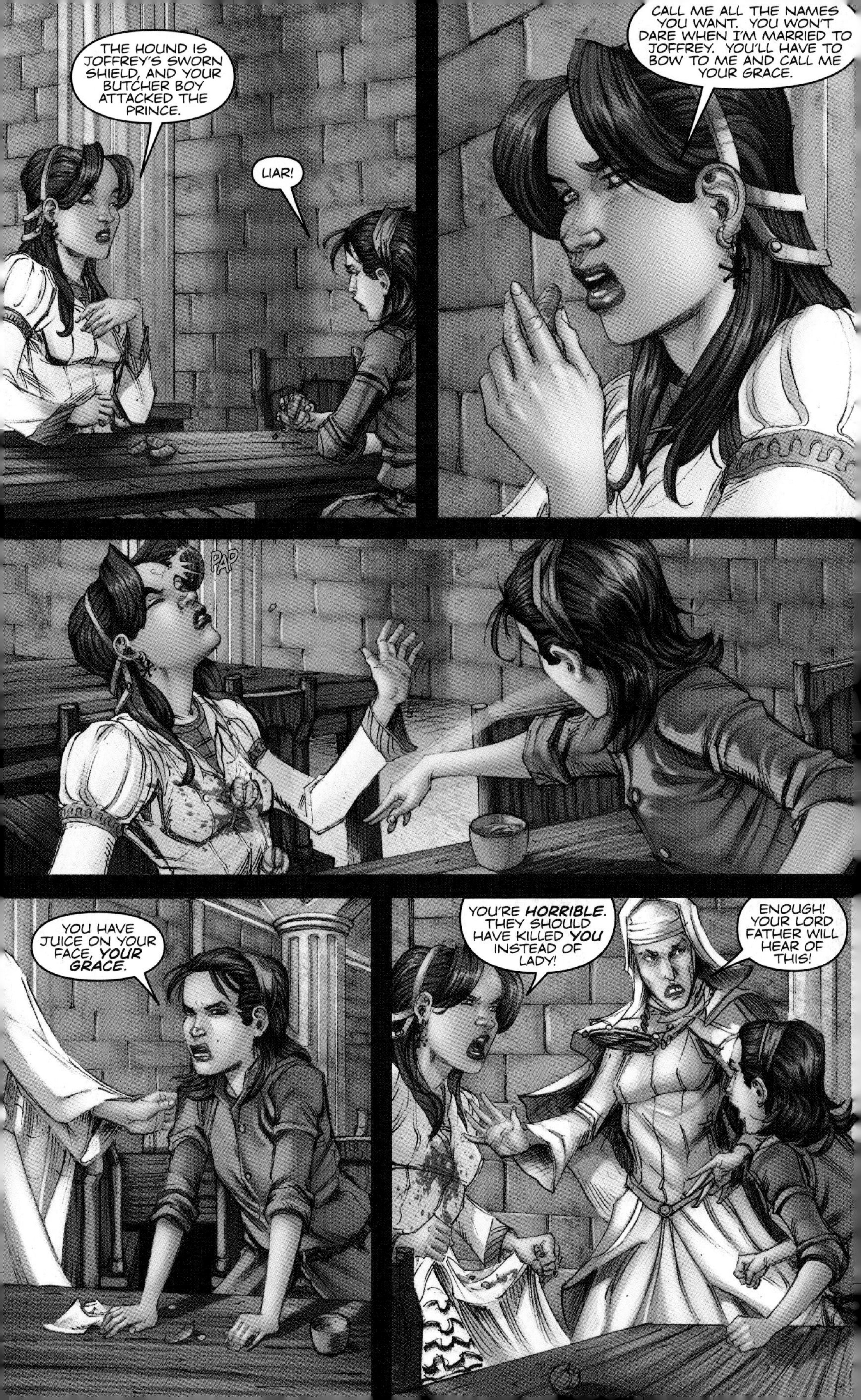
THE HOUND IS JOFFREY'S SWORN SHIELD, AND YOUR BUTCHER BOY ATTACKED THE PRINCE.
LIAR!
CALL ME ALL THE NAMES YOU WANT. YOU WON'T DARE WHEN I'M MARRIED TO JOFFREY. YOU'LL HAVE TO BOW TO ME AND CALL ME YOUR GRACE.
PAP
YOU HAVE JUICE ON YOUR FACE, **YOUR GRACE**.
YOU'RE **HORRIBLE**. THEY SHOULD HAVE KILLED **YOU** INSTEAD OF LADY!
ENOUGH! YOUR LORD FATHER WILL HEAR OF THIS!

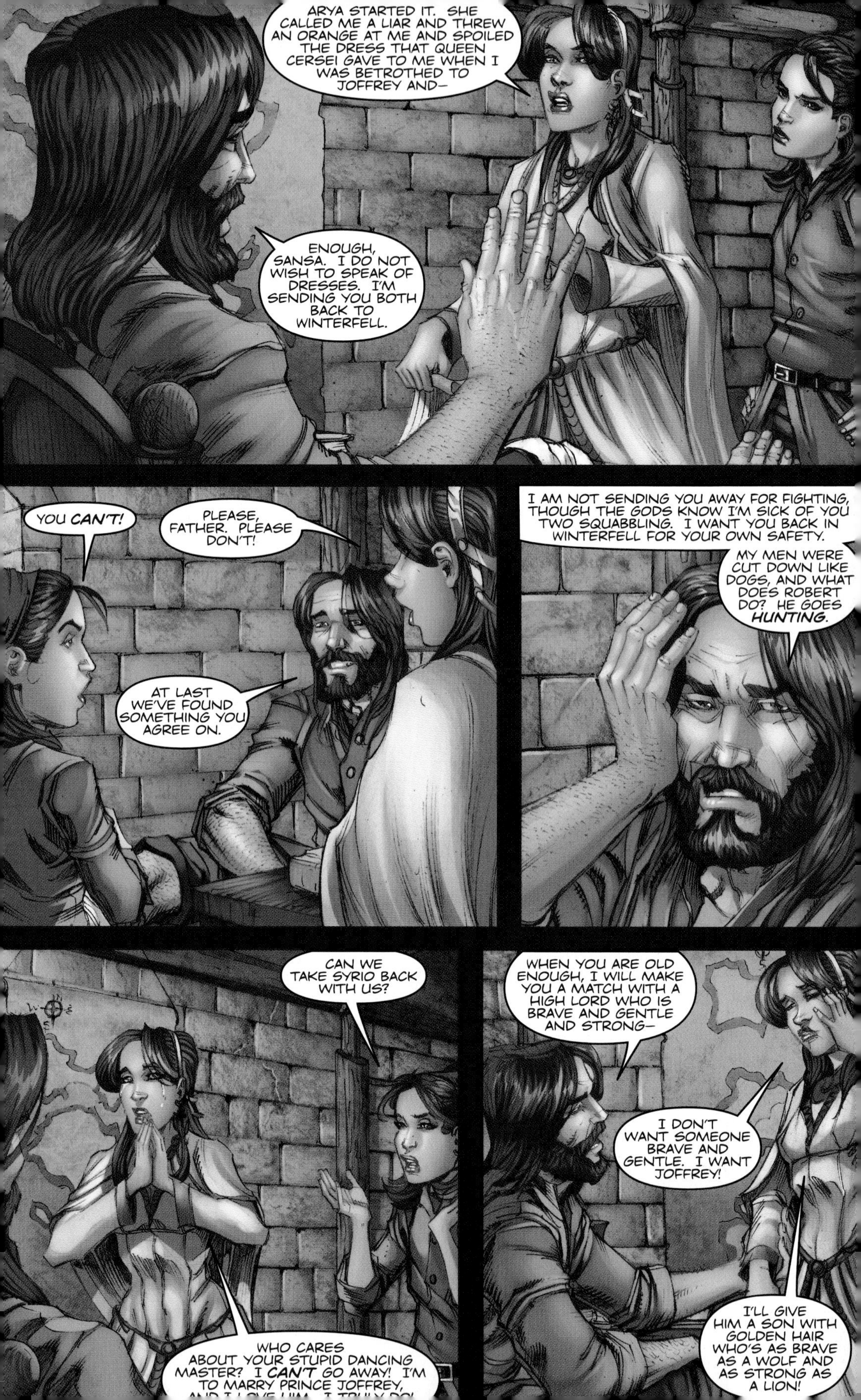
ARYA STARTED IT. SHE CALLED ME A LIAR AND THREW AN ORANGE AT ME AND SPOILED THE DRESS THAT QUEEN CERSEI GAVE TO ME WHEN I WAS BETROTHED TO JOFFREY AND—
ENOUGH, SANSA. I DO NOT WISH TO SPEAK OF DRESSES. I'M SENDING YOU BOTH BACK TO WINTERFELL.
YOU *CAN'T!*
PLEASE, FATHER. PLEASE DON'T!
AT LAST WE'VE FOUND SOMETHING YOU AGREE ON.
I AM NOT SENDING YOU AWAY FOR FIGHTING, THOUGH THE GODS KNOW I'M SICK OF YOU TWO SQUABBLING. I WANT YOU BACK IN WINTERFELL FOR YOUR OWN SAFETY.
MY MEN WERE CUT DOWN LIKE DOGS, AND WHAT DOES ROBERT DO? HE GOES *HUNTING*.
CAN WE TAKE SYRIO BACK WITH US?
WHO CARES ABOUT YOUR STUPID DANCING MASTER? I *CAN'T* GO AWAY! I'M TO MARRY PRINCE JOFFREY,
WHEN YOU ARE OLD ENOUGH, I WILL MAKE YOU A MATCH WITH A HIGH LORD WHO IS BRAVE AND GENTLE AND STRONG—
I DON'T WANT SOMEONE BRAVE AND GENTLE. I WANT JOFFREY!
I'LL GIVE HIM A SON WITH GOLDEN HAIR WHO'S AS BRAVE AS A WOLF AND AS STRONG AS A LION!

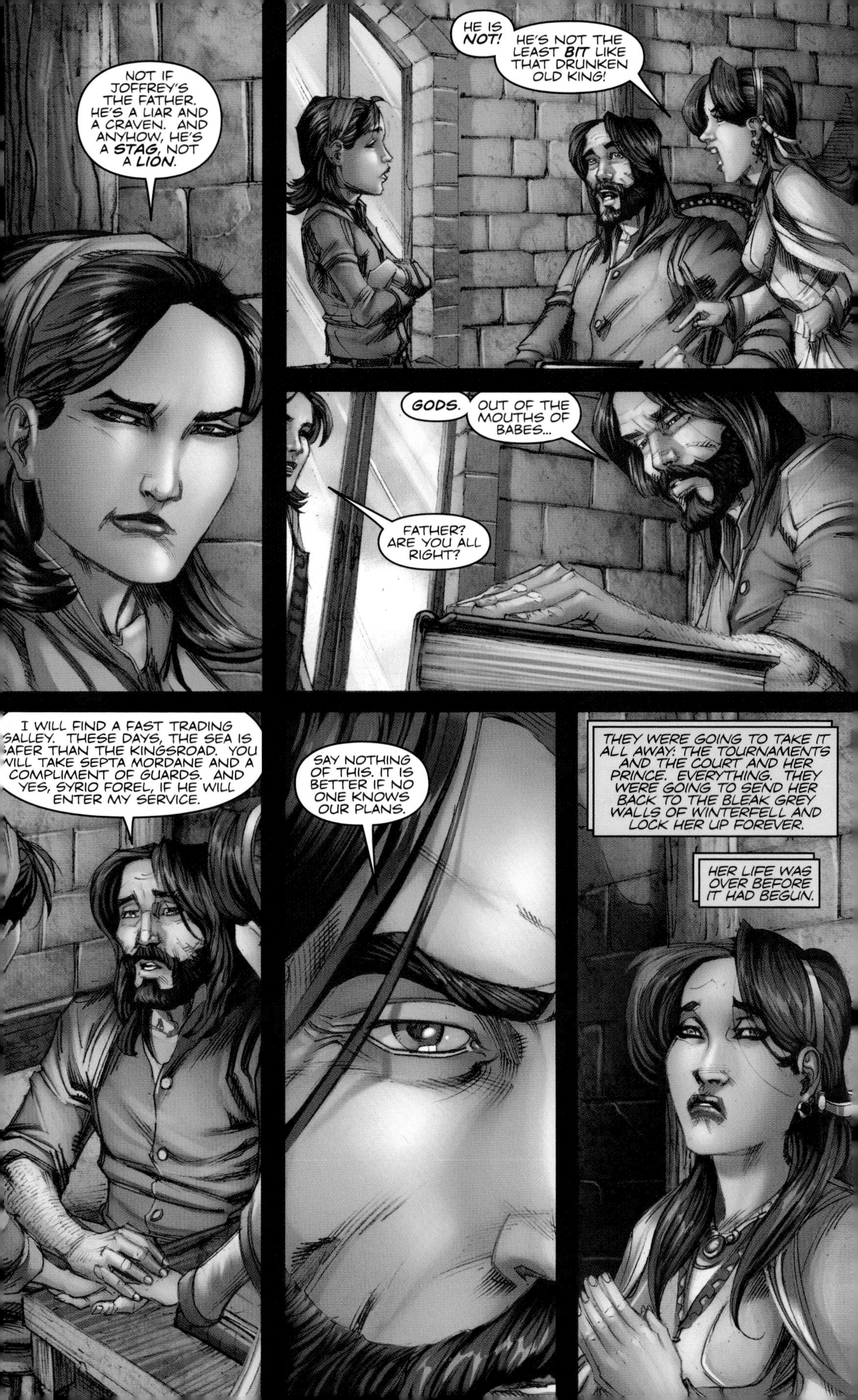
NOT IF JOFFREY'S THE FATHER. HE'S A LIAR AND A CRAVEN. AND ANYHOW, HE'S A **STAG**, NOT A **LION**.
HE IS **NOT**!
HE'S NOT THE LEAST **BIT** LIKE THAT DRUNKEN OLD KING!
**GODS**.
OUT OF THE MOUTHS OF BABES...
FATHER? ARE YOU ALL RIGHT?
I WILL FIND A FAST TRADING GALLEY. THESE DAYS, THE SEA IS SAFER THAN THE KINGSROAD. YOU WILL TAKE SEPTA MORDANE AND A COMPLIMENT OF GUARDS. AND YES, SYRIO FOREL, IF HE WILL ENTER MY SERVICE.
SAY NOTHING OF THIS. IT IS BETTER IF NO ONE KNOWS OUR PLANS.
THEY WERE GOING TO TAKE IT ALL AWAY: THE TOURNAMENTS AND THE COURT AND HER PRINCE. EVERYTHING. THEY WERE GOING TO SEND HER BACK TO THE BLEAK GREY WALLS OF WINTERFELL AND LOCK HER UP FOREVER.
HER LIFE WAS OVER BEFORE IT HAD BEGUN.

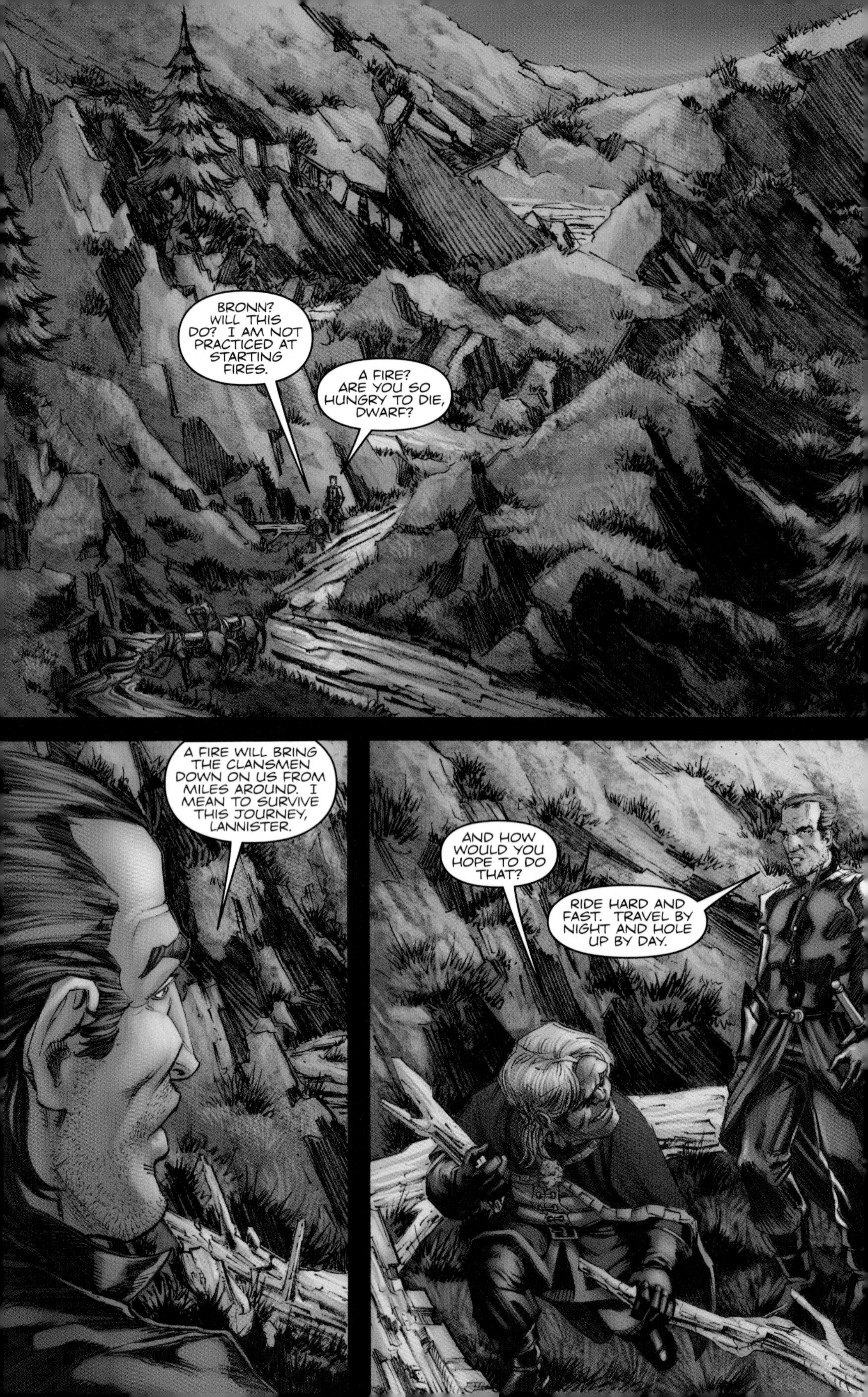
BRONN? WILL THIS DO? I AM NOT PRACTICED AT STARTING FIRES.
A FIRE? ARE YOU SO HUNGRY TO DIE, DWARF?
A FIRE WILL BRING THE CLANSMEN DOWN ON US FROM MILES AROUND. I MEAN TO SURVIVE THIS JOURNEY, LANNISTER.
AND HOW WOULD YOU HOPE TO DO THAT?
RIDE HARD AND FAST. TRAVEL BY NIGHT AND HOLE UP BY DAY.

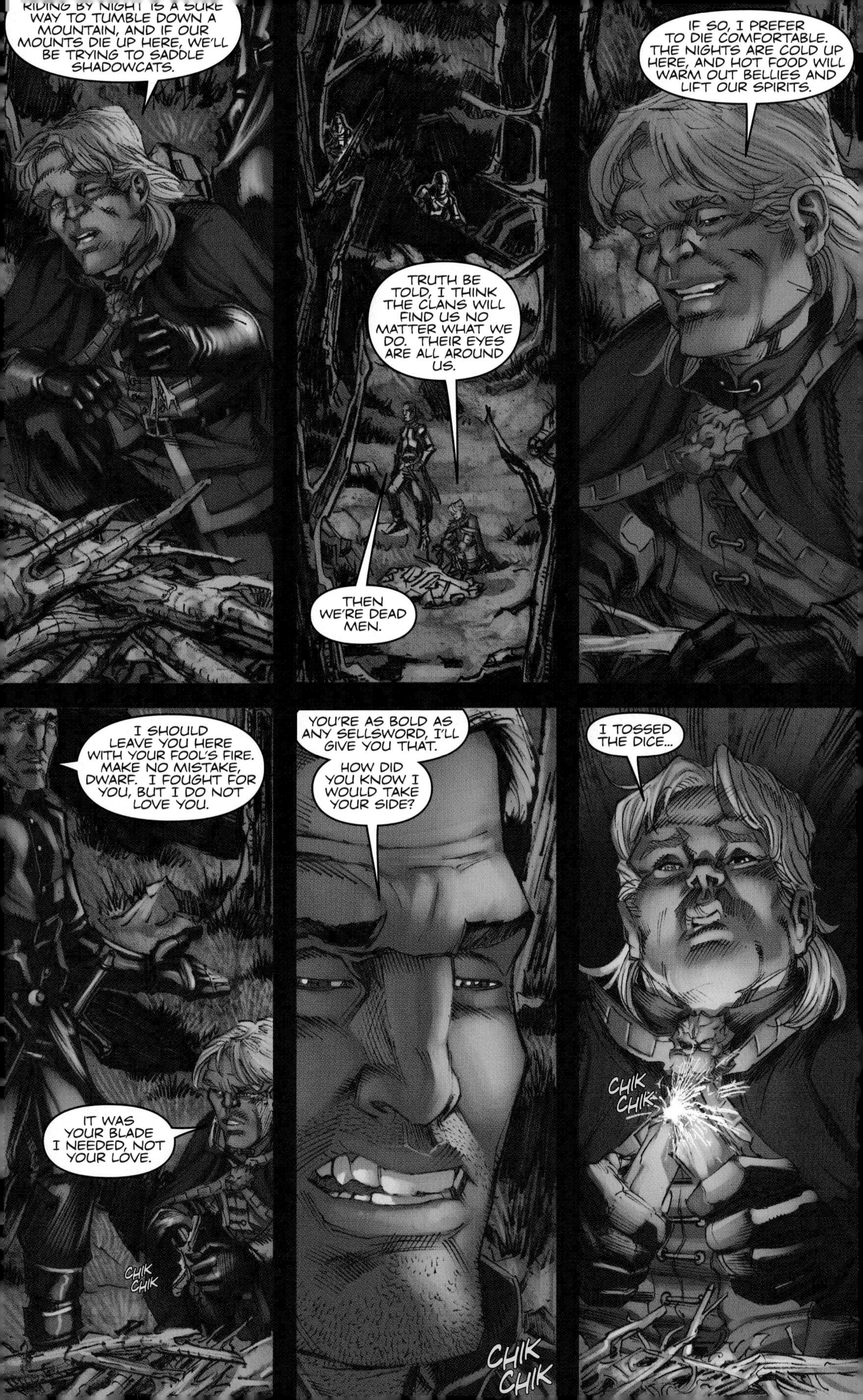
RIDING BY NIGHT IS A SURE WAY TO TUMBLE DOWN A MOUNTAIN, AND IF OUR MOUNTS DIE UP HERE, WE'LL BE TRYING TO SADDLE SHADOWCATS.
TRUTH BE TOLD, I THINK THE CLANS WILL FIND US NO MATTER WHAT WE DO. THEIR EYES ARE ALL AROUND US.
THEN WE'RE DEAD MEN.
IF SO, I PREFER TO DIE COMFORTABLE. THE NIGHTS ARE COLD UP HERE, AND HOT FOOD WILL WARM OUT BELLIES AND LIFT OUR SPIRITS.
I SHOULD LEAVE YOU HERE WITH YOUR FOOL'S FIRE. MAKE NO MISTAKE, DWARF. I FOUGHT FOR YOU, BUT I DO NOT LOVE YOU.
IT WAS YOUR BLADE I NEEDED, NOT YOUR LOVE.
CHIK CHIK
YOU'RE AS BOLD AS ANY SELLSWORD, I'LL GIVE YOU THAT.
HOW DID YOU KNOW I WOULD TAKE YOUR SIDE?
CHIK CHIK
I TOSSED THE DICE...
CHIK CHIK

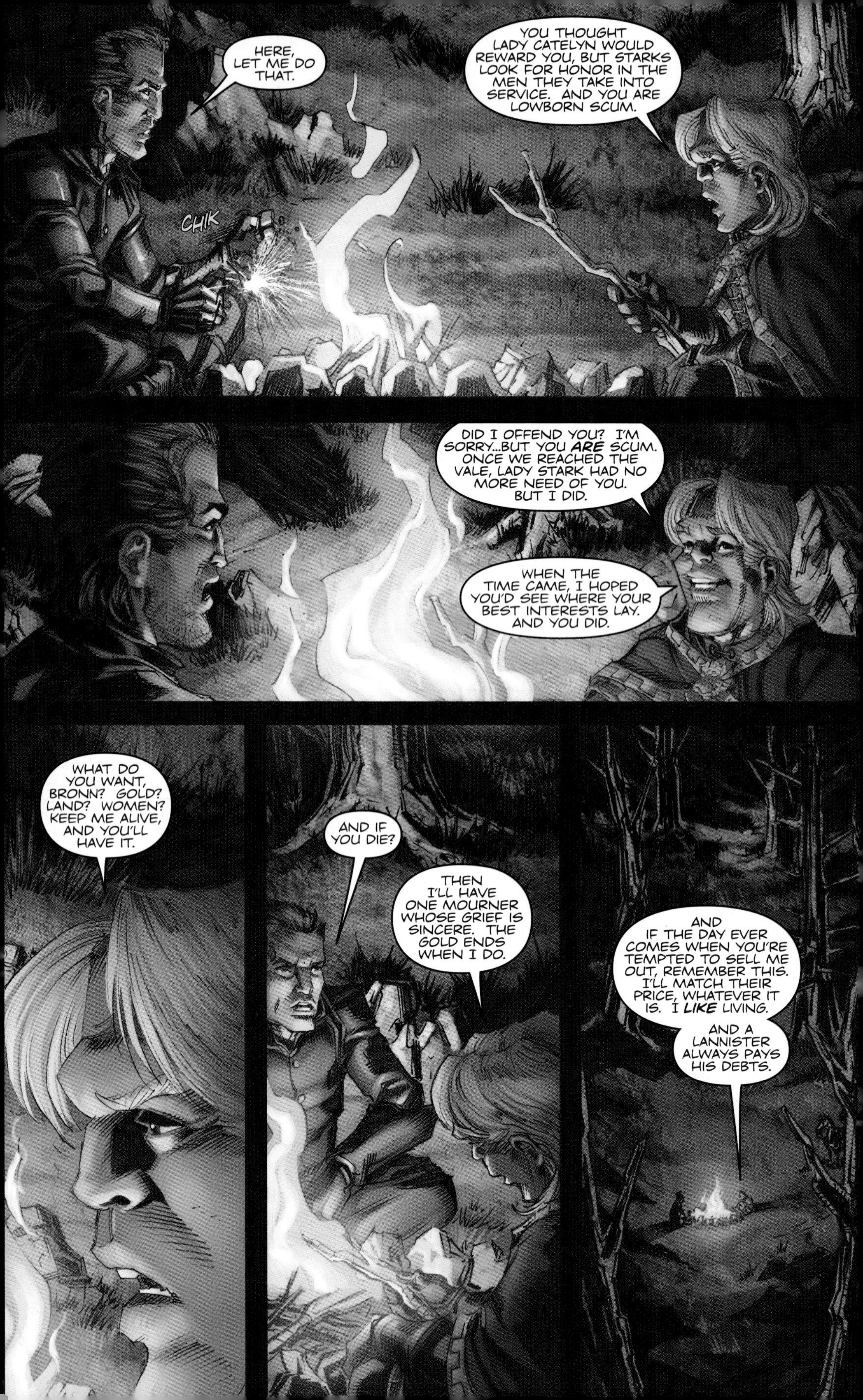
HERE, LET ME DO THAT.
YOU THOUGHT LADY CATELYN WOULD REWARD YOU, BUT STARKS LOOK FOR HONOR IN THE MEN THEY TAKE INTO SERVICE. AND YOU ARE LOWBORN SCUM.
CHIK
DID I OFFEND YOU? I'M SORRY...BUT YOU **ARE** SCUM. ONCE WE REACHED THE VALE, LADY STARK HAD NO MORE NEED OF YOU. BUT I DID.
WHEN THE TIME CAME, I HOPED YOU'D SEE WHERE YOUR BEST INTERESTS LAY. AND YOU DID.
WHAT DO YOU WANT, BRONN? GOLD? LAND? WOMEN? KEEP ME ALIVE, AND YOU'LL HAVE IT.
AND IF YOU DIE?
THEN I'LL HAVE ONE MOURNER WHOSE GRIEF IS SINCERE. THE GOLD ENDS WHEN I DO.
AND IF THE DAY EVER COMES WHEN YOU'RE TEMPTED TO SELL ME OUT, REMEMBER THIS. I'LL MATCH THEIR PRICE, WHATEVER IT IS. I **LIKE** LIVING.
AND A LANNISTER ALWAYS PAYS HIS DEBTS.

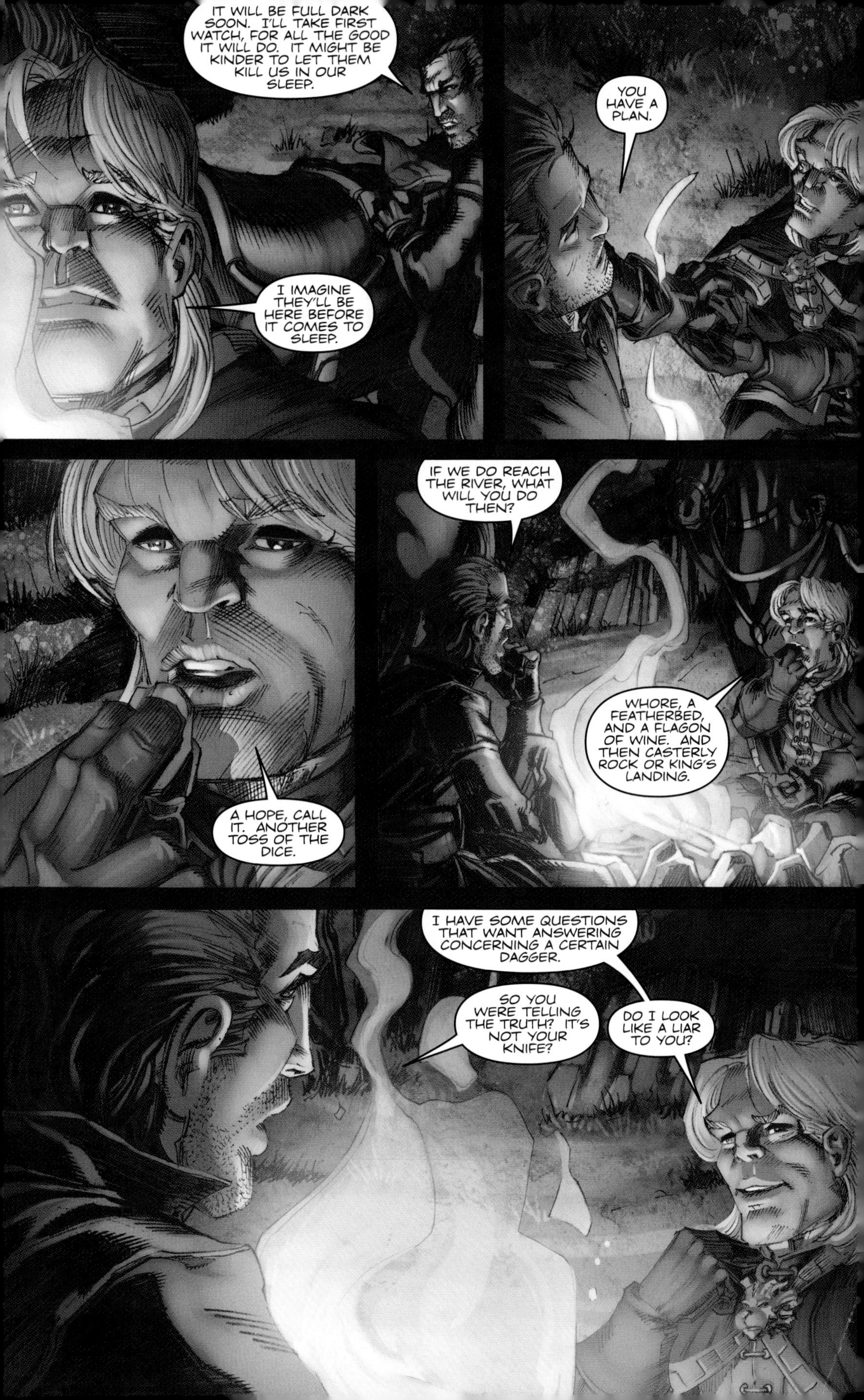
IT WILL BE FULL DARK SOON. I'LL TAKE FIRST WATCH, FOR ALL THE GOOD IT WILL DO. IT MIGHT BE KINDER TO LET THEM KILL US IN OUR SLEEP.
I IMAGINE THEY'LL BE HERE BEFORE IT COMES TO SLEEP.
YOU HAVE A PLAN.
A HOPE, CALL IT. ANOTHER TOSS OF THE DICE.
IF WE DO REACH THE RIVER, WHAT WILL YOU DO THEN?
WHORE, A FEATHERBED, AND A FLAGON OF WINE. AND THEN CASTERLY ROCK OR KING'S LANDING.
I HAVE SOME QUESTIONS THAT WANT ANSWERING CONCERNING A CERTAIN DAGGER.
SO YOU WERE TELLING THE TRUTH? IT'S NOT YOUR KNIFE?
DO I LOOK LIKE A LIAR TO YOU?

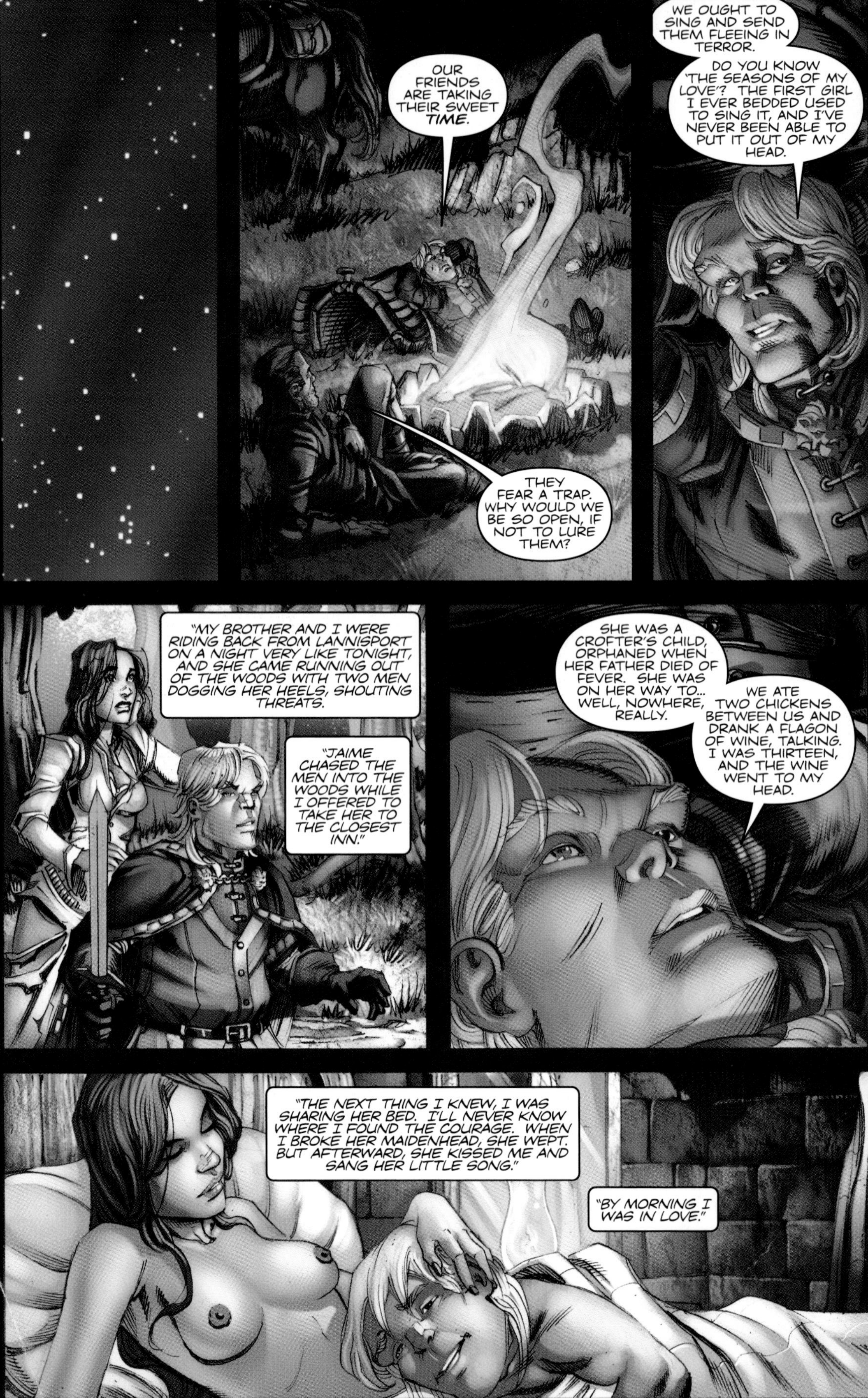
OUR FRIENDS ARE TAKING THEIR SWEET *TIME*.
THEY FEAR A TRAP. WHY WOULD WE BE SO OPEN, IF NOT TO LURE THEM?
WE OUGHT TO SING AND SEND THEM FLEEING IN TERROR.
DO YOU KNOW 'THE SEASONS OF MY LOVE'? THE FIRST GIRL I EVER BEDDED USED TO SING IT, AND I'VE NEVER BEEN ABLE TO PUT IT OUT OF MY HEAD.
"MY BROTHER AND I WERE RIDING BACK FROM LANNISPORT ON A NIGHT VERY LIKE TONIGHT, AND SHE CAME RUNNING OUT OF THE WOODS WITH TWO MEN DOGGING HER HEELS, SHOUTING THREATS.
"JAIME CHASED THE MEN INTO THE WOODS WHILE I OFFERED TO TAKE HER TO THE CLOSEST INN."
SHE WAS A CROFTER'S CHILD, ORPHANED WHEN HER FATHER DIED OF FEVER. SHE WAS ON HER WAY TO... WELL, NOWHERE, REALLY.
WE ATE TWO CHICKENS BETWEEN US AND DRANK A FLAGON OF WINE, TALKING. I WAS THIRTEEN, AND THE WINE WENT TO MY HEAD.
"THE NEXT THING I KNEW, I WAS SHARING HER BED. I'LL NEVER KNOW WHERE I FOUND THE COURAGE. WHEN I BROKE HER MAIDENHEAD, SHE WEPT. BUT AFTERWARD, SHE KISSED ME AND SANG HER LITTLE SONG."
"BY MORNING I WAS IN LOVE."

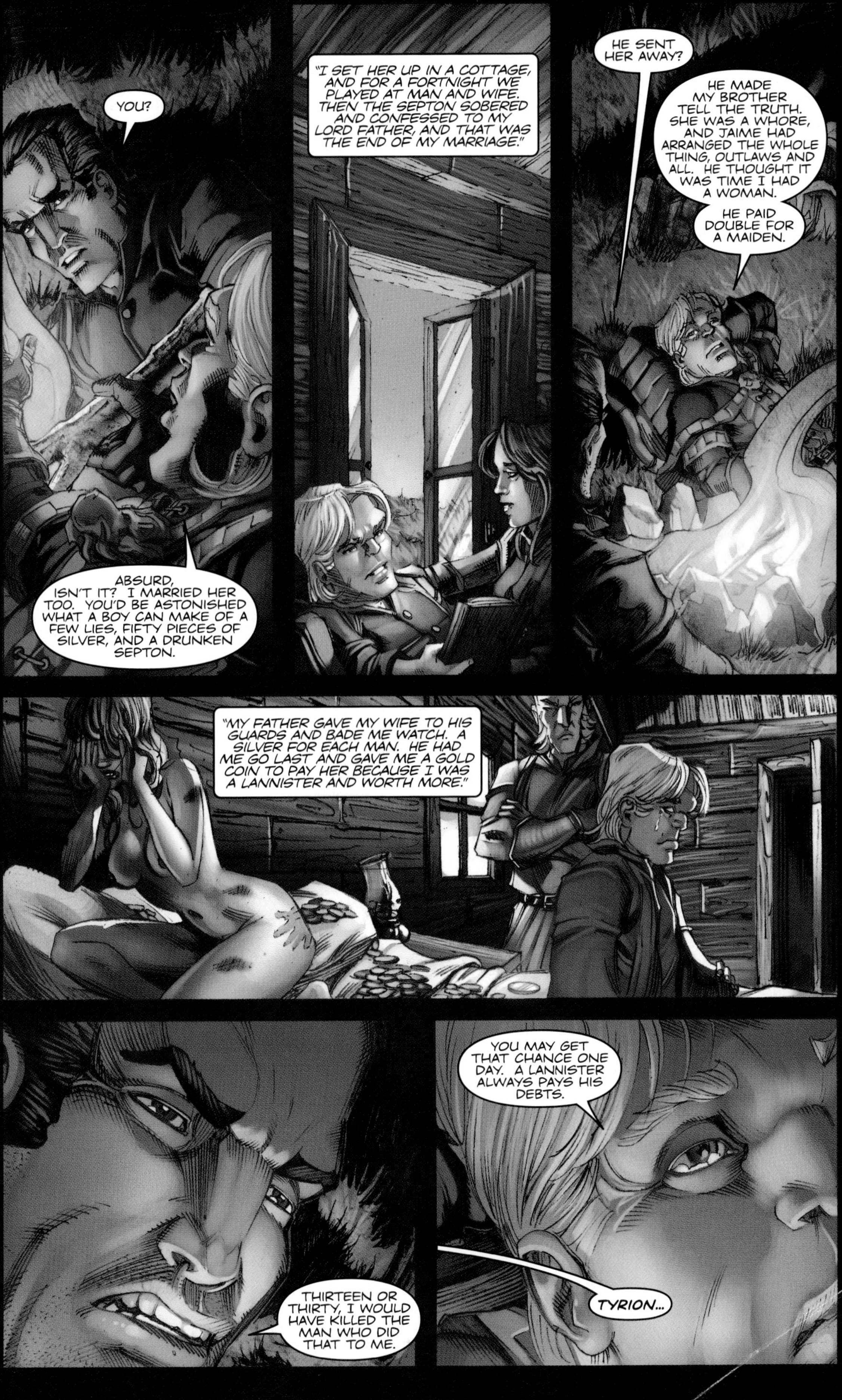
YOU?
ABSURD, ISN'T IT? I MARRIED HER TOO. YOU'D BE ASTONISHED WHAT A BOY CAN MAKE OF A FEW LIES, FIFTY PIECES OF SILVER, AND A DRUNKEN SEPTON.
"I SET HER UP IN A COTTAGE, AND FOR A FORTNIGHT WE PLAYED AT MAN AND WIFE. THEN THE SEPTON SOBERED AND CONFESSED TO MY LORD FATHER, AND THAT WAS THE END OF MY MARRIAGE."
HE SENT HER AWAY?
HE MADE MY BROTHER TELL THE TRUTH. SHE WAS A WHORE, AND JAIME HAD ARRANGED THE WHOLE THING, OUTLAWS AND ALL. HE THOUGHT IT WAS TIME I HAD A WOMAN.
HE PAID DOUBLE FOR A MAIDEN.
"MY FATHER GAVE MY WIFE TO HIS GUARDS AND BADE ME WATCH. A SILVER FOR EACH MAN. HE HAD ME GO LAST AND GAVE ME A GOLD COIN TO PAY HER BECAUSE I WAS A LANNISTER AND WORTH MORE."
THIRTEEN OR THIRTY, I WOULD HAVE KILLED THE MAN WHO DID THAT TO ME.
YOU MAY GET THAT CHANCE ONE DAY. A LANNISTER ALWAYS PAYS HIS DEBTS.
TYRION...

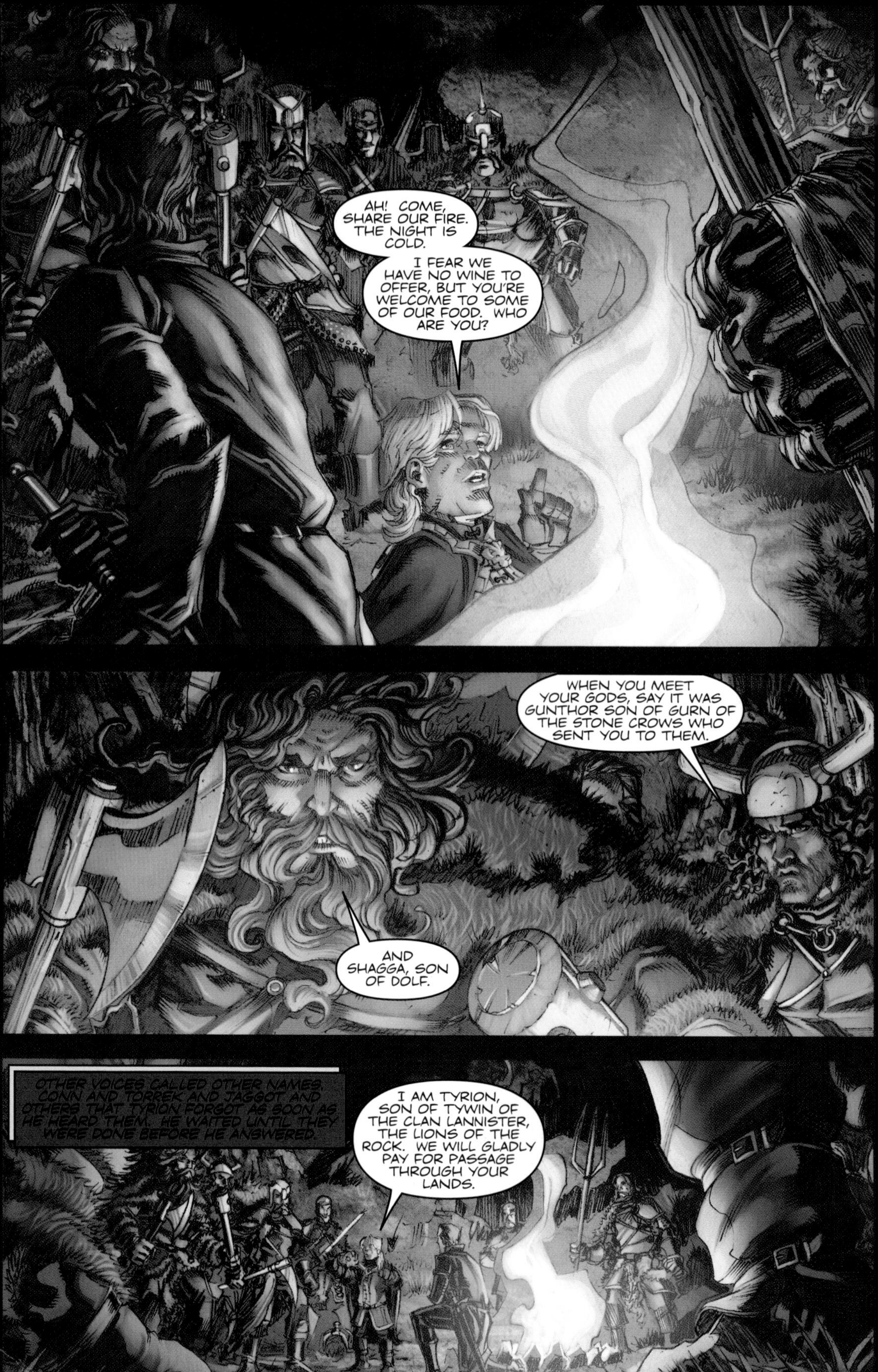
AH! COME, SHARE OUR FIRE. THE NIGHT IS COLD.
I FEAR WE HAVE NO WINE TO OFFER, BUT YOU'RE WELCOME TO SOME OF OUR FOOD. WHO ARE YOU?
WHEN YOU MEET YOUR GODS, SAY IT WAS GUNTHOR SON OF GURN OF THE STONE CROWS WHO SENT YOU TO THEM.
AND SHAGGA, SON OF DOLF.
OTHER VOICES CALLED OTHER NAMES. CONN AND TORREK AND JAGGOT AND OTHERS THAT TYRION FORGOT AS SOON AS HE HEARD THEM. HE WAITED UNTIL THEY WERE DONE BEFORE HE ANSWERED.
I AM TYRION, SON OF TYWIN OF THE CLAN LANNISTER, THE LIONS OF THE ROCK. WE WILL GLADLY PAY FOR PASSAGE THROUGH YOUR LANDS.

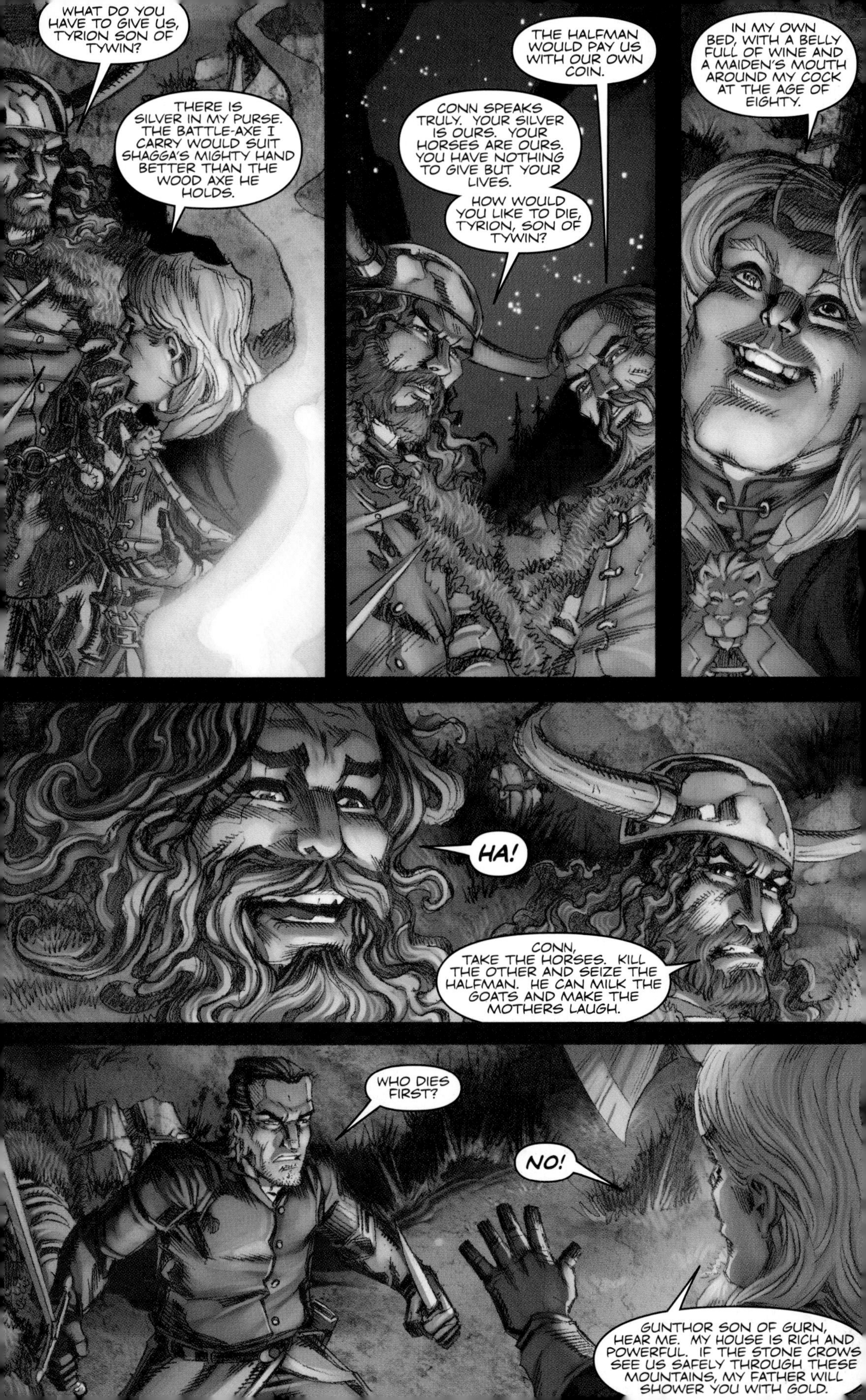
WHAT DO YOU HAVE TO GIVE US, TYRION SON OF TYWIN?
THERE IS SILVER IN MY PURSE. THE BATTLE-AXE I CARRY WOULD SUIT SHAGGA'S MIGHTY HAND BETTER THAN THE WOOD AXE HE HOLDS.
THE HALFMAN WOULD PAY US WITH OUR OWN COIN.
CONN SPEAKS TRULY. YOUR SILVER IS OURS. YOUR HORSES ARE OURS. YOU HAVE NOTHING TO GIVE BUT YOUR LIVES.
HOW WOULD YOU LIKE TO DIE, TYRION, SON OF TYWIN?
IN MY OWN BED, WITH A BELLY FULL OF WINE AND A MAIDEN'S MOUTH AROUND MY COCK AT THE AGE OF EIGHTY.
HA!
CONN, TAKE THE HORSES. KILL THE OTHER AND SEIZE THE HALFMAN. HE CAN MILK THE GOATS AND MAKE THE MOTHERS LAUGH.
WHO DIES FIRST?
NO!
GUNTHOR SON OF GURN, HEAR ME. MY HOUSE IS RICH AND POWERFUL. IF THE STONE CROWS SEE US SAFELY THROUGH THESE MOUNTAINS, MY FATHER WILL SHOWER YOU WITH GOLD.

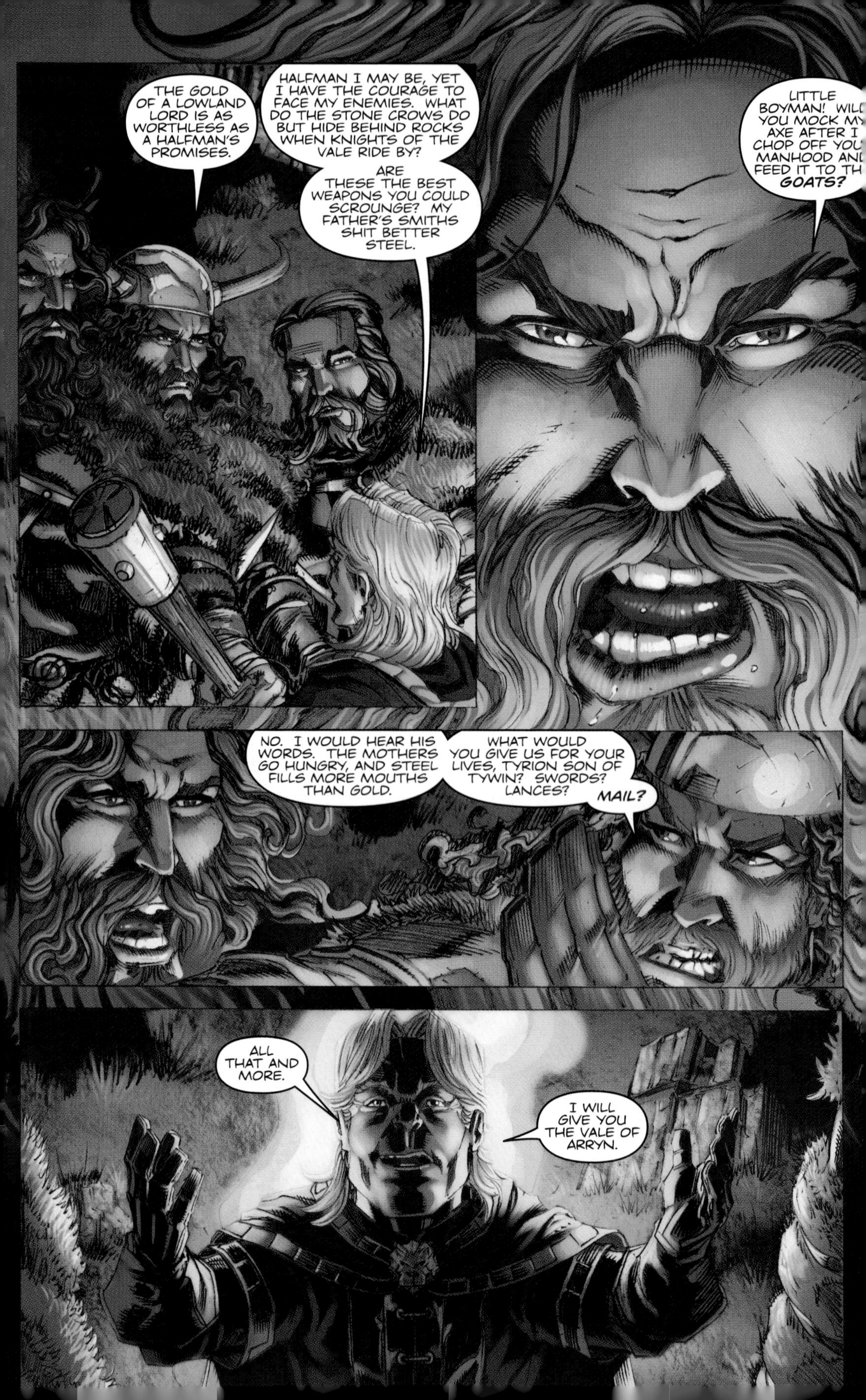
THE GOLD OF A LOWLAND LORD IS AS WORTHLESS AS A HALFMAN'S PROMISES.
HALFMAN I MAY BE, YET I HAVE THE COURAGE TO FACE MY ENEMIES. WHAT DO THE STONE CROWS DO BUT HIDE BEHIND ROCKS WHEN KNIGHTS OF THE VALE RIDE BY?
ARE THESE THE BEST WEAPONS YOU COULD SCROUNGE? MY FATHER'S SMITHS SHIT BETTER STEEL.
LITTLE BOYMAN! WILL YOU MOCK MY AXE AFTER I CHOP OFF YOUR MANHOOD AND FEED IT TO THE GOATS?
NO. I WOULD HEAR HIS WORDS. THE MOTHERS GO HUNGRY, AND STEEL FILLS MORE MOUTHS THAN GOLD.
WHAT WOULD YOU GIVE US FOR YOUR LIVES, TYRION SON OF TYWIN? SWORDS? LANCES? MAIL?
ALL THAT AND MORE.
I WILL GIVE YOU THE VALE OF ARRYN.

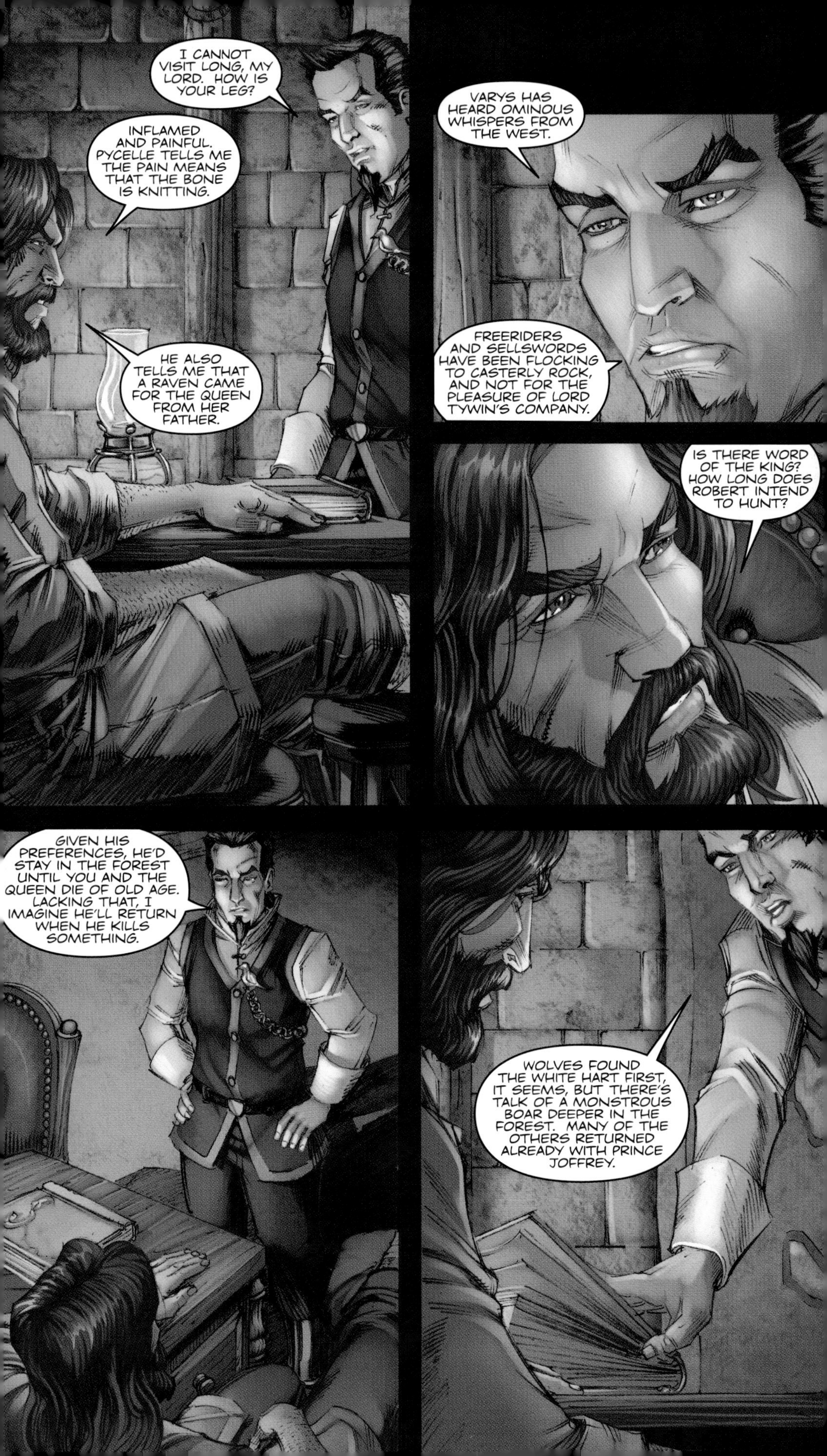
I CANNOT VISIT LONG, MY LORD. HOW IS YOUR LEG?
INFLAMED AND PAINFUL. PYCELLE TELLS ME THE PAIN MEANS THAT THE BONE IS KNITTING.
HE ALSO TELLS ME THAT A RAVEN CAME FOR THE QUEEN FROM HER FATHER.
VARYS HAS HEARD OMINOUS WHISPERS FROM THE WEST.
FREERIDERS AND SELLSWORDS HAVE BEEN FLOCKING TO CASTERLY ROCK, AND NOT FOR THE PLEASURE OF LORD TYWIN'S COMPANY.
IS THERE WORD OF THE KING? HOW LONG DOES ROBERT INTEND TO HUNT?
GIVEN HIS PREFERENCES, HE'D STAY IN THE FOREST UNTIL YOU AND THE QUEEN DIE OF OLD AGE. LACKING THAT, I IMAGINE HE'LL RETURN WHEN HE KILLS SOMETHING.
WOLVES FOUND THE WHITE HART FIRST, IT SEEMS, BUT THERE'S TALK OF A MONSTROUS BOAR DEEPER IN THE FOREST. MANY OF THE OTHERS RETURNED ALREADY WITH PRINCE JOFFREY.

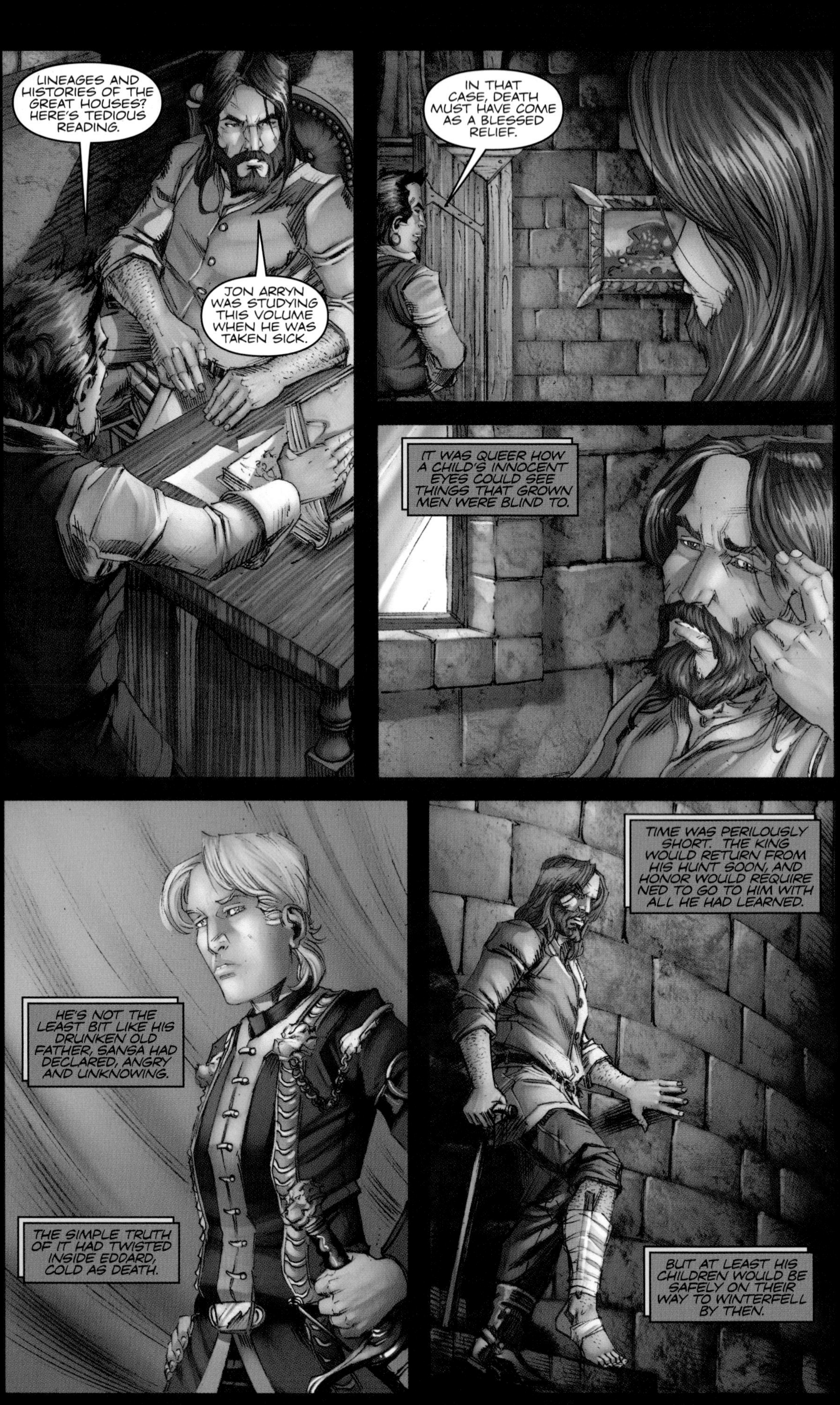
LINEAGES AND HISTORIES OF THE GREAT HOUSES? HERE'S TEDIOUS READING.
JON ARRYN WAS STUDYING THIS VOLUME WHEN HE WAS TAKEN SICK.
IN THAT CASE, DEATH MUST HAVE COME AS A BLESSED RELIEF.
IT WAS QUEER HOW A CHILD'S INNOCENT EYES COULD SEE THINGS THAT GROWN MEN WERE BLIND TO.
HE'S NOT THE LEAST BIT LIKE HIS DRUNKEN OLD FATHER, SANSA HAD DECLARED, ANGRY AND UNKNOWING.
THE SIMPLE TRUTH OF IT HAD TWISTED INSIDE EDDARD, COLD AS DEATH.
TIME WAS PERILOUSLY SHORT. THE KING WOULD RETURN FROM HIS HUNT SOON, AND HONOR WOULD REQUIRE NED TO GO TO HIM WITH ALL HE HAD LEARNED.
BUT AT LEAST HIS CHILDREN WOULD BE SAFELY ON THEIR WAY TO WINTERFELL BY THEN.

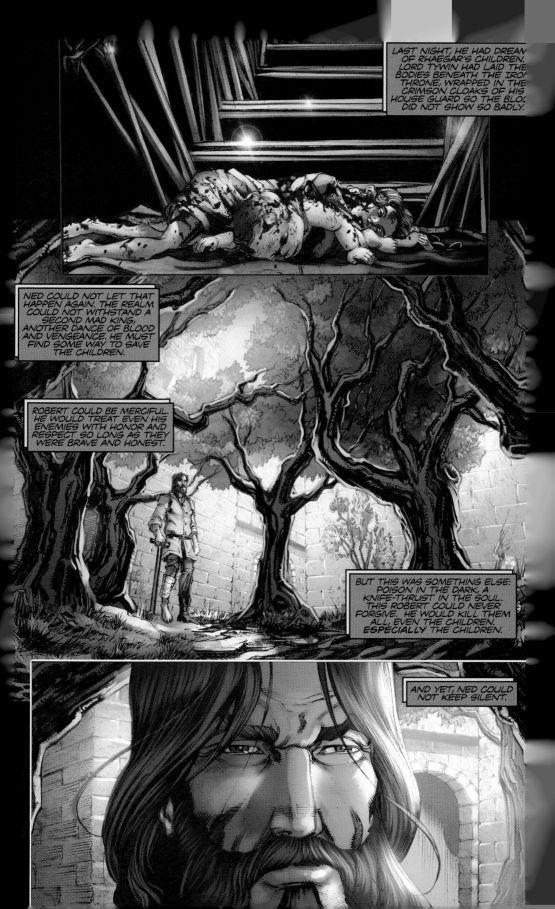

LAST NIGHT, HE HAD DREAM[ED] OF RHAEGAR'S CHILDREN. LORD TYWIN HAD LAID THE[IR] BODIES BENEATH THE IRO[N] THRONE, WRAPPED IN THE CRIMSON CLOAKS OF HIS HOUSE GUARD SO THE BLOO[D] DID NOT SHOW SO BADLY.

NED COULD NOT LET THAT HAPPEN AGAIN. THE REALM COULD NOT WITHSTAND A SECOND MAD KING, ANOTHER DANCE OF BLOOD AND VENGEANCE. HE MUST FIND SOME WAY TO SAVE THE CHILDREN.

ROBERT COULD BE MERCIFUL. HE WOULD TREAT EVEN HIS ENEMIES WITH HONOR AND RESPECT SO LONG AS THEY WERE BRAVE AND HONEST.

BUT THIS WAS SOMETHING ELSE: POISON IN THE DARK, A KNIFE-THRUST IN THE SOUL. THIS ROBERT COULD NEVER FORGIVE. HE WOULD KILL THEM ALL, EVEN THE CHILDREN. ESPECIALLY THE CHILDREN.

AND YET, NED COULD NOT KEEP SILENT.

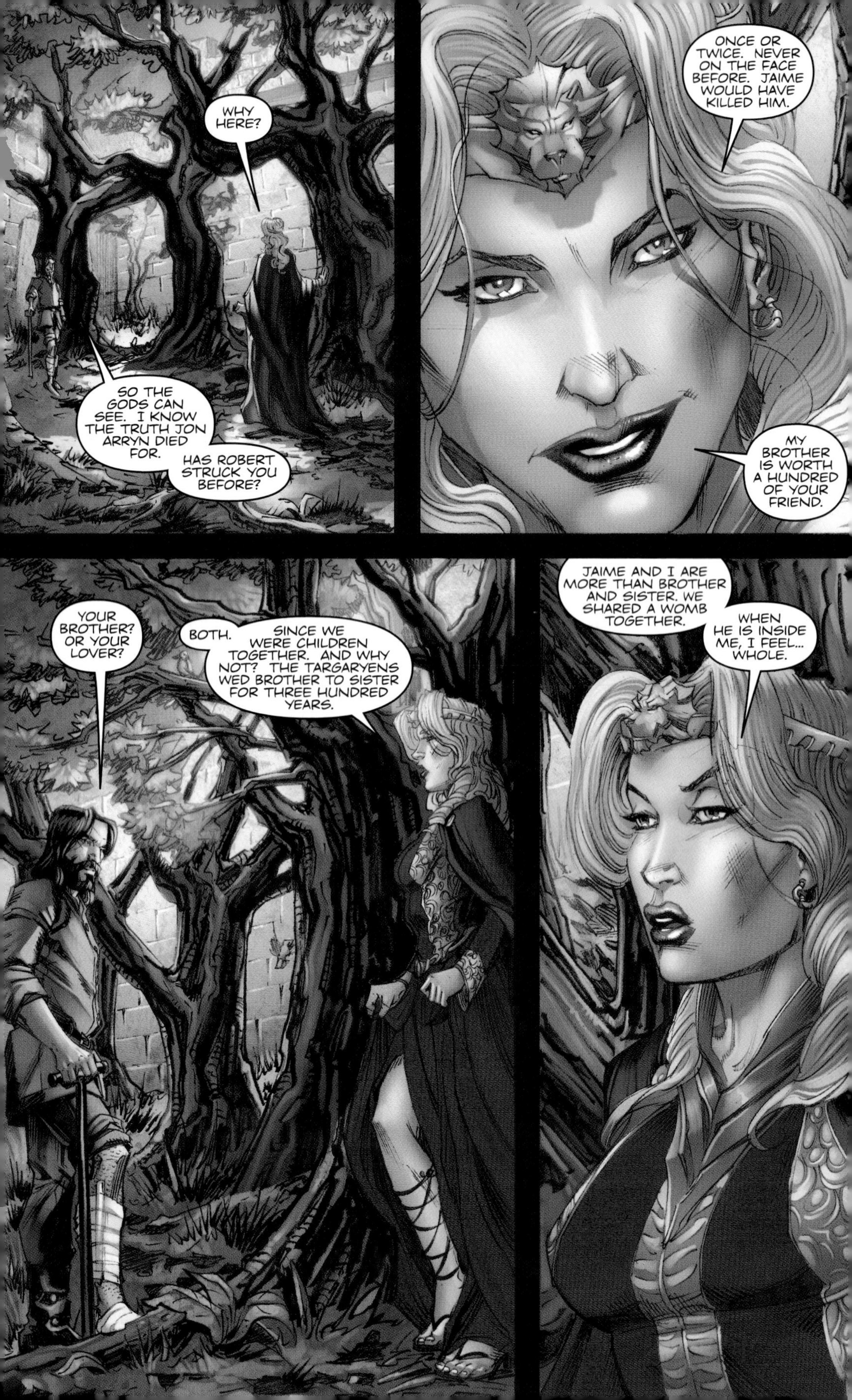
WHY HERE?
SO THE GODS CAN SEE. I KNOW THE TRUTH JON ARRYN DIED FOR.
HAS ROBERT STRUCK YOU BEFORE?
ONCE OR TWICE. NEVER ON THE FACE BEFORE. JAIME WOULD HAVE KILLED HIM.
MY BROTHER IS WORTH A HUNDRED OF YOUR FRIEND.
YOUR BROTHER? OR YOUR LOVER?
BOTH.
SINCE WE WERE CHILDREN TOGETHER. AND WHY NOT? THE TARGARYENS WED BROTHER TO SISTER FOR THREE HUNDRED YEARS.
JAIME AND I ARE MORE THAN BROTHER AND SISTER. WE SHARED A WOMB TOGETHER.
WHEN HE IS INSIDE ME, I FEEL... WHOLE.

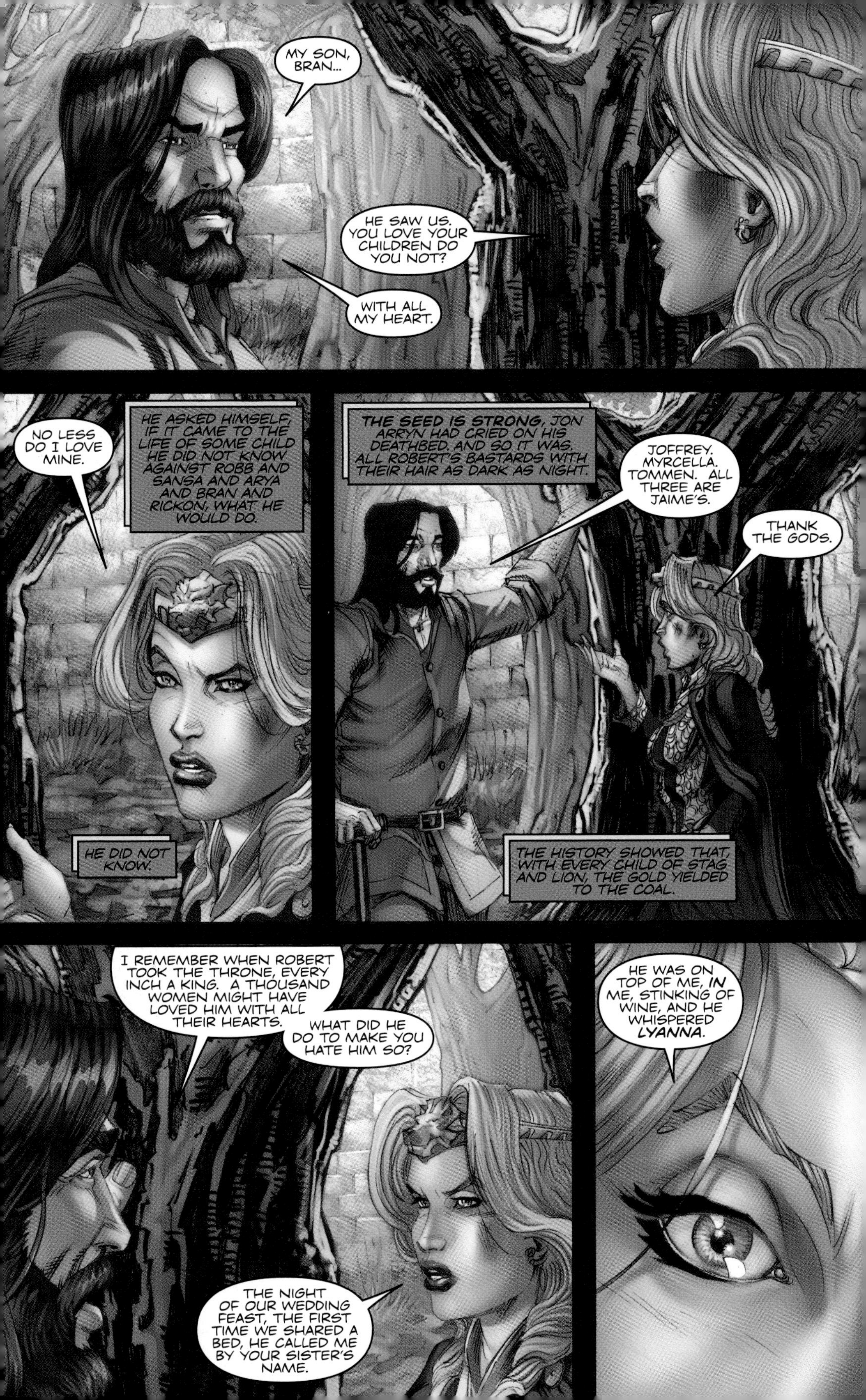
MY SON, BRAN...
HE SAW US. YOU LOVE YOUR CHILDREN DO YOU NOT?
WITH ALL MY HEART.
NO LESS DO I LOVE MINE.
HE ASKED HIMSELF, IF IT CAME TO THE LIFE OF SOME CHILD HE DID NOT KNOW AGAINST ROBB AND SANSA AND ARYA AND BRAN AND RICKON, WHAT HE WOULD DO.
HE DID NOT KNOW.
THE SEED IS STRONG, JON ARRYN HAD CRIED ON HIS DEATHBED. AND SO IT WAS. ALL ROBERT'S BASTARDS WITH THEIR HAIR AS DARK AS NIGHT.
JOFFREY. MYRCELLA. TOMMEN. ALL THREE ARE JAIME'S.
THANK THE GODS.
THE HISTORY SHOWED THAT, WITH EVERY CHILD OF STAG AND LION, THE GOLD YIELDED TO THE COAL.
I REMEMBER WHEN ROBERT TOOK THE THRONE, EVERY INCH A KING. A THOUSAND WOMEN MIGHT HAVE LOVED HIM WITH ALL THEIR HEARTS.
WHAT DID HE DO TO MAKE YOU HATE HIM SO?
THE NIGHT OF OUR WEDDING FEAST, THE FIRST TIME WE SHARED A BED, HE CALLED ME BY YOUR SISTER'S NAME.
HE WAS ON TOP OF ME, IN ME, STINKING OF WINE, AND HE WHISPERED LYANNA.

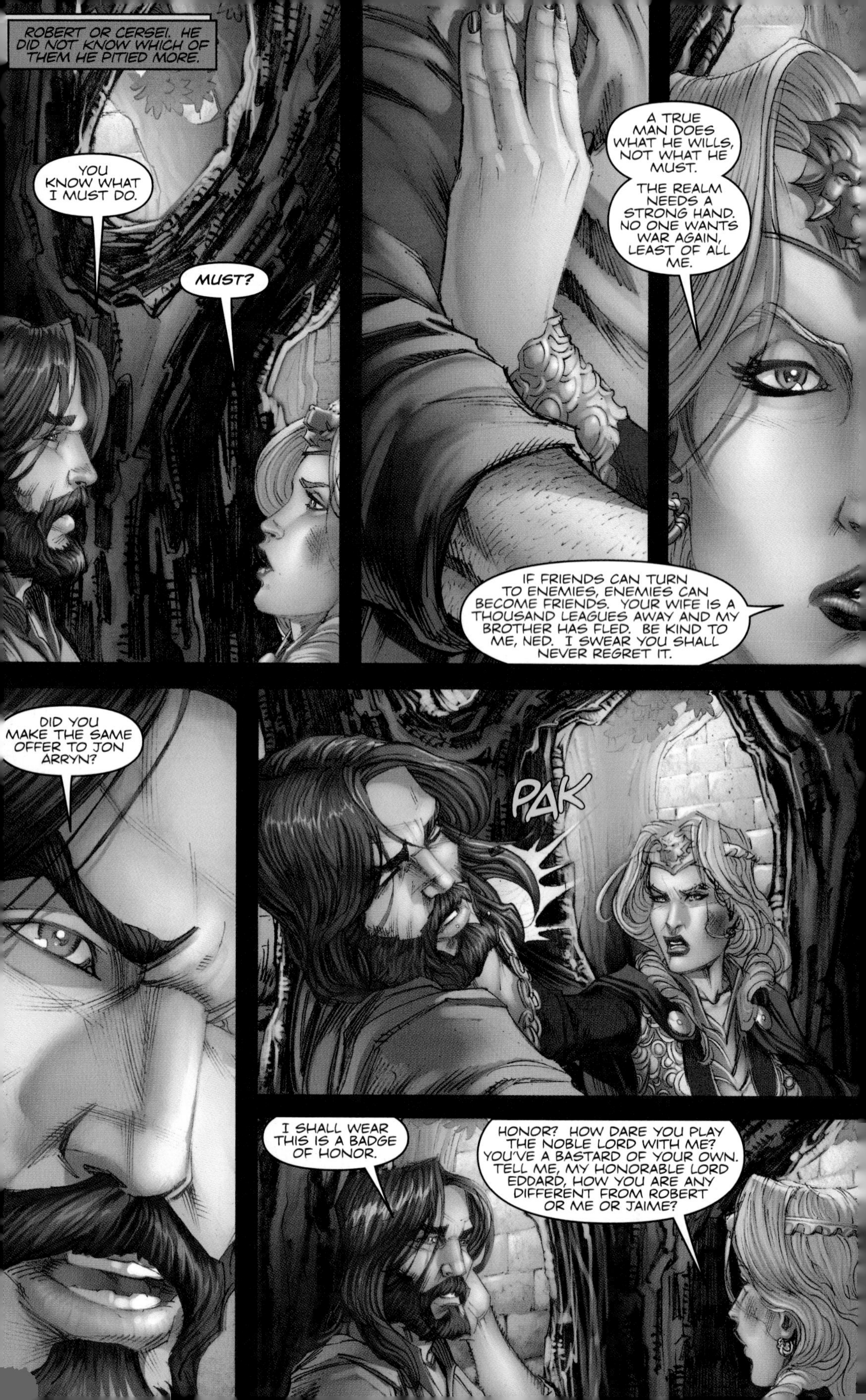
ROBERT OR CERSEI. HE DID NOT KNOW WHICH OF THEM HE PITIED MORE.
YOU KNOW WHAT I MUST DO.
MUST?
A TRUE MAN DOES WHAT HE WILLS, NOT WHAT HE MUST.
THE REALM NEEDS A STRONG HAND. NO ONE WANTS WAR AGAIN, LEAST OF ALL ME.
IF FRIENDS CAN TURN TO ENEMIES, ENEMIES CAN BECOME FRIENDS. YOUR WIFE IS A THOUSAND LEAGUES AWAY AND MY BROTHER HAS FLED. BE KIND TO ME, NED. I SWEAR YOU SHALL NEVER REGRET IT.
DID YOU MAKE THE SAME OFFER TO JON ARRYN?
PAK
I SHALL WEAR THIS IS A BADGE OF HONOR.
HONOR? HOW DARE YOU PLAY THE NOBLE LORD WITH ME? YOU'VE A BASTARD OF YOUR OWN. TELL ME, MY HONORABLE LORD EDDARD, HOW YOU ARE ANY DIFFERENT FROM ROBERT OR ME OR JAIME?

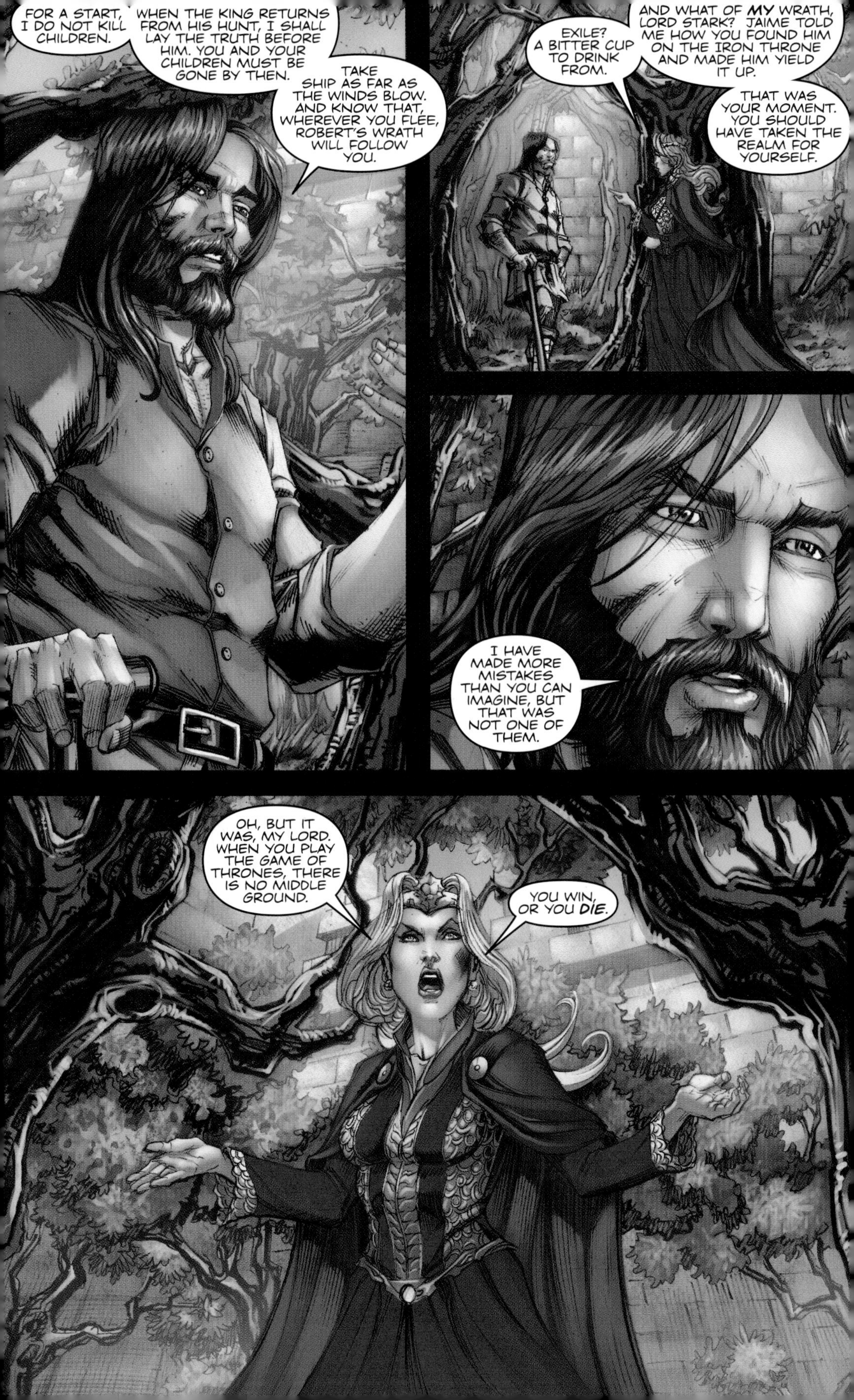
FOR A START, I DO NOT KILL CHILDREN.
WHEN THE KING RETURNS FROM HIS HUNT, I SHALL LAY THE TRUTH BEFORE HIM. YOU AND YOUR CHILDREN MUST BE GONE BY THEN.
TAKE SHIP AS FAR AS THE WINDS BLOW. AND KNOW THAT, WHEREVER YOU FLEE, ROBERT'S WRATH WILL FOLLOW YOU.
EXILE? A BITTER CUP TO DRINK FROM.
AND WHAT OF MY WRATH, LORD STARK? JAIME TOLD ME HOW YOU FOUND HIM ON THE IRON THRONE AND MADE HIM YIELD IT UP.
THAT WAS YOUR MOMENT. YOU SHOULD HAVE TAKEN THE REALM FOR YOURSELF.
I HAVE MADE MORE MISTAKES THAN YOU CAN IMAGINE, BUT THAT WAS NOT ONE OF THEM.
OH, BUT IT WAS, MY LORD. WHEN YOU PLAY THE GAME OF THRONES, THERE IS NO MIDDLE GROUND.
YOU WIN, OR YOU DIE.

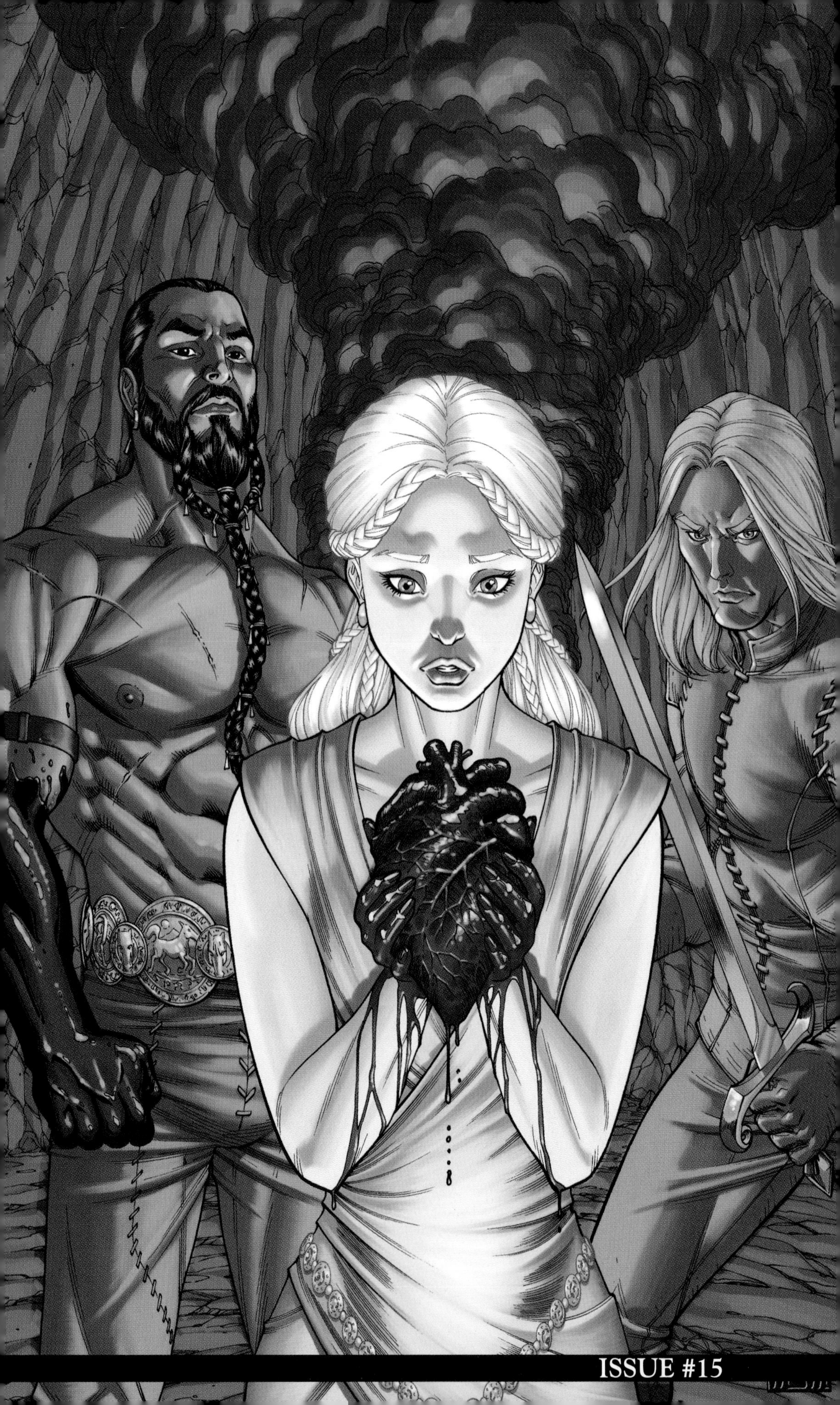
ISSUE #15

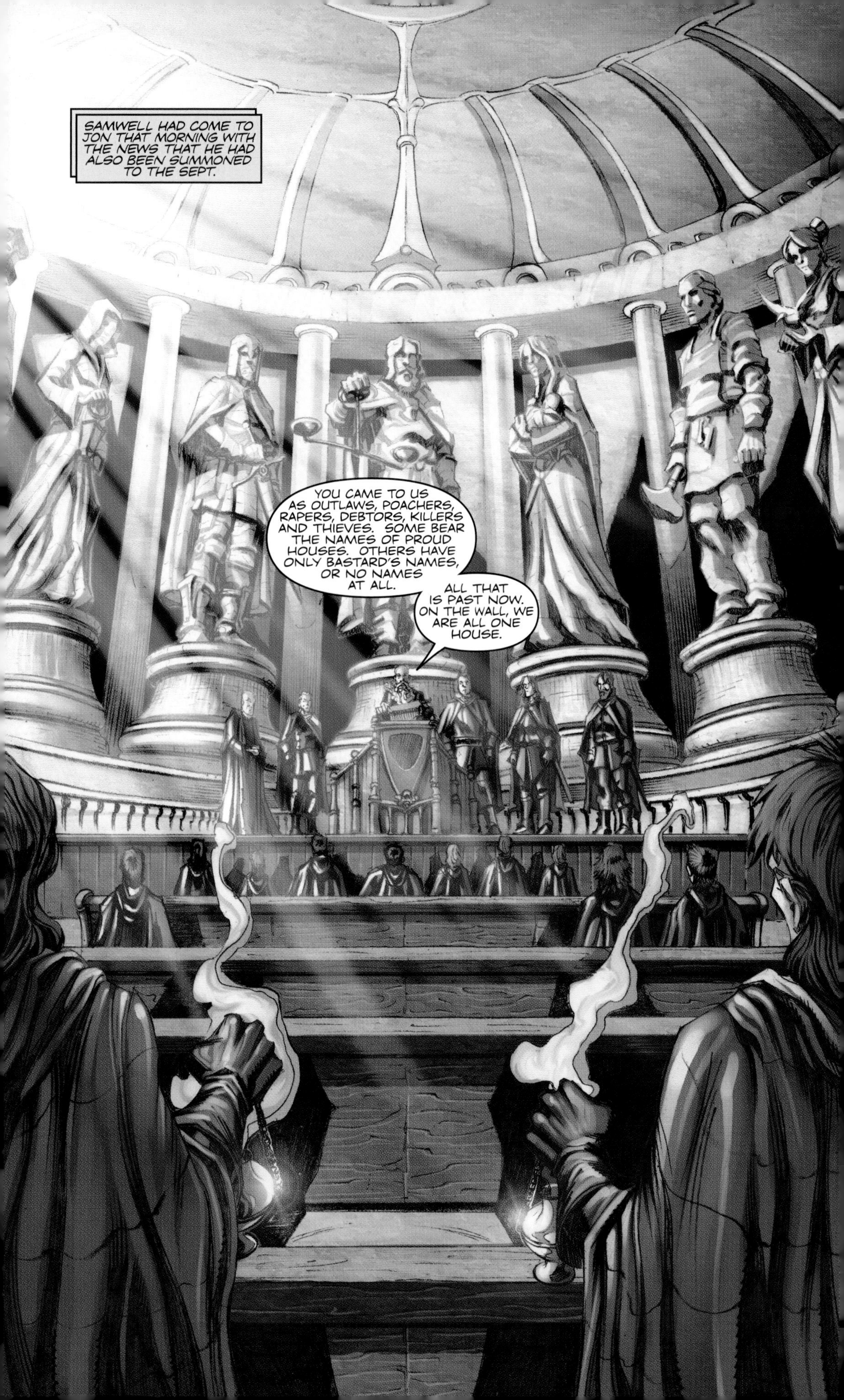
SAMWELL HAD COME TO JON THAT MORNING WITH THE NEWS THAT HE HAD ALSO BEEN SUMMONED TO THE SEPT.
YOU CAME TO US AS OUTLAWS, POACHERS, RAPERS, DEBTORS, KILLERS AND THIEVES. SOME BEAR THE NAMES OF PROUD HOUSES. OTHERS HAVE ONLY BASTARD'S NAMES, OR NO NAMES AT ALL.
ALL THAT IS PAST NOW. ON THE WALL, WE ARE ALL ONE HOUSE.

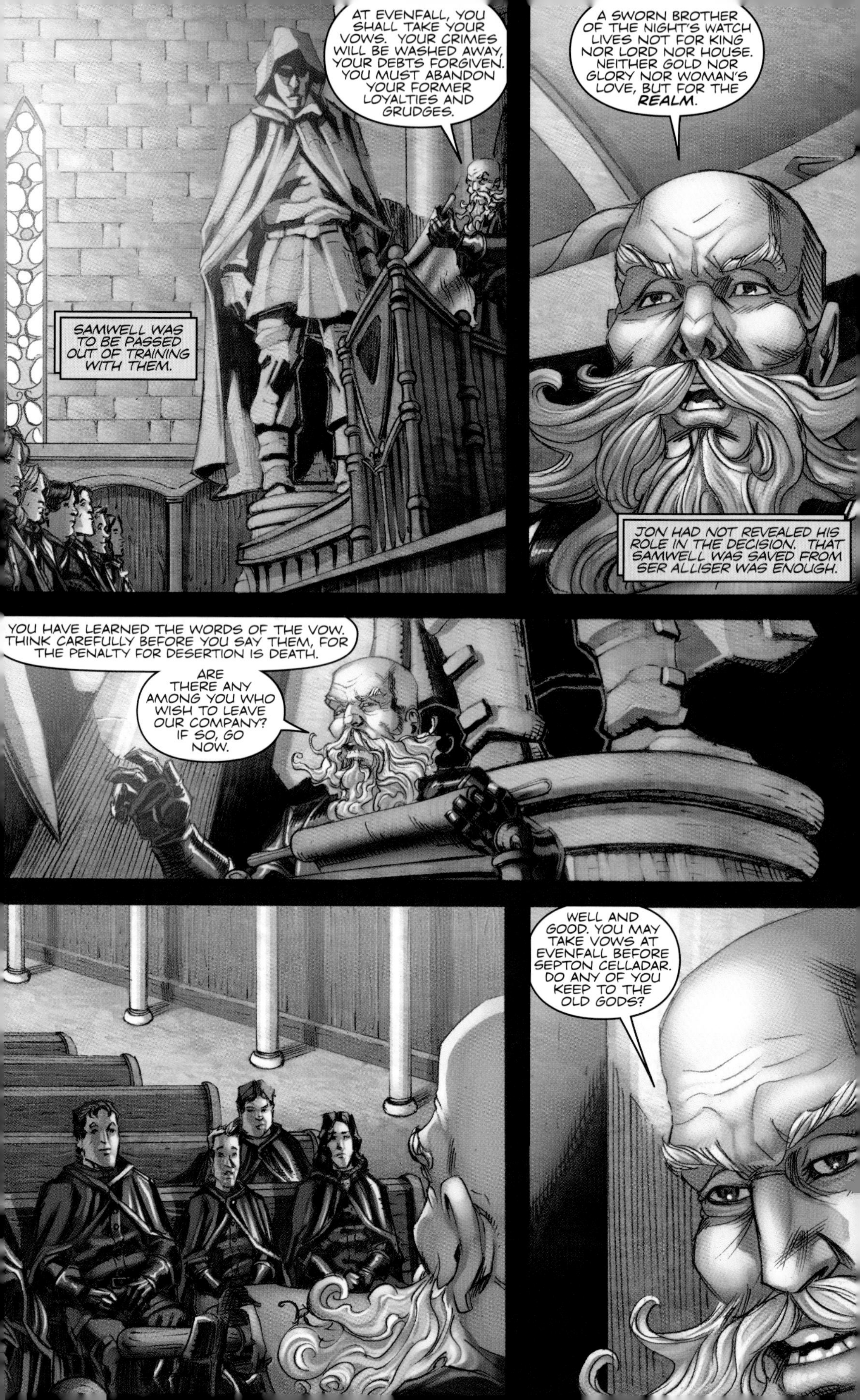
AT EVENFALL, YOU SHALL TAKE YOUR VOWS. YOUR CRIMES WILL BE WASHED AWAY, YOUR DEBTS FORGIVEN. YOU MUST ABANDON YOUR FORMER LOYALTIES AND GRUDGES.
SAMWELL WAS TO BE PASSED OUT OF TRAINING WITH THEM.
A SWORN BROTHER OF THE NIGHT'S WATCH LIVES NOT FOR KING NOR LORD NOR HOUSE. NEITHER GOLD NOR GLORY NOR WOMAN'S LOVE, BUT FOR THE REALM.
JON HAD NOT REVEALED HIS ROLE IN THE DECISION. THAT SAMWELL WAS SAVED FROM SER ALLISER WAS ENOUGH.
YOU HAVE LEARNED THE WORDS OF THE VOW. THINK CAREFULLY BEFORE YOU SAY THEM, FOR THE PENALTY FOR DESERTION IS DEATH.
ARE THERE ANY AMONG YOU WHO WISH TO LEAVE OUR COMPANY? IF SO, GO NOW.
WELL AND GOOD. YOU MAY TAKE VOWS AT EVENFALL BEFORE SEPTON CELLADAR. DO ANY OF YOU KEEP TO THE OLD GODS?

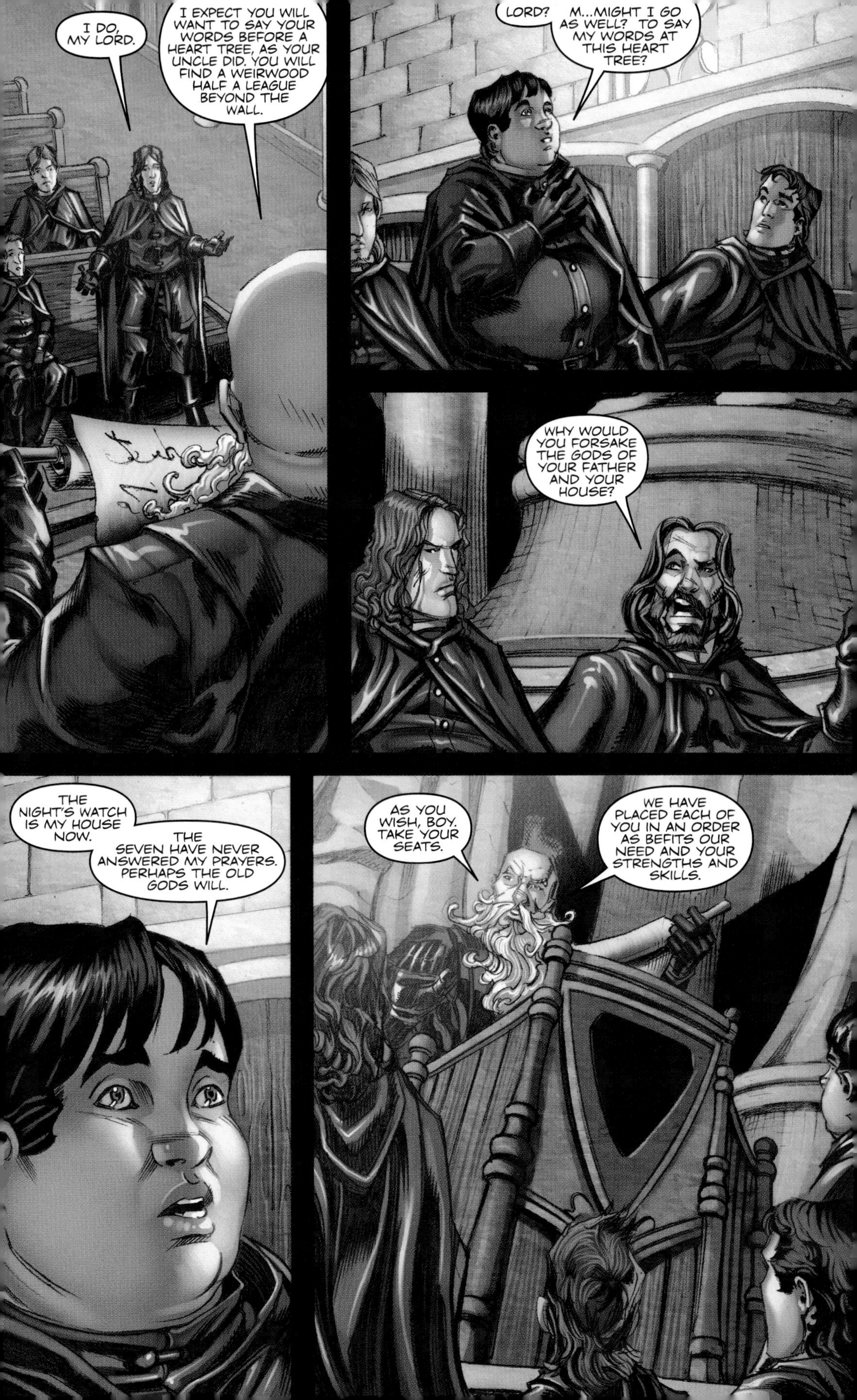
I DO, MY LORD.
I EXPECT YOU WILL WANT TO SAY YOUR WORDS BEFORE A HEART TREE, AS YOUR UNCLE DID. YOU WILL FIND A WEIRWOOD HALF A LEAGUE BEYOND THE WALL.
LORD?
M...MIGHT I GO AS WELL? TO SAY MY WORDS AT THIS HEART TREE?
WHY WOULD YOU FORSAKE THE GODS OF YOUR FATHER AND YOUR HOUSE?
THE NIGHT'S WATCH IS MY HOUSE NOW.
THE SEVEN HAVE NEVER ANSWERED MY PRAYERS. PERHAPS THE OLD GODS WILL.
AS YOU WISH, BOY. TAKE YOUR SEATS.
WE HAVE PLACED EACH OF YOU IN AN ORDER AS BEFITS OUR NEED AND YOUR STRENGTHS AND SKILLS.

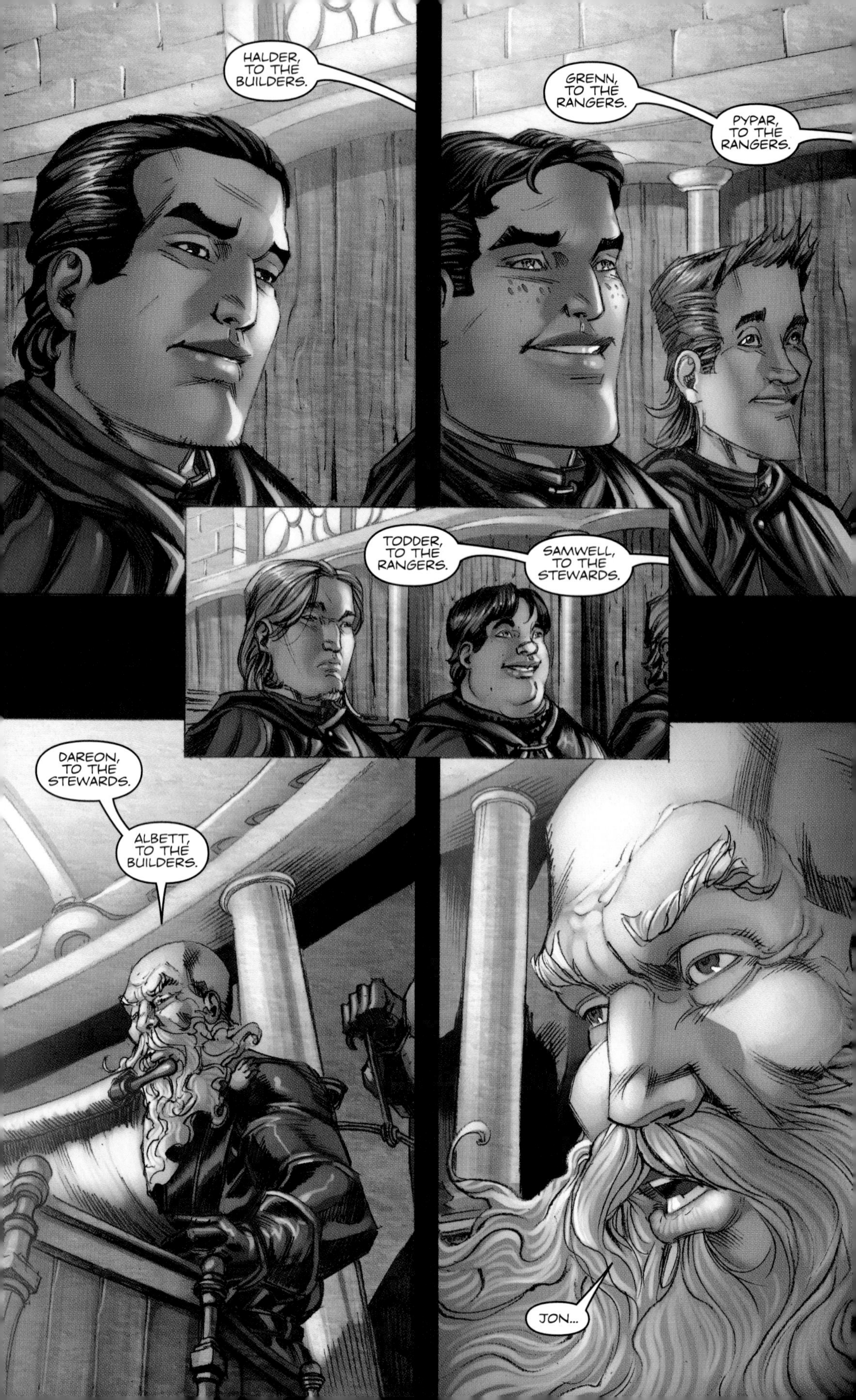
HALDER, TO THE BUILDERS.
GRENN, TO THE RANGERS.
PYPAR, TO THE RANGERS.
TODDER, TO THE RANGERS.
SAMWELL, TO THE STEWARDS.
DAREON, TO THE STEWARDS.
ALBETT, TO THE BUILDERS.
JON...

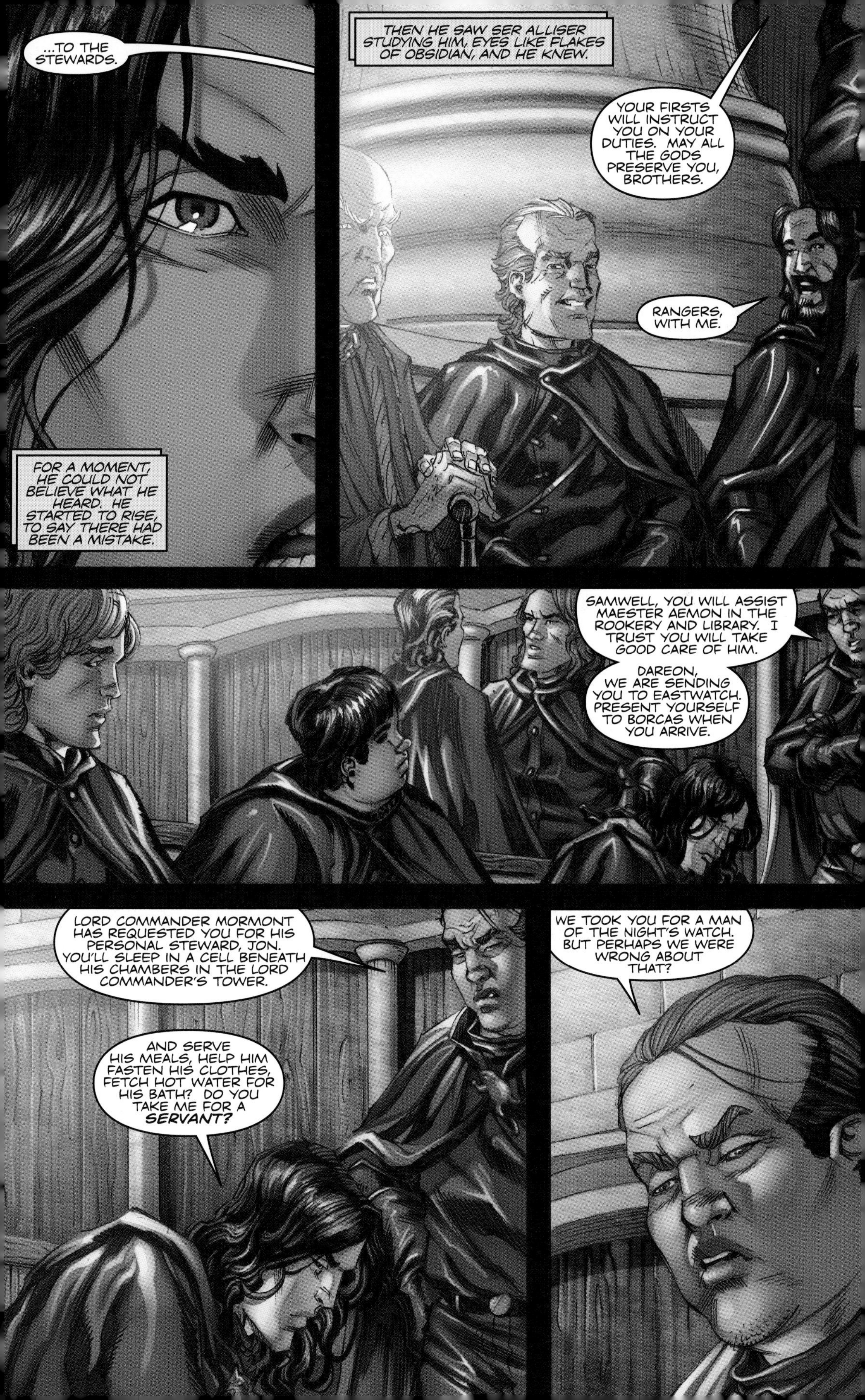
...TO THE STEWARDS.
FOR A MOMENT, HE COULD NOT BELIEVE WHAT HE HEARD. HE STARTED TO RISE, TO SAY THERE HAD BEEN A MISTAKE.
THEN HE SAW SER ALLISER STUDYING HIM, EYES LIKE FLAKES OF OBSIDIAN, AND HE KNEW.
YOUR FIRSTS WILL INSTRUCT YOU ON YOUR DUTIES. MAY ALL THE GODS PRESERVE YOU, BROTHERS.
RANGERS, WITH ME.
SAMWELL, YOU WILL ASSIST MAESTER AEMON IN THE ROOKERY AND LIBRARY. I TRUST YOU WILL TAKE GOOD CARE OF HIM.
DAREON, WE ARE SENDING YOU TO EASTWATCH. PRESENT YOURSELF TO BORCAS WHEN YOU ARRIVE.
LORD COMMANDER MORMONT HAS REQUESTED YOU FOR HIS PERSONAL STEWARD, JON. YOU'LL SLEEP IN A CELL BENEATH HIS CHAMBERS IN THE LORD COMMANDER'S TOWER.
AND SERVE HIS MEALS, HELP HIM FASTEN HIS CLOTHES, FETCH HOT WATER FOR HIS BATH? DO YOU TAKE ME FOR A **SERVANT?**
WE TOOK YOU FOR A MAN OF THE NIGHT'S WATCH. BUT PERHAPS WE WERE WRONG ABOUT THAT?

JON! WAIT! DON'T YOU SEE WHAT THEY'RE DOING?

I SEE SER ALLISER'S BLOODY HAND. HE WANTED TO SHAME ME, AND HE HAS.

THERE IS NO SHAME IN BEING A STEWARD.

DO YOU THINK I WANT TO SPEND MY LIFE WASHING AN OLD MAN'S SMALL CLOTHES?

I AM A BETTER SWORDSMAN AND RIDER THAN ANY OF YOU!

BUT THE OLD MAN IS THE LORD COMMANDER. YOU'LL TAKE HIS LETTERS. SQUIRE FOR HIM IN BATTLE. YOU'LL KNOW EVERYTHING, AND MORMONT ASKED FOR YOU HIMSELF.

DON'T YOU SEE? HE WANTS TO GROOM YOU FOR COMMAND.

I NEVER ASKED FOR THIS.

NONE OF US ARE HERE FOR ASKING.

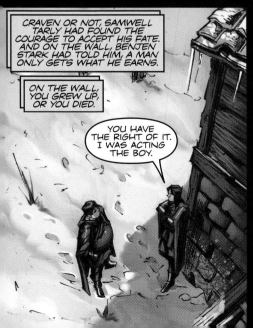

CRAVEN OR NOT, SAMWELL TARLY HAD FOUND THE COURAGE TO ACCEPT HIS FATE. AND ON THE WALL, BENJEN STARK HAD TOLD HIM, A MAN ONLY GETS WHAT HE EARNS.

ON THE WALL, YOU GREW UP, OR YOU DIED.

YOU HAVE THE RIGHT OF IT. I WAS ACTING THE BOY.

THEN YOU'LL STAY AND SAY WORDS WITH ME?

THE OLD GODS WILL BE EXPECTING US.

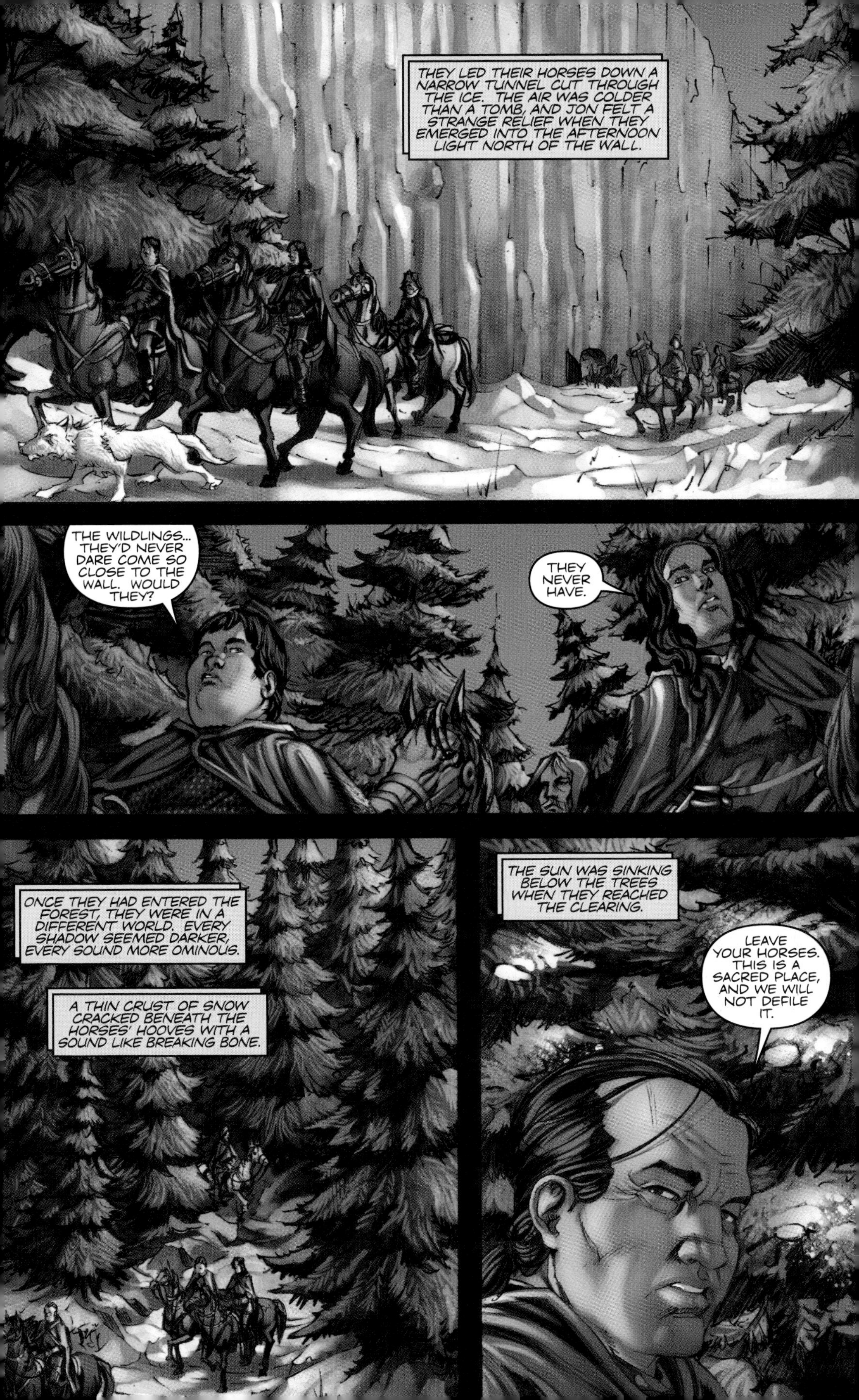
THEY LED THEIR HORSES DOWN A NARROW TUNNEL CUT THROUGH THE ICE. THE AIR WAS COLDER THAN A TOMB, AND JON FELT A STRANGE RELIEF WHEN THEY EMERGED INTO THE AFTERNOON LIGHT NORTH OF THE WALL.
THE WILDLINGS... THEY'D NEVER DARE COME SO CLOSE TO THE WALL. WOULD THEY?
THEY NEVER HAVE.
ONCE THEY HAD ENTERED THE FOREST, THEY WERE IN A DIFFERENT WORLD. EVERY SHADOW SEEMED DARKER, EVERY SOUND MORE OMINOUS.
A THIN CRUST OF SNOW CRACKED BENEATH THE HORSES' HOOVES WITH A SOUND LIKE BREAKING BONE.
THE SUN WAS SINKING BELOW THE TREES WHEN THEY REACHED THE CLEARING.
LEAVE YOUR HORSES. THIS IS A SACRED PLACE, AND WE WILL NOT DEFILE IT.

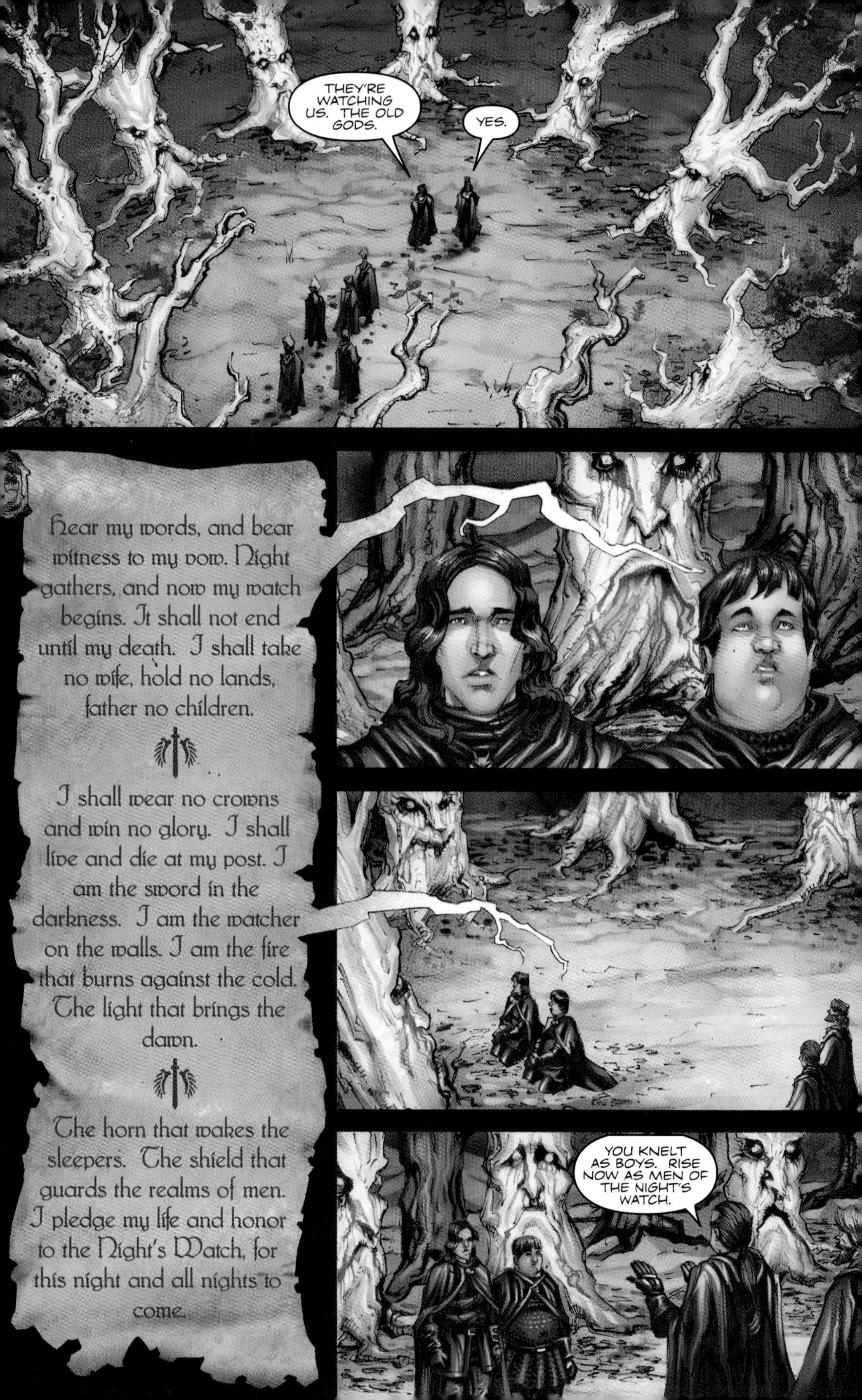
THEY'RE WATCHING US. THE OLD GODS.
YES.
Hear my words, and bear witness to my vow. Night gathers, and now my watch begins. It shall not end until my death. I shall take no wife, hold no lands, father no children.
I shall wear no crowns and win no glory. I shall live and die at my post. I am the sword in the darkness. I am the watcher on the walls. I am the fire that burns against the cold. The light that brings the dawn.
The horn that wakes the sleepers. The shield that guards the realms of men. I pledge my life and honor to the Night's Watch, for this night and all nights to come.
YOU KNELT AS BOYS. RISE NOW AS MEN OF THE NIGHT'S WATCH.

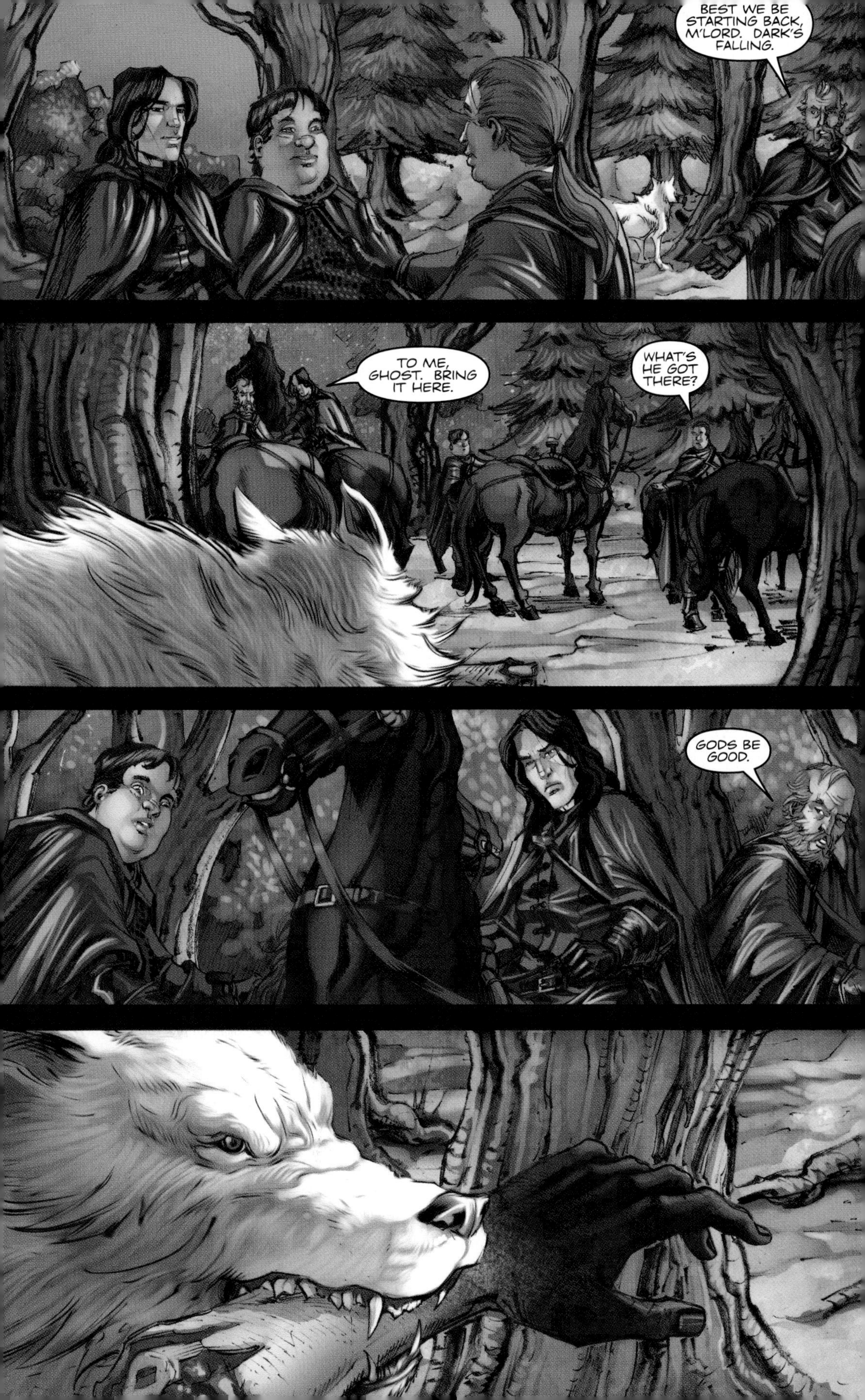
BEST WE BE STARTING BACK, M'LORD. DARK'S FALLING.
TO ME, GHOST. BRING IT HERE.
WHAT'S HE GOT THERE?
GODS BE GOOD.

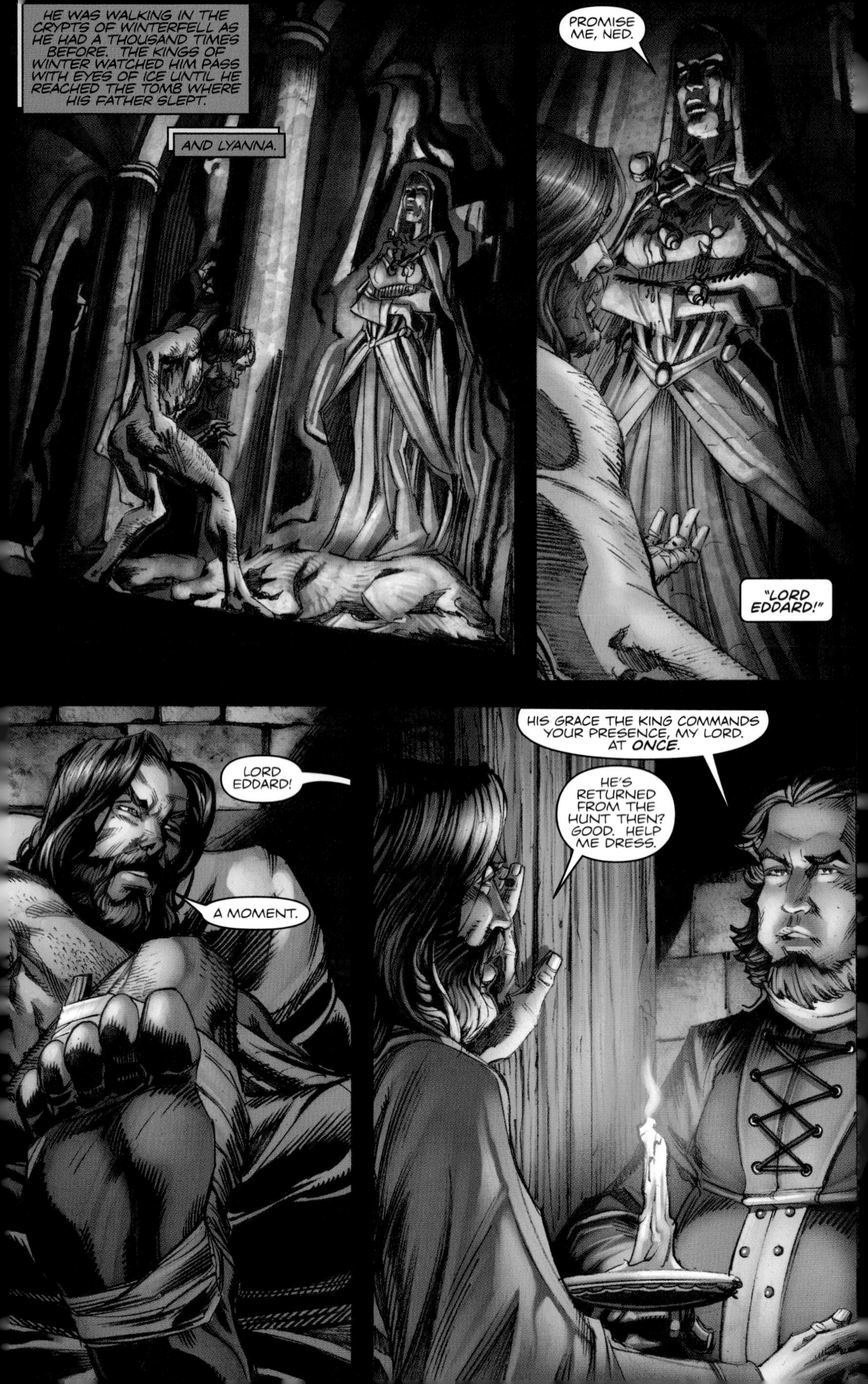
HE WAS WALKING IN THE CRYPTS OF WINTERFELL AS HE HAD A THOUSAND TIMES BEFORE. THE KINGS OF WINTER WATCHED HIM PASS WITH EYES OF ICE UNTIL HE REACHED THE TOMB WHERE HIS FATHER SLEPT.
AND LYANNA.
PROMISE ME, NED.
"LORD EDDARD!"
LORD EDDARD!
A MOMENT.
HIS GRACE THE KING COMMANDS YOUR PRESENCE, MY LORD. AT ONCE.
HE'S RETURNED FROM THE HUNT THEN? GOOD. HELP ME DRESS.

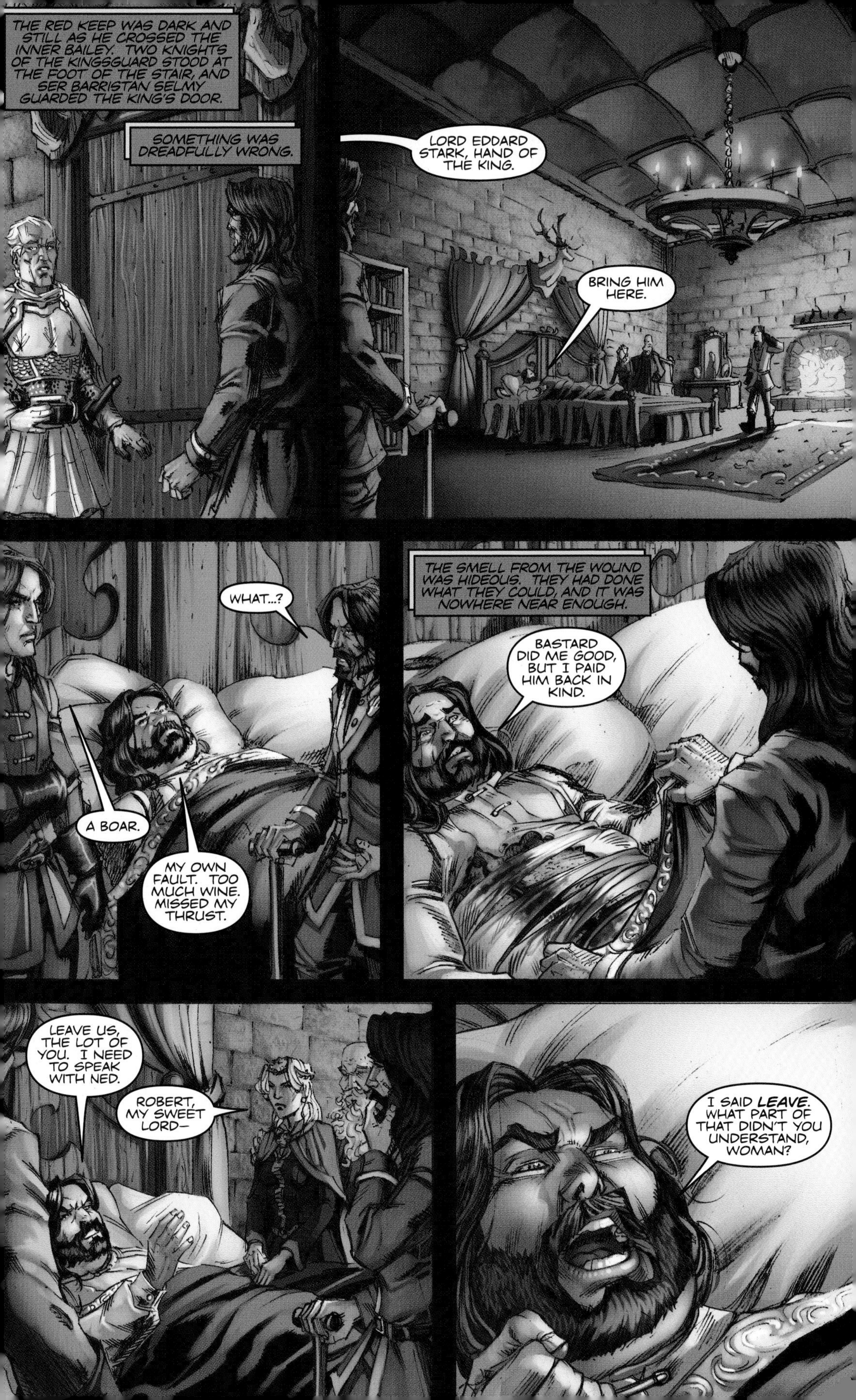
THE RED KEEP WAS DARK AND STILL AS HE CROSSED THE INNER BAILEY. TWO KNIGHTS OF THE KINGSGUARD STOOD AT THE FOOT OF THE STAIR, AND SER BARRISTAN SELMY GUARDED THE KING'S DOOR.
SOMETHING WAS DREADFULLY WRONG.
LORD EDDARD STARK, HAND OF THE KING.
BRING HIM HERE.
WHAT...?
A BOAR.
MY OWN FAULT. TOO MUCH WINE. MISSED MY THRUST.
THE SMELL FROM THE WOUND WAS HIDEOUS. THEY HAD DONE WHAT THEY COULD, AND IT WAS NOWHERE NEAR ENOUGH.
BASTARD DID ME GOOD, BUT I PAID HIM BACK IN KIND.
LEAVE US, THE LOT OF YOU. I NEED TO SPEAK WITH NED.
ROBERT, MY SWEET LORD–
I SAID ***LEAVE***. WHAT PART OF THAT DIDN'T YOU UNDERSTAND, WOMAN?

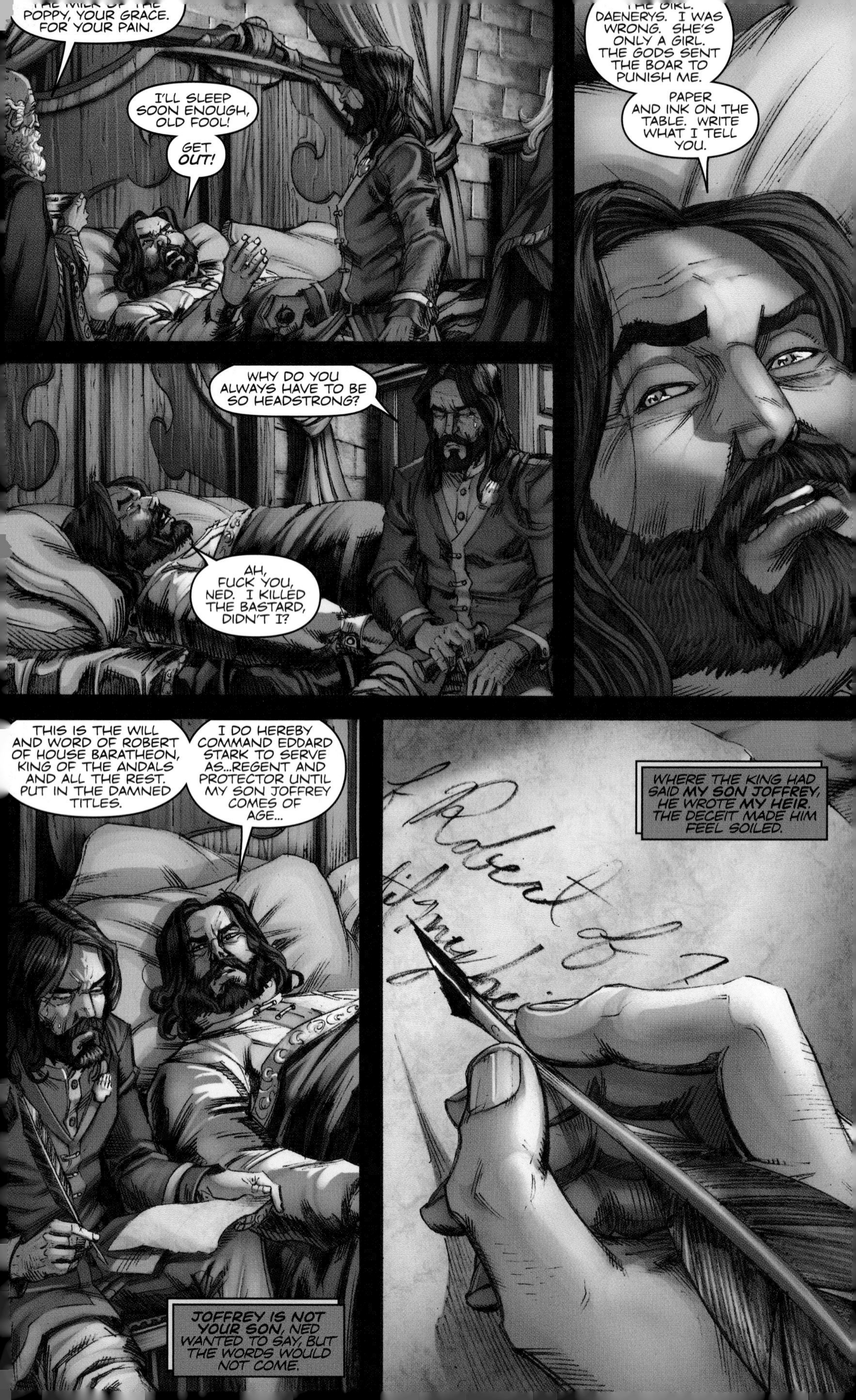
POPPY, YOUR GRACE. FOR YOUR PAIN.
I'LL SLEEP SOON ENOUGH, OLD FOOL!
GET OUT!
DAENERYS. I WAS WRONG. SHE'S ONLY A GIRL. THE GODS SENT THE BOAR TO PUNISH ME.
PAPER AND INK ON THE TABLE. WRITE WHAT I TELL YOU.
WHY DO YOU ALWAYS HAVE TO BE SO HEADSTRONG?
AH, FUCK YOU, NED. I KILLED THE BASTARD, DIDN'T I?
THIS IS THE WILL AND WORD OF ROBERT OF HOUSE BARATHEON, KING OF THE ANDALS AND ALL THE REST. PUT IN THE DAMNED TITLES.
I DO HEREBY COMMAND EDDARD STARK TO SERVE AS...REGENT AND PROTECTOR UNTIL MY SON JOFFREY COMES OF AGE...
JOFFREY IS NOT YOUR SON, NED WANTED TO SAY, BUT THE WORDS WOULD NOT COME.
WHERE THE KING HAD SAID MY SON JOFFREY, HE WROTE MY HEIR. THE DECEIT MADE HIM FEEL SOILED.

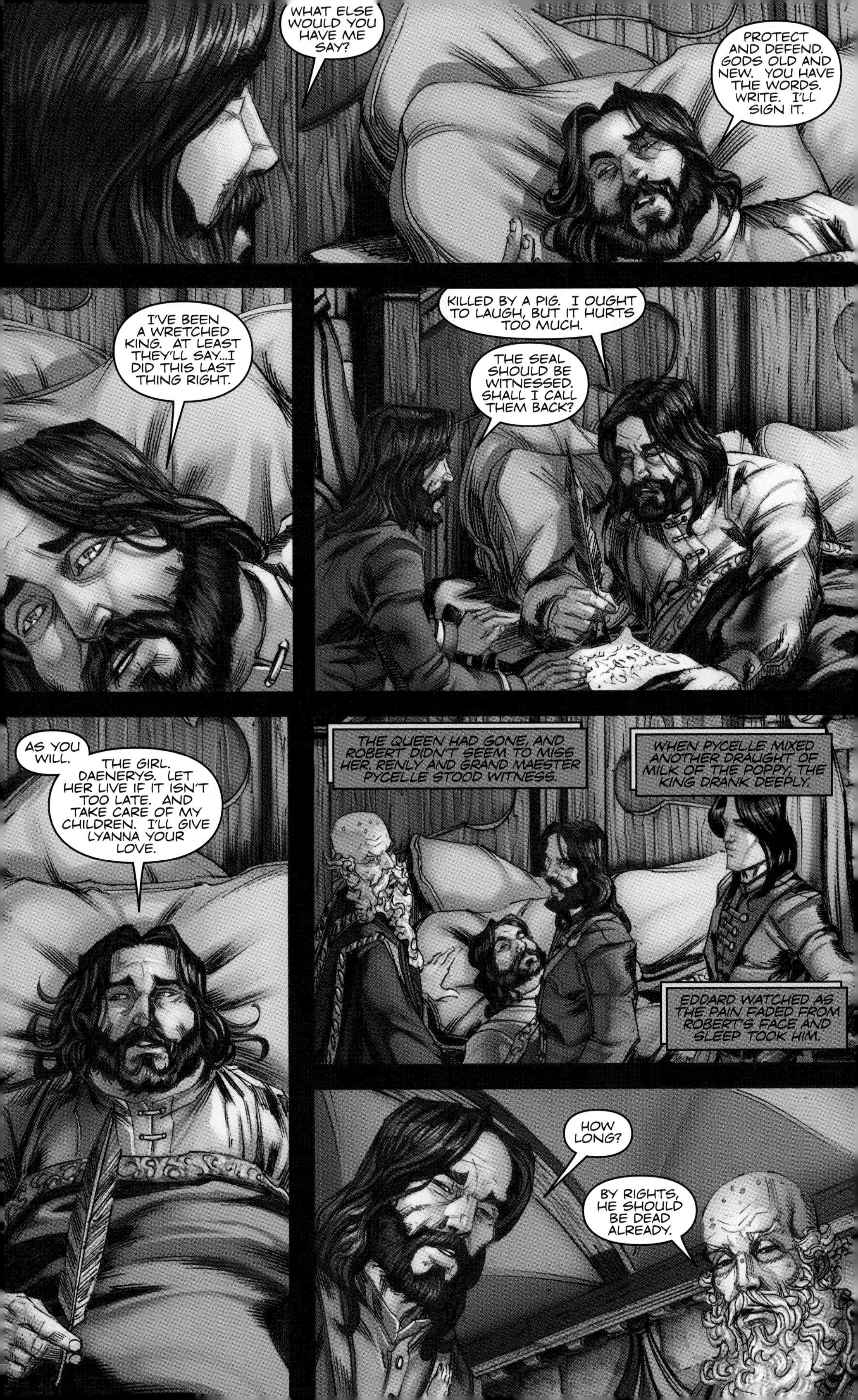
WHAT ELSE WOULD YOU HAVE ME SAY?
PROTECT AND DEFEND. GODS OLD AND NEW. YOU HAVE THE WORDS. WRITE. I'LL SIGN IT.
I'VE BEEN A WRETCHED KING. AT LEAST THEY'LL SAY...I DID THIS LAST THING RIGHT.
KILLED BY A PIG. I OUGHT TO LAUGH, BUT IT HURTS TOO MUCH.
THE SEAL SHOULD BE WITNESSED. SHALL I CALL THEM BACK?
AS YOU WILL.
THE GIRL. DAENERYS. LET HER LIVE IF IT ISN'T TOO LATE. AND TAKE CARE OF MY CHILDREN. I'LL GIVE LYANNA YOUR LOVE.
THE QUEEN HAD GONE, AND ROBERT DIDN'T SEEM TO MISS HER. RENLY AND GRAND MAESTER PYCELLE STOOD WITNESS.
WHEN PYCELLE MIXED ANOTHER DRAUGHT OF MILK OF THE POPPY, THE KING DRANK DEEPLY.
EDDARD WATCHED AS THE PAIN FADED FROM ROBERT'S FACE AND SLEEP TOOK HIM.
HOW LONG?
BY RIGHTS, HE SHOULD BE DEAD ALREADY.

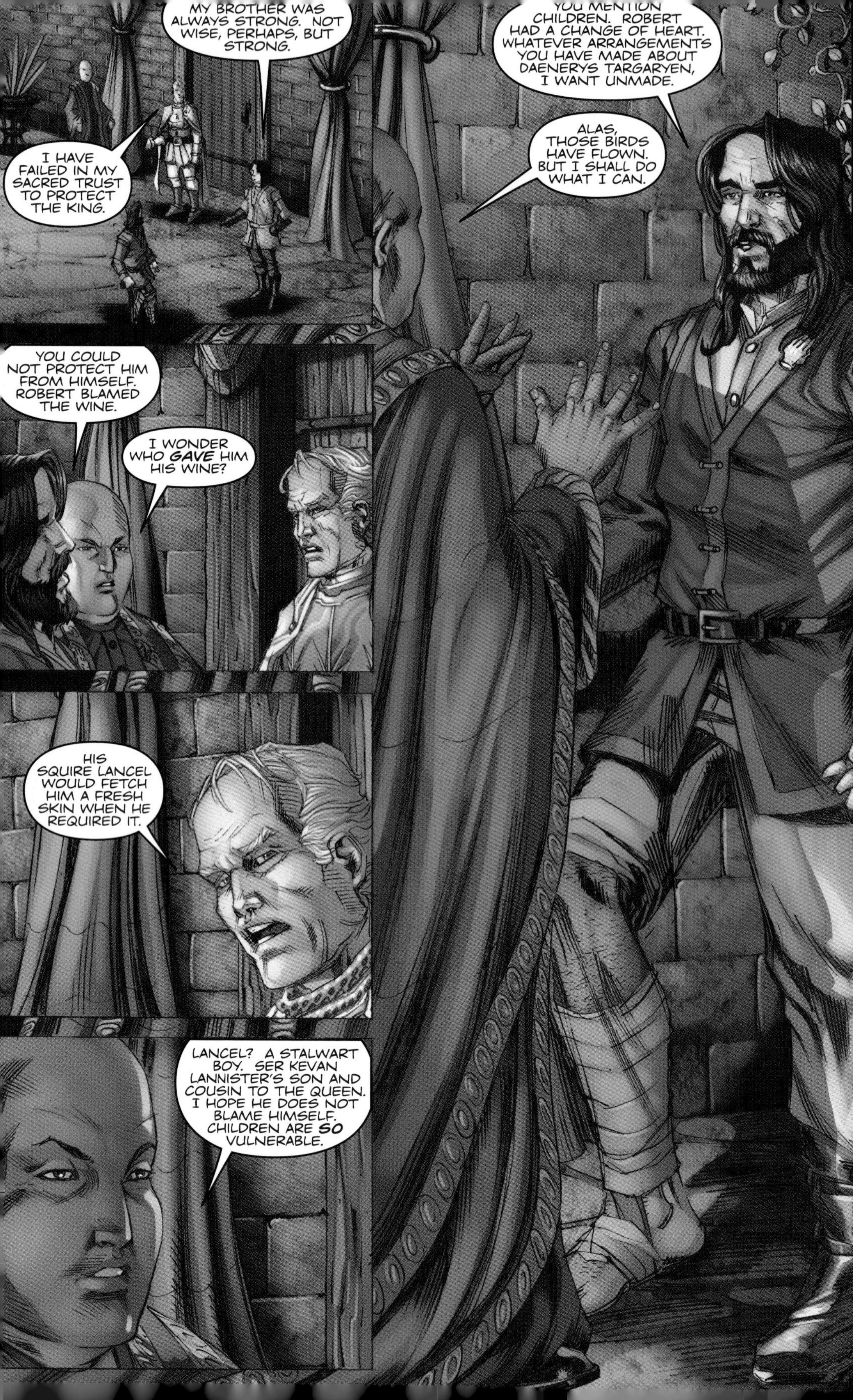
MY BROTHER WAS ALWAYS STRONG. NOT WISE, PERHAPS, BUT STRONG.
I HAVE FAILED IN MY SACRED TRUST TO PROTECT THE KING.
YOU COULD NOT PROTECT HIM FROM HIMSELF. ROBERT BLAMED THE WINE.
I WONDER WHO GAVE HIM HIS WINE?
HIS SQUIRE LANCEL WOULD FETCH HIM A FRESH SKIN WHEN HE REQUIRED IT.
LANCEL? A STALWART BOY. SER KEVAN LANNISTER'S SON AND COUSIN TO THE QUEEN. I HOPE HE DOES NOT BLAME HIMSELF. CHILDREN ARE SO VULNERABLE.
YOU MENTION CHILDREN. ROBERT HAD A CHANGE OF HEART. WHATEVER ARRANGEMENTS YOU HAVE MADE ABOUT DAENERYS TARGARYEN, I WANT UNMADE.
ALAS, THOSE BIRDS HAVE FLOWN. BUT I SHALL DO WHAT I CAN.

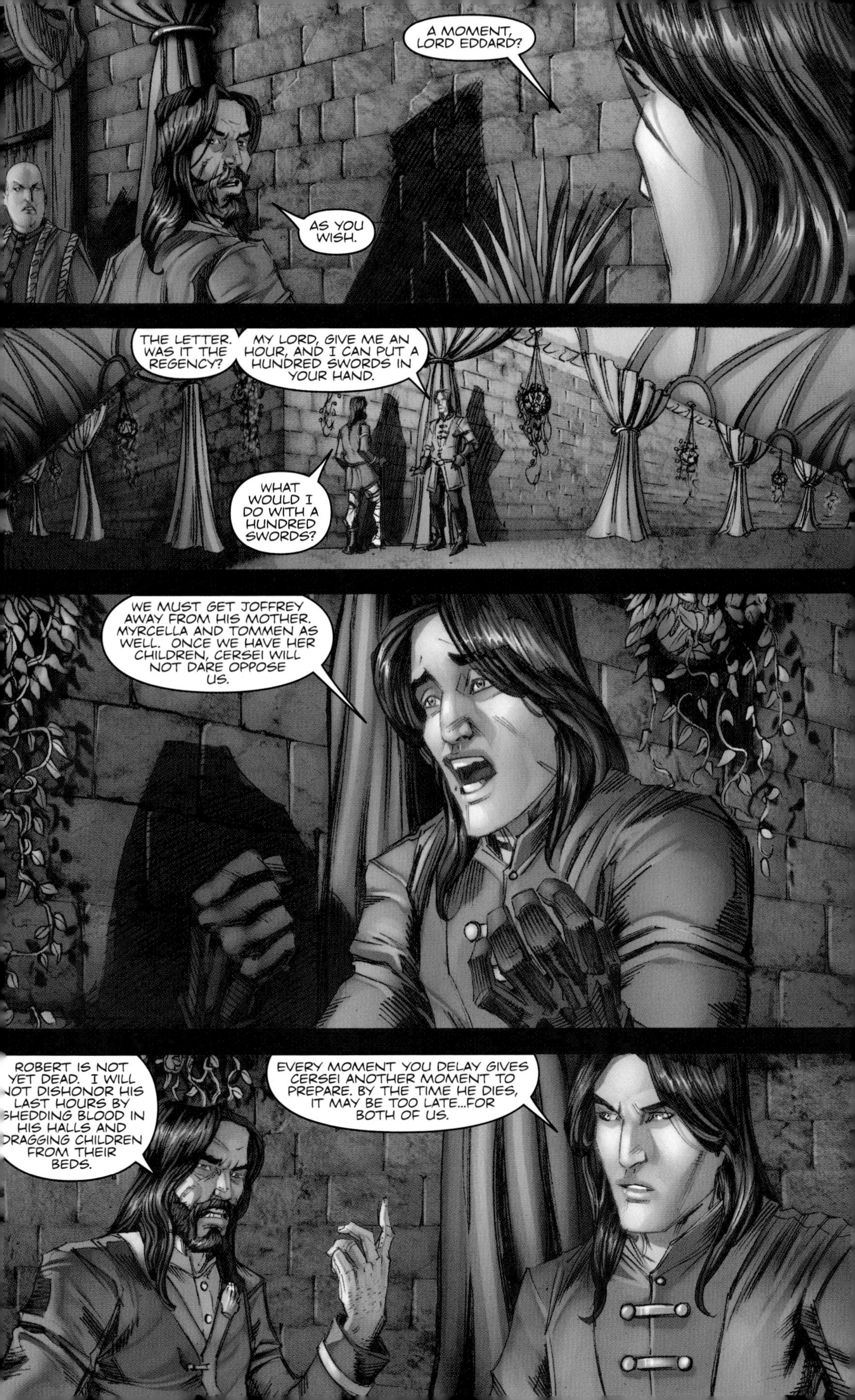
A MOMENT, LORD EDDARD?
AS YOU WISH.
THE LETTER. WAS IT THE REGENCY?
MY LORD, GIVE ME AN HOUR, AND I CAN PUT A HUNDRED SWORDS IN YOUR HAND.
WHAT WOULD I DO WITH A HUNDRED SWORDS?
WE MUST GET JOFFREY AWAY FROM HIS MOTHER. MYRCELLA AND TOMMEN AS WELL. ONCE WE HAVE HER CHILDREN, CERSEI WILL NOT DARE OPPOSE US.
ROBERT IS NOT YET DEAD. I WILL NOT DISHONOR HIS LAST HOURS BY SHEDDING BLOOD IN HIS HALLS AND DRAGGING CHILDREN FROM THEIR BEDS.
EVERY MOMENT YOU DELAY GIVES CERSEI ANOTHER MOMENT TO PREPARE. BY THE TIME HE DIES, IT MAY BE TOO LATE...FOR BOTH OF US.

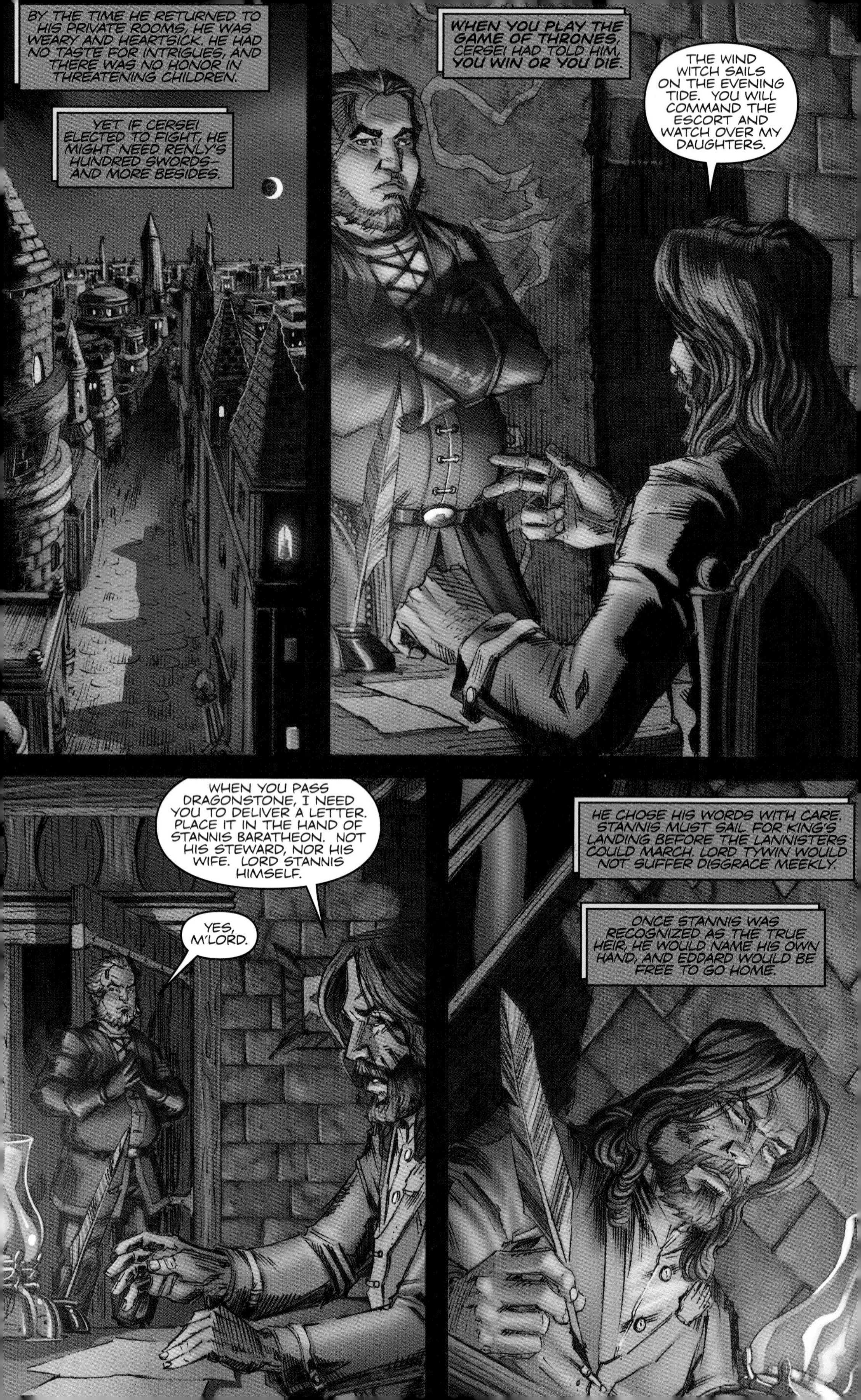
BY THE TIME HE RETURNED TO HIS PRIVATE ROOMS, HE WAS WEARY AND HEARTSICK. HE HAD NO TASTE FOR INTRIGUES, AND THERE WAS NO HONOR IN THREATENING CHILDREN.
YET IF CERSEI ELECTED TO FIGHT, HE MIGHT NEED RENLY'S HUNDRED SWORDS--AND MORE BESIDES.
WHEN YOU PLAY THE GAME OF THRONES, CERSEI HAD TOLD HIM, YOU WIN OR YOU DIE.
THE WIND WITCH SAILS ON THE EVENING TIDE. YOU WILL COMMAND THE ESCORT AND WATCH OVER MY DAUGHTERS.
WHEN YOU PASS DRAGONSTONE, I NEED YOU TO DELIVER A LETTER. PLACE IT IN THE HAND OF STANNIS BARATHEON. NOT HIS STEWARD, NOR HIS WIFE. LORD STANNIS HIMSELF.
YES, M'LORD.
HE CHOSE HIS WORDS WITH CARE. STANNIS MUST SAIL FOR KING'S LANDING BEFORE THE LANNISTERS COULD MARCH. LORD TYWIN WOULD NOT SUFFER DISGRACE MEEKLY.
ONCE STANNIS WAS RECOGNIZED AS THE TRUE HEIR, HE WOULD NAME HIS OWN HAND, AND EDDARD WOULD BE FREE TO GO HOME.

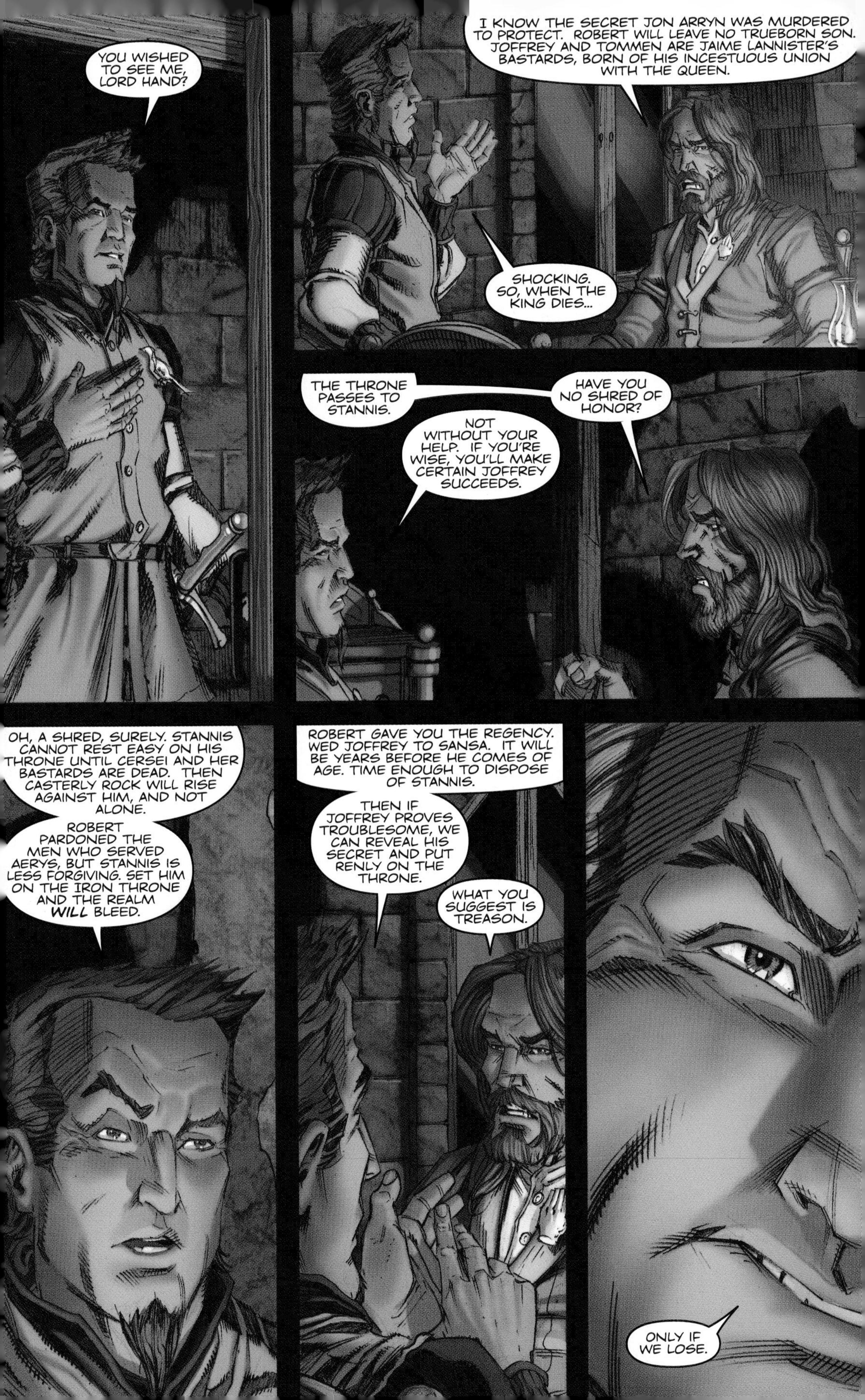
YOU WISHED TO SEE ME, LORD HAND?
I KNOW THE SECRET JON ARRYN WAS MURDERED TO PROTECT. ROBERT WILL LEAVE NO TRUEBORN SON. JOFFREY AND TOMMEN ARE JAIME LANNISTER'S BASTARDS, BORN OF HIS INCESTUOUS UNION WITH THE QUEEN.
SHOCKING. SO, WHEN THE KING DIES...
THE THRONE PASSES TO STANNIS.
HAVE YOU NO SHRED OF HONOR?
NOT WITHOUT YOUR HELP. IF YOU'RE WISE, YOU'LL MAKE CERTAIN JOFFREY SUCCEEDS.
OH, A SHRED, SURELY. STANNIS CANNOT REST EASY ON HIS THRONE UNTIL CERSEI AND HER BASTARDS ARE DEAD. THEN CASTERLY ROCK WILL RISE AGAINST HIM, AND NOT ALONE.
ROBERT PARDONED THE MEN WHO SERVED AERYS, BUT STANNIS IS LESS FORGIVING. SET HIM ON THE IRON THRONE AND THE REALM **WILL** BLEED.
ROBERT GAVE YOU THE REGENCY. WED JOFFREY TO SANSA. IT WILL BE YEARS BEFORE HE COMES OF AGE. TIME ENOUGH TO DISPOSE OF STANNIS.
THEN IF JOFFREY PROVES TROUBLESOME, WE CAN REVEAL HIS SECRET AND PUT RENLY ON THE THRONE.
WHAT YOU SUGGEST IS TREASON.
ONLY IF WE LOSE.

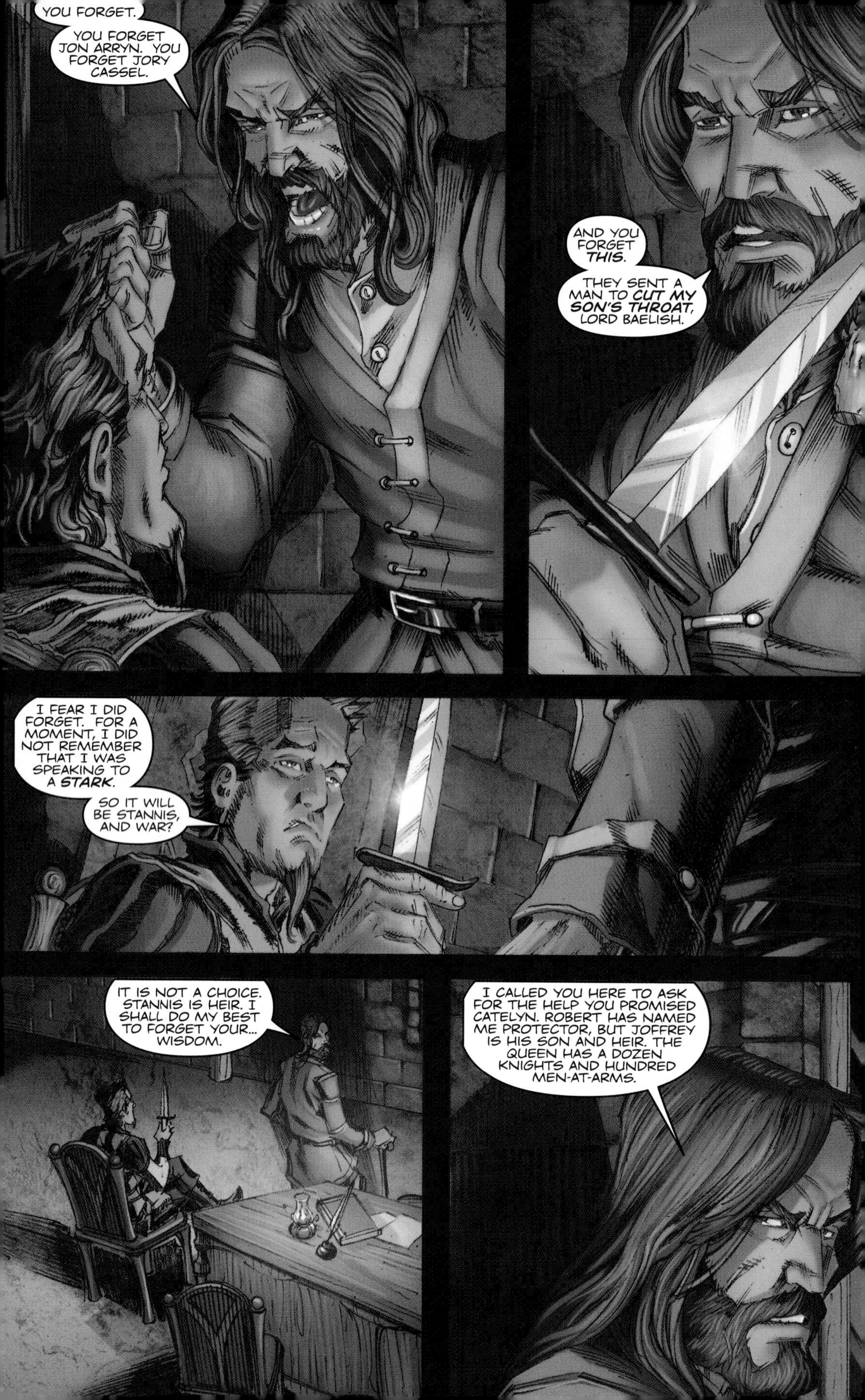
YOU FORGET.
YOU FORGET JON ARRYN. YOU FORGET JORY CASSEL.
AND YOU FORGET THIS.
THEY SENT A MAN TO CUT MY SON'S THROAT, LORD BAELISH.
I FEAR I DID FORGET. FOR A MOMENT, I DID NOT REMEMBER THAT I WAS SPEAKING TO A STARK.
SO IT WILL BE STANNIS, AND WAR?
IT IS NOT A CHOICE. STANNIS IS HEIR. I SHALL DO MY BEST TO FORGET YOUR... WISDOM.
I CALLED YOU HERE TO ASK FOR THE HELP YOU PROMISED CATELYN. ROBERT HAS NAMED ME PROTECTOR, BUT JOFFREY IS HIS SON AND HEIR. THE QUEEN HAS A DOZEN KNIGHTS AND HUNDRED MEN-AT-ARMS.

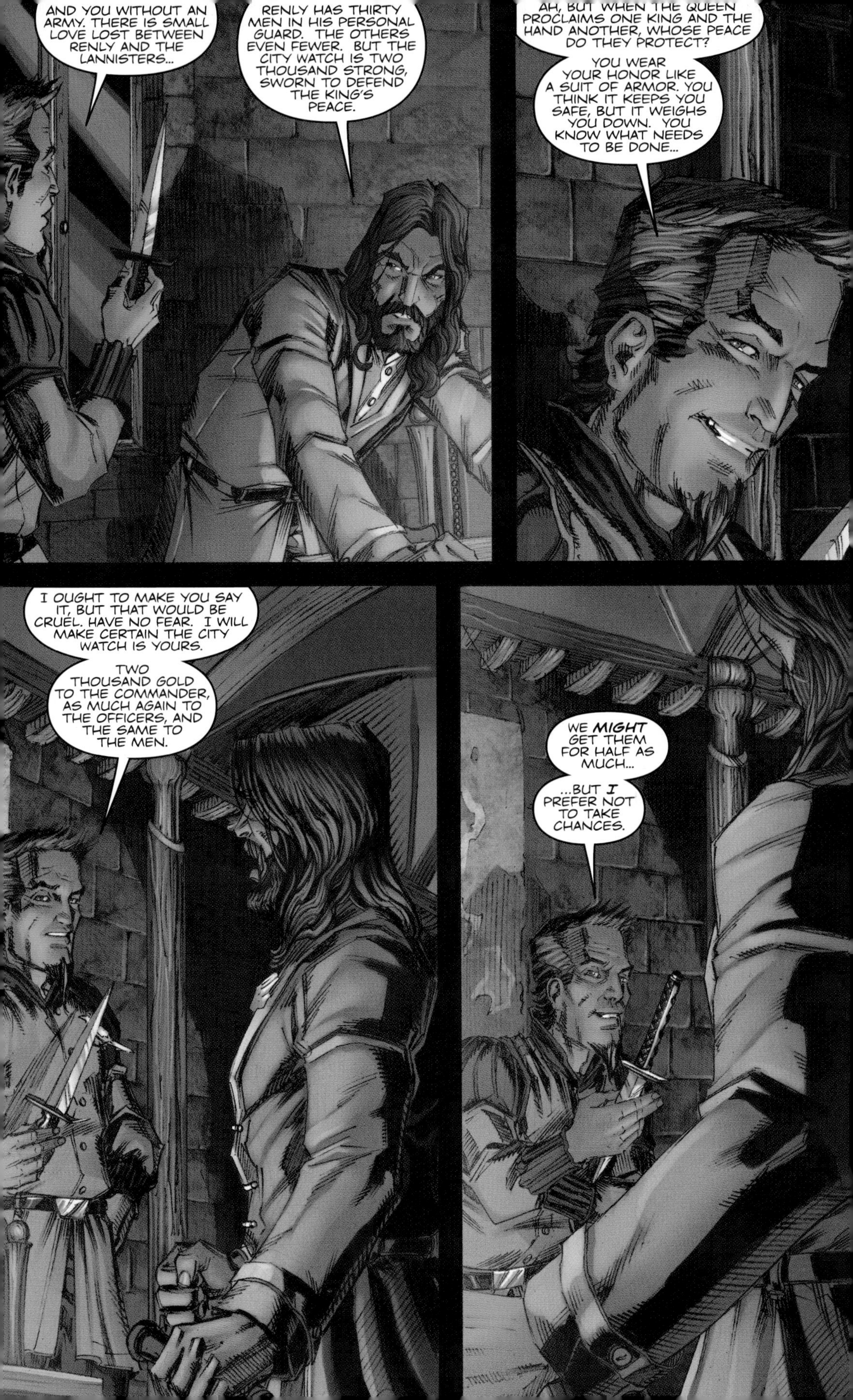
AND YOU WITHOUT AN ARMY. THERE IS SMALL LOVE LOST BETWEEN RENLY AND THE LANNISTERS...
RENLY HAS THIRTY MEN IN HIS PERSONAL GUARD. THE OTHERS EVEN FEWER. BUT THE CITY WATCH IS TWO THOUSAND STRONG, SWORN TO DEFEND THE KING'S PEACE.
AH, BUT WHEN THE QUEEN PROCLAIMS ONE KING AND THE HAND ANOTHER, WHOSE PEACE DO THEY PROTECT?
YOU WEAR YOUR HONOR LIKE A SUIT OF ARMOR. YOU THINK IT KEEPS YOU SAFE, BUT IT WEIGHS YOU DOWN. YOU KNOW WHAT NEEDS TO BE DONE...
I OUGHT TO MAKE YOU SAY IT, BUT THAT WOULD BE CRUEL. HAVE NO FEAR. I WILL MAKE CERTAIN THE CITY WATCH IS YOURS.
TWO THOUSAND GOLD TO THE COMMANDER, AS MUCH AGAIN TO THE OFFICERS, AND THE SAME TO THE MEN.
WE **MIGHT** GET THEM FOR HALF AS MUCH...
...BUT ***I*** PREFER NOT TO TAKE CHANCES.

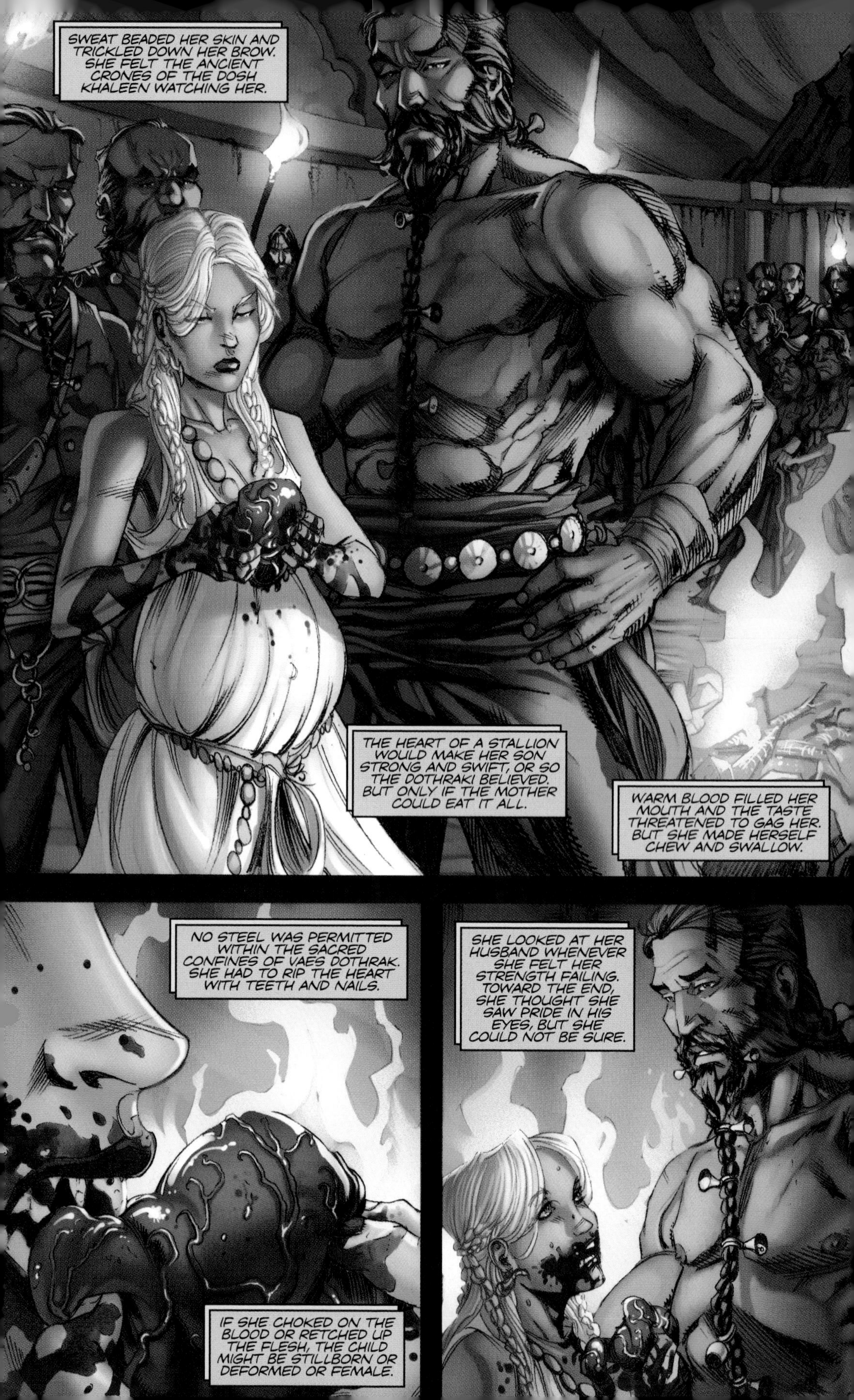
SWEAT BEADED HER SKIN AND TRICKLED DOWN HER BROW. SHE FELT THE ANCIENT CRONES OF THE DOSH KHALEEN WATCHING HER.
THE HEART OF A STALLION WOULD MAKE HER SON STRONG AND SWIFT, OR SO THE DOTHRAKI BELIEVED. BUT ONLY IF THE MOTHER COULD EAT IT ALL.
WARM BLOOD FILLED HER MOUTH AND THE TASTE THREATENED TO GAG HER. BUT SHE MADE HERSELF CHEW AND SWALLOW.
NO STEEL WAS PERMITTED WITHIN THE SACRED CONFINES OF VAES DOTHRAK. SHE HAD TO RIP THE HEART WITH TEETH AND NAILS.
IF SHE CHOKED ON THE BLOOD OR RETCHED UP THE FLESH, THE CHILD MIGHT BE STILLBORN OR DEFORMED OR FEMALE.
SHE LOOKED AT HER HUSBAND WHENEVER SHE FELT HER STRENGTH FAILING. TOWARD THE END, SHE THOUGHT SHE SAW PRIDE IN HIS EYES, BUT SHE COULD NOT BE SURE.

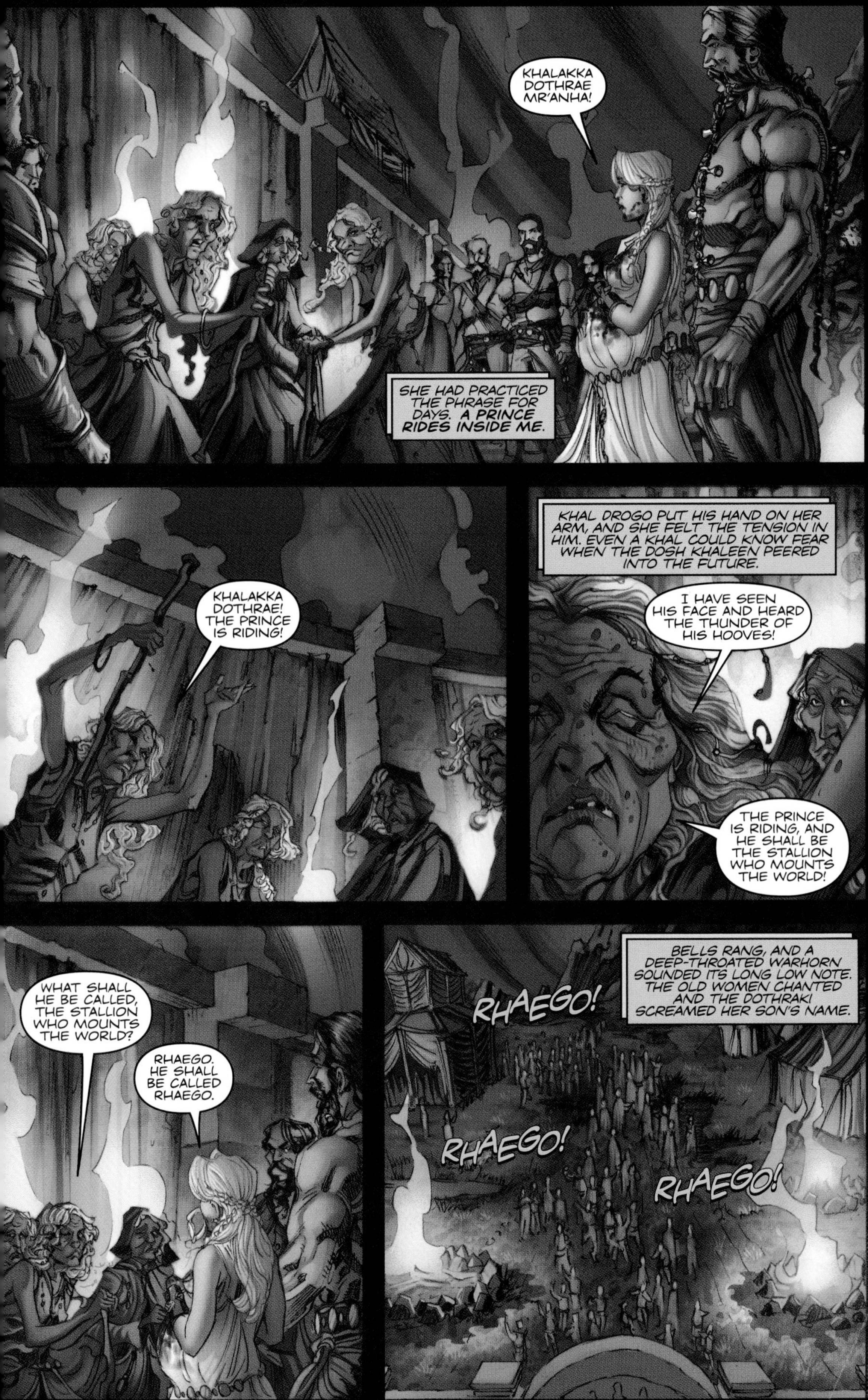
KHALAKKA DOTHRAE MR'ANHA!
SHE HAD PRACTICED THE PHRASE FOR DAYS. A PRINCE RIDES INSIDE ME.
KHALAKKA DOTHRAE! THE PRINCE IS RIDING!
KHAL DROGO PUT HIS HAND ON HER ARM, AND SHE FELT THE TENSION IN HIM. EVEN A KHAL COULD KNOW FEAR WHEN THE DOSH KHALEEN PEERED INTO THE FUTURE.
I HAVE SEEN HIS FACE AND HEARD THE THUNDER OF HIS HOOVES!
THE PRINCE IS RIDING, AND HE SHALL BE THE STALLION WHO MOUNTS THE WORLD!
WHAT SHALL HE BE CALLED, THE STALLION WHO MOUNTS THE WORLD?
RHAEGO. HE SHALL BE CALLED RHAEGO.
BELLS RANG, AND A DEEP-THROATED WARHORN SOUNDED ITS LONG LOW NOTE. THE OLD WOMEN CHANTED AND THE DOTHRAKI SCREAMED HER SON'S NAME.
RHAEGO!
RHAEGO!
RHAEGO!

THE NAME WAS STILL RINGING IN HER EARS AS THE PROCESSION FOLLOWED THEM DOWN THE GODSWAY.

THE CRONES OF THE DOSH KHALEEN CAME FIRST. EACH HAD ONCE BEEN KHALEESI, AND IT GAVE DANY THE SHIVERS TO THINK THAT ONE DAY SHE MIGHT JOIN THEM.

WHAT IS MEANING, NAME RHAEGO?

MY BROTHER RHAEGAR WAS A FIERCE WARRIOR, MY SUN-AND-STARS. HE DIED BEFORE I WAS BORN.

SER JORAH SAYS HE WAS THE LAST OF THE DRAGONS.

IS GOOD NAME, DAN ARES, MOON OF MY LIFE.

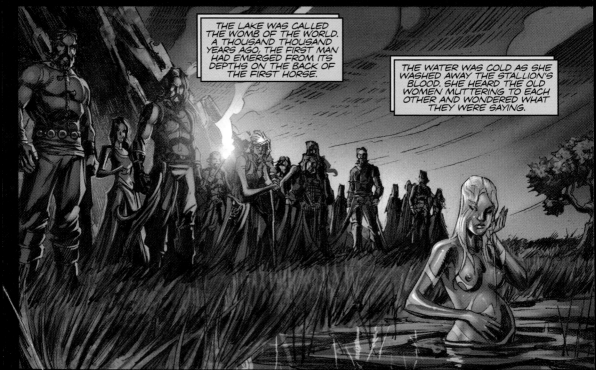

THE LAKE WAS CALLED THE WOMB OF THE WORLD. A THOUSAND THOUSAND YEARS AGO, THE FIRST MAN HAD EMERGED FROM ITS DEPTHS ON THE BACK OF THE FIRST HORSE.

THE WATER WAS COLD AS SHE WASHED AWAY THE STALLION'S BLOOD. SHE HEARD THE OLD WOMEN MUTTERING TO EACH OTHER AND WONDERED WHAT THEY WERE SAYING.

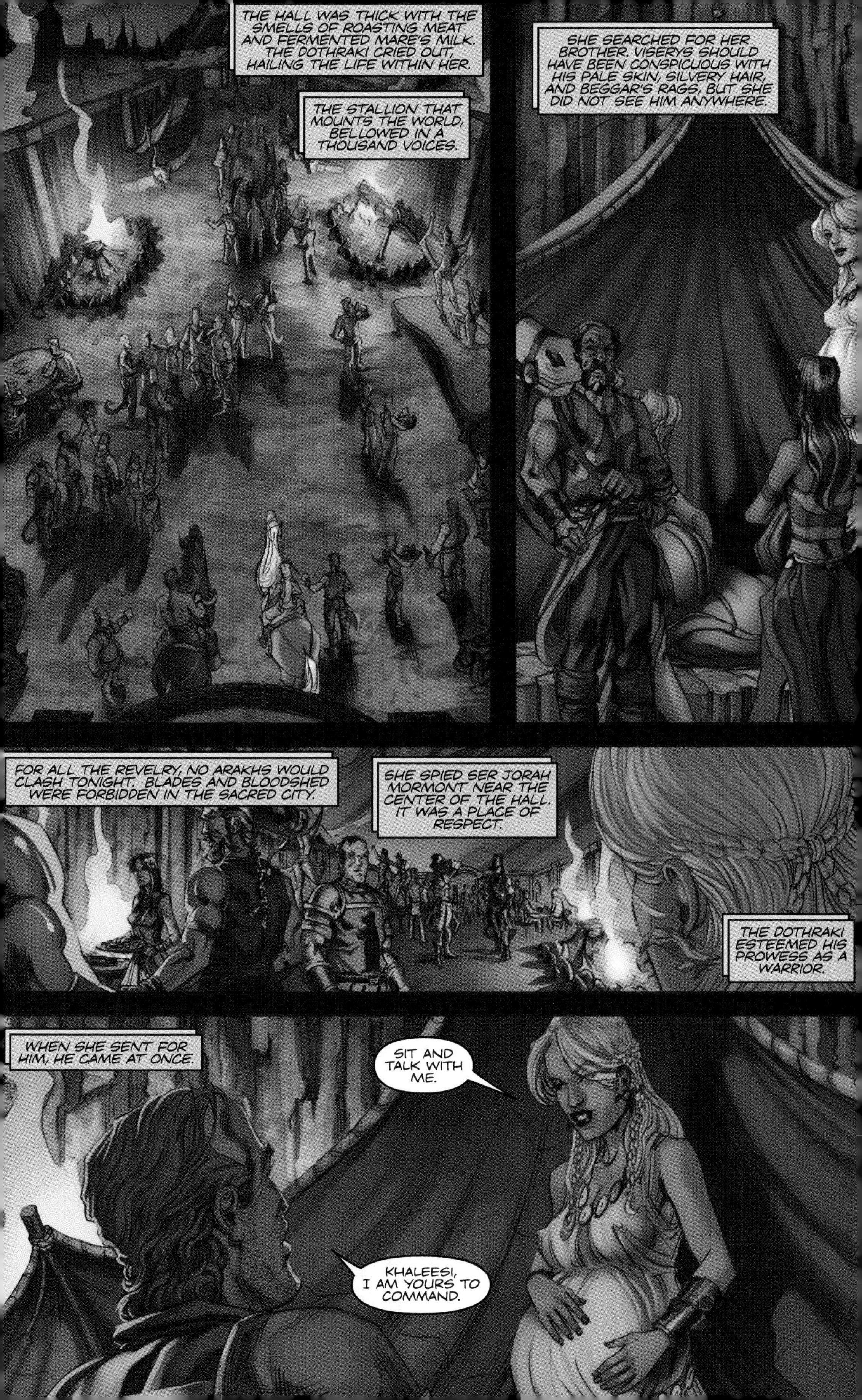
THE HALL WAS THICK WITH THE SMELLS OF ROASTING MEAT AND FERMENTED MARE'S MILK. THE DOTHRAKI CRIED OUT, HAILING THE LIFE WITHIN HER.
THE STALLION THAT MOUNTS THE WORLD, BELLOWED IN A THOUSAND VOICES.
SHE SEARCHED FOR HER BROTHER. VISERYS SHOULD HAVE BEEN CONSPICUOUS WITH HIS PALE SKIN, SILVERY HAIR, AND BEGGAR'S RAGS, BUT SHE DID NOT SEE HIM ANYWHERE.
FOR ALL THE REVELRY, NO ARAKHS WOULD CLASH TONIGHT. BLADES AND BLOODSHED WERE FORBIDDEN IN THE SACRED CITY.
SHE SPIED SER JORAH MORMONT NEAR THE CENTER OF THE HALL. IT WAS A PLACE OF RESPECT.
THE DOTHRAKI ESTEEMED HIS PROWESS AS A WARRIOR.
WHEN SHE SENT FOR HIM, HE CAME AT ONCE.
SIT AND TALK WITH ME.
KHALEESI, I AM YOURS TO COMMAND.

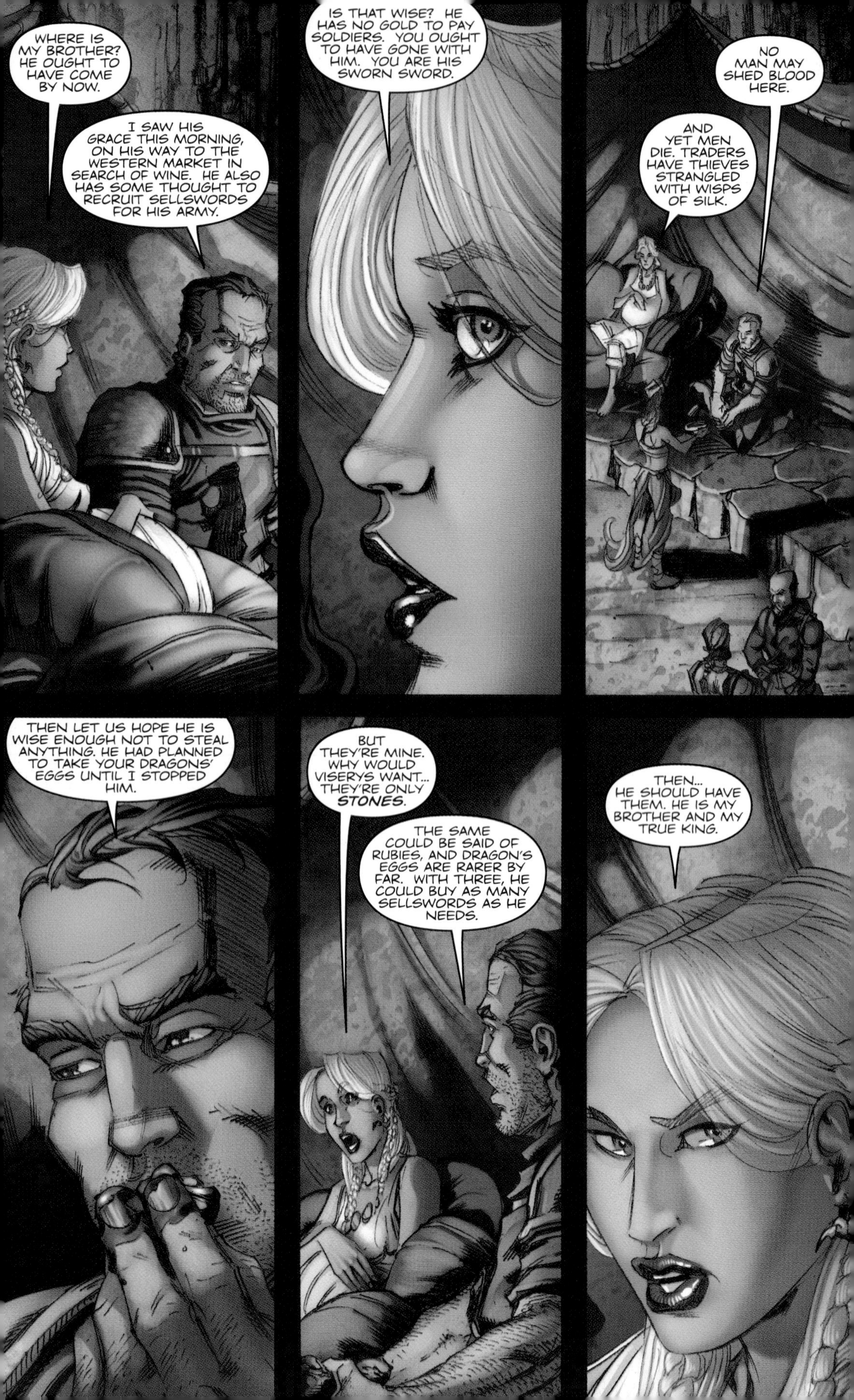
WHERE IS MY BROTHER? HE OUGHT TO HAVE COME BY NOW.
I SAW HIS GRACE THIS MORNING, ON HIS WAY TO THE WESTERN MARKET IN SEARCH OF WINE. HE ALSO HAS SOME THOUGHT TO RECRUIT SELLSWORDS FOR HIS ARMY.
IS THAT WISE? HE HAS NO GOLD TO PAY SOLDIERS. YOU OUGHT TO HAVE GONE WITH HIM. YOU ARE HIS SWORN SWORD.
NO MAN MAY SHED BLOOD HERE.
AND YET MEN DIE. TRADERS HAVE THIEVES STRANGLED WITH WISPS OF SILK.
THEN LET US HOPE HE IS WISE ENOUGH NOT TO STEAL ANYTHING. HE HAD PLANNED TO TAKE YOUR DRAGONS' EGGS UNTIL I STOPPED HIM.
BUT THEY'RE MINE. WHY WOULD VISERYS WANT... THEY'RE ONLY STONES.
THE SAME COULD BE SAID OF RUBIES, AND DRAGON'S EGGS ARE RARER BY FAR. WITH THREE, HE COULD BUY AS MANY SELLSWORDS AS HE NEEDS.
THEN... HE SHOULD HAVE THEM. HE IS MY BROTHER AND MY TRUE KING.

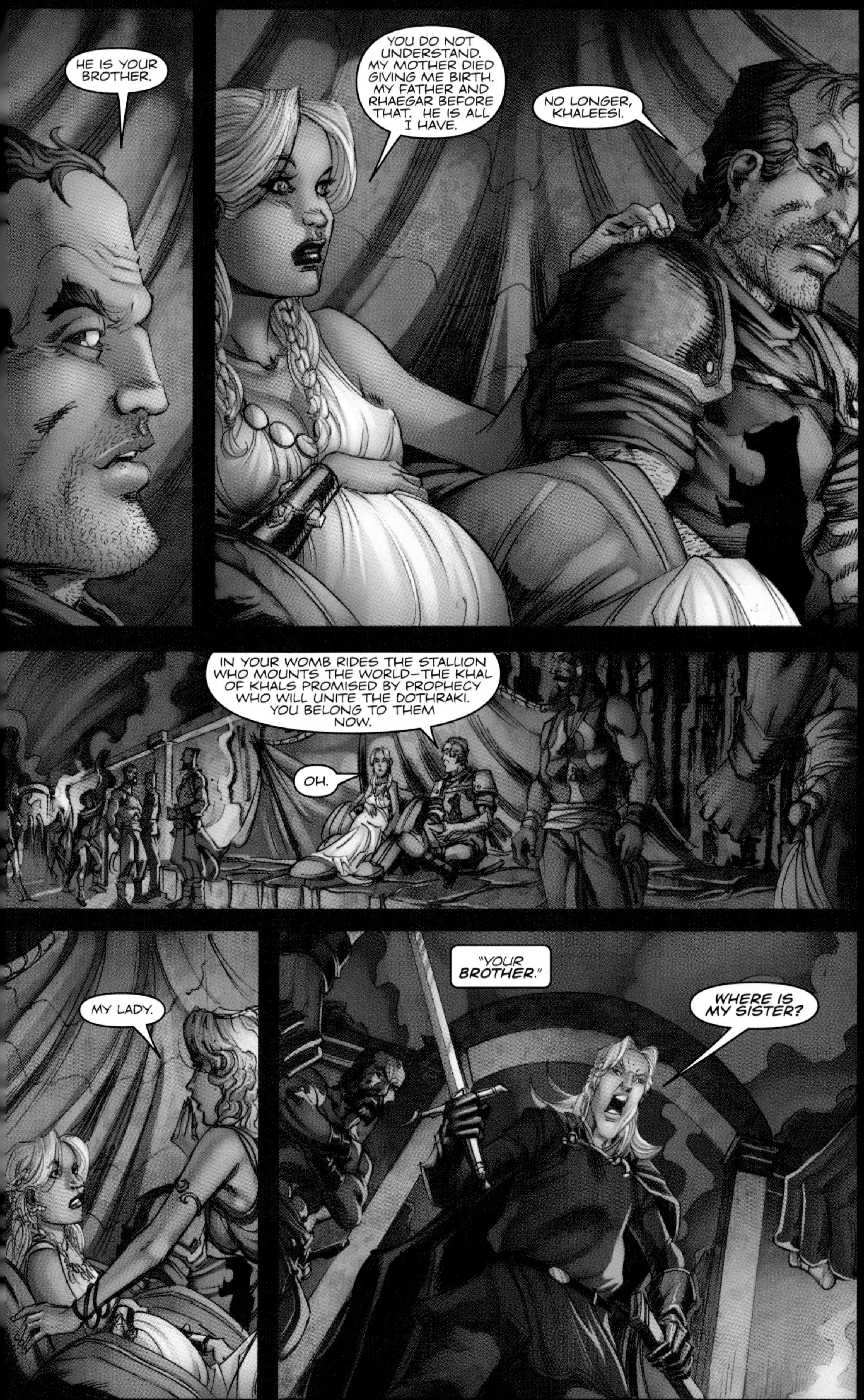
HE IS YOUR BROTHER.
YOU DO NOT UNDERSTAND. MY MOTHER DIED GIVING ME BIRTH. MY FATHER AND RHAEGAR BEFORE THAT. HE IS ALL I HAVE.
NO LONGER, KHALEESI.
IN YOUR WOMB RIDES THE STALLION WHO MOUNTS THE WORLD—THE KHAL OF KHALS PROMISED BY PROPHECY WHO WILL UNITE THE DOTHRAKI. YOU BELONG TO THEM NOW.
OH.
MY LADY.
"YOUR BROTHER."
WHERE IS MY SISTER?

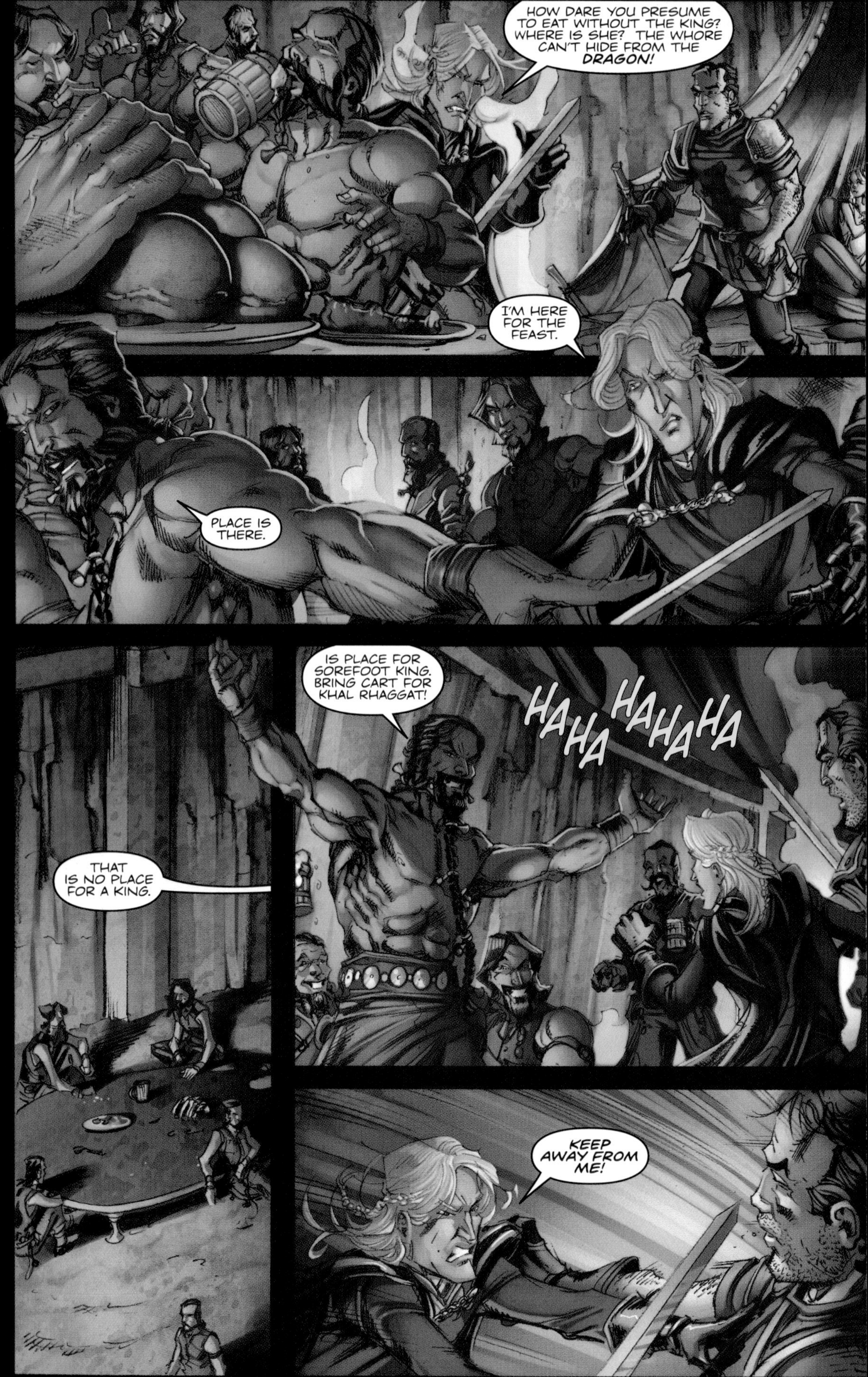
HOW DARE YOU PRESUME TO EAT WITHOUT THE KING? WHERE IS SHE? THE WHORE CAN'T HIDE FROM THE DRAGON!
I'M HERE FOR THE FEAST.
PLACE IS THERE.
IS PLACE FOR SOREFOOT KING. BRING CART FOR KHAL RHAGGAT!
HAHA HAHAHAHA
THAT IS NO PLACE FOR A KING.
KEEP AWAY FROM ME!

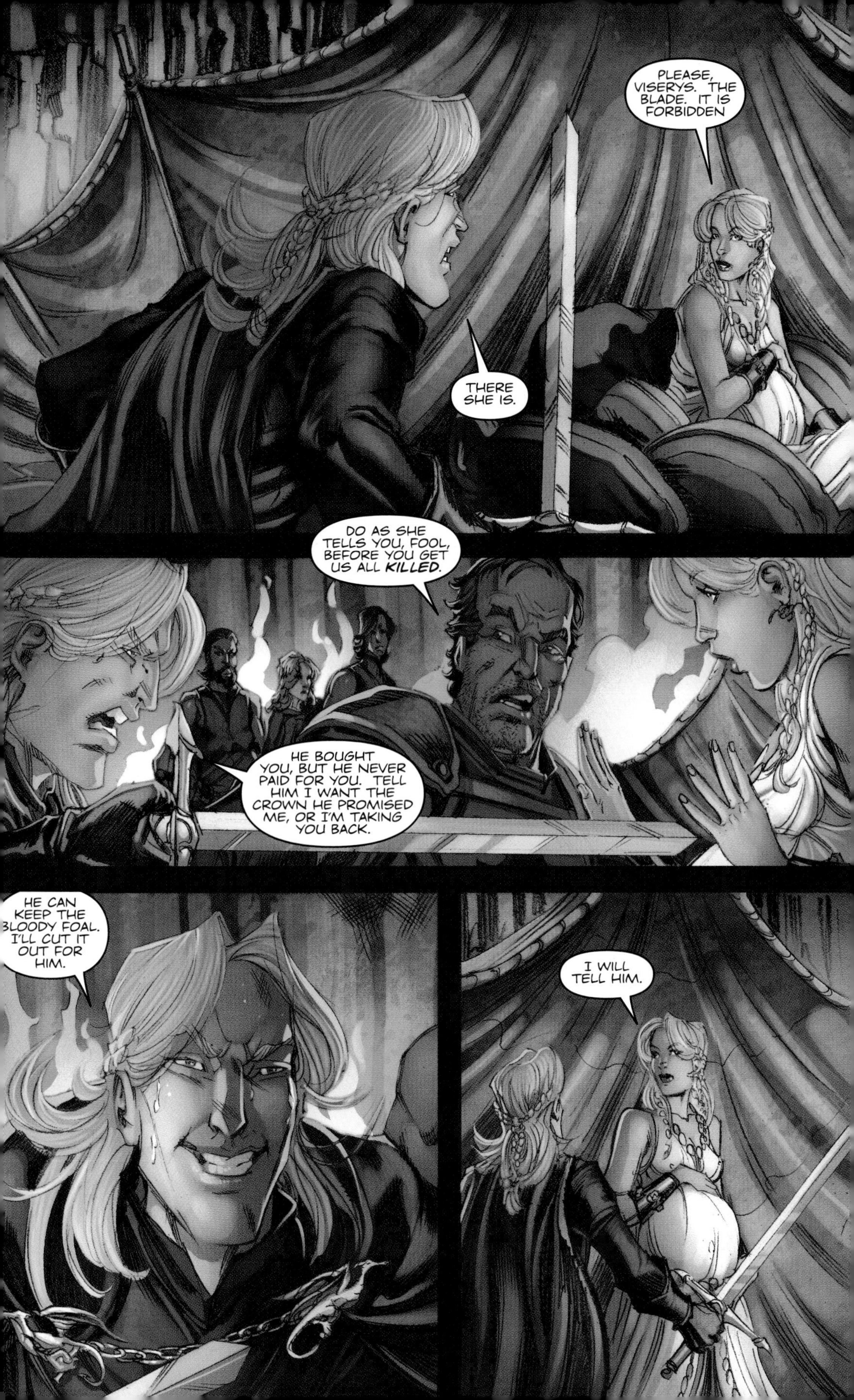
PLEASE, VISERYS. THE BLADE. IT IS FORBIDDEN
THERE SHE IS.
DO AS SHE TELLS YOU, FOOL, BEFORE YOU GET US ALL KILLED.
HE BOUGHT YOU, BUT HE NEVER PAID FOR YOU. TELL HIM I WANT THE CROWN HE PROMISED ME, OR I'M TAKING YOU BACK.
HE CAN KEEP THE BLOODY FOAL. I'LL CUT IT OUT FOR HIM.
I WILL TELL HIM.

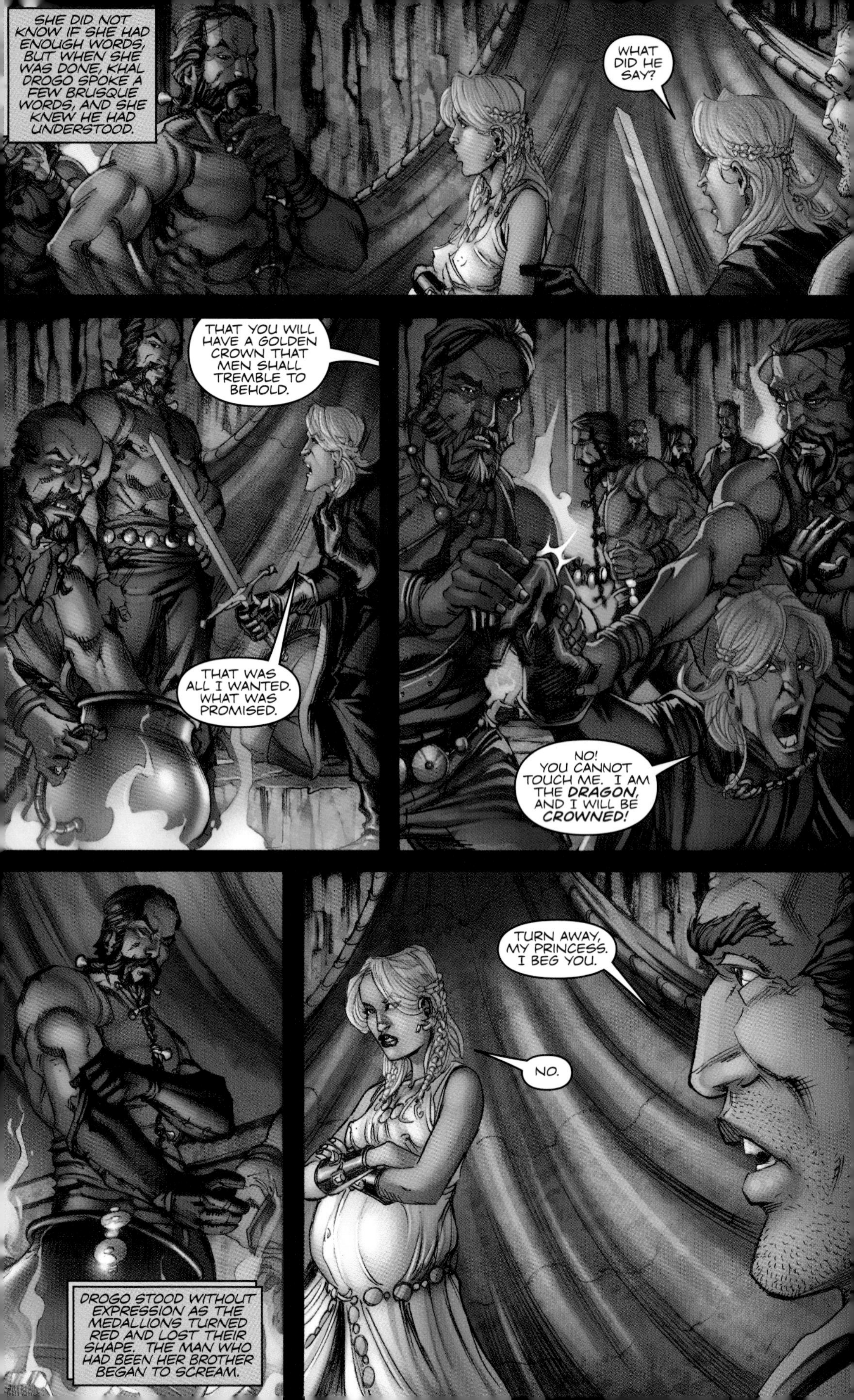
SHE DID NOT KNOW IF SHE HAD ENOUGH WORDS, BUT WHEN SHE WAS DONE, KHAL DROGO SPOKE A FEW BRUSQUE WORDS, AND SHE KNEW HE HAD UNDERSTOOD.
WHAT DID HE SAY?
THAT YOU WILL HAVE A GOLDEN CROWN THAT MEN SHALL TREMBLE TO BEHOLD.
THAT WAS ALL I WANTED. WHAT WAS PROMISED.
NO! YOU CANNOT TOUCH ME. I AM THE *DRAGON*, AND I WILL BE *CROWNED*!
DROGO STOOD WITHOUT EXPRESSION AS THE MEDALLIONS TURNED RED AND LOST THEIR SHAPE. THE MAN WHO HAD BEEN HER BROTHER BEGAN TO SCREAM.
TURN AWAY, MY PRINCESS. I BEG YOU.
NO.

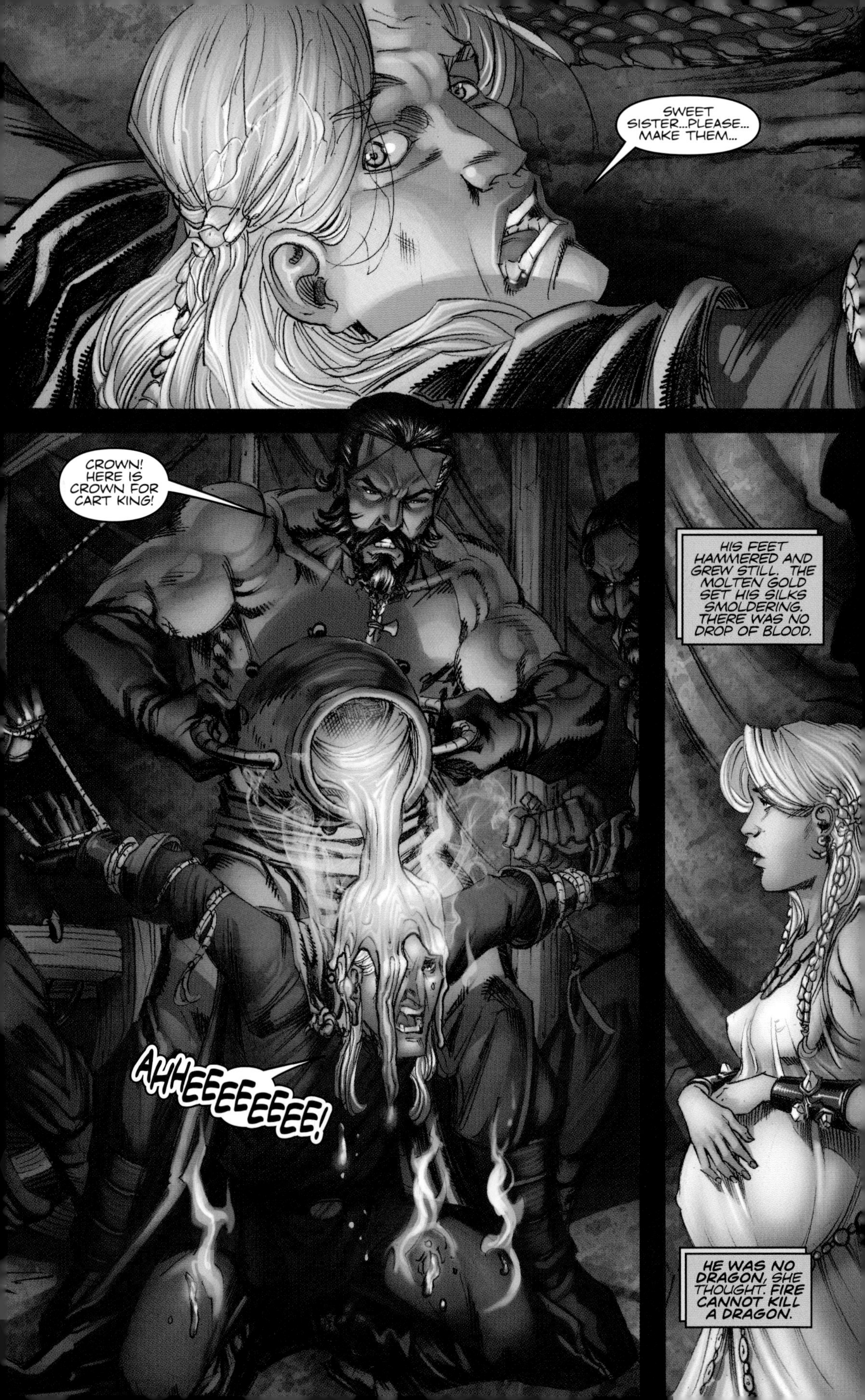
SWEET SISTER...PLEASE... MAKE THEM...
CROWN! HERE IS CROWN FOR CART KING!
AHHEEEEEEEEEE!
HIS FEET HAMMERED AND GREW STILL. THE MOLTEN GOLD SET HIS SILKS SMOLDERING. THERE WAS NO DROP OF BLOOD.
HE WAS NO DRAGON, SHE THOUGHT. FIRE CANNOT KILL A DRAGON.

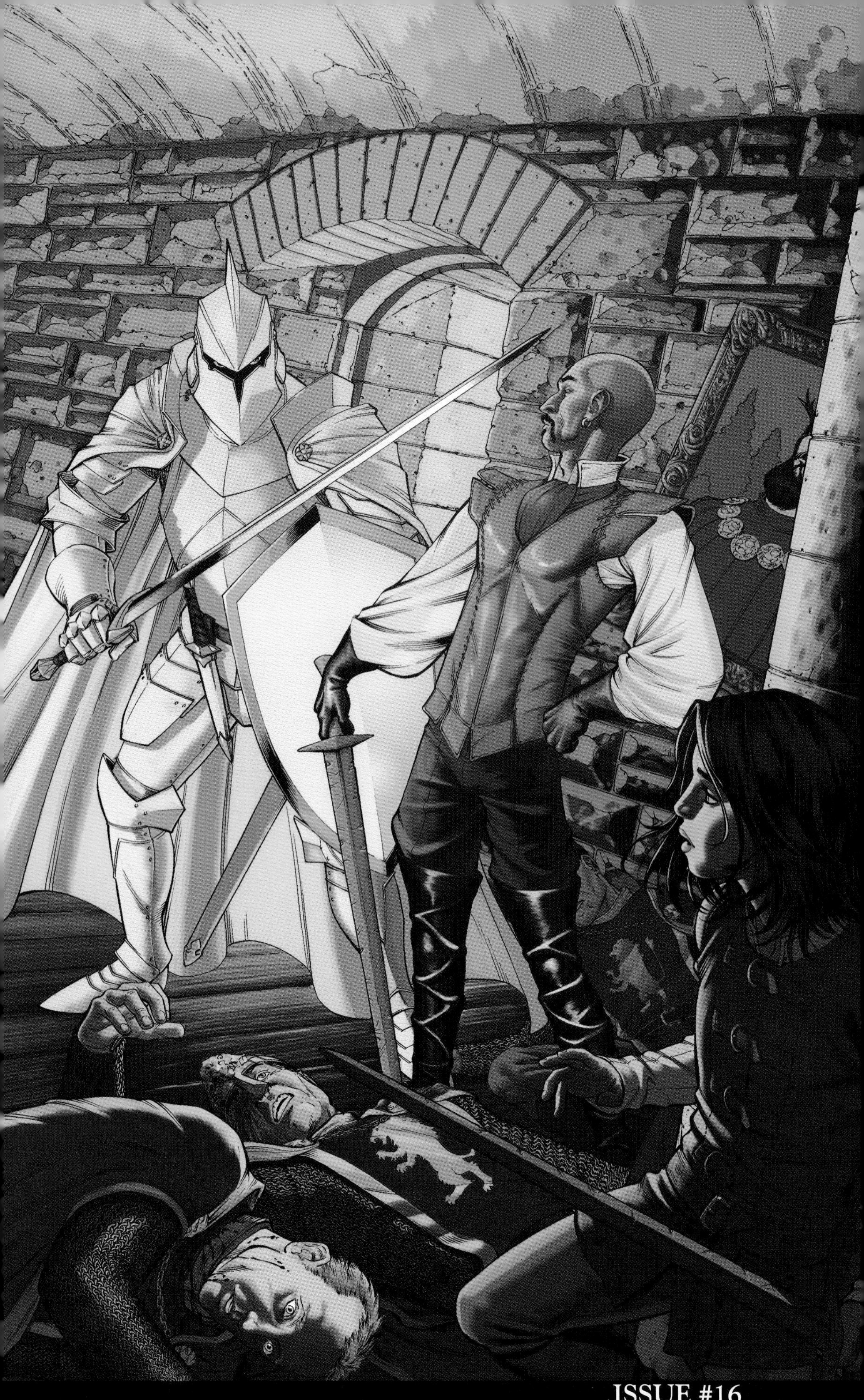

ISSUE #16

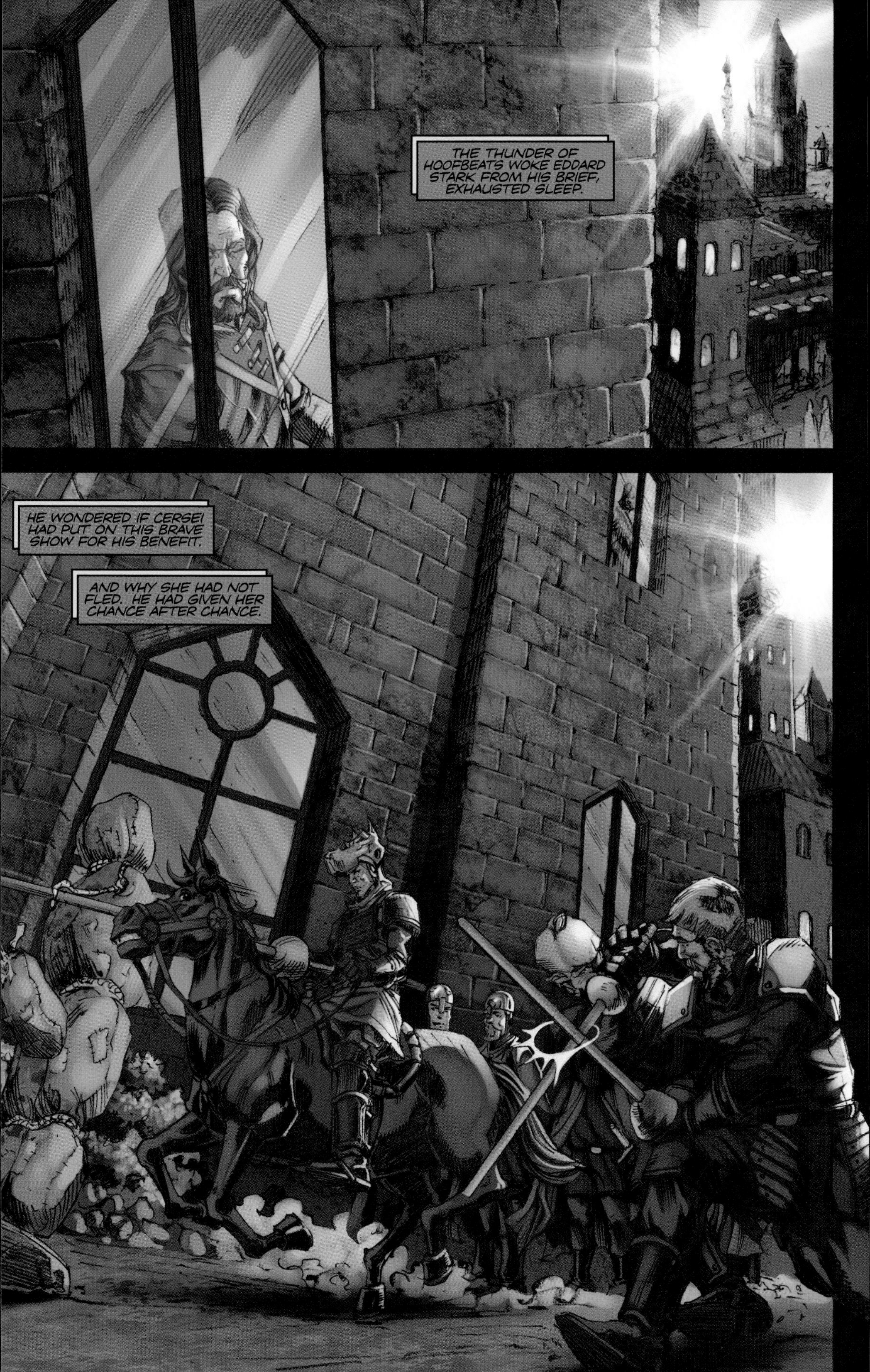
THE THUNDER OF HOOFBEATS WOKE EDDARD STARK FROM HIS BRIEF, EXHAUSTED SLEEP.
HE WONDERED IF CERSEI HAD PUT ON THIS BRAVE SHOW FOR HIS BENEFIT.
AND WHY SHE HAD NOT FLED. HE HAD GIVEN HER CHANCE AFTER CHANCE.

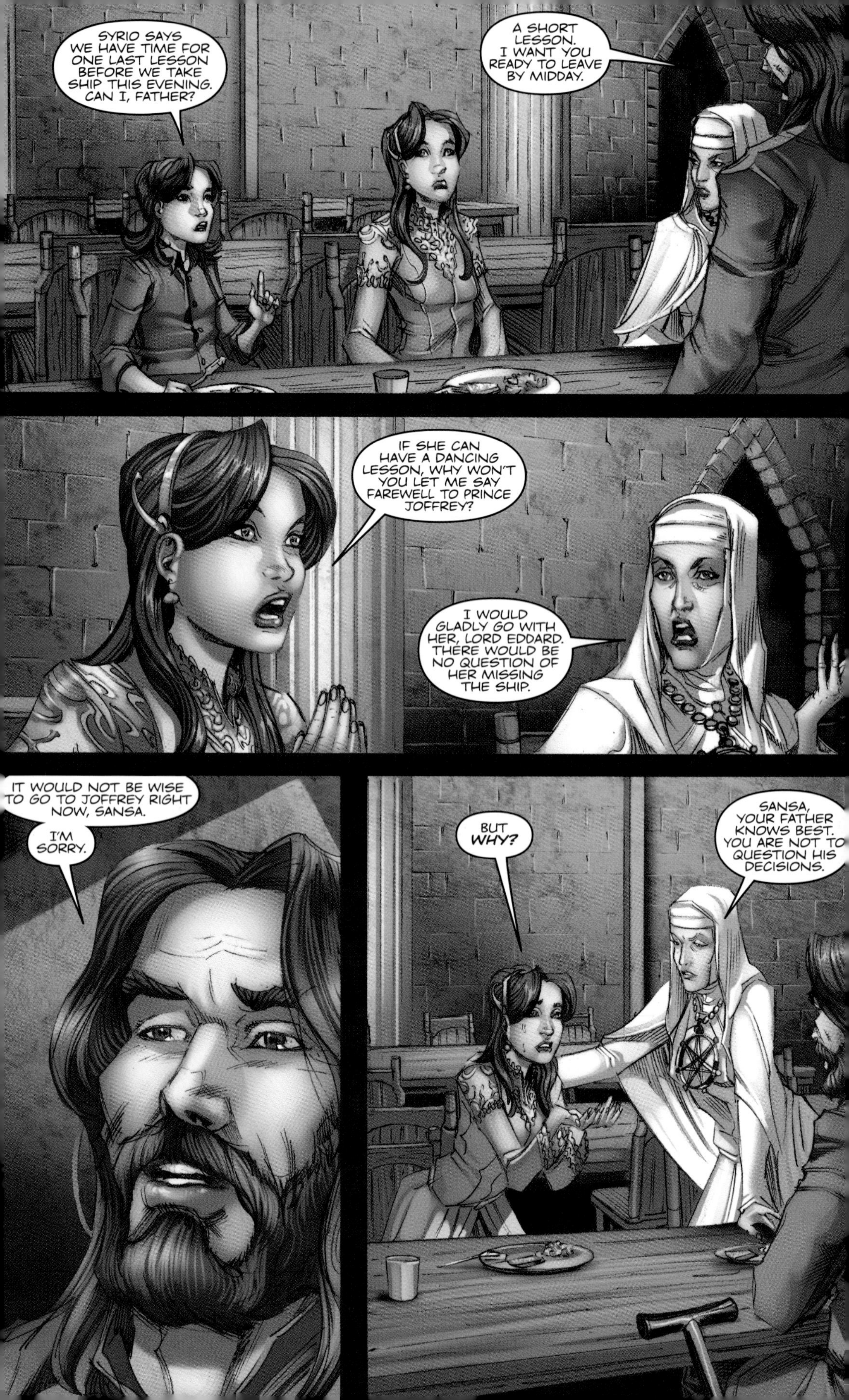
SYRIO SAYS WE HAVE TIME FOR ONE LAST LESSON BEFORE WE TAKE SHIP THIS EVENING. CAN I, FATHER?
A SHORT LESSON. I WANT YOU READY TO LEAVE BY MIDDAY.
IF SHE CAN HAVE A DANCING LESSON, WHY WON'T YOU LET ME SAY FAREWELL TO PRINCE JOFFREY?
I WOULD GLADLY GO WITH HER, LORD EDDARD. THERE WOULD BE NO QUESTION OF HER MISSING THE SHIP.
IT WOULD NOT BE WISE TO GO TO JOFFREY RIGHT NOW, SANSA.
I'M SORRY.
BUT *WHY?*
SANSA, YOUR FATHER KNOWS BEST. YOU ARE NOT TO QUESTION HIS DECISIONS.

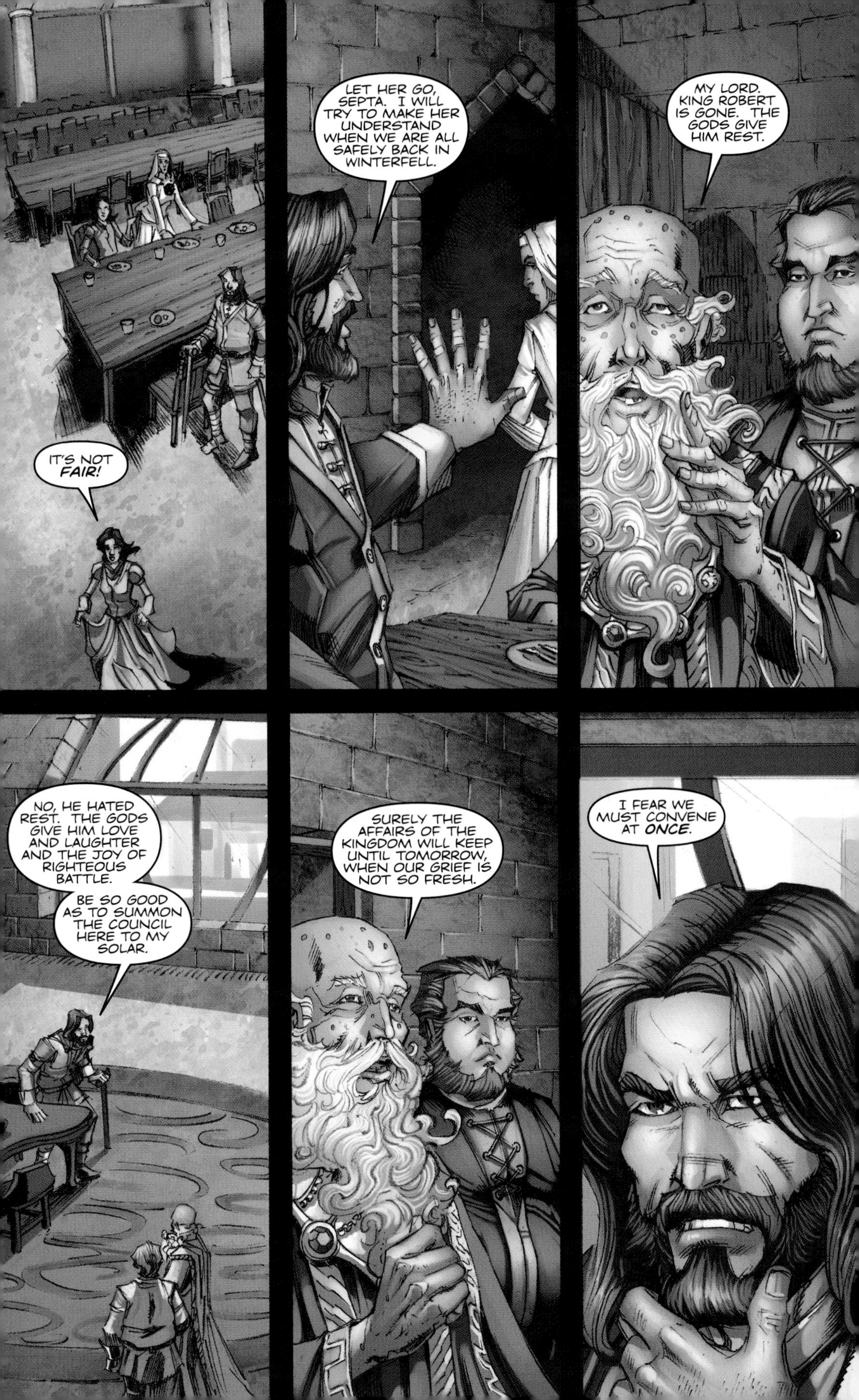
IT'S NOT FAIR!
LET HER GO, SEPTA. I WILL TRY TO MAKE HER UNDERSTAND WHEN WE ARE ALL SAFELY BACK IN WINTERFELL.
MY LORD. KING ROBERT IS GONE. THE GODS GIVE HIM REST.
NO, HE HATED REST. THE GODS GIVE HIM LOVE AND LAUGHTER AND THE JOY OF RIGHTEOUS BATTLE.
BE SO GOOD AS TO SUMMON THE COUNCIL HERE TO MY SOLAR.
SURELY THE AFFAIRS OF THE KINGDOM WILL KEEP UNTIL TOMORROW, WHEN OUR GRIEF IS NOT SO FRESH.
I FEAR WE MUST CONVENE AT ONCE.

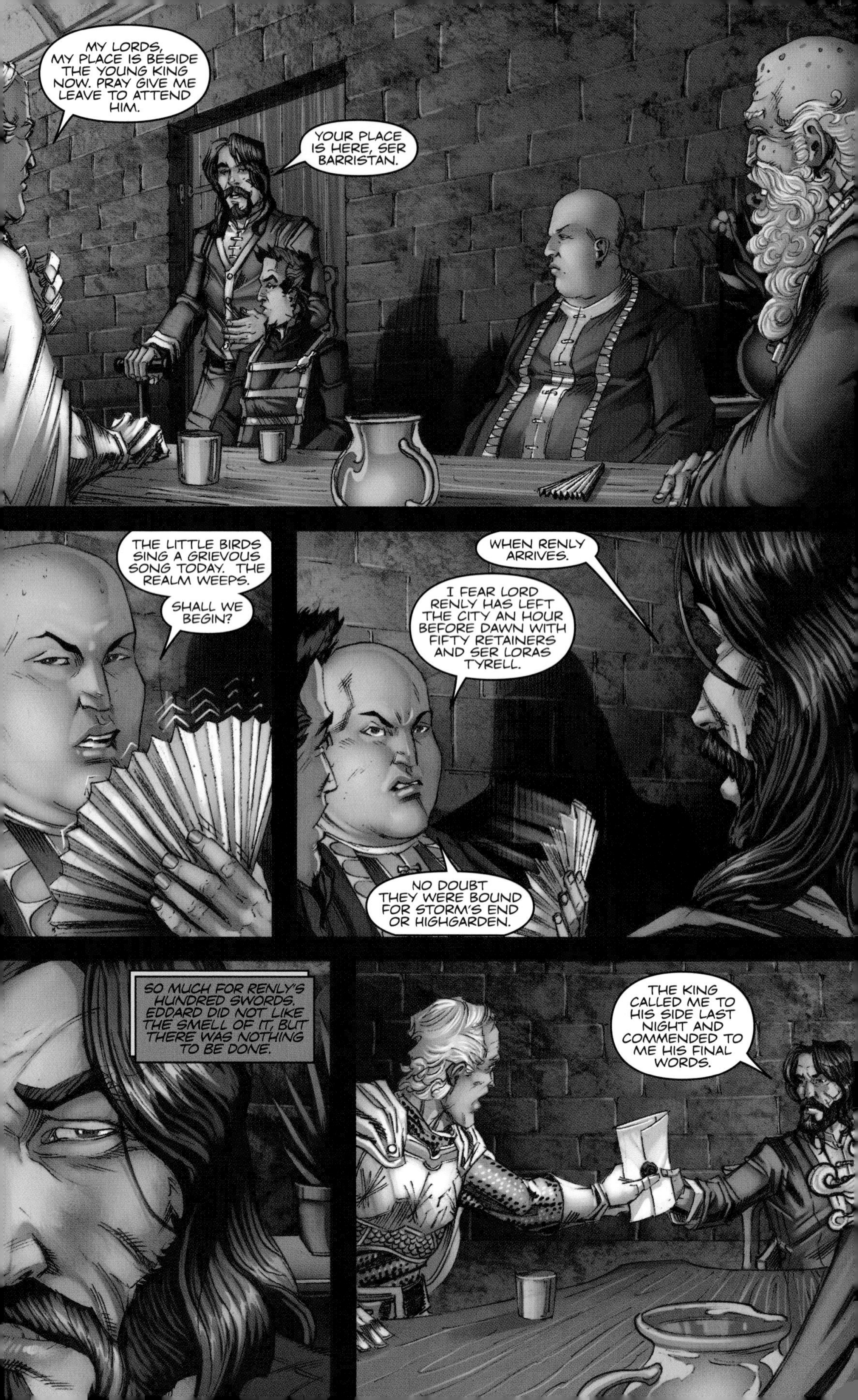
MY LORDS, MY PLACE IS BESIDE THE YOUNG KING NOW. PRAY GIVE ME LEAVE TO ATTEND HIM.
YOUR PLACE IS HERE, SER BARRISTAN.
THE LITTLE BIRDS SING A GRIEVOUS SONG TODAY. THE REALM WEEPS.
SHALL WE BEGIN?
WHEN RENLY ARRIVES.
I FEAR LORD RENLY HAS LEFT THE CITY AN HOUR BEFORE DAWN WITH FIFTY RETAINERS AND SER LORAS TYRELL.
NO DOUBT THEY WERE BOUND FOR STORM'S END OR HIGHGARDEN.
SO MUCH FOR RENLY'S HUNDRED SWORDS. EDDARD DID NOT LIKE THE SMELL OF IT, BUT THERE WAS NOTHING TO BE DONE.
THE KING CALLED ME TO HIS SIDE LAST NIGHT AND COMMENDED TO ME HIS FINAL WORDS.

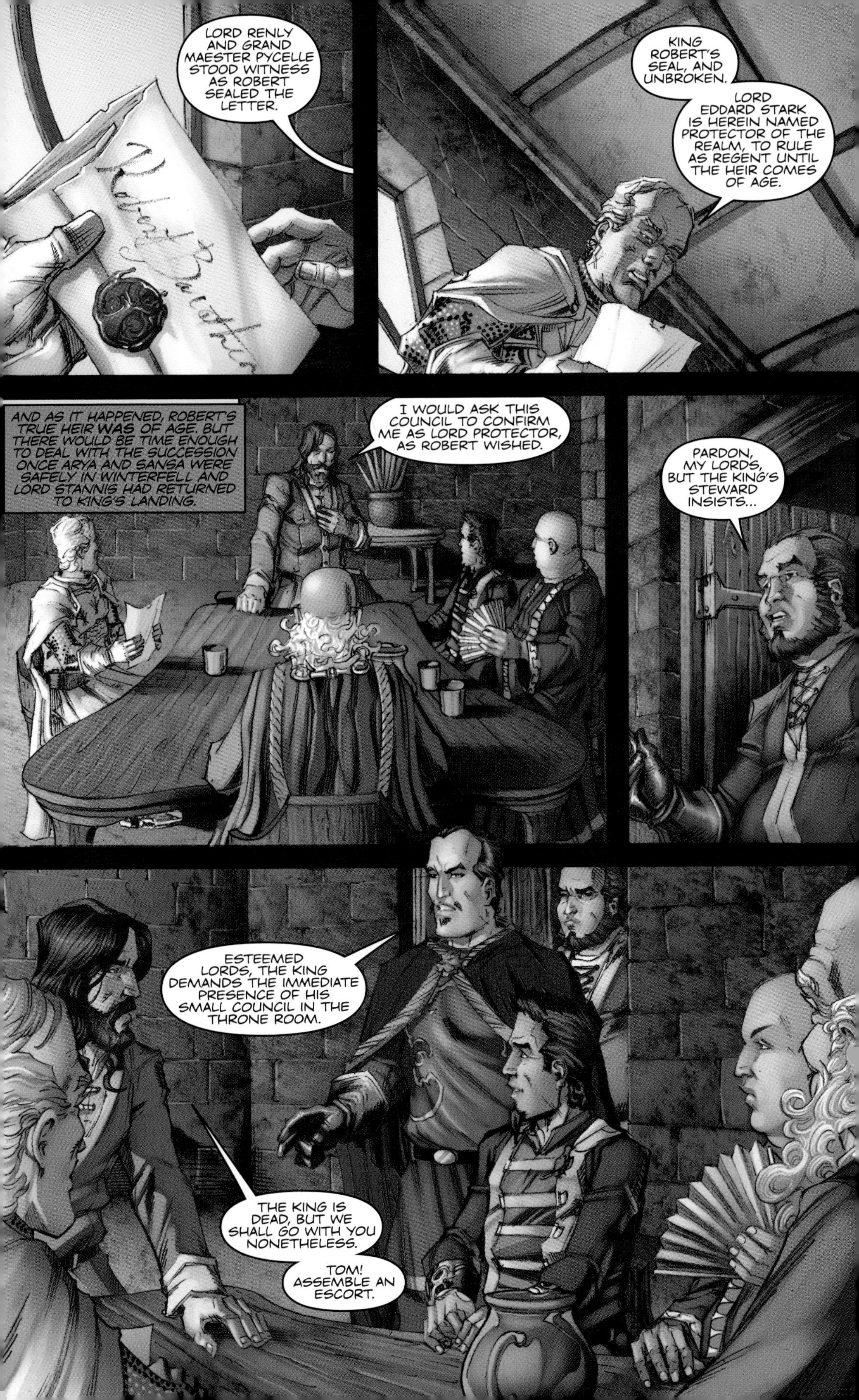
LORD RENLY AND GRAND MAESTER PYCELLE STOOD WITNESS AS ROBERT SEALED THE LETTER.
KING ROBERT'S SEAL, AND UNBROKEN.
LORD EDDARD STARK IS HEREIN NAMED PROTECTOR OF THE REALM, TO RULE AS REGENT UNTIL THE HEIR COMES OF AGE.
AND AS IT HAPPENED, ROBERT'S TRUE HEIR WAS OF AGE. BUT THERE WOULD BE TIME ENOUGH TO DEAL WITH THE SUCCESSION ONCE ARYA AND SANSA WERE SAFELY IN WINTERFELL AND LORD STANNIS HAD RETURNED TO KING'S LANDING.
I WOULD ASK THIS COUNCIL TO CONFIRM ME AS LORD PROTECTOR, AS ROBERT WISHED.
PARDON, MY LORDS, BUT THE KING'S STEWARD INSISTS...
ESTEEMED LORDS, THE KING DEMANDS THE IMMEDIATE PRESENCE OF HIS SMALL COUNCIL IN THE THRONE ROOM.
THE KING IS DEAD, BUT WE SHALL GO WITH YOU NONETHELESS.
TOM! ASSEMBLE AN ESCORT.

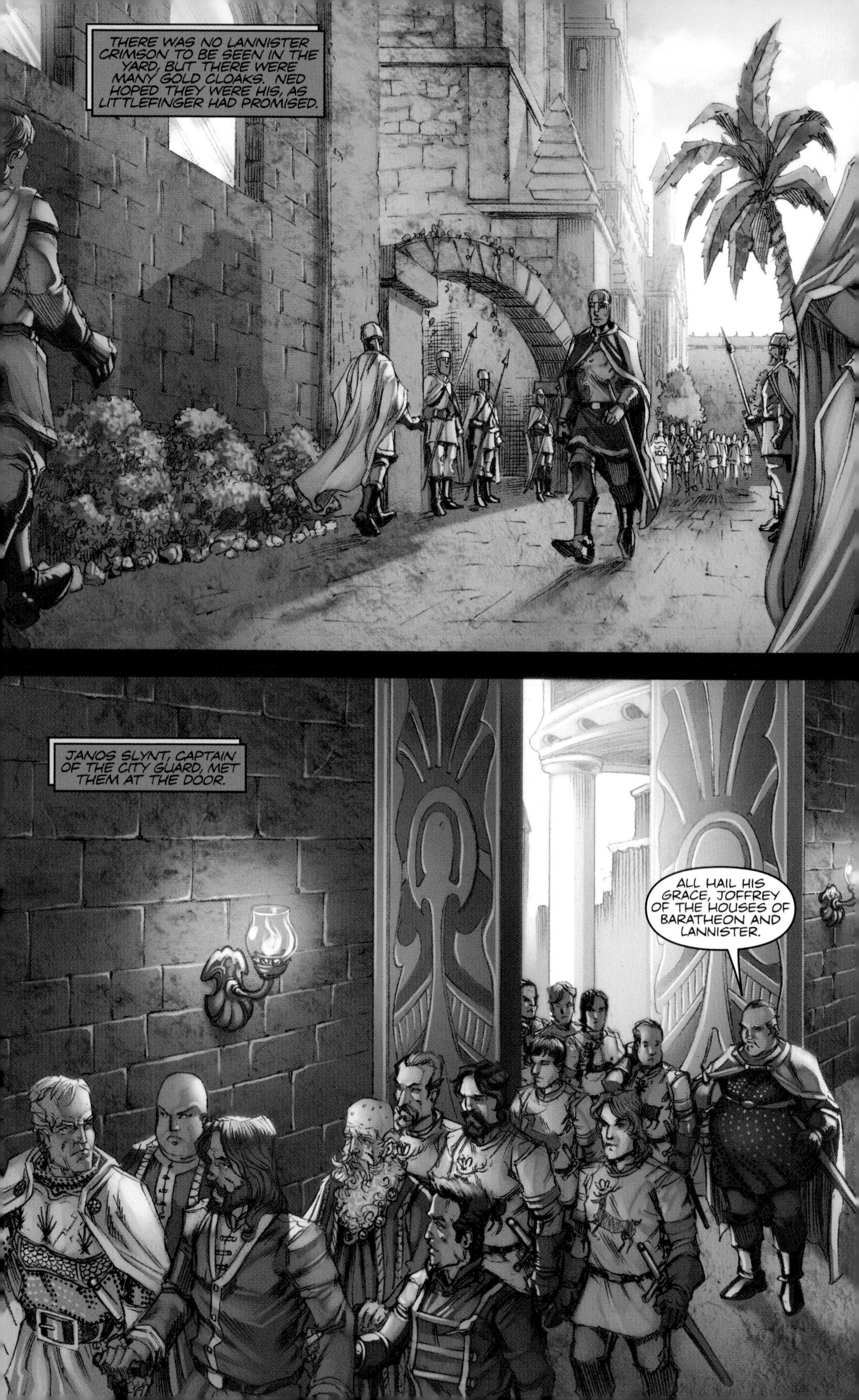
THERE WAS NO LANNISTER CRIMSON TO BE SEEN IN THE YARD, BUT THERE WERE MANY GOLD CLOAKS. NED HOPED THEY WERE HIS, AS LITTLEFINGER HAD PROMISED.
JANOS SLYNT, CAPTAIN OF THE CITY GUARD, MET THEM AT THE DOOR.
ALL HAIL HIS GRACE, JOFFREY OF THE HOUSES OF BARATHEON AND LANNISTER.

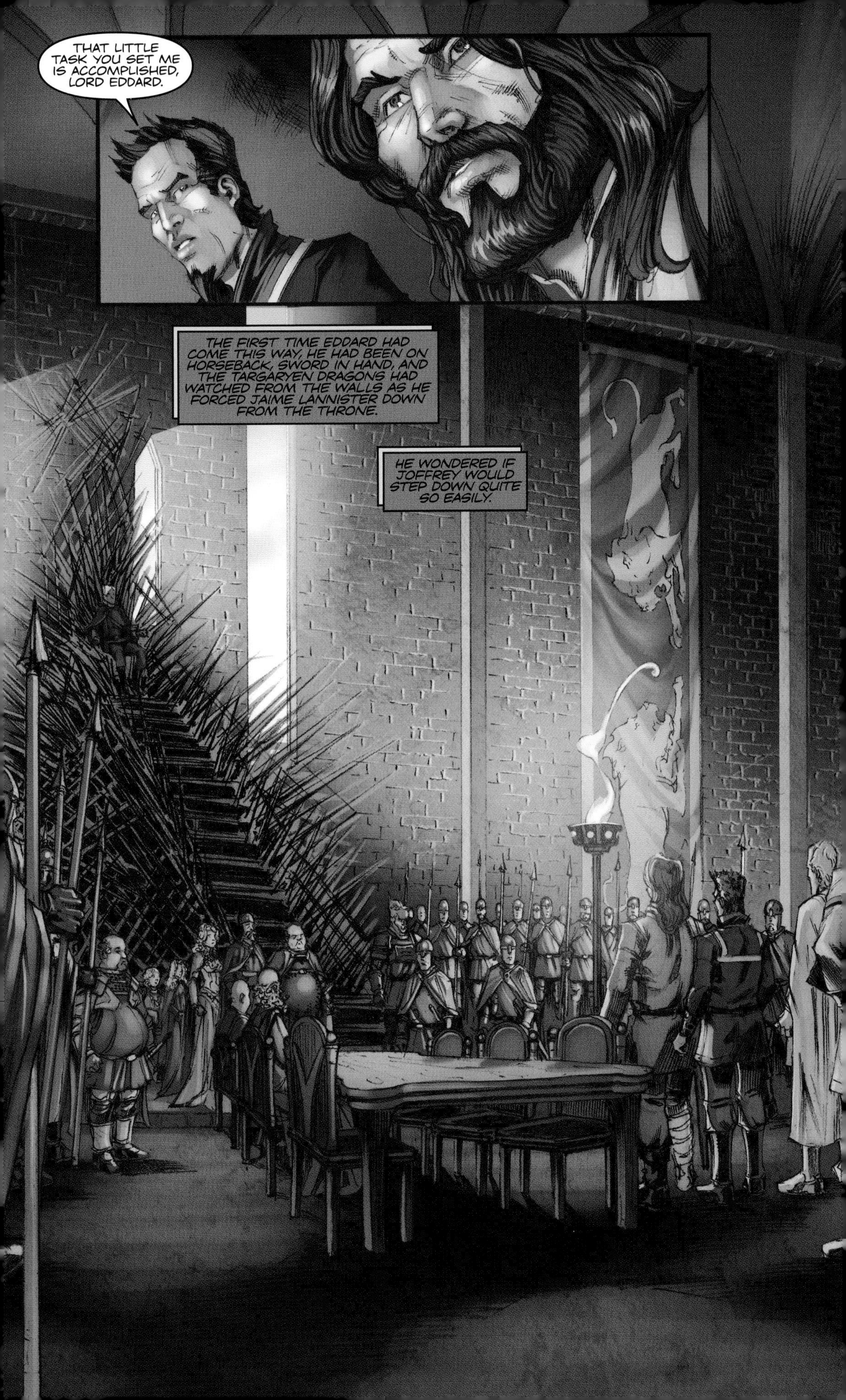
THAT LITTLE TASK YOU SET ME IS ACCOMPLISHED, LORD EDDARD.
THE FIRST TIME EDDARD HAD COME THIS WAY, HE HAD BEEN ON HORSEBACK, SWORD IN HAND, AND THE TARGARYEN DRAGONS HAD WATCHED FROM THE WALLS AS HE FORCED JAIME LANNISTER DOWN FROM THE THRONE.
HE WONDERED IF JOFFREY WOULD STEP DOWN QUITE SO EASILY.

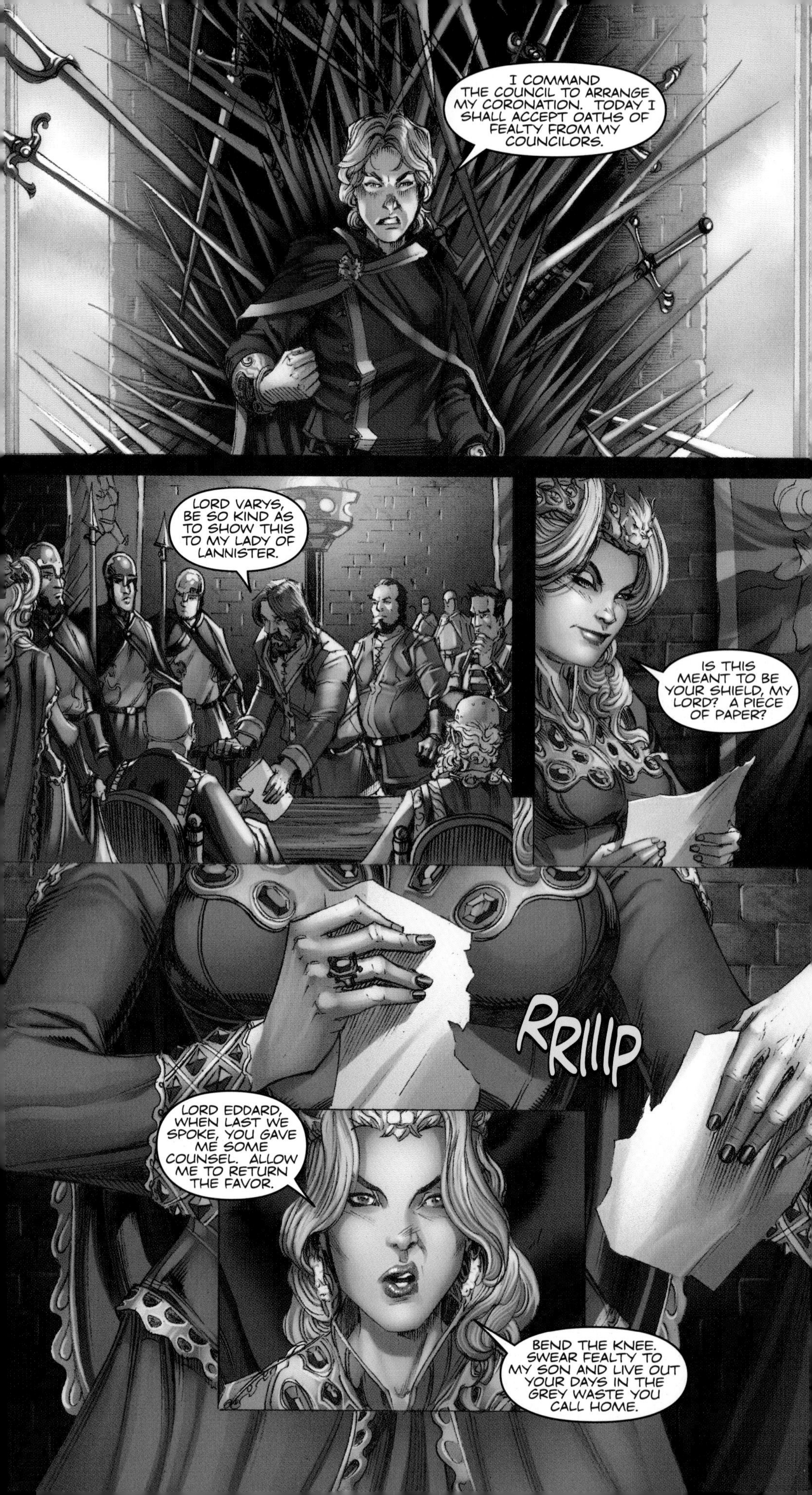

I COMMAND THE COUNCIL TO ARRANGE MY CORONATION. TODAY I SHALL ACCEPT OATHS OF FEALTY FROM MY COUNCILORS.
LORD VARYS, BE SO KIND AS TO SHOW THIS TO MY LADY OF LANNISTER.
IS THIS MEANT TO BE YOUR SHIELD, MY LORD? A PIECE OF PAPER?
RRIIIP
LORD EDDARD, WHEN LAST WE SPOKE, YOU GAVE ME SOME COUNSEL. ALLOW ME TO RETURN THE FAVOR.
BEND THE KNEE. SWEAR FEALTY TO MY SON AND LIVE OUT YOUR DAYS IN THE GREY WASTE YOU CALL HOME.

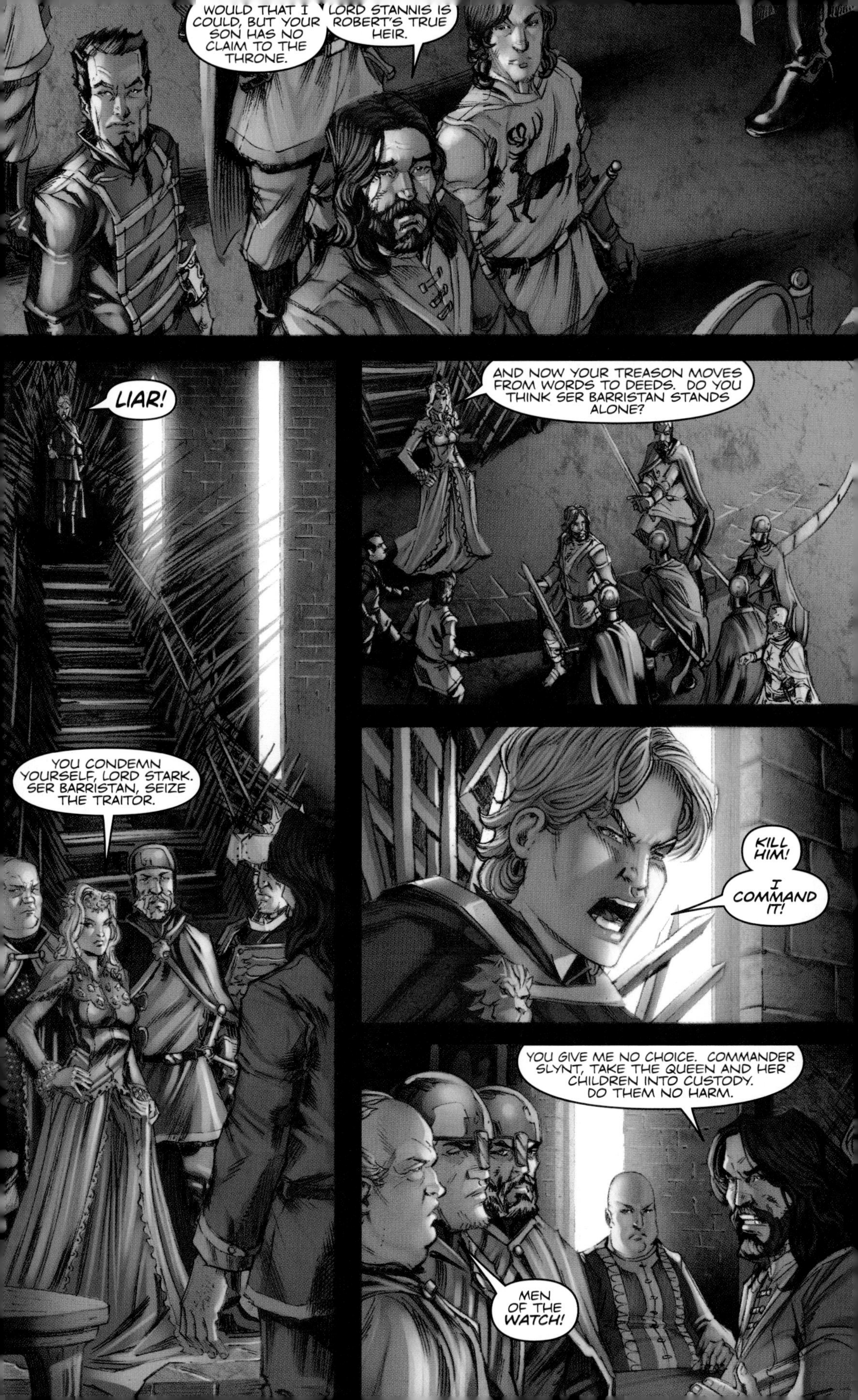
WOULD THAT I COULD, BUT YOUR SON HAS NO CLAIM TO THE THRONE.
LORD STANNIS IS ROBERT'S TRUE HEIR.
LIAR!
YOU CONDEMN YOURSELF, LORD STARK. SER BARRISTAN, SEIZE THE TRAITOR.
AND NOW YOUR TREASON MOVES FROM WORDS TO DEEDS. DO YOU THINK SER BARRISTAN STANDS ALONE?
KILL HIM!
I COMMAND IT!
YOU GIVE ME NO CHOICE. COMMANDER SLYNT, TAKE THE QUEEN AND HER CHILDREN INTO CUSTODY. DO THEM NO HARM.
MEN OF THE WATCH!

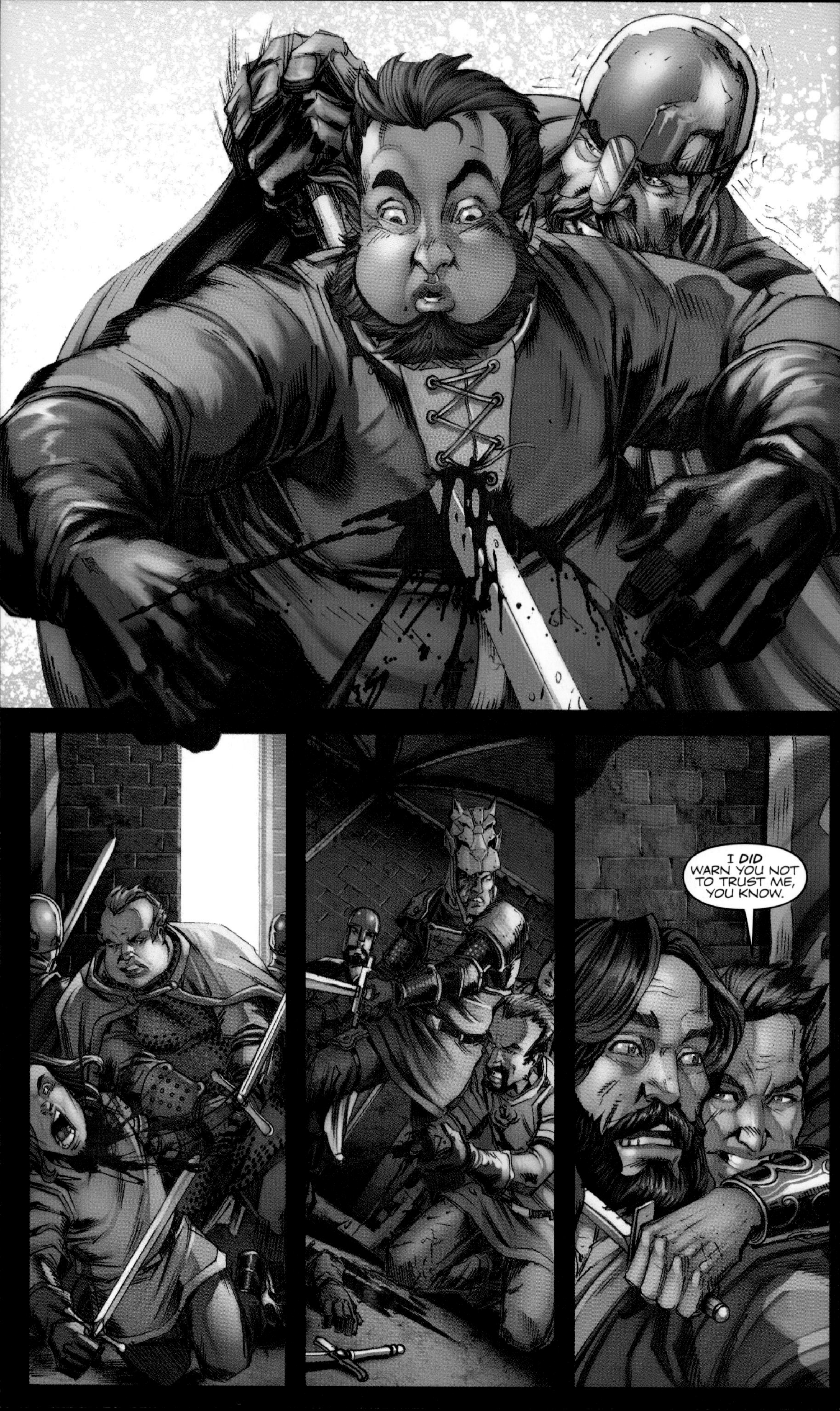
I *DID* WARN YOU NOT TO TRUST ME, YOU KNOW.

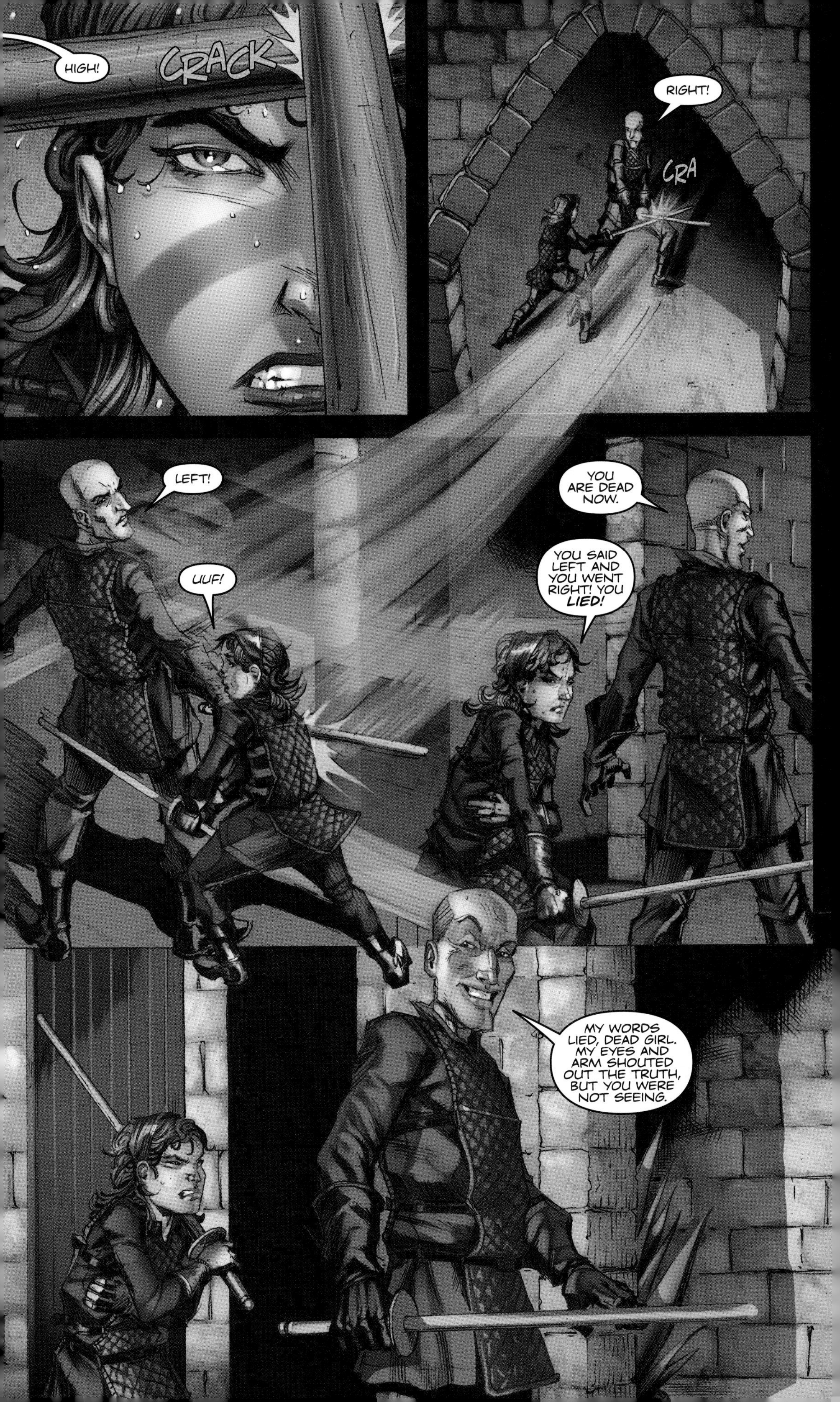

HIGH!
CRACK
RIGHT!
CRA
LEFT!
UUF!
YOU ARE DEAD NOW.
YOU SAID LEFT AND YOU WENT RIGHT! YOU **LIED!**
MY WORDS LIED, DEAD GIRL. MY EYES AND ARM SHOUTED OUT THE TRUTH, BUT YOU WERE NOT SEEING.

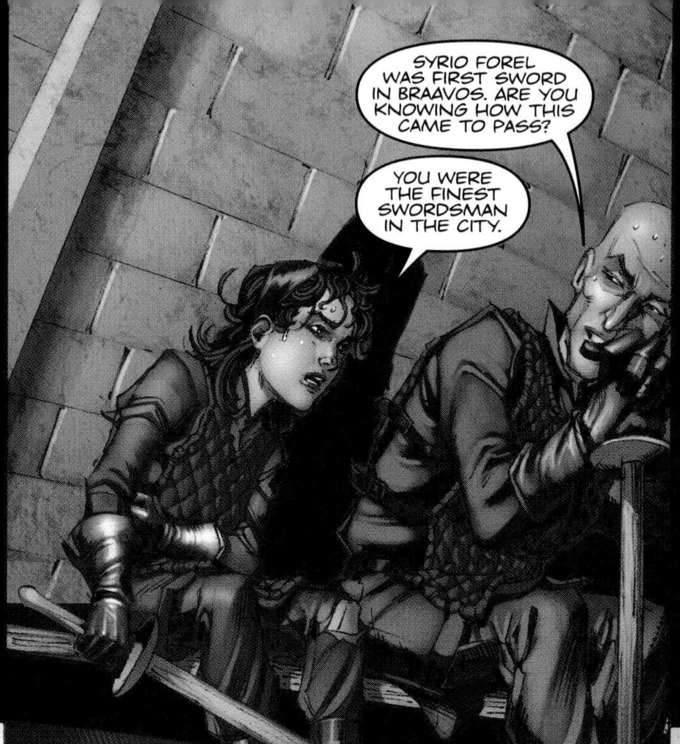

SYRIO FOREL WAS FIRST SWORD IN BRAAVOS. ARE YOU KNOWING HOW THIS CAME TO PASS?
YOU WERE THE FINEST SWORDSMAN IN THE CITY.

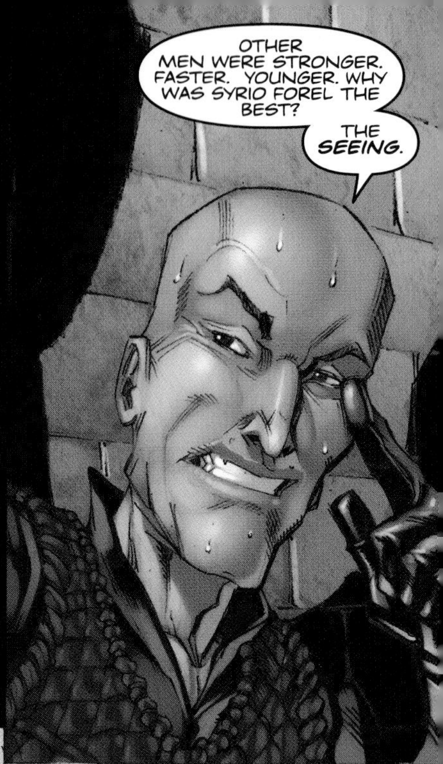

OTHER MEN WERE STRONGER. FASTER. YOUNGER. WHY WAS SYRIO FOREL THE BEST?
THE SEEING.

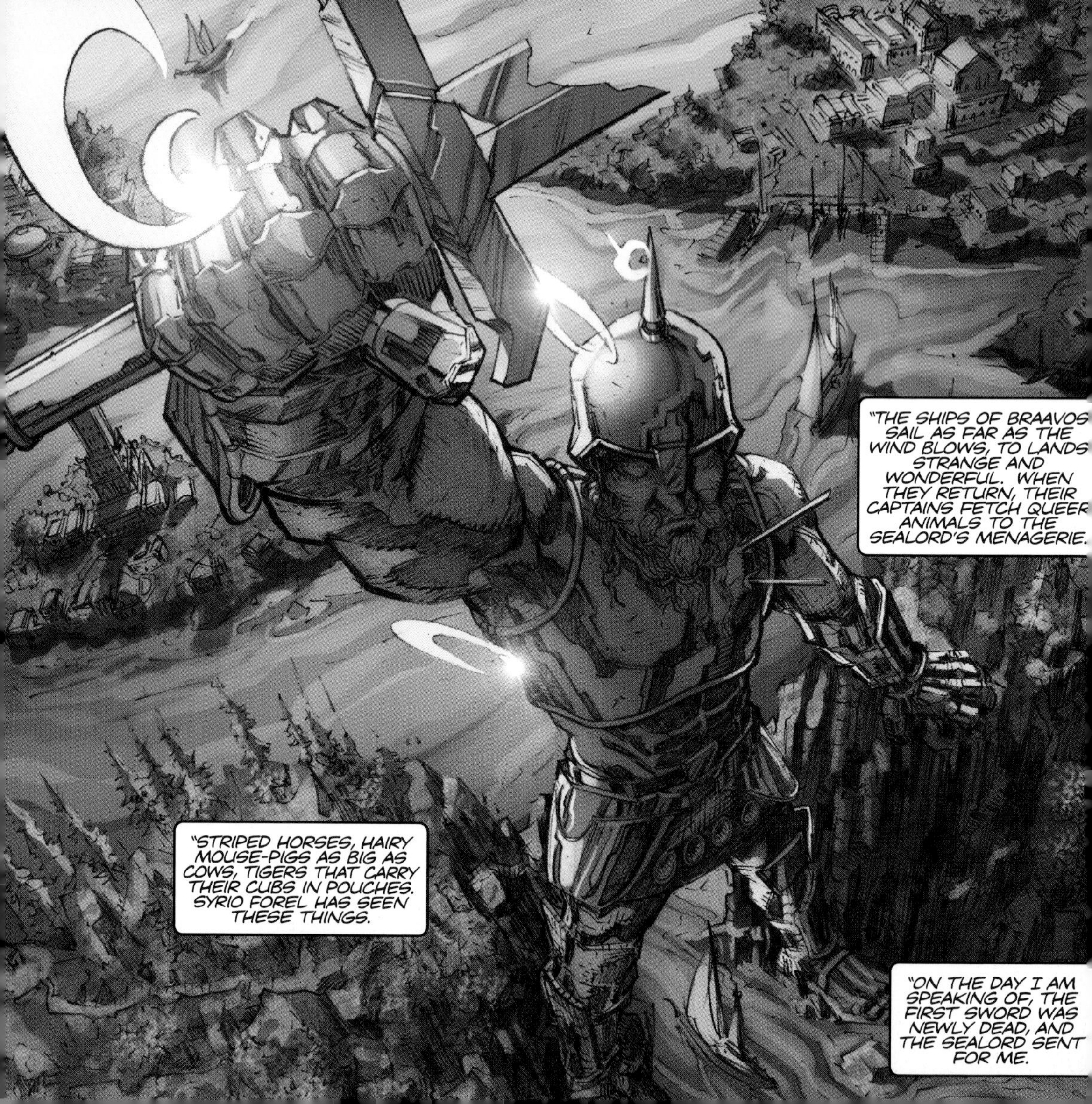

"THE SHIPS OF BRAAVOS SAIL AS FAR AS THE WIND BLOWS, TO LANDS STRANGE AND WONDERFUL. WHEN THEY RETURN, THEIR CAPTAINS FETCH QUEER ANIMALS TO THE SEALORD'S MENAGERIE.
"STRIPED HORSES, HAIRY MOUSE-PIGS AS BIG AS COWS, TIGERS THAT CARRY THEIR CUBS IN POUCHES. SYRIO FOREL HAS SEEN THESE THINGS.
"ON THE DAY I AM SPEAKING OF, THE FIRST SWORD WAS NEWLY DEAD, AND THE SEALORD SENT FOR ME.

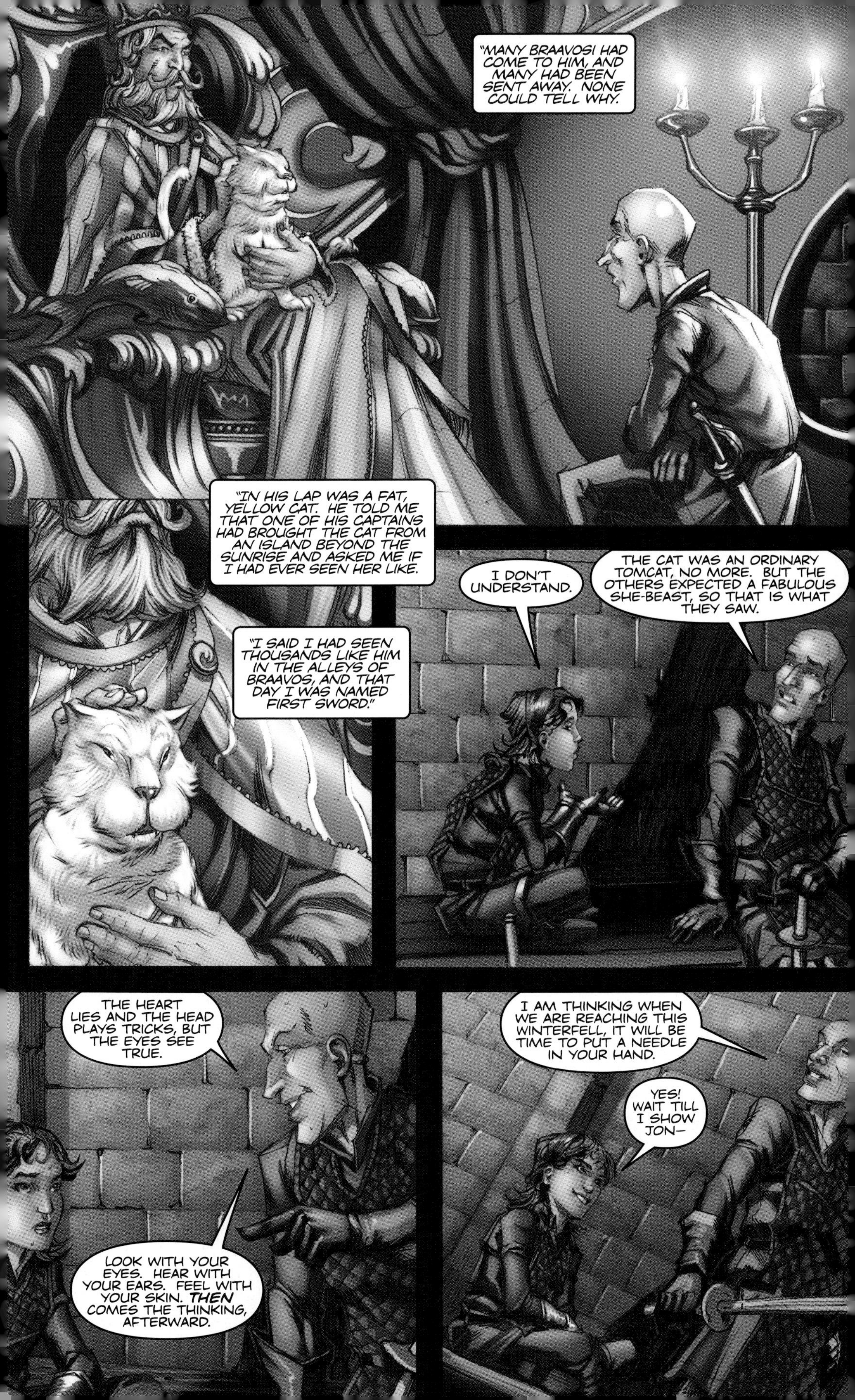
"MANY BRAAVOSI HAD COME TO HIM, AND MANY HAD BEEN SENT AWAY. NONE COULD TELL WHY.
"IN HIS LAP WAS A FAT, YELLOW CAT. HE TOLD ME THAT ONE OF HIS CAPTAINS HAD BROUGHT THE CAT FROM AN ISLAND BEYOND THE SUNRISE AND ASKED ME IF I HAD EVER SEEN HER LIKE.
"I SAID I HAD SEEN THOUSANDS LIKE HIM IN THE ALLEYS OF BRAAVOS, AND THAT DAY I WAS NAMED FIRST SWORD."
I DON'T UNDERSTAND.
THE CAT WAS AN ORDINARY TOMCAT, NO MORE. BUT THE OTHERS EXPECTED A FABULOUS SHE-BEAST, SO THAT IS WHAT THEY SAW.
THE HEART LIES AND THE HEAD PLAYS TRICKS, BUT THE EYES SEE TRUE.
LOOK WITH YOUR EYES. HEAR WITH YOUR EARS. FEEL WITH YOUR SKIN. THEN COMES THE THINKING, AFTERWARD.
I AM THINKING WHEN WE ARE REACHING THIS WINTERFELL, IT WILL BE TIME TO PUT A NEEDLE IN YOUR HAND.
YES! WAIT TILL I SHOW JON—

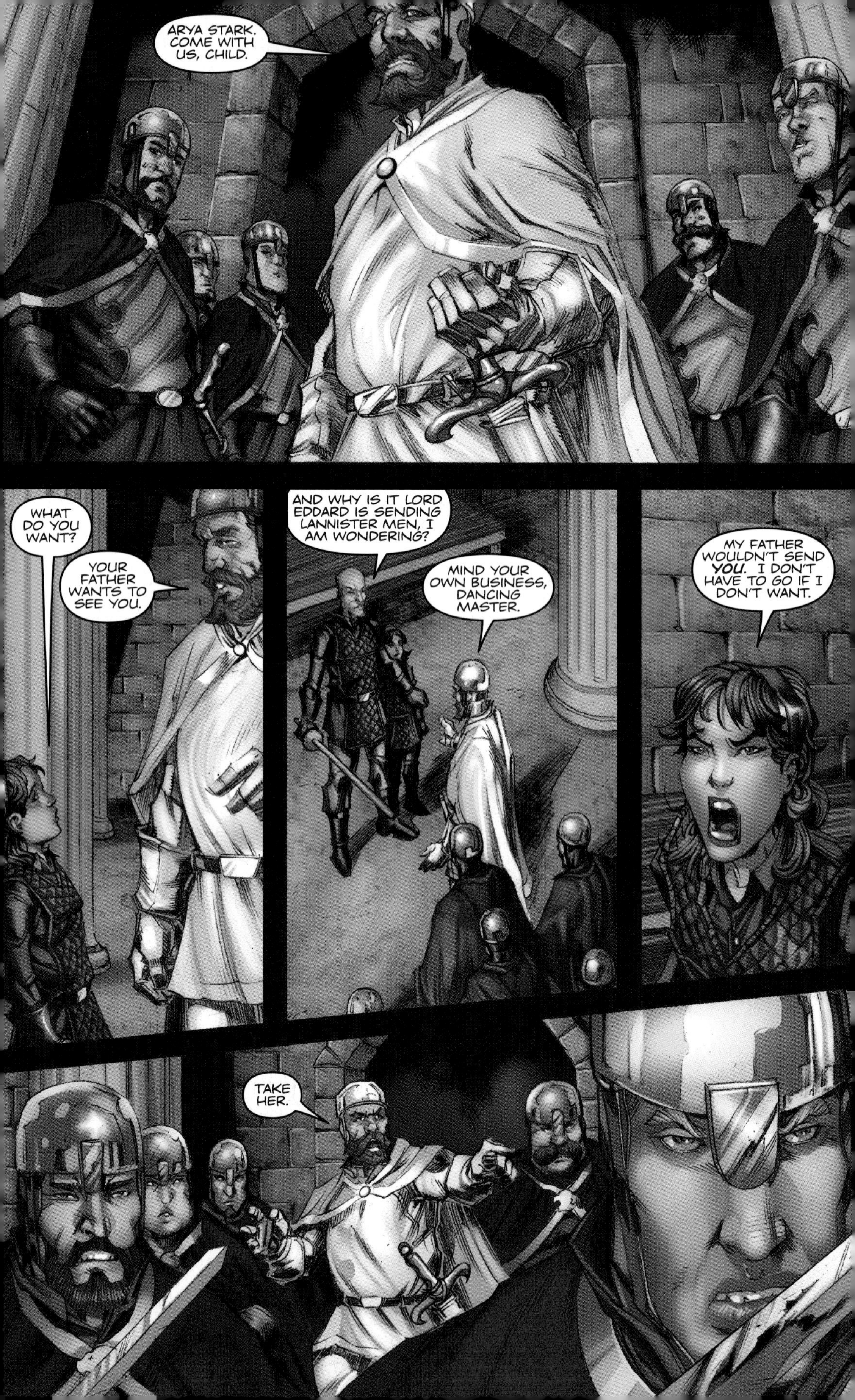
ARYA STARK. COME WITH US, CHILD.
WHAT DO YOU WANT?
YOUR FATHER WANTS TO SEE YOU.
AND WHY IS IT LORD EDDARD IS SENDING LANNISTER MEN, I AM WONDERING?
MIND YOUR OWN BUSINESS, DANCING MASTER.
MY FATHER WOULDN'T SEND **YOU**. I DON'T HAVE TO GO IF I DON'T WANT.
TAKE HER.

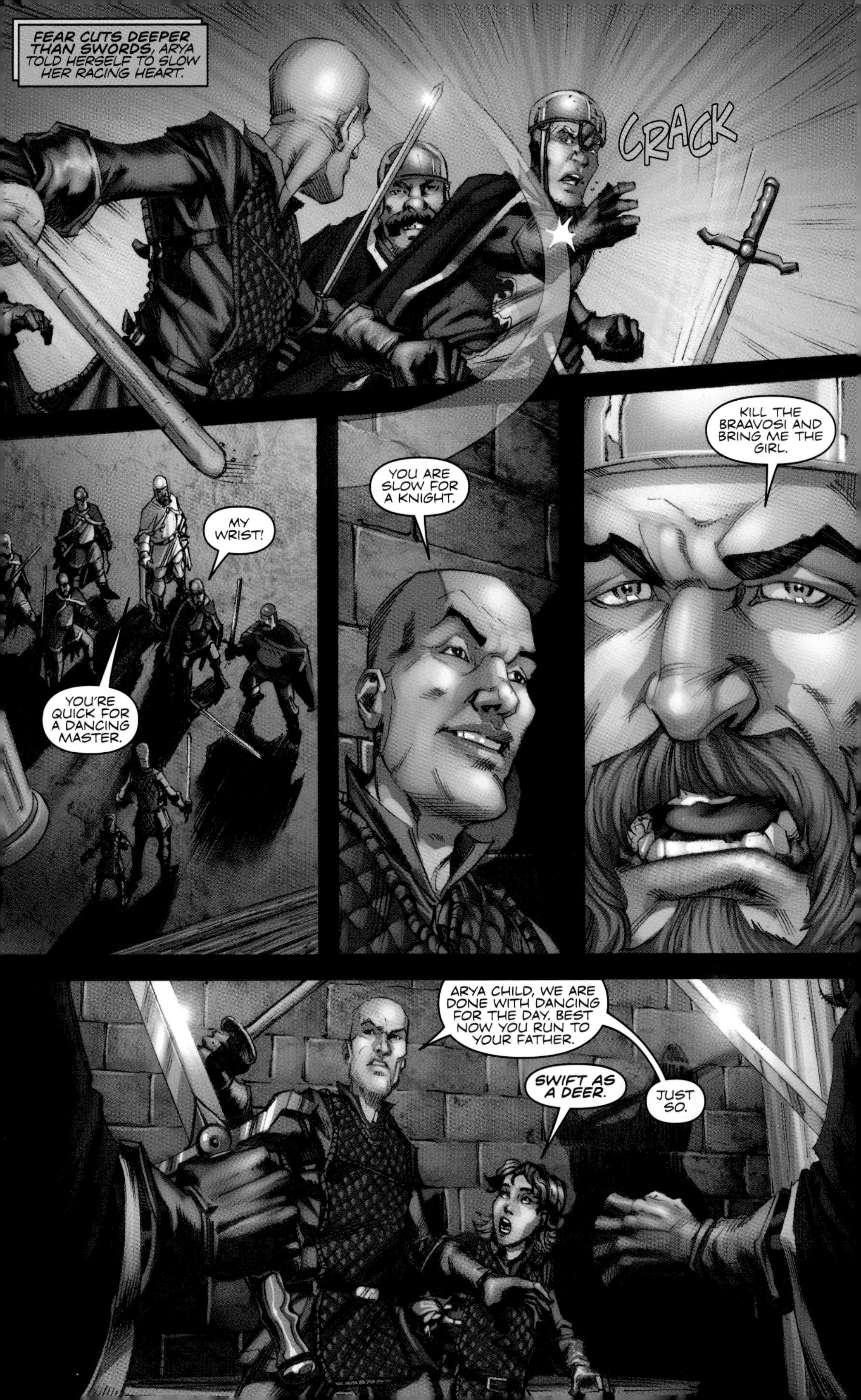
FEAR CUTS DEEPER THAN SWORDS, ARYA TOLD HERSELF TO SLOW HER RACING HEART.
CRACK
MY WRIST!
YOU'RE QUICK FOR A DANCING MASTER.
YOU ARE SLOW FOR A KNIGHT.
KILL THE BRAAVOSI AND BRING ME THE GIRL.
ARYA CHILD, WE ARE DONE WITH DANCING FOR THE DAY. BEST NOW YOU RUN TO YOUR FATHER.
SWIFT AS A DEER.
JUST SO.

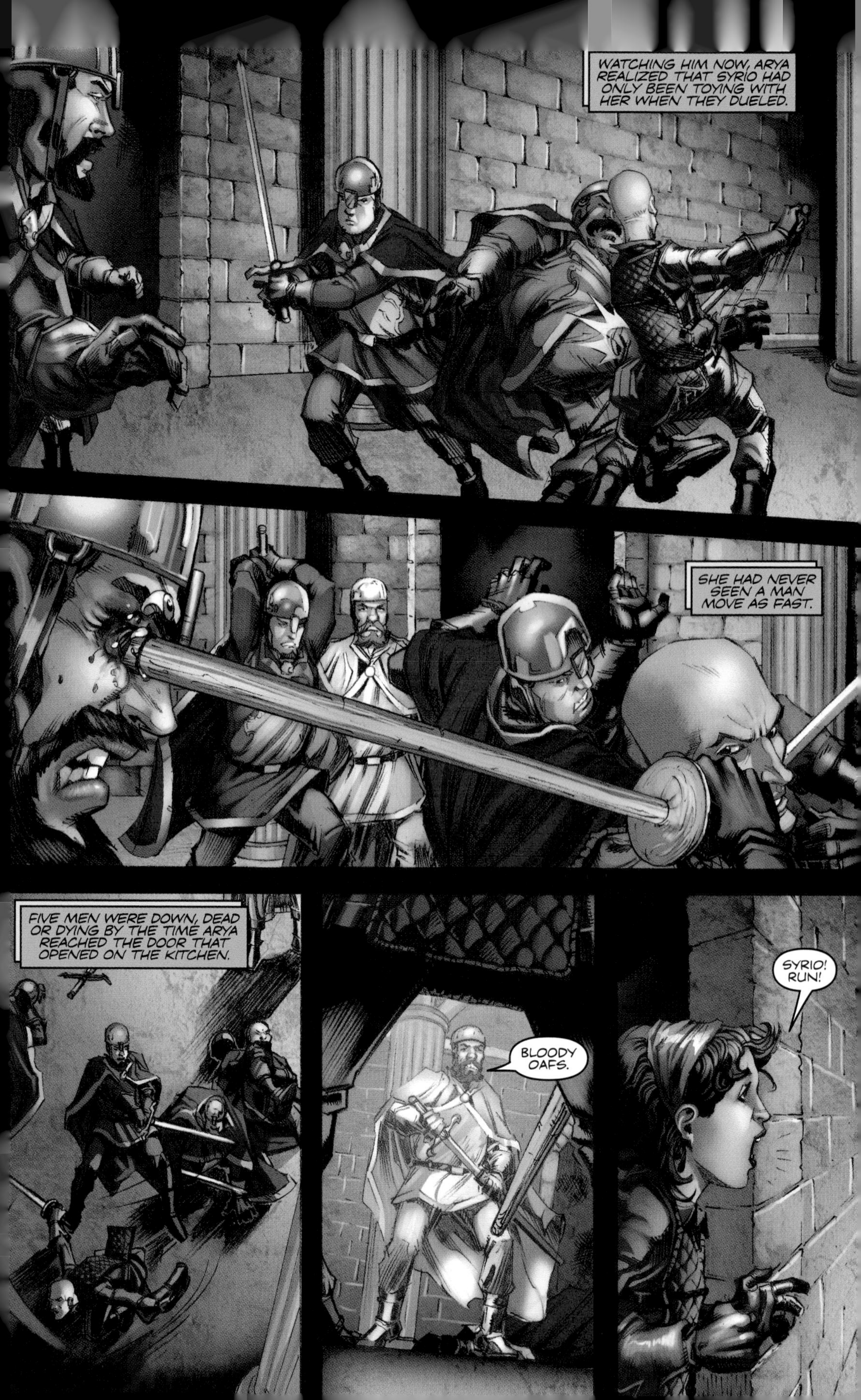
WATCHING HIM NOW, ARYA REALIZED THAT SYRIO HAD ONLY BEEN TOYING WITH HER WHEN THEY DUELED.
SHE HAD NEVER SEEN A MAN MOVE AS FAST.
FIVE MEN WERE DOWN, DEAD OR DYING BY THE TIME ARYA REACHED THE DOOR THAT OPENED ON THE KITCHEN.
BLOODY OAFS.
SYRIO! RUN!

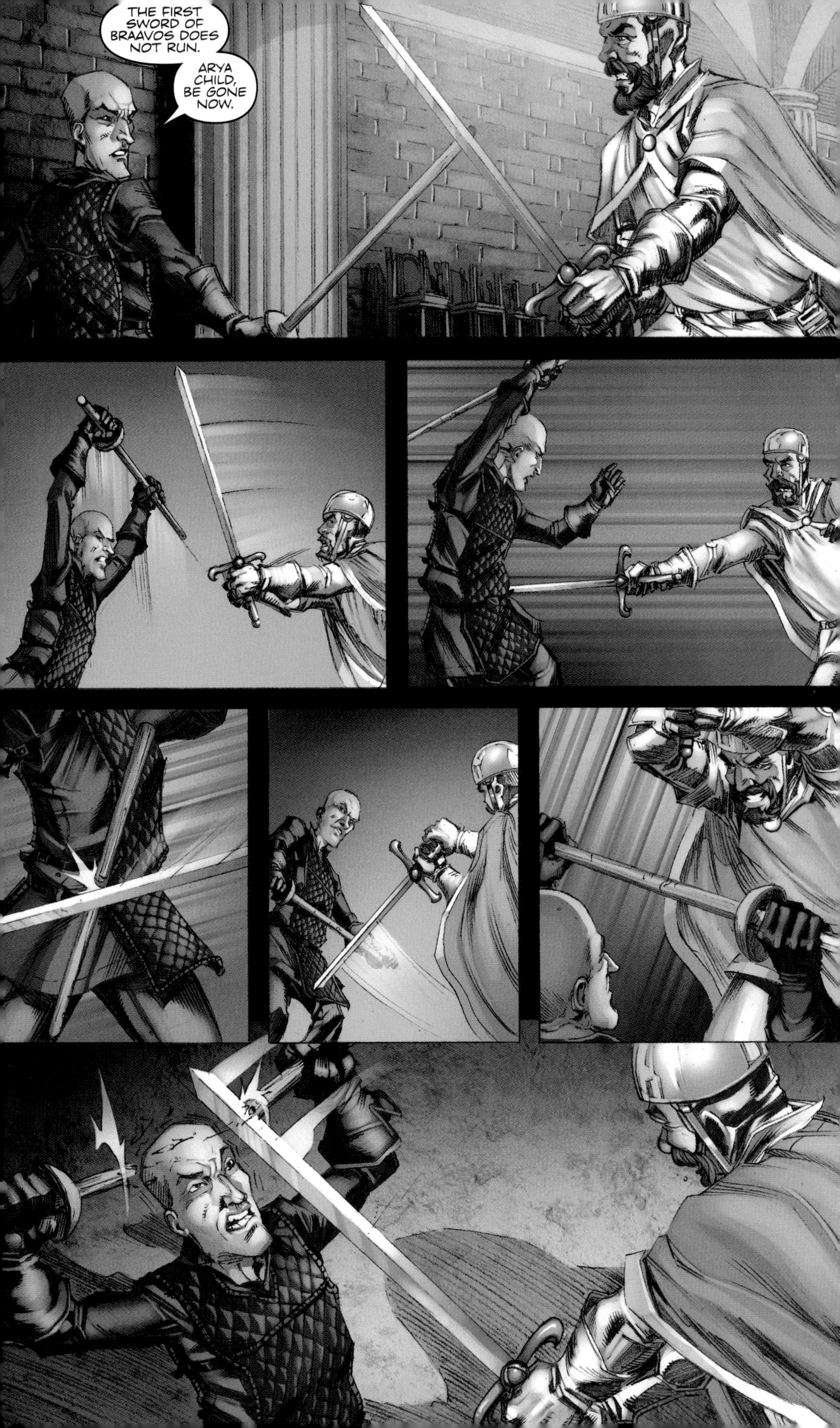
THE FIRST SWORD OF BRAAVOS DOES NOT RUN.
ARYA CHILD, BE GONE NOW.

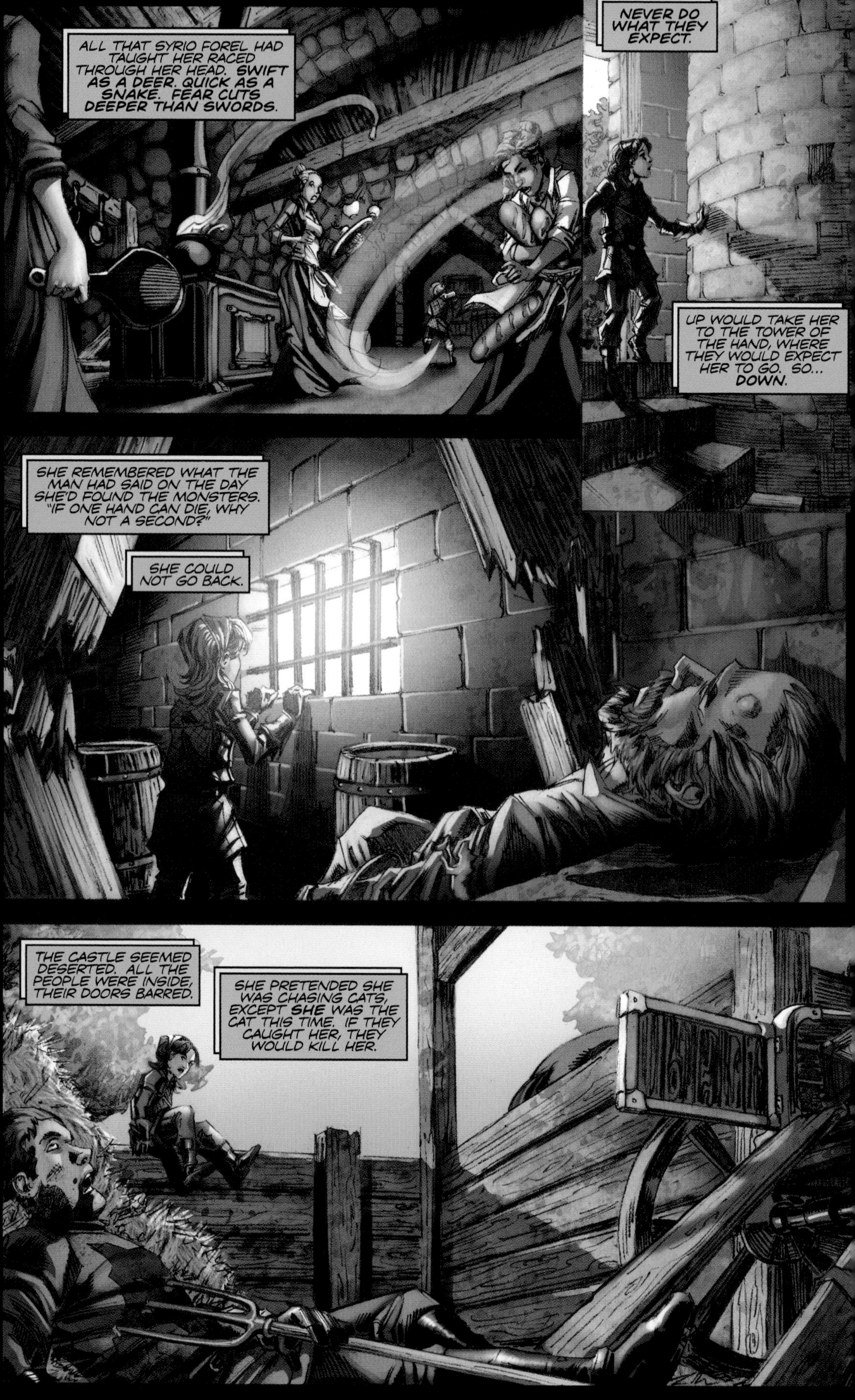
ALL THAT SYRIO FOREL HAD TAUGHT HER RACED THROUGH HER HEAD. SWIFT AS A DEER. QUICK AS A SNAKE. FEAR CUTS DEEPER THAN SWORDS.
NEVER DO WHAT THEY EXPECT.
UP WOULD TAKE HER TO THE TOWER OF THE HAND, WHERE THEY WOULD EXPECT HER TO GO. SO... **DOWN.**
SHE REMEMBERED WHAT THE MAN HAD SAID ON THE DAY SHE'D FOUND THE MONSTERS. "IF ONE HAND CAN DIE, WHY NOT A SECOND?"
SHE COULD NOT GO BACK.
THE CASTLE SEEMED DESERTED. ALL THE PEOPLE WERE INSIDE, THEIR DOORS BARRED.
SHE PRETENDED SHE WAS CHASING CATS, EXCEPT **SHE** WAS THE CAT THIS TIME. IF THEY CAUGHT HER, THEY WOULD KILL HER.

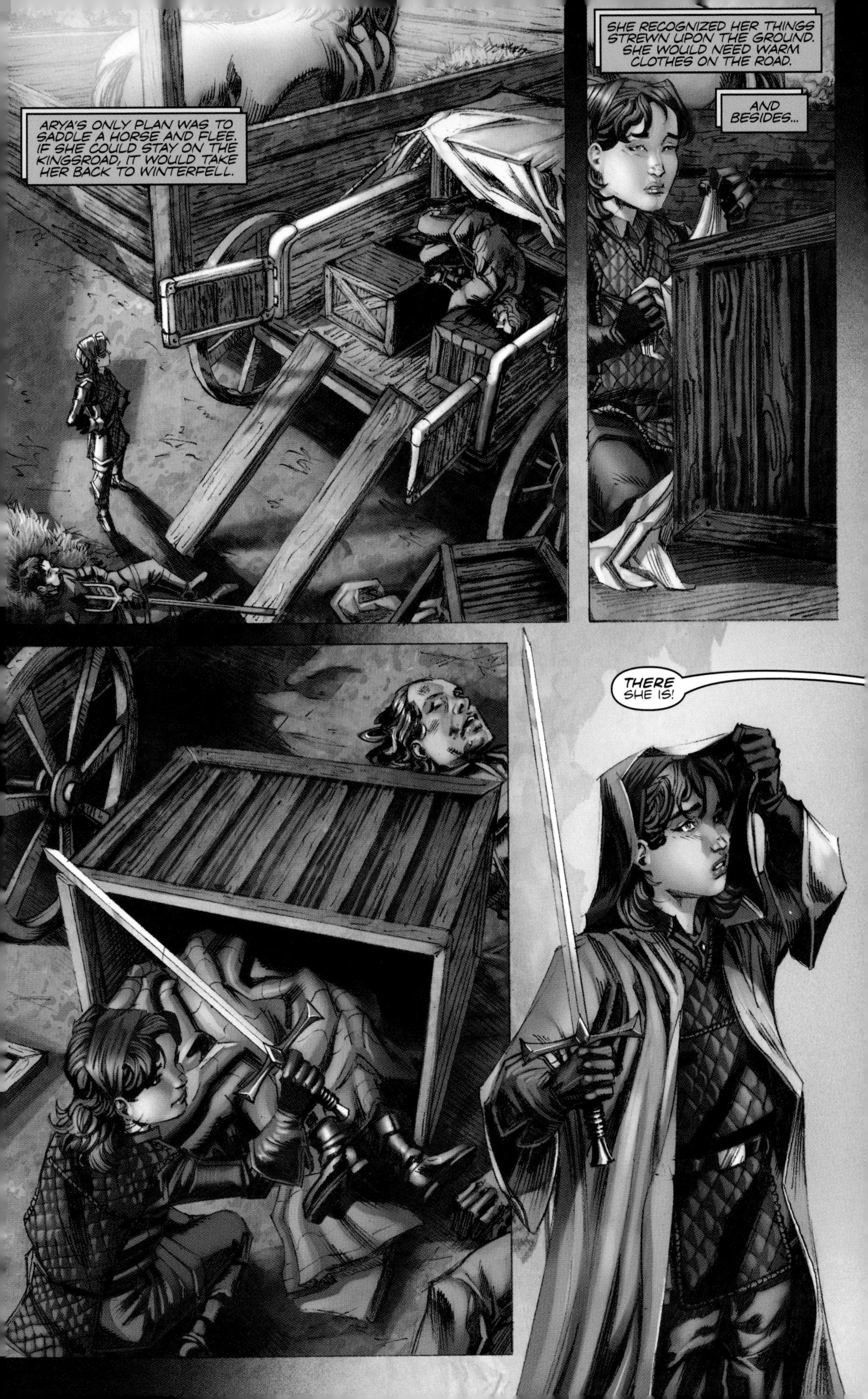
ARYA'S ONLY PLAN WAS TO SADDLE A HORSE AND FLEE. IF SHE COULD STAY ON THE KINGSROAD, IT WOULD TAKE HER BACK TO WINTERFELL.
SHE RECOGNIZED HER THINGS STREWN UPON THE GROUND. SHE WOULD NEED WARM CLOTHES ON THE ROAD.
AND BESIDES...
THERE SHE IS!

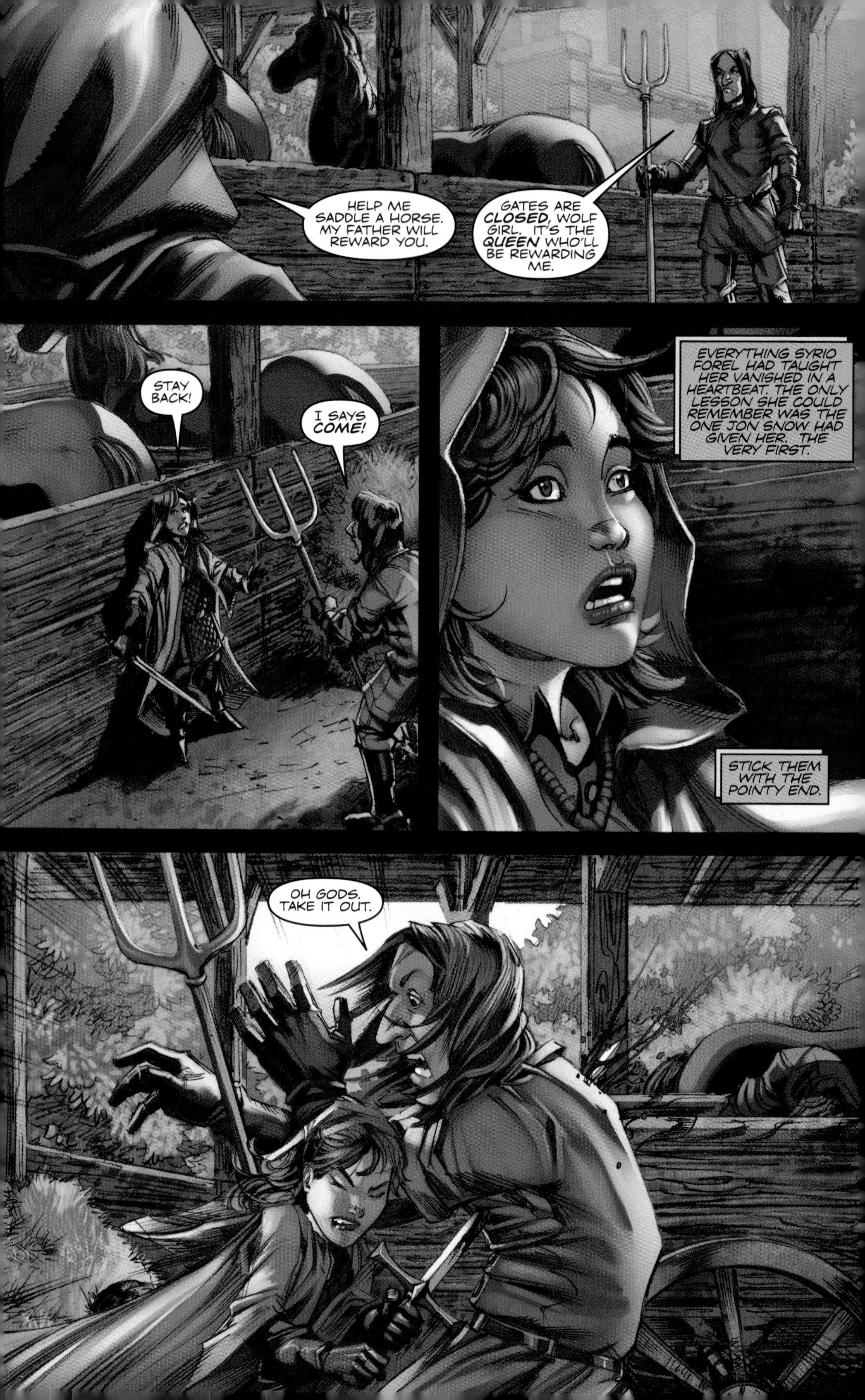
HELP ME SADDLE A HORSE. MY FATHER WILL REWARD YOU.
GATES ARE **CLOSED**, WOLF GIRL. IT'S THE **QUEEN** WHO'LL BE REWARDING ME.
STAY BACK!
I SAYS **COME!**
EVERYTHING SYRIO FOREL HAD TAUGHT HER VANISHED IN A HEARTBEAT. THE ONLY LESSON SHE COULD REMEMBER WAS THE ONE JON SNOW HAD GIVEN HER. THE VERY FIRST.
STICK THEM WITH THE POINTY END.
OH GODS. TAKE IT OUT.

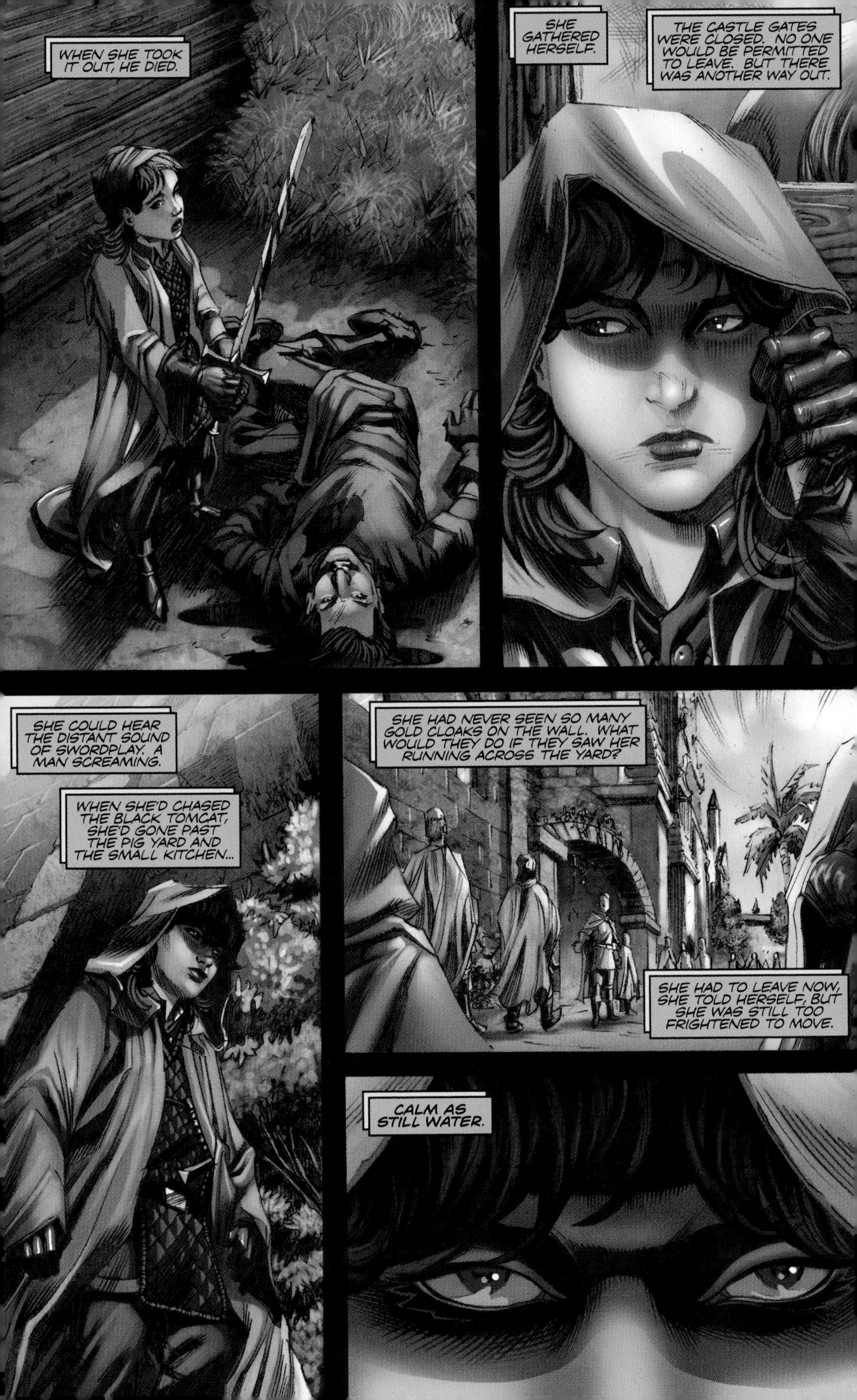
WHEN SHE TOOK IT OUT, HE DIED.
SHE GATHERED HERSELF.
THE CASTLE GATES WERE CLOSED. NO ONE WOULD BE PERMITTED TO LEAVE. BUT THERE WAS ANOTHER WAY OUT.
SHE COULD HEAR THE DISTANT SOUND OF SWORDPLAY. A MAN SCREAMING.
WHEN SHE'D CHASED THE BLACK TOMCAT, SHE'D GONE PAST THE PIG YARD AND THE SMALL KITCHEN...
SHE HAD NEVER SEEN SO MANY GOLD CLOAKS ON THE WALL. WHAT WOULD THEY DO IF THEY SAW HER RUNNING ACROSS THE YARD?
SHE HAD TO LEAVE NOW, SHE TOLD HERSELF, BUT SHE WAS STILL TOO FRIGHTENED TO MOVE.
CALM AS STILL WATER.

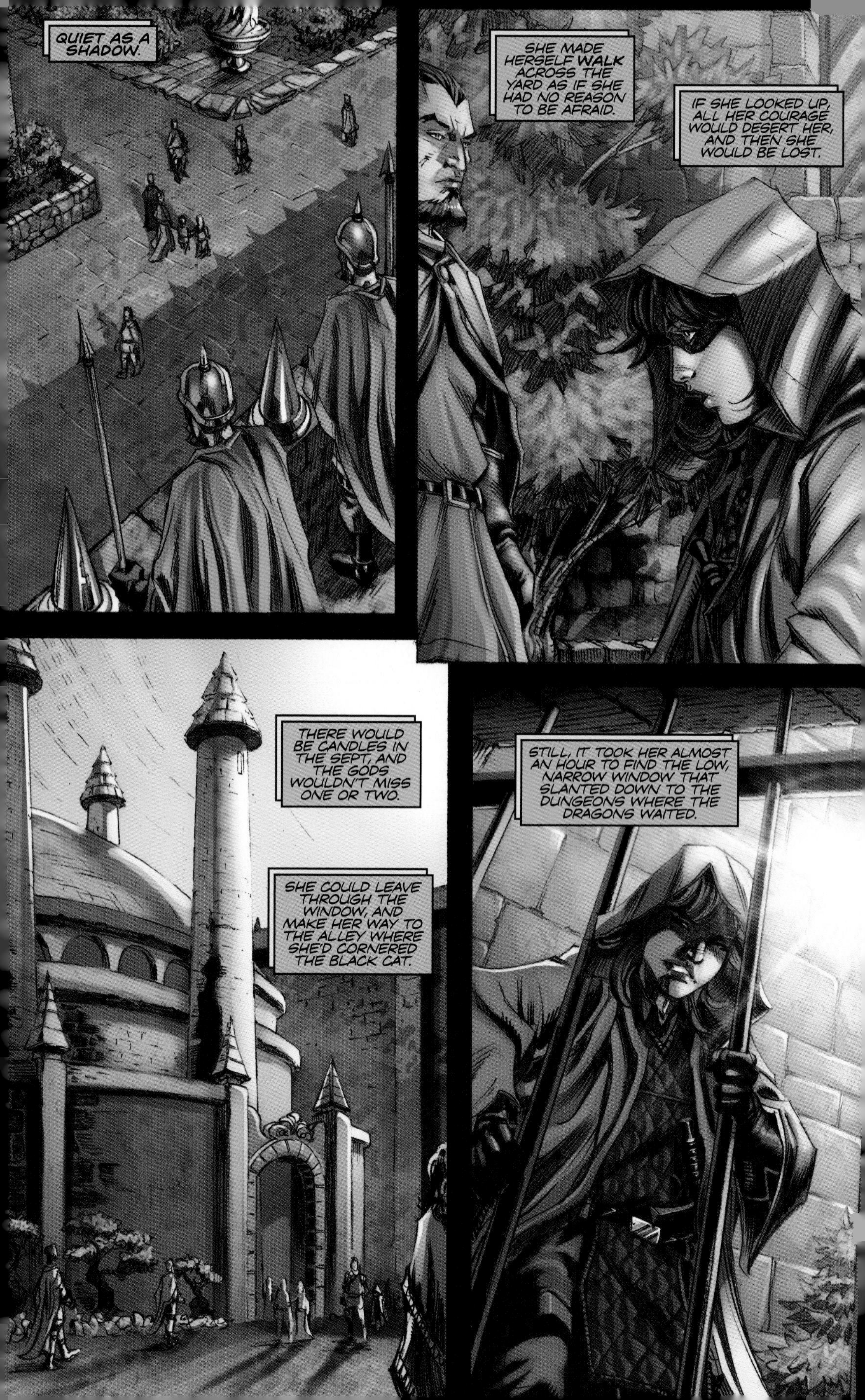

QUIET AS A SHADOW.
SHE MADE HERSELF WALK ACROSS THE YARD AS IF SHE HAD NO REASON TO BE AFRAID.
IF SHE LOOKED UP, ALL HER COURAGE WOULD DESERT HER, AND THEN SHE WOULD BE LOST.
THERE WOULD BE CANDLES IN THE SEPT, AND THE GODS WOULDN'T MISS ONE OR TWO.
SHE COULD LEAVE THROUGH THE WINDOW, AND MAKE HER WAY TO THE ALLEY WHERE SHE'D CORNERED THE BLACK CAT.
STILL, IT TOOK HER ALMOST AN HOUR TO FIND THE LOW, NARROW WINDOW THAT SLANTED DOWN TO THE DUNGEONS WHERE THE DRAGONS WAITED.

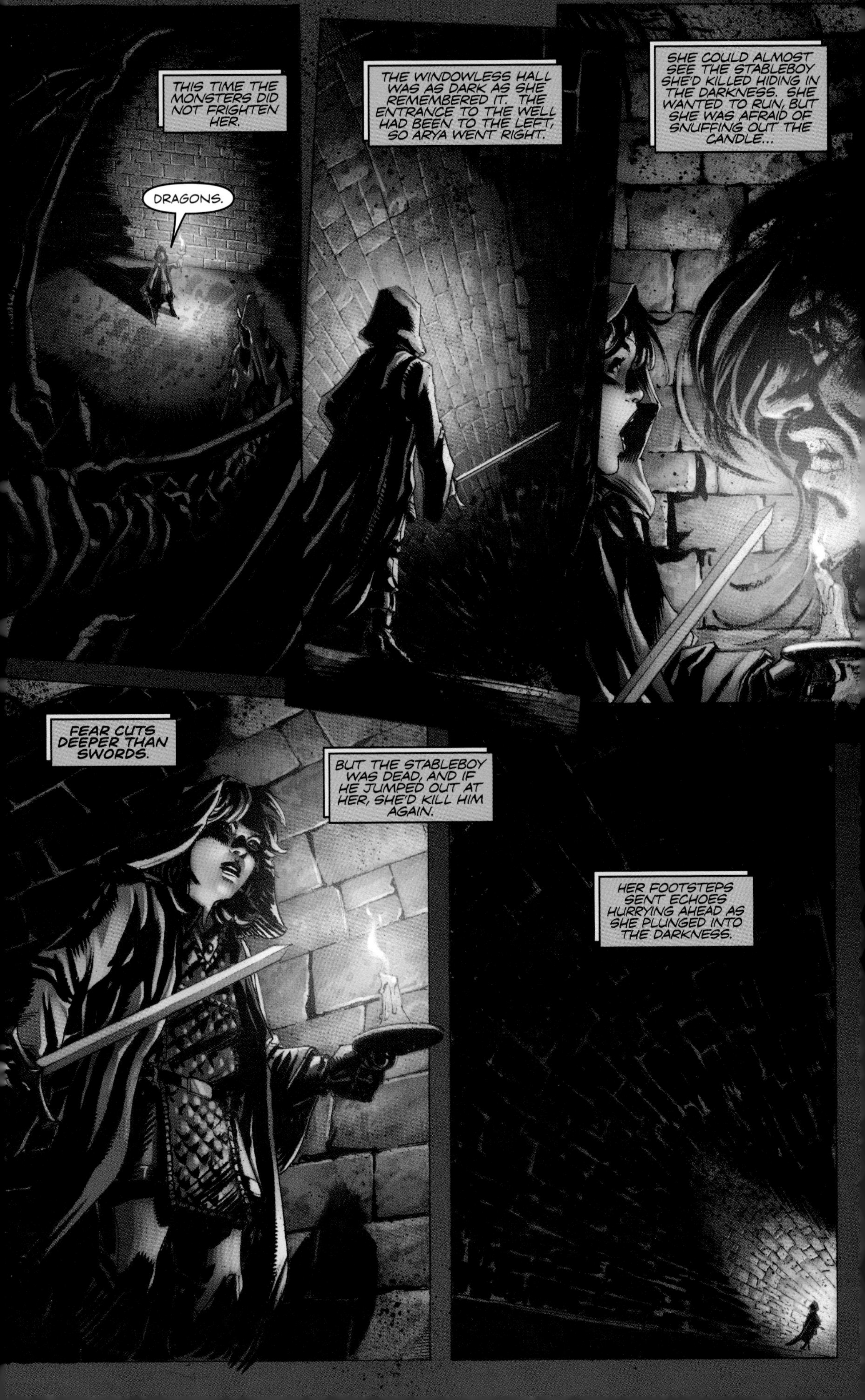
THIS TIME THE MONSTERS DID NOT FRIGHTEN HER.
DRAGONS.
THE WINDOWLESS HALL WAS AS DARK AS SHE REMEMBERED IT. THE ENTRANCE TO THE WELL HAD BEEN TO THE LEFT, SO ARYA WENT RIGHT.
SHE COULD ALMOST SEE THE STABLEBOY SHE'D KILLED HIDING IN THE DARKNESS. SHE WANTED TO RUN, BUT SHE WAS AFRAID OF SNUFFING OUT THE CANDLE...
FEAR CUTS DEEPER THAN SWORDS.
BUT THE STABLEBOY WAS DEAD, AND IF HE JUMPED OUT AT HER, SHE'D KILL HIM AGAIN.
HER FOOTSTEPS SENT ECHOES HURRYING AHEAD AS SHE PLUNGED INTO THE DARKNESS.

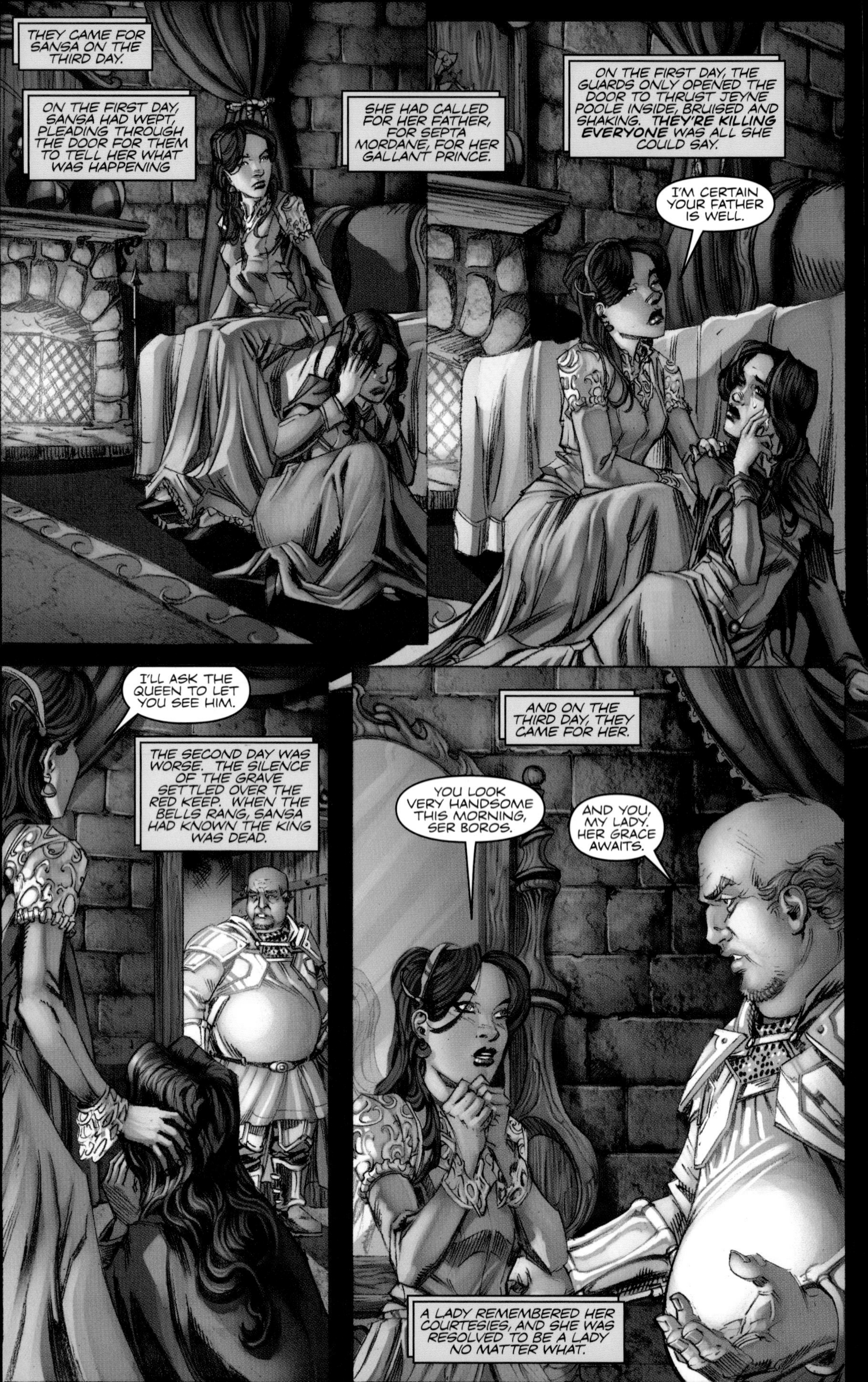
THEY CAME FOR SANSA ON THE THIRD DAY.
ON THE FIRST DAY, SANSA HAD WEPT, PLEADING THROUGH THE DOOR FOR THEM TO TELL HER WHAT WAS HAPPENING
SHE HAD CALLED FOR HER FATHER, FOR SEPTA MORDANE, FOR HER GALLANT PRINCE.
ON THE FIRST DAY, THE GUARDS ONLY OPENED THE DOOR TO THRUST JEYNE POOLE INSIDE, BRUISED AND SHAKING. **THEY'RE KILLING EVERYONE** WAS ALL SHE COULD SAY.
I'M CERTAIN YOUR FATHER IS WELL.
I'LL ASK THE QUEEN TO LET YOU SEE HIM.
THE SECOND DAY WAS WORSE. THE SILENCE OF THE GRAVE SETTLED OVER THE RED KEEP. WHEN THE BELLS RANG, SANSA HAD KNOWN THE KING WAS DEAD.
AND ON THE THIRD DAY, THEY CAME FOR HER.
YOU LOOK VERY HANDSOME THIS MORNING, SER BOROS.
AND YOU, MY LADY. HER GRACE AWAITS.
A LADY REMEMBERED HER COURTESIES, AND SHE WAS RESOLVED TO BE A LADY NO MATTER WHAT.

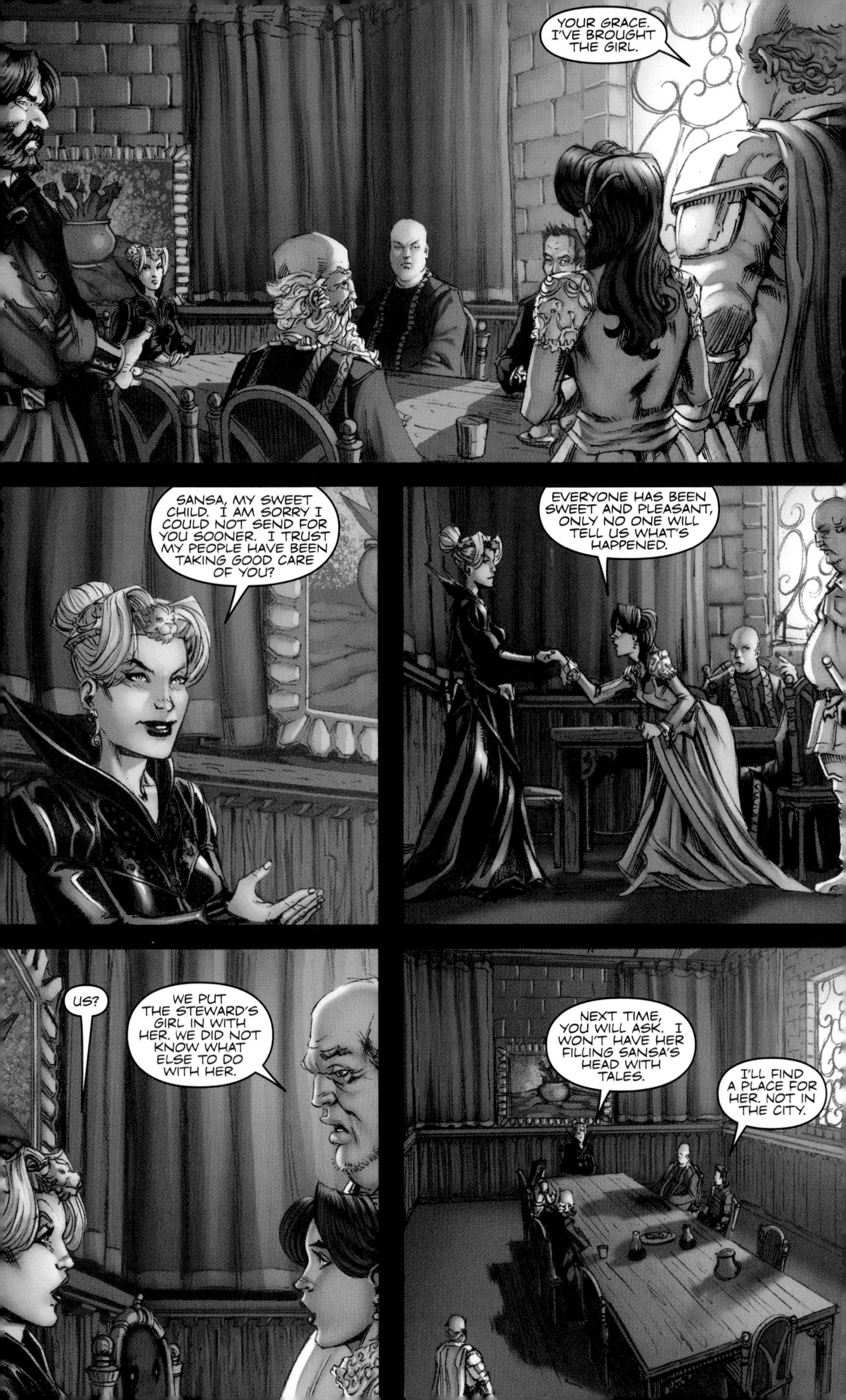
YOUR GRACE. I'VE BROUGHT THE GIRL.
SANSA, MY SWEET CHILD. I AM SORRY I COULD NOT SEND FOR YOU SOONER. I TRUST MY PEOPLE HAVE BEEN TAKING GOOD CARE OF YOU?
EVERYONE HAS BEEN SWEET AND PLEASANT, ONLY NO ONE WILL TELL US WHAT'S HAPPENED.
US?
WE PUT THE STEWARD'S GIRL IN WITH HER. WE DID NOT KNOW WHAT ELSE TO DO WITH HER.
NEXT TIME, YOU WILL ASK. I WON'T HAVE HER FILLING SANSA'S HEAD WITH TALES.
I'LL FIND A PLACE FOR HER. NOT IN THE CITY.

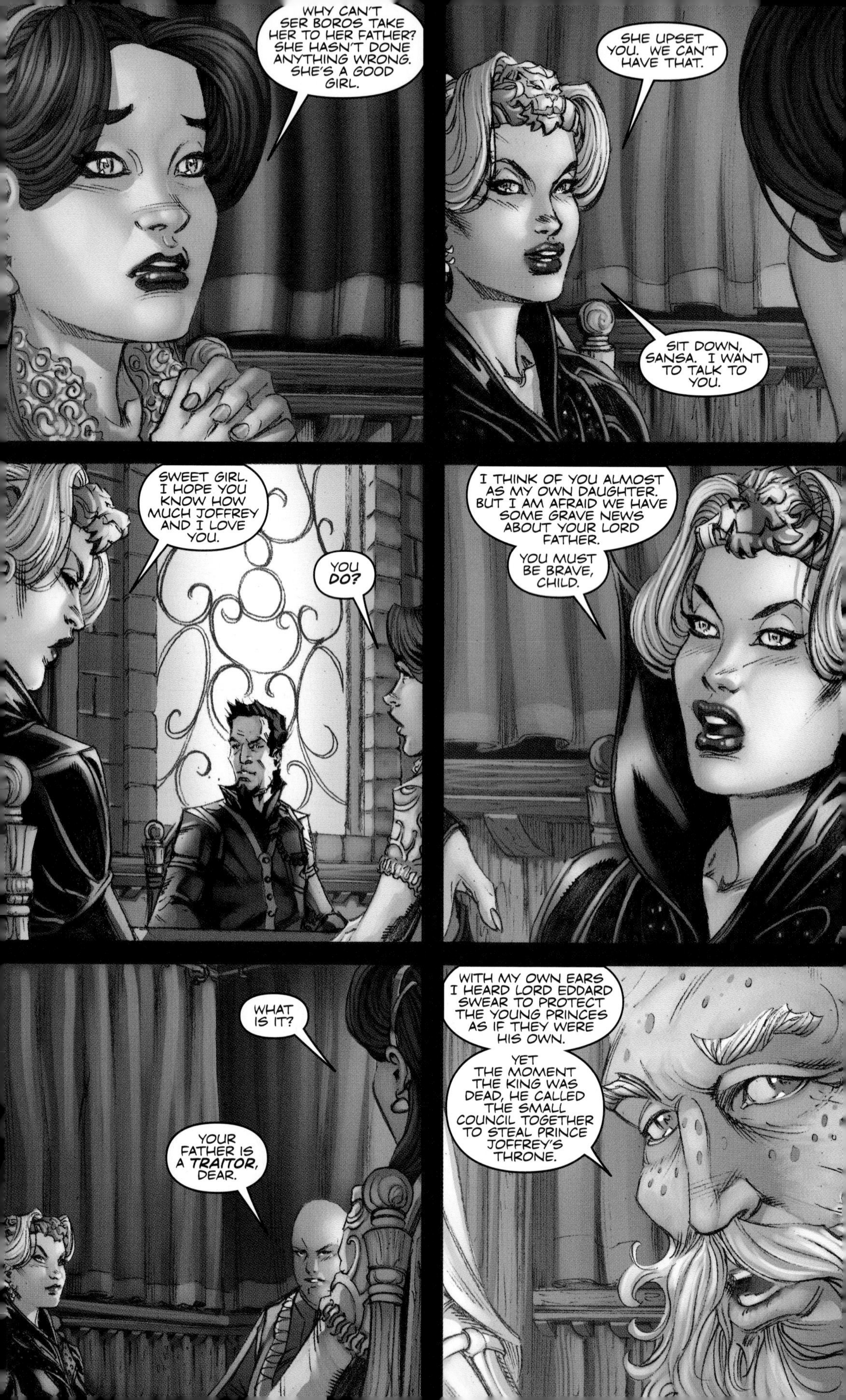
WHY CAN'T SER BOROS TAKE HER TO HER FATHER? SHE HASN'T DONE ANYTHING WRONG. SHE'S A GOOD GIRL.
SHE UPSET YOU. WE CAN'T HAVE THAT.
SIT DOWN, SANSA. I WANT TO TALK TO YOU.
SWEET GIRL. I HOPE YOU KNOW HOW MUCH JOFFREY AND I LOVE YOU.
YOU *DO?*
I THINK OF YOU ALMOST AS MY OWN DAUGHTER. BUT I AM AFRAID WE HAVE SOME GRAVE NEWS ABOUT YOUR LORD FATHER.
YOU MUST BE BRAVE, CHILD.
WHAT IS IT?
YOUR FATHER IS A *TRAITOR*, DEAR.
WITH MY OWN EARS I HEARD LORD EDDARD SWEAR TO PROTECT THE YOUNG PRINCES AS IF THEY WERE HIS OWN.
YET THE MOMENT THE KING WAS DEAD, HE CALLED THE SMALL COUNCIL TOGETHER TO STEAL PRINCE JOFFREY'S THRONE.

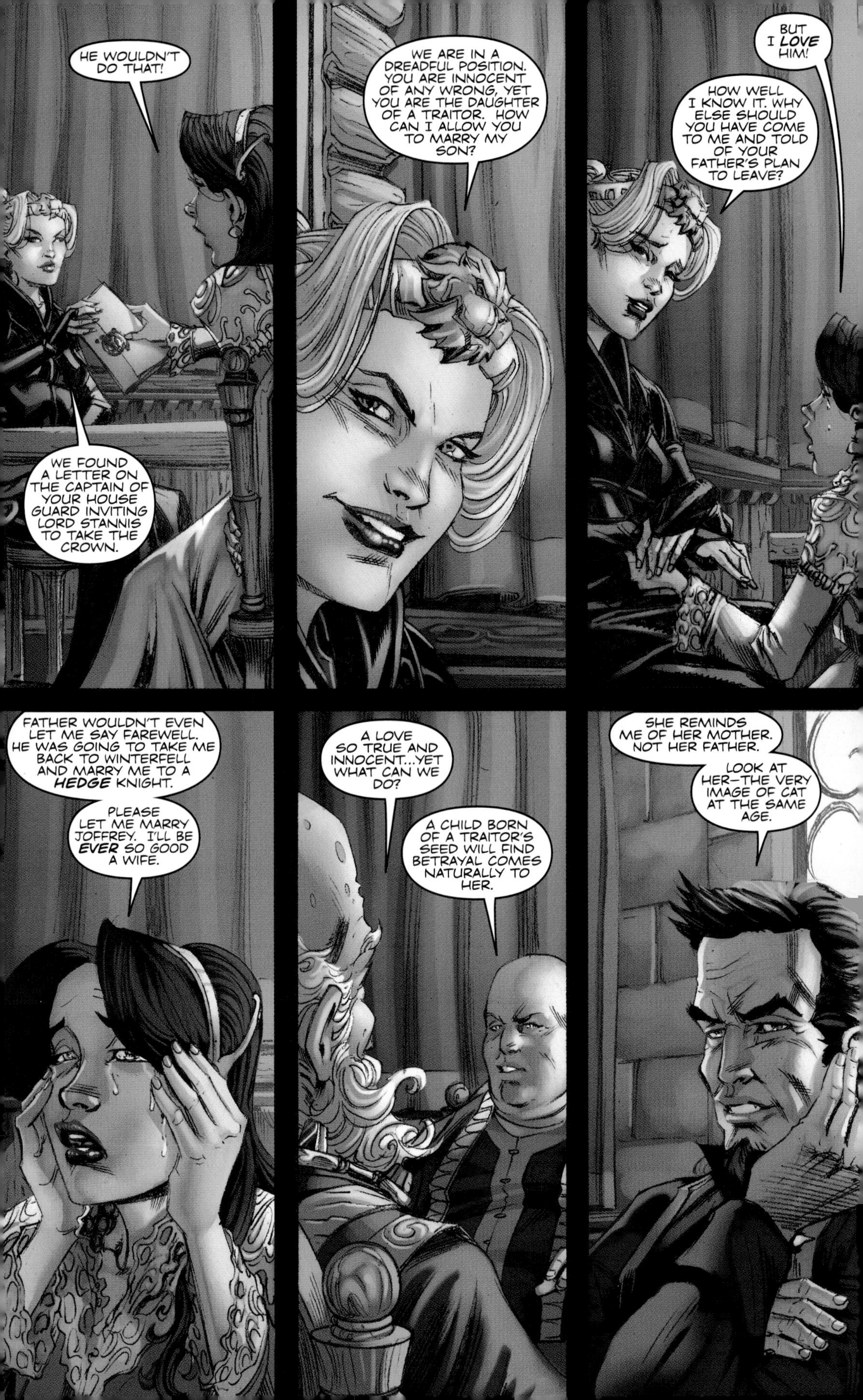
HE WOULDN'T DO THAT!
WE FOUND A LETTER ON THE CAPTAIN OF YOUR HOUSE GUARD INVITING LORD STANNIS TO TAKE THE CROWN.
WE ARE IN A DREADFUL POSITION. YOU ARE INNOCENT OF ANY WRONG, YET YOU ARE THE DAUGHTER OF A TRAITOR. HOW CAN I ALLOW YOU TO MARRY MY SON?
BUT I **LOVE** HIM!
HOW WELL I KNOW IT. WHY ELSE SHOULD YOU HAVE COME TO ME AND TOLD OF YOUR FATHER'S PLAN TO LEAVE?
FATHER WOULDN'T EVEN LET ME SAY FAREWELL. HE WAS GOING TO TAKE ME BACK TO WINTERFELL AND MARRY ME TO A **HEDGE** KNIGHT.
PLEASE LET ME MARRY JOFFREY. I'LL BE **EVER** SO GOOD A WIFE.
A LOVE SO TRUE AND INNOCENT...YET WHAT CAN WE DO?
A CHILD BORN OF A TRAITOR'S SEED WILL FIND BETRAYAL COMES NATURALLY TO HER.
SHE REMINDS ME OF HER MOTHER. NOT HER FATHER.
LOOK AT HER—THE VERY IMAGE OF CAT AT THE SAME AGE.

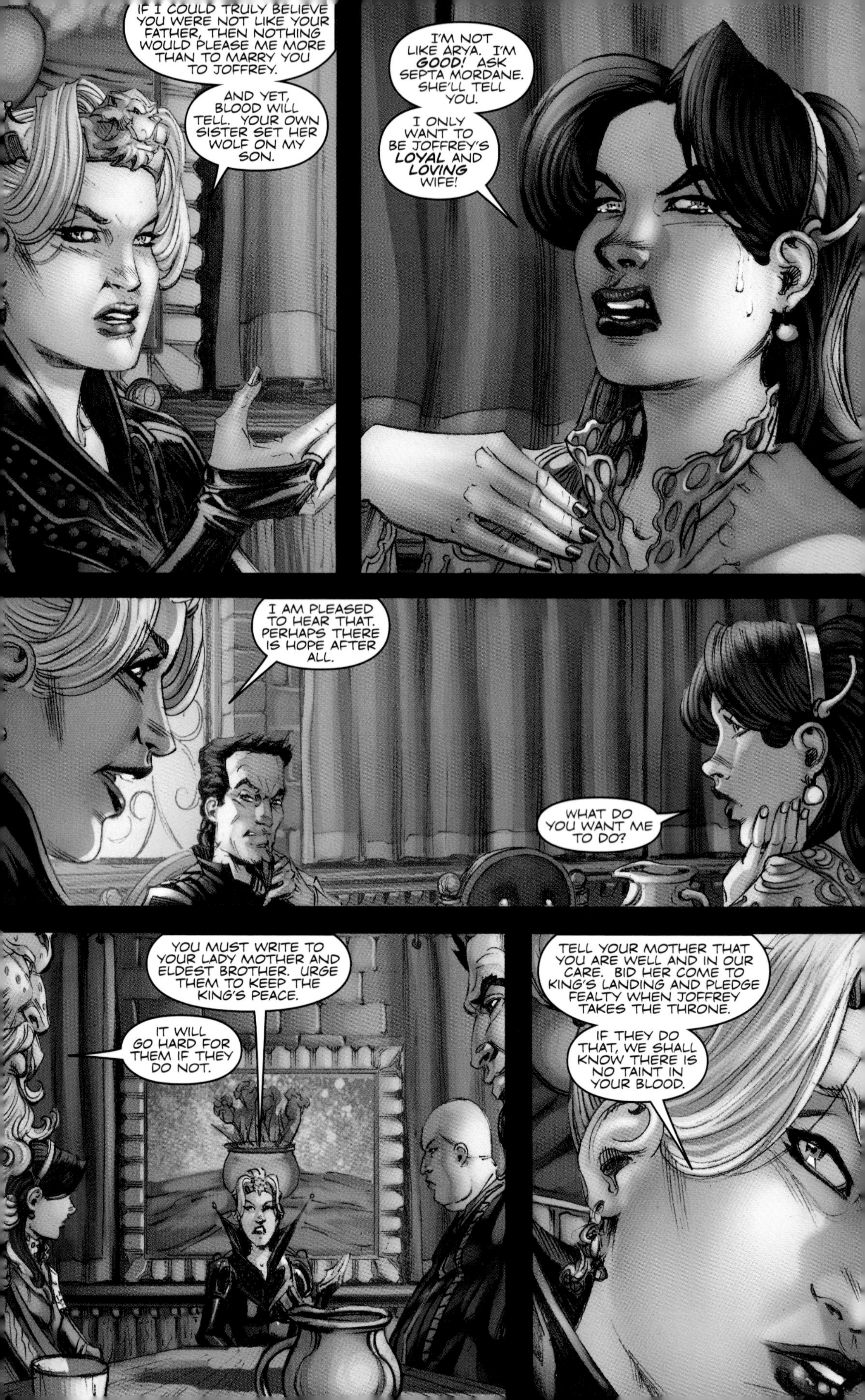
IF I COULD TRULY BELIEVE YOU WERE NOT LIKE YOUR FATHER, THEN NOTHING WOULD PLEASE ME MORE THAN TO MARRY YOU TO JOFFREY.
AND YET, BLOOD WILL TELL. YOUR OWN SISTER SET HER WOLF ON MY SON.
I'M NOT LIKE ARYA. I'M **GOOD!** ASK SEPTA MORDANE. SHE'LL TELL YOU.
I ONLY WANT TO BE JOFFREY'S **LOYAL** AND **LOVING** WIFE!
I AM PLEASED TO HEAR THAT. PERHAPS THERE IS HOPE AFTER ALL.
WHAT DO YOU WANT ME TO DO?
YOU MUST WRITE TO YOUR LADY MOTHER AND ELDEST BROTHER. URGE THEM TO KEEP THE KING'S PEACE.
IT WILL GO HARD FOR THEM IF THEY DO NOT.
TELL YOUR MOTHER THAT YOU ARE WELL AND IN OUR CARE. BID HER COME TO KING'S LANDING AND PLEDGE FEALTY WHEN JOFFREY TAKES THE THRONE.
IF THEY DO THAT, WE SHALL KNOW THERE IS NO TAINT IN YOUR BLOOD.

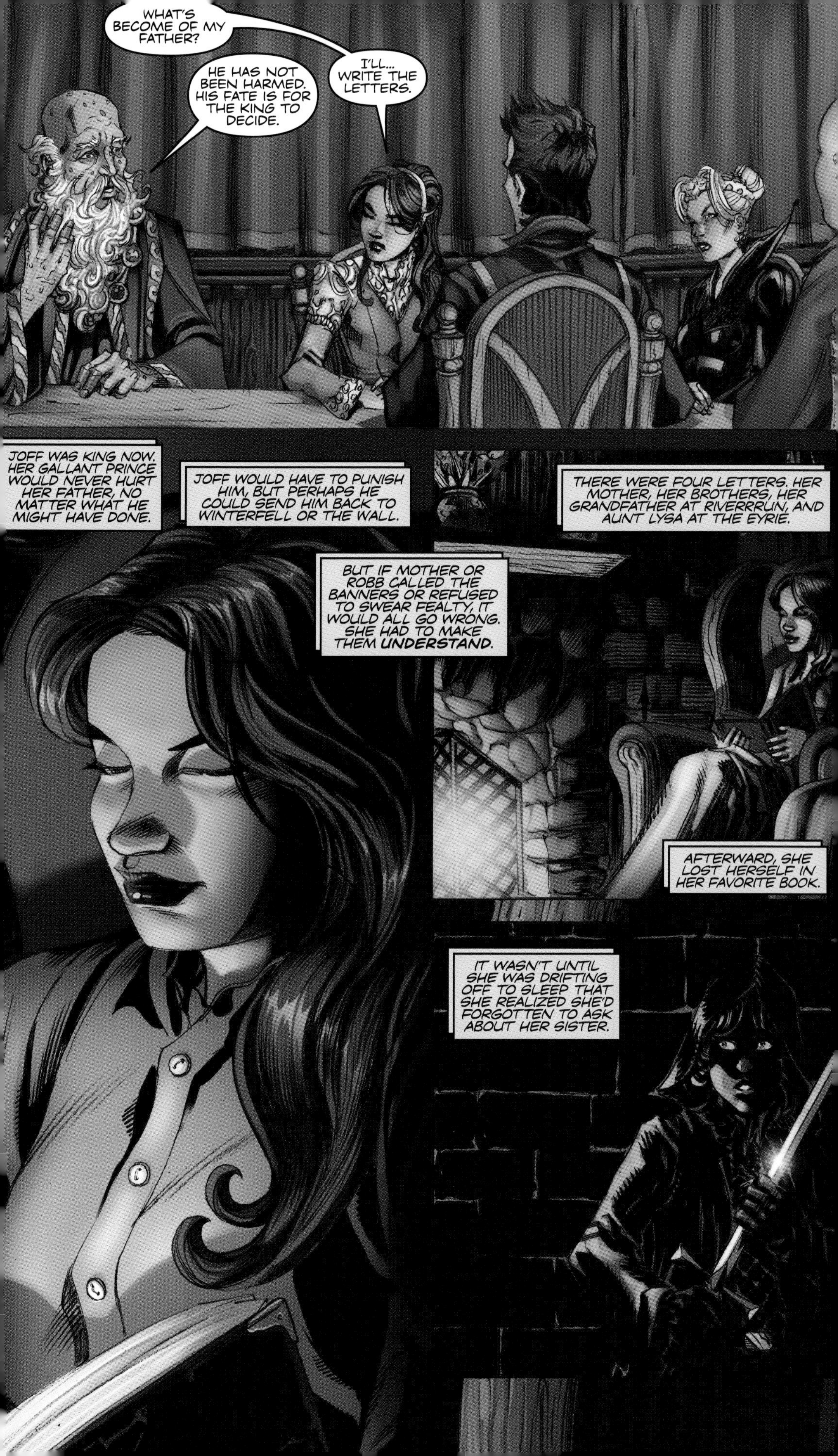

WHAT'S BECOME OF MY FATHER?
HE HAS NOT BEEN HARMED. HIS FATE IS FOR THE KING TO DECIDE.
I'LL... WRITE THE LETTERS.
JOFF WAS KING NOW. HER GALLANT PRINCE WOULD NEVER HURT HER FATHER, NO MATTER WHAT HE MIGHT HAVE DONE.
JOFF WOULD HAVE TO PUNISH HIM, BUT PERHAPS HE COULD SEND HIM BACK TO WINTERFELL OR THE WALL.
BUT IF MOTHER OR ROBB CALLED THE BANNERS OR REFUSED TO SWEAR FEALTY, IT WOULD ALL GO WRONG. SHE HAD TO MAKE THEM UNDERSTAND.
THERE WERE FOUR LETTERS. HER MOTHER, HER BROTHERS, HER GRANDFATHER AT RIVERRUN, AND AUNT LYSA AT THE EYRIE.
AFTERWARD, SHE LOST HERSELF IN HER FAVORITE BOOK.
IT WASN'T UNTIL SHE WAS DRIFTING OFF TO SLEEP THAT SHE REALIZED SHE'D FORGOTTEN TO ASK ABOUT HER SISTER.

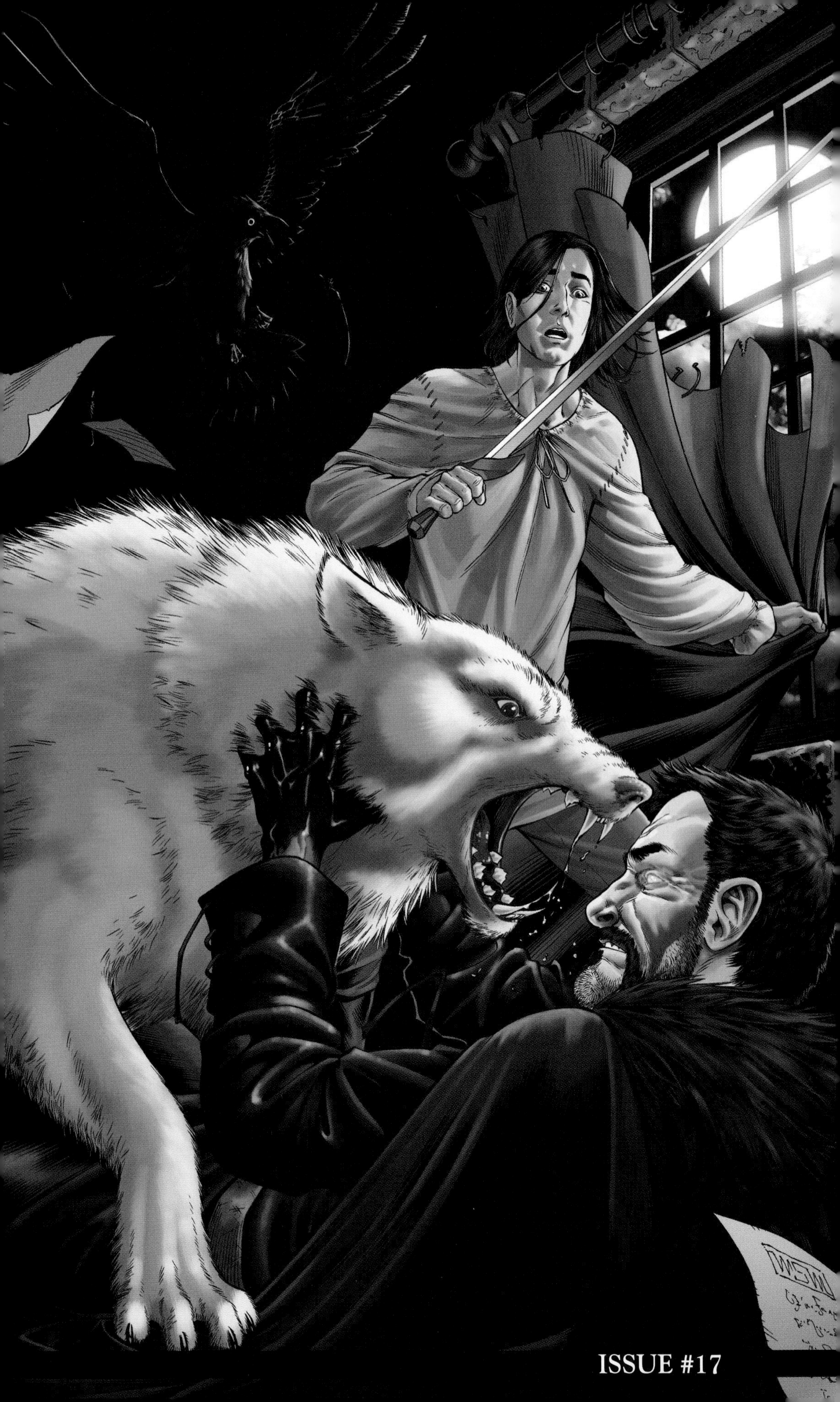

ISSUE #17

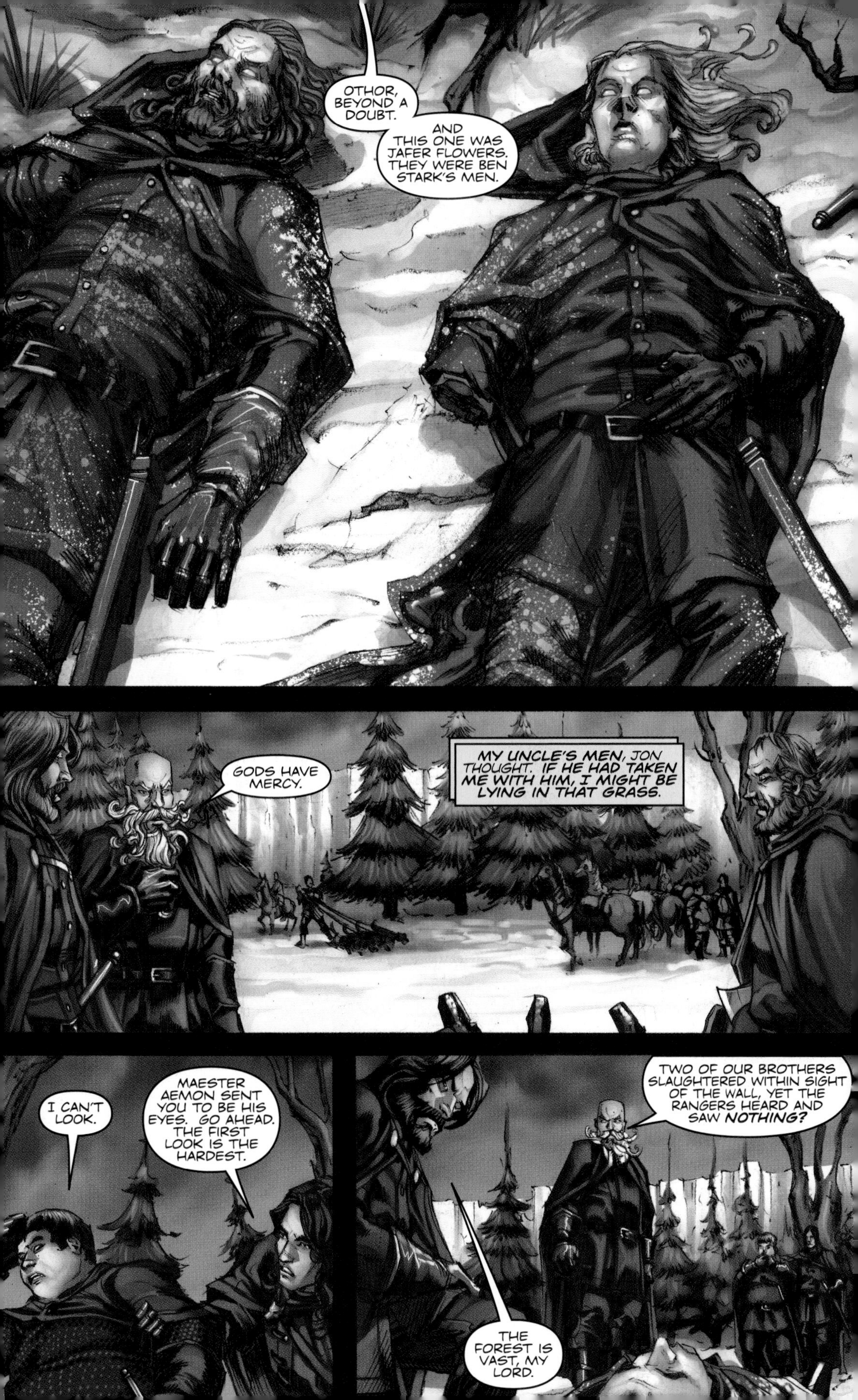
OTHOR, BEYOND A DOUBT.
AND THIS ONE WAS JAFER FLOWERS. THEY WERE BEN STARK'S MEN.
GODS HAVE MERCY.
MY UNCLE'S MEN, JON THOUGHT. IF HE HAD TAKEN ME WITH HIM, I MIGHT BE LYING IN THAT GRASS.
I CAN'T LOOK.
MAESTER AEMON SENT YOU TO BE HIS EYES. GO AHEAD. THE FIRST LOOK IS THE HARDEST.
TWO OF OUR BROTHERS SLAUGHTERED WITHIN SIGHT OF THE WALL, YET THE RANGERS HEARD AND SAW NOTHING?
THE FOREST IS VAST, MY LORD.

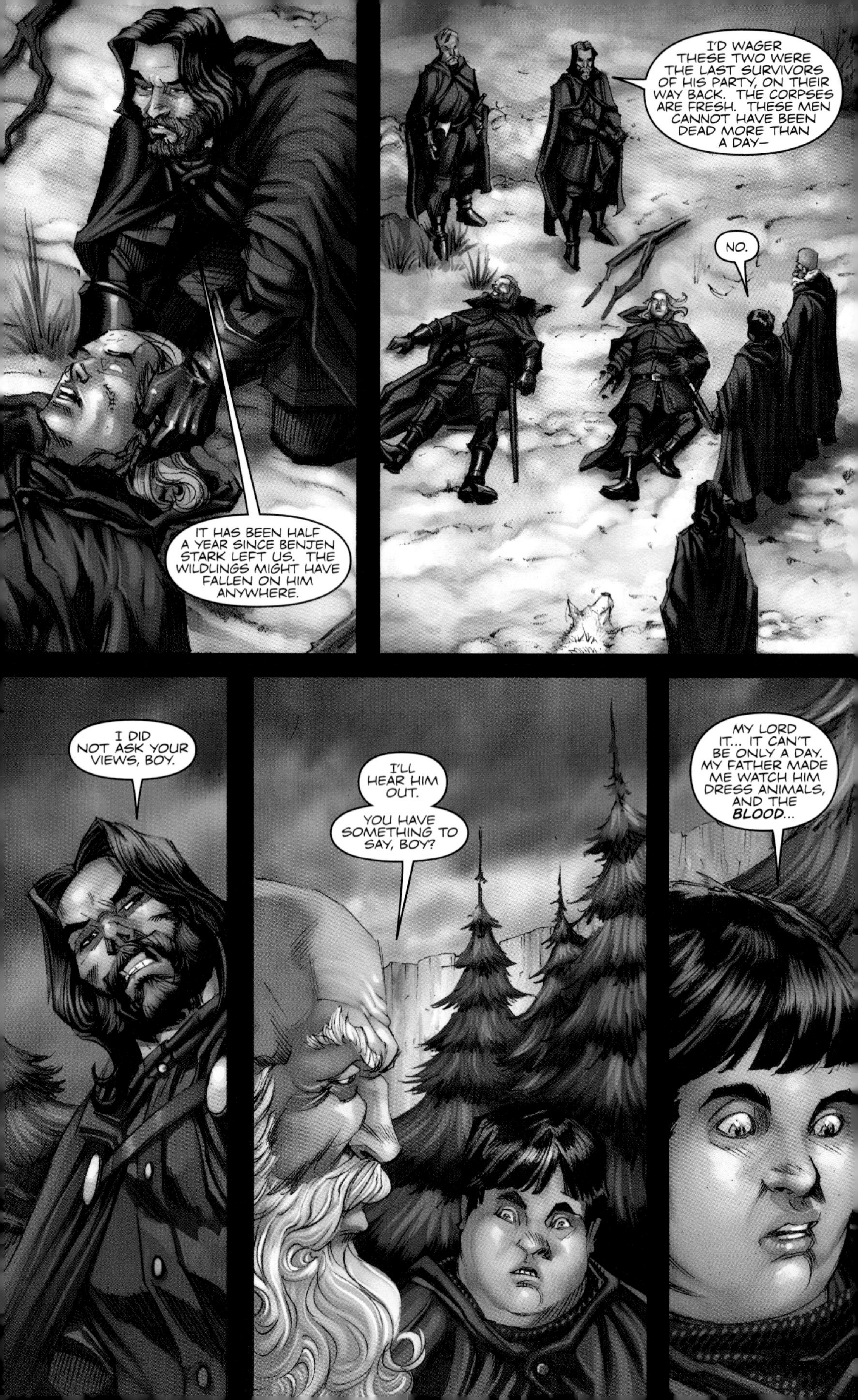
IT HAS BEEN HALF A YEAR SINCE BENJEN STARK LEFT US. THE WILDLINGS MIGHT HAVE FALLEN ON HIM ANYWHERE.
I'D WAGER THESE TWO WERE THE LAST SURVIVORS OF HIS PARTY, ON THEIR WAY BACK. THE CORPSES ARE FRESH. THESE MEN CANNOT HAVE BEEN DEAD MORE THAN A DAY–
NO.
I DID NOT ASK YOUR VIEWS, BOY.
I'LL HEAR HIM OUT.
YOU HAVE SOMETHING TO SAY, BOY?
MY LORD IT... IT CAN'T BE ONLY A DAY. MY FATHER MADE ME WATCH HIM DRESS ANIMALS, AND THE BLOOD...

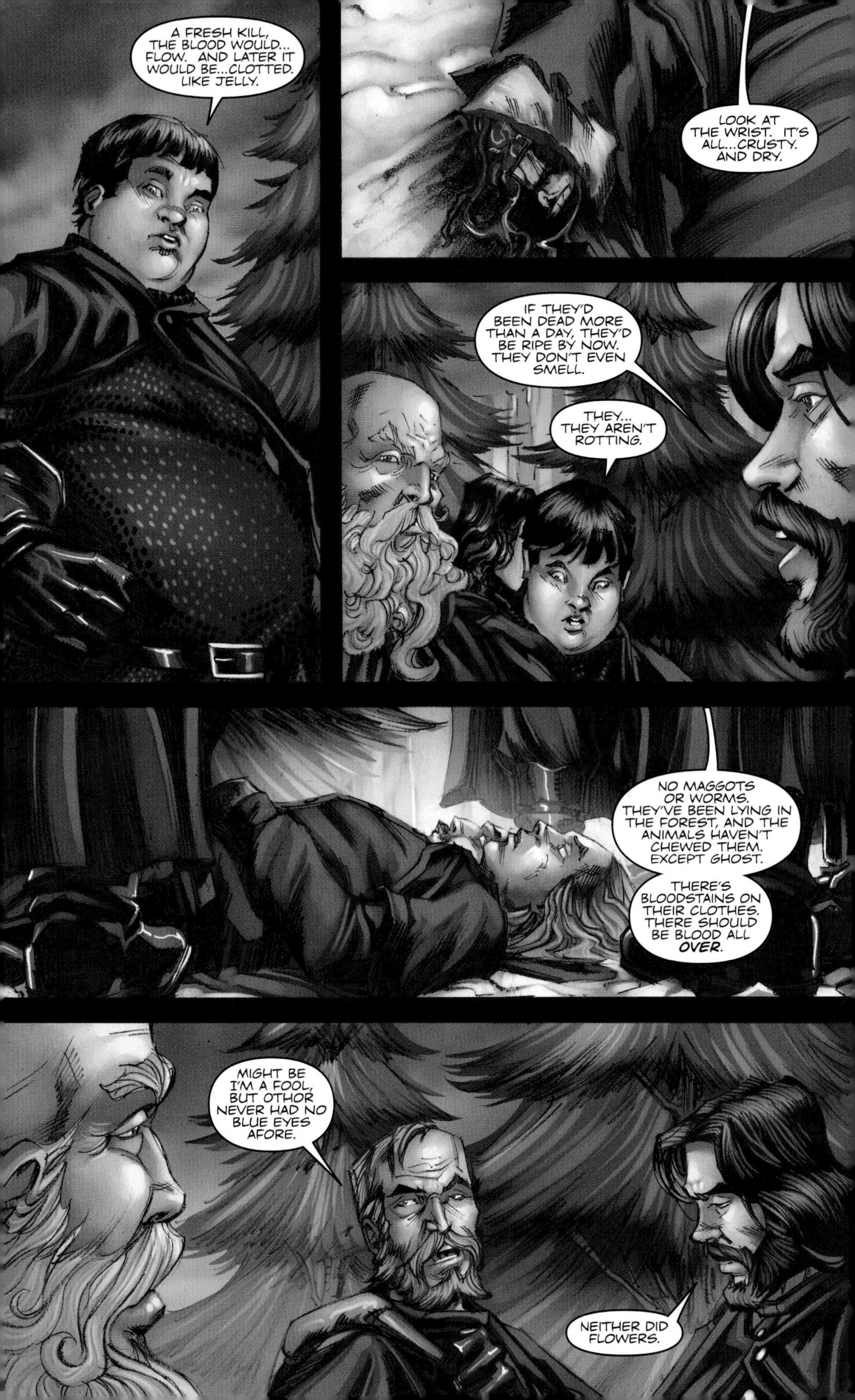
A FRESH KILL, THE BLOOD WOULD... FLOW. AND LATER IT WOULD BE...CLOTTED. LIKE JELLY.
LOOK AT THE WRIST. IT'S ALL...CRUSTY. AND DRY.
IF THEY'D BEEN DEAD MORE THAN A DAY, THEY'D BE RIPE BY NOW. THEY DON'T EVEN SMELL.
THEY... THEY AREN'T ROTTING.
NO MAGGOTS OR WORMS. THEY'VE BEEN LYING IN THE FOREST, AND THE ANIMALS HAVEN'T CHEWED THEM. EXCEPT GHOST.
THERE'S BLOODSTAINS ON THEIR CLOTHES. THERE SHOULD BE BLOOD ALL OVER.
MIGHT BE I'M A FOOL, BUT OTHOR NEVER HAD NO BLUE EYES AFORE.
NEITHER DID FLOWERS.

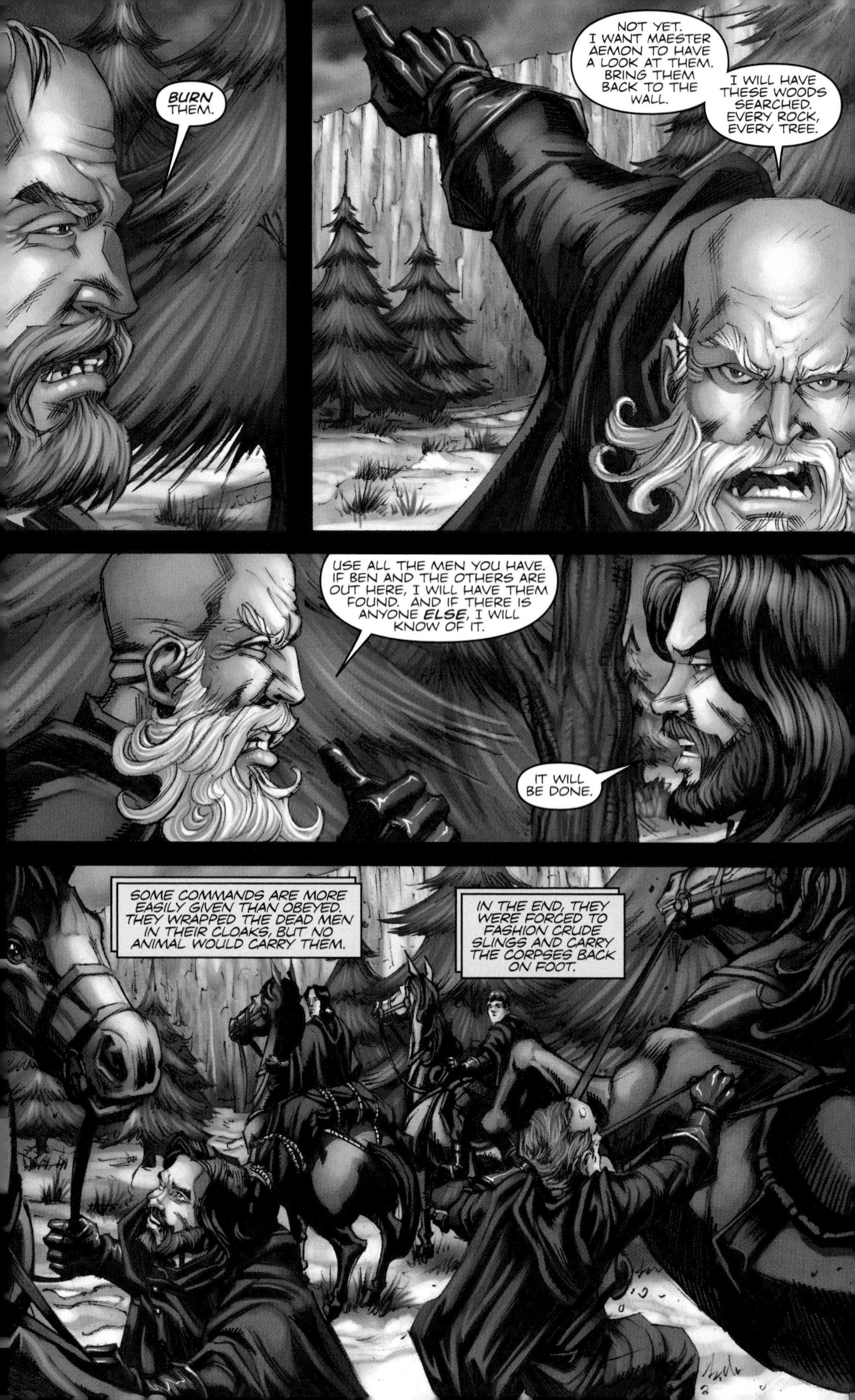
BURN THEM.
NOT YET. I WANT MAESTER AEMON TO HAVE A LOOK AT THEM. BRING THEM BACK TO THE WALL.
I WILL HAVE THESE WOODS SEARCHED. EVERY ROCK, EVERY TREE.
USE ALL THE MEN YOU HAVE. IF BEN AND THE OTHERS ARE OUT HERE, I WILL HAVE THEM FOUND. AND IF THERE IS ANYONE ELSE, I WILL KNOW OF IT.
IT WILL BE DONE.
SOME COMMANDS ARE MORE EASILY GIVEN THAN OBEYED. THEY WRAPPED THE DEAD MEN IN THEIR CLOAKS, BUT NO ANIMAL WOULD CARRY THEM.
IN THE END, THEY WERE FORCED TO FASHION CRUDE SLINGS AND CARRY THE CORPSES BACK ON FOOT.

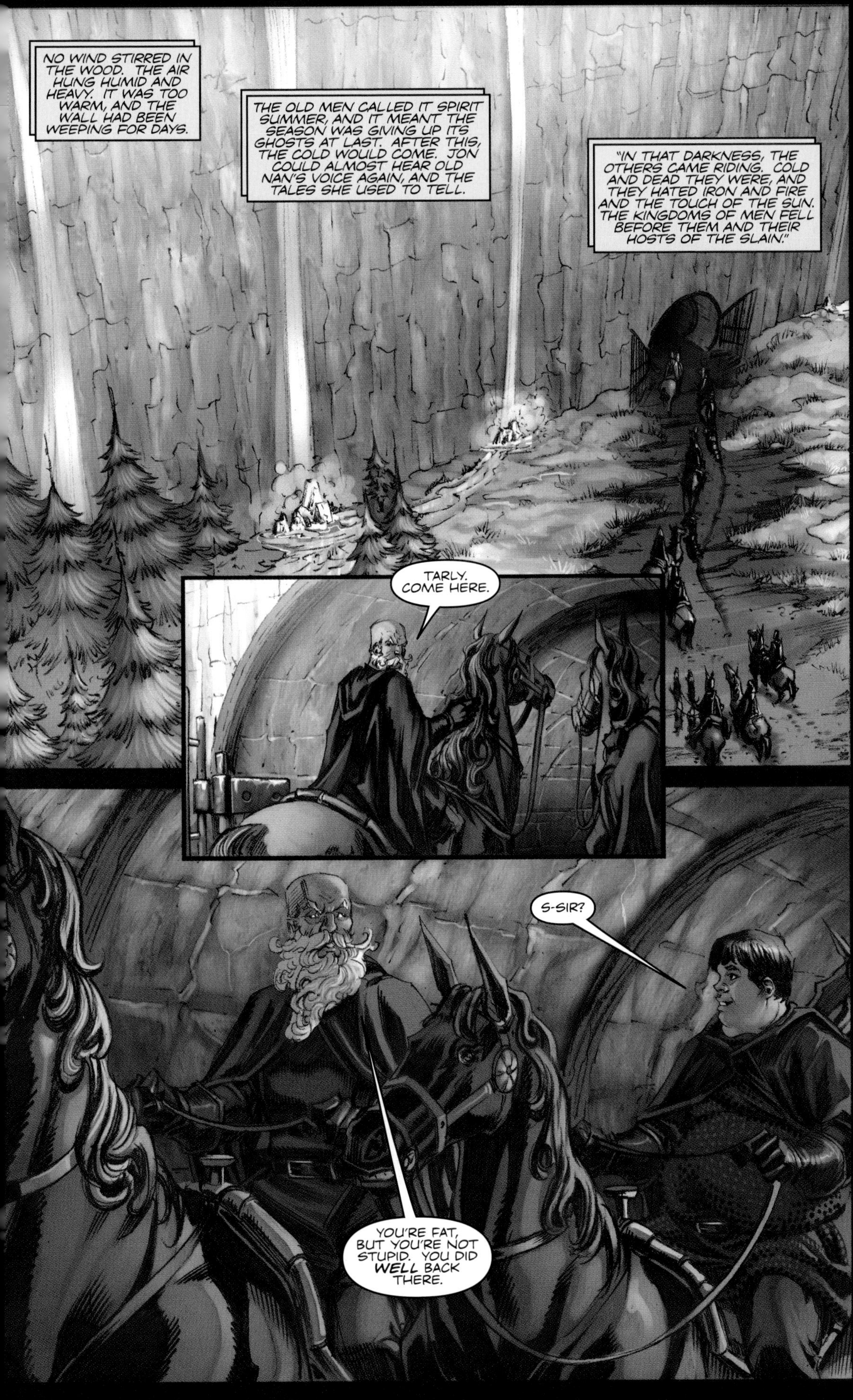
NO WIND STIRRED IN THE WOOD. THE AIR HUNG HUMID AND HEAVY. IT WAS TOO WARM, AND THE WALL HAD BEEN WEEPING FOR DAYS.
THE OLD MEN CALLED IT SPIRIT SUMMER, AND IT MEANT THE SEASON WAS GIVING UP ITS GHOSTS AT LAST. AFTER THIS, THE COLD WOULD COME. JON COULD ALMOST HEAR OLD NAN'S VOICE AGAIN, AND THE TALES SHE USED TO TELL.
"IN THAT DARKNESS, THE OTHERS CAME RIDING. COLD AND DEAD THEY WERE, AND THEY HATED IRON AND FIRE AND THE TOUCH OF THE SUN. THE KINGDOMS OF MEN FELL BEFORE THEM AND THEIR HOSTS OF THE SLAIN."
TARLY. COME HERE.
S-SIR?
YOU'RE FAT, BUT YOU'RE NOT STUPID. YOU DID WELL BACK THERE.

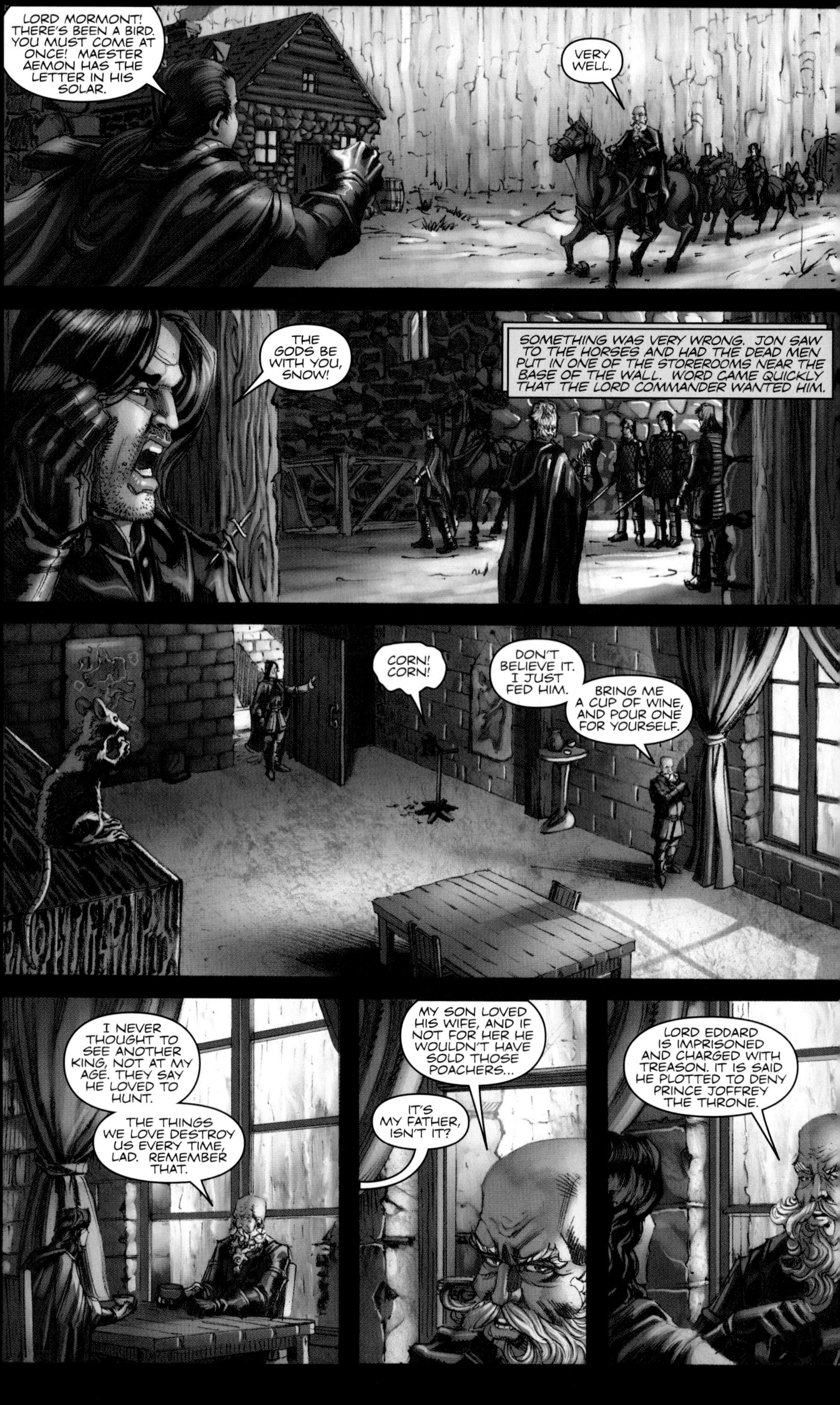
LORD MORMONT! THERE'S BEEN A BIRD. YOU MUST COME AT ONCE! MAESTER AEMON HAS THE LETTER IN HIS SOLAR.
VERY WELL.
THE GODS BE WITH YOU, SNOW!
SOMETHING WAS VERY WRONG. JON SAW TO THE HORSES AND HAD THE DEAD MEN PUT IN ONE OF THE STOREROOMS NEAR THE BASE OF THE WALL. WORD CAME QUICKLY THAT THE LORD COMMANDER WANTED HIM.
CORN! CORN!
DON'T BELIEVE IT. I JUST FED HIM.
BRING ME A CUP OF WINE, AND POUR ONE FOR YOURSELF.
I NEVER THOUGHT TO SEE ANOTHER KING, NOT AT MY AGE. THEY SAY HE LOVED TO HUNT.
THE THINGS WE LOVE DESTROY US EVERY TIME, LAD. REMEMBER THAT.
MY SON LOVED HIS WIFE, AND IF NOT FOR HER HE WOULDN'T HAVE SOLD THOSE POACHERS...
IT'S MY FATHER, ISN'T IT?
LORD EDDARD IS IMPRISONED AND CHARGED WITH TREASON. IT IS SAID HE PLOTTED TO DENY PRINCE JOFFREY THE THRONE.

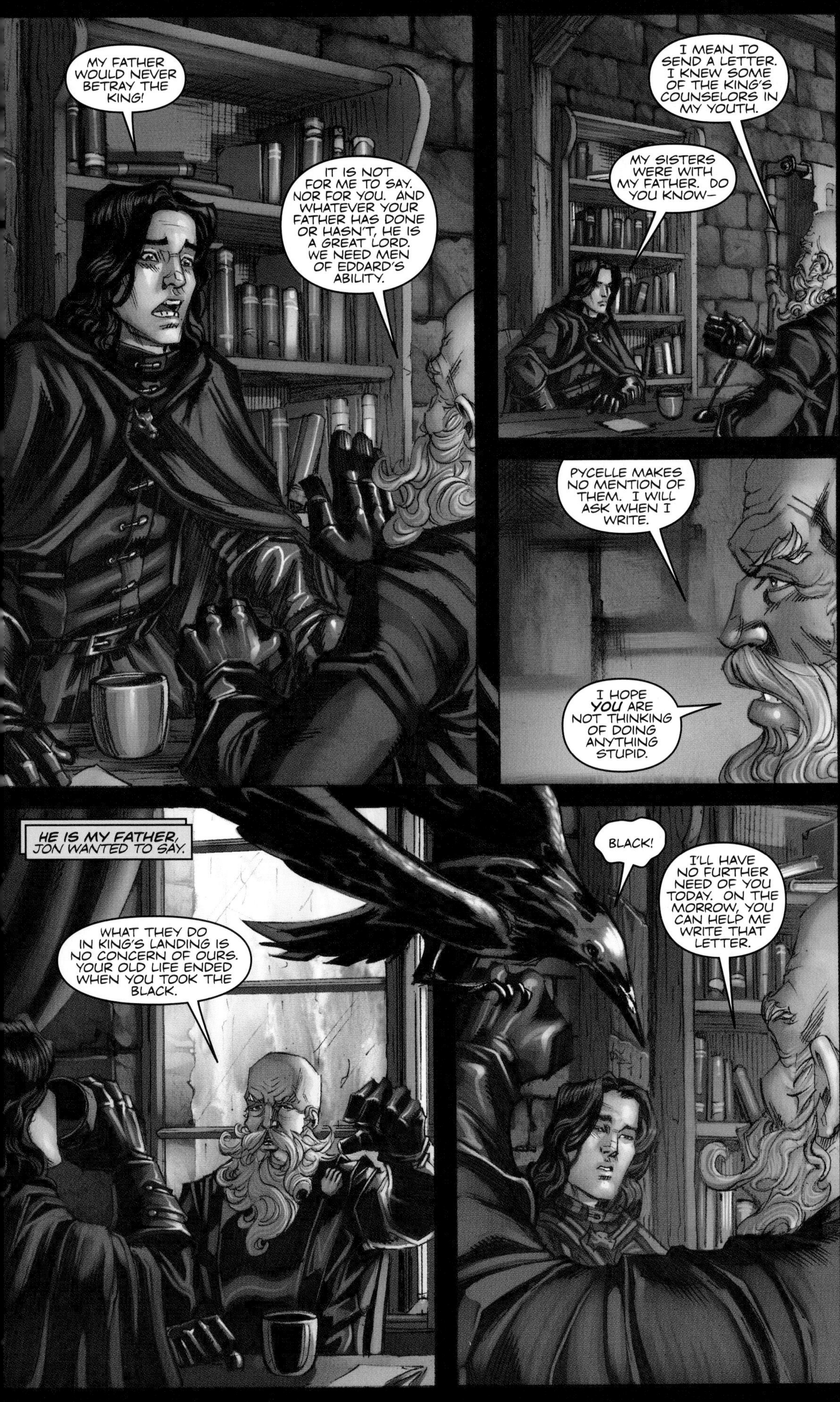
MY FATHER WOULD NEVER BETRAY THE KING!
IT IS NOT FOR ME TO SAY. NOR FOR YOU. AND WHATEVER YOUR FATHER HAS DONE OR HASN'T, HE IS A GREAT LORD. WE NEED MEN OF EDDARD'S ABILITY.
I MEAN TO SEND A LETTER. I KNEW SOME OF THE KING'S COUNSELORS IN MY YOUTH.
MY SISTERS WERE WITH MY FATHER. DO YOU KNOW—
PYCELLE MAKES NO MENTION OF THEM. I WILL ASK WHEN I WRITE.
I HOPE *YOU* ARE NOT THINKING OF DOING ANYTHING STUPID.
*HE IS MY FATHER,* JON WANTED TO SAY.
WHAT THEY DO IN KING'S LANDING IS NO CONCERN OF OURS. YOUR OLD LIFE ENDED WHEN YOU TOOK THE BLACK.
BLACK!
I'LL HAVE NO FURTHER NEED OF YOU TODAY. ON THE MORROW, YOU CAN HELP ME WRITE THAT LETTER.

BE STRONG, BOY. THE GODS ARE CRUEL.
THEY KNEW.
THEY ALL KNEW.
WE ASKED THE SEPTON TO LIGHT A CANDLE FOR YOUR FATHER. IT'S A LIE. EVEN GRENN KNOWS IT'S A LIE.
YOU'RE MY BROTHER NOW, SO HE'S MY FATHER TOO. IF YOU WANT TO PRAY AT THE WEIRWOOD, I'LL GO WITH YOU.
THE WEIRWOODS WERE BEYOND THE WALL, YET HE KNEW SAM MEANT WHAT HE'D SAID. THESE WERE HIS BROTHERS TOO, AS MUCH AS ROBB OR BRAN OR RICKON...
HA HA HA!
...NOT ONLY A BASTARD, BUT A TRAITOR'S BASTARD...
RRHHHAAGGH!
"I THOUGHT I TOLD YOU NOT TO DO ANYTHING STUPID, BOY."

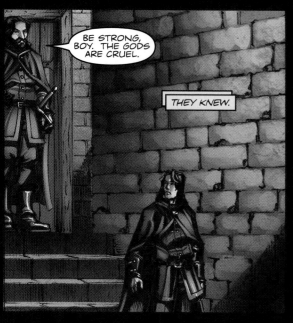

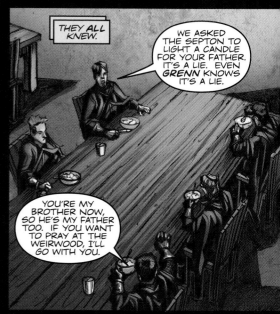

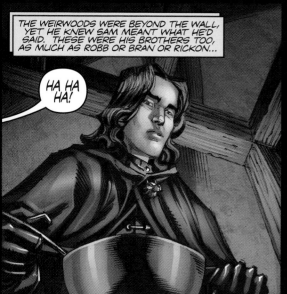

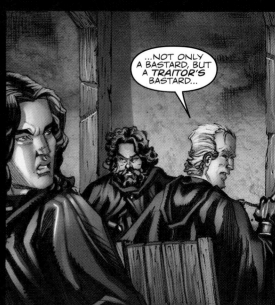

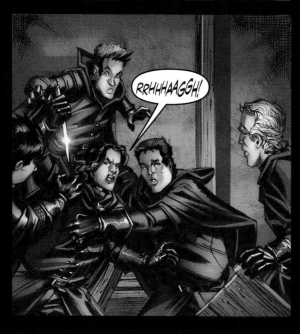

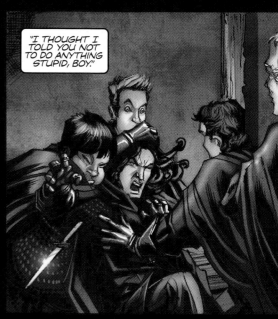

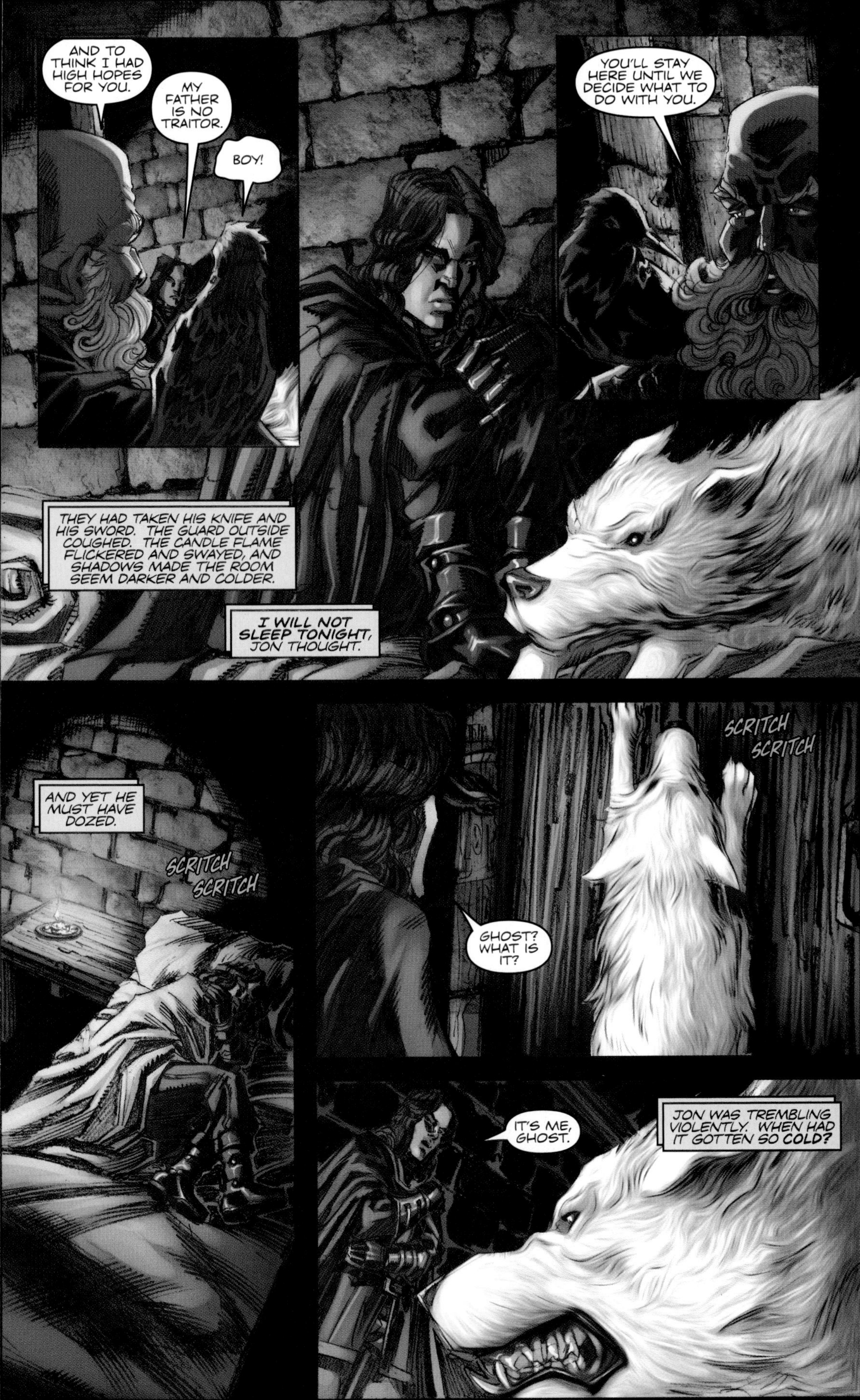
AND TO THINK I HAD HIGH HOPES FOR YOU.
MY FATHER IS NO TRAITOR.
BOY!
YOU'LL STAY HERE UNTIL WE DECIDE WHAT TO DO WITH YOU.
THEY HAD TAKEN HIS KNIFE AND HIS SWORD. THE GUARD OUTSIDE COUGHED. THE CANDLE FLAME FLICKERED AND SWAYED, AND SHADOWS MADE THE ROOM SEEM DARKER AND COLDER.
I WILL NOT SLEEP TONIGHT, JON THOUGHT.
AND YET HE MUST HAVE DOZED.
SCRITCH SCRITCH
SCRITCH SCRITCH
GHOST? WHAT IS IT?
IT'S ME, GHOST.
JON WAS TREMBLING VIOLENTLY. WHEN HAD IT GOTTEN SO COLD?

THERE'S SOMEONE OUT THERE, ISN'T THERE?

THE GUARD AT THE DOOR, JON THOUGHT. GHOST SMELLS HIM THROUGH THE DOOR, THAT'S ALL.

CREEEK

THE LORD COMMANDER'S TOWER WAS GUARDED DAY AND NIGHT. THIS COULD NOT HAPPEN. IT HAD TO BE A DREAM. A NIGHTMARE.

HE HEARD IT. THE SOFT SCRAPE OF A BOOT ON STONE, THE SOUND OF A LATCH TURNING. THEY CAME FROM ABOVE.

FROM THE LORD COMMANDER'S ROOM.

A NIGHTMARE THIS MIGHT BE, BUT IT WAS NO DREAM.

CORN!

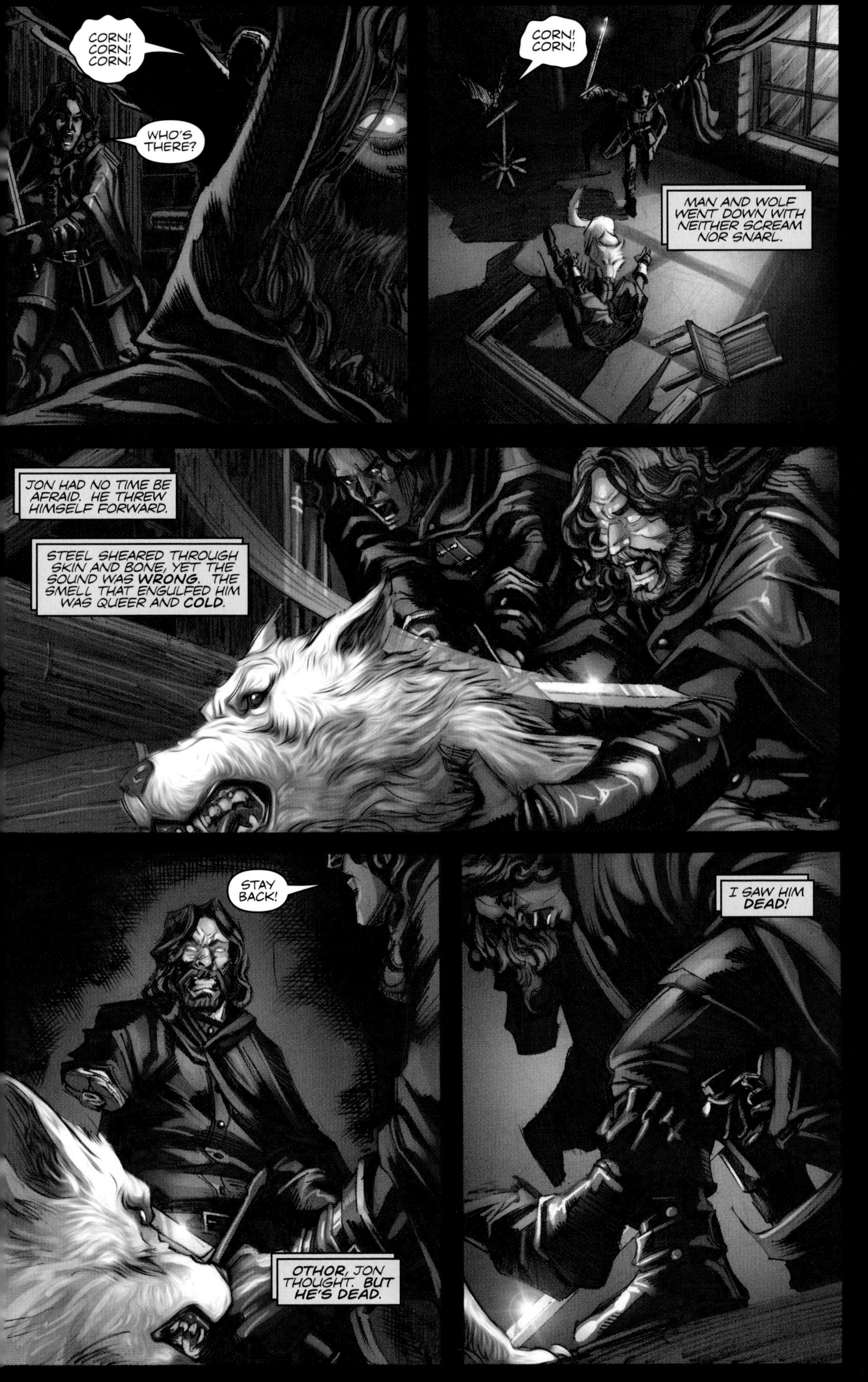
CORN! CORN! CORN!
WHO'S THERE?
CORN! CORN!
MAN AND WOLF WENT DOWN WITH NEITHER SCREAM NOR SNARL.
JON HAD NO TIME BE AFRAID. HE THREW HIMSELF FORWARD.
STEEL SHEARED THROUGH SKIN AND BONE, YET THE SOUND WAS **WRONG**. THE SMELL THAT ENGULFED HIM WAS QUEER AND **COLD**.
STAY BACK!
**OTHOR**, JON THOUGHT. **BUT HE'S DEAD.**
I SAW HIM **DEAD!**

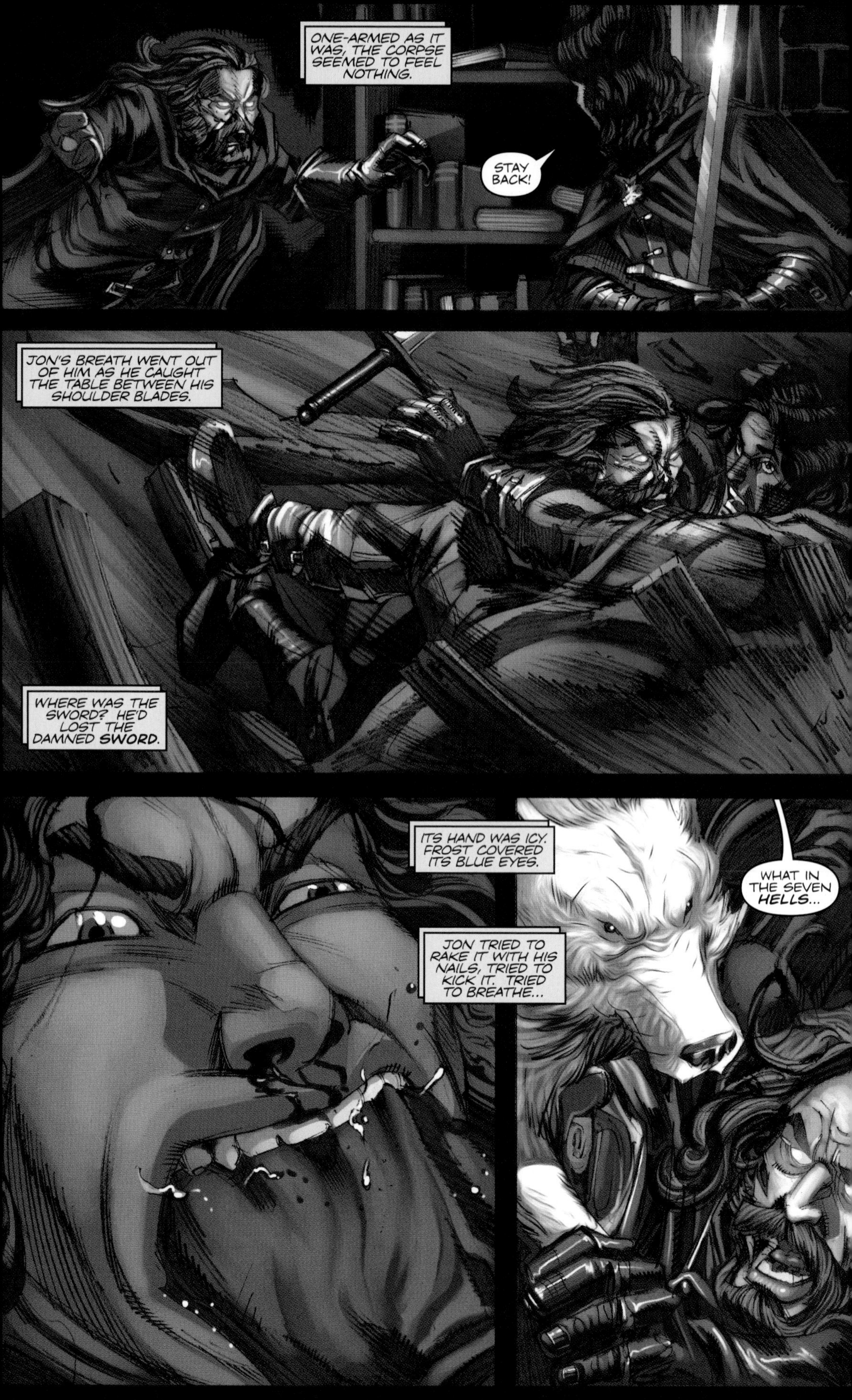
ONE-ARMED AS IT WAS, THE CORPSE SEEMED TO FEEL NOTHING.
STAY BACK!
JON'S BREATH WENT OUT OF HIM AS HE CAUGHT THE TABLE BETWEEN HIS SHOULDER BLADES.
WHERE WAS THE SWORD? HE'D LOST THE DAMNED **SWORD**.
ITS HAND WAS ICY. FROST COVERED ITS BLUE EYES.
JON TRIED TO RAKE IT WITH HIS NAILS, TRIED TO KICK IT. TRIED TO BREATHE...
WHAT IN THE SEVEN **HELLS**...

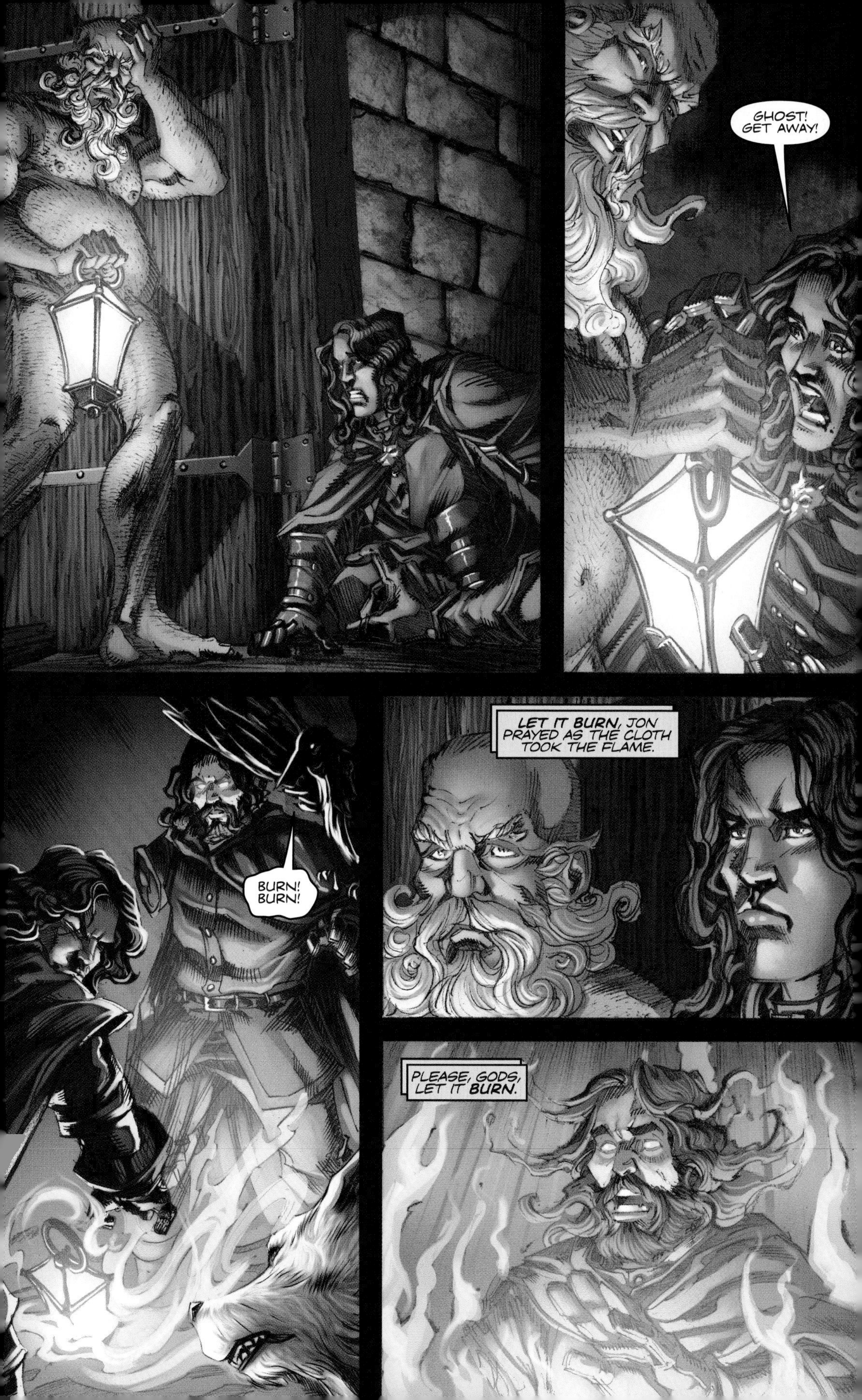
GHOST! GET AWAY!
BURN! BURN!
LET IT BURN, JON PRAYED AS THE CLOTH TOOK THE FLAME.
PLEASE, GODS, LET IT BURN.

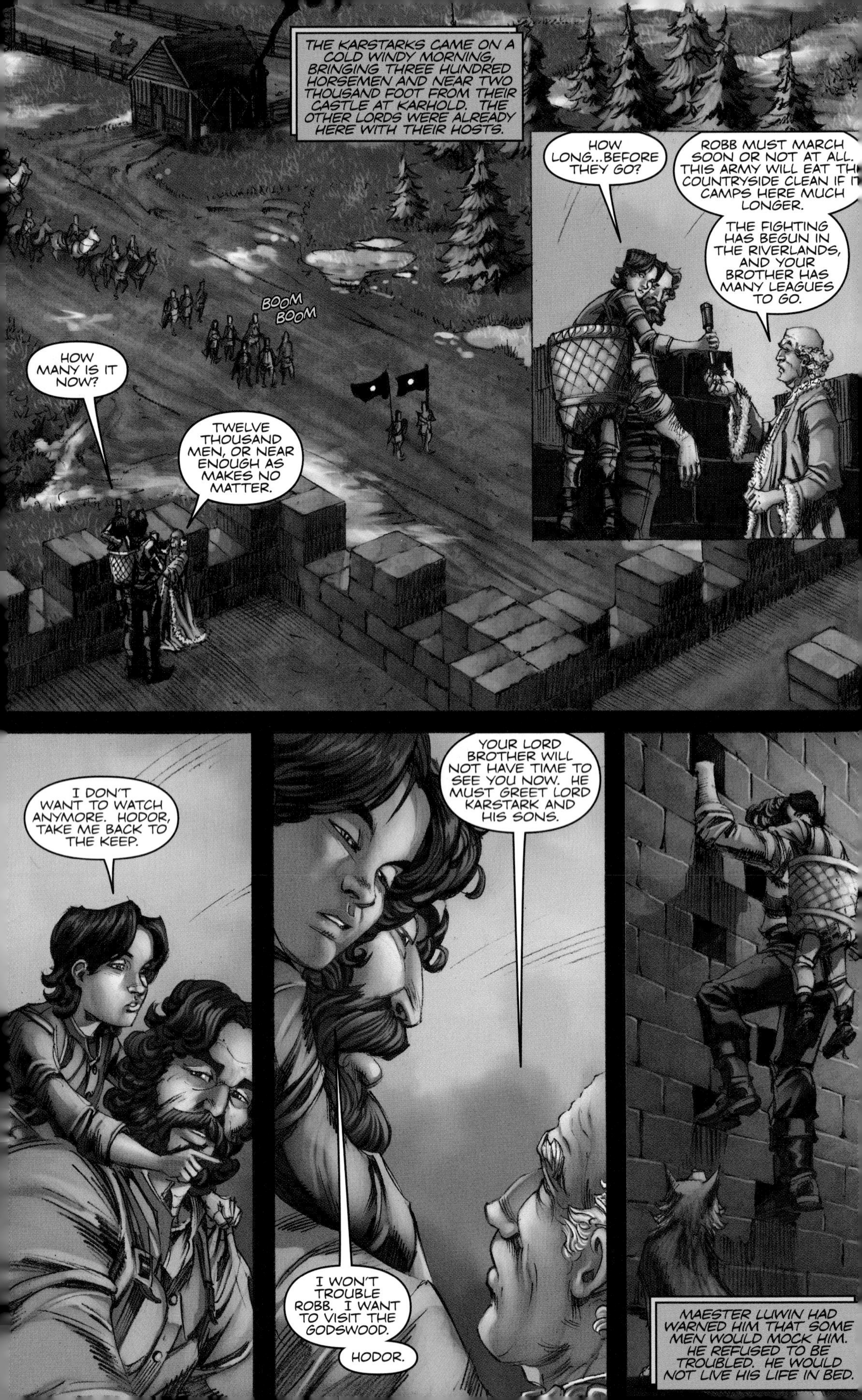
THE KARSTARKS CAME ON A COLD WINDY MORNING, BRINGING THREE HUNDRED HORSEMEN AND NEAR TWO THOUSAND FOOT FROM THEIR CASTLE AT KARHOLD. THE OTHER LORDS WERE ALREADY HERE WITH THEIR HOSTS.
BOOM BOOM
HOW MANY IS IT NOW?
TWELVE THOUSAND MEN, OR NEAR ENOUGH AS MAKES NO MATTER.
HOW LONG...BEFORE THEY GO?
ROBB MUST MARCH SOON OR NOT AT ALL. THIS ARMY WILL EAT THE COUNTRYSIDE CLEAN IF IT CAMPS HERE MUCH LONGER.
THE FIGHTING HAS BEGUN IN THE RIVERLANDS, AND YOUR BROTHER HAS MANY LEAGUES TO GO.
I DON'T WANT TO WATCH ANYMORE. HODOR, TAKE ME BACK TO THE KEEP.
YOUR LORD BROTHER WILL NOT HAVE TIME TO SEE YOU NOW. HE MUST GREET LORD KARSTARK AND HIS SONS.
I WON'T TROUBLE ROBB. I WANT TO VISIT THE GODSWOOD.
HODOR.
MAESTER LUWIN HAD WARNED HIM THAT SOME MEN WOULD MOCK HIM. HE REFUSED TO BE TROUBLED. HE WOULD NOT LIVE HIS LIFE IN BED.

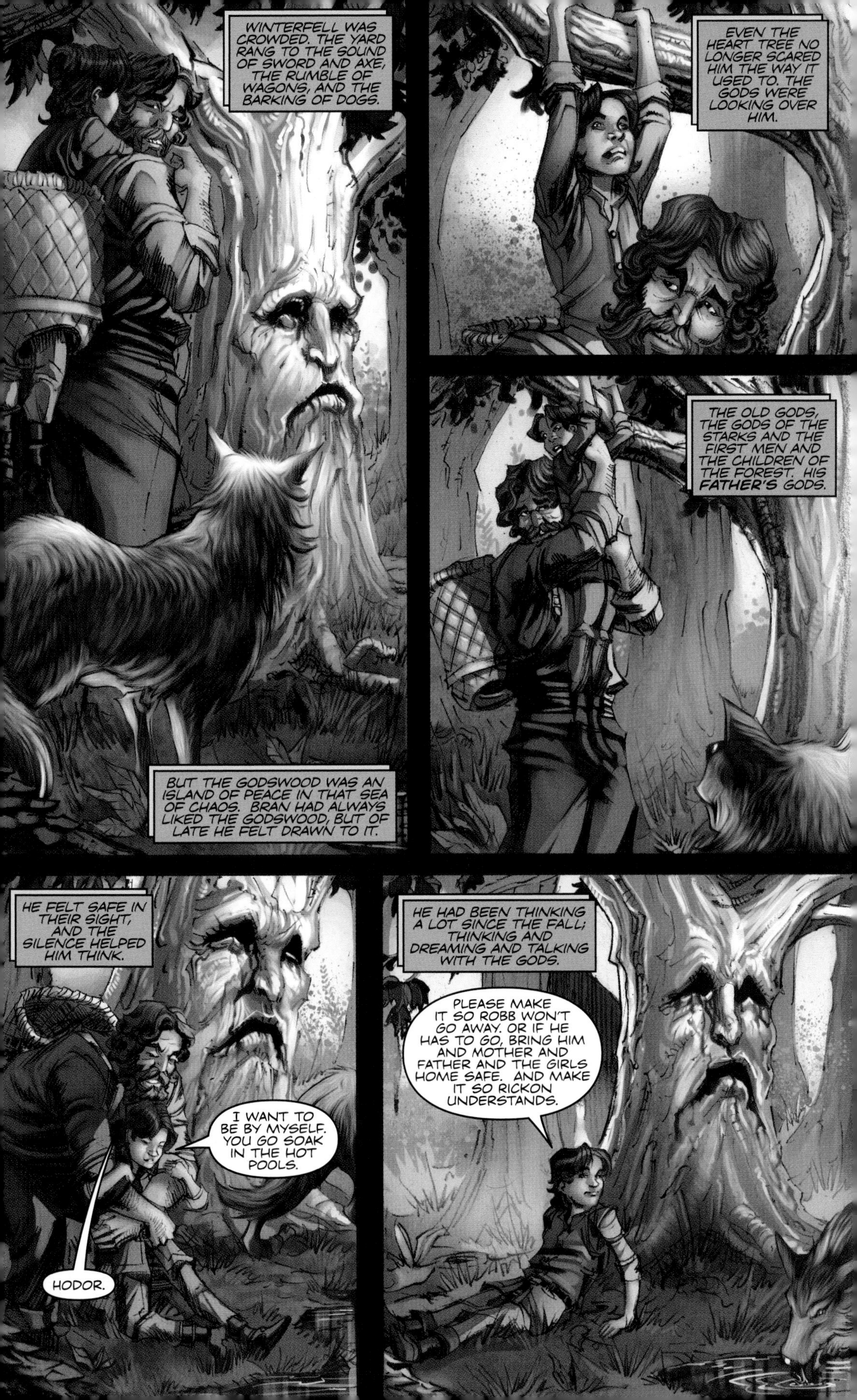
WINTERFELL WAS CROWDED. THE YARD RANG TO THE SOUND OF SWORD AND AXE, THE RUMBLE OF WAGONS, AND THE BARKING OF DOGS.
BUT THE GODSWOOD WAS AN ISLAND OF PEACE IN THAT SEA OF CHAOS. BRAN HAD ALWAYS LIKED THE GODSWOOD, BUT OF LATE HE FELT DRAWN TO IT.
EVEN THE HEART TREE NO LONGER SCARED HIM THE WAY IT USED TO. THE GODS WERE LOOKING OVER HIM.
THE OLD GODS, THE GODS OF THE STARKS AND THE FIRST MEN AND THE CHILDREN OF THE FOREST. HIS FATHER'S GODS.
HE FELT SAFE IN THEIR SIGHT, AND THE SILENCE HELPED HIM THINK.
I WANT TO BE BY MYSELF. YOU GO SOAK IN THE HOT POOLS.
HODOR.
HE HAD BEEN THINKING A LOT SINCE THE FALL; THINKING AND DREAMING AND TALKING WITH THE GODS.
PLEASE MAKE IT SO ROBB WON'T GO AWAY. OR IF HE HAS TO GO, BRING HIM AND MOTHER AND FATHER AND THE GIRLS HOME SAFE. AND MAKE IT SO RICKON UNDERSTANDS.

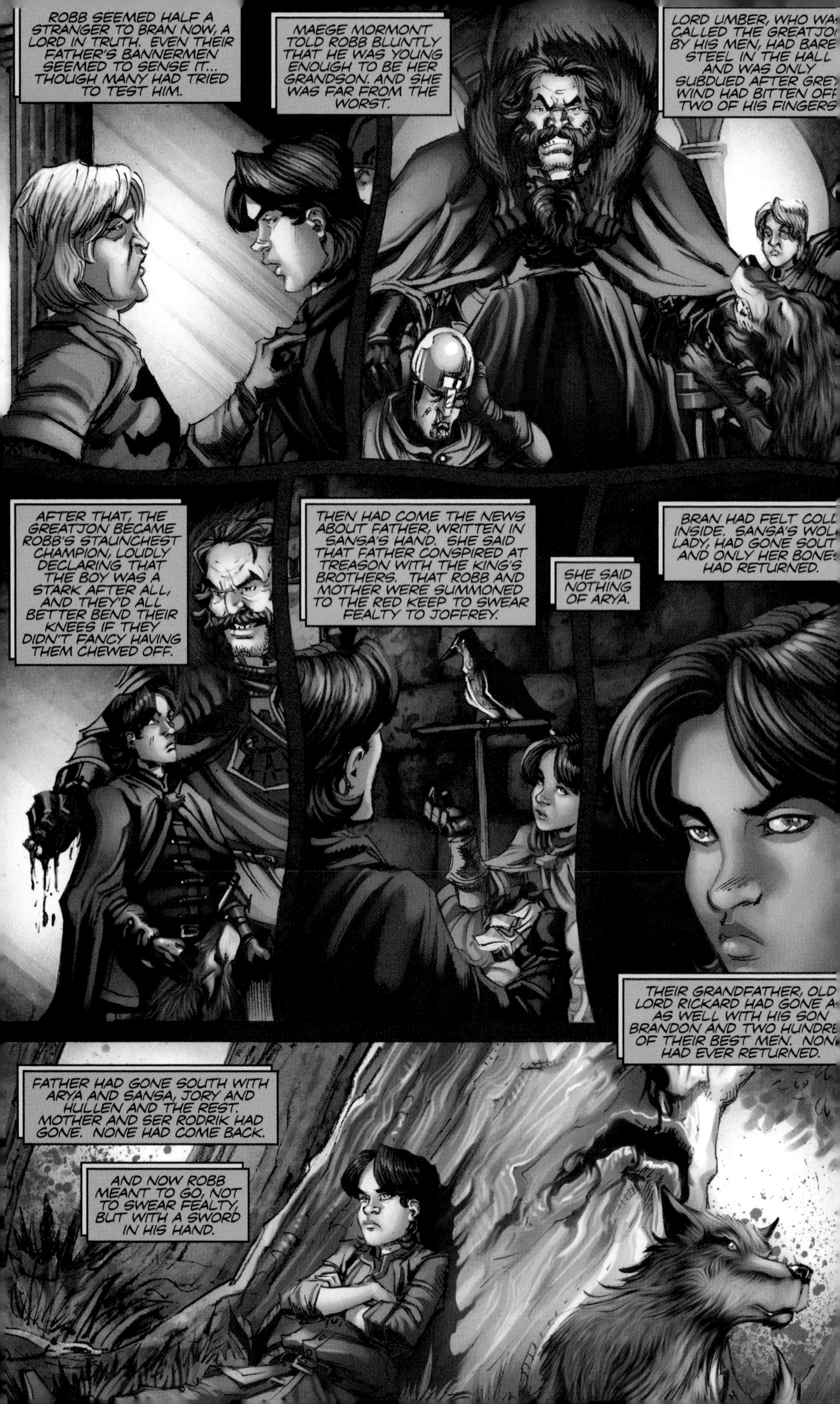
ROBB SEEMED HALF A STRANGER TO BRAN NOW, A LORD IN TRUTH. EVEN THEIR FATHER'S BANNERMEN SEEMED TO SENSE IT... THOUGH MANY HAD TRIED TO TEST HIM.
MAEGE MORMONT TOLD ROBB BLUNTLY THAT HE WAS YOUNG ENOUGH TO BE HER GRANDSON. AND SHE WAS FAR FROM THE WORST.
LORD UMBER, WHO WA CALLED THE GREATJO BY HIS MEN, HAD BARE STEEL IN THE HALL AND WAS ONLY SUBDUED AFTER GREY WIND HAD BITTEN OFF TWO OF HIS FINGERS
AFTER THAT, THE GREATJON BECAME ROBB'S STAUNCHEST CHAMPION, LOUDLY DECLARING THAT THE BOY WAS A STARK AFTER ALL, AND THEY'D ALL BETTER BEND THEIR KNEES IF THEY DIDN'T FANCY HAVING THEM CHEWED OFF.
THEN HAD COME THE NEWS ABOUT FATHER, WRITTEN IN SANSA'S HAND. SHE SAID THAT FATHER CONSPIRED AT TREASON WITH THE KING'S BROTHERS. THAT ROBB AND MOTHER WERE SUMMONED TO THE RED KEEP TO SWEAR FEALTY TO JOFFREY.
SHE SAID NOTHING OF ARYA.
BRAN HAD FELT COL INSIDE. SANSA'S WOL LADY, HAD GONE SOUT AND ONLY HER BONE HAD RETURNED.
THEIR GRANDFATHER, OLD LORD RICKARD HAD GONE A AS WELL WITH HIS SON BRANDON AND TWO HUNDR OF THEIR BEST MEN. NON HAD EVER RETURNED.
FATHER HAD GONE SOUTH WITH ARYA AND SANSA, JORY AND HULLEN AND THE REST. MOTHER AND SER RODRIK HAD GONE. NONE HAD COME BACK.
AND NOW ROBB MEANT TO GO, NOT TO SWEAR FEALTY, BUT WITH A SWORD IN HIS HAND.

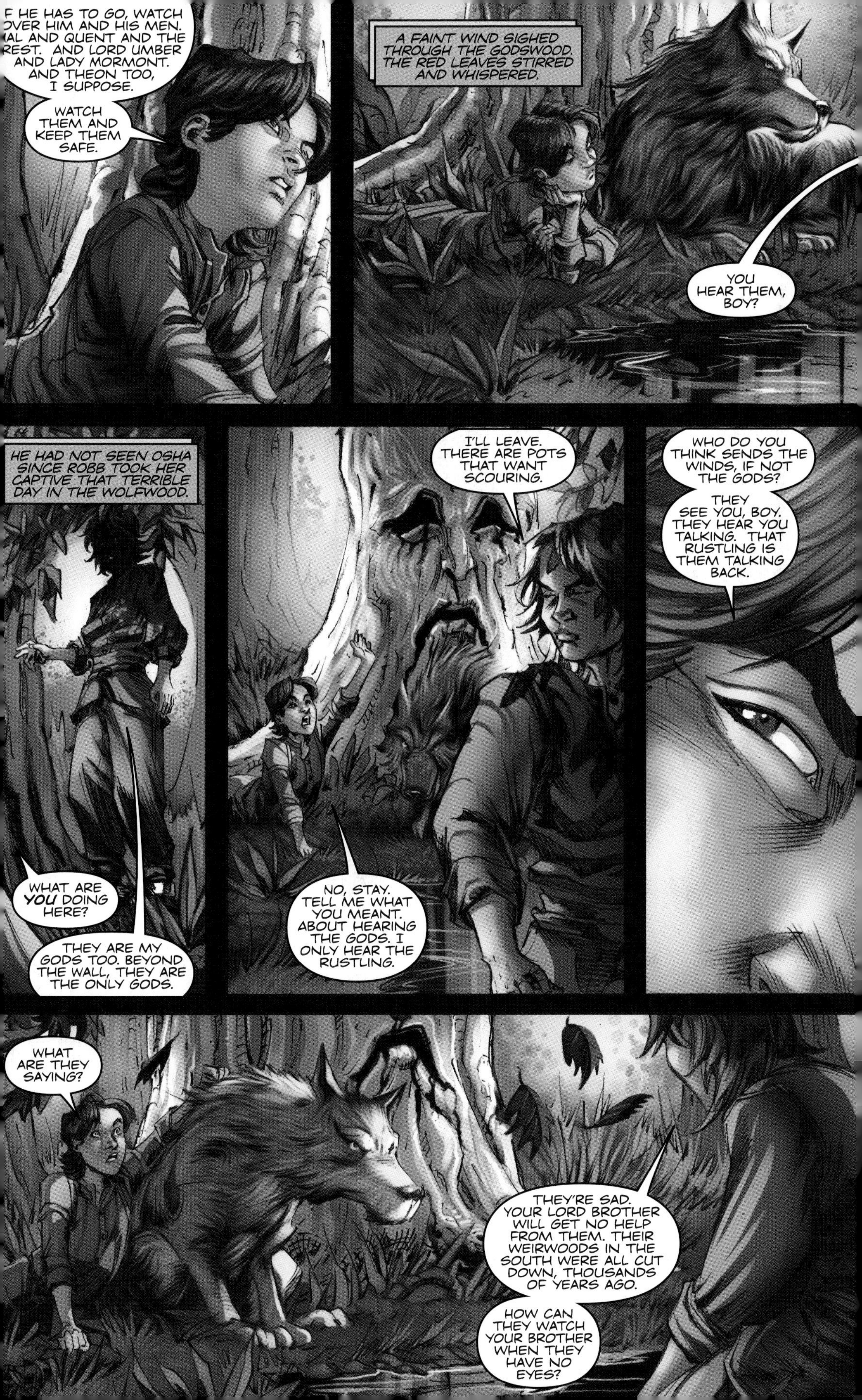
F HE HAS TO GO, WATCH OVER HIM AND HIS MEN. AL AND QUENT AND THE REST. AND LORD UMBER AND LADY MORMONT. AND THEON TOO, I SUPPOSE.
WATCH THEM AND KEEP THEM SAFE.
A FAINT WIND SIGHED THROUGH THE GODSWOOD. THE RED LEAVES STIRRED AND WHISPERED.
YOU HEAR THEM, BOY?
HE HAD NOT SEEN OSHA SINCE ROBB TOOK HER CAPTIVE THAT TERRIBLE DAY IN THE WOLFWOOD.
WHAT ARE ***YOU*** DOING HERE?
THEY ARE MY GODS TOO. BEYOND THE WALL, THEY ARE THE ONLY GODS.
I'LL LEAVE. THERE ARE POTS THAT WANT SCOURING.
NO, STAY. TELL ME WHAT YOU MEANT. ABOUT HEARING THE GODS. I ONLY HEAR THE RUSTLING.
WHO DO YOU THINK SENDS THE WINDS, IF NOT THE GODS?
THEY SEE YOU, BOY. THEY HEAR YOU TALKING. THAT RUSTLING IS THEM TALKING BACK.
WHAT ARE THEY SAYING?
THEY'RE SAD. YOUR LORD BROTHER WILL GET NO HELP FROM THEM. THEIR WEIRWOODS IN THE SOUTH WERE ALL CUT DOWN, THOUSANDS OF YEARS AGO.
HOW CAN THEY WATCH YOUR BROTHER WHEN THEY HAVE NO EYES?

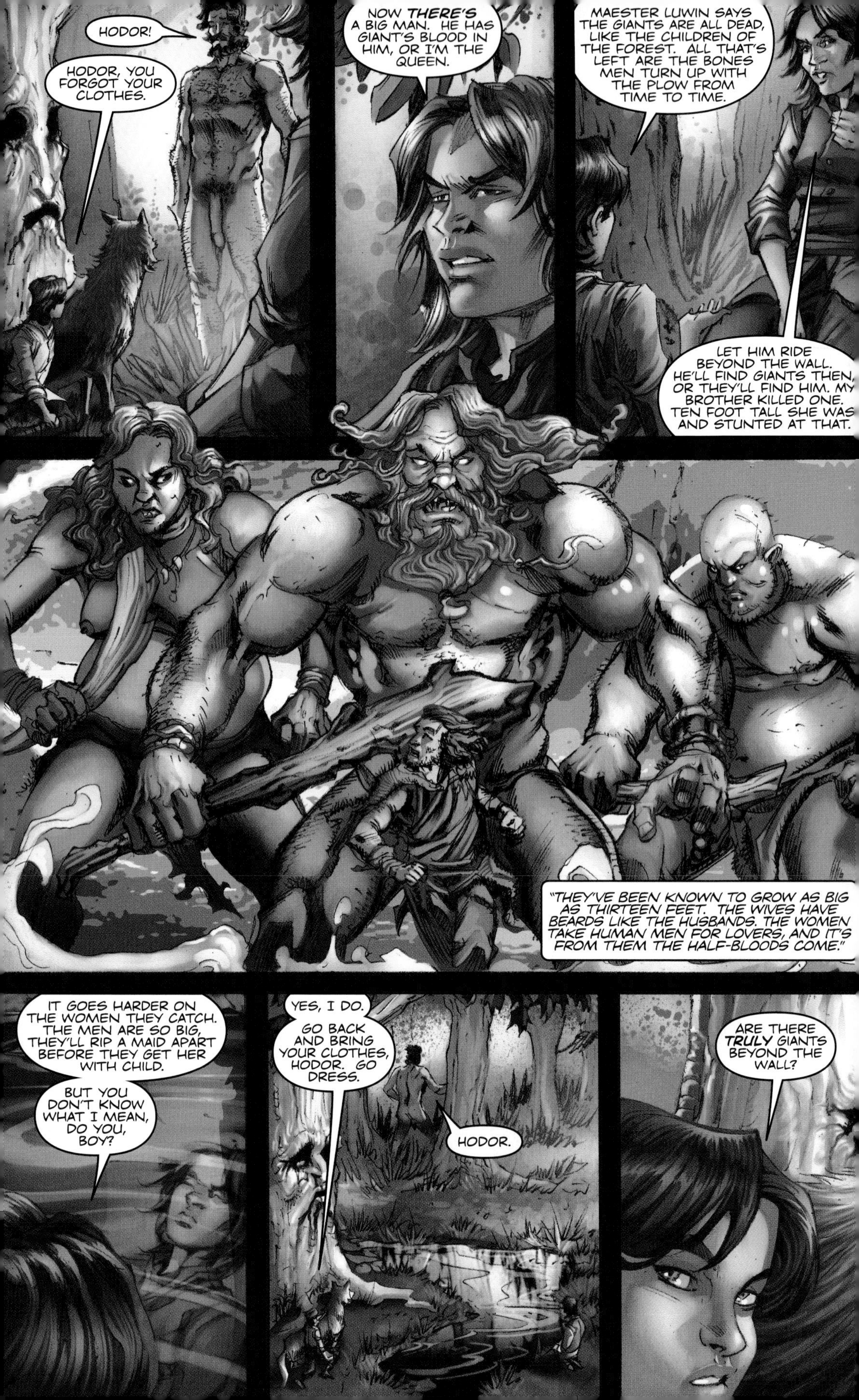
HODOR!
HODOR, YOU FORGOT YOUR CLOTHES.
NOW THERE'S A BIG MAN. HE HAS GIANT'S BLOOD IN HIM, OR I'M THE QUEEN.
MAESTER LUWIN SAYS THE GIANTS ARE ALL DEAD, LIKE THE CHILDREN OF THE FOREST. ALL THAT'S LEFT ARE THE BONES MEN TURN UP WITH THE PLOW FROM TIME TO TIME.
LET HIM RIDE BEYOND THE WALL. HE'LL FIND GIANTS THEN, OR THEY'LL FIND HIM. MY BROTHER KILLED ONE. TEN FOOT TALL SHE WAS AND STUNTED AT THAT.
"THEY'VE BEEN KNOWN TO GROW AS BIG AS THIRTEEN FEET. THE WIVES HAVE BEARDS LIKE THE HUSBANDS. THE WOMEN TAKE HUMAN MEN FOR LOVERS, AND IT'S FROM THEM THE HALF-BLOODS COME."
IT GOES HARDER ON THE WOMEN THEY CATCH. THE MEN ARE SO BIG, THEY'LL RIP A MAID APART BEFORE THEY GET HER WITH CHILD.
BUT YOU DON'T KNOW WHAT I MEAN, DO YOU, BOY?
YES, I DO.
GO BACK AND BRING YOUR CLOTHES, HODOR. GO DRESS.
HODOR.
ARE THERE TRULY GIANTS BEYOND THE WALL?

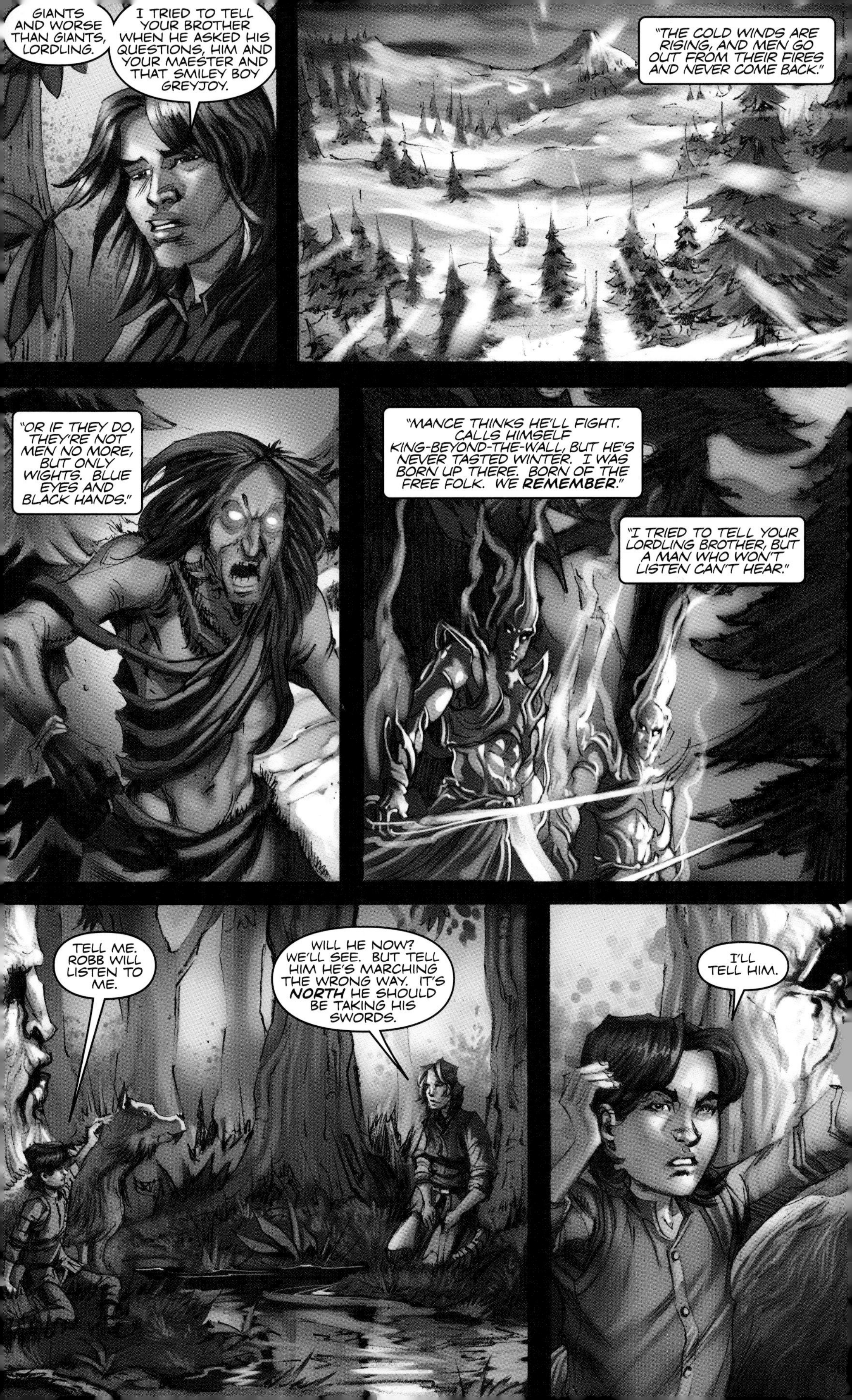
GIANTS AND WORSE THAN GIANTS, LORDLING.
I TRIED TO TELL YOUR BROTHER WHEN HE ASKED HIS QUESTIONS, HIM AND YOUR MAESTER AND THAT SMILEY BOY GREYJOY.
"THE COLD WINDS ARE RISING, AND MEN GO OUT FROM THEIR FIRES AND NEVER COME BACK."
"OR IF THEY DO, THEY'RE NOT MEN NO MORE, BUT ONLY WIGHTS. BLUE EYES AND BLACK HANDS."
"MANCE THINKS HE'LL FIGHT. CALLS HIMSELF KING-BEYOND-THE-WALL, BUT HE'S NEVER TASTED WINTER. I WAS BORN UP THERE. BORN OF THE FREE FOLK. WE REMEMBER."
"I TRIED TO TELL YOUR LORDLING BROTHER, BUT A MAN WHO WON'T LISTEN CAN'T HEAR."
TELL ME. ROBB WILL LISTEN TO ME.
WILL HE NOW? WE'LL SEE. BUT TELL HIM HE'S MARCHING THE WRONG WAY. IT'S NORTH HE SHOULD BE TAKING HIS SWORDS.
I'LL TELL HIM.

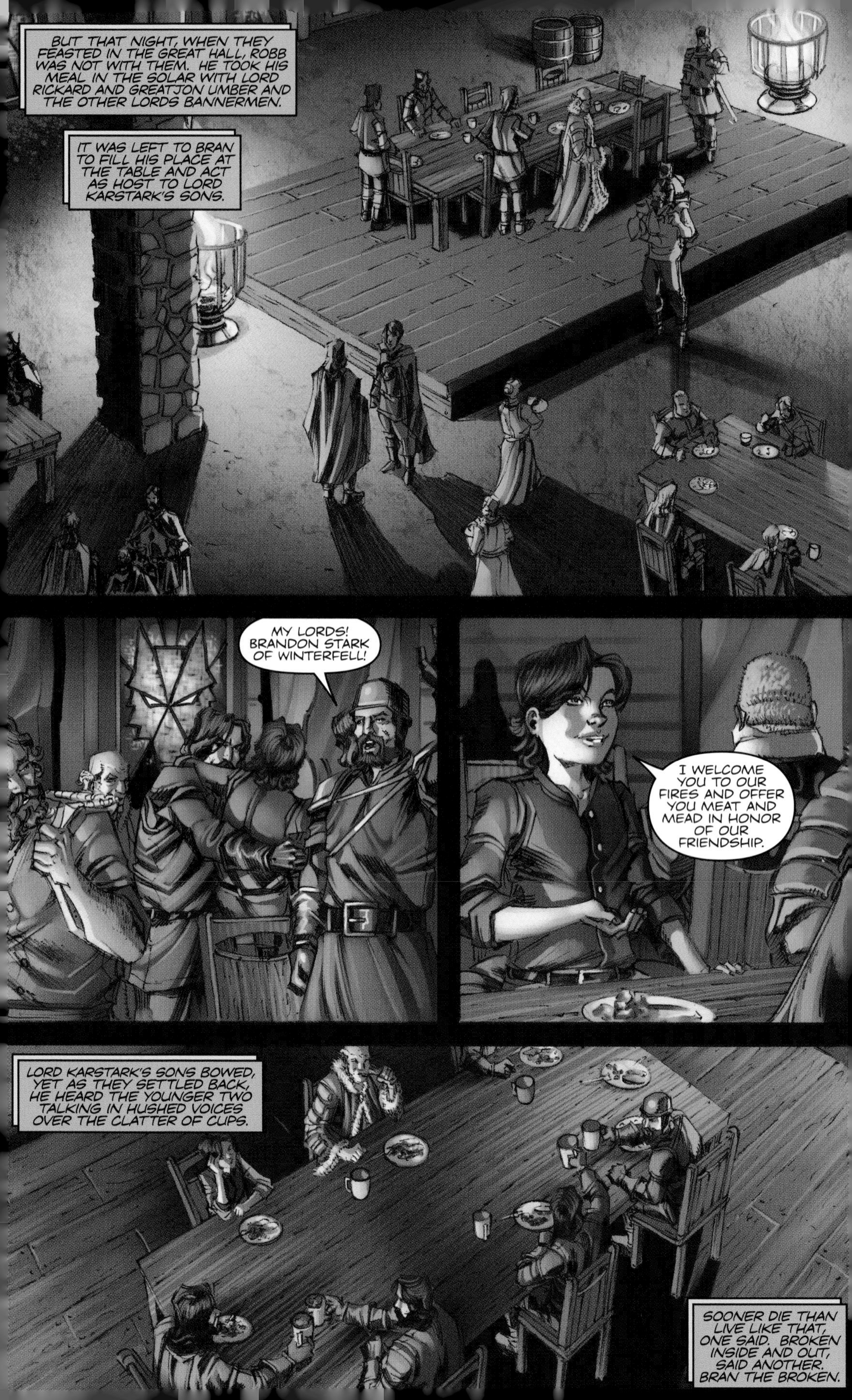
BUT THAT NIGHT, WHEN THEY FEASTED IN THE GREAT HALL, ROBB WAS NOT WITH THEM. HE TOOK HIS MEAL IN THE SOLAR WITH LORD RICKARD AND GREATJON UMBER AND THE OTHER LORDS BANNERMEN.
IT WAS LEFT TO BRAN TO FILL HIS PLACE AT THE TABLE AND ACT AS HOST TO LORD KARSTARK'S SONS.
MY LORDS! BRANDON STARK OF WINTERFELL!
I WELCOME YOU TO OUR FIRES AND OFFER YOU MEAT AND MEAD IN HONOR OF OUR FRIENDSHIP.
LORD KARSTARK'S SONS BOWED, YET AS THEY SETTLED BACK, HE HEARD THE YOUNGER TWO TALKING IN HUSHED VOICES OVER THE CLATTER OF CUPS.
SOONER DIE THAN LIVE LIKE THAT, ONE SAID. BROKEN INSIDE AND OUT, SAID ANOTHER. BRAN THE BROKEN.

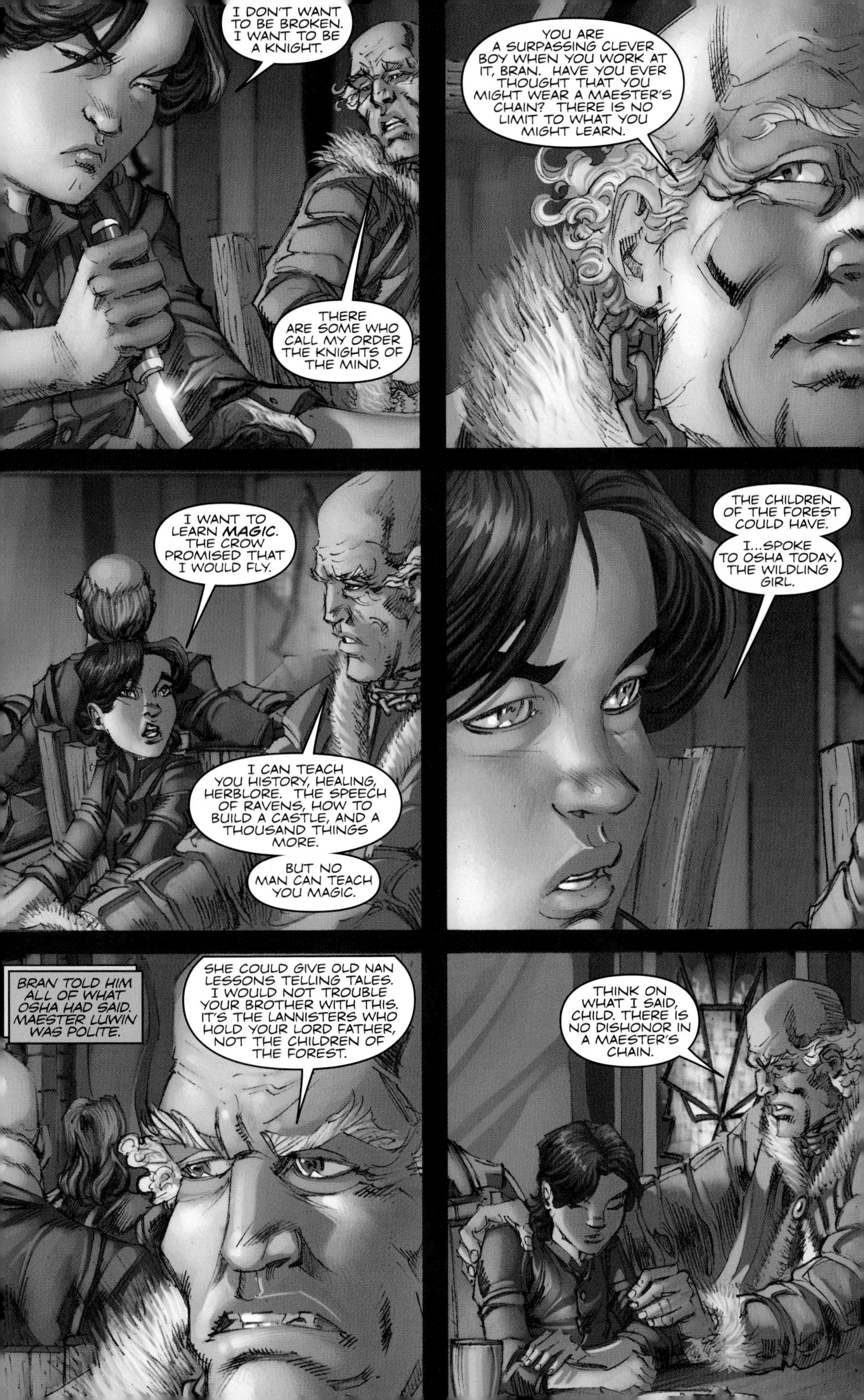
I DON'T WANT TO BE BROKEN. I WANT TO BE A KNIGHT.
THERE ARE SOME WHO CALL MY ORDER THE KNIGHTS OF THE MIND.
YOU ARE A SURPASSING CLEVER BOY WHEN YOU WORK AT IT, BRAN. HAVE YOU EVER THOUGHT THAT YOU MIGHT WEAR A MAESTER'S CHAIN? THERE IS NO LIMIT TO WHAT YOU MIGHT LEARN.
I WANT TO LEARN MAGIC. THE CROW PROMISED THAT I WOULD FLY.
I CAN TEACH YOU HISTORY, HEALING, HERBLORE. THE SPEECH OF RAVENS, HOW TO BUILD A CASTLE, AND A THOUSAND THINGS MORE.
BUT NO MAN CAN TEACH YOU MAGIC.
THE CHILDREN OF THE FOREST COULD HAVE.
I...SPOKE TO OSHA TODAY. THE WILDLING GIRL.
BRAN TOLD HIM ALL OF WHAT OSHA HAD SAID. MAESTER LUWIN WAS POLITE.
SHE COULD GIVE OLD NAN LESSONS TELLING TALES. I WOULD NOT TROUBLE YOUR BROTHER WITH THIS. IT'S THE LANNISTERS WHO HOLD YOUR LORD FATHER, NOT THE CHILDREN OF THE FOREST.
THINK ON WHAT I SAID, CHILD. THERE IS NO DISHONOR IN A MAESTER'S CHAIN.

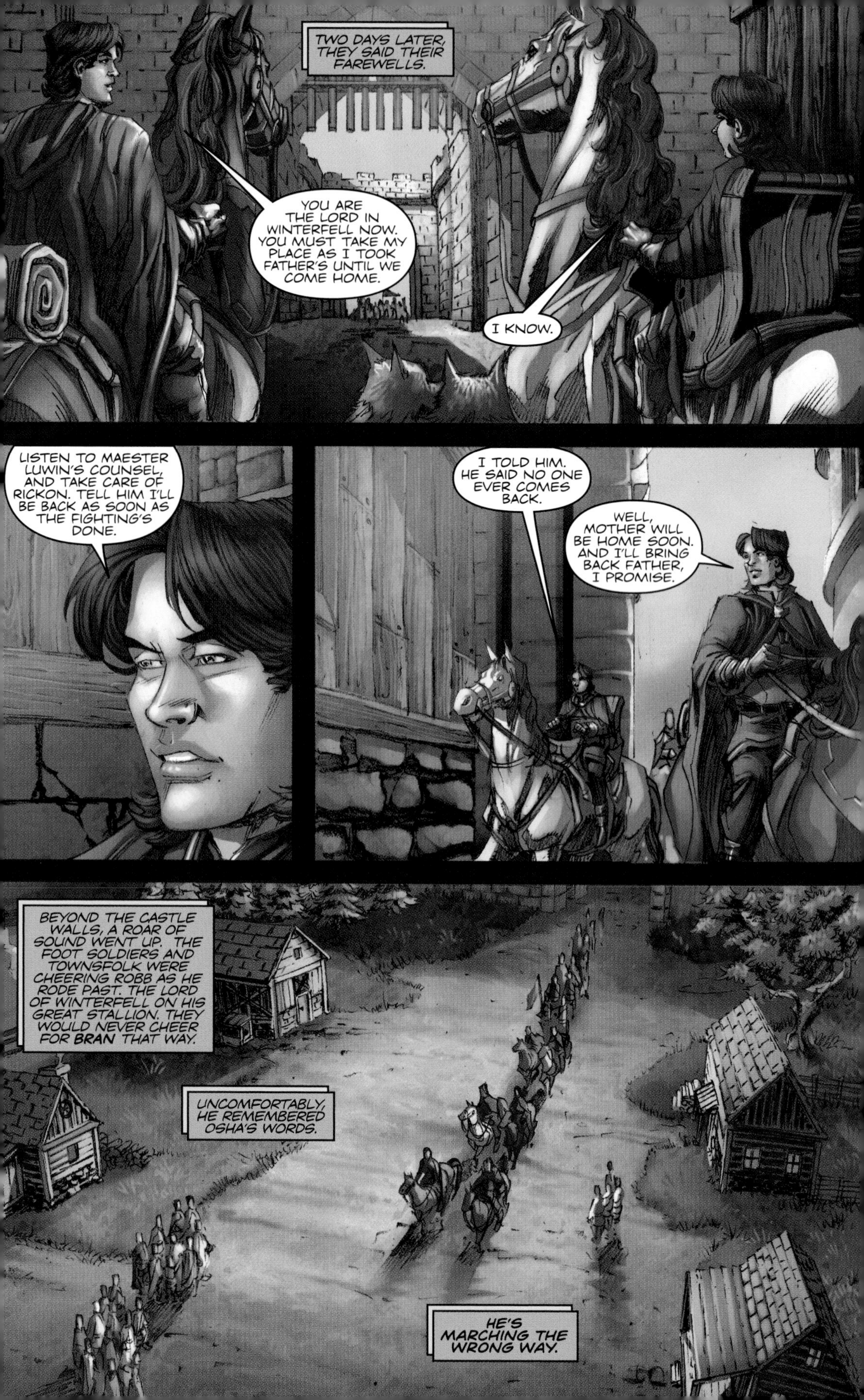

TWO DAYS LATER, THEY SAID THEIR FAREWELLS.
YOU ARE THE LORD IN WINTERFELL NOW. YOU MUST TAKE MY PLACE AS I TOOK FATHER'S UNTIL WE COME HOME.
I KNOW.
LISTEN TO MAESTER LUWIN'S COUNSEL, AND TAKE CARE OF RICKON. TELL HIM I'LL BE BACK AS SOON AS THE FIGHTING'S DONE.
I TOLD HIM. HE SAID NO ONE EVER COMES BACK.
WELL, MOTHER WILL BE HOME SOON. AND I'LL BRING BACK FATHER, I PROMISE.
BEYOND THE CASTLE WALLS, A ROAR OF SOUND WENT UP. THE FOOT SOLDIERS AND TOWNSFOLK WERE CHEERING ROBB AS HE RODE PAST. THE LORD OF WINTERFELL ON HIS GREAT STALLION. THEY WOULD NEVER CHEER FOR BRAN THAT WAY.
UNCOMFORTABLY, HE REMEMBERED OSHA'S WORDS.
HE'S MARCHING THE WRONG WAY.

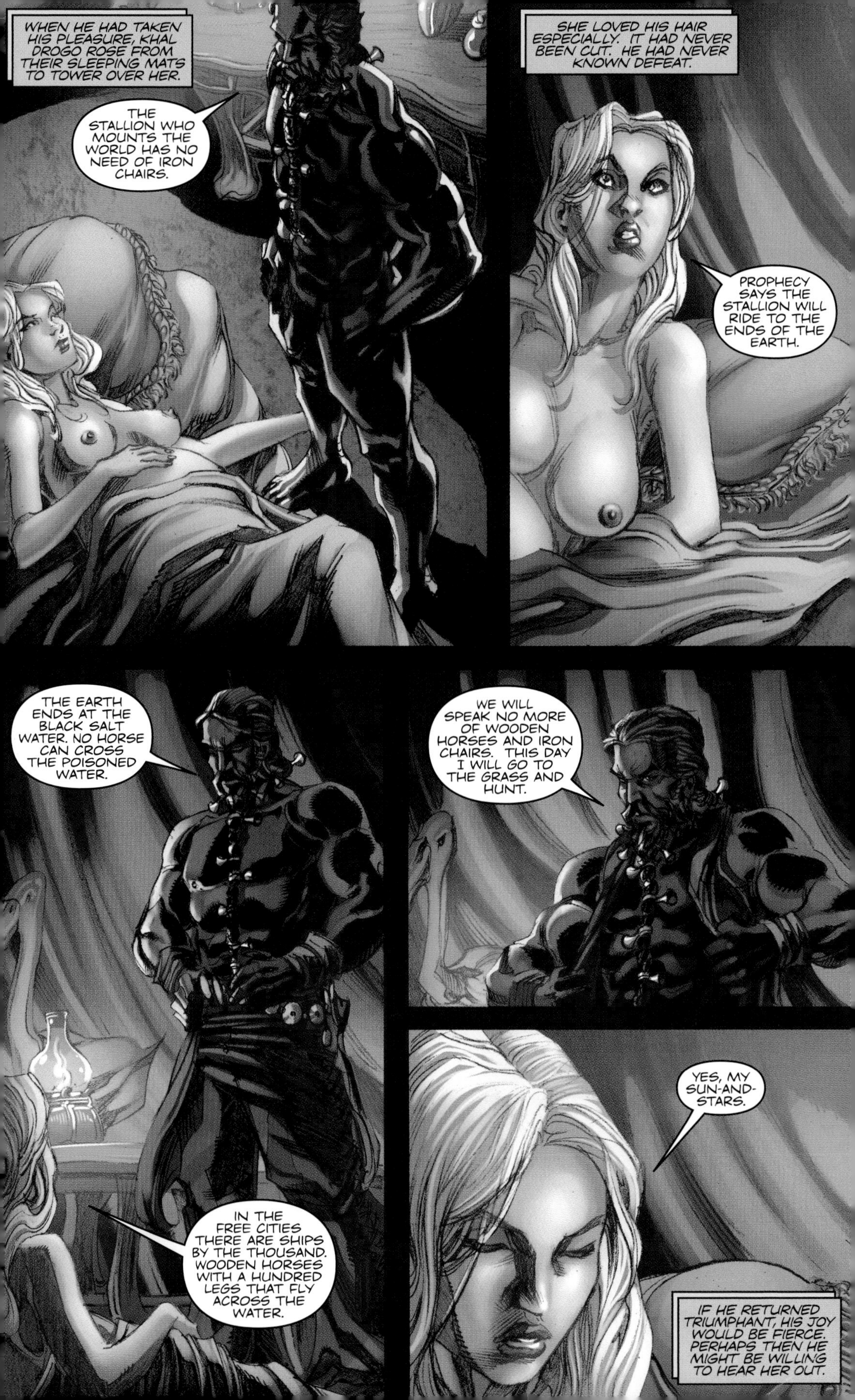
WHEN HE HAD TAKEN HIS PLEASURE, KHAL DROGO ROSE FROM THEIR SLEEPING MATS TO TOWER OVER HER.
THE STALLION WHO MOUNTS THE WORLD HAS NO NEED OF IRON CHAIRS.
SHE LOVED HIS HAIR ESPECIALLY. IT HAD NEVER BEEN CUT. HE HAD NEVER KNOWN DEFEAT.
PROPHECY SAYS THE STALLION WILL RIDE TO THE ENDS OF THE EARTH.
THE EARTH ENDS AT THE BLACK SALT WATER. NO HORSE CAN CROSS THE POISONED WATER.
IN THE FREE CITIES THERE ARE SHIPS BY THE THOUSAND. WOODEN HORSES WITH A HUNDRED LEGS THAT FLY ACROSS THE WATER.
WE WILL SPEAK NO MORE OF WOODEN HORSES AND IRON CHAIRS. THIS DAY I WILL GO TO THE GRASS AND HUNT.
YES, MY SUN-AND-STARS.
IF HE RETURNED TRIUMPHANT, HIS JOY WOULD BE FIERCE. PERHAPS THEN HE MIGHT BE WILLING TO HEAR HER OUT.

AFTER THE KHAL AND HIS BLOODRIDERS HAD RIDDEN OFF, SHE SENT JHIQUI TO FETCH SER JORAH MORMONT

MY PRINCESS. HOW MAY I SERVE YOU?

DROGO TALKS OF LEADING HIS KHALASAR EAST AFTER RHAEGO IS BORN TO PLUNDER THE LANDS AROUND THE JADE SEA, BUT HE MUST RIDE *WEST*.

THE KHAL HAS NEVER SEEN THE SEVEN KINGDOMS. THEY ARE NOTHING TO HIM.

PLEASE. HELP ME MAKE HIM UNDERSTAND.

SHE HAD NEVER SEEN THE SEVEN KINGDOMS EITHER, YET SHE FELT SHE KNEW THEM FROM THE TALES HER BROTHER TOLD. BUT HE WAS DEAD NOW, AND HIS PROMISES WITH HIM.

THE DOTHRAKI DO THINGS IN THEIR OWN TIME. HAVE PATIENCE. WE WILL GO HOME, I PROMISE YOU.

HOME? WHAT WAS HOME TO HER? A FEW TALES, THE FADING MEMORY OF A RED DOOR.

A GREAT CARAVAN ARRIVED IN THE NIGHT, KHALEESI. ILLYRIO MAY HAVE SENT A LETTER. WOULD YOU CARE TO VISIT THE WESTERN MARKET?

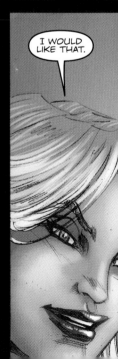

I WOULD LIKE THAT.

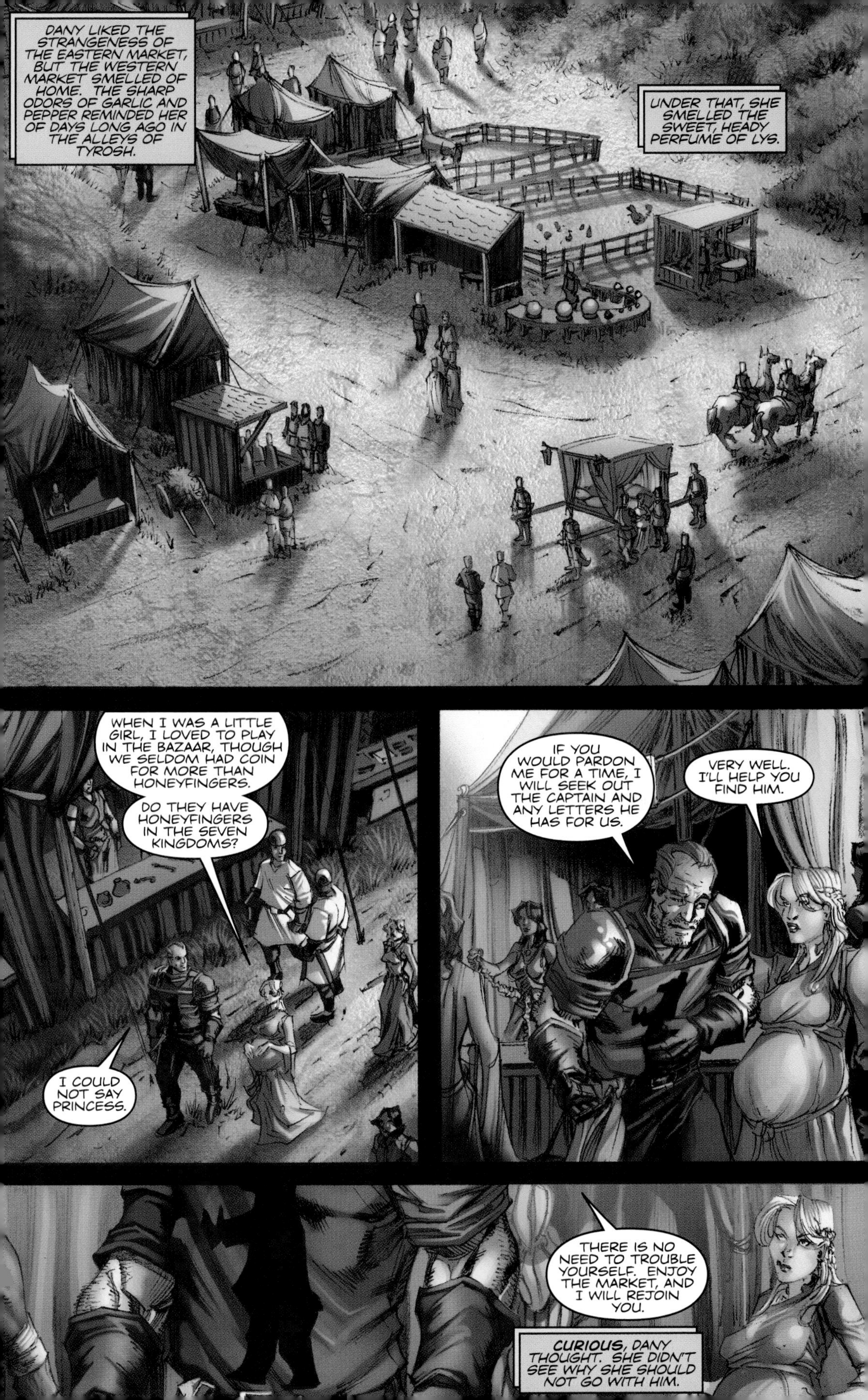
DANY LIKED THE STRANGENESS OF THE EASTERN MARKET, BUT THE WESTERN MARKET SMELLED OF HOME. THE SHARP ODORS OF GARLIC AND PEPPER REMINDED HER OF DAYS LONG AGO IN THE ALLEYS OF TYROSH.
UNDER THAT, SHE SMELLED THE SWEET, HEADY PERFUME OF LYS.
WHEN I WAS A LITTLE GIRL, I LOVED TO PLAY IN THE BAZAAR, THOUGH WE SELDOM HAD COIN FOR MORE THAN HONEYFINGERS.
DO THEY HAVE HONEYFINGERS IN THE SEVEN KINGDOMS?
I COULD NOT SAY PRINCESS.
IF YOU WOULD PARDON ME FOR A TIME, I WILL SEEK OUT THE CAPTAIN AND ANY LETTERS HE HAS FOR US.
VERY WELL. I'LL HELP YOU FIND HIM.
THERE IS NO NEED TO TROUBLE YOURSELF. ENJOY THE MARKET, AND I WILL REJOIN YOU.
CURIOUS, DANY THOUGHT. SHE DIDN'T SEE WHY SHE SHOULD NOT GO WITH HIM.

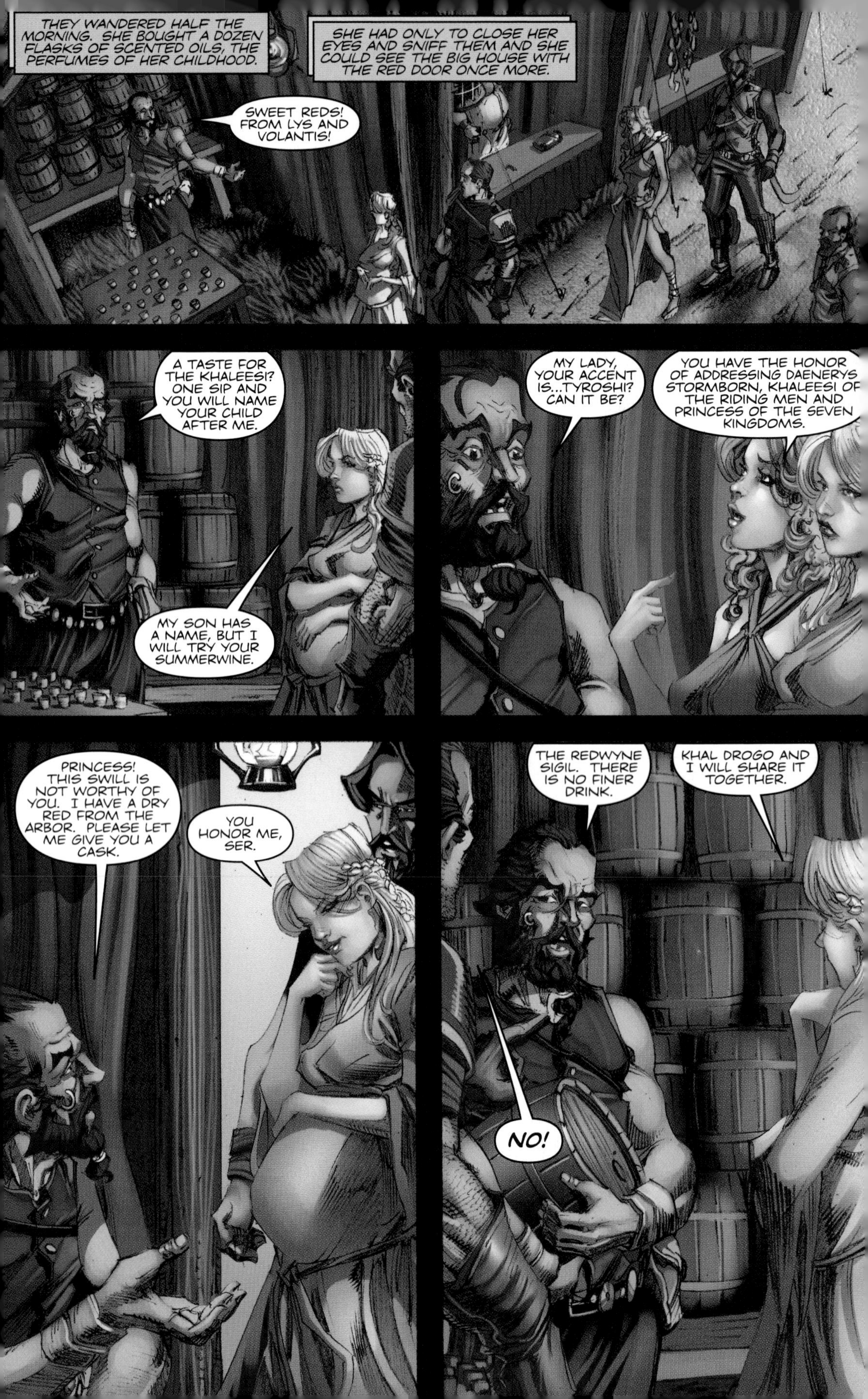
THEY WANDERED HALF THE MORNING. SHE BOUGHT A DOZEN FLASKS OF SCENTED OILS, THE PERFUMES OF HER CHILDHOOD.
SHE HAD ONLY TO CLOSE HER EYES AND SNIFF THEM AND SHE COULD SEE THE BIG HOUSE WITH THE RED DOOR ONCE MORE.
SWEET REDS! FROM LYS AND VOLANTIS!
A TASTE FOR THE KHALEESI? ONE SIP AND YOU WILL NAME YOUR CHILD AFTER ME.
MY SON HAS A NAME, BUT I WILL TRY YOUR SUMMERWINE.
MY LADY, YOUR ACCENT IS...TYROSHI? CAN IT BE?
YOU HAVE THE HONOR OF ADDRESSING DAENERYS STORMBORN, KHALEESI OF THE RIDING MEN AND PRINCESS OF THE SEVEN KINGDOMS.
PRINCESS! THIS SWILL IS NOT WORTHY OF YOU. I HAVE A DRY RED FROM THE ARBOR. PLEASE LET ME GIVE YOU A CASK.
YOU HONOR ME, SER.
THE REDWYNE SIGIL. THERE IS NO FINER DRINK.
KHAL DROGO AND I WILL SHARE IT TOGETHER.
NO!

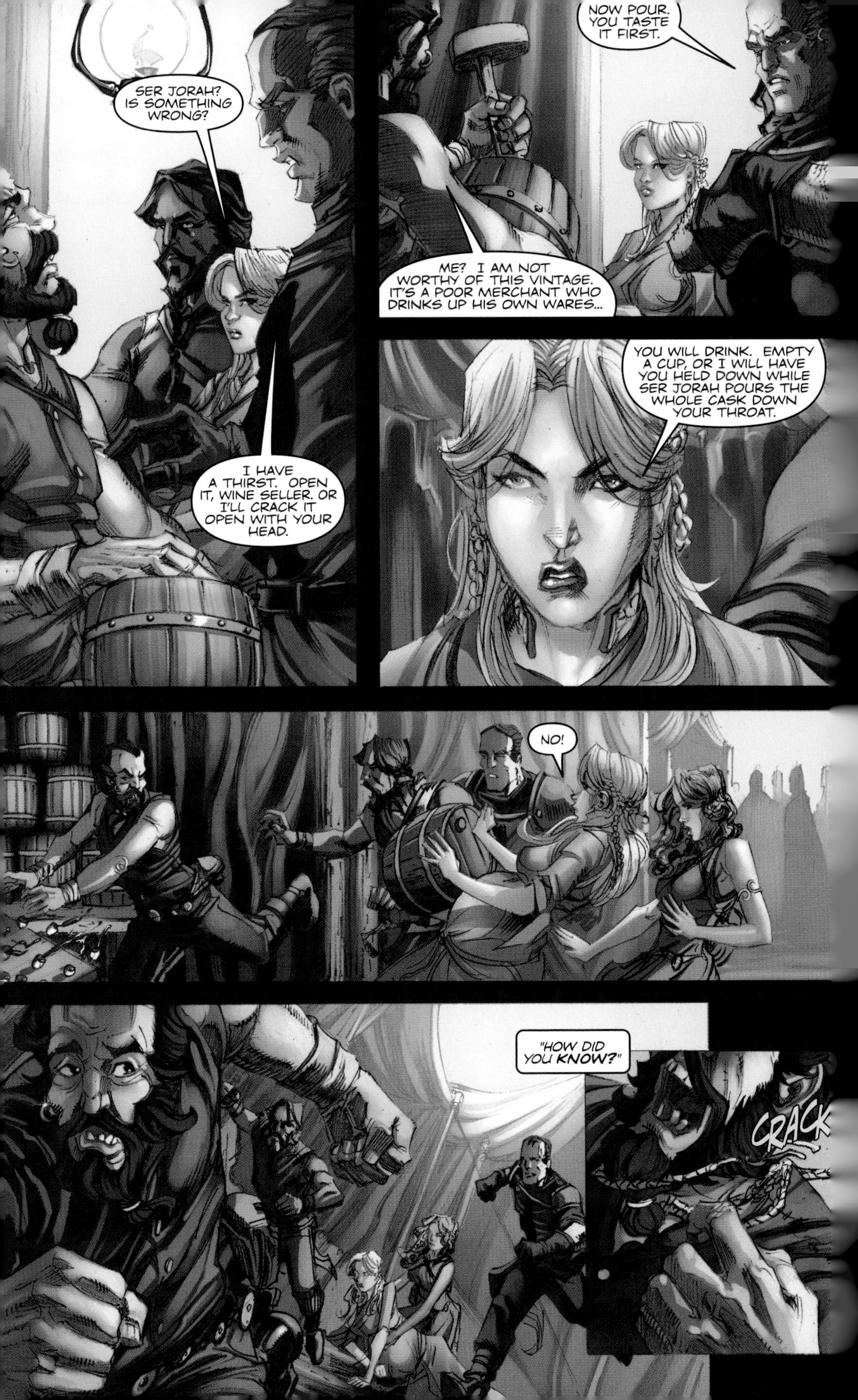

SER JORAH? IS SOMETHING WRONG?
I HAVE A THIRST. OPEN IT, WINE SELLER. OR I'LL CRACK IT OPEN WITH YOUR HEAD.
NOW POUR. YOU TASTE IT FIRST.
ME? I AM NOT WORTHY OF THIS VINTAGE. IT'S A POOR MERCHANT WHO DRINKS UP HIS OWN WARES...
YOU WILL DRINK. EMPTY A CUP, OR I WILL HAVE YOU HELD DOWN WHILE SER JORAH POURS THE WHOLE CASK DOWN YOUR THROAT.
NO!
"HOW DID YOU KNOW?"
CRACK

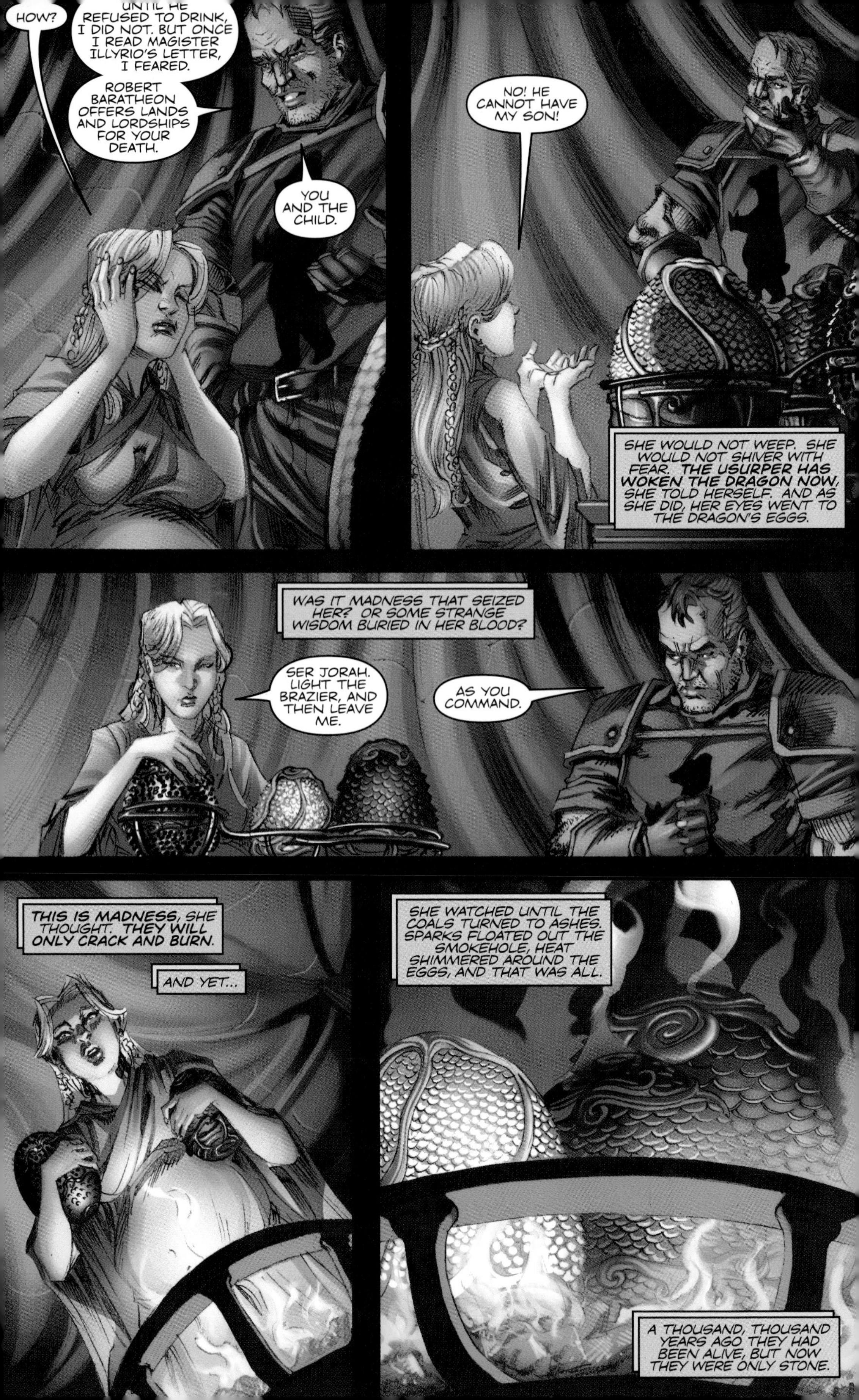
HOW?
UNTIL HE REFUSED TO DRINK, I DID NOT. BUT ONCE I READ MAGISTER ILLYRIO'S LETTER, I FEARED.
ROBERT BARATHEON OFFERS LANDS AND LORDSHIPS FOR YOUR DEATH.
YOU AND THE CHILD.
NO! HE CANNOT HAVE MY SON!
SHE WOULD NOT WEEP. SHE WOULD NOT SHIVER WITH FEAR. THE USURPER HAS WOKEN THE DRAGON NOW, SHE TOLD HERSELF. AND AS SHE DID, HER EYES WENT TO THE DRAGON'S EGGS.
WAS IT MADNESS THAT SEIZED HER? OR SOME STRANGE WISDOM BURIED IN HER BLOOD?
SER JORAH. LIGHT THE BRAZIER, AND THEN LEAVE ME.
AS YOU COMMAND.
THIS IS MADNESS, SHE THOUGHT. THEY WILL ONLY CRACK AND BURN.
AND YET...
SHE WATCHED UNTIL THE COALS TURNED TO ASHES. SPARKS FLOATED OUT THE SMOKEHOLE, HEAT SHIMMERED AROUND THE EGGS, AND THAT WAS ALL.
A THOUSAND, THOUSAND YEARS AGO THEY HAD BEEN ALIVE, BUT NOW THEY WERE ONLY STONE.

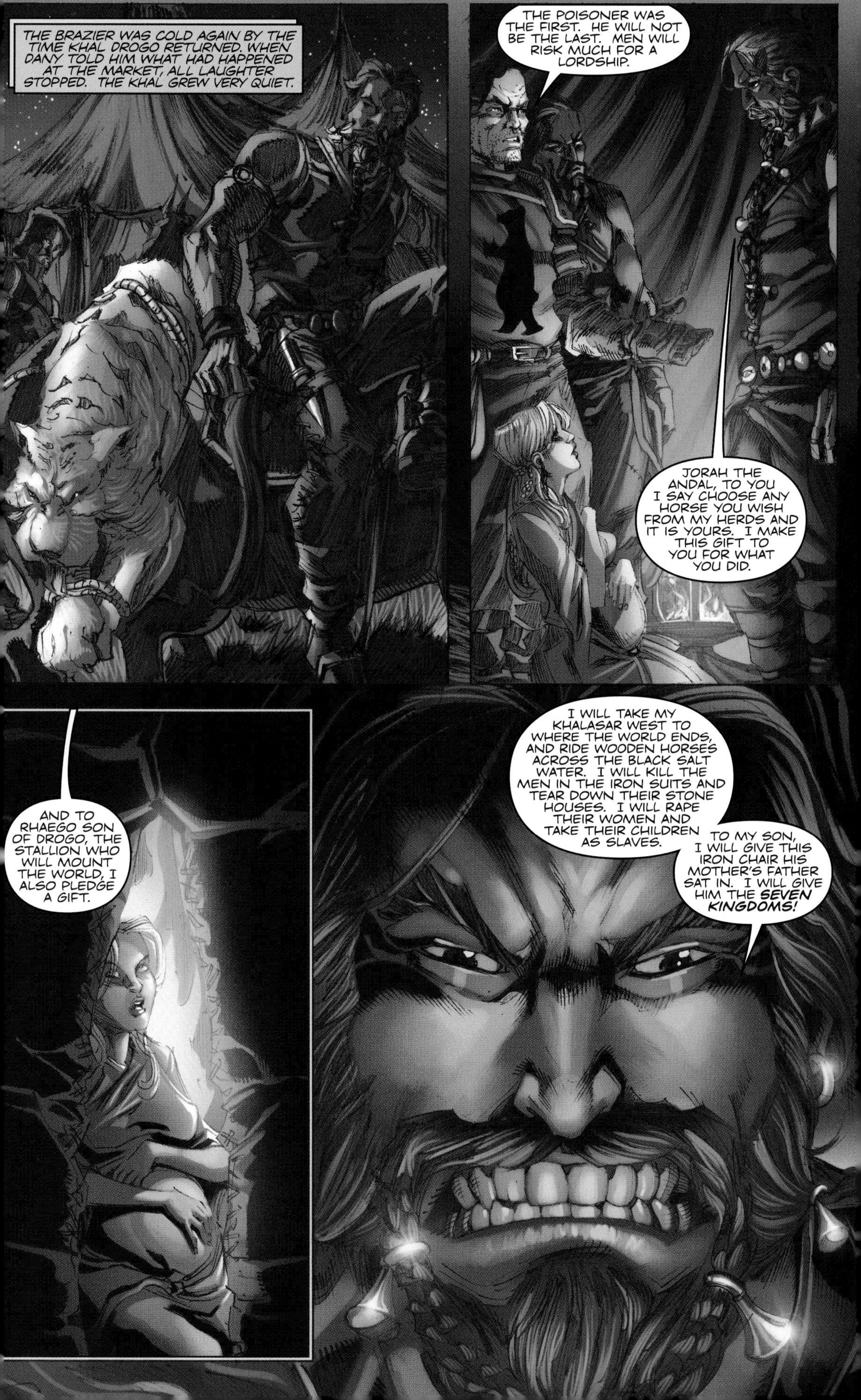
THE BRAZIER WAS COLD AGAIN BY THE TIME KHAL DROGO RETURNED. WHEN DANY TOLD HIM WHAT HAD HAPPENED AT THE MARKET, ALL LAUGHTER STOPPED. THE KHAL GREW VERY QUIET.
THE POISONER WAS THE FIRST. HE WILL NOT BE THE LAST. MEN WILL RISK MUCH FOR A LORDSHIP.
JORAH THE ANDAL, TO YOU I SAY CHOOSE ANY HORSE YOU WISH FROM MY HERDS AND IT IS YOURS. I MAKE THIS GIFT TO YOU FOR WHAT YOU DID.
AND TO RHAEGO SON OF DROGO, THE STALLION WHO WILL MOUNT THE WORLD, I ALSO PLEDGE A GIFT.
I WILL TAKE MY KHALASAR WEST TO WHERE THE WORLD ENDS, AND RIDE WOODEN HORSES ACROSS THE BLACK SALT WATER. I WILL KILL THE MEN IN THE IRON SUITS AND TEAR DOWN THEIR STONE HOUSES. I WILL RAPE THEIR WOMEN AND TAKE THEIR CHILDREN AS SLAVES.
TO MY SON, I WILL GIVE THIS IRON CHAIR HIS MOTHER'S FATHER SAT IN. I WILL GIVE HIM THE **SEVEN KINGDOMS!**

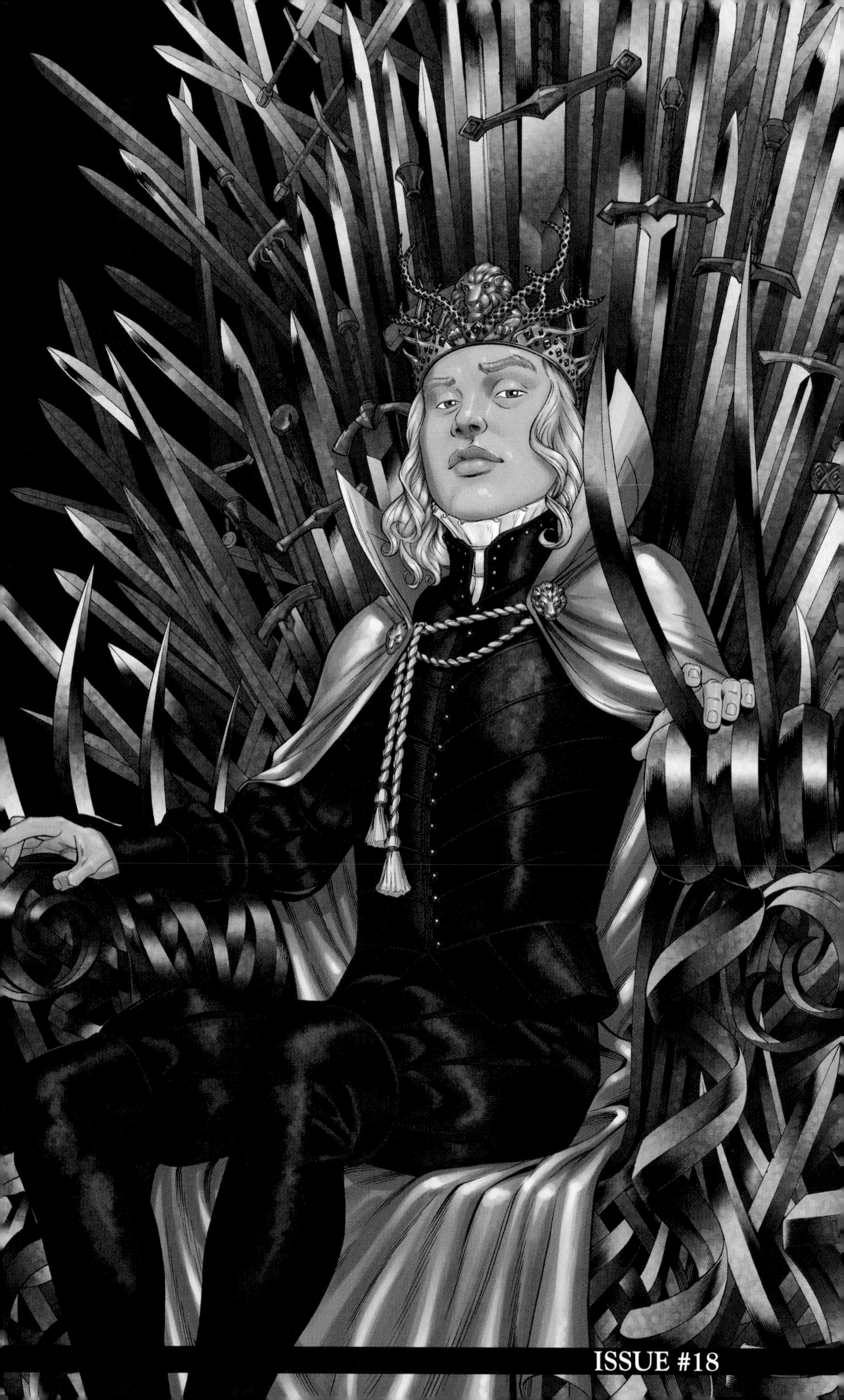

ISSUE #18

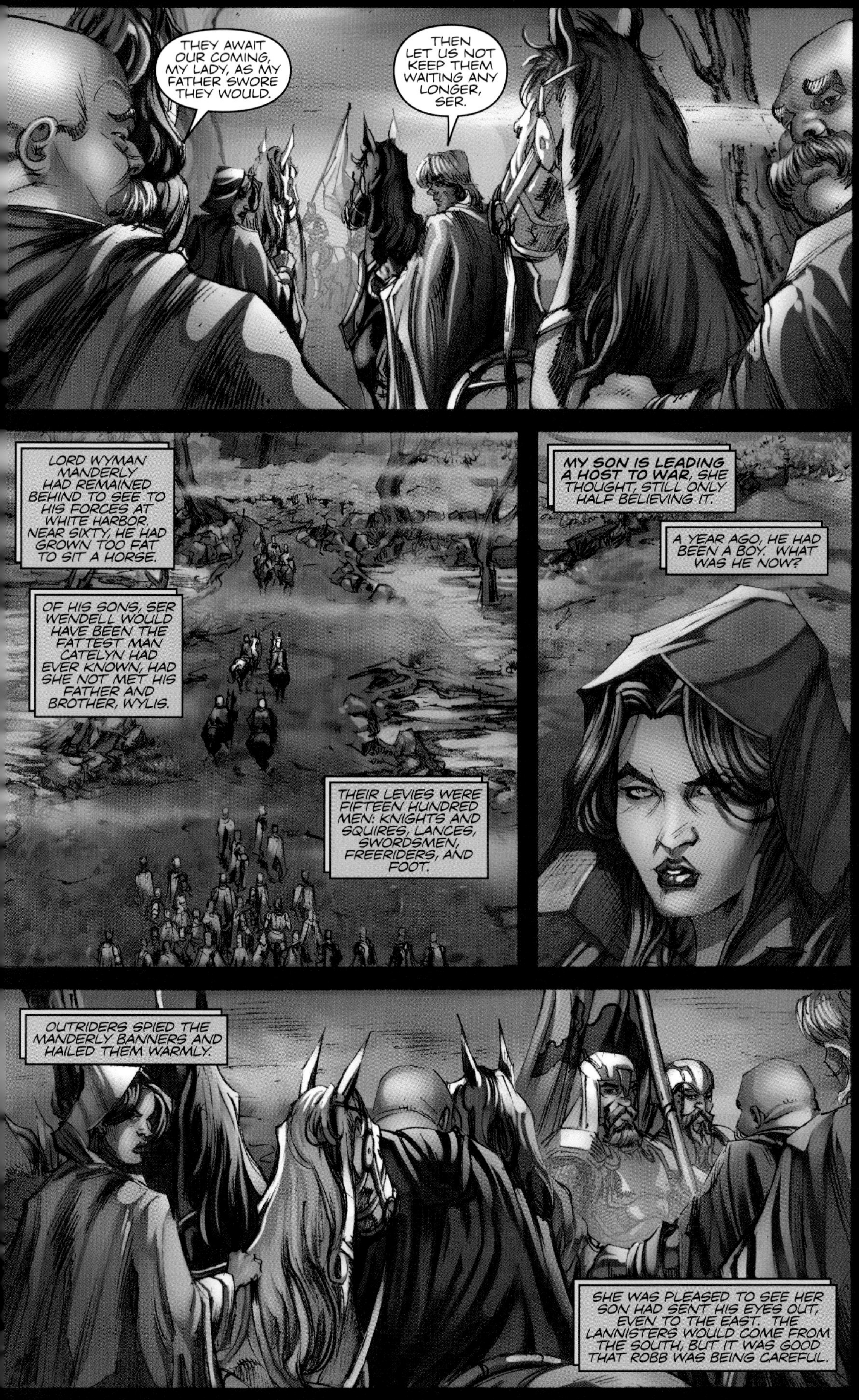

THEY AWAIT OUR COMING, MY LADY, AS MY FATHER SWORE THEY WOULD.
THEN LET US NOT KEEP THEM WAITING ANY LONGER, SER.
LORD WYMAN MANDERLY HAD REMAINED BEHIND TO SEE TO HIS FORCES AT WHITE HARBOR. NEAR SIXTY, HE HAD GROWN TOO FAT TO SIT A HORSE.
OF HIS SONS, SER WENDELL WOULD HAVE BEEN THE FATTEST MAN CATELYN HAD EVER KNOWN, HAD SHE NOT MET HIS FATHER AND BROTHER, WYLIS.
THEIR LEVIES WERE FIFTEEN HUNDRED MEN: KNIGHTS AND SQUIRES, LANCES, SWORDSMEN, FREERIDERS, AND FOOT.
MY SON IS LEADING A HOST TO WAR, SHE THOUGHT, STILL ONLY HALF BELIEVING IT.
A YEAR AGO, HE HAD BEEN A BOY. WHAT WAS HE NOW?
OUTRIDERS SPIED THE MANDERLY BANNERS AND HAILED THEM WARMLY.
SHE WAS PLEASED TO SEE HER SON HAD SENT HIS EYES OUT, EVEN TO THE EAST. THE LANNISTERS WOULD COME FROM THE SOUTH, BUT IT WAS GOOD THAT ROBB WAS BEING CAREFUL.

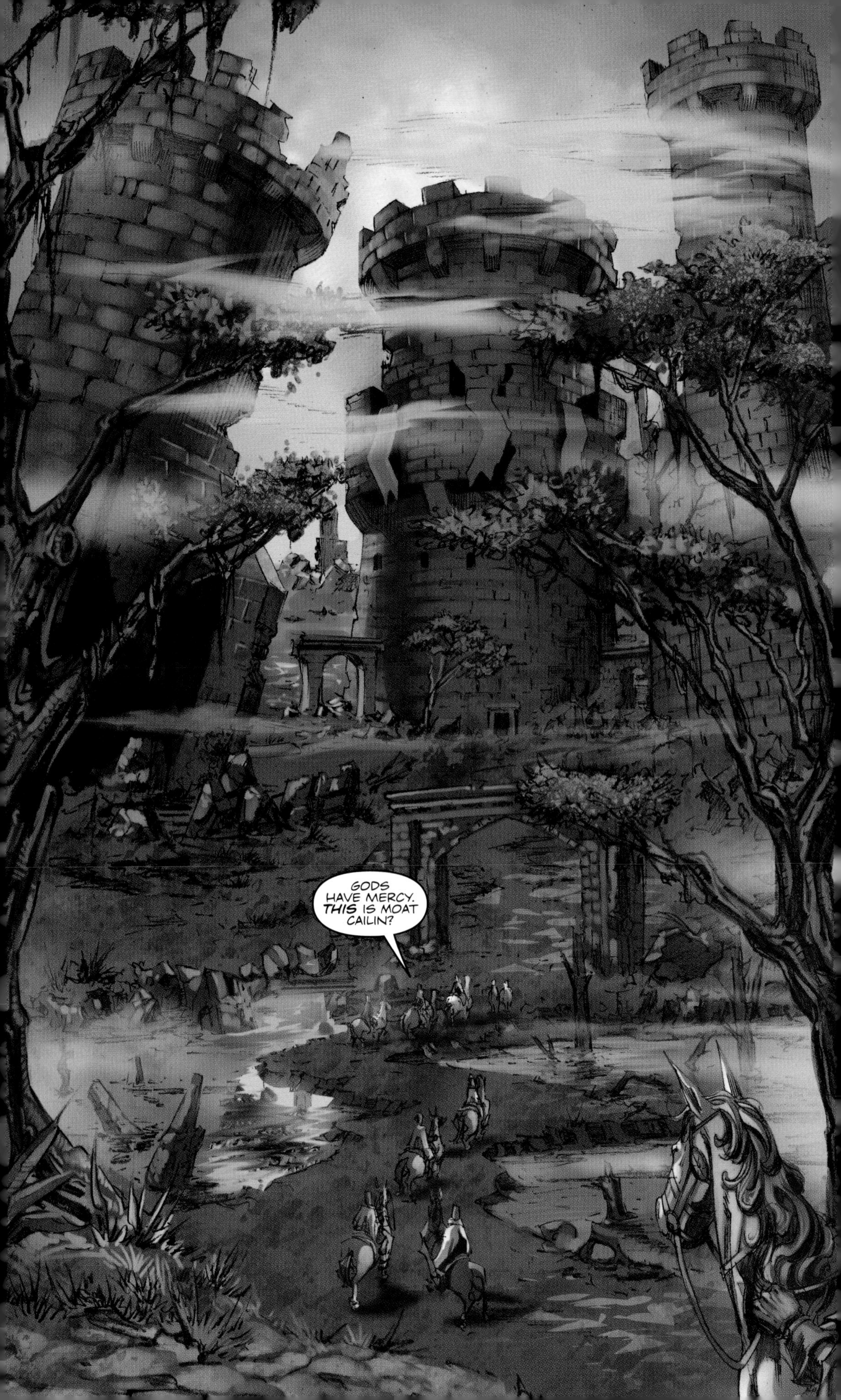
GODS HAVE MERCY. THIS IS MOAT CAILIN?

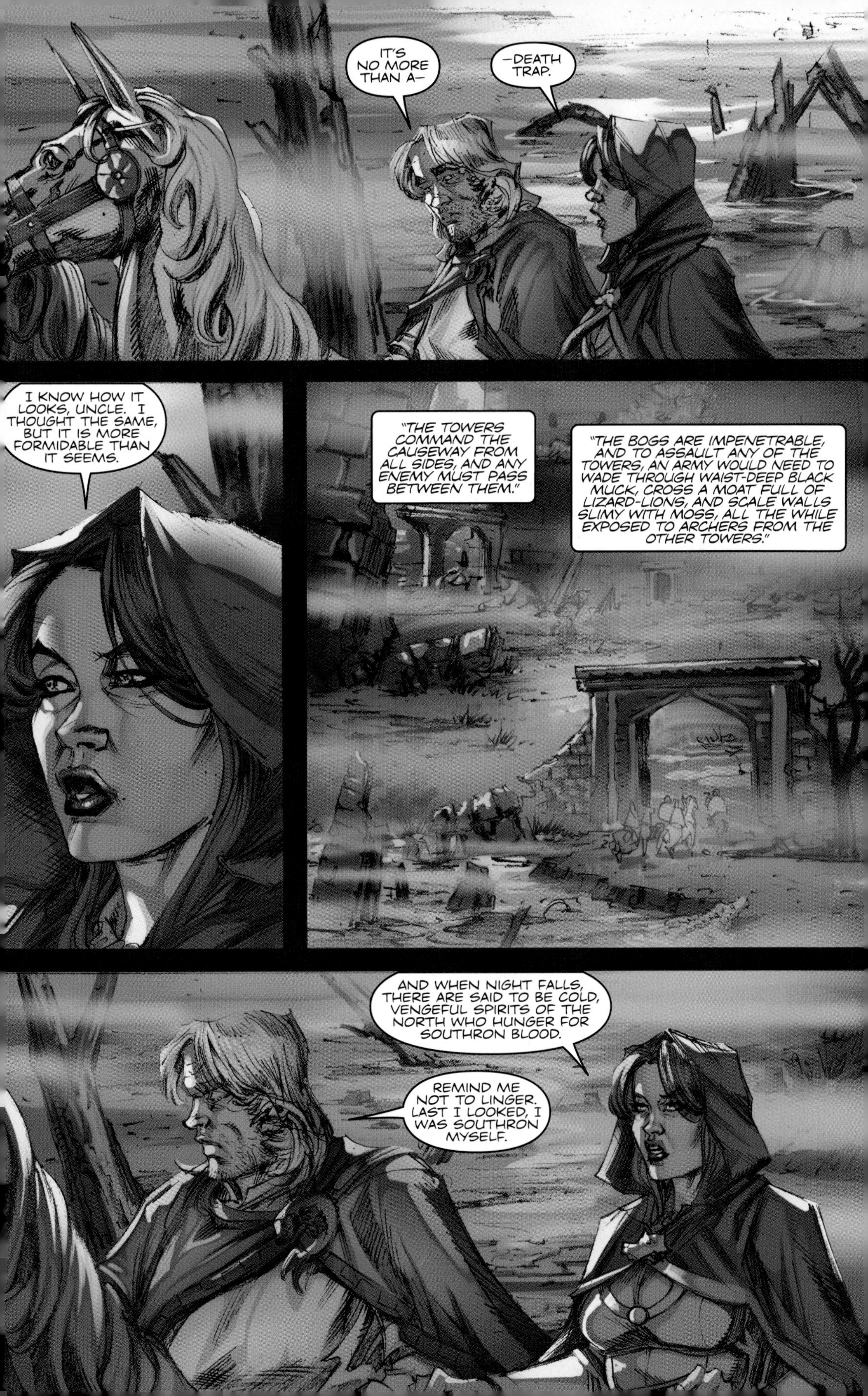
IT'S NO MORE THAN A—
—DEATH TRAP.
I KNOW HOW IT LOOKS, UNCLE. I THOUGHT THE SAME, BUT IT IS MORE FORMIDABLE THAN IT SEEMS.
"THE TOWERS COMMAND THE CAUSEWAY FROM ALL SIDES, AND ANY ENEMY MUST PASS BETWEEN THEM."
"THE BOGS ARE IMPENETRABLE, AND TO ASSAULT ANY OF THE TOWERS, AN ARMY WOULD NEED TO WADE THROUGH WAIST-DEEP BLACK MUCK, CROSS A MOAT FULL OF LIZARD-LIONS, AND SCALE WALLS SLIMY WITH MOSS, ALL THE WHILE EXPOSED TO ARCHERS FROM THE OTHER TOWERS."
AND WHEN NIGHT FALLS, THERE ARE SAID TO BE COLD, VENGEFUL SPIRITS OF THE NORTH WHO HUNGER FOR SOUTHRON BLOOD.
REMIND ME NOT TO LINGER. LAST I LOOKED, I WAS SOUTHRON MYSELF.

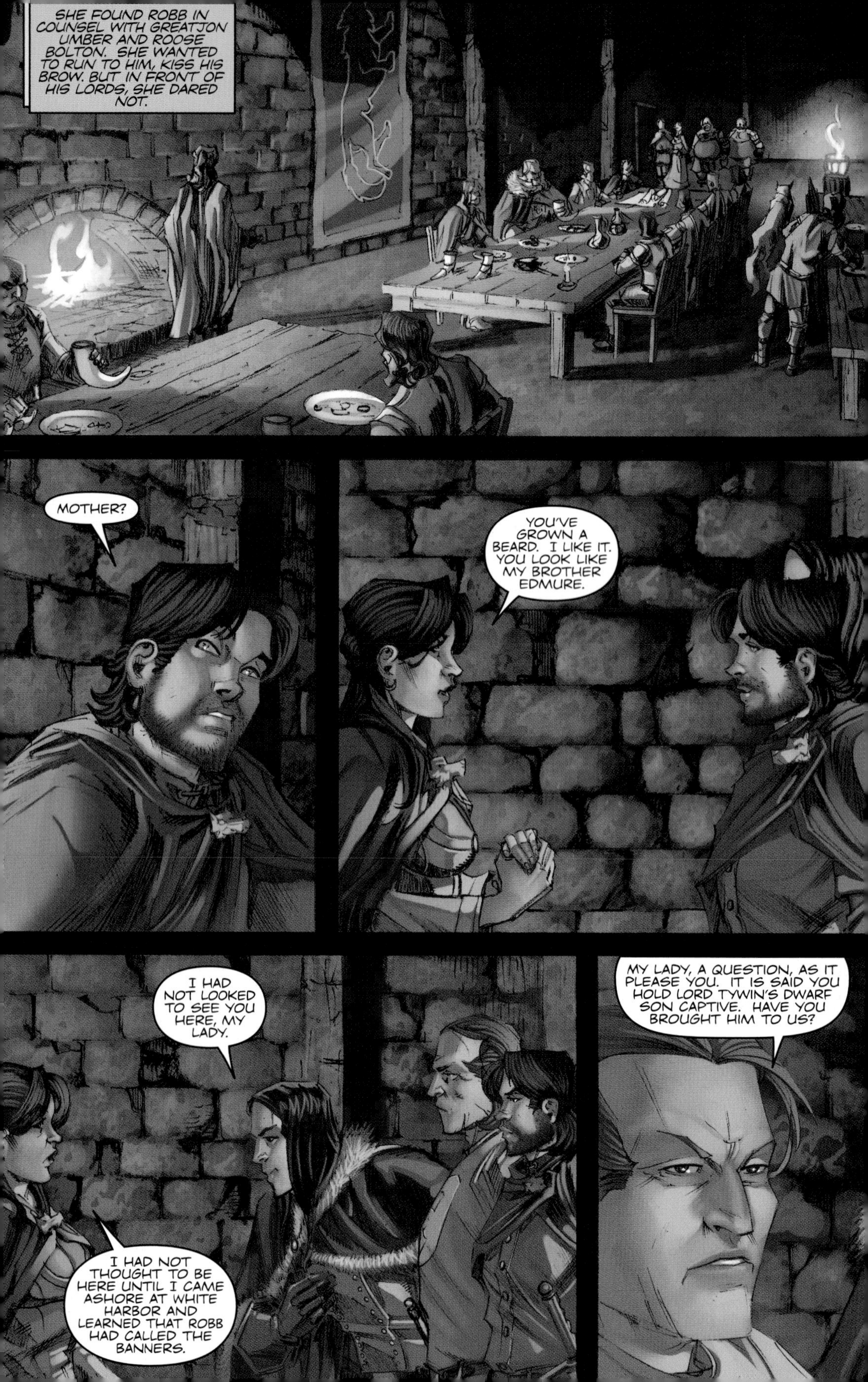
SHE FOUND ROBB IN COUNSEL WITH GREATJON UMBER AND ROOSE BOLTON. SHE WANTED TO RUN TO HIM, KISS HIS BROW. BUT IN FRONT OF HIS LORDS, SHE DARED NOT.
MOTHER?
YOU'VE GROWN A BEARD. I LIKE IT. YOU LOOK LIKE MY BROTHER EDMURE.
I HAD NOT LOOKED TO SEE YOU HERE, MY LADY.
I HAD NOT THOUGHT TO BE HERE UNTIL I CAME ASHORE AT WHITE HARBOR AND LEARNED THAT ROBB HAD CALLED THE BANNERS.
MY LADY, A QUESTION, AS IT PLEASE YOU. IT IS SAID YOU HOLD LORD TYWIN'S DWARF SON CAPTIVE. HAVE YOU BROUGHT HIM TO US?

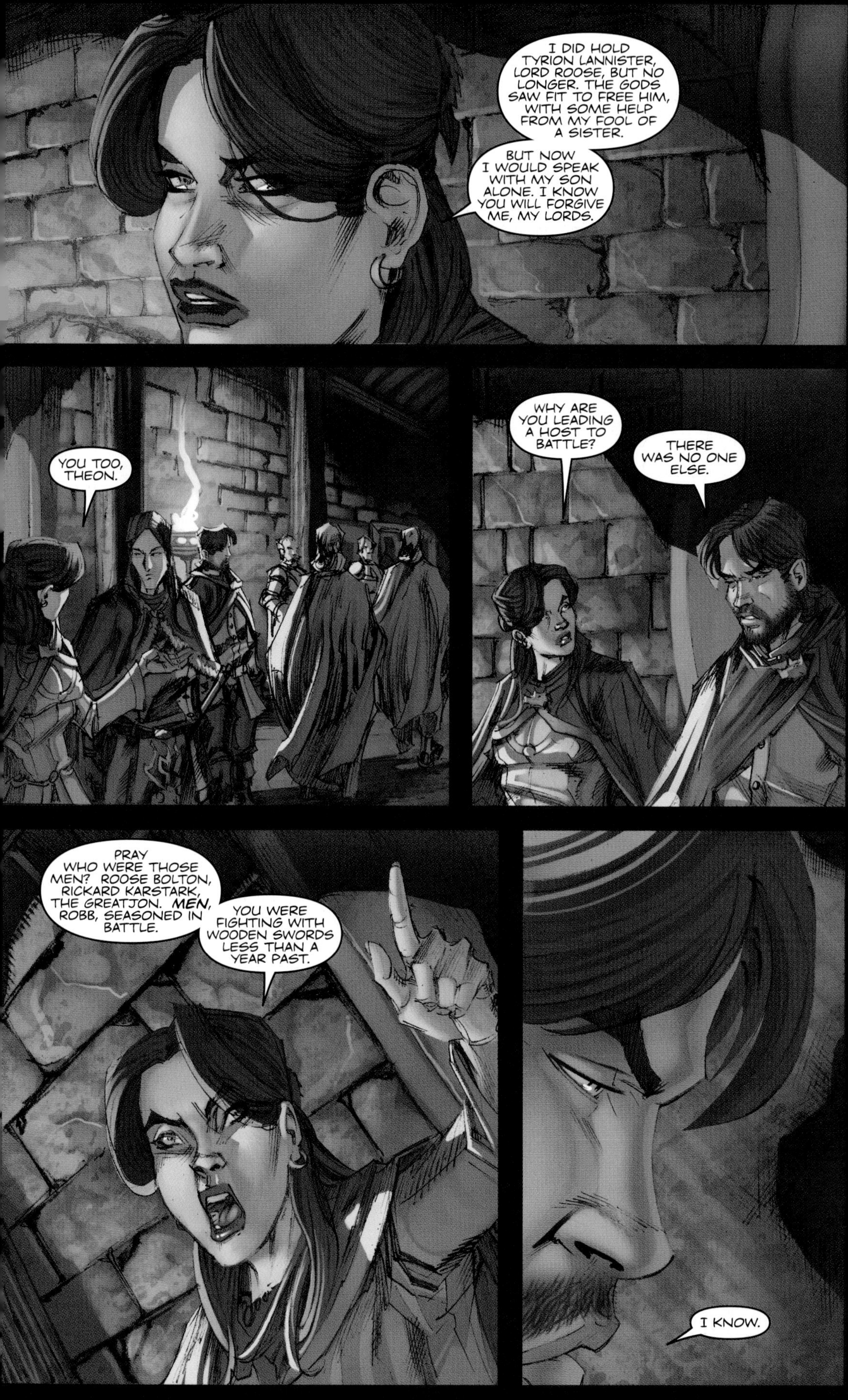
I DID HOLD TYRION LANNISTER, LORD ROOSE, BUT NO LONGER. THE GODS SAW FIT TO FREE HIM, WITH SOME HELP FROM MY FOOL OF A SISTER.
BUT NOW I WOULD SPEAK WITH MY SON ALONE. I KNOW YOU WILL FORGIVE ME, MY LORDS.
YOU TOO, THEON.
WHY ARE YOU LEADING A HOST TO BATTLE?
THERE WAS NO ONE ELSE.
PRAY WHO WERE THOSE MEN? ROOSE BOLTON, RICKARD KARSTARK, THE GREATJON. *MEN*, ROBB, SEASONED IN BATTLE.
YOU WERE FIGHTING WITH WOODEN SWORDS LESS THAN A YEAR PAST.
I KNOW.

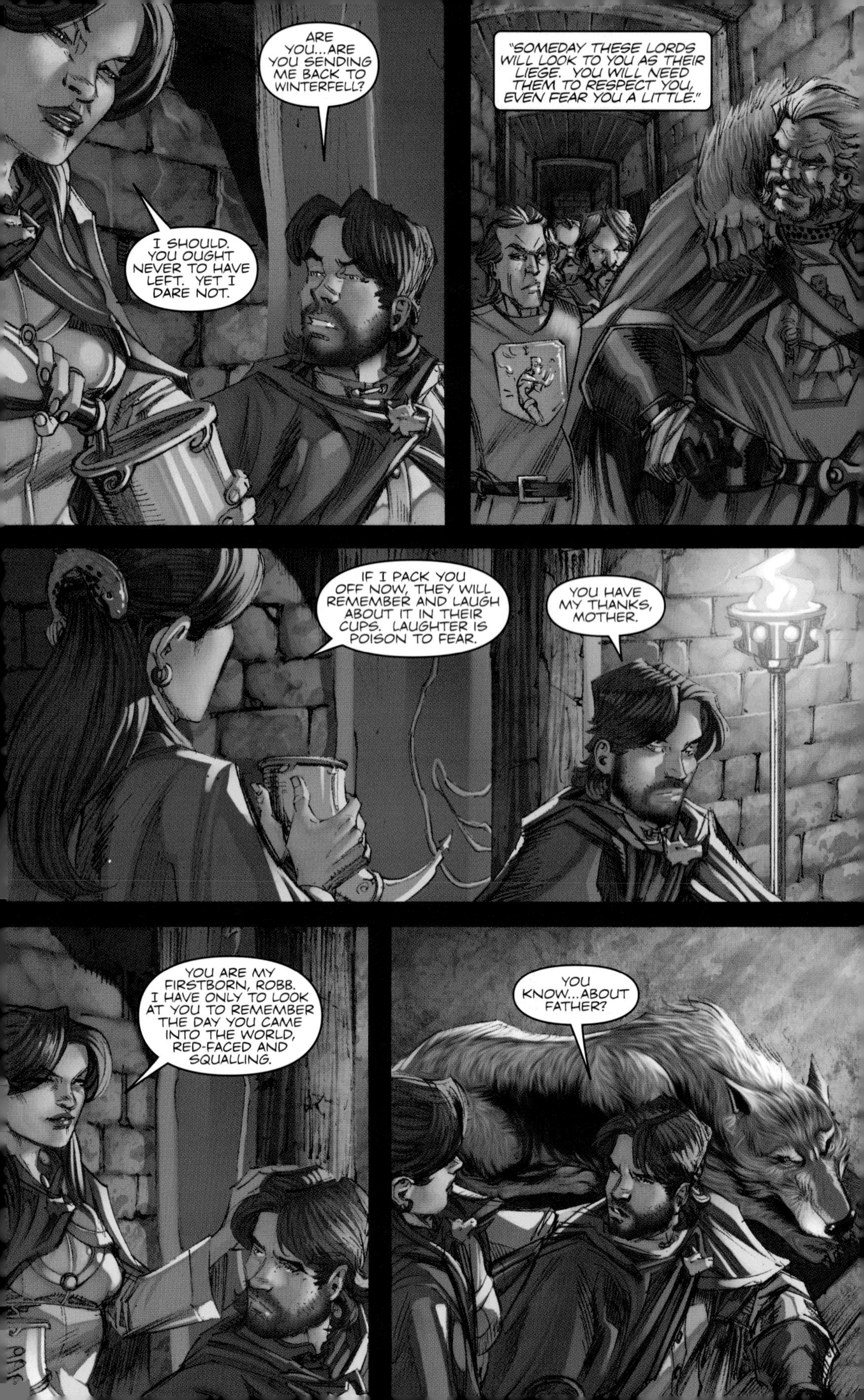
ARE YOU...ARE YOU SENDING ME BACK TO WINTERFELL?
I SHOULD. YOU OUGHT NEVER TO HAVE LEFT. YET I DARE NOT.
"SOMEDAY THESE LORDS WILL LOOK TO YOU AS THEIR LIEGE. YOU WILL NEED THEM TO RESPECT YOU, EVEN FEAR YOU A LITTLE."
IF I PACK YOU OFF NOW, THEY WILL REMEMBER AND LAUGH ABOUT IT IN THEIR CUPS. LAUGHTER IS POISON TO FEAR.
YOU HAVE MY THANKS, MOTHER.
YOU ARE MY FIRSTBORN, ROBB. I HAVE ONLY TO LOOK AT YOU TO REMEMBER THE DAY YOU CAME INTO THE WORLD, RED-FACED AND SQUALLING.
YOU KNOW...ABOUT FATHER?

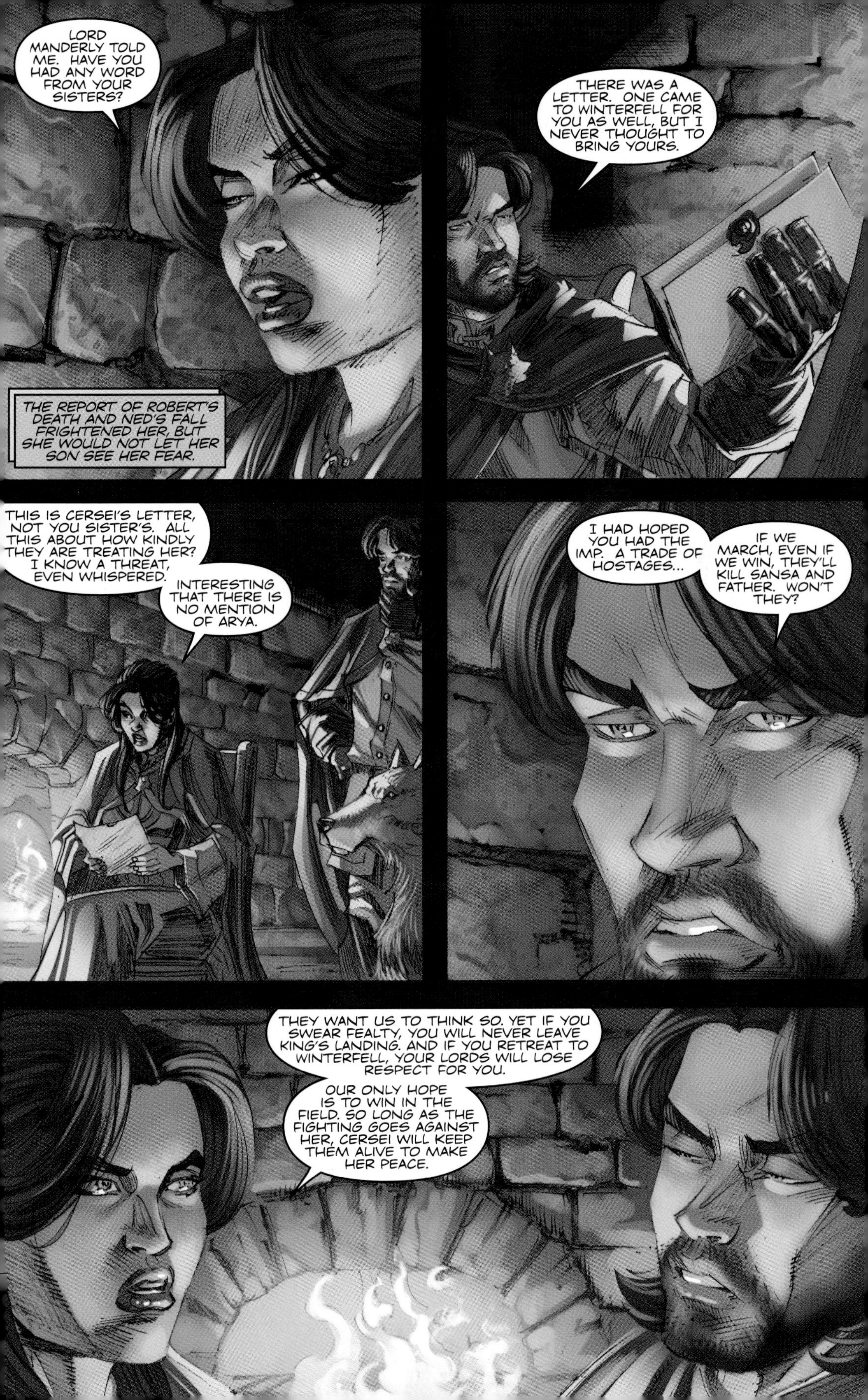
LORD MANDERLY TOLD ME. HAVE YOU HAD ANY WORD FROM YOUR SISTERS?
THE REPORT OF ROBERT'S DEATH AND NED'S FALL FRIGHTENED HER, BUT SHE WOULD NOT LET HER SON SEE HER FEAR.
THERE WAS A LETTER. ONE CAME TO WINTERFELL FOR YOU AS WELL, BUT I NEVER THOUGHT TO BRING YOURS.
THIS IS CERSEI'S LETTER, NOT YOU SISTER'S. ALL THIS ABOUT HOW KINDLY THEY ARE TREATING HER? I KNOW A THREAT, EVEN WHISPERED.
INTERESTING THAT THERE IS NO MENTION OF ARYA.
I HAD HOPED YOU HAD THE IMP. A TRADE OF HOSTAGES...
IF WE MARCH, EVEN IF WE WIN, THEY'LL KILL SANSA AND FATHER. WON'T THEY?
THEY WANT US TO THINK SO. YET IF YOU SWEAR FEALTY, YOU WILL NEVER LEAVE KING'S LANDING. AND IF YOU RETREAT TO WINTERFELL, YOUR LORDS WILL LOSE RESPECT FOR YOU.
OUR ONLY HOPE IS TO WIN IN THE FIELD. SO LONG AS THE FIGHTING GOES AGAINST HER, CERSEI WILL KEEP THEM ALIVE TO MAKE HER PEACE.

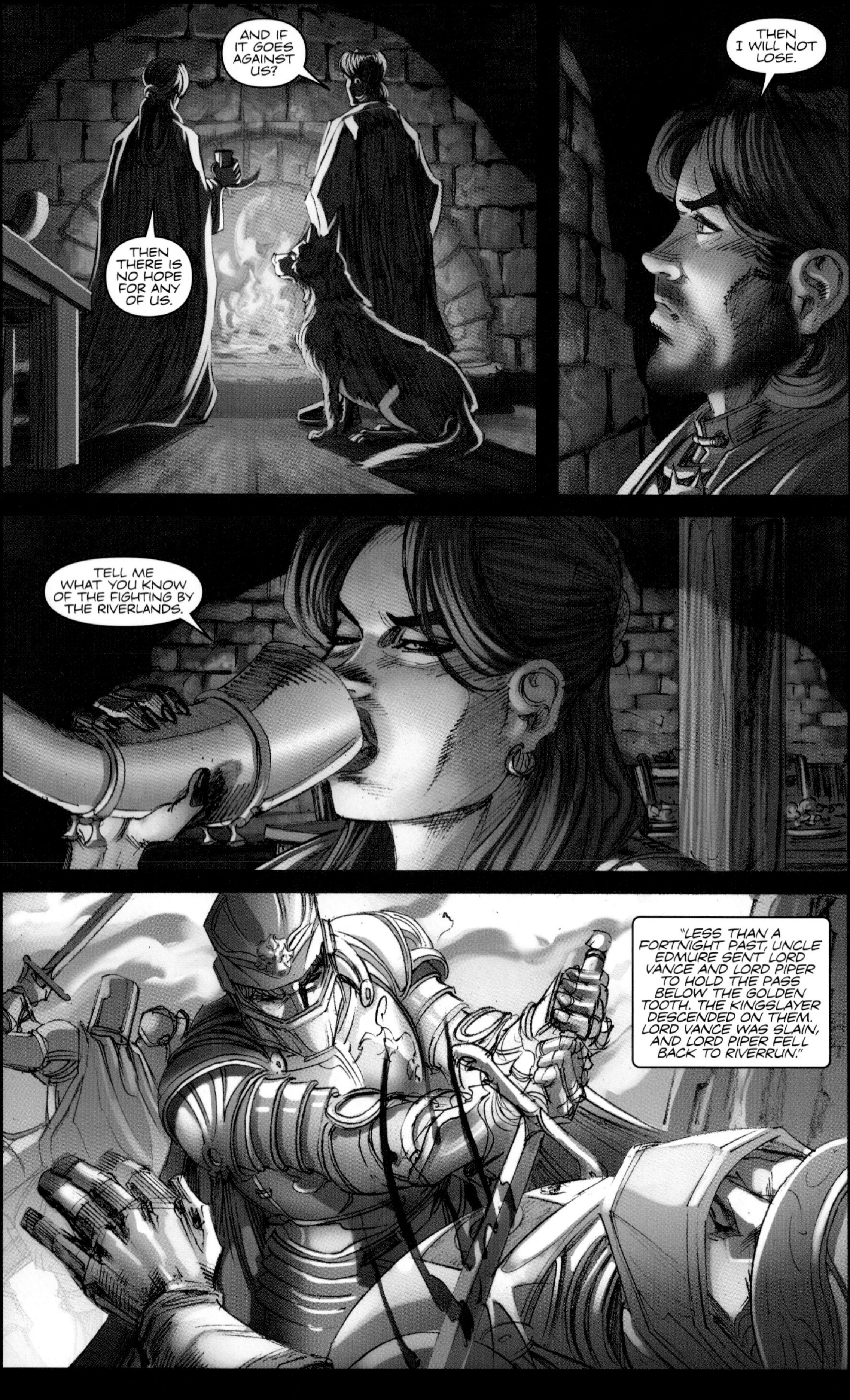
AND IF IT GOES AGAINST US?
THEN THERE IS NO HOPE FOR ANY OF US.
THEN I WILL NOT LOSE.
TELL ME WHAT YOU KNOW OF THE FIGHTING BY THE RIVERLANDS.
"LESS THAN A FORTNIGHT PAST, UNCLE EDMURE SENT LORD VANCE AND LORD PIPER TO HOLD THE PASS BELOW THE GOLDEN TOOTH. THE KINGSLAYER DESCENDED ON THEM. LORD VANCE WAS SLAIN, AND LORD PIPER FELL BACK TO RIVERRUN."

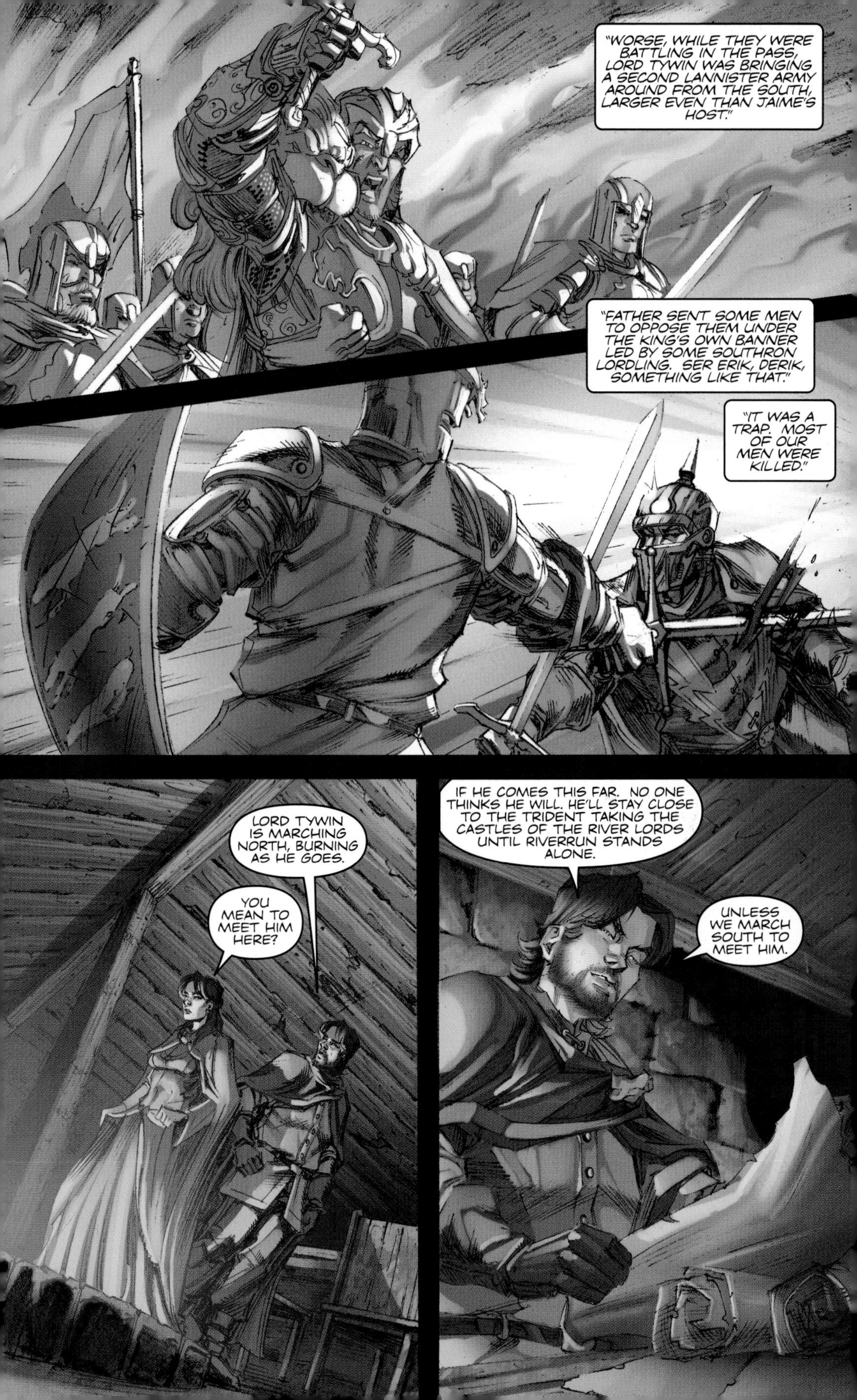
"WORSE, WHILE THEY WERE BATTLING IN THE PASS, LORD TYWIN WAS BRINGING A SECOND LANNISTER ARMY AROUND FROM THE SOUTH, LARGER EVEN THAN JAIME'S HOST."
"FATHER SENT SOME MEN TO OPPOSE THEM UNDER THE KING'S OWN BANNER LED BY SOME SOUTHRON LORDLING. SER ERIK, DERIK, SOMETHING LIKE THAT."
"IT WAS A TRAP. MOST OF OUR MEN WERE KILLED."
LORD TYWIN IS MARCHING NORTH, BURNING AS HE GOES.
YOU MEAN TO MEET HIM HERE?
IF HE COMES THIS FAR. NO ONE THINKS HE WILL. HE'LL STAY CLOSE TO THE TRIDENT TAKING THE CASTLES OF THE RIVER LORDS UNTIL RIVERRUN STANDS ALONE.
UNLESS WE MARCH SOUTH TO MEET HIM.

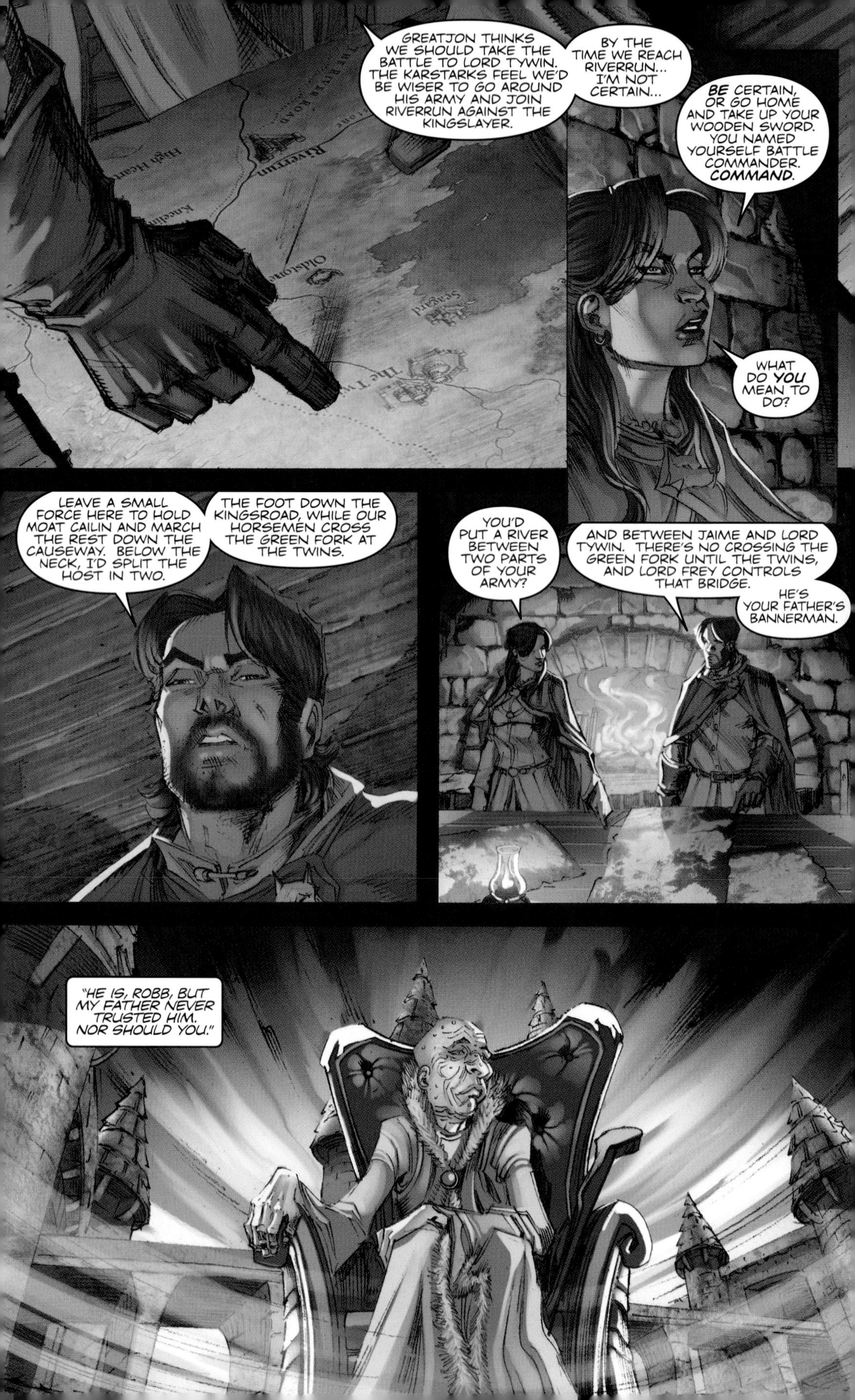
GREATJON THINKS WE SHOULD TAKE THE BATTLE TO LORD TYWIN. THE KARSTARKS FEEL WE'D BE WISER TO GO AROUND HIS ARMY AND JOIN RIVERRUN AGAINST THE KINGSLAYER.
BY THE TIME WE REACH RIVERRUN... I'M NOT CERTAIN...
**BE** CERTAIN, OR GO HOME AND TAKE UP YOUR WOODEN SWORD. YOU NAMED YOURSELF BATTLE COMMANDER. ***COMMAND***.
WHAT DO **YOU** MEAN TO DO?
LEAVE A SMALL FORCE HERE TO HOLD MOAT CAILIN AND MARCH THE REST DOWN THE CAUSEWAY. BELOW THE NECK, I'D SPLIT THE HOST IN TWO.
THE FOOT DOWN THE KINGSROAD, WHILE OUR HORSEMEN CROSS THE GREEN FORK AT THE TWINS.
YOU'D PUT A RIVER BETWEEN TWO PARTS OF YOUR ARMY?
AND BETWEEN JAIME AND LORD TYWIN. THERE'S NO CROSSING THE GREEN FORK UNTIL THE TWINS, AND LORD FREY CONTROLS THAT BRIDGE.
HE'S YOUR FATHER'S BANNERMAN.
*"HE IS, ROBB, BUT MY FATHER NEVER TRUSTED HIM. NOR SHOULD YOU."*

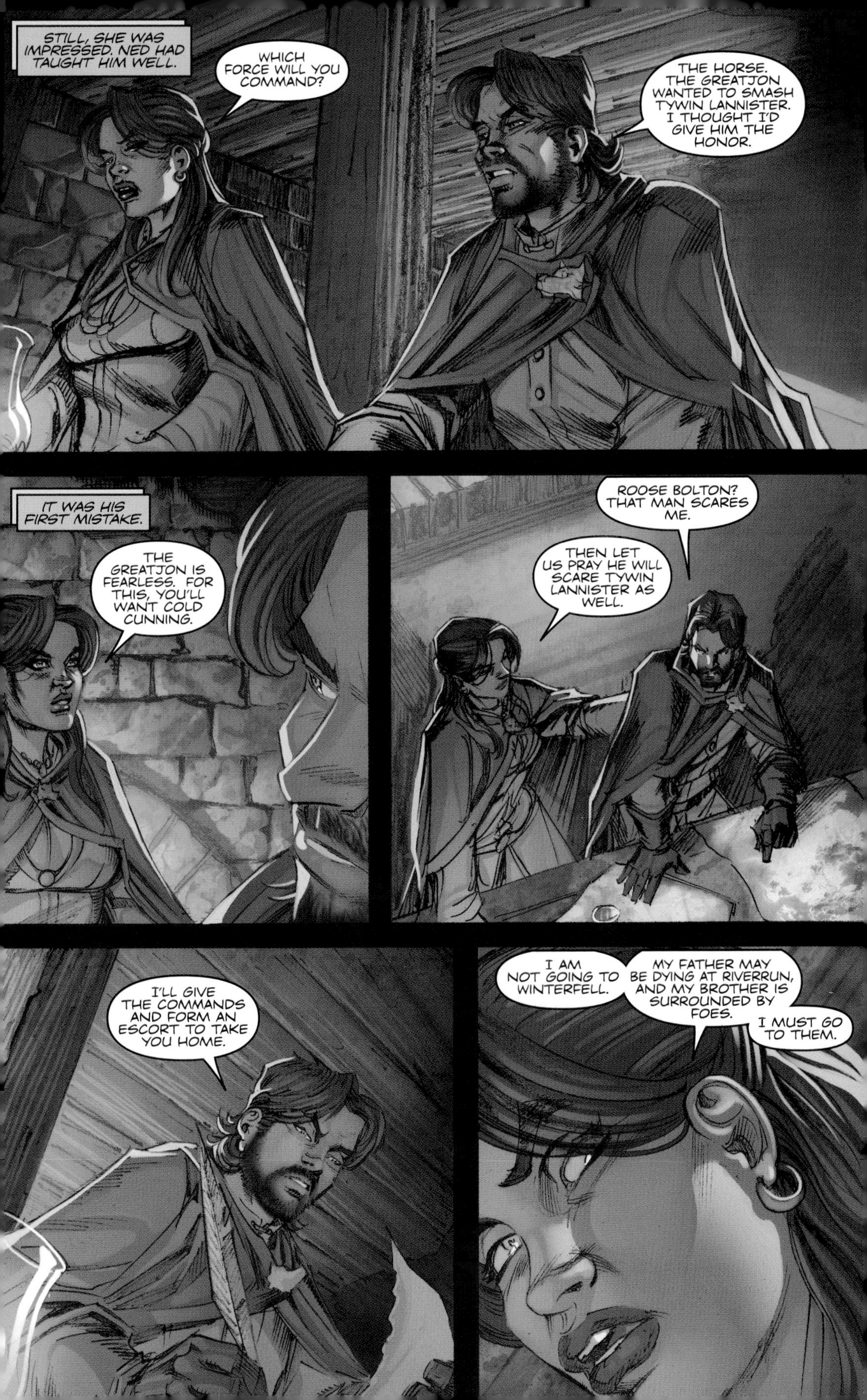
STILL, SHE WAS IMPRESSED. NED HAD TAUGHT HIM WELL.
WHICH FORCE WILL YOU COMMAND?
THE HORSE. THE GREATJON WANTED TO SMASH TYWIN LANNISTER. I THOUGHT I'D GIVE HIM THE HONOR.
IT WAS HIS FIRST MISTAKE.
THE GREATJON IS FEARLESS. FOR THIS, YOU'LL WANT COLD CUNNING.
ROOSE BOLTON? THAT MAN SCARES ME.
THEN LET US PRAY HE WILL SCARE TYWIN LANNISTER AS WELL.
I'LL GIVE THE COMMANDS AND FORM AN ESCORT TO TAKE YOU HOME.
I AM NOT GOING TO WINTERFELL.
MY FATHER MAY BE DYING AT RIVERRUN, AND MY BROTHER IS SURROUNDED BY FOES.
I MUST GO TO THEM.

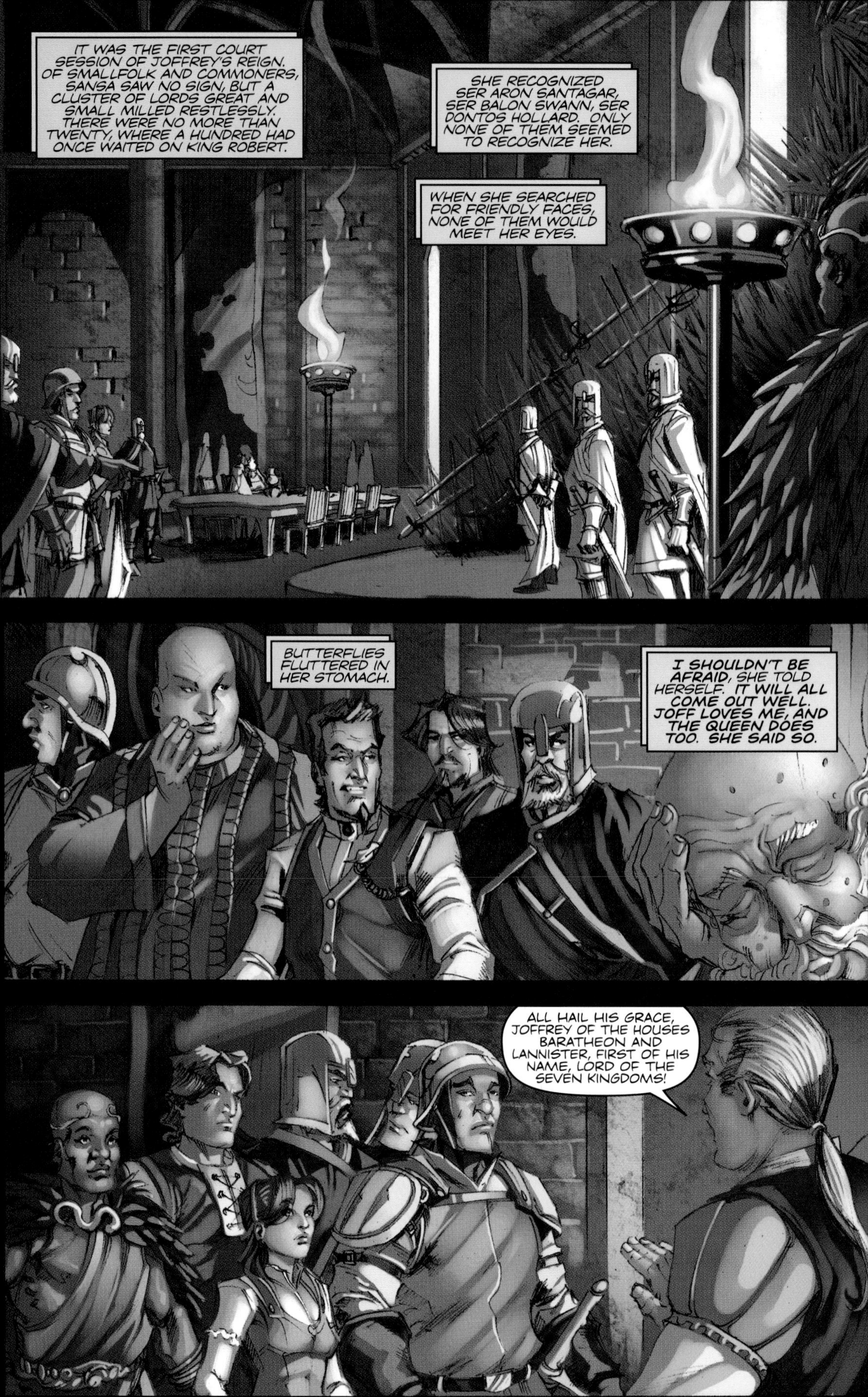
IT WAS THE FIRST COURT SESSION OF JOFFREY'S REIGN. OF SMALLFOLK AND COMMONERS, SANSA SAW NO SIGN, BUT A CLUSTER OF LORDS GREAT AND SMALL MILLED RESTLESSLY. THERE WERE NO MORE THAN TWENTY, WHERE A HUNDRED HAD ONCE WAITED ON KING ROBERT.
SHE RECOGNIZED SER ARON SANTAGAR, SER BALON SWANN, SER DONTOS HOLLARD. ONLY NONE OF THEM SEEMED TO RECOGNIZE HER.
WHEN SHE SEARCHED FOR FRIENDLY FACES, NONE OF THEM WOULD MEET HER EYES.
BUTTERFLIES FLUTTERED IN HER STOMACH.
I SHOULDN'T BE AFRAID, SHE TOLD HERSELF. IT WILL ALL COME OUT WELL. JOFF LOVES ME, AND THE QUEEN DOES TOO. SHE SAID SO.
ALL HAIL HIS GRACE, JOFFREY OF THE HOUSES BARATHEON AND LANNISTER, FIRST OF HIS NAME, LORD OF THE SEVEN KINGDOMS!

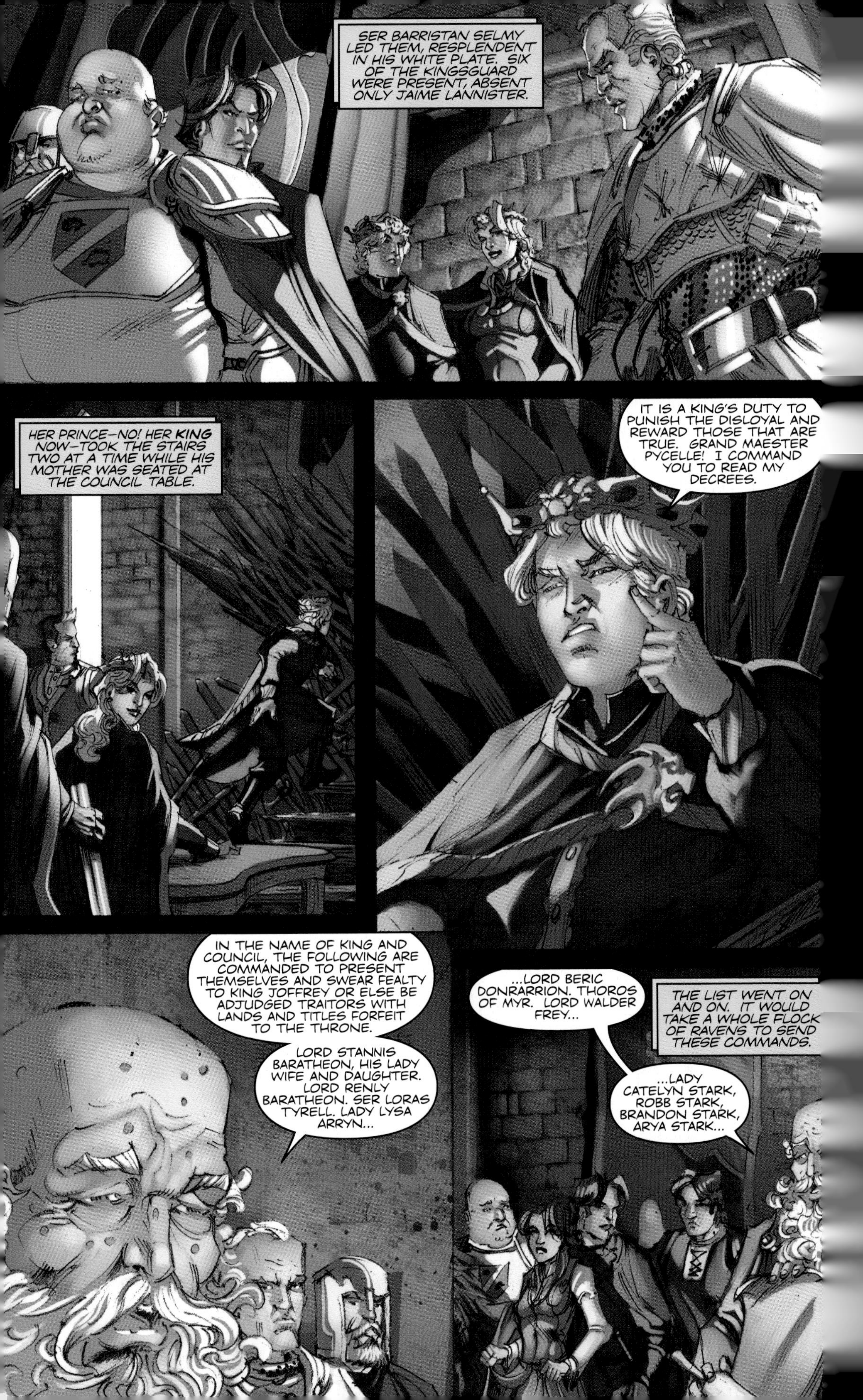
SER BARRISTAN SELMY LED THEM, RESPLENDENT IN HIS WHITE PLATE. SIX OF THE KINGSGUARD WERE PRESENT, ABSENT ONLY JAIME LANNISTER.
HER PRINCE—NO! HER KING NOW—TOOK THE STAIRS TWO AT A TIME WHILE HIS MOTHER WAS SEATED AT THE COUNCIL TABLE.
IT IS A KING'S DUTY TO PUNISH THE DISLOYAL AND REWARD THOSE THAT ARE TRUE. GRAND MAESTER PYCELLE! I COMMAND YOU TO READ MY DECREES.
IN THE NAME OF KING AND COUNCIL, THE FOLLOWING ARE COMMANDED TO PRESENT THEMSELVES AND SWEAR FEALTY TO KING JOFFREY OR ELSE BE ADJUDGED TRAITORS WITH LANDS AND TITLES FORFEIT TO THE THRONE.
LORD STANNIS BARATHEON, HIS LADY WIFE AND DAUGHTER. LORD RENLY BARATHEON. SER LORAS TYRELL. LADY LYSA ARRYN...
...LORD BERIC DONRARRION. THOROS OF MYR. LORD WALDER FREY...
...LADY CATELYN STARK, ROBB STARK, BRANDON STARK, ARYA STARK...
THE LIST WENT ON AND ON. IT WOULD TAKE A WHOLE FLOCK OF RAVENS TO SEND THESE COMMANDS.

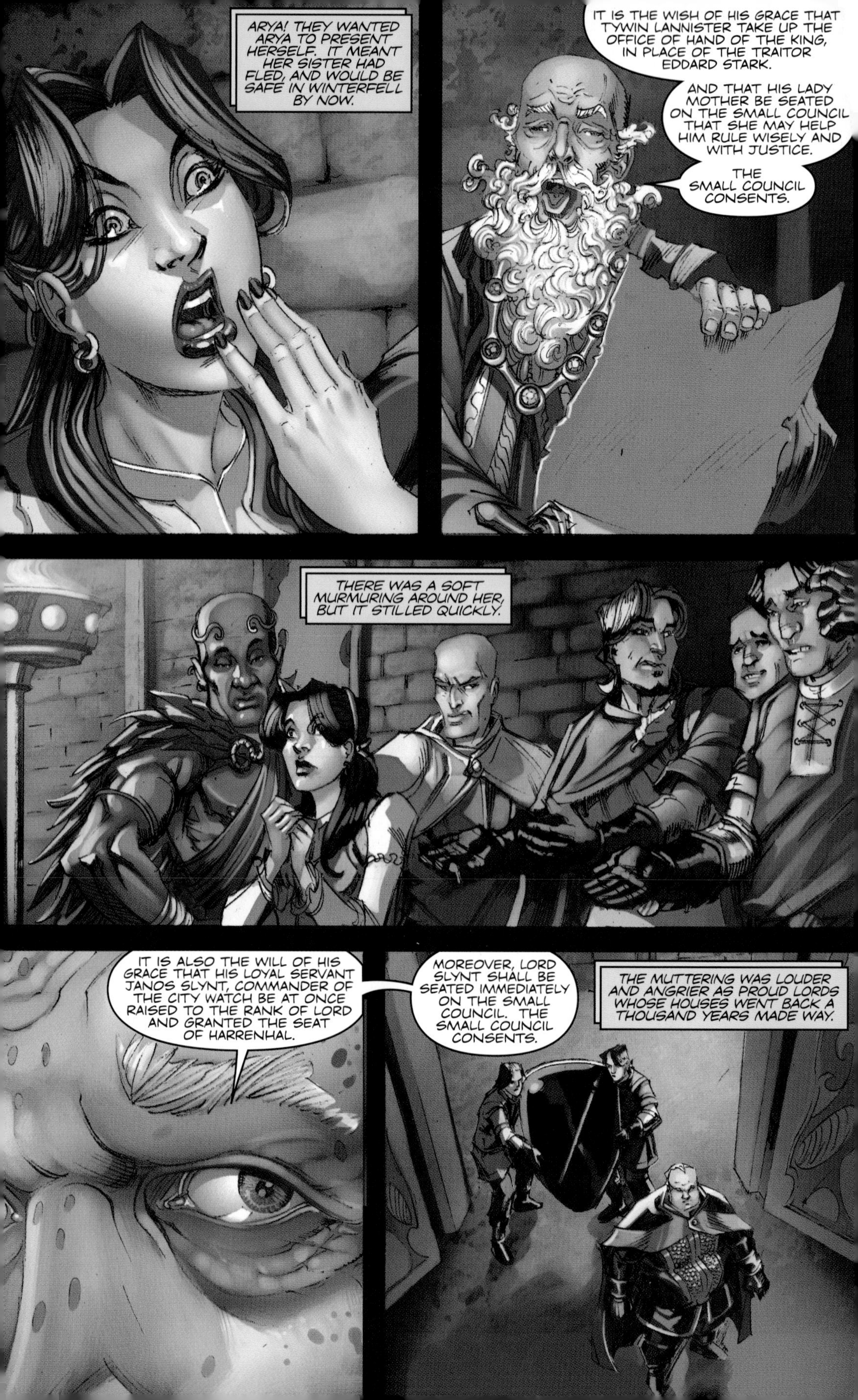
ARYA! THEY WANTED ARYA TO PRESENT HERSELF. IT MEANT HER SISTER HAD FLED, AND WOULD BE SAFE IN WINTERFELL BY NOW.
IT IS THE WISH OF HIS GRACE THAT TYWIN LANNISTER TAKE UP THE OFFICE OF HAND OF THE KING, IN PLACE OF THE TRAITOR EDDARD STARK.
AND THAT HIS LADY MOTHER BE SEATED ON THE SMALL COUNCIL THAT SHE MAY HELP HIM RULE WISELY AND WITH JUSTICE.
THE SMALL COUNCIL CONSENTS.
THERE WAS A SOFT MURMURING AROUND HER, BUT IT STILLED QUICKLY.
IT IS ALSO THE WILL OF HIS GRACE THAT HIS LOYAL SERVANT JANOS SLYNT, COMMANDER OF THE CITY WATCH BE AT ONCE RAISED TO THE RANK OF LORD AND GRANTED THE SEAT OF HARRENHAL.
MOREOVER, LORD SLYNT SHALL BE SEATED IMMEDIATELY ON THE SMALL COUNCIL. THE SMALL COUNCIL CONSENTS.
THE MUTTERING WAS LOUDER AND ANGRIER AS PROUD LORDS WHOSE HOUSES WENT BACK A THOUSAND YEARS MADE WAY.

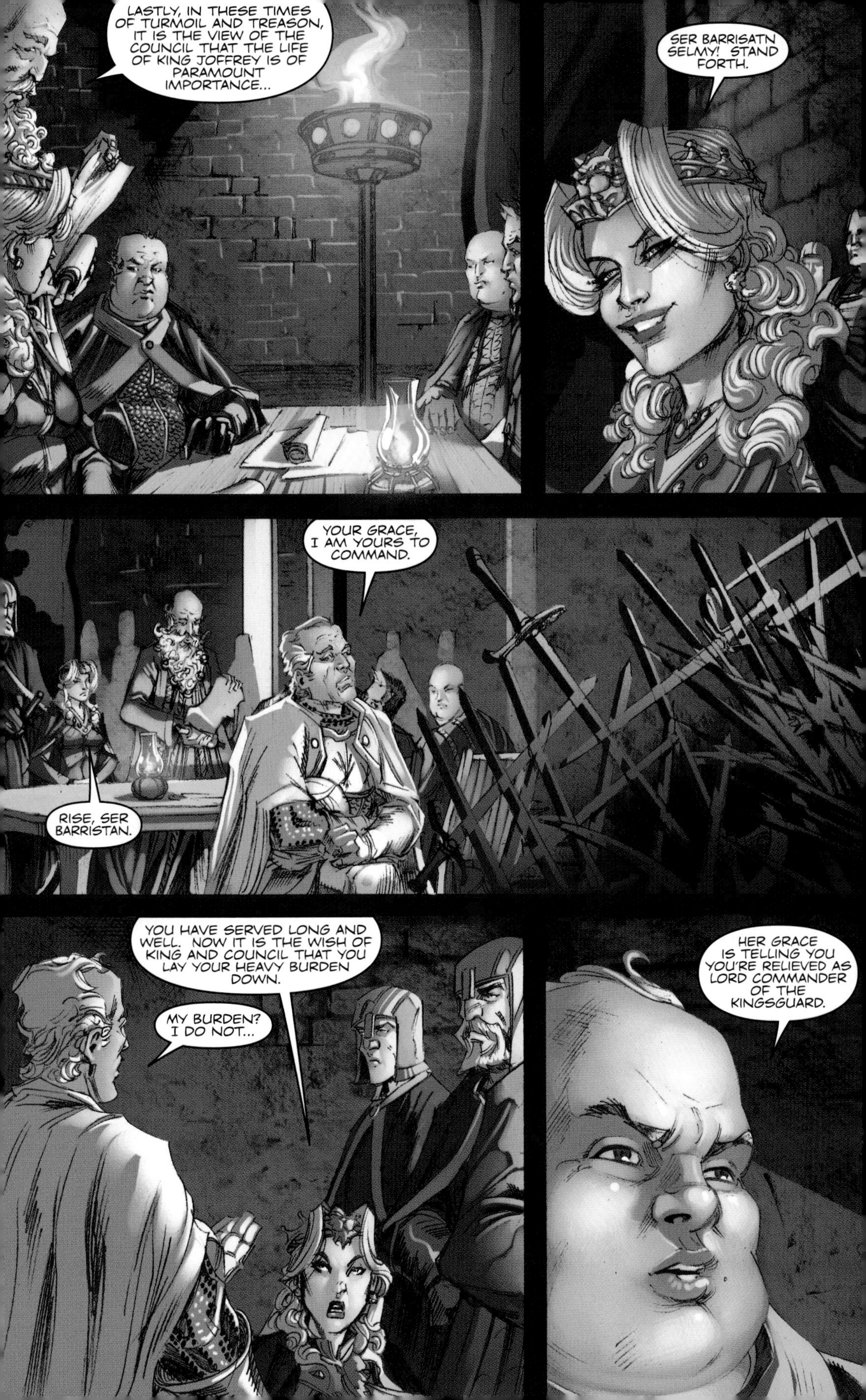
LASTLY, IN THESE TIMES OF TURMOIL AND TREASON, IT IS THE VIEW OF THE COUNCIL THAT THE LIFE OF KING JOFFREY IS OF PARAMOUNT IMPORTANCE...
SER BARRISATN SELMY! STAND FORTH.
YOUR GRACE, I AM YOURS TO COMMAND.
RISE, SER BARRISTAN.
YOU HAVE SERVED LONG AND WELL. NOW IT IS THE WISH OF KING AND COUNCIL THAT YOU LAY YOUR HEAVY BURDEN DOWN.
MY BURDEN? I DO NOT...
HER GRACE IS TELLING YOU YOU'RE RELIEVED AS LORD COMMANDER OF THE KINGSGUARD.

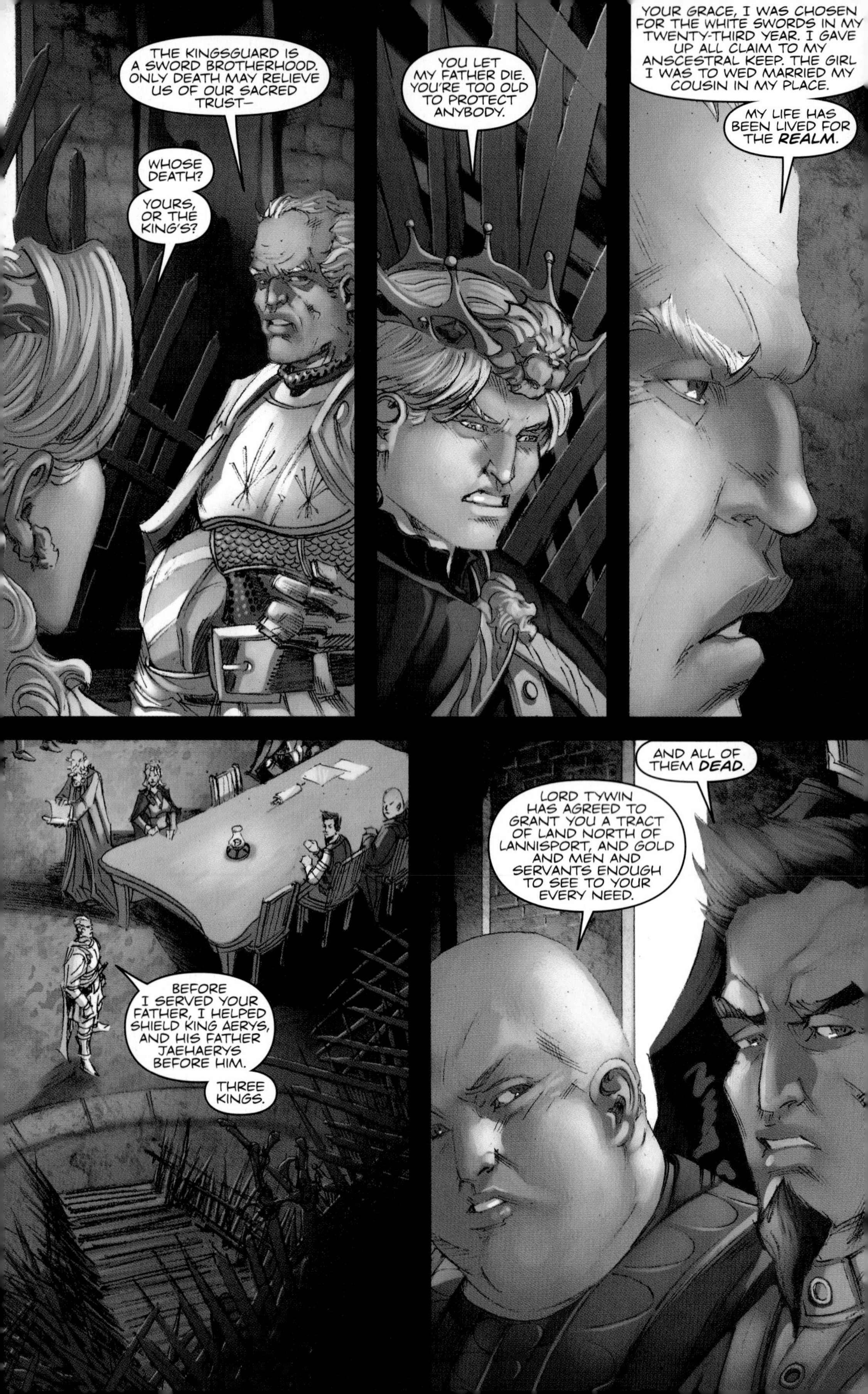
THE KINGSGUARD IS A SWORD BROTHERHOOD. ONLY DEATH MAY RELIEVE US OF OUR SACRED TRUST–
WHOSE DEATH?
YOURS, OR THE KING'S?
YOU LET MY FATHER DIE. YOU'RE TOO OLD TO PROTECT ANYBODY.
YOUR GRACE, I WAS CHOSEN FOR THE WHITE SWORDS IN MY TWENTY-THIRD YEAR. I GAVE UP ALL CLAIM TO MY ANSCESTRAL KEEP. THE GIRL I WAS TO WED MARRIED MY COUSIN IN MY PLACE.
MY LIFE HAS BEEN LIVED FOR THE **REALM**.
BEFORE I SERVED YOUR FATHER, I HELPED SHIELD KING AERYS, AND HIS FATHER JAEHAERYS BEFORE HIM.
THREE KINGS.
AND ALL OF THEM **DEAD**.
LORD TYWIN HAS AGREED TO GRANT YOU A TRACT OF LAND NORTH OF LANNISPORT, AND GOLD AND MEN AND SERVANTS ENOUGH TO SEE TO YOUR EVERY NEED.

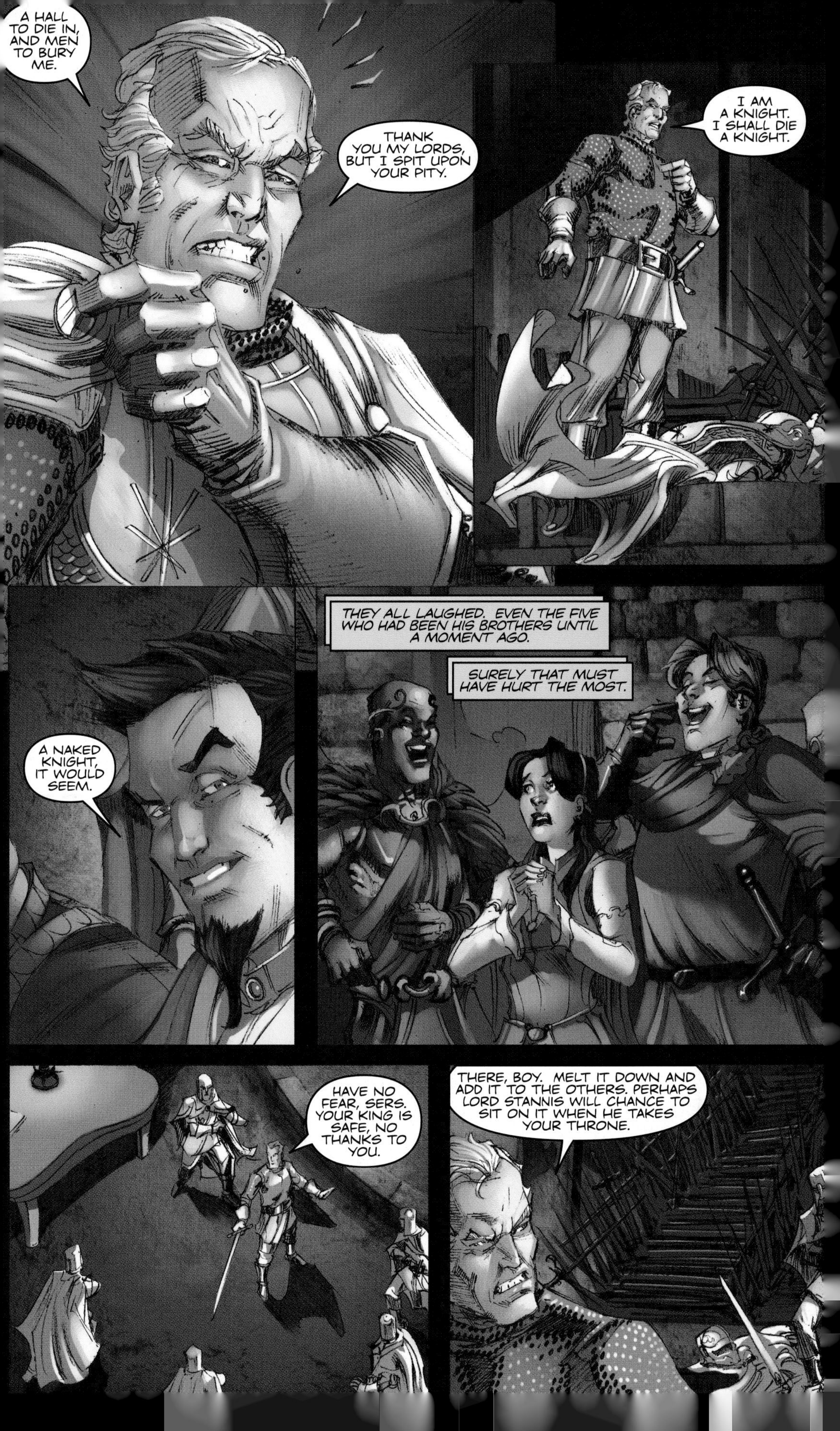

A HALL TO DIE IN, AND MEN TO BURY ME.
THANK YOU MY LORDS, BUT I SPIT UPON YOUR PITY.
I AM A KNIGHT. I SHALL DIE A KNIGHT.
A NAKED KNIGHT, IT WOULD SEEM.
THEY ALL LAUGHED. EVEN THE FIVE WHO HAD BEEN HIS BROTHERS UNTIL A MOMENT AGO.
SURELY THAT MUST HAVE HURT THE MOST.
HAVE NO FEAR, SERS. YOUR KING IS SAFE, NO THANKS TO YOU.
THERE, BOY. MELT IT DOWN AND ADD IT TO THE OTHERS. PERHAPS LORD STANNIS WILL CHANCE TO SIT ON IT WHEN HE TAKES YOUR THRONE.

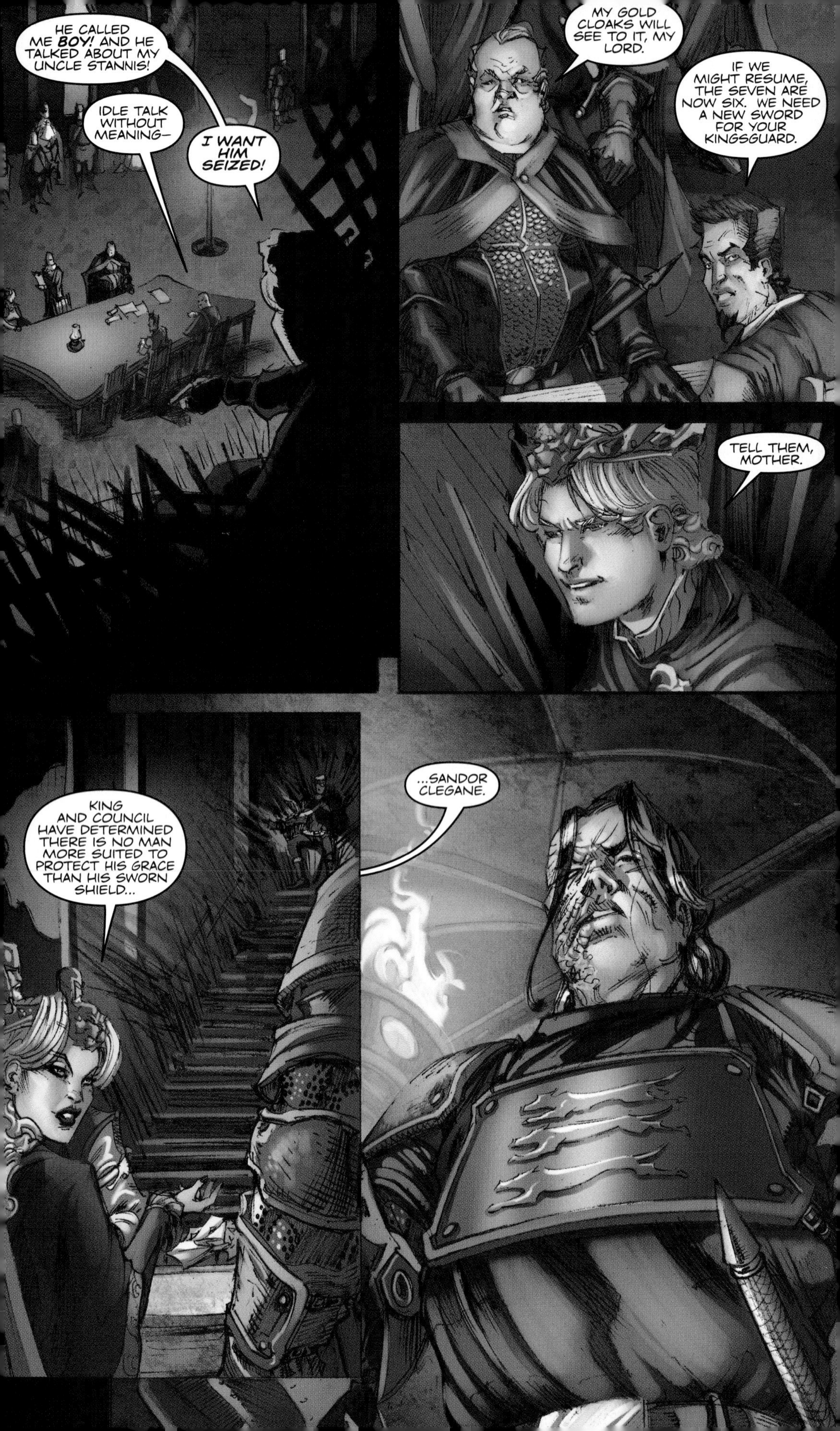
HE CALLED ME BOY! AND HE TALKED ABOUT MY UNCLE STANNIS!
IDLE TALK WITHOUT MEANING—
I WANT HIM SEIZED!
MY GOLD CLOAKS WILL SEE TO IT, MY LORD.
IF WE MIGHT RESUME, THE SEVEN ARE NOW SIX. WE NEED A NEW SWORD FOR YOUR KINGSGUARD.
TELL THEM, MOTHER.
KING AND COUNCIL HAVE DETERMINED THERE IS NO MAN MORE SUITED TO PROTECT HIS GRACE THAN HIS SWORN SHIELD...
...SANDOR CLEGANE.

HOW DO YOU FEEL ABOUT THAT, DOG?

WHY NOT?

I HAVE NO WIFE OR LAND TO FORSAKE. BUT I WARN YOU, I'LL SAY NO KNIGHT'S VOWS.

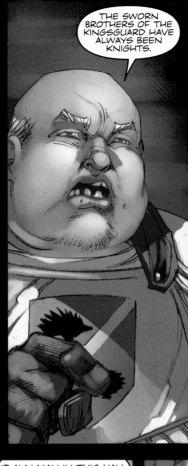

THE SWORN BROTHERS OF THE KINGSGUARD HAVE ALWAYS BEEN KNIGHTS.

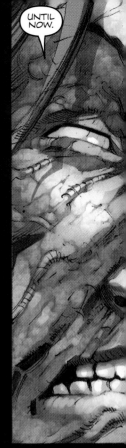

UNTIL NOW.

IF ANY MAN IN THIS HALL HAS OTHER MATTERS TO SET BEFORE HIS GRACE, SPEAK NOW OR HOLD TO SILENCE.

NOW, SHE THOUGHT. I MUST DO IT NOW. GODS, GIVE ME STRENGTH.

YOUR GRACE.

COME FORWARD, MY LADY.

HE DOES LOVE ME. SANSA TOLD HERSELF. HE DOES.

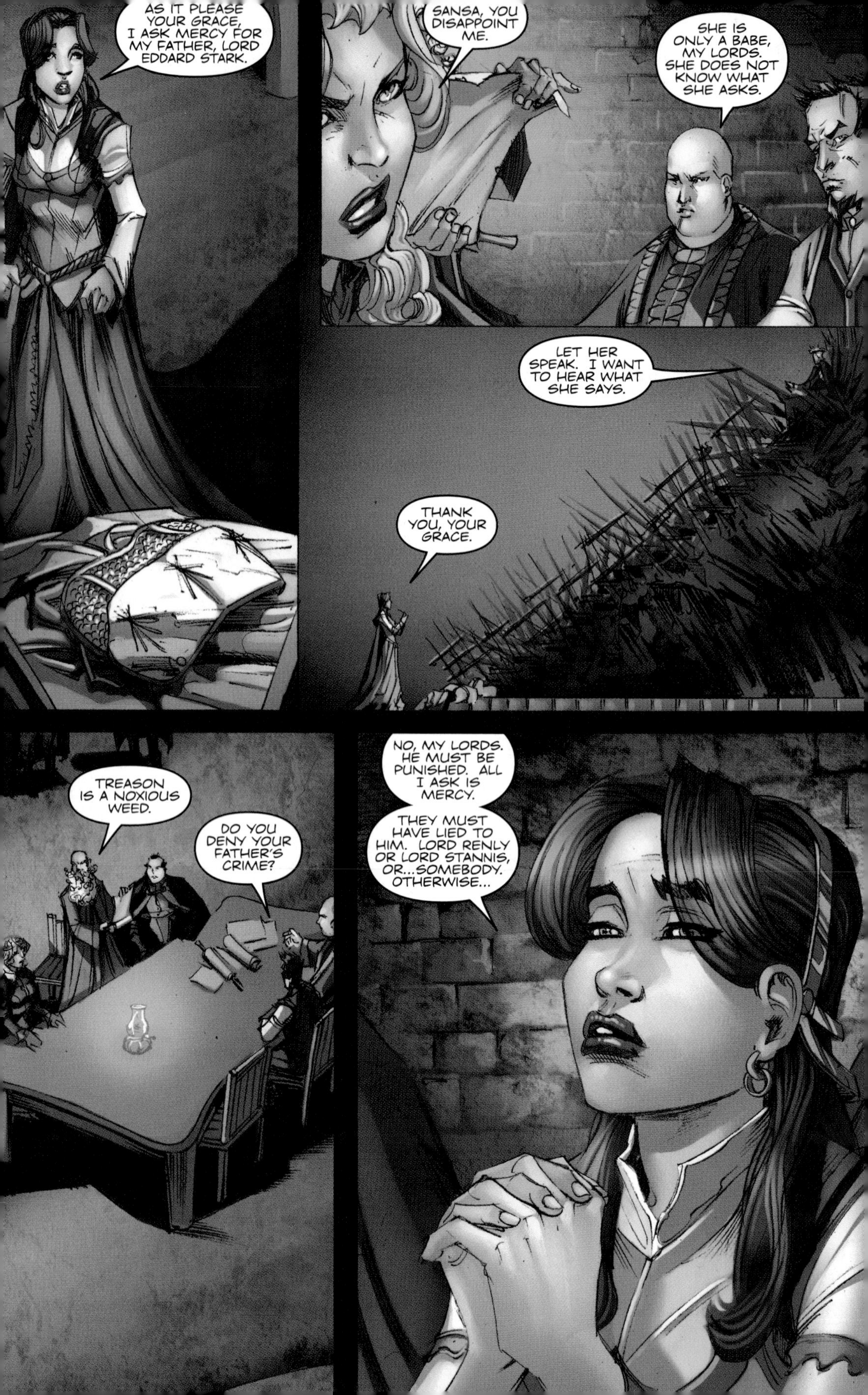
AS IT PLEASE YOUR GRACE, I ASK MERCY FOR MY FATHER, LORD EDDARD STARK.
SANSA, YOU DISAPPOINT ME.
SHE IS ONLY A BABE, MY LORDS. SHE DOES NOT KNOW WHAT SHE ASKS.
LET HER SPEAK. I WANT TO HEAR WHAT SHE SAYS.
THANK YOU, YOUR GRACE.
TREASON IS A NOXIOUS WEED.
DO YOU DENY YOUR FATHER'S CRIME?
NO, MY LORDS. HE MUST BE PUNISHED. ALL I ASK IS MERCY.
THEY MUST HAVE LIED TO HIM. LORD RENLY OR LORD STANNIS, OR...SOMEBODY. OTHERWISE...

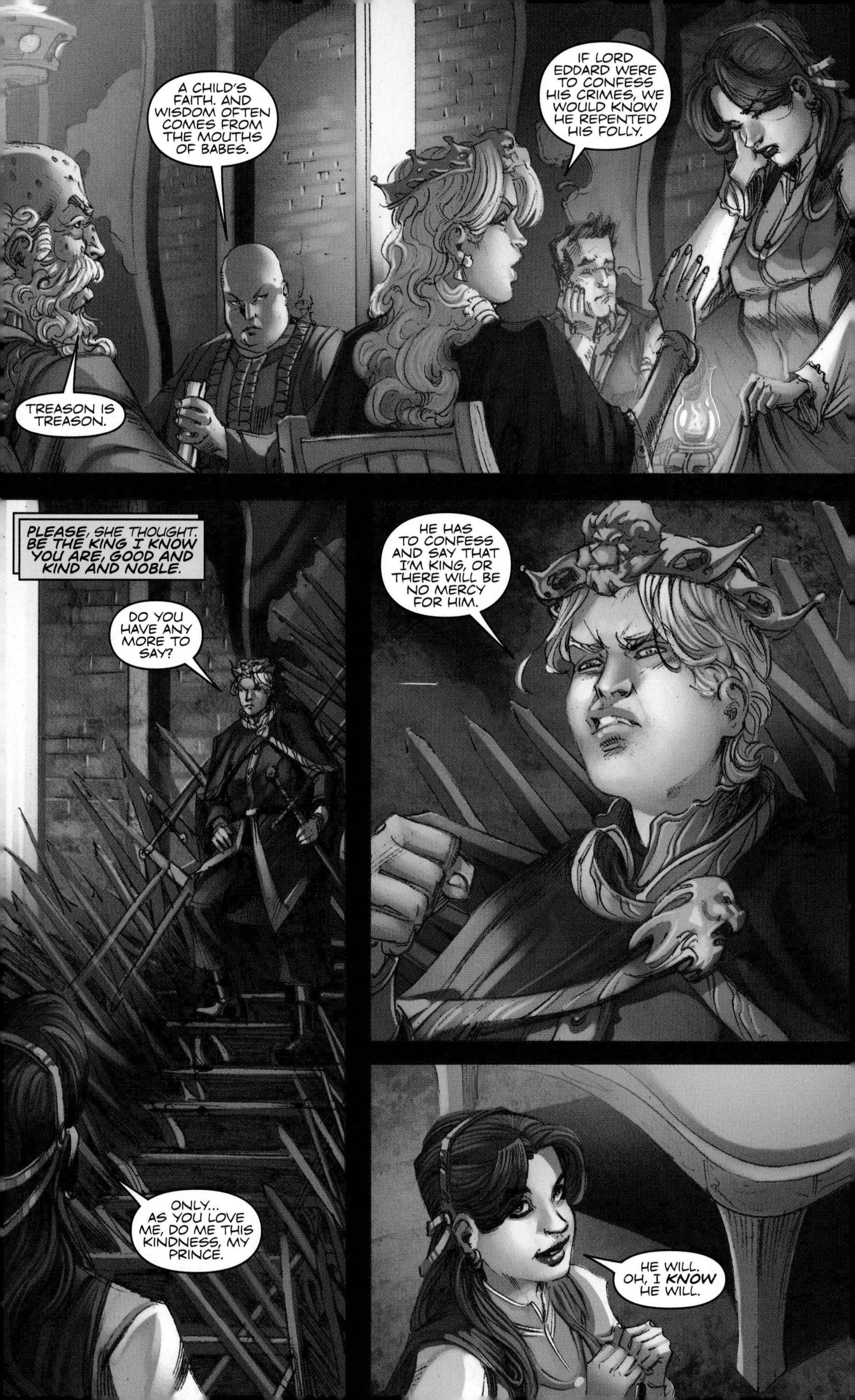
A CHILD'S FAITH. AND WISDOM OFTEN COMES FROM THE MOUTHS OF BABES.
TREASON IS TREASON.
IF LORD EDDARD WERE TO CONFESS HIS CRIMES, WE WOULD KNOW HE REPENTED HIS FOLLY.
PLEASE, SHE THOUGHT. BE THE KING I KNOW YOU ARE, GOOD AND KIND AND NOBLE.
DO YOU HAVE ANY MORE TO SAY?
ONLY... AS YOU LOVE ME, DO ME THIS KINDNESS, MY PRINCE.
HE HAS TO CONFESS AND SAY THAT I'M KING, OR THERE WILL BE NO MERCY FOR HIM.
HE WILL. OH, I KNOW HE WILL.

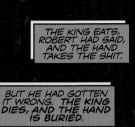

THE KING EATS, ROBERT HAD SAID, AND THE HAND TAKES THE SHIT.

BUT HE HAD GOTTEN IT WRONG. THE KING DIES, AND THE HAND IS BURIED.

WHEN HE KEPT VERY STILL, HIS LEG DIDN'T HURT SO MUCH. HE DID HIS BEST LIE UNMOVING.

THERE WAS NO SUN AND NO MOON. HE SLEPT AND WOKE AND SLEPT AGAIN. THE DARKNESS WAS ABSOLUTE.

NED WAS HALF ASLEEP WHEN THE FOOTSTEPS CAME DOWN THE HALL.

HE WAS FEVERISH BY THEN, HIS LEG A DULL AGONY, HIS LIPS PARCHED AND CRACKED.

THE SUDDEN LIGHT WAS PAINFUL.

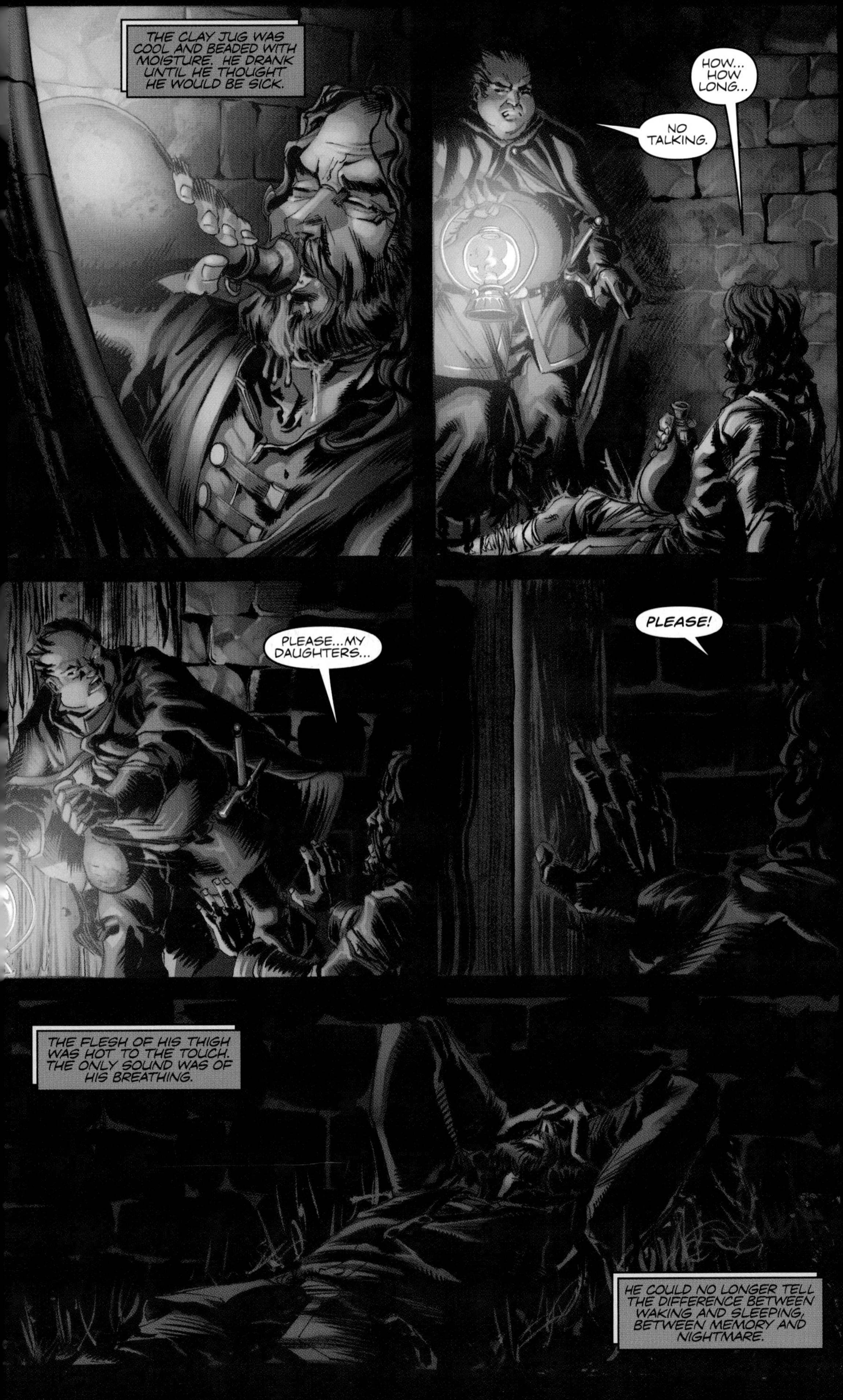
THE CLAY JUG WAS COOL AND BEADED WITH MOISTURE. HE DRANK UNTIL HE THOUGHT HE WOULD BE SICK.
HOW... HOW LONG...
NO TALKING.
PLEASE...MY DAUGHTERS...
PLEASE!
THE FLESH OF HIS THIGH WAS HOT TO THE TOUCH. THE ONLY SOUND WAS OF HIS BREATHING.
HE COULD NO LONGER TELL THE DIFFERENCE BETWEEN WAKING AND SLEEPING, BETWEEN MEMORY AND NIGHTMARE.

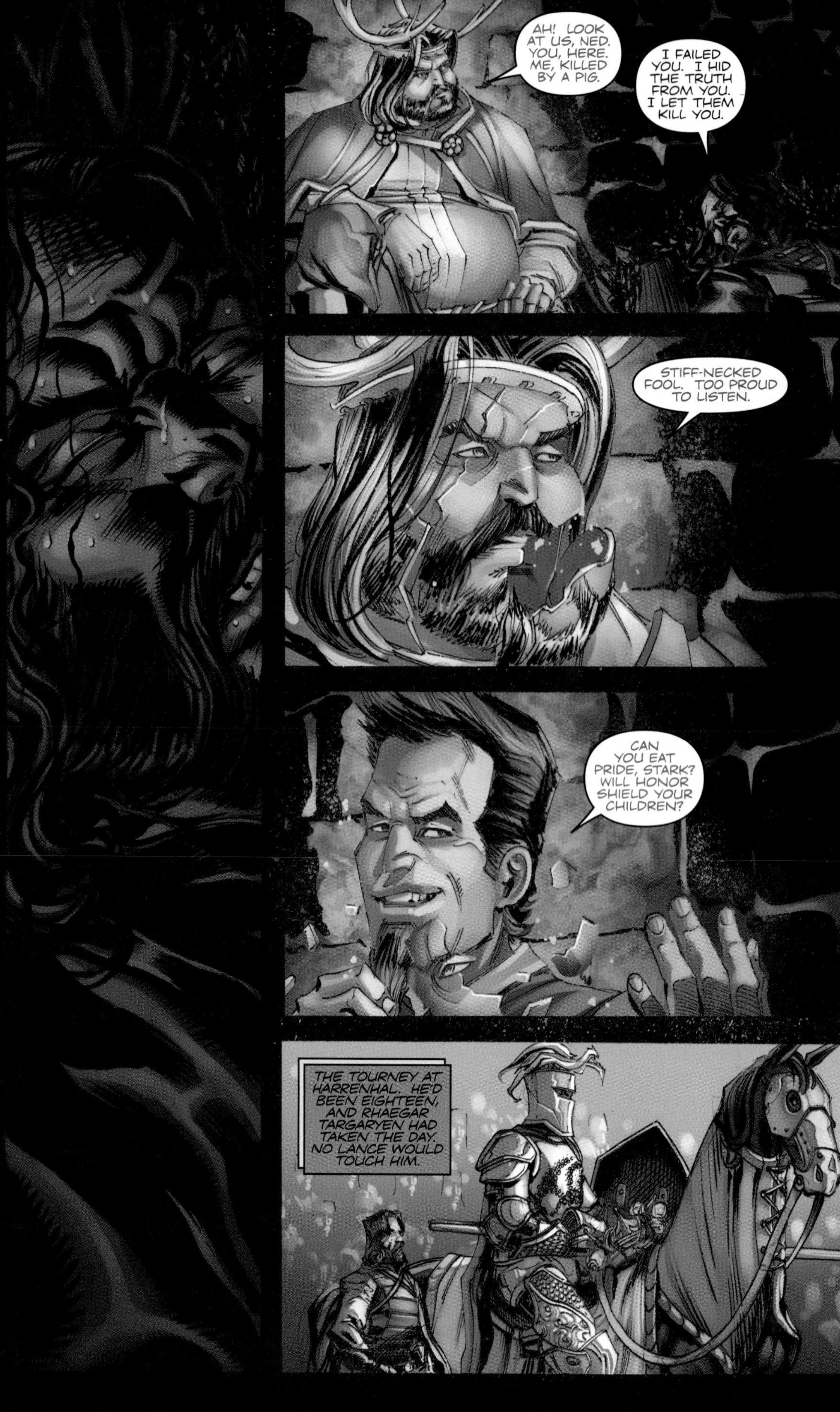
AH! LOOK AT US, NED. YOU, HERE. ME, KILLED BY A PIG.
I FAILED YOU. I HID THE TRUTH FROM YOU. I LET THEM KILL YOU.
STIFF-NECKED FOOL. TOO PROUD TO LISTEN.
CAN YOU EAT PRIDE, STARK? WILL HONOR SHIELD YOUR CHILDREN?
THE TOURNEY AT HARRENHAL. HE'D BEEN EIGHTEEN, AND RHAEGAR TARGARYEN HAD TAKEN THE DAY. NO LANCE WOULD TOUCH HIM.

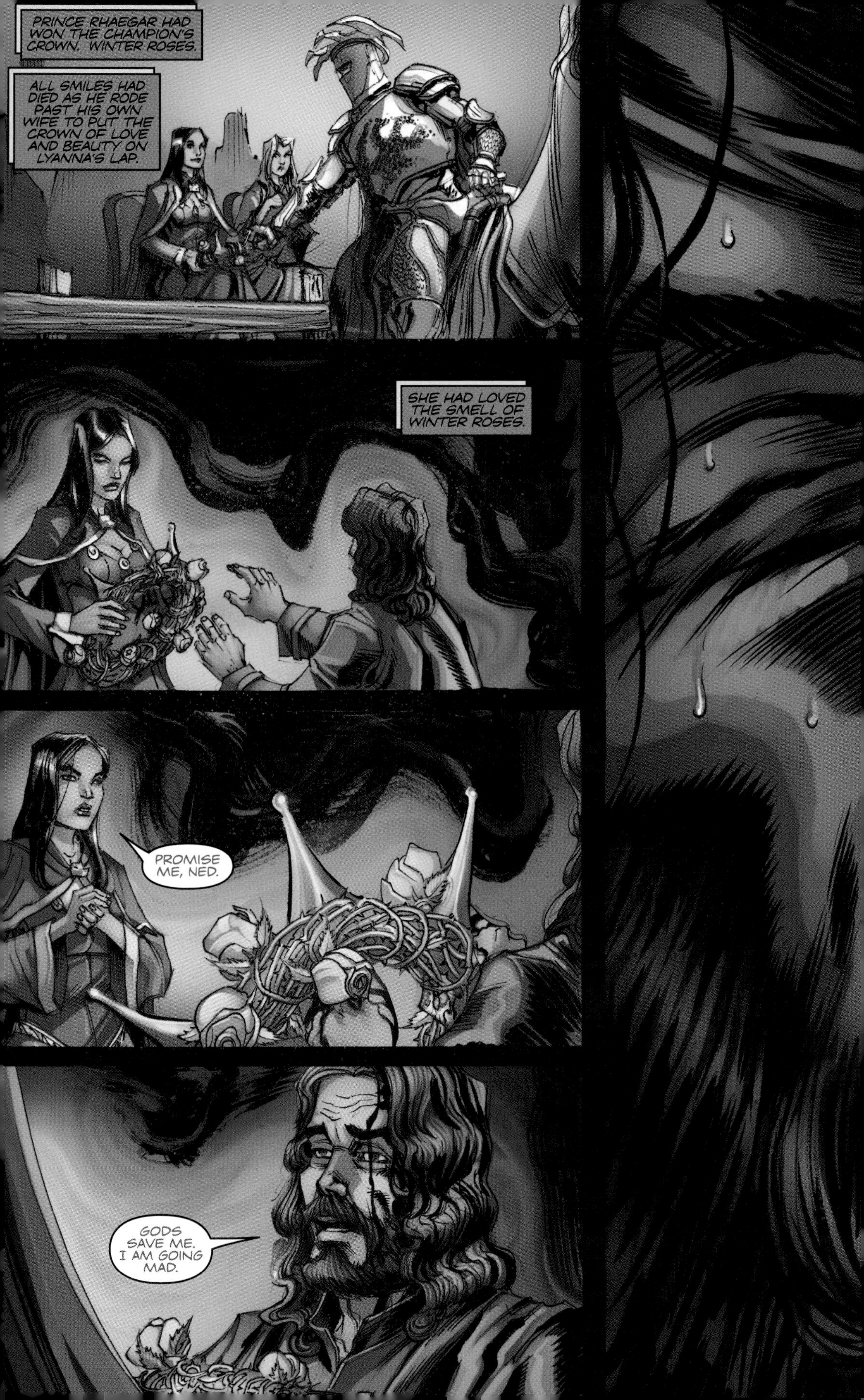
PRINCE RHAEGAR HAD WON THE CHAMPION'S CROWN. WINTER ROSES.
ALL SMILES HAD DIED AS HE RODE PAST HIS OWN WIFE TO PUT THE CROWN OF LOVE AND BEAUTY ON LYANNA'S LAP.
SHE HAD LOVED THE SMELL OF WINTER ROSES.
PROMISE ME, NED.
GODS SAVE ME. I AM GOING MAD.

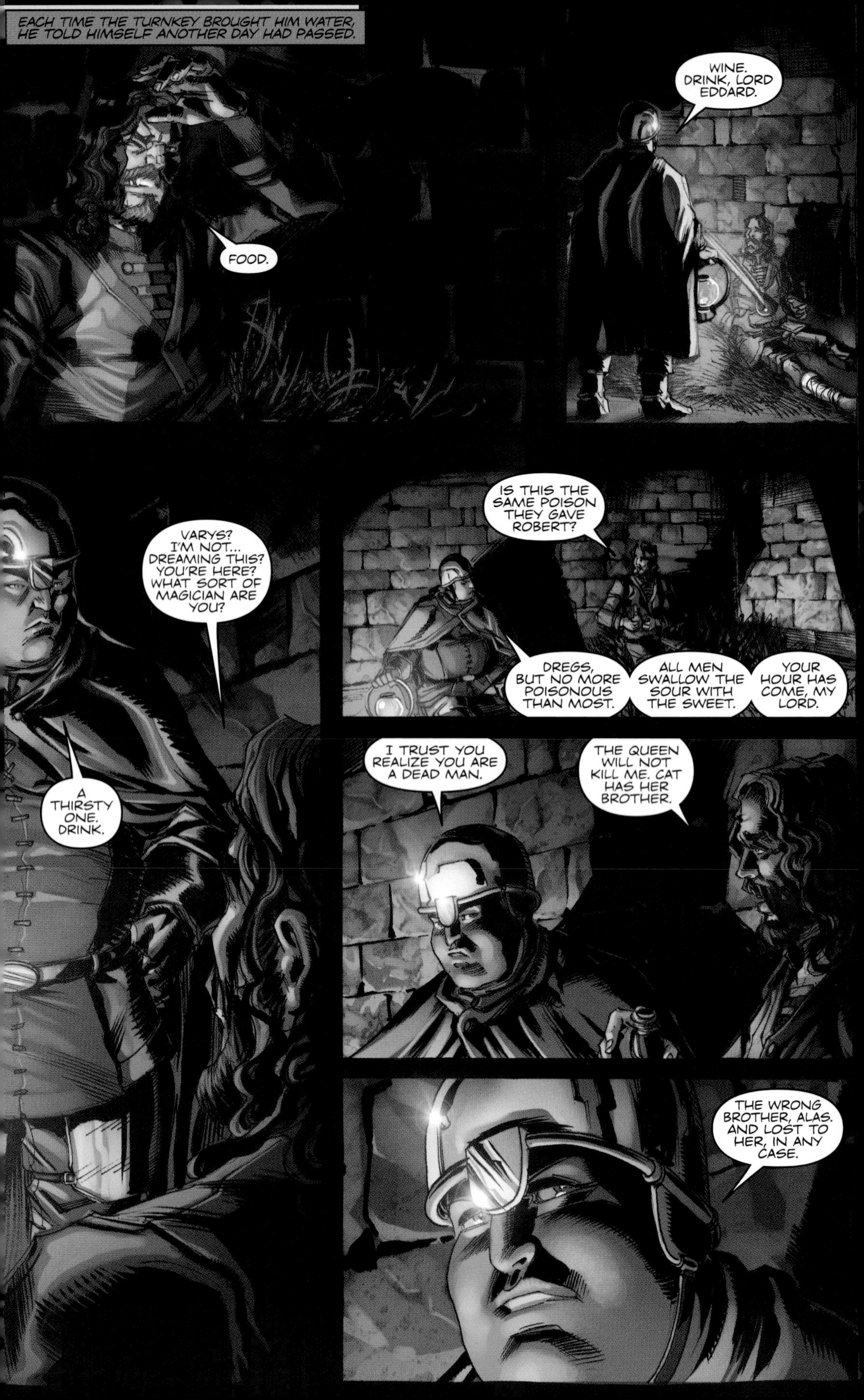
EACH TIME THE TURNKEY BROUGHT HIM WATER, HE TOLD HIMSELF ANOTHER DAY HAD PASSED.
FOOD.
WINE. DRINK, LORD EDDARD.
VARYS? I'M NOT... DREAMING THIS? YOU'RE HERE? WHAT SORT OF MAGICIAN ARE YOU?
A THIRSTY ONE. DRINK.
IS THIS THE SAME POISON THEY GAVE ROBERT?
DREGS, BUT NO MORE POISONOUS THAN MOST.
ALL MEN SWALLOW THE SOUR WITH THE SWEET.
YOUR HOUR HAS COME, MY LORD.
I TRUST YOU REALIZE YOU ARE A DEAD MAN.
THE QUEEN WILL NOT KILL ME. CAT HAS HER BROTHER.
THE WRONG BROTHER, ALAS. AND LOST TO HER, IN ANY CASE.

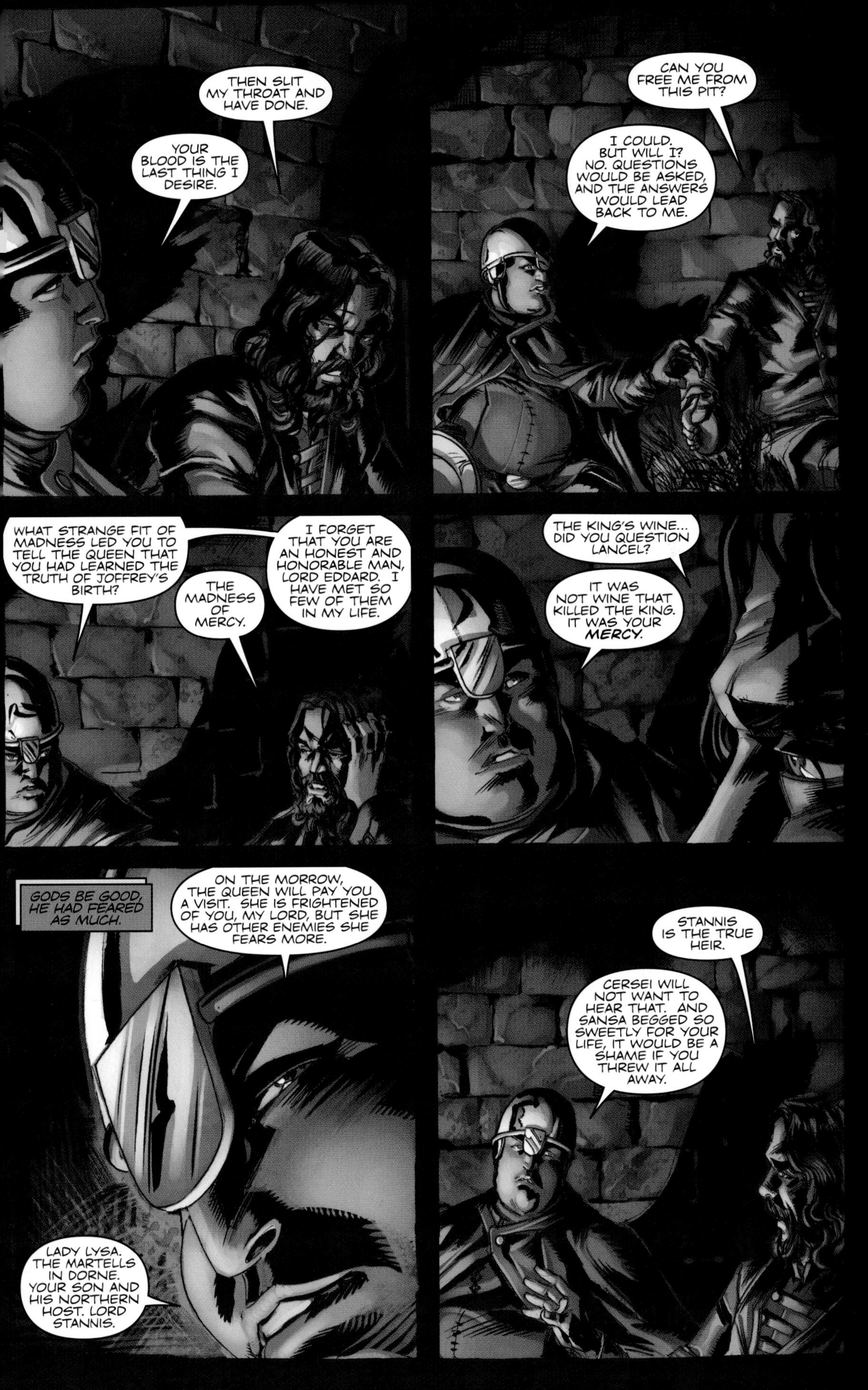

THEN SLIT MY THROAT AND HAVE DONE.
YOUR BLOOD IS THE LAST THING I DESIRE.
CAN YOU FREE ME FROM THIS PIT?
I COULD. BUT WILL I? NO. QUESTIONS WOULD BE ASKED, AND THE ANSWERS WOULD LEAD BACK TO ME.
WHAT STRANGE FIT OF MADNESS LED YOU TO TELL THE QUEEN THAT YOU HAD LEARNED THE TRUTH OF JOFFREY'S BIRTH?
THE MADNESS OF MERCY.
I FORGET THAT YOU ARE AN HONEST AND HONORABLE MAN, LORD EDDARD. I HAVE MET SO FEW OF THEM IN MY LIFE.
THE KING'S WINE... DID YOU QUESTION LANCEL?
IT WAS NOT WINE THAT KILLED THE KING. IT WAS YOUR MERCY.
GODS BE GOOD, HE HAD FEARED AS MUCH.
ON THE MORROW, THE QUEEN WILL PAY YOU A VISIT. SHE IS FRIGHTENED OF YOU, MY LORD, BUT SHE HAS OTHER ENEMIES SHE FEARS MORE.
LADY LYSA. THE MARTELLS IN DORNE. YOUR SON AND HIS NORTHERN HOST. LORD STANNIS.
STANNIS IS THE TRUE HEIR.
CERSEI WILL NOT WANT TO HEAR THAT. AND SANSA BEGGED SO SWEETLY FOR YOUR LIFE, IT WOULD BE A SHAME IF YOU THREW IT ALL AWAY.

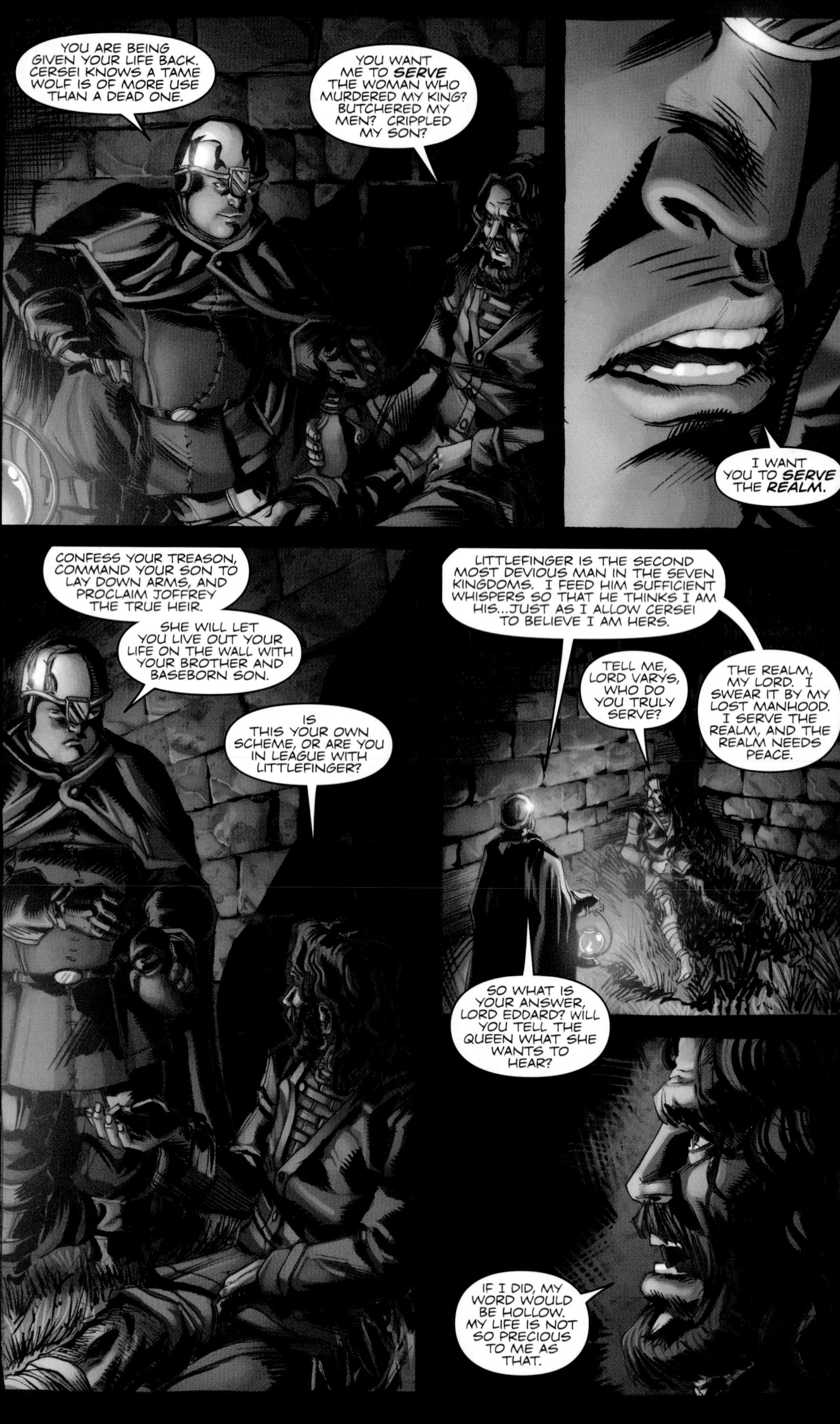
YOU ARE BEING GIVEN YOUR LIFE BACK. CERSEI KNOWS A TAME WOLF IS OF MORE USE THAN A DEAD ONE.
YOU WANT ME TO SERVE THE WOMAN WHO MURDERED MY KING? BUTCHERED MY MEN? CRIPPLED MY SON?
I WANT YOU TO SERVE THE REALM.
CONFESS YOUR TREASON, COMMAND YOUR SON TO LAY DOWN ARMS, AND PROCLAIM JOFFREY THE TRUE HEIR.
SHE WILL LET YOU LIVE OUT YOUR LIFE ON THE WALL WITH YOUR BROTHER AND BASEBORN SON.
IS THIS YOUR OWN SCHEME, OR ARE YOU IN LEAGUE WITH LITTLEFINGER?
LITTLEFINGER IS THE SECOND MOST DEVIOUS MAN IN THE SEVEN KINGDOMS. I FEED HIM SUFFICIENT WHISPERS SO THAT HE THINKS I AM HIS...JUST AS I ALLOW CERSEI TO BELIEVE I AM HERS.
TELL ME, LORD VARYS, WHO DO YOU TRULY SERVE?
THE REALM, MY LORD. I SWEAR IT BY MY LOST MANHOOD. I SERVE THE REALM, AND THE REALM NEEDS PEACE.
SO WHAT IS YOUR ANSWER, LORD EDDARD? WILL YOU TELL THE QUEEN WHAT SHE WANTS TO HEAR?
IF I DID, MY WORD WOULD BE HOLLOW. MY LIFE IS NOT SO PRECIOUS TO ME AS THAT.

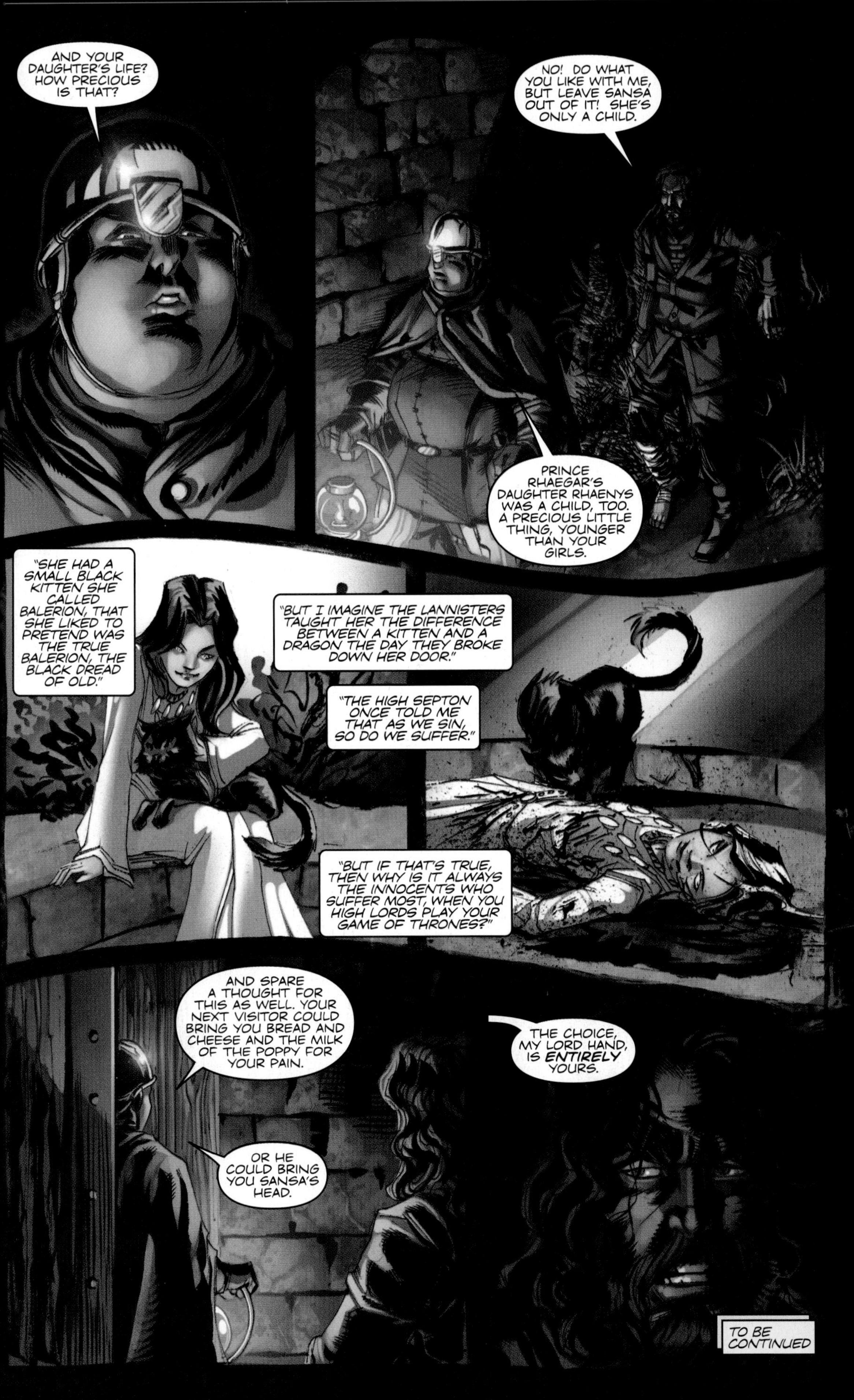
AND YOUR DAUGHTER'S LIFE? HOW PRECIOUS IS THAT?
NO! DO WHAT YOU LIKE WITH ME, BUT LEAVE SANSA OUT OF IT! SHE'S ONLY A CHILD.
PRINCE RHAEGAR'S DAUGHTER RHAENYS WAS A CHILD, TOO. A PRECIOUS LITTLE THING, YOUNGER THAN YOUR GIRLS.
"SHE HAD A SMALL BLACK KITTEN SHE CALLED BALERION, THAT SHE LIKED TO PRETEND WAS THE TRUE BALERION, THE BLACK DREAD OF OLD."
"BUT I IMAGINE THE LANNISTERS TAUGHT HER THE DIFFERENCE BETWEEN A KITTEN AND A DRAGON THE DAY THEY BROKE DOWN HER DOOR."
"THE HIGH SEPTON ONCE TOLD ME THAT AS WE SIN, SO DO WE SUFFER."
"BUT IF THAT'S TRUE, THEN WHY IS IT ALWAYS THE INNOCENTS WHO SUFFER MOST, WHEN YOU HIGH LORDS PLAY YOUR GAME OF THRONES?"
AND SPARE A THOUGHT FOR THIS AS WELL. YOUR NEXT VISITOR COULD BRING YOU BREAD AND CHEESE AND THE MILK OF THE POPPY FOR YOUR PAIN.
OR HE COULD BRING YOU SANSA'S HEAD.
THE CHOICE, MY LORD HAND, IS ENTIRELY YOURS.
TO BE CONTINUED

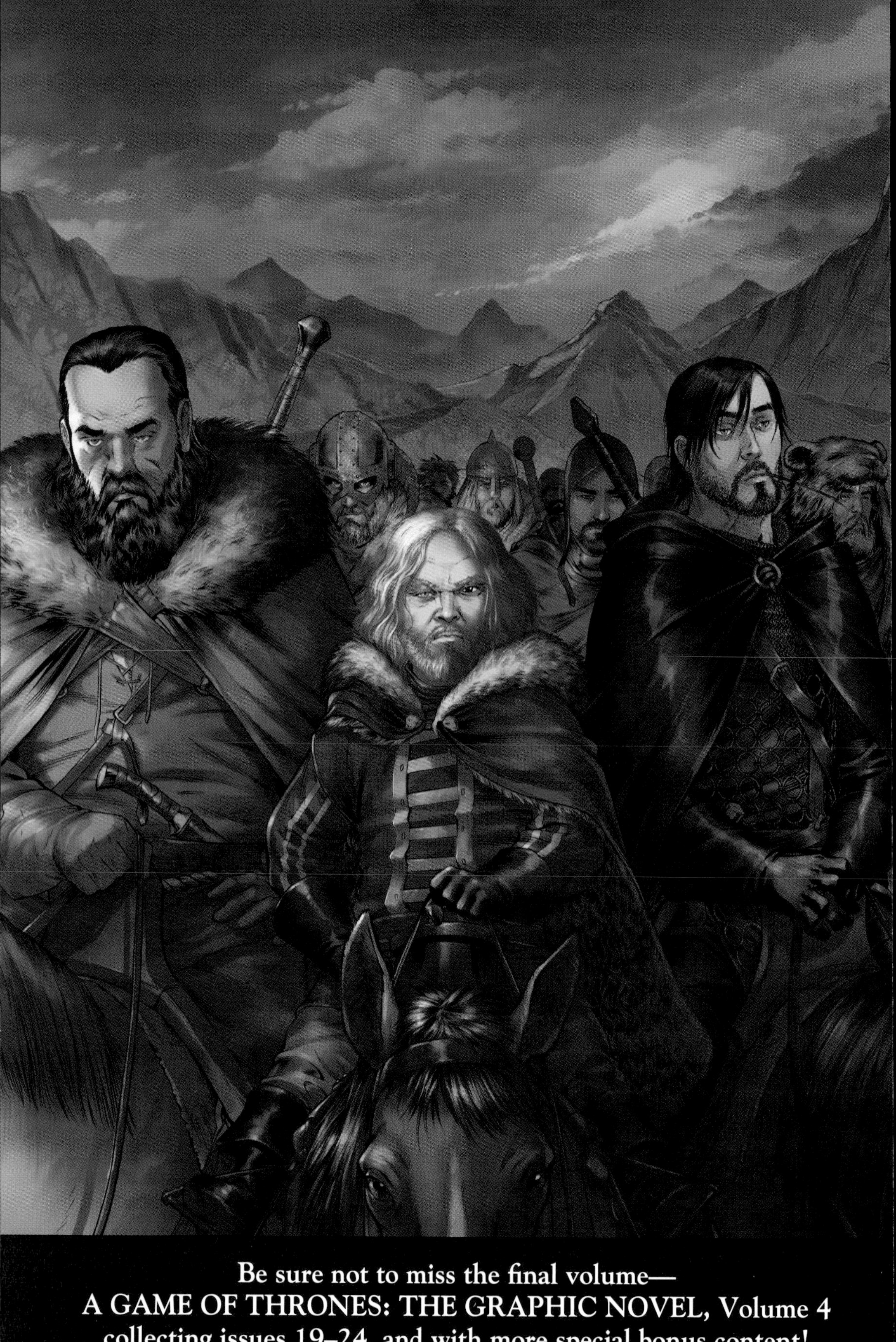

AND NOW...
HERE IS A SPECIAL INSIDER'S LOOK AT

THE MAKING OF

# A GAME OF THRONES

# THRONES

THE GRAPHIC NOVEL

VOLUME 3

WITH COMMENTARY BY
ANNE GROELL (SERIES EDITOR)

# THE CHARACTERS
## (Oh, the characters!)

In addition to drawing every panel of every issue—a massive undertaking in and of itself—the amazing Tommy Patterson has one more major job that happens very much behind the scenes, and that is designing the literally hundred-plus characters that populate George's vast and rich world. And since, in a visual format, we can't easily tag characters with their names, they need to look individual enough to be easily recognizable from one issue to the next—especially for the more major characters.

Just think about the task of sitting down to draw a bunch of very-different-looking people. Man or woman; okay, that's two choices. Add in some ages, maybe old, middle-aged, or young; that's six. Weight classes: fat, medium, skinny. Now you have eighteen. A few different hair options could get you up into the sixties. Now add forty more people, and you begin to understand the scope of the undertaking.

To help me keep track of all the various bits of this project, I have five large notebooks on the go at any one time. In my Script Notebook, I keep copies of all the finished scripts, to compare against the pencils and lettered proofs as they come in. Then I have an Issue Progress Notebook, into which I file all the various stages of each issue—initial pencils, final pencils, lettered proof, colors, and colors and letters together. Then I have my Issue Notebook, which contains the final version of each issue, for reference. And finally, I have two separate Character Notebooks—one subdivided by issue number, and one alphabetically, in which all the approved and finalized characters are stowed by name.

For each issue that we do, I check to see which characters are showing up for the first time, then Daniel and I decide which characters we think George will need to look at and approve before we can officially put them on the page. Once we have that list, I create a separate character document for each issue—in addition to whatever descriptions Daniel put in the script—subdivided by POV Characters, Major Non-POV Characters, More Minor but Recurring Characters, and Most Minor Characters. I then slot each character under their appropriate heading, pull up my searchable pdfs of the Ice and Fire series, and start trolling the text for descriptions.

And—as I talked about with the Iron Throne in volume 1—this is not always an easy task. Some characters have sizable descriptions, but some only have a line. Or half a line. Or one descriptive word. Or nothing at all. Sometimes Tommy hit the nail on the head, and we had approval on the first try. At other times, we had to go through two or three revisions to match the very specific vision that George had of that particular character.

To date, as we are finalizing issue 18, we have 119 characters that George has seen and approved—and this is not including all the many walk-on characters and scene fillers which we have not seen fit to show him.

So here, for your viewing pleasure, is a gallery of some of Tommy's favorite characters, along with, where relevant, the descriptive passages from the book that he had to work with.

## HOUSE STARK

Jon and Eddard were approved as part of Tommy's audition package, but here are the rest of the Stark clan—some of our earliest characters approved.

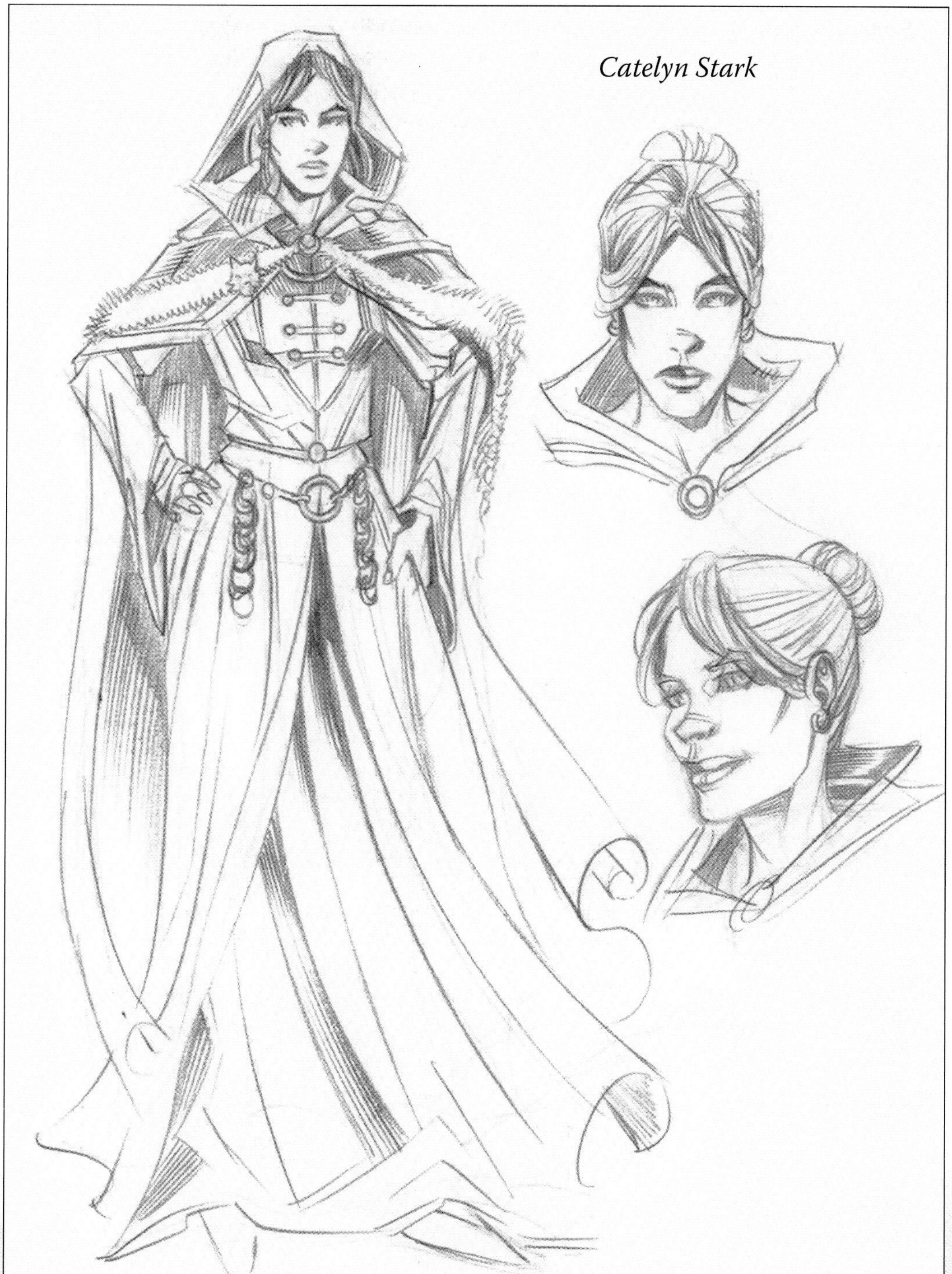

*Catelyn Stark*

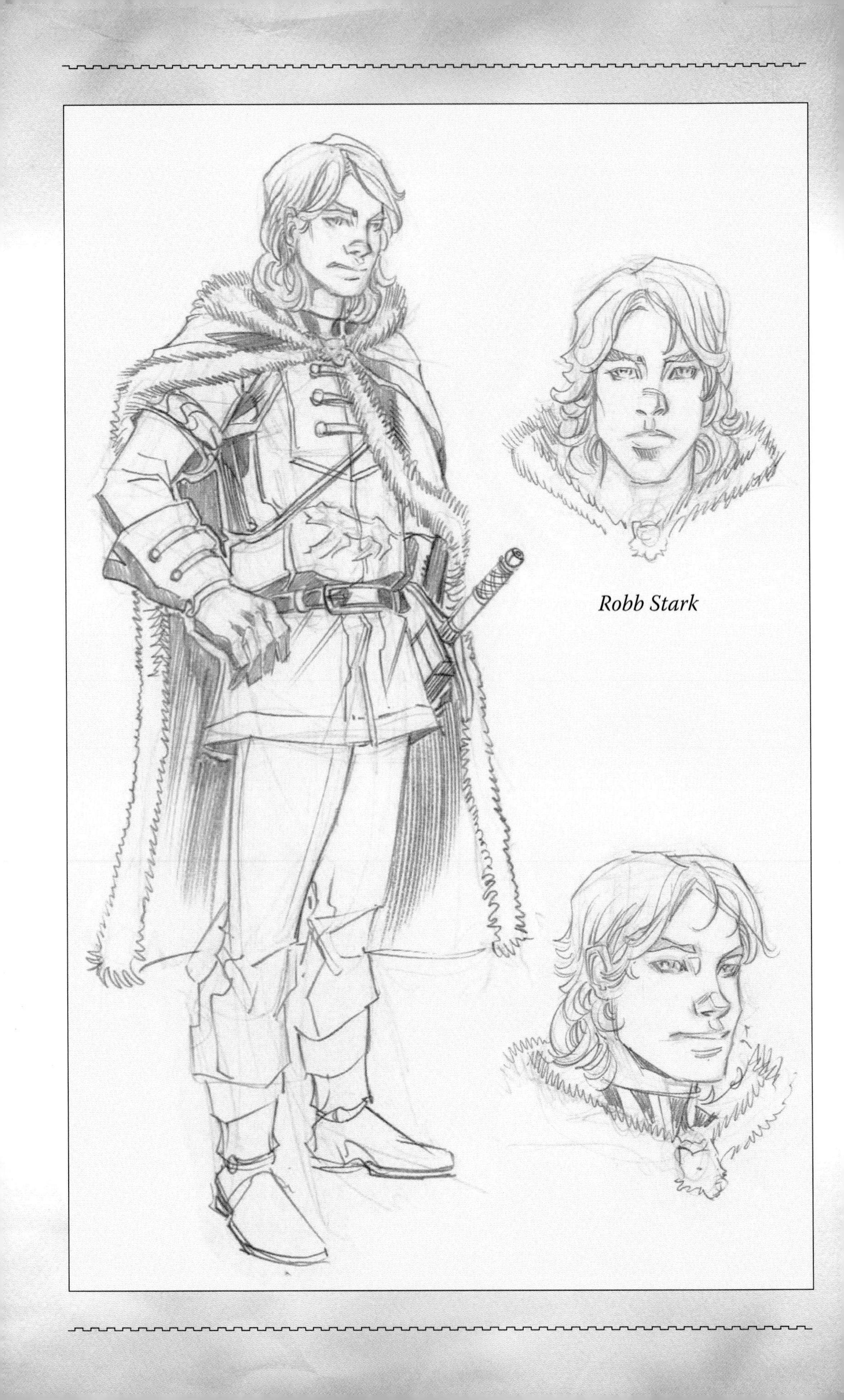

*Robb Stark*

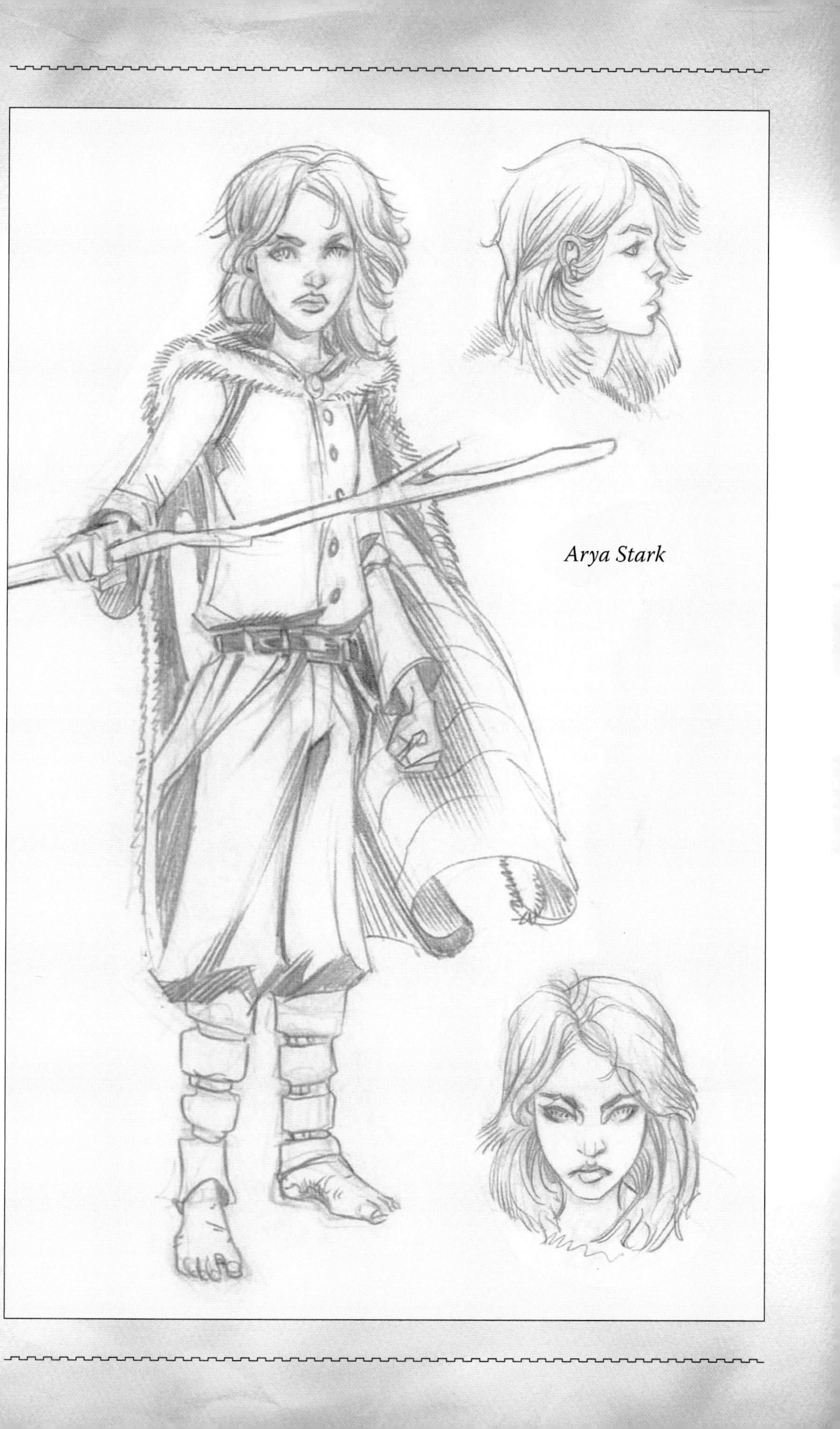

*Arya Stark*

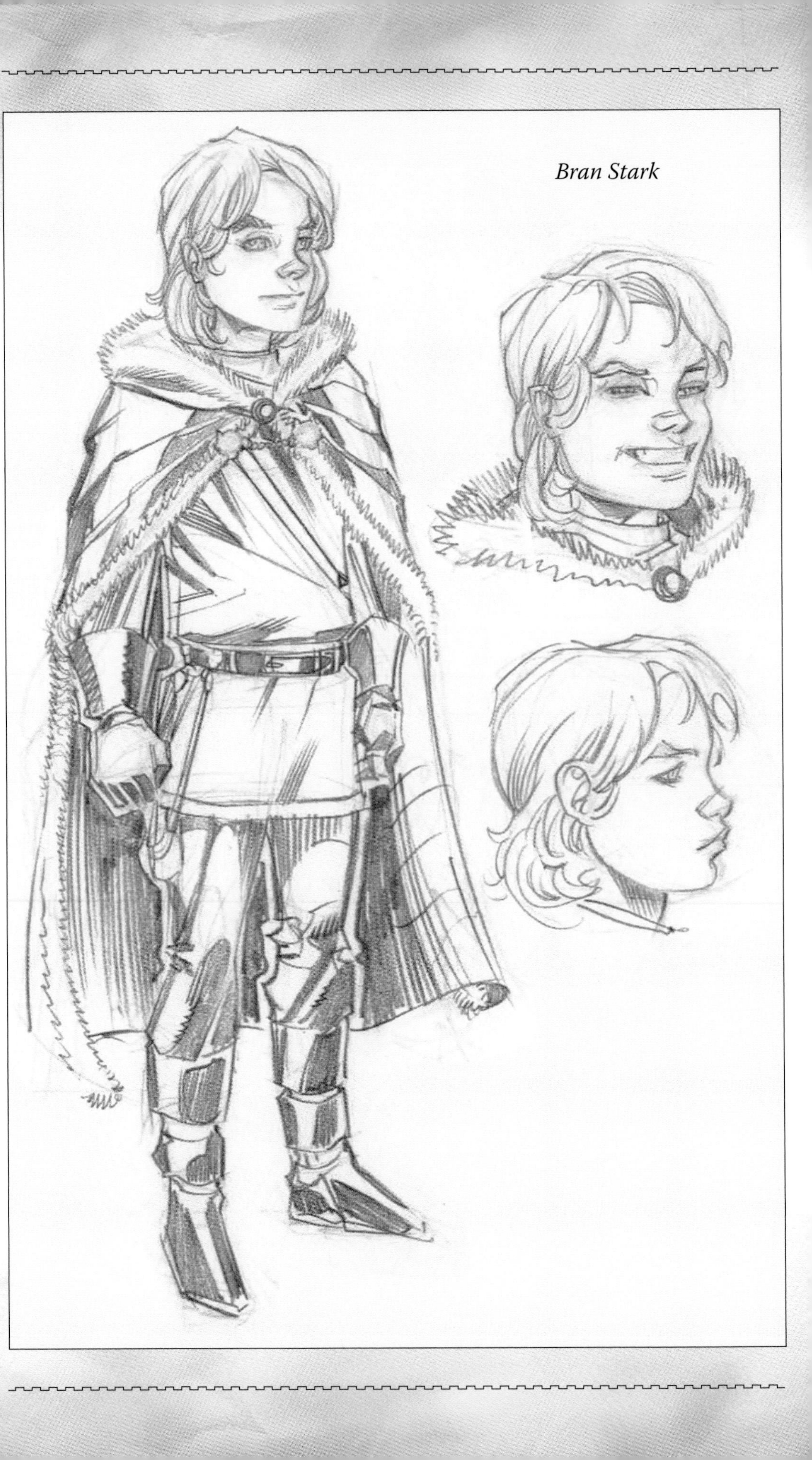
Bran Stark

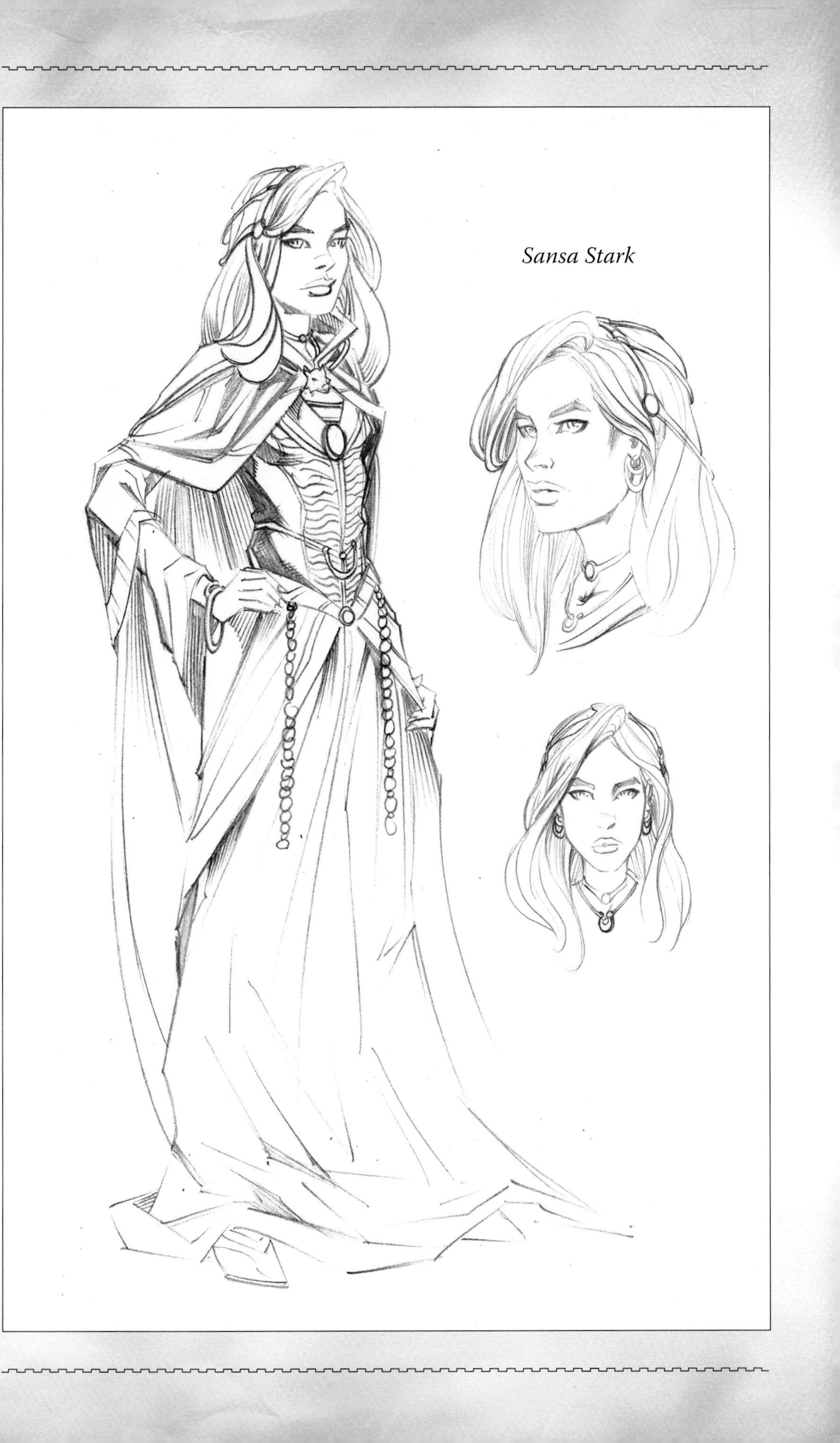
*Sansa Stark*

## AT WINTERFELL

Here are some of the Stark retainers.

Sansa's posse: Jeyne Poole and Beth Cassel. No concrete descriptions are given of either of these girls. All we know is that Sansa is prettier than Jeyne, and that Beth is younger than Sansa, and has curly hair.

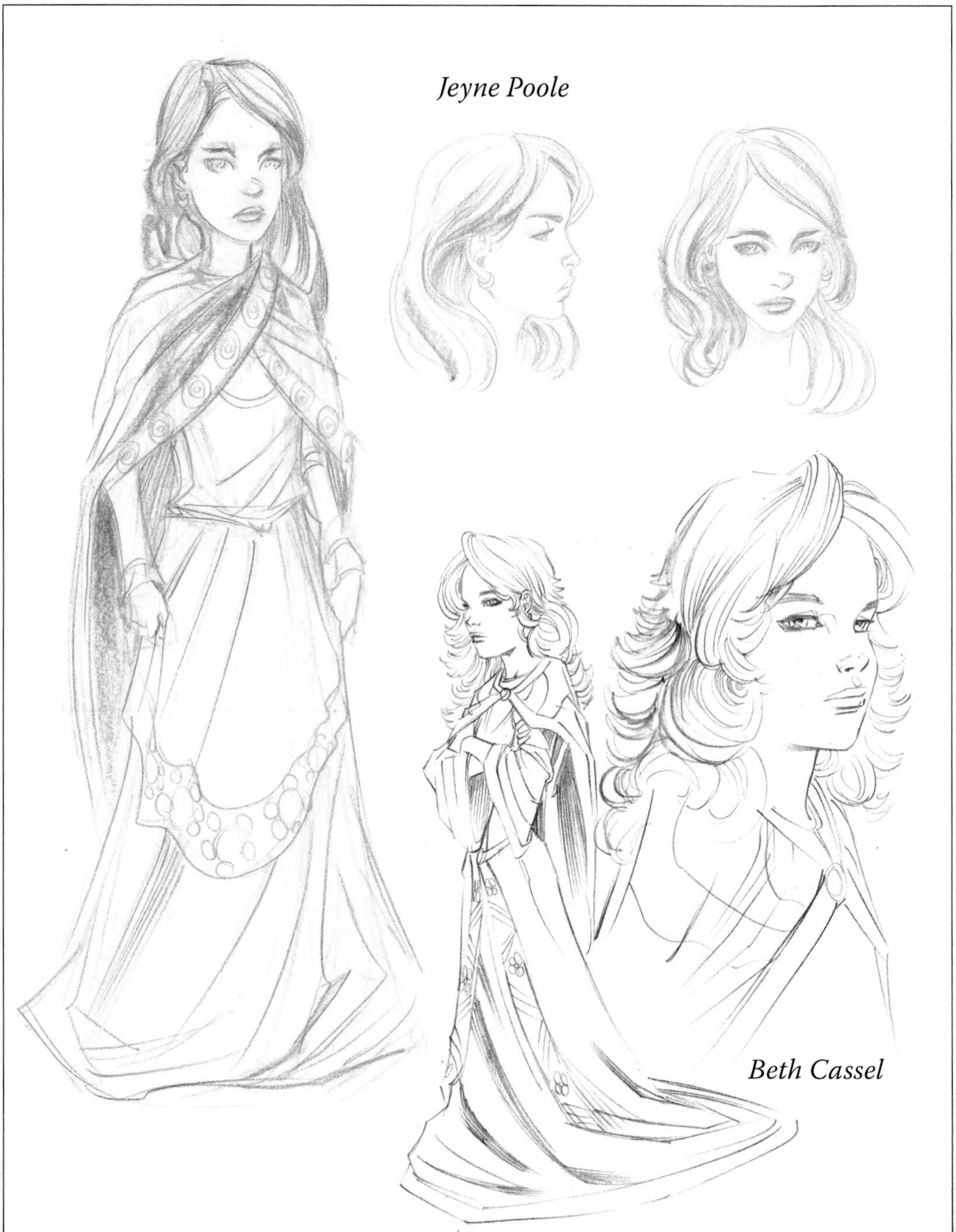

Jeyne Poole
Beth Cassel

Septa Mordane: "She had a bony face, sharp eyes, and a thin, lipless mouth made for frowning."

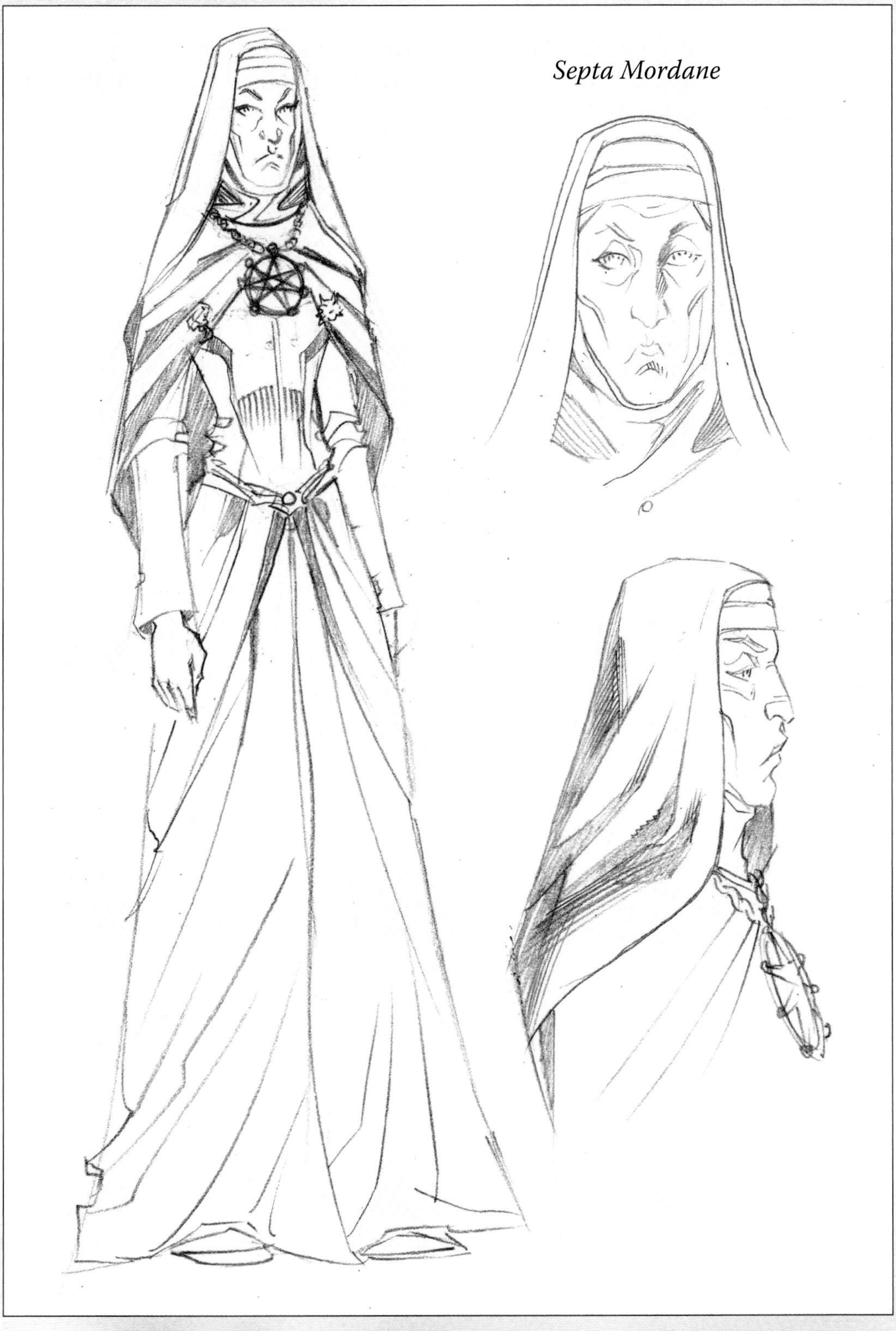
*Septa Mordane*

Ser Rodrik Cassel: Winterfell's master-at-arms and Beth's dad. "They were huffing and puffing and hitting at each other with padded wooden swords under the watchful eye of old Ser Rodrik Cassel, the master-at-arms, a great stout keg of a man with magnificent white cheek whiskers."

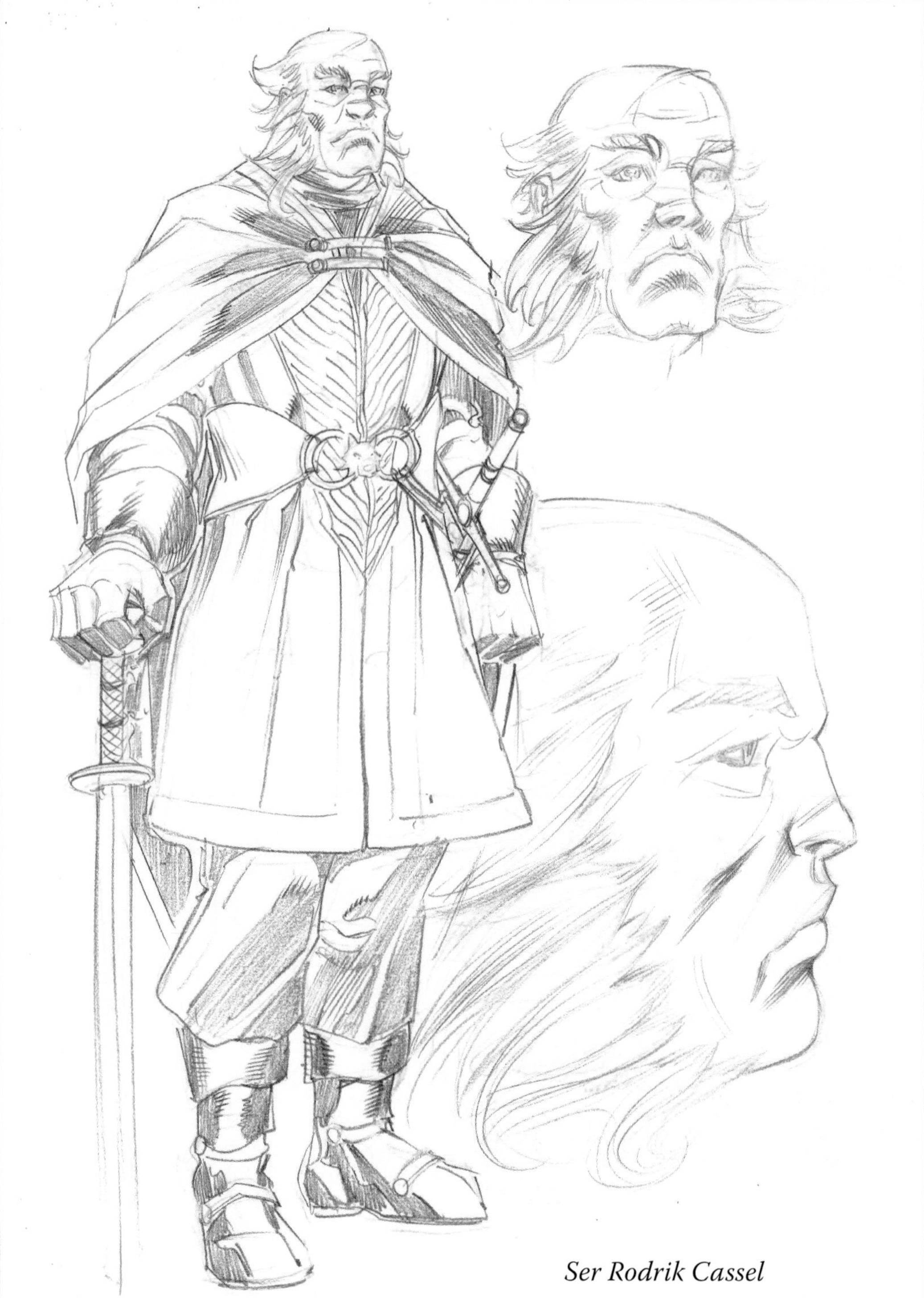

*Ser Rodrik Cassel*

Hodor: "He ducked to get his great shaggy head under the door. Hodor was nearly seven feet tall." And: "His arms were thick with muscle and matted with brown hair."

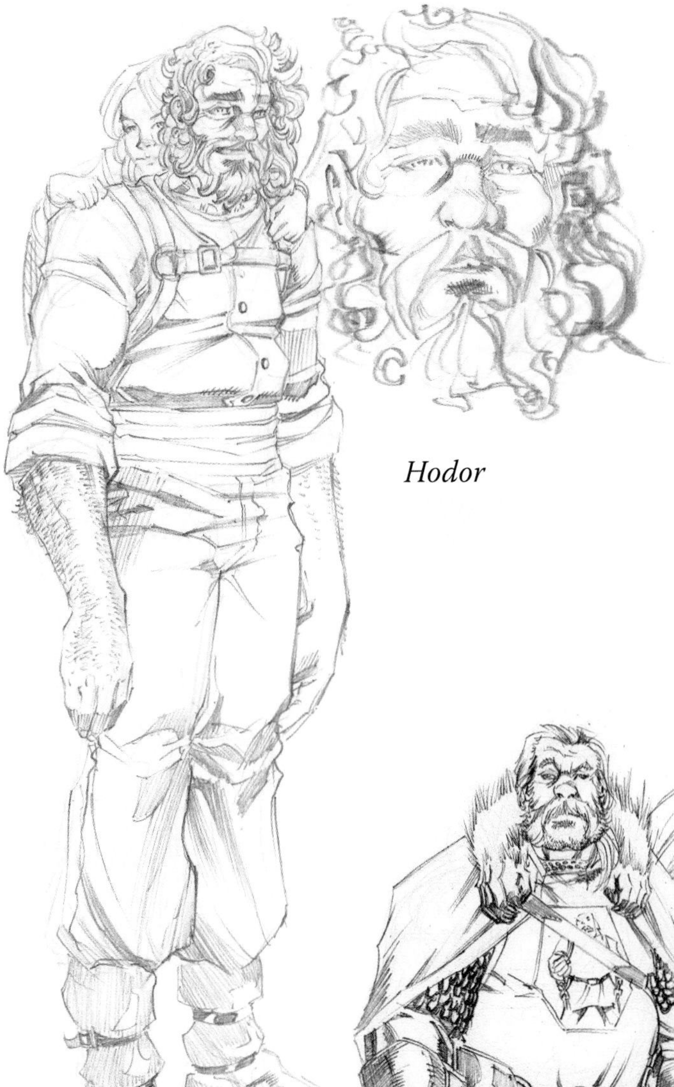

*Hodor*

And here is one of Robb's bannermen.

Greatjon Umber: "The loudest of Robb's northern bannermen . . . and the truest and fiercest as well, or so he insisted." And a man who: "stood as tall as Hodor and twice as wide."

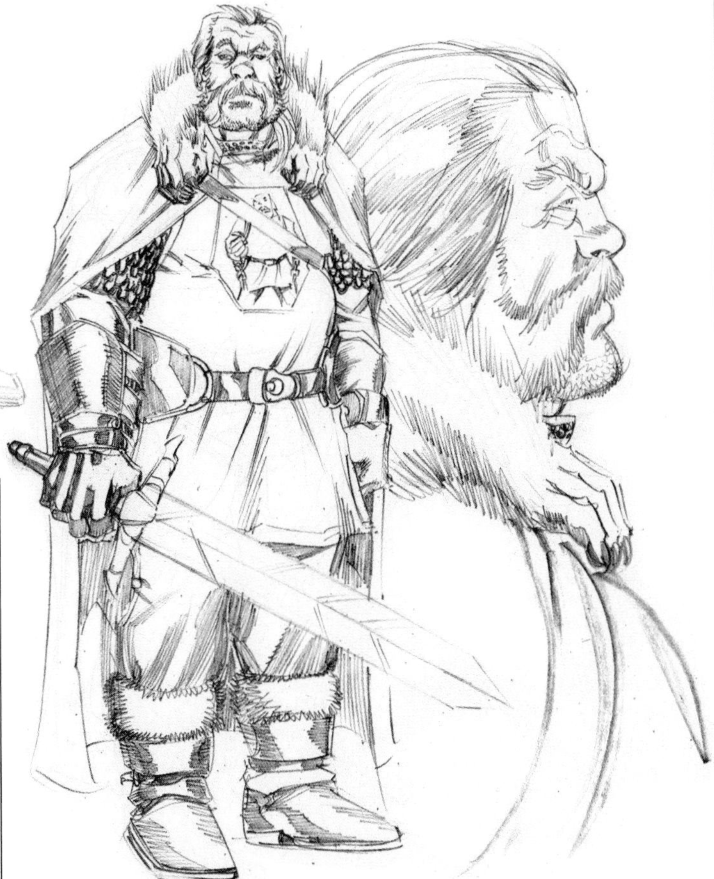

*Greatjon Umber*

## AT KING'S LANDING

King Aerys: Aerys does not appear save in flashbacks, but the Mad King dead at the foot of his throne is such a powerful image that we had to include it. Here is Tommy's take on Aerys, based on no more than the fact that he was a Targaryen, and mad.

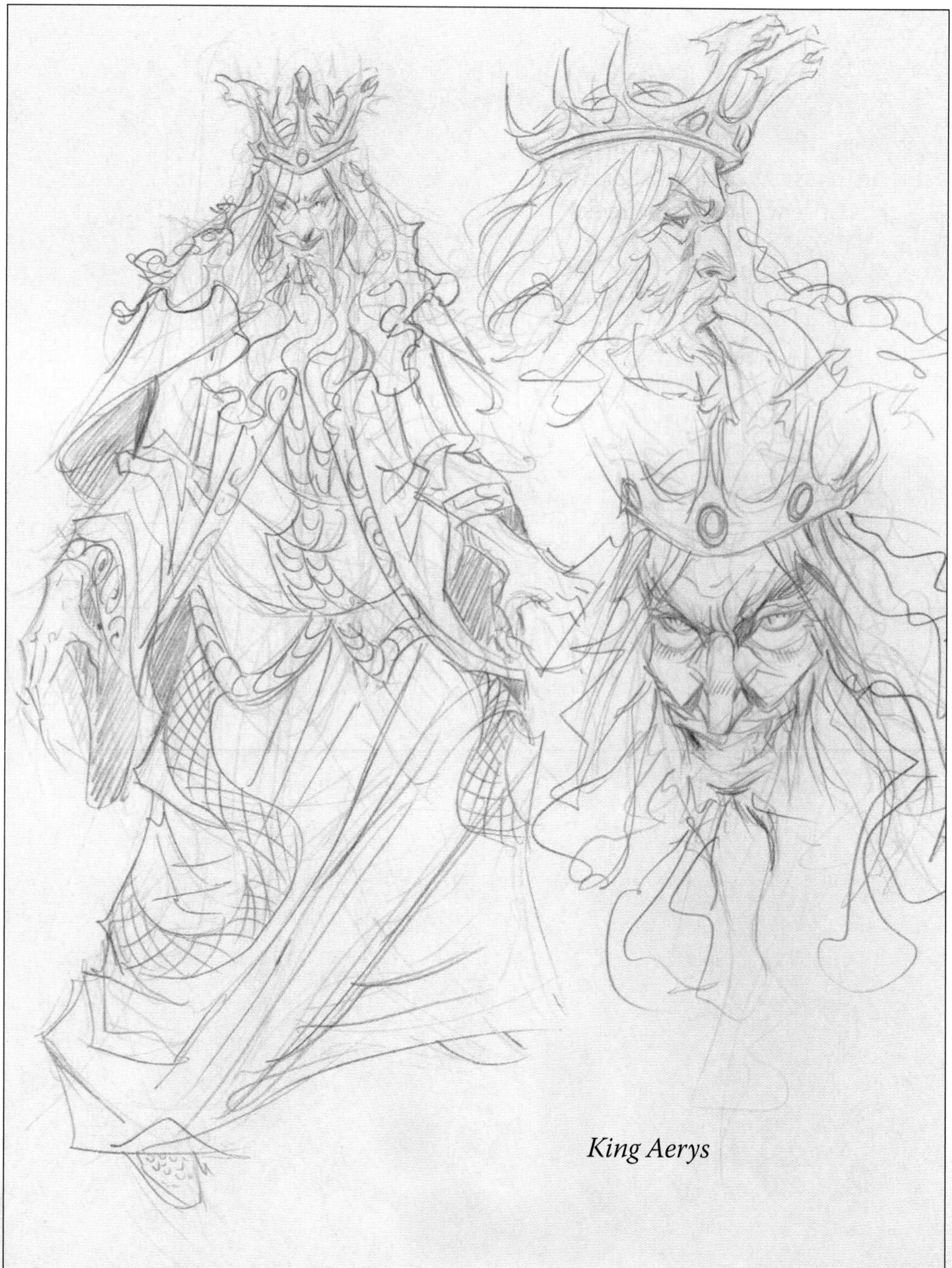

*King Aerys*

Tommen Baratheon: "Arya was paired with plump young Tommen, whose white-blond hair was longer than hers."

Below are a few of the Kingsguard.

Ser Boros Blount: "Boros was a bald man with a jowly face." And: "Ser Boros was an ugly man with a broad chest and short, bandy legs. His nose was flat, his cheeks baggy with jowls."

Ser Arys Oakheart: All I could find was: "Ser Arys had light brown hair and a face that was not unpleasant to look upon."

*Tommen Baratheon*

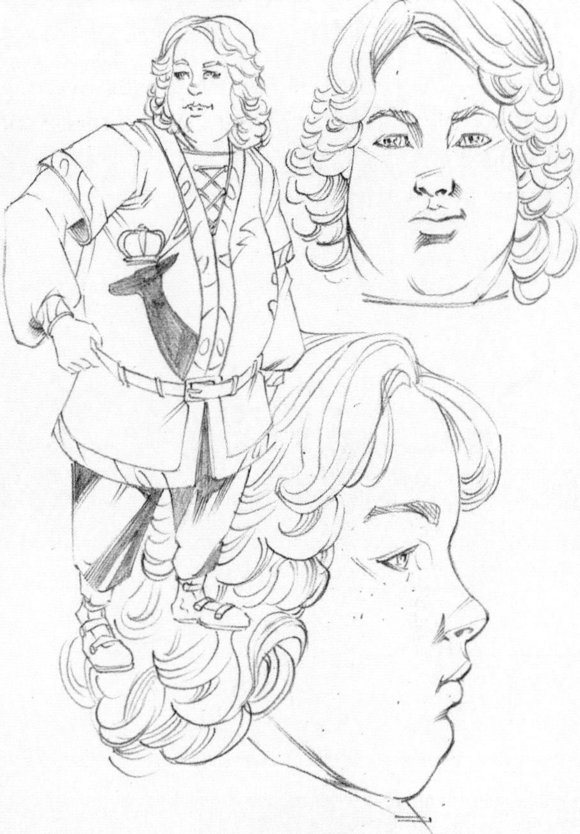

*Ser Boros Blount*

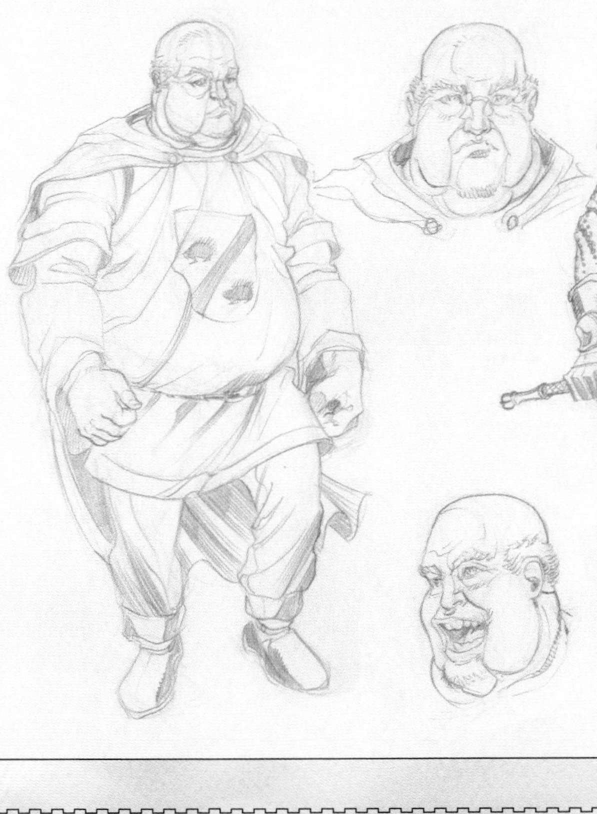

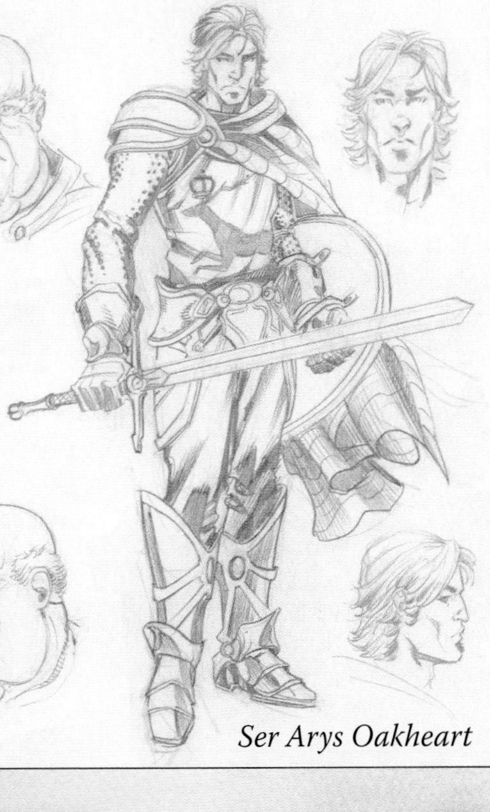

*Ser Arys Oakheart*

Here are some lords and knights of the court:

*Ser Loras Tyrell*

Ser Loras Tyrell: There are many descriptions of Loras's fabulous armor—both the one enameled with flowers and the one studded with sapphires. Of the man himself, we have: "Sansa had never seen anyone so beautiful…His hair was a mass of lazy brown curls, his eyes like liquid gold." And: "Ser Loras Tyrell was slender as a reed."

*Lancel Lannister*

Lancel Lannister: A "handsome boy, fair and well made, perhaps fifteen, sandy-haired, with a wisp of a mustache and the emerald-green eyes of the queen. He was cursed with all the certainty of youth, unleavened by any trace of humor or self-doubt, and wed to the arrogance that came so naturally to those born blond and strong and handsome."

Ser Hugh of the Vale: There is no description whatsoever of poor, doomed Ser Hugh.

Lord Beric Dondarrion: "Close behind came the young lord himself, a dashing figure on a black courser, with red-gold hair and a black satin cloak dusted with stars."

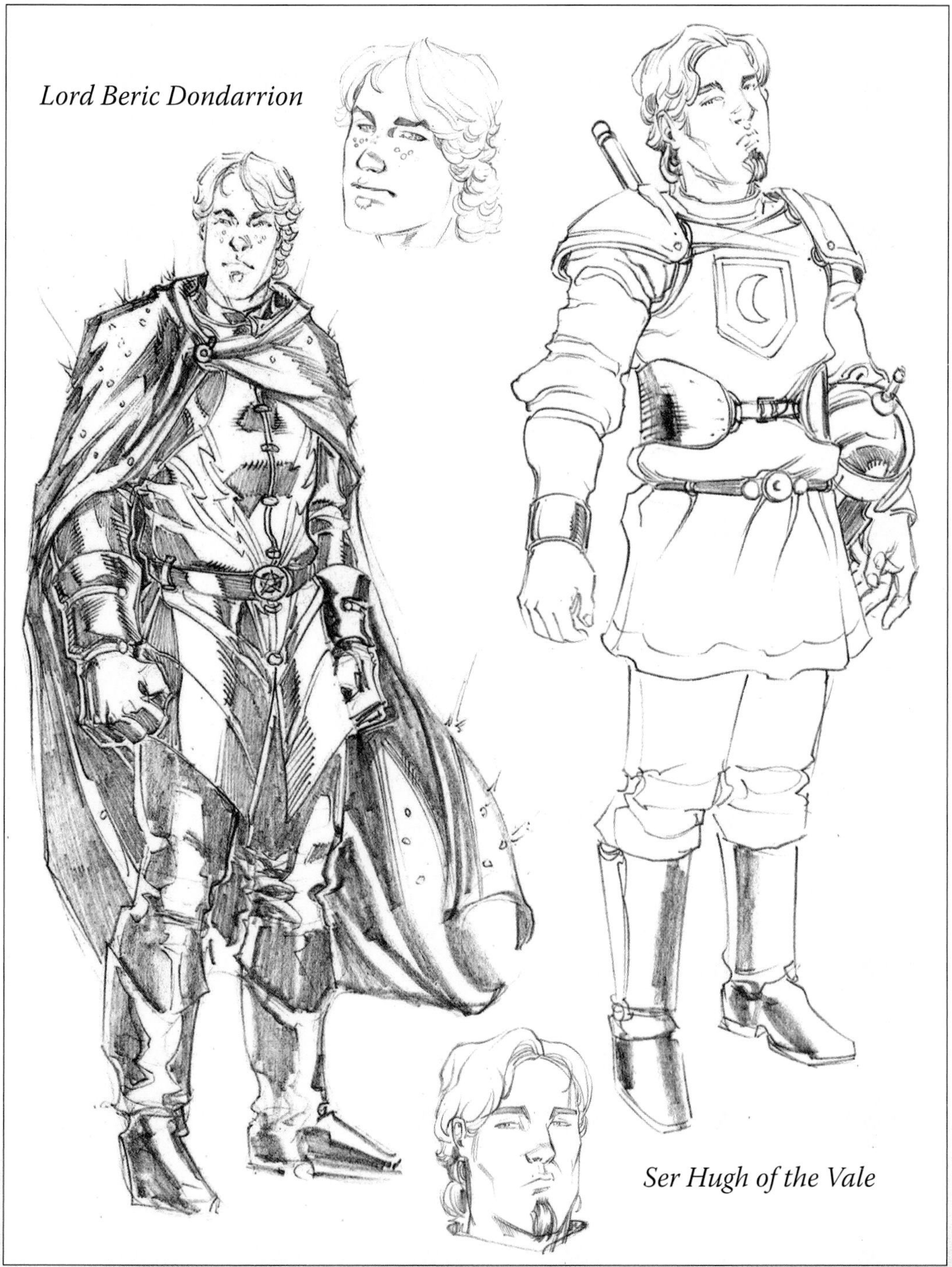

*Lord Beric Dondarrion*
*Ser Hugh of the Vale*

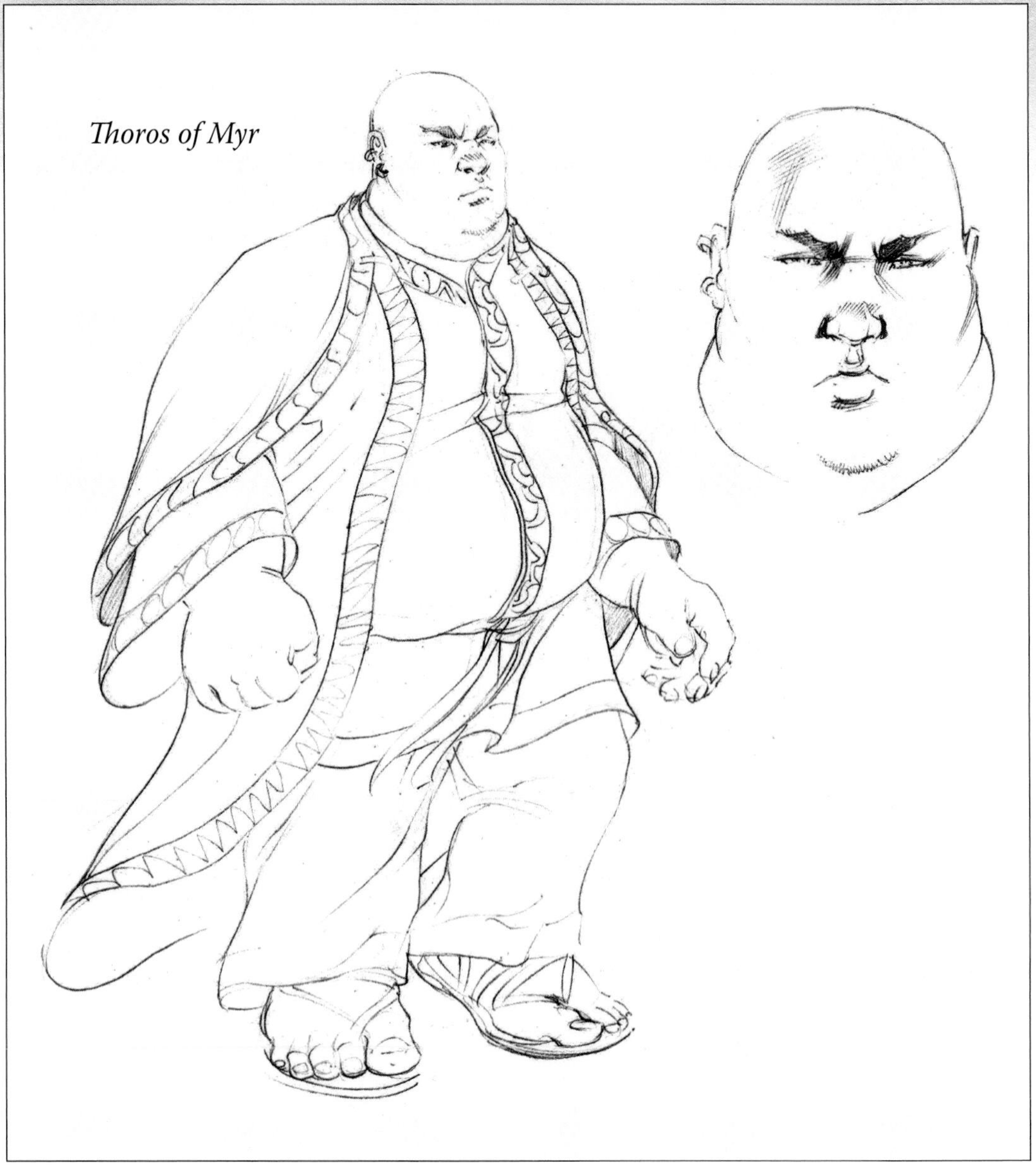
Thoros of Myr

Thoros of Myr: "The girls giggled over the warrior priest Thoros of Myr, with his flapping red robes and shaven head, until the septa told them that he had once scaled the walls of Pyke with a flaming sword in hand." And: "The victor was the red priest, Thoros of Myr, a madman who shaved his head and fought with a flaming sword." We also know he is fat.

*Ser Marq Piper*

Ser Marq Piper: He was a swaggering bantam rooster of a youth, too young and too hot-blooded for Ned's taste, though a fast friend of Catelyn's brother, Edmure Tully." And: "Young, hot-tempered Marq Piper urged a strike west at Casterly Rock instead. Still others counseled patience."

Ser Karyl Vance: "Sad-eyed Ser Karyl Vance, who would have been handsome but for the winestain birthmark that discolored his face, gestured at the kneeling villagers."

*Ser Karyl Vance*

And some people from the wider city.

Tobho Mott: No physical description of the man, just his clothes.

Gendry: "The master called over a tall lad about Robb's age, his arms and chest corded with muscle. 'This is Lord Stark, the new Hand of the King,' he told him as the boy looked at Ned through sullen blue eyes and pushed back sweat-soaked hair with his fingers. Thick hair, shaggy and unkempt and black as ink. The shadow of a new beard darkened his jaw…Ned studied the shape of his jaw, the eyes like blue ice. Yes, he thought, I see it."

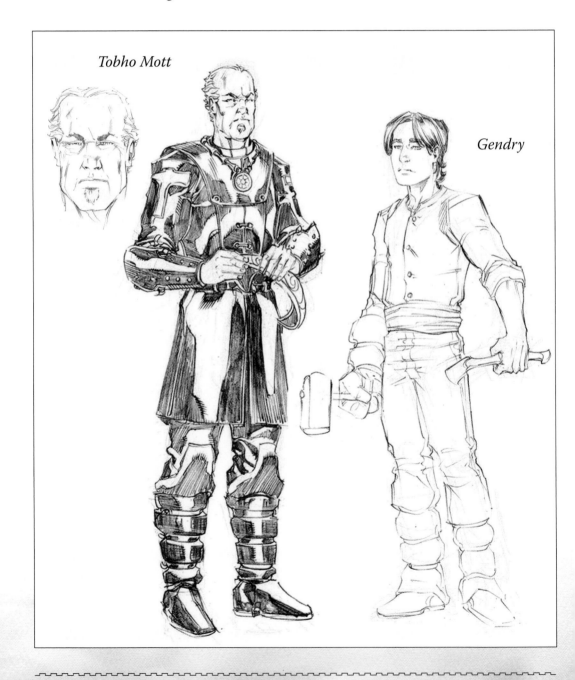

*Tobho Mott*

*Gendry*

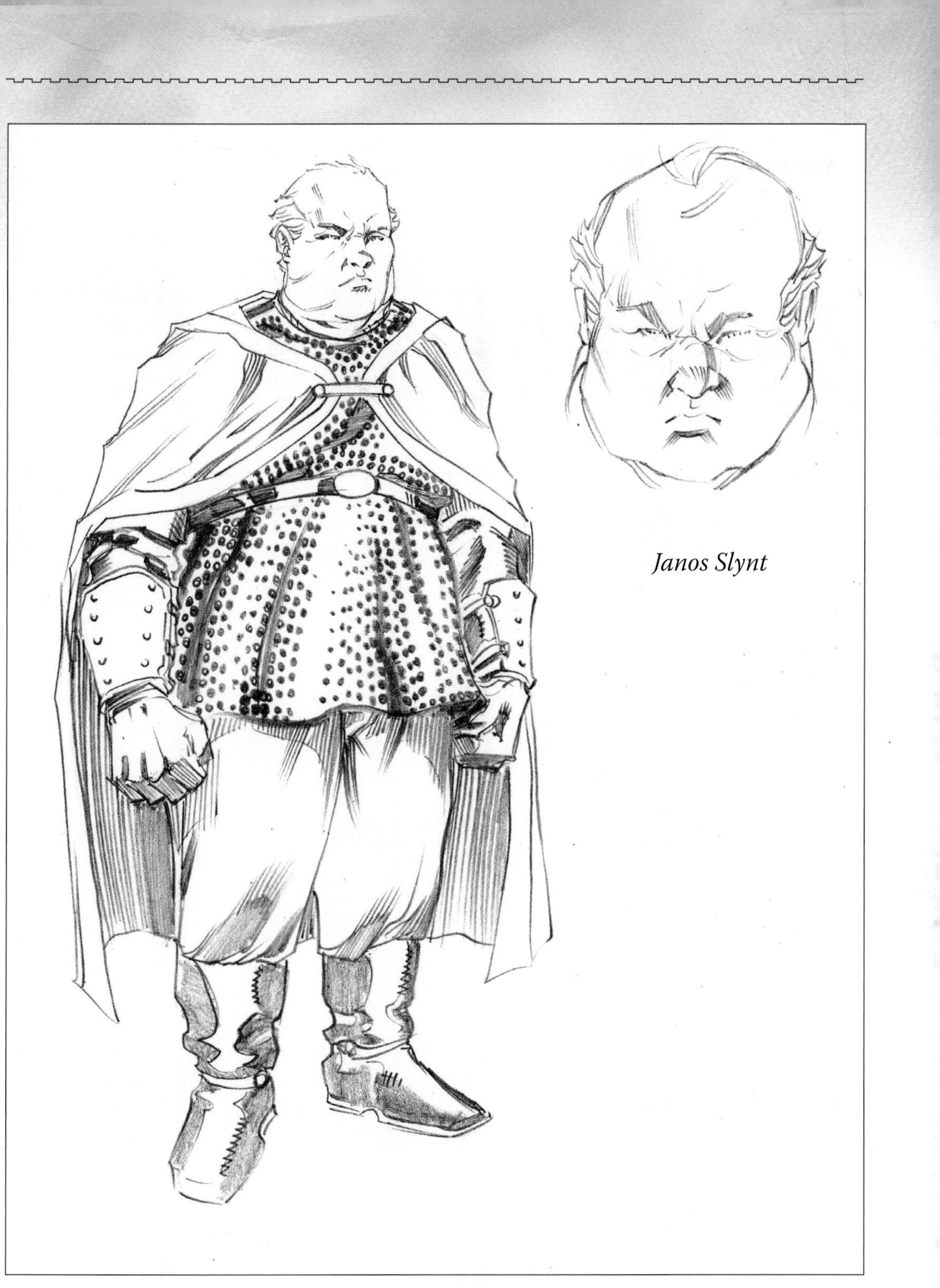

*Janos Slynt*

Janos Slynt: "Stout, jowly Janos Slynt puffed himself up like an angry frog, his bald pate reddening." And: "When Slynt scowled, his jowls quivered. He was as broad as the Old Bear had been, and no doubt would be as bald if he lived to Mormont's age. Half his hair was gone already, though he could not have been more than forty." And: "Jowly, balding Janos Slynt looked rather like a frog, a smug frog who had gotten rather above himself."

## AT THE WALL

Samwell Tarly: "Jon turned. Through the eye slit of his helm, he beheld the fattest boy he had ever seen standing in the door of the armory. By the look of him, he must have weighed twenty stone. The fur collar of his embroidered surcoat was lost beneath his chins. Pale eyes moved nervously in a great round moon of a face, and plump sweaty fingers wiped themselves on the velvet of his doublet."

*Samwell Tarly*

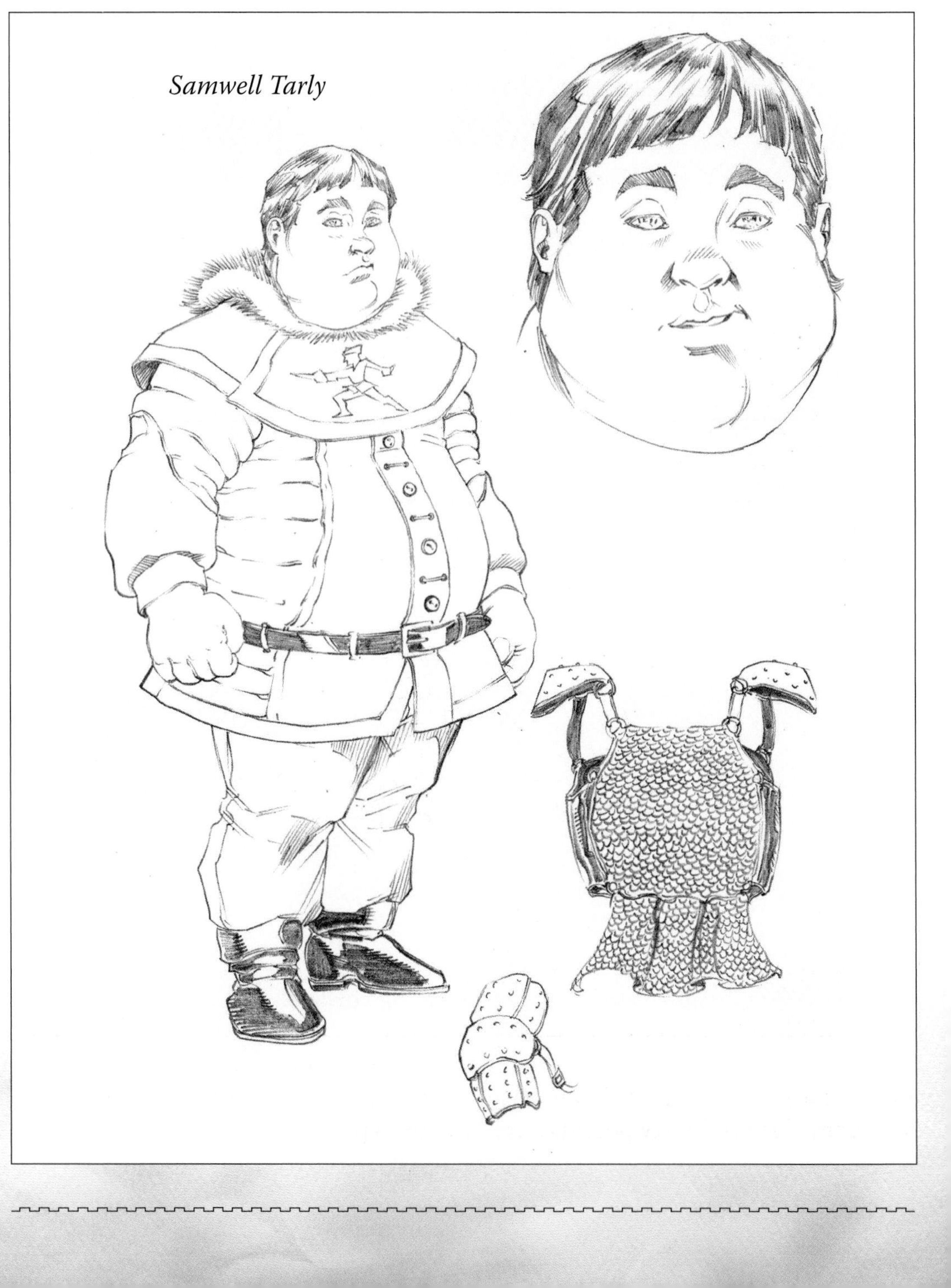

Pyp: "The mummer's boy with the big ears was a born liar with a hundred different voices, and he did not tell his tales so much as live them, playing all the parts as needed, a king one moment and a swineherd the next. When he turned into an alehouse girl or a virgin princess, he used a high falsetto voice that reduced them all to tears of helpless laughter, and his eunuchs were always eerily accurate caricatures of Ser Alliser."

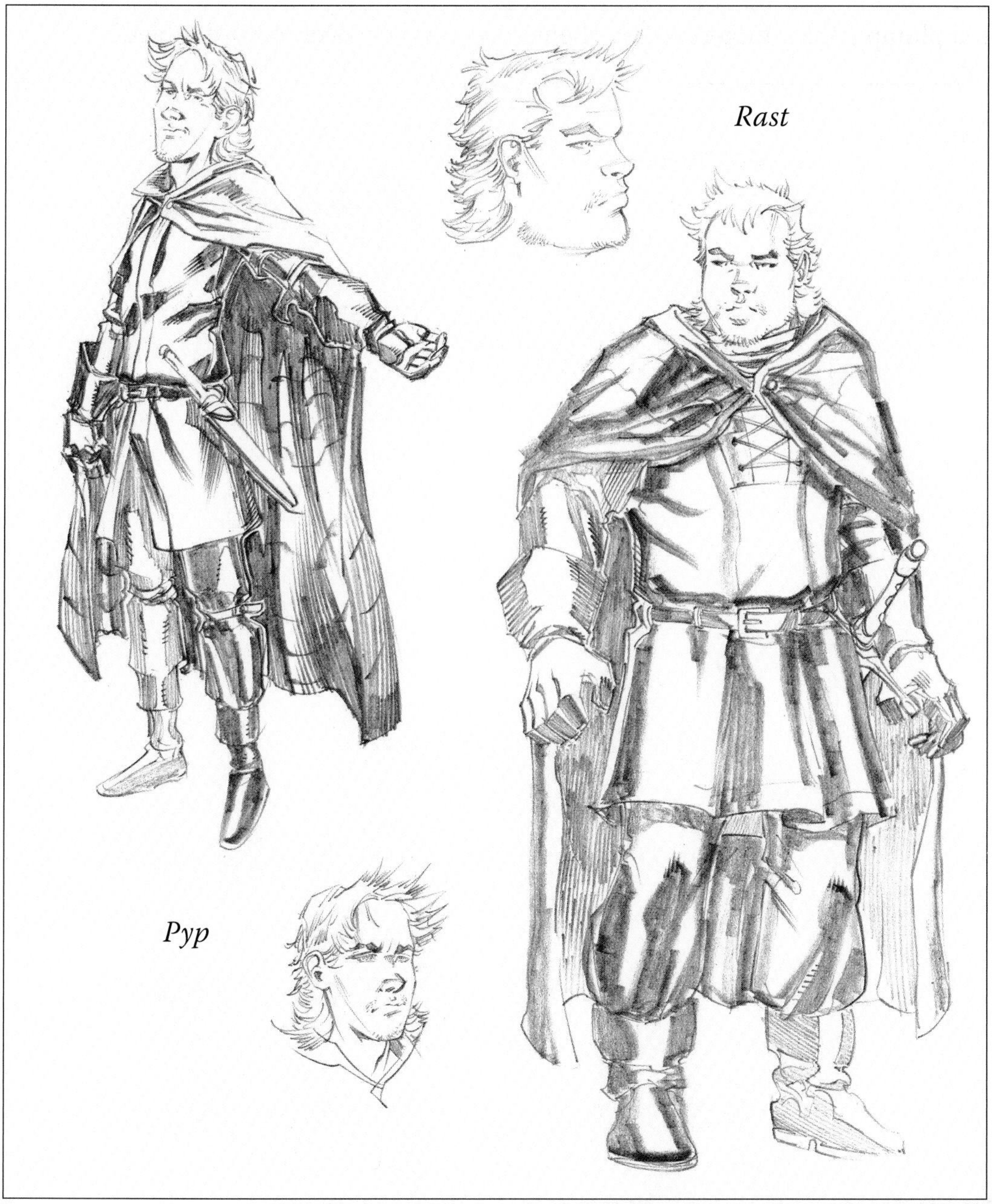
Rast
Pyp

Rast: All we know is that he is known as "Rat," probably for obvious reasons. He is two years older and forty pounds heavier than Pyp.

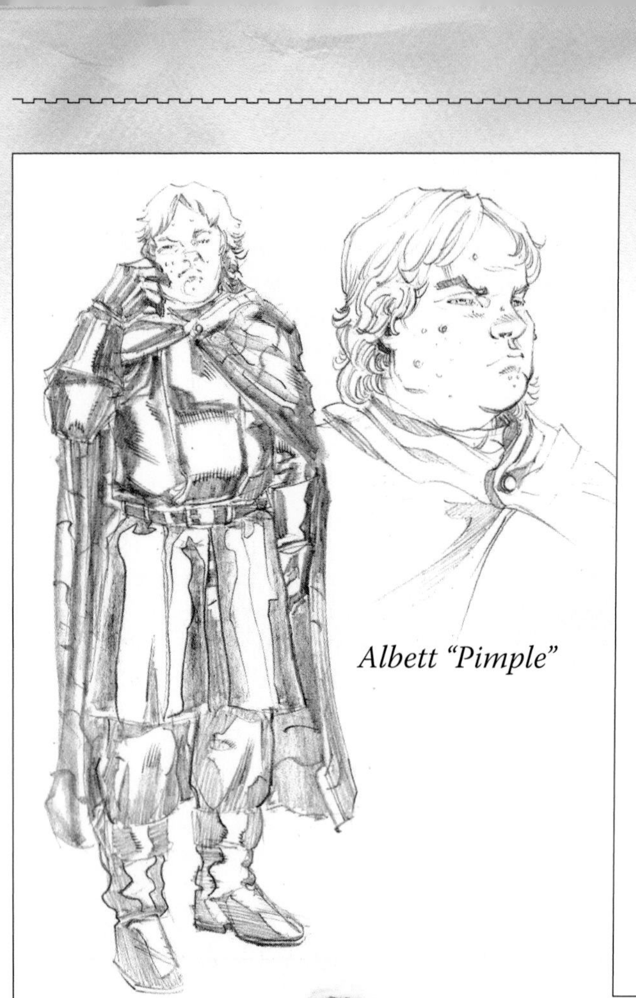

*Albett "Pimple"*

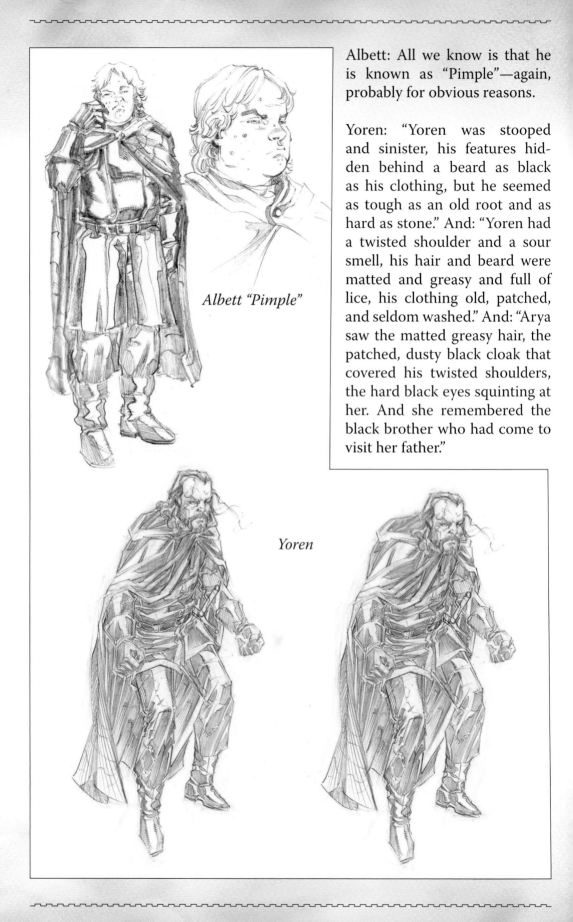

Albett: All we know is that he is known as "Pimple"—again, probably for obvious reasons.

Yoren: "Yoren was stooped and sinister, his features hidden behind a beard as black as his clothing, but he seemed as tough as an old root and as hard as stone." And: "Yoren had a twisted shoulder and a sour smell, his hair and beard were matted and greasy and full of lice, his clothing old, patched, and seldom washed." And: "Arya saw the matted greasy hair, the patched, dusty black cloak that covered his twisted shoulders, the hard black eyes squinting at her. And she remembered the black brother who had come to visit her father."

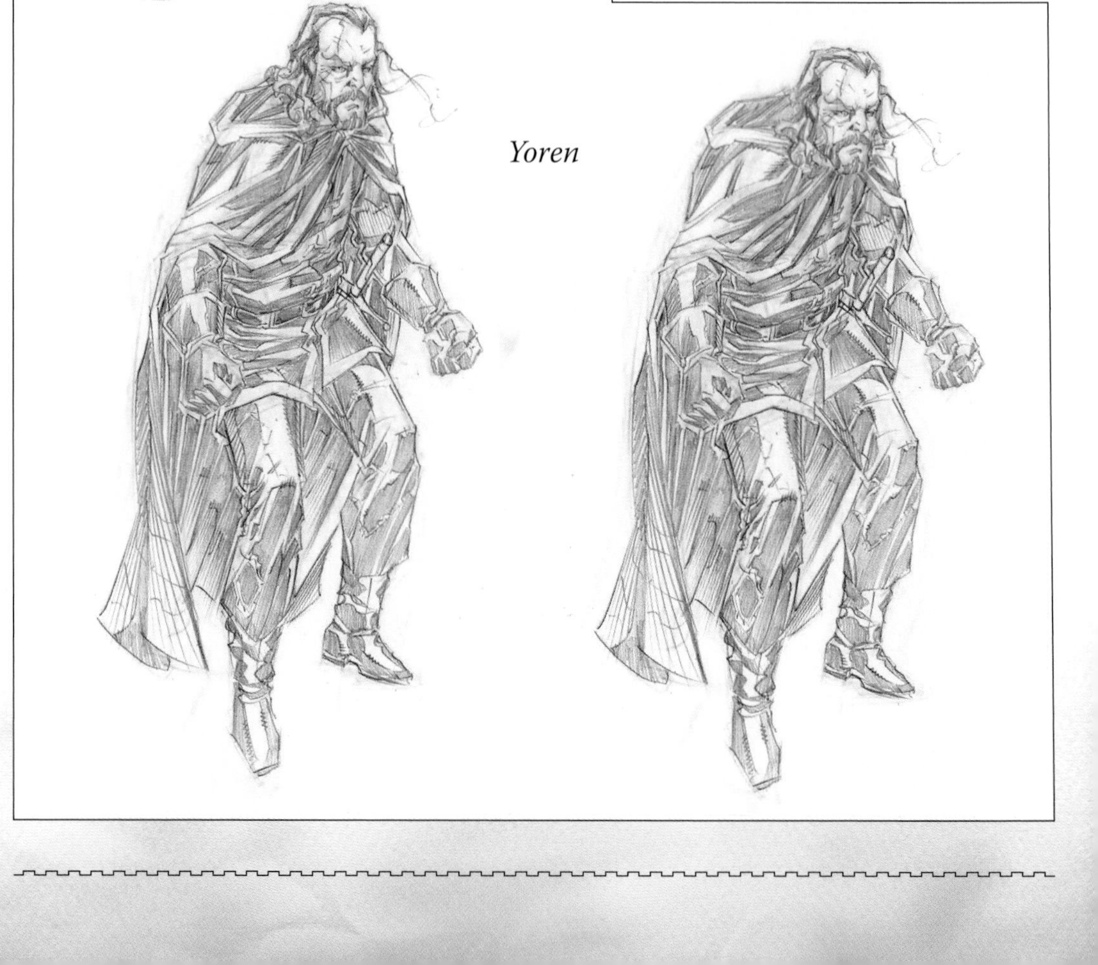

*Yoren*

Othell Yarwyck: Othell is described as "lantern-jawed" and big.

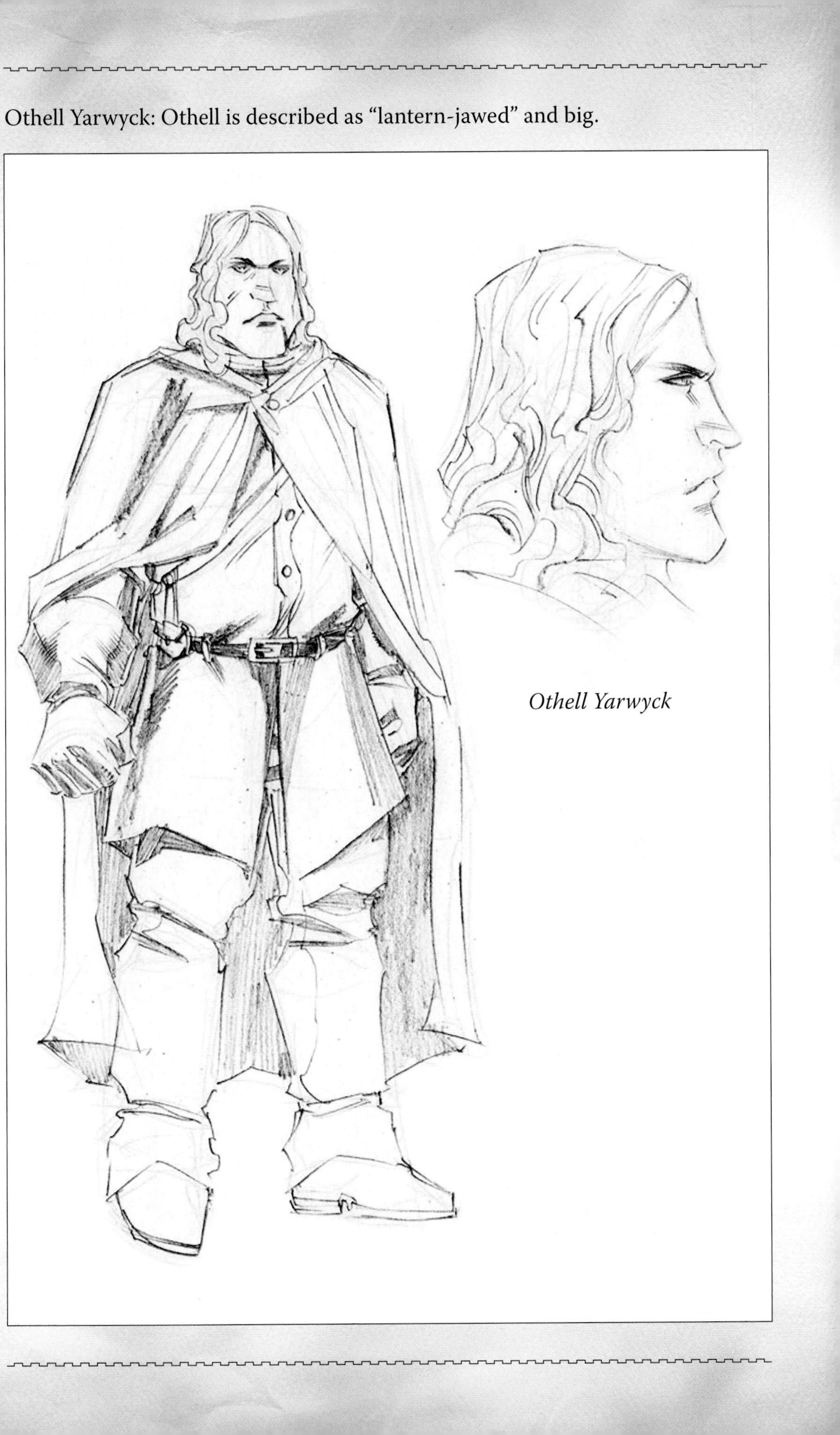

*Othell Yarwyck*

Dywen: Dywen is described as a "gnarled old forester." And: "Dywen smiled an oaken smile; his teeth were carved of wood, and fit badly."

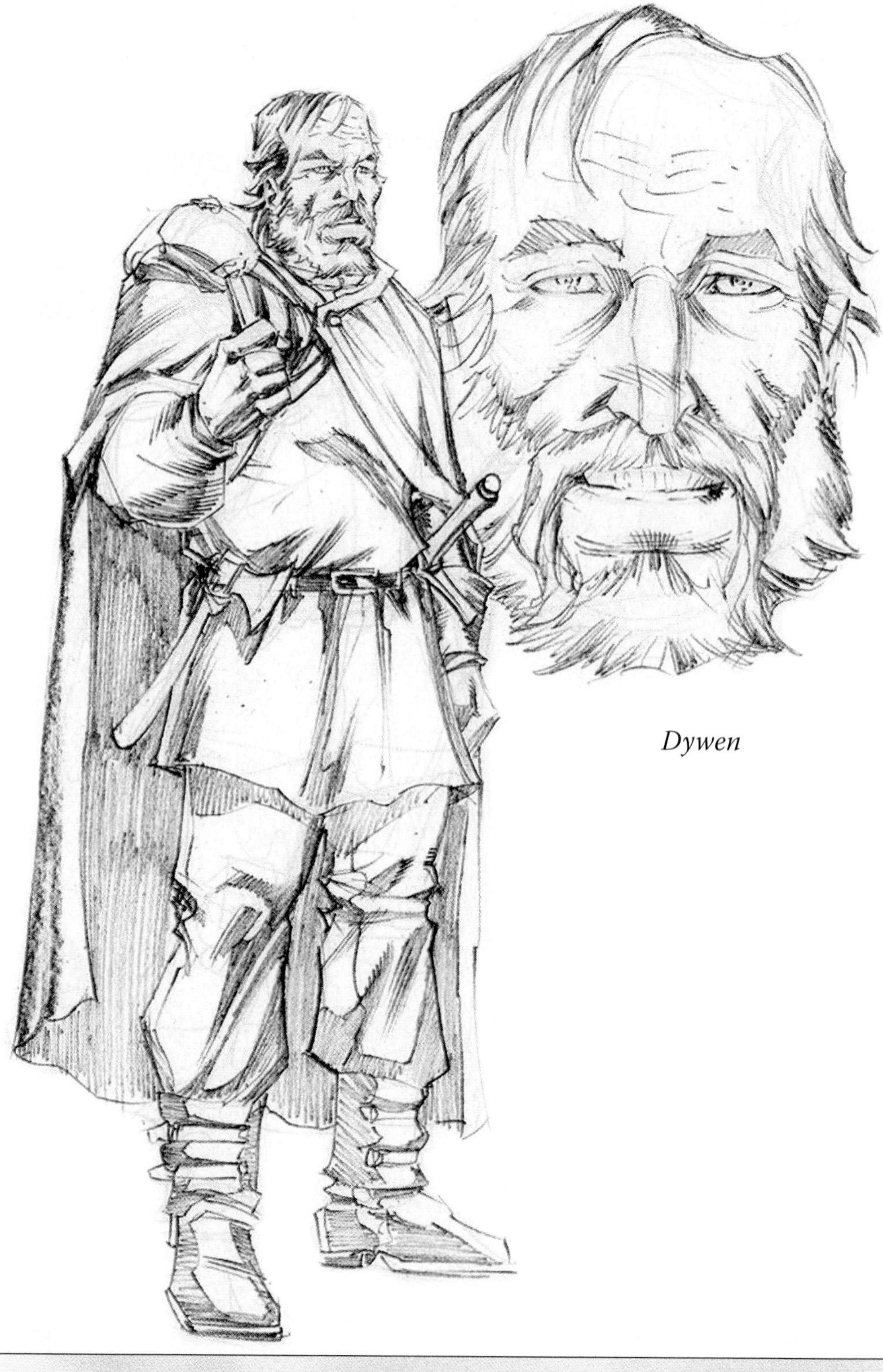

*Dywen*

## WITH DANY

Irri and Jhiqui: These two handmaidens share the same description, which is: "Irri and Jhiqui were copper-skinned Dothraki with black hair and almond-shaped eyes." So here is how Tommy distinguished them.

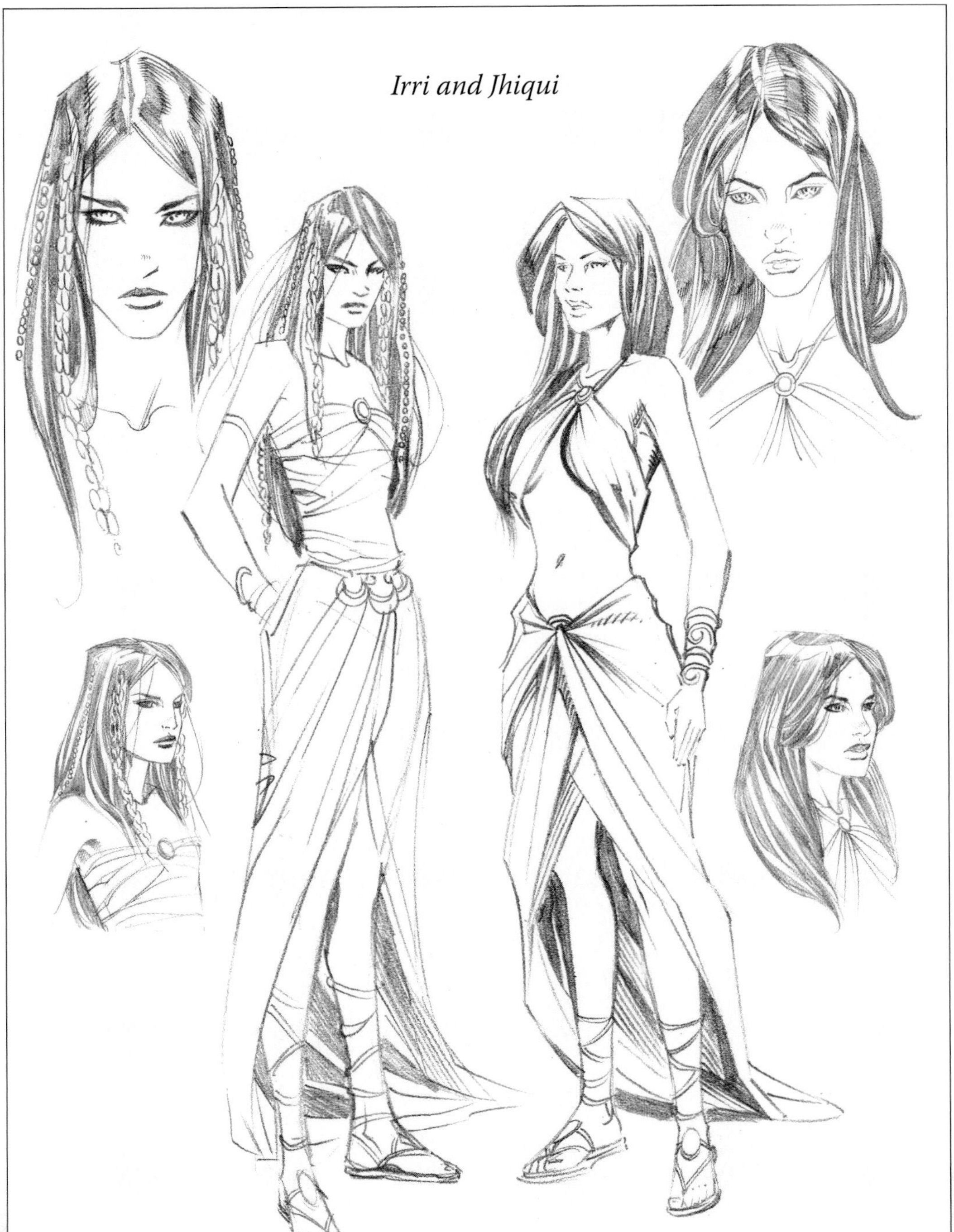

*Irri and Jhiqui*

The Dragon Eggs: "They were the most beautiful things she had ever seen, each different than the others, patterned in such rich colors that at first she thought they were crusted with jewels, and so large it took both of her hands to hold one. She lifted it delicately, expecting that it would be made of some fine porcelain or delicate enamel, or even blown glass, but it was much heavier than that, as if it were all of solid stone. The surface of the shell was covered with tiny scales, and as she turned the egg between her fingers, they shimmered like polished metal in the light of the setting sun. One egg was a deep green, with burnished bronze flecks that came and went depending on how Dany turned it. Another was pale cream streaked with gold. The last was black, as black as a midnight sea, yet alive with scarlet ripples and swirls."

# WITH TYRION

All of these are characters Tyrion encountered while taken captive by Catelyn Stark and immediately after his release from the Eyrie.

Masha Heddle: The innkeeper. The best description I could find was the one Daniel compiled in the script: a fat, grey, middle-aged woman with a fondness of chewing sourleaf, which has stained her teeth bright red.

*Masha Heddle*

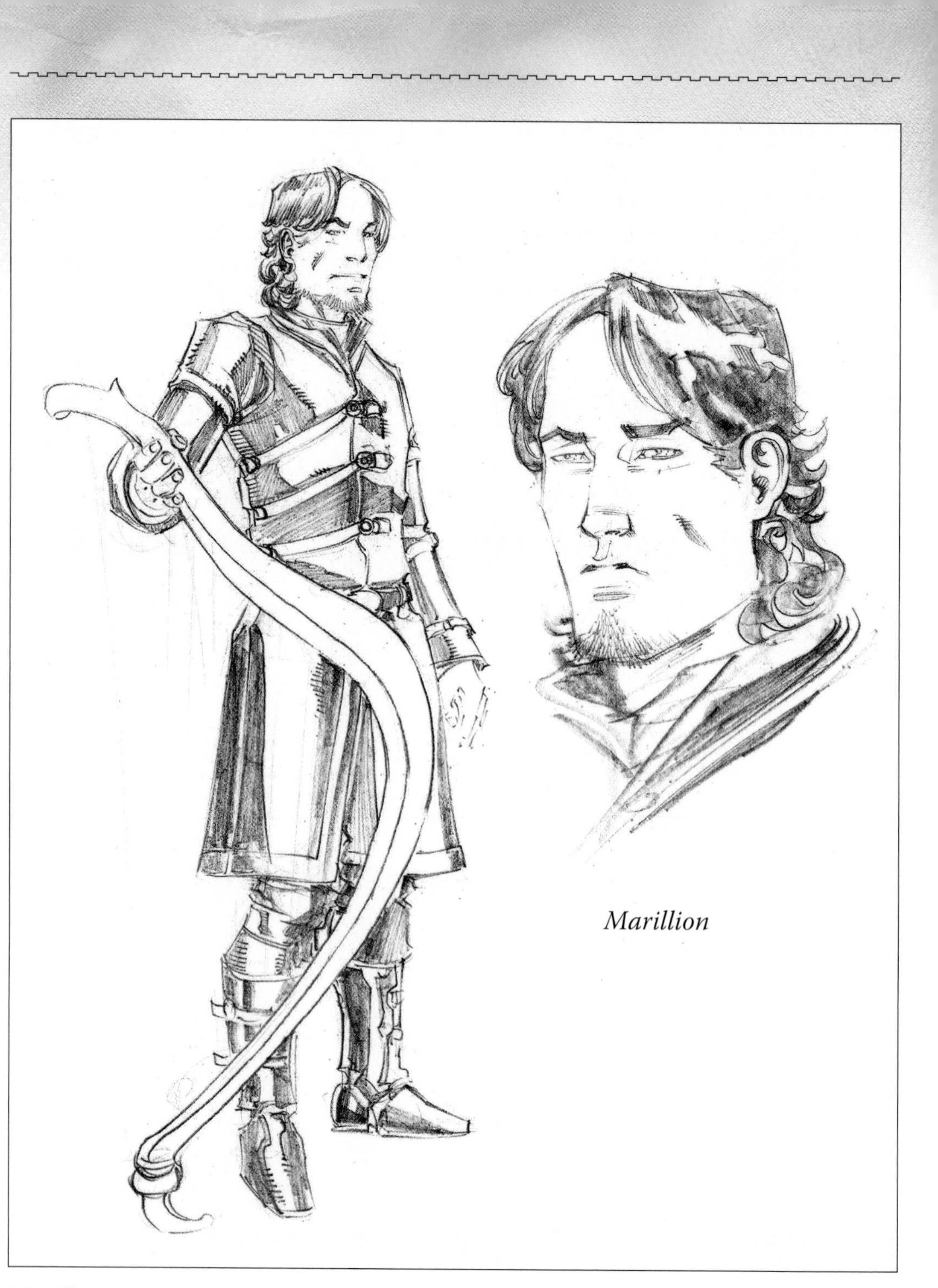

*Marillion*

Marillion: A singer, who carries a woodharp. Described as "a handsome youth." Young, slender, handsome, and boyish, with sandy hair and a charming smile.

Maester Colemon: "Beside him stood Maester Colemon, thin and nervous, with too little hair and too much neck." We also know that he has a prominent Adam's apple, and Maester Pycelle describes him as a young man, so they are probably about a generation apart, though Colemon is no spring chicken.

*Maester Colemon*

Conn of the Stone Crows: "Conn might have been handsome if you washed him."

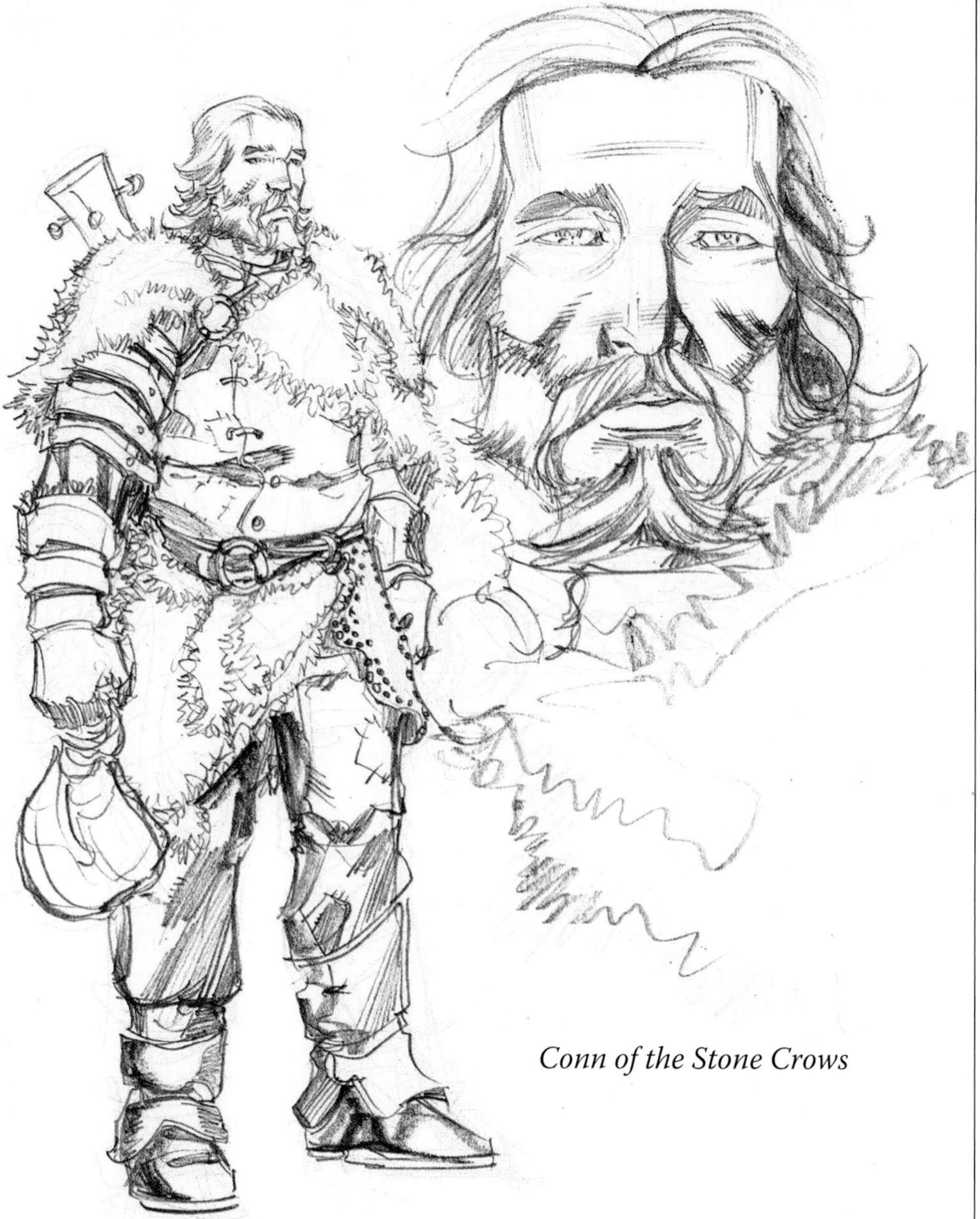

*Conn of the Stone Crows*

Shagga son of Dolf: "A boulder shifted to their left, and stood, and became a man. Massive and slow and strong he seemed, dressed all in skins, with a club in his right hand and an axe in his left. He smashed them together as he lumbered closer." And: "Shagga son of Dolf is the one who looks like Casterly Rock with hair."

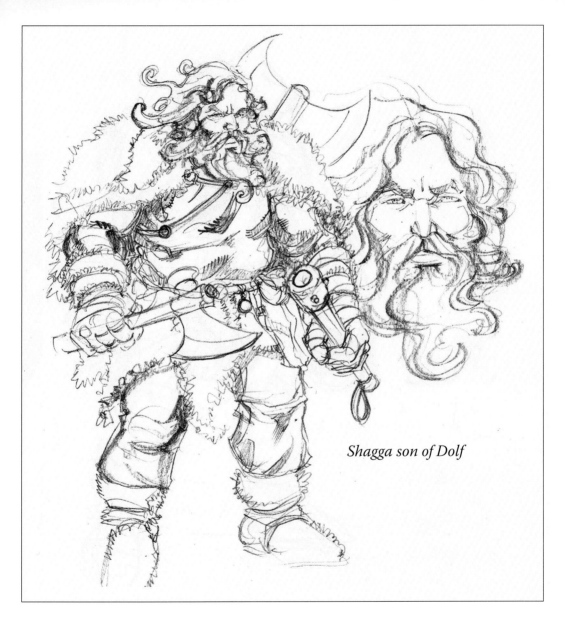

*Shagga son of Dolf*

**GEORGE R. R. MARTIN** is the #1 *New York Times* bestselling author of many novels, including the acclaimed series A Song of Ice and Fire—*A Game of Thrones, A Clash of Kings, A Storm of Swords, A Feast for Crows,* and *A Dance with Dragons.* As a writer-producer, he has worked on *The Twilight Zone, Beauty and the Beast,* and various feature films and pilots that were never made. He lives with the lovely Parris in Santa Fe, New Mexico.

**DANIEL ABRAHAM** is the author of the critically acclaimed fantasy novels *The Long Price Quartet* and *The Dagger and The Coin.* He's been nominated for the Hugo, Nebula, and World Fantasy awards, and has won the International Horror Guild award. He also writes as M. L. N. Hanover and (with Ty Franck) as James S. A. Corey.

**TOMMY PATTERSON**'S illustrator credits include *Farscape* for Boom! Studios, the movie adaptation *The Warriors* for Dynamite Entertainment, and *Tales from Wonderland: The White Night, The Red Rose,* and *Stingers* for Zenescope Entertainment.